LAWRENCE BLOCK
Five Great Novels

Lawrence Block
Five Great Novels

Coward's Kiss
Grifter's Game
You Could Call It Murder
The Girl With The Long Green Heart
Deadly Honeymoon

ORION

This omnibus edition first published in Great Britain in 2005 by Orion,
an imprint of the Orion Publishing Group Ltd.

A CIP catalogue record for this book is
available from the British Library.

ISBN 0 75287 314 8 (trade paperback)

Typeset by Deltatype Ltd, Birkenhead, Merseyside

Set in Minion

Printed in Great Britain by
Clays Ltd, St Ives Plc

The Orion Publishing Group Ltd
Orion House
5 Upper Saint Martin's Lane
London, WC2H 9EA

www.orionbooks.co.uk

Contents

Coward's Kiss

1

It was the right kind of night for it.

The afternoon had been tattletale gray that slowly turned to black. It had been warm and it got warmer, with humidity hanging in the air like crepe. All afternoon New York had crouched under a dark sky and waited for the rain to come.

I ate a quick and tasteless supper at the delicatessen around the corner, then went back to my apartment and stacked records on the hi-fi. I sat in a chair by the window, smoking a pipe and listening to the music and watching the night roll in like smoky fog.

It was a dark night, a coat of flat black paint that masked the moon and stars. Somewhere between eleven and twelve it started to rain. By that time the winds were ready. They came in behind the rain and brought it down hard and fast. I took Mozart off the hi-fi and put on a Bartók quartet – the slashing dissonance matched the mood of the turbulent weather outside. It was the kind of night nice people stayed safe and sound in their own apartments, stared at television sets and went to sleep early.

I hoped all the nice people who lived on East Fifty-first Street would do just that.

When the record ended I turned off the hi-fi and went to the closet. I put on the trench coat and slouch hat that every good private detective picks up the day he gets his license. Then I rolled up the oriental rug in the front hall and took it out of the apartment with me. I walked down a flight of stairs and out of my brownstone into the rain.

The weather was even worse than I had thought. Drops of water bounced off my trench coat. Others rolled off the hat. Still others found their way into the bowl of my pipe and put it out for me. I stuffed my pipe into a pocket and started walking. I had the rug under my arm like a king-size pumpernickel.

I keep my car in a garage around the corner on Third between Eighty-fourth and Eighty-fifth. The kid on duty there has a bad case of acne, plus some adenoids that get in his way when he tries to talk.

'Mr London,' he said. 'You want your car on a night like this?'

I told him I did. He put down a Batman comic and ran off to find it while I brushed raindrops off the roll of rug. He brought the Chevy around and presented me with the keys with what was supposed to be a flourish.

'You better keep the top up,' he said. 'Convertible's not much fun in this kind of rain. Man, you put the top down and you'll drown in there.'

I gave him a quarter and hoped he'd put it toward an operation. I dropped the rug in the back seat and got behind the wheel. I glanced over at the kid to see whether he was busy wondering where the hell I was carrying a rug at twelve-thirty in the morning. He didn't seem to care. His nose was buried in the comic book and he was off in a private world inhabited by Batman, Robin and the Joker. I started the car and drove away feeling more like the Joker than Batman.

I took Second Avenue downtown and headed for Fifty-first Street – the address Jack Enright had given me – 111 East Fifty-first Street. The address was impressive. I guess if you're going to keep a mistress you might as well do it in style. Jack's mistress was a blonde named Sheila Kane and I was on my way to meet her.

Traffic was light on Second Avenue. A handful of cabs cruised slowly, waiting to be hailed by the drinkers and drunks who use the avenue's cocktail lounges as a home away from home. There were very few pedestrians. New York stays awake twenty-four hours a day, even in the middle of the week, but that only holds for a few sections of the city. Times Square, bits of Greenwich Village, parts of Harlem. The residential neighborhoods go to bed early.

Fifty-first Street was already going to bed. A few hours later all the lights would be out and all eyes would be closed. When everyone's asleep, a single walking man is cause for suspicion. This was the best time to pass un-noticed.

I drove past number 111 slowly. There was no doorman; no flunkey on duty. I circled the block and found a parking space two doors east of the building. I got out of the Chevy and left it there, lugging the carpet roll to the building's doorway.

I stood for a moment or two in the vestibule, studying the names of the tenants. Three others shared the fourth floor with Miss S. Kane. There was a P.D. Huber, an Angela Weeks, a Mrs Aaron Clyman. I hoped they were all sleeping peacefully. I wasn't worried about Sheila Kane. It was a hell of an hour to pay a call on her, but I knew she couldn't care less.

She was dead.

One of the keys Jack Enright had given me fit the outer door. I let myself in, carried the carpet to the elevator. It was a self-service affair and it was slower than a retarded child. I piloted it to the fourth floor, got out of it, then left my own keycase wedged between the door and the jamb. That way nobody could steal it away from me. I wanted it to be there waiting when I was ready for it.

One of the doors had a neat brass nameplate that told me Sheila Kane lived there, which wasn't exactly true. I stuck Jack's other key into the lock and turned it. The door opened silently. I walked inside, closed the door, then felt around for the light switch. The room was very dark. Somewhere, in another apartment, someone was listening to 'Death and Transfiguration.' It was in tune with everything else.

When I switched on the light I knew how Jack must have felt. It was quite a shock.

The living room was large and the thick gray carpeting that ran wall-to-wall made it look still larger. Well-chosen pieces of French Provincial furniture rimmed the room and left a large oval of carpeted floor in the middle. In the precise center of the oval was the girl.

She wore stockings and a garter belt and nothing else and she looked nuder than nude. The full effect was surrealistic, a grisly joke by Dali in three dimensions. The room itself was too neat to be true. Nothing was out of place. There were no ashes in the ashtrays, no empty glasses on the table tops. There was just a girl, flat on her back, arms outstretched, almost nude, with a hole in her face. A little blood reddened the carpet near her head and matted her blonde hair.

She must have been pretty. She wasn't now, because the face is the center of beauty and there was nothing beautiful about that face now. Death was its only expression and death is not beautiful. Corpses do not look as though they are sleeping. They look dead.

Her body tried to deny that death. It was so young and rounded and firm and pink it almost looked alive. The breasts were firm, the waist slender, the legs long and lovely.

I left her and looked around the apartment. I checked the other rooms – a bedroom, a bathroom, a tiny kitchen. The neatness was almost overpowering. The bed was made, the sink scrubbed, the dishes washed and put away. I wondered why the killer had stripped her, or half-stripped her, and I wondered what he had done with her clothes. Carried them away with him, maybe. As souvenirs of death.

It didn't make much sense. When one gangster shoots down another gangster it doesn't matter a hell of a lot and the world doesn't lose by the killing. This was something else. It doesn't make sense when someone kills a pretty girl.

What I had to do was tasteless. I didn't want to do it. I wanted to go home and pretend I didn't know anybody named Jack Enright, that I had never been to a fourth-floor apartment on East Fifty-first Street. That there was no girl named Sheila Kane, that she wasn't lying dead on her living room floor.

I went back to the living room and stood looking at her for too many seconds. Then I grabbed the rug I'd brought and rolled it out next to her. It was just the right size. I kneeled down next to her and rolled a-little-over-a-hundred pounds of carbon and hydrogen onto the rug. Her flesh was cold and she was heavy now, cold and heavy with death. I got her onto the rug and rolled her and the carpet together until I wound up with a package that looked like nothing more than a thick roll of carpet.

Then I went to her bathroom, her very neat and very immaculate bathroom. I lifted the lid of a spotless toilet and threw up. I felt a little better after that.

I gave the apartment a once-over before leaving it forever. While I walked around the place I had the feeling it was a waste of time, that I wouldn't find anything. I was right.

There couldn't have been anything to see there. It was a good apartment, a pleasant apartment, but I got the impression that no one could possibly have lived there. Everything was put together like a stage set. There was nothing extraneous, nothing without a purpose. A desk on stage which is never opened will have empty drawers. Sheila Kane's apartment radiated this feeling. Her personality had left no stamp on the place. The apartment stood alone, well-furnished and well-arranged, waiting for a rental agent to show it to prospective tenants. But some fool had been dumb enough to leave a corpse in the middle of the living room.

I found a throw rug in a closet and covered the bloody part of the carpet with it. That would do unless someone searched the apartment carefully, and when that happened the bloodstains would be found no matter what I did to hide them. Then I picked up the roll of rug with the girl's body in it and carried it to the doorway. It was heavier now. Too heavy.

I turned off the light again, opened the door. My key case still held the elevator for me. Somewhere somebody was ringing for it impatiently. I carried my package into it, pushed the button. The door closed and we rode slowly down to the first floor.

A woman was waiting for the elevator. A gray, fifty-ish woman with a sable stole and a lorgnette. She held a closed umbrella in one hand.

'That rain,' she said. 'Terrible.'

'Is it still raining?'

She smiled at me. Everything about her told me that her husband had had the decency to die well-insured. 'Just a drizzle,' she said. 'But these elevators. They should have a boy to run them. So slow.'

I smiled back at her. She got into the elevator and rode to the third floor, which meant she probably hadn't known Sheila Kane. I left the building knowing that she wouldn't remember me. She was a woman who lived in a world of her own. That rain and that elevator were her major problems.

The rain had eased up, but the night was as dark as ever. Streetlights tried to brighten things and failed. I carried the rug through the gloom to the car. It went in the back seat. I went in the front seat and the car went to Fifth Avenue, then uptown to Central Park. Traffic was even thinner now. I checked the mirror now and then to make sure nobody was following me. Nobody was.

Central Park is an oasis in a desert or a wilderness in the middle of a jungle, depending on how you look at it. I drove through it, left the wide roads for the twisting lanes, let the Chevy follow its nose. I found a spot and pulled off onto the grass at the side of the road. I killed the engine and climbed out onto grass that was soft and wet from all that rain. The air was so fresh and clean that it didn't seem like New York at all.

That much was good. If she had to lie dead, at least she should do so in a fresh clean spot. But it was a shame about the rain. There was something very indecent about spilling her out nude and dead in the dampness. There was something . . .

I opened the back door and picked up the rug again, and by this time I was beginning to feel like an Armenian delivery boy. I held onto one end of the rug and let it spill out. The rug unwound neatly and what was left of Sheila Kane hit the ground, rolled over twice and came to rest face down on the grass.

There was a flashlight in the Chevy's glove compartment. I got it; took a last look at the girl. The bullet hadn't lodged in her head. There was a small and neatly rounded hole in the back of her head where it had made its exit. I thought about modern police methods and scientific laboratory techniques and decided they would figure out that she had been killed by a white male between thirty and thirty-two years of age, wearing a blue pea jacket and favoring his right foot when he walked. Science is wonderful. All I could tell from the hole was that the killer had picked up the bullet from the apartment, and I'd guessed that all along.

I turned off the flashlight. I rolled up the damned rug and tossed it back in the car, feeling very sick of rugs and corpses, of the smell of Central Park and of the smell of death. I thought about Sheila Kane, shrouded in darkness in tall wet grass. I thought about Newton's law of inertia. Bodies at rest were supposed to remain at rest, but the dead girl had broken that law. She wasn't supposed to be moving around. And how long would it be before they let her rest? A quick ride to the morgue. An autopsy. And then another ride, slow and sedate, and a final home under the ground.

I got back into the Chevy, put it in low and got the hell out of Central Park. I dropped the rug at my apartment – there was no point shoving it in the garage kid's nose – and ran the car back to the garage. I turned it over to Adenoids and Pimples.

'Crazy night,' he told me.

'Crazy?'

'That's where it's at.' He shifted a wad of gum from one side of his mouth to the other, knocked ashes off a filter-tipped cigarette. He gave me a grin that he could have kept to himself.

'A night to get killed on,' he said. 'That type night.'

I didn't have an answer handy.

'Spooky-kooky, what I mean. Me, I'm happy. I live right, Mr London. I don't cut work until the sun comes up. Midnight to dawn, that's my scene. I wouldn't walk around on a night like this. I couldn't make it.'

'I'm walking home.'

'Take a hack,' he told me. 'You live far?'

'Not far.'

'You could get hit on the head. Knifed, even. How far do you live?'

'Around the corner,' I said. 'I think I'll chance it.'

'Ruck, anyway.'

I looked at him.

'Rotsa Ruck. Like they say in China.'

They don't, but I wasn't going to argue with him. I left him there and walked back to the apartment. Nobody knifed me and nobody hit me over the head, which wasn't much of a surprise. I put my rug back in the hall where it belonged and sponged a few drops of caked blood from it. There were probably traces of blood in the thing but I wasn't going to stay up nights worrying about them. Nobody would come to look at my rug. Because nobody would connect me with Sheila Kane. Because there was no connection.

Now it was time to relax, time to unwind. I found a pipe and stuffed tobacco into it. I lit it evenly all around and smoked. I poured cognac into a glass and sipped it. It was smooth and it went all the way down and left a pleasant glow in its path.

It was time to relax, but I couldn't manage it. There was a picture that stayed in my mind – a picture of a nude blonde, dead and cold, all dolled up in stockings and garter belt, with her face shot up and her hair bloody, lying in the very middle of a room that was the essence of neatness and order.

An ugly picture. A hard one to forget and a hard one to think about.

But I managed to think about something else, finally. I managed to think about my sister, whose name is Kaye. A very nice person, my sister. A lovely woman. A sweet woman.

I thought about her for a few minutes. Then I thought about her husband. His name is Jack Enright.

2

He had leaned on my doorbell around three that afternoon. I had been doing the Times crossword puzzle. I stopped trying to think of a twelve-letter word for 'Son of Jocasta,' put down the paper and went to answer the door. I pushed the buzzer to unlock the downstairs door, then waited in the hallway while he worked his way up a flight of stairs. He climbed quickly and he was panting before he hit the top.

Jack Enright. My sister's husband. A tall man, forty-two or forty-three, with a reddish complexion and a little too much weight on a broad frame. A good handball player and a fair hand at squash, even though he didn't look the part. Now he didn't look the part at all.

His shoulders sagged like an antique mattress. His face was drawn, his eyes hollow. His tie was loose and his jacket was unbuttoned. He looked like hell.

He said: 'I have to talk to you, Ed.'

'Something the matter?'

'Everything. I have to talk to you. I'm in trouble.'

I motioned him inside. He followed me into the living room like a domesticated zombie. I found a chair for him and he sat down heavily in it.

'Go ahead,' I said. 'What's up?'

'Ed . . .'

He said my name and let it hang there. He didn't even manage to close his mouth. I found a bottle of cognac and poured three fingers of it into an Old Fashioned glass. I gave it to him and he looked at it vacantly. I don't think he saw it.

'Drink, it Jack.'

'It's not four o'clock,' he said stupidly. 'A gentleman never drinks before four o'clock. And it's—'

'It's four o'clock somewhere,' I told him. 'Go ahead and drink it, Jack.'

He emptied the glass in a single swallow and I'm sure he never tasted it at all. Then he put down the glass and looked at me through empty eyes.

'Is something wrong with Kaye?'

'Why?'

I shrugged. 'She's your wife and my sister. Why else would you come to me?'

'Kaye's fine,' he said. 'There's nothing wrong with Kaye.'

I waited.

'I'm the one who needs some help, Ed. Badly.'

'Want to tell me about it?'

He looked away. 'I suppose so,' he said. 'I don't even know where to begin.'

The drink was helping but it had its work cut out for it. It unnerved me to see a steady guy like Jack Enright that badly shaken up. He's a doctor – a very good one – a very successful one. He's got a wife who loves him and two daughters who adore him. I'd always thought of him as a strong man, a Rock-of-Gibraltar type, for my not-too-strong sister to lean on. Now he was ready to fall apart at the seams.

'Let's have it, Jack.'

He said: 'You've got to help me.'

'I have to hear about it first.'

He sighed, nodded, reached for a cigarette. His hands were shaking but he managed to get it lit. He drew a lot of smoke into his lungs and blew it out in a long thin column. I watched his eyes narrow to focus on the end of the cigarette.

'Fifty-first Street,' he said. '111 East Fifty-first Street. An apartment on the fourth floor.'

I waited.

'There's a girl in there, Ed. A dead girl. Somebody shot her in the . . . in the face. At close range, I think. Most of her . . . most of her face is missing. Blown off.'

He shuddered.

'You didn't—'

'No!' His eyes screamed at me. 'No, of course not. I didn't kill her. That's what you were going to ask, isn't it?'

'I suppose so. Why the hell else would you be so jumpy? You're a doctor. You've seen death before.'

'Not like this.'

I picked up my pipe and crammed tobacco into the bowl. I took my time lighting up while he got ready to talk some more. By the time the pipe was lit he was off again.

'I didn't kill her, Ed. I discovered the body. It was . . . a shock. Opening the door. Walking inside. Looking around, not seeing her at first. She was on the floor, Ed. How often do you look at the floor when you walk into a room. I almost . . . almost fell on her. I looked down and there she was. She was lying on her back. I looked at her and saw her and she had a hole where her face was supposed to be.'

I poured more brandy into his glass. He looked at it for a second or two. Then he tossed it off.

'You called the police?'

'I couldn't.'

I looked hard at him. 'All right,' I said evenly. 'You can stumble around for the next half hour and it won't do either of us any good. Get to the point, Jack.'

He looked at the rug. It's a Bokhara, a much better oriental than the length of rug in the hallway. But Jack Enright isn't especially interested in oriental rugs.

He found this one fascinating now.

'Who was she?'

'Sheila Kane.'

'And—?'

'And I've been paying her rent for the past three months now,' he said. He was still looking at the rug. His voice was steady, the tone slightly defiant. 'I've been paying her rent, and I've been buying her clothes and I've been giving her spending money. I've been keeping her, Ed. And now she's dead.'

He stopped talking. We both sat there and listened to the silence.

He laughed. His laughter had no humor to it. 'It happens to other men,' he said. 'You've got a perfectly good marriage; you love your wife and she loves you. Then you listen to the song of the sirens. You meet a beautiful blonde. Why are they always blondes, Ed?'

'Sheila Kane was a blonde?'

'Sort of a dirty blonde originally. She tinted it. Her hair was all yellow-gold. She wore it long and it would cascade over her bare shoulders and—'

He stopped for another sigh. 'I didn't kill her, Ed. God, I couldn't kill anybody. I'm not a killer. And I don't even own a damn gun. But I can't call the police. Christ, you know what would happen. They'd have me on the carpet for hours with the bright lights in my eyes and the questions coming over and over. They'd work me six ways and backwards. They'd rake me over the coals.'

'And then they'd let you go.'

'And so would Kaye.' His eyes turned meek, helpless. 'Your sister's a wonderful woman, Ed. I love her. I don't want to lose her.'

'If you love her so much—'

'Then why did I play around? I don't know, Ed. God knows I don't make a habit of it.'

'Did you love this Sheila?'

'No. Yes. Maybe . . . I don't know.'

That was a big help. 'How did it start?'

He hung his head. 'I don't know that either. It just happened, damn it. She came to my office one day. Just wandered in off the street, picked my name out of the yellow pages. She thought she was pregnant, wanted me to examine her.'

'Was she?'

'No. She'd missed a period or two and she was worried. Hell, it happens all the time. Just worrying can make a girl miss. I gave her an examination

11

and told her she was all right. She wanted to be sure, asked me to run a test. I took a urine sample and told her I'd run it through the lab and give her a call. She said she didn't have a phone, she'd be back in two days.'

'And?'

'And that was that. For the time being, anyway. The test went to the lab. It was negative, of course. She wasn't pregnant. That's what I told her when she came back.'

I told him it was a funny way to start an affair.

'I suppose so,' he said. He was getting steadier now, pulling himself back together again. It seemed to me that his adultery was nagging him more than the simple fact of the girl's death. Now that it was out in the open, now that he'd let his hair down in front of me, he could start to relax a little.

'She was broke, Ed. Couldn't pay me. I told her the hell with it, she could pay me when she got the chance. Or not at all. I've got a rich practice. East Side clientele. I can afford to miss out on an occasional fifteen-dollar fee. But she seemed so bothered about it that I felt sorry for her. I took her to a decent restaurant and bought her a lunch. She was a kid in a candy store, Ed. She said she'd been eating all her meals in cafeterias.'

I grimaced appropriately.

'So that's how it started, Ed. Silly, isn't it? Affairs aren't supposed to start with a pelvic examination.'

'They can end with one,' I suggested.

He didn't laugh. 'I guess I was just in the right mood for it, if you know what I mean. I was in a rut. The girls are growing up, Kaye has her women's groups, my practice is so safe and secure that it's duller than dishwater. I've got a good life and a good marriage and that's that. So I decided I was missing something. Why do men climb mountains? Because they're there. That's the way I heard it.'

'And that's why you climbed Sheila Kane?'

'Just about.' He lit another cigarette while I knocked the dottle out of my pipe. 'I was a different person when I was with her, Ed. I was young and fresh and alive. I wasn't the old man in a rut. Hell, she had me pegged as some sort of romantic figure. I took her to a matinee or two on Broadway. I gave her books to read and records to listen to. This made me a God.'

He drew on the cigarette. 'It's nice, being a God. Your sister sees me as I am. That's the way a marriage has to be – firm understanding, genuine acceptance, all of that. But . . . oh, the hell with it. I'm a damned fool, Ed.'

'You went with her for three months. Then what happened?'

He looked at me.

'Did she start angling for marriage?'

'Oh,' he said. 'No, nothing like that. I was cold-blooded about it, Ed. I made up my mind that one word from her about marriage would mean it was time to walk out on her. You've got to understand that – I never stopped loving Kaye, never thought about a divorce. But Sheila was the perfect paramour, happy to sit in the shade and be there when I wanted her. It was almost terrifying, having that kind of hold over a person.'

I nodded. 'And now she's dead.'

'Now she's dead.' He made the word sound colder than dry ice.

'And you won't call the police.'

'Ed . . .'

'Anonymously,' I suggested. 'So they can look for the killer.'

He was shaking his head so hard I thought he'd lose it. 'I paid her rent,' he said. 'I gave her checks; I spent plenty of time up at her apartment. Her neighbors would remember me and her landlord would recognize my name.'

He was sweating now. He wiped sweat from his forehead with one hand. His eyes were angry and frightened at once.

'So the police will find me, Ed. They'll find me and they'll drag me in. And then they'll be sure I did it. That I killed her, that I found a gun somewhere and got rid of it somewhere. Isn't that what they'll say?'

'Probably.'

'And Kaye will find out,' he finished. 'And you know what that will do to her.'

I knew damn well what it would do to her. The marriage that seemed like a rut to Jack was Kaye's whole life. She lived in a sweet little world where the sun was always shining, where charge accounts bloomed on every bush, where the worst peril was going down two doubled in an afternoon bridge session. Where her husband loved her, and loved her faithfully, and where God was in his heaven and all was right with the world.

'What do I do, Ed?'

'Let's turn that one around. What am I supposed to do for you, Jack?'

'Help me.'

'How?'

He avoided my eyes. 'Suppose I were a client,' he said. 'Suppose I came to you and—'

'I'd throw you out on your ear. Or call the cops. Or both.'

'But I'm not a client. I'm you're brother-in-law.'

He went on talking but I wasn't listening any more. Hell, if he was a client I had no problems. I turned him in and avoided being an accessory after the fact to murder. Because if I didn't know him, if he weren't my brother-in-law, I would have to figure him for the killer. He didn't have a gun? A hundred dollars buys you an unregistered gun in half the pawnshops in New York. On every street corner there's a sewer to toss it into when you're done with it. So he didn't have much of a case at all. A good prosecutor would tie him in Gordian knots.

'She can't be found at the apartment,' I said slowly. 'Or they'll connect the two of you. That's how it boils down.'

He blinked, then nodded.

'Which means they can't identify her at all,' I went on. 'If they do, they trace her to the apartment. Then they trace her to you, all of which makes things difficult. Was she from New York?'

He shook his head.

'Know many people in town?'

'Hardly anybody. But . . .'

'Go on.'

'I was just going to say that I wasn't with her all the time. She could have had some other interests. We didn't talk much about the time we spent apart.'

I didn't say anything.

'I don't know, Ed. I think she was trying to get into the theater. She never had a part, never talked about it. But I got the idea somewhere. She might know . . . might have known some theater people.'

I said it was possible. 'Still, the police would have a tough time making a positive identification. Not if she didn't wind up in her own apartment. Her fingerprints probably aren't on file anywhere. If she were found, say, in Central Park, she'd go as an unidentified victim. They might never find out her name, let alone yours. At any rate it would give you time to stall. Your checks would clear the bank and the landlord would forget your name.'

'And the real killer—'

'Would go scot free,' I finished for him. 'Not necessarily. In the first place, you're the real killer. No, hold on – I know you didn't do it. But the police would stop looking once they hit you. They'd have enough circumstantial evidence to get an indictment without looking any farther. Meanwhile, the killer would cover his tracks.'

I paused for breath. 'This way they won't have you on hand as a convenient dummy. They'll have to start from scratch and they just might come up with the real killer.'

He brightened visibly.

'That's not all. I'll know things they won't know. I'll be able to run my own check on Sheila Kane. Maybe somebody had a damn good reason to shoot a hole in her head. I can look around, see what I can find out.'

'Do you think—'

'I don't think much of anything, to tell you the truth. I don't want your marriage to fall in. I don't want Kaye to get hurt and I don't want to see you tried for murder. So it looks as though I'll have to move a body for you.'

He got up from the chair and started to pace the floor. I watched him ball one hand into a fist and smack it into the palm of the other hand. He was still a collection of loose nerves but they were starting to tighten up again.

I looked at him and tried to hate him. He married my sister and cheated on her and that ought to be cause for hatred. It didn't work out that way. You can't coin an ersatz double standard and apply it to brothers-in-law. He fell on his face for a pretty blonde; hell, I'd taken a few falls for the same type of thing myself. He was married and I wasn't, but the state of matrimony doesn't alter body chemistry. He was a guy in a jam and I had to help him.

'Can I do anything, Ed?'

I shook my head. 'I'll do it alone,' I told him. 'Not now. Later this evening when it's dark and the streets are empty. It's chancey but I'll take the chance. I'll need a key, if you've got one handy.'

He fished in a pocket and came up with a set of keys. I took them from him and set them on the coffee table.

'Go on home,' I said. 'Try to relax.'

He nodded but I don't think he heard me. 'The hard part comes later,' he said. 'When I realize that she's really dead. Now she's part of a mess that I've gotten myself into. But in a few hours she'll turn back into a person. A person I knew well and cared a great deal about. And then it's going to be tough. I'll think about you picking her body up like a sack of flour and dumping her in the park and ... I'm sorry. I'm going on and on like a damned fool.'

I didn't say anything.

'This'll sound silly as hell, Ed. But ... be gentle with her, will you? She was a very nice person. You would have liked her, I think.'

'Jack ...'

He brushed my hand away. 'Hell with it,' he said. 'I'm all right. Look, give me a ring tomorrow at the office if you get the chance. And be careful.'

I walked him to the door. Then I went to the front window and watched him walk a few doors down the block to his big black Buick. He sat in it for a moment, then started the motor and drove away. I looked up at the clouds and watched them get darker.

The cognac was gone. I filled the glass again and listened to words that went through my mind. 'Be gentle with her, will you?' Gentle. Roll her gently in a rug and toss her gently in a car and drop her gently in the wet grass. And leave her there.

It was a mess. A private detective doesn't solve a crime by suppressing evidence. He doesn't launch a murder investigation by transporting a body illegally. Instead he plays ball with the police, keeps his nose clean and collects his fees. That way he can pay too much rent for a floor-through apartment loaded with heavy furniture and Victorian charm. He can drive a convertible and smoke expensive tobacco and drink expensive cognac.

I like my apartment and my car and my tobacco and my cognac. So I make a point of playing ball with cops and keeping a clean nose.

Most of the time.

But now I had a brother-in-law instead of a client and a mess instead of a case. That shot the rule book out the window. It gave me a dirty nose.

I looked at my watch. It was four in the morning. And at four a gentleman can drink. It's nice to be a gentleman. It puts you at peace with the world. And, although my glass was empty, there was plenty of cognac left in the bottle.

When it was empty I went to sleep.

3

Dawn was a gray lady with red eyes and a cigarette cough. She shook me awake by the eyelids and hauled me out of bed. I called her nasty names, stumbled into the kitchen to boil water for coffee. I washed up, brushed my teeth and shaved. I spooned instant coffee into a cup and poured boiling water over it, then lit a cigarette and tried to convince myself that I was really awake.

It was a hard selling-job. My mind was overflowing with blondes and they were all dead. There was a blonde with her face shot away, another blonde in stockings and garter belt in a surrealistic living room, a third blonde bundled snug as a corpse in a rug, a fourth blonde sprawled headlong in Central Park's wet grass.

I scalded my mouth with coffee, anesthetized it with cigarette smoke. It was time to start turning over flat rocks to find a killer and I didn't know where the rocks were. Sheila Kane was dead and I had been her undertaker, but that was all I knew about the girl. She was blonde, she was dead, she had been Jack Enright's mistress. Nothing more.

So Jack was the logical place to start. There were things I had to know and he could fill me in. I wondered how much he had left out, how much he had lied, how much he had forgotten.

And how much he had never known in the first place.

I turned the burner on under the water and dumped more instant coffee into the cup. The water boiled and I made more coffee. I was stirring it when the phone rang.

It was Jack.

'Did you—?'

'Everything's all right,' I told him. 'You can relax now. It's all taken care of.'

His breath came like a tire blowing out. His words followed it just as fast. 'I don't know how to thank you, Ed. You sure as hell saved my bacon. We'll have to get together . . .'

'That's an understatement.'

He hesitated and I knew why. In the Age of the Wiretap the telephone's an instrument of torture. It's like talking with an extra person in the room. I looked around for a better way to phrase things.

'I've been having trouble with my back,' I said. 'Been planning to drop by. Think you can fit me in sometime this afternoon?'

'Just a minute.'

I waited. He came back, his tone easy, his manner professional now. 'I'm all booked up but I can squeeze you in, Ed. Make it around two-thirty. Good enough?'

I looked at the clock. It was a few minutes after ten. I'd be seeing him in four and a half hours.

'Fine,' I said. 'I'll see you then. Take it easy, Jack.'

He told me he would, mumbled something pleasant, and rang off. I stood there for a second or two with the phone in my hand, looking at the receiver and waiting for it to start talking all by itself.

Then I cradled it and went back to my coffee.

The *Times* had what story there was but you had to look hard to find it. In New York they don't stick an unidentified corpse on the front page. There are too many bodies floating around for them to do that. The tabloids might have found room for Sheila on page three or four, but the *Times* was too high-minded. They printed the full texts of speeches by Khrushchev and Castro and Adenauer and my blonde didn't even make the first section. I found her on the second page from the end under two decks of sedate eighteen-point type.

GIRL FOUND DEAD
IN CENTRAL PARK

It went on from there, straight and cold and to the point. The body of a young woman in her late teens or early twenties had been found partially nude and shot to death on the eastern edge of Central Park near 91st Street. A preliminary medical examination disclosed that the girl had not been sexually attacked and that the fatal shot had been fired at relatively close range. The slug had not been recovered, but police guessed it had come from a .32 or .38-calibre handgun. Police theorized the victim had been killed elsewhere and then transported to the park, where she was found by a night laborer on his way home from work.

There were a few more lines but they didn't have anything vital to say. I killed time thumbing through the rest of the paper, reading the world news and the national news and the local news, filling myself with vital information. Asian cholera was at epidemic strength in northern India. Reform Democrats were pushing for the over-throw of Tammany Hall. A military junta had ousted the government of El Salvador; Jersey Standard was off an eighth of a point; Telephone was up three-eighths, Polaroid down five and a half. An obscure play by Strindberg had been exhumed for presentation off-Broadway and the critics had cremated it.

At ten-thirty I folded the paper and stuck it in a wastebasket. I took a shower and got dressed. This made me officially awake, so I filled a pipe with tobacco and lit it.

And the phone rang.

I picked up the receiver and said hello to the mouth-piece. That was all I had a chance to say. The voice that bounced back at me was low and raspy. It was thick heavy New York with echoes of Brownsville or Mulberry Street beneath it.

'This London? Listen good. You got the stuff and we want it. We're not playing games.'

I asked him what the hell he was talking about.

His laugh was short and unpleasant. 'Play it anyway you want, London. I know where you been and what you picked up. If you got a price, fine. It's reasonable and we pay it.'

'Who is this, anyway?'

No laughter this time. 'Don't play hard to get, London. You got a reputation as a smart boy so be smart. You're just a private eye, smart or stupid. You're on your own. We got an organization. We can find things out and we can get things done. We know you were at the broad's apartment. We know you picked her up and dumped her. Jesus, you think you're playing tag with amateurs? We can go hard or soft, baby. You don't want to be too cute. You can get paid nice or you can get hit in the head. Anyway you want it, it's up to you.'

'What do I get if I sell?'

'More than you get anywhere else.' He chuckled. 'We can hand you a better deal. We got—'

'An organization,' I said, tired of the game. 'I know all about it. You told me.'

He toughened up. 'We hit the broad,' he said, his voice grating. 'We can hit you the same way. It gets messy. You might as well be smart about it.'

'Go to hell.'

'We'll be in touch, London. You know how they say it: Don't call us, we'll call you.'

The phone clicked in my ear.

I was getting pretty damned sick of holding a dead phone in my hand. I put it down hard, stuck my pipe in my mouth. It had gone dead. I scratched a match for it and found a chair to sit in.

Things were taking their own kind of shape. I had to know a motive and I had to know a killer, and in a cockeyed way I now knew both. The motive was whatever my mystery man wanted me to hand over to him. The killer was my mystery man. All I had to do was fill in the blanks.

What the hell was the stuff? Something worth money, but something you needed the right connections to handle properly. It could be dope or it could be spy secrets or it could be blackmail information or it could be . . .

To hell with it. It could be anything.

There was no way to get a line on the package, no way to figure out why

Sheila Kane had a hole in her head. There was no way to dope out the name and face that went with the raspy voice I'd talked to, no way to figure out how he'd connected me with Sheila. I might get something from Enright, but I wasn't seeing him until two-thirty and I had a few hours to kill. The only open avenue of approach was Sheila herself . . . what had Jack told me about her?

Damned little. She wasn't from New York, and if she knew a soul in town Jack didn't know about it. But she might have had something to do with the theater. Maybe.

And that much would fit in with the young-and-almost-innocent small-town girl on the loose in the big city. That type is drawn to the grease paint circuit like moths to a flame.

Not Broadway, not the way I saw it. Not the bright lights and the high-priced tickets. Sheila would have been more likely to have made her small inroads on the off-Broadway scene, where Equity minimum is a hot $45 a week and the ars comes gratis artist.

Which meant I should call Maddy Parson.

I had to look her number up in my notebook – it had been a long time. Then I picked up the damned phone again and dialed a Chelsea number. While the phone rang three times I thought about Madeleine Parson, a small and slender brunette with the kind of oval face and long neck that Modigliani would have loved to paint. Not a pretty girl by Hollywood's silly standards. A very beautiful one by mine.

An actress. An undiscovered thing who earned her forty-five bucks a week when she was lucky enough to catch a part and who prayed that whatever turkey she was in would run twenty weeks to put her in line for unemployment insurance when it finally gave up the ghost and folded. A girl who loved the theater with a capital T; a girl who waited for the one big break and who had fun while she waited. Not a Bohemian; not a fraud. An actress.

She answered midway through the fourth ring. Her hello was heartbreak-ingly hopeful.

'Relax,' I told her. 'Not an agent, not a producer, not a director. Just a dilettante.'

'Ed! Ed London!' She sounded delighted. But that's the trouble with theater people. They're on stage twenty-four hours a day. It's hard to tell what's real.

'Are you working these days, Maddy?'

'Are you dreaming, Ed? I've had nibbles. Grinnell was going to cast me for the Agatha part in *A Sound of Distant Drums* but the angel decided that oil stocks looked better than off-Broadway ventures. Then I ran second in the last three auditions. But they don't pay off for second place.'

'Then you're free tonight?'

'As the air we breathe. Why?'

'I'd like to see you. I'll buy you a dinner and we'll talk far into the night. Sound good?'.

'Sounds too good,' she said. 'So good there's a catch in it somewhere. Is this purely pleasure or is there some business on the agenda?'

I found myself smiling. 'A little business, Maddy. We'll play questions and answers.'

'I thought we would.'

'No good?'

I could see her faking a pout into the telephone. 'Well,' she said, 'I'd like to think you want to see me for my charm and beauty alone. But I don't really mind. I'll make you pay dearly for my company, sirrah. I'll force you to buy me a very expensive steak with at least two cocktails beforehand. To teach you a lesson.'

'It's deductible. Seven o'clock all right?'

'I'll be too hungry by then. Make it six-thirty?'

We made it six-thirty. I told her I'd pick her up, then hung up and got out of the apartment. All that talk about steak had me hungry. I went down the block for a belated breakfast.

The air was warm outside and the waitress at the little restaurant was cheerful. I had shirred eggs and chicken livers with two cups of coffee. Real coffee, not instant. It was so good I almost forgot about the dead girl I'd dropped in Central Park and the raspy-voiced man who wanted to kill me.

Jack Enright's office was on Park Avenue at the corner of Eighty-eighth. A towering brick building. The liveried doorman opened my cab door, then hurried to yank open the building door for me. I walked straight to Jack's office on the first floor in the rear. I knew the way.

The receptionist looked as though someone had starched her to match her bright white uniform. She smiled at me without showing a single tooth and asked me who I was. I told her.

She repeated my name twice to commit it to memory. Then she got up from a blonde free-form desk and vanished through a heavy windowless door. I stood by her desk and studied the glut of patients waiting for the doctor. A sallow little man squinted through bifocals at the *New Yorker*. Appropriately, a pregnant young woman had her nose buried in *Parent's Magazine*. Four or five others sat around in the overstuffed chairs and stared at each other and at me. Their stares were pure envy when the woman in white came back and announced that the great man would see me.

I went through the door she pointed at, walked down a little hallway to Jack's private office. He was sitting behind a massive leather-topped wooden desk. Bookshelves which held medical texts and a smattering of classics lined the walls. There was a set of Trollope bound in morocco and a good Dickens in buckram.

A chair waited for me at the side of the desk. A pony of brandy was on the desk-top in front of the chair.

He said: 'Courvoisier. Is it all right?'

It was more than all right. I took a sip and felt the taste buds on my tongue enjoying themselves.

'Well?'

I set down the glass and shrugged. 'You're pretty well out of it,' I said. 'For the time being they've got nothing to tie you in.'

'Thank God.'

'But not completely out of it. As long as the killer's free, there's a chance that you'll get dragged into the picture. The police won't let go of it for awhile. The papers are playing with it. I saw a copy of the *Post* on the way over. The early edition. A sex angle, a pretty girl, a shooting-and-dumping. It makes nice copy.'

He nodded. 'And you're going to look for the murderer?'

'I have to.' I started to tell him I'd spoken to the killer, then changed my mind. 'I came here to ask you some questions, Jack. I need a lot of answers.'

'What do you want to know?'

'Everything you know. Everything, whether it seems important to you or not. People she knew, places she went to, anything she ever mentioned or did that'll give me a place to start digging. Whatever it is, I want to know about it.'

I fished a pipe out of one pocket and a tobacco pouch from another. While I filled and lit the pipe he sat at his desk and thought. He ran the fingers of one hand through his dark hair. He drummed the leather desk-top with the fingers of the other hand. I shook out my match and dropped it into a heavy brass ashtray. He looked down at the match, then back at me.

'There's not a hell of a lot to tell, Ed. I've been trying to figure out how I could have been so damned close to a girl and know so little about her. She was from some little town in the sticks. Pennsylvania, I think. Maybe Ohio. I don't remember. She never mentioned her parents. If she had any brothers or sisters I never heard about them.'

'Anything about the town?'

'Not a thing. That's how it went, Ed . . . when she was with me she was a girl without a past. She acted as if . . . as if she hadn't existed until we met.'

I looked at him. 'Isn't that a little romantic?'

'You know what I mean. She never mentioned anything that happened before we started our . . . affair. Here's an example – she came to me thinking she was pregnant. But she never mentioned any other man, or that there had been other men. Sometimes I felt I was only seeing a small part of her.'

'The part she wanted you to see?'

'Maybe. She was like an iceberg. I saw the part above the water line.'

I drew on the pipe, sipped more of the cognac. 'Then let's forget her past,' I said. 'She's what you said. A girl without a past.'

'And without a future. Ed—'

He was loosening up. 'Steady,' I said. 'Let's take it from another angle. She must have had some friends in town, a guy or a girl she saw when you weren't around. And she couldn't have spent twenty-four hours a day in the apartment.'

'You're probably right, but—'

'You mentioned something about show business. Was she looking for a part in a play? Hungry for bright lights?'

'I don't think so.' He paused. 'It was just an impression I got, Ed. Something in the way she talked and acted. Nothing concrete, nothing you could put your finger on. Just a vague notion, that's all.'

'Then she didn't talk about it?'

'Not directly.'

I was getting tired of it. 'Damn it, what in hell did you talk about? You didn't discuss past or present or future. You didn't talk about her friends or her family or anything at all. Did you spend every damn minute in the hay?'

His mouth fell open and his face turned redder than blood. He looked as though he'd been kicked in the stomach.

'I'm sorry,' I said honestly. 'It came out wrong.'

He nodded very slowly. 'We talked,' he said. 'We talked about art and literature and the state of the universe. We had deep philosophical discussions that would have fit in perfectly in a Village coffee house. I could tell you a lot about her, Ed. She's an interesting person. Was an interesting person. It's hard to keep the tenses straight, hard to remember that she's dead.'

He got up and came out from behind the desk. He started walking around the office, clenching and unclenching his fingers, pacing like a lion in a tiny cage. I didn't say anything.

'She preferred Brahms to Wagner and Mozart to Haydn. She didn't like stereo because you have to sit in one spot to listen to it and she likes – liked – to move around. She wasn't religious exactly but she believed in God. A vague God who created the universe and then let it run by itself. She preferred long novels to short ones because once she got interested in a set of characters she wanted to spend some time with them.'

He put out one cigarette and lit another. 'She liked the color red,' he went on. 'One time I bought her a loud red-plaid bathrobe and she loved to lounge around the apartment in it. She liked good food – she was a hopeless cook but she liked to fool around in the kitchen. One night she broiled steaks for the two of us and we opened a bottle of '57 Beaujolais and ate by candlelight. I can tell you a million things like that, Ed. Nothing about her past, nothing about what she did or who she did it with. But I could fill volumes with the sort of person she was.'

There was nothing to say because he couldn't have heard me. He was wrapped up in memories of a girl he would never see again, a girl he had loved. I wondered how he could be the kind of person he was, able to turn emotions on and off so easily. From Devoted Husband to Ardent Lover in nothing flat, and back again. He said he loved Kaye and I believed him. And I believed he loved Sheila.

'Let's try another angle,' I suggested. 'I know you don't want to hash over it. But let's go back to the apartment. Yesterday, when you found the body.'

'She was dead.' His voice was empty. 'That's all ... she was dead.'

'I mean—'

A long sigh. 'I know what you mean. Hell, what's the point? You saw everything I saw. You were there, weren't you? What more is there to say?'

'We saw it through different eyes. You may have caught something that I missed.'

'I don't think so. I didn't see much of anything, Ed. Just her, dead. Everything was a mess and she was in the middle of it. I looked at the apartment and wondered what cyclone had hit it. I looked at her and I felt sick. I ran like a bat out of hell and went straight to you and ... what's the matter?'

'The apartment,' I snapped at him. 'You said it was messy.'

He looked at me strangely. 'Sure,' he said. 'Hell, you saw it. Chairs knocked over, papers all over the floor – either she put up a fight or the bastard who killed her turned the place upside-down. You must have ... what's wrong? Why are you staring like that?'

4

I told him why I was staring at him. I told him just how the apartment had looked, just how neat it had been. I watched him while I talked. His eyes were open wide and his mouth was open wider. My description of neatness was as jarring to him as his talk of disorder was to me.

'God,' he said finally. 'Then you didn't strip her.'

I just looked at him.

'In the papers,' he said. 'I read that she was . . . half-naked when they found her. I thought you stripped her to keep them from identifying her from her clothes.'

'I didn't have to. She wasn't wearing any.'

He shook his head. 'She was fully dressed when I found her, Ed. A sweater and a skirt, I think. I don't remember too well, my mind was swimming all over the place. But I would have remembered if she had been naked, wouldn't I?'

'It's a hard sight to forget.'

'That's what I mean. When I read the paper . . . but I couldn't believe you stripped her, not really. I didn't think you would do something like that. It's sort of sacrilegious, taking the clothes from a dead body.' He paused for breath. 'Then I thought some sex fiend found her in the park before the police got there. Or that the papers were trying to make livelier copy out of it. Hell, I wasn't sure what to think. But if she was nude when you found her—'

I finished the sentence for him. 'Then somebody got there after you left and before I arrived. That's what happened. Some clown cleaned her apartment from floor to ceiling, took off her clothes and sneaked off into the night.'

'But why?'

I couldn't answer that one.

'It's senseless,' he exploded. 'Nothing makes any sense. Killing Sheila didn't make any sense and neither does any of the rest of it. It's crazy.'

He looked ready to blow up. I said: 'Physician, heal thyself,' and pointed to the bottle of Courvoisier. He poured us each a shot of brandy and we drank it.

I got out of there as fast as I could, but first I made him give me the only picture he had of the dead girl. I wanted to show it to Maddy. I put it in my wallet, said something cheerful to him, and left him to his patients.

The sallow little man peered myopically at me over his *New Yorker*, the expectant mother put her magazine on her ample belly, and all of them looked happy as hell to see me. I said good-bye to the starched receptionist and walked out of the building.

The sun was shining and the air was clear and clean enough to breathe. I filled my lungs and headed for home. It was walking weather and I was glad – I was sick of sitting around waiting for things to happen. The walk gave me something to do, anyway. I winked at pretty girls and one or two of them even smiled back.

I didn't notice anybody following me. But that may have been because I didn't look.

Maybe I should have.

I didn't hear the bullet until it passed me.

I was in my building, on the way up the stairs. When I was a few steps from the landing there was a loud noise behind me. I was already falling on my face when the bullet buried itself in the wall. Plaster flew at my face.

Instinct said: Stay still, don't move. Instinct gave bad advice. Whoever he was, he was behind me and he was shooting at me and I made a hell of a good target.

But instinct's got a compelling voice. By the time I managed to spin around – it's tricky when you're on your hands and knees on a staircase – he was gone. A door closed behind him and I looked at nothing.

'Mr London?'

I looked up. Mrs Glendower was leaning a gray head over the railing. Her expression was mildly puzzled.

'That wasn't a gunshot, was it? Or didn't you hear the noise?'

I got straightened out on my feet and tried to look sheepish. 'Just a truck backfiring,' I told her.

'It frightened me, Mr London.'

I managed to grin. 'You're not the only one, Mrs Glendower. It startled me so badly I nearly fell over. I've been nervous lately.'

That was the perfect explanation as far as Mrs Glendower was concerned. She smiled vaguely and pleasantly. Then she went away.

I went into my apartment and had a shot of cognac, then I went back into the hallway and looked at the hole in the wall. When I sighted from the bullet hole to the doorway I knew the gunman hadn't been trying to kill me at all. The bullet was way out of line. He must have missed me by five feet.

He could have been a lousy shot. But he didn't even make a second try – just one shot and away he went.

So it was a warning. A little message from the guy on the phone, the one with the raspy voice.

Fine.

I found a can of spackling paste in a drawer and patched up the hole in the wall, giving the bullet a permanent home. I let the paste dry, which didn't take long, and dabbed a little paint over it. It wasn't a perfect match but I didn't figure everybody in the world was going to come staring at my wall.

Then I went back inside and sat down.

It was an algebraic equation with too many unknowns. X was the killer, the voice on the phone. He shot the girl, searched the apartment and ran. Then Jack came in, looked around and ran. Then somebody else came, rearranged things, stripped the girl and ran. Then I came, carted off the body – and now everything was happening.

It didn't add up. And, like an algebraic equation, it wouldn't add up. Not until I knew all the unknowns.

In the meantime I had nothing to do, no place to go. There was a bullet in the wall outside my door and it wasn't worth the trouble to dig it out. What the hell was it going to prove? It might be a .32 or .38 slug. So what? I couldn't find out anything one way or the other, not that way.

So to hell with it.

I took a book from the bookcase and sat down with it. I read three pages, looked up suddenly and realized I didn't remember a word that I'd read. I put the book back on the shelf and poured more cognac. Nothing was working out.

And I was tied in deep. Jack was clear – I'd seen to that, rushing around like a goddam hero. But I was hanging by my thumbs. The bastard who shot a hole in Sheila knew who I was and where I lived and I didn't know a thing about him. And he had some damn fool idea that I had a package that he wanted. I was supposed to sell it to him.

There was only one catch. I didn't have it. I didn't even know what the hell it was.

Which complicated things. Jack was free and clear – he could go back to his wife, back to my sister. He could pretend that everything was all right with the world.

I couldn't.

I put music on the hi-fi and tried to listen to it. I hauled out my wallet and found the picture of Sheila Kane that Jack had given me. It was just a snapshot, probably taken with a box camera. The background – trees and open space – was out of focus. But the background wasn't important when you saw the girl.

Her long blonde hair was caught up in a pony tail. Her head was thrown back, her eyes bright. She was laughing. She wore a bulky turtle-neck sweater and a loose plaid skirt and she looked like the queen of the homecoming game.

I studied the picture and remembered everything Jack Enright had told me about her. I tried to imagine the kind of girl she must have been, tried to mesh that image with the image I got from the photograph. I came up with a person.

Poor Sheila, I kept thinking. Poor, poor Sheila.

'Poor Ed.'

I looked across the table at Maddy Parson's pretty face. She was grinning at me over the brim of her second Daiquiri. Her eyes were sparkling. The two drinks had her high as a Chinese kite.

'Poor Ed,' she said again. 'You didn't know you'd get stuck for a dinner like this one. This is going to run you twenty dollars before we get out of here.'

'It's worth it.'

'I hope so,' she said. 'I hope you have some darn good questions to ask.'

'I hope you know the answers.'

We were at McGraw's on Forty-fifth near Third. There are girls who prefer the haute cuisine of French cookery; there are girls who will go anyplace to eat as long as it's fashionable; there are girls who like to sample out-of-the-way restaurants where not even the waiter can understand the menu. And there are still other girls – a few of them, anyhow – who like lean red meat and plenty of it with a big baked potato on the side. Maddy Parson belonged in the last group and that explains our presence at McGraw's.

McGraw's is a steakhouse. Which is a little like saying that the Grand Canyon is a hole in the ground. It's true enough but it doesn't tell the whole story. McGraw's is an institution.

The front window facing out on Forty-fifth Street opens on a cold room where hunks of steak hang and ripen. In the dining room the decor is unobtrusive nineteenth-century American male – heavy oak panelling, a thick wine-red carpet, massive leather chairs. They don't have a menu. All you do is tell your white-haired waiter how you want your sirloin and what you're drinking with it. If you don't order your meat rare he looks unhappy. We didn't disappoint the old gentleman.

'It's been a long time,' Madeleine Parson was saying. 'Almost too long. I don't know where to start talking.'

'Start with yourself.'

She rolled her eyes. 'An actor's lot is not a happy one. Nor is an actress'. I almost took a job, Ed. Can you imagine that? Not even a semi-theatrical job that lets you kid yourself along. All the girls do that. They sell tickets in a box office or follow a producer around and sharpen his pencils for him and think they're learning the business from the ground up. But I almost took a job selling hats. Can you imagine that? I thought to myself how easy it would be, just sell hats and earn a steady $72.50 a week before taxes and move up gradually, maybe be a buyer in time, and—'

She saw the expression on my face. Her eyes danced and she laughed. 'Then my agent called me and told me Schwerner was auditioning for *Love*

Among The Falling Stars and I stuffed my mental hats into a mental hat-box and went away singing. I didn't get the part. I read miserably and it wasn't right for me to begin with. But I forgot all about selling hats.'

'You'll get your break, Maddy.'

'Of course I will. And I'll need it, Ed. I came to New York ready to take Broadway by storm. I was the best damn actress in the country and it was only a question of time before the rest of the world figured it out for themselves. And I was lousy, Ed. I'm not too good even now. Hayes and Cornell have nothing to worry about.'

Her eyes were challenging. 'And suppose I don't get that damn break, Ed? Then what do I do? Sell hats?'

I shook my head. 'Meet some lucky guy and marry him. Live in a house and make babies. It's better than selling hats.'

'Uh-huh.' A smile that was not altogether happy spread slowly over her face. 'It's funny, Ed. I had an offer not long ago.'

'That's not funny. You should get lots of offers.'

'This one was different. He wasn't a jerk or a square or a Philistine. He was a hell of a nice guy. Thirty-six years old, associate editor at a properly respectable publishing house, with a yen to buy one of those wonderful stone houses in Bucks County and fill it with children. He was a good talker and a good listener and good in bed. God, I'm talking like a successful actress, telling one man what another one's like in bed. I hate me when I talk like that. But you know what I'm driving at, Ed. He was nice. I think you would have liked him – I know I did, and he wanted me to marry him.'

'But you didn't.'

'Nope.'

'How come?'

She closed her eyes. 'I thought about being married,' she said softly. 'And I thought about waking up every single morning with somebody else in bed with me. And I thought maybe one day I'd want to take a trip somewhere, or maybe I'd get sick of the house and want to live someplace else, or I'd meet some guy and get an itch to go out with him and find out what he was like. And I thought that I'd have to pass up all these things, and how it would be, being tied to one man and one home and one way of life that you live with until you die. So much freedom out the window, so much responsibility around your neck like the albatross in that poem everybody had to read in the tenth grade. And I thought, God, you'd have to love somebody a hell of a lot to put up with such a load of crap. And I just didn't love him that much. I loved him, but not enough.'

I didn't say anything. The oval face was a mask now. The eyes were opaque. A good actress can conceal emotions, just as she can portray them.

'So here I am,' she said. 'Free and white and twenty-seven. That's not so young any more, Ed. Pretty soon some other nice guy'll ask me to follow him to the nearest altar and I won't love him enough either and it won't be so important any more and I'll say yes. I'm a tragic figure, Ed. Too old to play games and too young to admit it. It's a hell of a thing.' She looked over her shoulder and smiled. 'Here come the steaks,' she said. 'Now we can stop talking.'

The steaks came and we stopped talking. Conversation is the wrong accompaniment to a meal at McGraw's. The meat has to be approached quietly, reverently. Talk comes later. We attacked the steaks like tigers. They were black with charcoal on the outside and raw in the middle and nothing ever tasted better.

Afterward she had Drambuie and I had cognac. I leaned forward to light her cigarette, then put the match to my pipe. I watched her draw the smoke deep into her lungs and let it escape slowly between slightly parted lips. She used very little lipstick. Her shade was a very dark red.

'What time is it, Ed?'

'A few minutes past nine.'

'God! That late?'

'I didn't pick you up until quarter of seven. It took us another fifteen minutes to get out of your apartment. We had to wait for a table. Two drinks before dinner, a leisurely meal—'

'The time flew.' She sighed. 'Well, I suppose it's time for the business side of things. You have questions to ask me, sir. Want to ask them here or go elsewhere?'

'Elsewhere sounds good,' I said. 'Where do you want to go?'

'Obviously a very exclusive and most expensive cafe in the east Fifties, of course. That's what I should suggest. But I'm going to be a considerate young lady and a forward wench at the same time. Let's go back to my apartment.'

'Fine.'

'After all,' she said, 'you've been there before.'

She lived in a third-floor loft on West Twenty-fourth just east of Eighth. Her building had been condemned years ago and it wasn't legal to live there, but Maddy and the landlord had taken care of all that. According to the lease, she used the loft to give acting lessons and didn't live there at all. The landlord paid the trustworthy firemen so much a month and everybody was happy. Maddy would go on living there until the building came down around her little ears.

A rusty machine shop took up the ground floor of the old brick building. An ancient palmist and crystal-gazer named Madame Sindra held court on the second floor. We climbed to the third floor on an unlit and shaky wooden staircase. I stood by while Maddy unlocked the door.

The apartment inside looked as though it belonged in a different building in a different part of town. The living room was huge, with a false fireplace along one wall and a massive studio couch on the other. All the furniture was expensive-looking, but Maddy had picked it up, a little at a time, at the University Place auction houses and she made a few dollars go a long way.

There were a few bookcases, all of them crammed with paperbacks and covered with Moselle bottles topped with candle-drippings.

Now she waved small hands at everything. 'Be it ever so affected, there's no place like home. Sit down, Ed. Relax. I don't have a thing to drink, but relax anyway.'

I sat down on the couch. She kicked off her shoes and curled up next to me with her legs tucked neatly under her pretty little behind. 'Now,' she said. 'Fire away, Mr London, sir. Be a devastatingly direct detective and detect like mad. I'll oblige with all my heart.'

I took Sheila's picture from my wallet. I looked at it and she peered over my shoulder.

'Who's she?'

'Her name's Sheila Kane. Does it ring a bell?'

'I don't think so. Should it?'

'Just a hunch,' I said. 'Somebody thought she might be a show biz nut one way or another.'

'An actress?'

'Maybe. Or some outsider in the theatrical in-group. Or the guy who told me this has rocks in his head, which isn't impossible. I had an idea you might have run into her somewhere.'

'The name doesn't sound familiar.' She tossed her head. 'But then one meets so many exciting people in this mad and wonderful life—'

I laughed. 'Give it a good look,' I suggested. 'You might have met her without an introduction. Make sure.'

She craned her neck to look more closely over my shoulder and her soft black hair brushed my face. I could smell the sweetness of her. She wore no perfume, only the healthy vibrance of a well-scrubbed young woman. Which was enough.

'No pony tail,' she said suddenly. 'Her hair loose and flowing. And this must have been taken awhile ago, if it's the same gal. She didn't look so damned Betty Co-ed when I saw her. And her name wasn't Sheila Kane.'

'Are you sure?'

'Almost. Gosh, you're excited, aren't you? It's nice to see a real detective in action.'

I growled at her. 'Talk.'

'Not much to talk about.' She shrugged her pretty shoulders. 'I don't know much. I met her only once and that was about . . . oh, say six or seven weeks ago. I could find out the exact date easily enough. It was the night *Hungry Wedding* opened. Did you see it?'

I hadn't.

'You didn't have much chance. It closed after five performances, to the surprise of practically no one and to the delight of many. It was a gold-plated turkey.'

'You weren't in it, were you?'

'No such luck. That's usually the kind of show I wind up in, the type that fights to last a week. But I missed this one. Anyway, I was tight with a few kids in the cast and I got an invite to the cast party. It was sort of a wake. Everybody in the show knew they were going to get a roasting. But no actor passes up a party with free drinks. We all got quietly loaded.'

'And Sheila Kane was there?'

'With one of the angels,' she said. 'She wasn't an actress. She waltzed in on the arm of a very grim-looking man with a cigar in his mouth. His name was Clay and her name was Alicia and that's all I found out about either of them. I didn't particularly want to know more, to tell you the truth. He looked like a Hollywood heavy and she looked like Whore Row Goes To College and I just wasn't interested.'

'Clay—'

'Clay and Alicia, and don't ask me her last name or his first name. I don't know how much money he wasted on the show but he didn't seem to give a damn. He smoked his cigars and nursed one glass of sour red wine and ignored everybody. She spent her time watching everybody very carefully. Like a rich tourist taking a walk on the Bowery, curious about everything but careful not to get her precious hands dirty. I took an instant dislike to her. I suppose it was bitchy of me but that's the way I am. I make quick judgments. I didn't like her at all.'

'Anyone else with either of them?'

'Not that I noticed. And no, I don't remember who the other backers were. Lee Brougham produced the play – he could tell you who put up the money, I suppose. Unless he thought you were trying to steal his angels for a dog of your own. But he'll be tough to find. I heard he went to the coast. You can't blame him after *Hungry Wedding*. A genuinely terrible play. An abortion.'

She didn't have anything more to tell me. She hadn't seen the girl again, never heard anything more about her. I tried to fit the new picture with what I knew about Sheila Kane. Now her name was Alicia, and she sounded a little less like Jack Enright's mistress, a little less like the girl in the snapshot.

And I had another name now. Mr Clay. Joe Clay? Sam Clay? Tom, Dick or Harry Clay?

To hell with it. It was another scrap and it would fit into place eventually. In the meantime we could switch to another topic of conversation.

But I forgot I was talking to Maddy Parson.

'Now,' she said dramatically, 'give.'

I tried to look blank.

'It is now my turn to play detective, Mr London, sir. If you think you can pump me blind without telling me a damn thing—'

'Pump you dry, you mean.'

'That sounds dirty, sort of. And don't change the subject. You are now going to tell me all about Sheila or Alicia or whoever the hell she is. Come clean, Mr London, sir.'

'Maddy—'

'About the girl,' she said heavily. 'Talk.'

I said: 'She's dead, Maddy.'

'Oh. I sort of thought so. Now I'm sorry I didn't like her. I mean—'

'I know.'

'Tell me the whole thing, Ed. I'll be very quiet and I won't repeat a thing to a soul. I'll be good. But tell me.'

I told her. There was no reason to keep secrets from her. She wasn't involved, didn't know any of the people involved, and made a good sounding board for the ideas that were rattling around in my head. I gave her the full summary, from the minute Jack Enright walked through my door to the moment I picked her up for dinner. I didn't leave anything out.

She shivered properly when I told her how I got shot at. She made a face when I described the scene in the blonde girl's apartment. And she listened intently all the way through.

'So here you are,' she said finally. 'Hunting a killer and dodging him at the same tune. You think Clay's the killer?'

I shrugged. 'He looks as good as anybody else, but I don't know who he is.'

'He looked capable of murder. Be careful, Ed.'

'I'm always careful. I'm a coward.'

She grinned at me. I grinned back, and we stood up together, both grinning foolishly. Somewhere along the way the grins gave way to deep long looks. Her eyes were not opaque at all now. I stared into them.

Then all at once she was in my arms and I was stroking silky hair. Her face buried itself against my chest and my arms were filled with the softness of her.

She pulled away from me. Her voice was very small. 'I'm going to be forward again,' she said. 'Very forward. You're not going home now, Ed. I don't want you to go.'

'I don't want to go.'

'I'm glad,' she said, taking my hand. 'I'm very glad, Ed. And I don't think we should stay in here. I think we should go to the bedroom.'

We started for the bedroom.

'It's right through that door,' she said, pointing. 'But you know that. After all, you've been there before.'

5

She was soft and warm and sweet. She moved beside me and her lips nuzzled my ear. 'Don't go,' she whispered. 'Stay all night. I'll make breakfast in the morning. I make good coffee, Ed.'

I drew her close and buried my face in the fragrance of her hair. Her body pressed against mine. Sleep was drowning me, dragging me under. The bed was warm, too warm to get out of. Sheila Kane and Jack Enright and a man called Clay were dull and trivial, a batch of mute ciphers swimming in charcoal gray water. I wanted to let them drown, to wink the world away with Maddy's fine female body beside me.

Something stopped me. 'I've got to go,' I said.

'Don't, Ed. See how shameless I am? Every sentence ends with a proposition. But stay here. It gets so lonely in this bed. It's a big bed. I rattle around in it all by myself. Don't go.'

She didn't say anything while I slipped out of bed and fumbled around for my clothes. I leaned over to kiss her cheek and she didn't move a muscle or speak a word. Then, while I was tying my shoelaces, she sat upright in the bed and talked to me. A half-light from the living room bathed her in yellow warmth. The sheet had fallen away from her small breasts and she looked like a primitive goddess with wild hair and sleepy eyes.

'Be careful, Ed. I'm not kidding; I like you; I like having you around, be careful, please. I don't like the way everything sounds. These people are dangerous. My God, one of them tried to kill you—'

'It was just a warning.'

'He shot at you. He could have killed you.'

'Please don't worry.'

'Of course I'll worry. It's a woman's prerogative to worry – you ought to know that. Worrying makes me feel all female and motherly and everything. If I only knew how to knit I'd make you a nice warm sweater. A warm wool sweater with a bullet-proof lining. Would you like that?'

I grinned. 'Sounds good.'

Her tone turned serious. 'You better call me tomorrow, you bastard. Otherwise I'll get mad. When I get mad I'm hell on wheels, Ed. There's no telling what I might do. I could sic the Mafia on you or something.' She frowned. 'So call me.'

'I will.'

'But not before noon.' A low sigh. 'I like to sleep late. I wish you could stay with me, Ed. We'd both sleep late and then I'd cook breakfast and feel as domestic as a pair of bedroom slippers. Maybe I'll knit you a pair of bedroom slippers.'

I laughed.

'Now kiss me good-bye. That's right. Now get the hell out of here before I start bawling, because this whole scene is so touching I can't take it. Did you know I can cry on cue? It's a valuable talent. Good-bye, Ed. And be careful. And call me. And . . .'

I kissed her again. Her lips were very soft, and when I kissed her she closed her eyes. Then I left her there and went out into the night.

On the way home the streets were almost empty. I took Eighth Avenue uptown to Columbus Circle where it turned into Central Park West, then angled the Chevy through the park and came out at Fifth and 67th. The ride through the park got to me – I remembered another trip the night before when I had a passenger in the car. A dead one.

I drove straight to the garage and got set for a session of playing straight man to the kid with the acne. It turned out to be his night off, which was wonderful. The guy taking over for him was a nautical type with a lantern jaw and tattooed forearms. One of the tattoos was a naked girl with impossible breasts; another I noticed was an anchor with 'Mother' etched across it. He was long and stringy and short of speech and I couldn't have been happier. I gave him the Chevy and walked home.

It was maybe two-thirty. The air was clear and it had a chill to it. My footsteps were hollow against the backdrop of a silent night. A taxi took a corner and its tires squealed. I looked around and made sure nobody was following me. It was a good thing. My building was solidly built, but too many holes in the wall could weaken it.

The brownstone waited for me. I unlocked the outer door and took the stairs two at a time. I stopped in front of my door, stuffed tobacco into a pipe and lit it. Then I stuck my key in the lock and opened the door.

I flicked on the light and saw him. He was sitting in my chair smoking a cigarette. He was neither smiling nor frowning. He looked nervous.

'Please close the door,' he said. 'And please sit down, Mr London. I have to talk with you.'

He was holding a small pistol in his left hand. It was not aimed at me. He held it almost apologetically, as if to say that he was sorry he had to hold a gun on me and he'd at least be enough of a gentleman to point it somewhere else.

I closed the door and moved into the center of the living room. He gestured with the gun, indicating a chair, and I sat in it.

'I'm very sorry about this,' he said. 'I really wanted to find the briefcase in your apartment and be gone before you returned. Wishful thinking, I fear.

A very thorough search revealed only that your taste in music and in literature is not coincident with mine. You prefer chamber music while I tend to favor crashing orchestral pieces. But the furnishings here are marvellous, simply marvellous. This rug is a Bokhara, isn't it?'

I nodded at him. He was a very small and very neat man. He wore black Italian loafers of pebble-grain leather with pointed toes. His suit was lampblack, continental cut. His tie was a very proper foulard and his shirt was crisply white. There was something indefinably foreign about him. His eyes had a vaguely oriental cast and his complexion was dark, close to olive. I couldn't pin down his accent but he had one. His head and face were round, his hair jet black and he was going bald in front. This made his face even rounder.

'We're both reasonable men,' he said. 'Rational individuals. I'm sure you realize I wouldn't have broken in if I could have avoided it. I did use a device which opened your lock without damaging it.'

'Thanks.'

He almost smiled. 'You resent me, don't you? It's easy to understand. But I hope to conquer your resentment. Since we'll be doing business together, Mr London . . .'

He let the sentence trail off. 'You're way ahead of me,' I said. 'You know my name.'

'You may call me Peter Armin. It will be meaningless to you, but it's as good a name as any.'

I didn't say anything.

'To return to the subject,' he said. 'The briefcase. It's really no good to you and I'm prepared to pay very well for it. A simple business transaction. I have a use for it and you do not. That's a natural foundation for economic cooperation, don't you think?'

Then the missing item was a briefcase. I wondered what was in it.

I said: 'You're not the only one who wants it.'

'Of course not. If I were, you'd sell it to me for next to nothing. But I'll pay handsomely for it. Five thousand dollars.'

'No sale.'

He shrugged. I caught a whiff of his cigarette. It smelled like Turkish or Egyptian tobacco. 'I don't blame you,' he said. 'I was being cheap and that's indecent. The briefcase is worth ten thousand dollars to me. I cannot afford to pay more and wouldn't if I could. That's my offer. Is it a good one?'

'Probably. What if I say I don't have the briefcase?'

'I don't think I would believe you.'

'Why not?'

His smile spread. 'It's hardly logical. After all, Mr Bannister doesn't have the briefcase. I'm certain of that. And I'm very glad of it as well. He's an unpleasant man, Mr Bannister is. Uncouth and uncultured. Boorish. You wouldn't like him at all, Mr London. You may dislike me, but you'd detest Mr Bannister.'

I looked at the gun in his left hand. It was a Beretta. A .22-calibre gun. I wondered if he killed Sheila with it.

'Bannister doesn't have it,' Armin went on. 'He wants it but he doesn't have it. And I doubt that he'd be willing to pay as much for it as I am. He'd probably try to take it away from you by force. A crude man. So you should sell it to me, you see.'

'Suppose I don't have it?'

'But you must. You were at the girl's apartment. So was the briefcase. It's not there now because you have it. It follows.'

'Like night follows day. Suppose someone else was at her place?'

He shrugged again. His face was very sad now. 'I was there,' he said. 'Really, I'm in a position to know that I don't have the thing. If I had it I wouldn't be here, much as I enjoy your company. And Mr Bannister was at the girl's apartment. But he doesn't have it either. That leaves you.'

'Eeny meeny miny moe?'

'More or less. Really, there's no reason for you to deny that you have the case. It's no use whatsoever to you, whereas no man lives who can't find a use for ten thousand dollars. And I need the case very badly. Desperately, you might say. Can't we do business?'

I relit my pipe and looked at Armin. I wondered who and what the hell he was. French or Greek or Italian or Spanish or Cuban. I couldn't place the accent.

'Fine,' I said. 'I've got the briefcase. So what's in it?'

He stroked his chin. 'If you have the case and know what's inside,' he said, 'it would be a waste of time to tell you. If you have the case and do not understand the significance of the contents, it would be foolish to tell you. And there must be a chance in a thousand that you are telling the truth, that you do not have the case. Why in the world should I tell you?'

'Who's Bannister? Who are you?'

He smiled.

'Who killed the girl? Why was she killed?'

He didn't answer.

'Who shot at me?'

He shrugged.

I let out a sigh. 'You're wasting your time,' I told him. 'And mine. I don't have the case.'

'Then it's not for sale?'

'Take it any way you want it. I don't have the briefcase and it's not for sale.'

His sigh was very unhappy. He got to his feet, still holding the gun loosely in his hand. 'If you want more money, I really can't help you. Ten thousand is my top price. I erred in offering five thousand first. I'm not generally that type of businessman. I quote one price and it is a firm price.' He managed a shrug. 'Perhaps you'll reconsider while there's still time. You may call me any hour, day or night. Let me give you my card.'

His right hand dipped into his inside jacket-pocket. We were both on our feet and the gun was pointed at the floor.

I picked that moment to hit him.

My right hand sank into his gut and my left hand closed around the gun. I hit him hard, harder than I planned, and he collapsed like a blown-out tire and folded up into the chair. The gun stayed in my hand, a light and cool piece of metal. I switched it to my right hand and pointed it at him.

His shoulders sagged and his eyes were pools of misery. He was massaging himself where I hit him. His face was a mask of infinite disappointment.

'You hit me,' he said thoughtfully. 'Now why did you do that?'

I didn't have an answer handy. 'The briefcase,' I snapped. 'Tell me about it. Tell me about yourself and about Bannister. Tell me who killed the girl.'

He sighed again. 'You don't seem to understand,' he said sadly. 'We're at a stalemate. We should be co-operating and we're at odds. I didn't threaten you with the gun, Mr London, for the simple reason that it would have accomplished nothing. Now you have the gun and you can't do a thing with it. Ask me all the questions you wish. I won't answer them. What can you do? Shoot me? Beat me? Call the police? You won't do any of those things. It's a stalemate, Mr London.'

The annoying thing was that he was right all the way. I stood there with the gun in my hand and felt like a clown. I was sorry I hit him. It was a waste of time, for one thing. For another, I was beginning to like the little weasel. I tried to picture myself beating him up or shooting him or calling the cops. The picture didn't look too sensible.

'You see what I mean, Mr London. We're similar men, you and I. Neither of us is unnecessarily violent. In that respect Mr Bannister has the advantage on us. He would beat us or have us beaten purely as a matter of course if we stood in his way. That's why you and I should be allies. But perhaps you'll come to your senses.'

He stood up stiffly, still holding himself where I slugged him. Once again his right hand dipped into his pocket. This time he came up with a pigskin pocket secretary. He flipped it open and took out a card which he handed to me. I read: Peter Armin . . . Hotel Ruskin . . . Room 1104 . . . Oxford 2–1560.

'The Ruskin,' he said. 'On West Forty-fourth Street. I'll be there for the next several days.'

I put the card in my pocket. He stood still and I realized I was still pointing the gun at him. I lowered it.

'Mr London,' he said. He lowered his eyes. 'May I have my gun back?'

'So you can shoot me with it?'

'Hardly. I just want my gun.'

'You don't need it,' I told him. 'You're not a violent man.'

'I might have to defend myself.'

'You're not the only one. Somebody shot at me today.'

'Mr Bannister?'

'Maybe. I think I'll hold onto your gun. I might need it sooner or later.' I shrugged. 'I didn't invite you here, anyway.'

His smile returned. 'As you wish,' he said. 'I have another at the hotel.'

'A thirty-two? The one you shot the girl with?'

He laughed now. 'I didn't kill her,' he said. 'And if I had, I'd hardly hold onto the gun. No, the other is a Beretta, the mate to the one you're holding. Good night, Mr London.'

I didn't move. He turned his back on me and walked past me to the door. He left the apartment quickly and closed the door after himself. I listened to his footsteps on the stairway, heard the front door slam behind him. I walked to the window and watched him cross the street and get into a maroon Ford a year or two old. He drove away.

Something kept me at the window, waiting for him to circle the block and come back for me. This didn't happen. After ten minutes, with no sight of him or his car, I went to the door and slid the bolt into place. The lock itself wasn't doing me a hell of a lot of good lately.

I spilled cognac into a glass and drank it. I juggled names like Peter Armin and Bannister and Alicia and Sheila and Clay and I tried to fit them into the human equation along with S, Y and Z. Nothing added up, nothing took form.

At least I knew what we were looking for now. A briefcase – but it didn't do me a hell of a lot of good to know that. First I had to figure out what was in the case.

Which was a good question.

Anyway, it was a good thing I hadn't given in to temptation and spent the rest of the night with Maddy. I would have missed Armin's visit.

Or would I have? I couldn't help smiling. The funny little guy probably would have sat in the darkness all night long, waiting for me with the little toy gun in his hand.

I looked at the gun, smelled the barrel. It hadn't been fired recently. I stuck it in a drawer and went to bed.

6

I sat in an overstuffed chair in the middle of a neat and spacious room. A healthy fire roared in the fireplace and animated figures of X, Y and Z danced in crackling flames. The man called Clay shuffled into the room with a girl on his arm. He wore a Broadway suit and a snap-brim hat. There was a cigar in the corner of his mouth and pale green smoke drifted from it to the ceiling. He did not have any eyes.

I looked from him to the girl. I saw she was a skeleton with long blonde hair. She wore only a pair of nylon stockings and a garter belt. She did a stripper's bump-and-grind, tossing loins of bone at me.

I turned and saw Bannister. He was built along the lines of an anthropoid ape. His arms were longer than his legs. He had a length of lead pipe in one hand and a baseball bat in the other. 'The briefcase,' he rasped. 'The briefcase the briefcase the briefcase the briefcase.'

I looked down. There was a briefcase on my lap. It smelled of good leather and death. I clutched it in both hands and hugged it to my chest.

When I looked up again Bannister had turned into Peter Armin. He was pointing a Beretta at the man called Clay, whose face had changed to Jack Enright's. 'Help me, Ed,' Jack was saying. And 'Help me,' chorus X, Y and Z. They were still dancing in the fireplace, skipping gaily in the flames.

Armin turned, pointed the Beretta at me. 'I, Mr London, am a reasonable man,' he said. 'And you, Mr London, are a reasonable man. We are not men of violence.'

Then he shot me.

I looked up at the skeleton. Her hair was black now and her face was Maddy Parson's face. She screamed a shrill, piercing scream. She stopped, then shrieked again.

The third scream wasn't a scream at all. It was the telephone ringing, ringing viciously, and it brought back reality in bits and pieces. I got oriented again – I was in bed, it was early morning, and the phone was going full blast. I picked up the receiver and growled at it.

'Ed? This is Jack, Ed.'

I asked him what time it was. It was the first thing I thought of.

'Time? Eight or so, a few minutes after. Ed, I'm calling from a pay phone. Can we talk?'

'Yes,' I said. 'What's wrong?'

'They've identified her.'

'They?'

'The police.'

'They identified Sheila Kane?'

'That's right.'

It didn't seem possible. I figured they might tag her eventually if they worked on it long enough, but it would be a few weeks, even with luck – not overnight.

'Do you have a newspaper handy, Ed?'

'I'll read it later,' I told him. 'Jack, you're in trouble. If they've got her labelled they'll have you in nothing flat. You better beat them to the punch. Get in touch with Homicide, tell them you're surrendering voluntarily, you didn't kill her, you're just guilty of withholding evidence. That way—'

'Ed.'

I stopped.

'Ed, do you get the *Times*?'

'Sure, but—'

'It can explain better than I can. I'll hold the line. Get your newspaper and read the story. Check page 34 – that's the second page of the second section. Go on – read it. Then you'll see what I mean.'

I was too foggy to argue with him. I managed to get out of bed, found a robe on a hook in the closet, slipped it on. I padded barefoot from the bedroom through the living room to the door, opened the door and picked up the paper. I carried it inside, shut the door and got rid of the first section on the way back to the phone. I ran my eyes over page 34 until I came to the right story. The headline said:

POLICE IDENTIFY CORPSE
FOUND IN CENTRAL PARK

The article ran seven paragraphs but the kicker was right there at the top in paragraph one. They had a make on the dead blonde, all right, but that was no reason for Jack to hand himself in at headquarters.

Not at all.

Because they had identified her as Alicia Arden, twenty-five, of 87 Bank Street in Greenwich Village. The identification was a pretty simple matter, too. Somebody sent her prints to the FBI's Washington office. Her prints were on file there – Alicia Arden had a record. She'd been arrested in Santa Monica four years back on a disorderly conduct charge, had drawn a suspended sentence and had vanished from the area – at least as far as the police records show.

The story ran downhill from there on to the finish. The possible identity of the killer was unknown. Clues were conspicuously absent. Miss Arden had no friends or relatives. Her Village apartment was one room plus a bath, and nobody in her building knew the first thing about her.

The police were pursuing all angles of the case thoroughly, according to the *Times* reporter. I read between the lines and saw that they were getting ready to write the murder off as unsolvable. A detective sergeant named Leon Taubler was quoted as saying that, although the girl hadn't been sexually molested, 'It looks like a sex crime.'

All the unsolved murders in Manhattan look like sex crimes. It helps the police and the tabloids at the same time. One hand washes the other.

I picked up the phone again. Jack's voice was hoarse. 'You read the story? You see what I mean?'

I answered yes to both questions.

'I can't believe it,' he said heavily. 'They must have made a mistake.'

'No mistake.'

'But—'

'Fingerprints don't make mistakes,' I said. 'And even if they did, it's a little too much to expect both gals to be missing at the same time. There's no mistake, Jack.'

'It doesn't seem possible.'

'It does to me. Sheila – Alicia – was living two lives at once. I more or less figured that much last night. A girl I know recognized her picture, met her once at a party. She was using the Alicia name at the time. So the newspaper story wasn't as much of a shock to me as it was to you.'

'Why would she give me a wrong name?'

'She went to you because she thought she was pregnant,' I improvised. 'She handed you a phony name automatically. Then she stayed with it. It was easier than admitting a lie.'

There was a long pause. 'What's disorderly conduct, Ed? What does it mean?'

'All things to all people. It's like vagrancy – a handy catch-all for the police. The New York cops use it for prostitutes. Easier to prove. God knows what it means in Santa Monica. Anything from keeping bad company to walking the streets in a tight skirt.'

'You heard me talk about her. About the type of person she was. Did she sound like that newspaper story?'

'No.'

'That just wasn't her, Ed. Maybe I didn't know who she was or where she came from, but I certainly knew the sort of girl she was. And, damn it, she wasn't a tramp!'

'Not when she was with you,' I said.

'She was still the same person, wasn't she?'

'Not necessarily.' I got a cigarette going and talked through a mouthful of smoke. 'Look at it this way. She was living two lives. Part of the time she was Bank Street's Alicia Arden and the rest of the time she was your girl Sheila.

She probably had two personalities, one to go with each name. You must have represented a better way of life to her, Jack. You told me about the first time you took her to lunch, how she stood there like a kid with her nose against a candy-store window. It wasn't the luxury that excited her. It was the respectability.'

'Is it so damned respectable to be a mistress?'

'It is if you used to be a prostitute.'

'Ed—'

'Hang on a minute. You were a cushion, Jack. A security blanket. A nice decent guy with a nice clean safe apartment in the fabulous Fifties. She was a little girl up to her neck in trouble with a batch of very unpleasant people. Hell, she was in over her head – that's why she was killed. But when she was with you she could pin her hair up and relax. She could be calm and cool and cultured. She was in a very lovely dream world and life was good to her. Naturally she was a different person in that world. You made her that way.'

'She seemed so honest, Ed.'

'She was honest enough,' I said. 'She could have lied to you, could have invented a background for herself. Instead she left the past blank. That's honest, isn't it?'

'I suppose you're right. It's . . . hard to accept the whole mess, Ed. I still don't know what's happening. You know how I felt when I saw the story this morning? First I read the headline and thought the police would be breaking down my door any minute. Then I read the first paragraph and I thought: God, the girl was somebody else and Sheila is still alive. It took me a few minutes to come to my senses again.'

I didn't say anything. Things were starting to take form in my mind and I wanted to get rid of Jack so that I could think straight. My human equation was setting itself up.

'You mentioned something about her being in over her head, Ed. Were you kidding?'

'No,' I said.

'What's it all about?'

'I don't know. Did she ever mention anything to you about a briefcase?'

'A briefcase?'

'Yeah.'

'No,' he said. 'Never.'

'Ever see one around the apartment?'

'No. Why?'

'Just wondered,' I said. 'Look, you're free as green stamps now. If the police have her under one name they won't look for another. If they've nailed her to one address they won't worry about a missing girl on Fifty-first Street. You can stop worrying and start living. Like the books say.'

For a moment or two he said nothing. Then: 'I see. What do I do now?'

I frowned at the phone. 'You pretend you're a family man,' I said. 'You take good care of your wife and your kids. You remove a lot of appendixes and split a lot of fees and have a ball.'

'Ed—'

'Give my best to my sister,' I told him. 'So long.'

I hung up on him before he could thank me or tell me any more of his problems or do whatever he was going to do. He was out of it now and I was bored with him. He had his small fling, got into a mess, and I helped him get out of it smelling of roses – which was more than he deserved. And in return for that I was getting warned, shot at and generally annoyed.

I decided to send the bastard a bill.

I went down the street for breakfast because it was too damned early to try stomaching instant coffee. I read the rest of the *Times* with breakfast but couldn't keep my mind on what I was reading. I had the names of all the characters now and things were setting themselves up.

The human equation – X and Y and Z. X killed Sheila, Y cleaned up her apartment and Z had the briefcase.

And I had the names to fit the letters.

Peter Armin. I couldn't figure him for X, the killer. He just didn't fit there at all. And I knew that he didn't have the briefcase because he wouldn't go to such a hell of a lot of trouble to get it from me if he did. That put him in the Y position – the joker who straightened things up, stripped Sheila and otherwise tampered with the scenery. I couldn't figure out why – that would come later, with luck – but it was in character. He'd given my apartment a thorough search the night before without disturbing a thing. It stood to reason that he'd be equally considerate of Sheila's apartment.

That left X and Z. Now—

'Nice morning,' the waitress said.

I looked up at her. 'Is it? I hadn't noticed.'

She started to laugh. I must have said something funny as hell because she was laughing hysterically. I tucked X and Z away for future reference, paid her, tipped her and went home.

I got there in time to answer the phone.

It was the man with the raspy voice again.

'You had time to think. Now you can go or get off the pot, London. How much?'

'How much for what?'

'The briefcase. Come on, quit stalling. What's the price?'

'I haven't got it,' I said.

There was a pregnant pause. 'That's your story? You haven't got it?'

'That's my story.'

'One last chance,' he said. His voice was supposed to sound coaxing. Try coaxing in a rasp. It doesn't come off. 'One last, chance, London. You're a smart boy. I play very rough. How much do you want for it?'

'Are you Bannister?'

'I'm Al Capone,' he said. 'What do you say, London?'

I said: 'Go to hell, Al.' And I hung up on him.

I made coffee, filled and lit a pipe, sat down to think. I was pretty sure it was Bannister on the phone. I was just as sure that Bannister was X – that he had killed Sheila-Alicia himself or had ordered the killing.

That left Z and it left Clay, so I put the two of them together. He was the one with the briefcase.

It played itself out that far and it hit a snag. I couldn't carry it any further. It looked as though Sheila-Alicia had teamed up with Clay to pull something on Bannister. Or as though Sheila-Alicia had something Bannister wanted, and she gave it to Clay, and then Bannister killed her. But there wasn't much point in listing possibilities. First I needed more facts.

Like Bannister's name. Like Clay's name.

Like an idea of what was in the briefcase.

I gave up for the time being, picked up the phone again and gave Maddy a ring. It was too early to call her, too early for her to be properly awake. I could have been polite, waited a few hours to call her, but I didn't feel polite to begin with. Too many people had called me early in the morning for me to take anybody else's sleep into consideration.

Still, Maddy was special. And I felt guilty, expecting her to answer the phone with sleep coating her tongue and clogging her pores. She surprised me. Her hello was fresh and happy and very much awake.

'Sleep well?'

'It's Ed,' she said gaily. 'Hello, Ed. Yes, I slept well. Like a hibernating bear, sort of. Then I woke up and saw my shadow. Or is that with groundhogs? I guess it is. Anyway, I slept soundly and awoke bright-eyed and hungry. You missed a phenomenal breakfast, sir. Fresh orange juice and pancakes with real maple syrup and crisp bacon.'

She said all this with one mouthful of air, then stopped and caught her breath. 'And then it was all topped off with a phone call from you. How sweet! You're still alive!'

I laughed, picturing her in my mind. Her phone was by the side of her bed. She would be sitting on the edge of the bed with a cigarette in one hand and the phone in the other. She'd be wearing old slacks and a man's shirt and she'd look lovely.

'Damn you,' she said suddenly.

'Why?'

'Because you wouldn't call at this hour just to be nice. I'm never awake this early and you know it. You've got some more detecting for me to do.'

'I'm afraid you're right.'

'Damn you again. What is it?'

'Clay.'

'Clay,' she said. 'You want more inside info on this off-Broadway

44

behemoth. You want the high-up way-out lowdown on this murky man of mystery, this heavyweight hotster, this—'

'You should be ghosting for Winchell.'

'I'm a gal of many talents,' she said. 'What do you want to know about him?'

'Who he is.'

'Oh,' she said heavily. 'It couldn't be something simple, like what he eats for breakfast or what brand of cigarettes he smokes. Cigars, I mean. It has to be—'

'Just who he is. All I've got now is a name. I'd like a first name to go with it. If you can find out.'

'Lee Brougham would know,' she said thoughtfully. 'But he's supposed to be in California. I told you that.'

'Uh-huh.'

She was silent for a minute. 'This,' she said, 'is going to be a bitch.'

'I'm afraid you're right.'

'Hell of a conversation. You keep being afraid and I keep being right. Let me think this out for a minute, Ed. I can find out who directed *Hungry Wedding*. Nobody would boast about it, but somebody must have directed the dog, and I can find out who. And he just might have a list of backers, which he just might let me look at. And Clay just might be on it. There's no guarantee, Ed. It's a shot in the dark.'

'That's the only kind there is.'

'So I'll fire away. It may take an hour and it may take six hours and it may take three weeks. Anything interesting happen last night?'

'Nothing much,' I lied. 'I spent a little time with a girl.'

'Who?'

'You,' I said. 'Remember?'

'Ed—'

'I'll have more to tell you,' I said. 'When you get over here.'

'Where?'

'Here,' I said.

'Your apartment? No, don't tell me you're afraid again and I'm right again. You don't want me to call with the precious information. You want me to trot it over. Right?'

'Right.'

She sighed. 'I'll take cabs all over the city,' she told me. 'And I have a hunch you're going to wind up shelling out for another dinner tonight, Mr London, sir.'

'It's all deductible,' I said. 'See what you can find out.'

I was lighting my pipe when the doorbell rang.

An hour had passed since I talked to Maddy. Maybe a little more than an hour – it was hard to say. I finished lighting the pipe and started for the door, then stopped when I was halfway there.

It was too soon for it to be Maddy. It could have been anybody else in the world, ranging from the Con Ed man coming to read my meter to a girl scout selling cookies. But I was feeling nervous. I went back for Armin's Beretta and hoped to God it wasn't a girl scout selling cookies.

I felt only halfway ridiculous holding the gun in one hand while I opened the door.

I felt completely ridiculous when the big one knocked it out of my hand.

There were two of them – a big one and a small one. The big one was very big, a little taller than I am and a hell of a lot wider. He had a boxer's flattened nose and a cretin idiot's fixed stare. His jacket was stretched tight across huge shoulders. His eyes were small and beady and his forehead was wide and dull.

The small one wasn't really that small – he looked small because he was standing next to a human mountain. He wore a hat and a suit and a tie. He had his hands in his pants pockets and he was smiling.

'Inside,' he said. 'Move.'

I didn't move. The big one gave me a shove, his arm hardly moving, and I moved. I backed up fast and damn near fell over. The big one reached out a paw and scooped up the Beretta. He pitched it at a chair. He seemed contemptuous of it, as if it was some kind of silly toy.

The small one turned, closed the door, slid the bolt across. He turned again, his eyes showing the same contempt for me that the big one had shown for the gun.

'Now,' he said, 'we talk. That briefcase.'

7

The big one held his hands in front of his chest and flexed his fingers. The small one had a bulge under his jacket that was either a gun or a lonely left breast. I remembered Peter Armin and thought about reasonable men. These two didn't look reasonable at all.

They didn't talk now. They were waiting me out, waiting for me to say something or do something. I wondered if I was supposed to offer them a drink.

'You're out in left field,' I said finally. 'I don't have the briefcase.'

'The boss said you'd say that.'

'It's the truth.'

Their faces told me nothing. 'The boss said to ask you nice,' the smaller one said. 'He said ask you nice, and if you didn't come up with the briefcase, then work you over.'

'He had to send two of you?'

They didn't get angry. 'Two of us,' the talker said. 'One to ask nice, the other to work you over. I'm asking nice. Billy takes care of the rest.'

'I don't have the briefcase.'

The little one considered that. He pursed his lips, narrowed his eyes, then made a small clucking sound with his tongue. 'Billy,' he said softly, 'hit him.'

Billy hit me in the stomach.

He wound up like a bush-league pitcher and telegraphed the punch all over the place. He had all the subtlety of a pneumatic hammer and I was too dumb to get out of the way. My legs turned to gelatin and I wound up on the floor. I opened my eyes, saw little black circles. I blinked the circles away and looked at Billy. His hands were in front of his chest again. He flexed them, smiling the smile of a competent workman who is proud of his craft.

Something made me get up. I wobbled around and wondered if he was going to hit me again. He didn't. I looked at him and watched his smile spread. I said a few words about Billy, and a few more about his mother, and still more about the probable relationship between the two of them.

He couldn't help understanding them. They were all about four letters long. He growled and moved at me.

'Billy!'

He grunted, stopped in his tracks. The hands that were balled into fists now unwound. He flexed his fingers.

'Don't get mad, Billy,' the little one said.

'Aw, Ralph—'

'Don't get mad. You know what happens when you get mad. You blow up, you hit too hard, you hurt somebody more than you should. You know what the boss said. You do that again, you go out on your ear.'

'He can't call me that kind of thing.'

Ralph shrugged. 'So his manners stink. It's not like he was saying the truth. Your mother's a wonderful woman.'

'I love her.'

'Of course you do,' Ralph said. 'Don't worry what this schmuck says. Forget about it.'

He turned to me again. His tone was conversational. 'Don't talk to Billy like that, London. He's an ex-pug. In the ring when he heard somebody call him a name, he went off his nut. Lost his control every time, swinging like a maniac. When he connected he won a lot of fights. Sometimes he missed. You he wouldn't miss, so don't talk dirty to him.'

I didn't say anything.

'You remember where that briefcase is?'

'I told you—'

'We got orders, London. Don't try to sell us anything. Just give us the case.'

'And if I don't? Are you going to beat me to death?'

He shook his head. 'We search the place. The boss figures if you got the stuff it's not here anyhow, but we look to make sure. Then we work you over so you know better. Just a light going-over. Not enough to put you in the hospital or anything. Just enough so next time the boss asks a favor you jump.'

They were a pair of fairly complex machines, primed to do a task and nothing more. Reasoning with them was like reasoning with IBM's latest product. It couldn't work.

'You could save yourself a beating,' Ralph said confidentially. 'Billy works you over, it don't kill you but it don't do you any good either. It's the same either way. You lose the briefcase whether you get hit or not. And the next hit might be in the head. The boss doesn't like to hit people in the head if he can help it. Sometimes he can't help it.'

I opened my mouth to tell him again that I didn't have the damned thing. I changed my mind before the sentence got going. I was starting to feel like a broken record.

Ralph shrugged at me again. 'You're calling the shots,' he said. 'You change your mind while Billy's taking you apart, you tell me. He'll stop if I tell him to. And I'll tell him to when you cough up the briefcase.' He turned his head slightly in Billy's direction. 'Now take it easy on him, Billy. Go gentle. But let him feel it a little.'

Billy heard the command and answered it like an old pug answering the bell. He moved toward me and all I could think was, dammit, this son of a bitch isn't going to hit me again. I stepped right at him and threw a right at his jaw.

He picked it off with his left, brushed it away like a cow's tail brushing flies.

Then he hit me in the stomach.

I didn't even have time to think about it. I went straight to my knees and used both hands to hold my guts together. This time I didn't try to get up. Billy helped me. He lifted me with one hand on my shirt front, hit me with the other hand, and I went down again.

'Prop him against the wall,' Ralph suggested. 'So he don't keep falling down. And pull the punches a little more. You're hitting a little too hard.'

'I ain't hitting that hard, Ralph.'

'A little easier,' Ralph said. 'His stomach's soft. He can't take too much punishment.'

Billy picked me up again and stood me up against one wall. He hit me three more times. He was supposed to be letting up on the punches. Maybe he was. I couldn't tell.

My stomach was on fire. When I opened my eyes the room rocked like teenager's music. When I closed them it didn't help at all. He held me with one paw and slugged me with the other and I stood there like a sap and took it.

Ralph said: 'Hold it.'

Billy let go of me and I started to slide down the wall. It was a scene out of a Chaplin movie with the humor left on the cutting-room floor. He caught me easily and propped me up again.

'You had enough, London? You want to open up?'

I told him to go to hell.

'A hero,' Ralph said.

I wasn't being a hero. I would have given him a brief-case full of H-bomb secrets without giving a damn at that point. But I didn't have it to give.

'Slap the hero, Billy. First take off your ring. We aren't supposed to mark him up.'

Billy took a large signet ring from the third finger of his right hand. Then he held onto me with his left hand and started slapping me with the right one. He slapped forehand, then backhand, and between my head bounced off the wall. There was a regular pattern to it: slap, bump, slap, bump—

The pain stopped after a little while. I stopped feeling things, stopped seeing and stopped hearing. There was the blue-gray monotony of the slap bump slap bump, a deading rhythm that went on forever.

A voice came through a filter: '—just won't talk,' it said. Then a few words were lost. Then: '—search the place. Won't find anything but the boss said take a look. Dump the schmuck and we'll look.'

I wondered what 'dump the schmuck' was supposed to mean. I opened my eyes and watched Billy cock a fist as big as a cannon ball. Then the fist exploded against my jaw and the universe went from gray to black.

It wasn't like waking up. The world came back into focus a little at a time, a broken series of short gray spasms in a world of black. A batch of disconnected scenes, vague and partially formed, breaking up long stretches of nothing in particular.

Someone talking in a low voice. The darkness again.

The phone ringing. I wanted to get up to answer it. Instead I stayed where I was and counted the rings. I kept losing count and starting over. Finally it stopped, or I didn't hear it any more. Then the black curtain fell and I was out again.

And then, very suddenly, I was awake.

I was lying on the floor against one wall – the wall Billy had used to prop me up against. My head ached dully and my jaw ached sharply and my stomach had a hole in it. The hole was about the size of a large human fist. It took me two tries to get to my feet. I staggered into the bathroom and poured my stomach out. Then I took four aspirins from the bottle in the medicine chest, carried them back to the living room, washed them down with a glassful of cognac.

The cognac was more important than the aspirins. The aspirins took a minimum of two seconds to dissolve, according to the ads. The cognac went to work instantly to relieve aches and pains caused by headache, neuritis and neuralgia.

It helped. My eyes focussed again and my knees worked and I didn't notice my stomach as much as before. I took another belt from the bottle.

Then I saw what they had done to the apartment.

It didn't look as though a cyclone had hit it. A cyclone isn't selective. It hits a whole area and knocks the hell out of anything that gets in the way. They had been more selective.

But just as destructive.

The Bokhara was rolled up in one corner of the room and the floor was bare. But even with the rug rolled up you couldn't see too much of the floor. It was covered with things.

It was covered with every book that had been in the bookcases. Maybe the bastards thought I hid the brief-case behind the books. Maybe they were just being thorough. I looked down at a collection of Stephen Crane first editions, picked up a copy of *The Little Regiment*. The spine was broken.

The cushions of the two leather chairs leaked their stuffing onto the floor. Ralph – or Billy, it didn't matter which one – had slashed them open with a knife. Two reproductions lay curling at the edges. The Miro had a footprint in the middle and the Tanguy was in shreds. They had been ripped from their frames.

I found a pack of cigarettes and got one going. There was more, plenty more, but I didn't feel like looking at it. I went to the bedroom and sat down on the edge of the bed. That room was a mess, too, but not quite as bad.

And the damnedest thing was that I knew they hadn't ruined anything on purpose. They weren't trying to do damage any more than they were trying to prevent it. They were machines, with a single job to do, and everything else was incidental. They were supposed to beat me up – not kill me, not send me to the hospital.

And they did just that. I was on my feet already, with nothing to show for it but a pain in the gut and an aching head. The headache would be gone in the morning, the rest wouldn't last much longer.

I ground out the cigarette. Who was I supposed to hate? Bannister, of course. He was the man who gave the order, the leading bastard who gave the order that sent the two minor bastards on my neck. He killed a blonde and had the crap knocked out of a private detective and he was going to get his.

And Ralph and Billy. Now how the hell could I hate Billy? He was a mongoloid with muscles and he practiced the only trade he knew. When he was a fighter he got paid for beating other fighters senseless. Now he did the same work without ropes or gloves. Do you hate a machine?

Or Ralph. He was a company man to the core, a junior executive, and he'd be the same guy underneath if he worked for General Motors or Jimmy Hoffa or the CIA. He even tried his best to save me from a beating. Hate him?

I didn't hate them, didn't hate Ralph and didn't hate Billy. They weren't the kind of people you hated.

But I was in their debt and I'm the kind of slob who likes to mark his debts paid. I owed them for a beating and a wrecked apartment. It was a debt I was going to pay.

I was going to kill them.

I went back to the living room and looked at wreckage for a few long minutes. A little of that goes a long way. I picked up the telephone and called a girl named Cora Johnson. She's a girl in her middle twenties, a very bright gal with a degree from City College. She is also a Negro, and she earns a small living doing housework. They do things strangely in the United States some of the time.

I asked her if she could come over in an hour or two and she said she could. I told her the place looked like hell with a hangover, that she should do whatever she could and not worry about it. 'Just set the books in the bookcases,' I told her. 'I can rearrange them later. Try to make the place livable again. I'll leave a key under the mat for you.'

She didn't ask what had happened. I knew she wouldn't ask, and that she'd keep her mouth shut. She was that sort of person.

I was still standing around, wondering where to go next and who to see next, when the bell rang. The doorbell.

And I knew right away who it was. Ralph and Billy, coming back to give me another spin through the old slap bump circuit, another chance to be a good little boy and give them a briefcase that I didn't have.

This time it was going to be different.

I must have been a little bit insane. I found the Beretta on the floor – they hadn't even bothered to take it with them. I picked it up and curled my index finger around the trigger. I walked to the door and stood there with my hand on the knob, ready to give the trigger a squeeze the minute I saw them. Billy wasn't going to knock the gun out of my hand this time, by George. I'd shoot him first.

I turned the knob. I gave the door a yank and stuck the gun in my visitor's face.

And Maddy Parson let out a small scream.

It took a few minutes to calm her down. 'You were joking,' she said uncertainly. 'It was your idea of a gag. Well, it wasn't very funny. I could have had a heart attack. Is that thing loaded, Ed?'

'I hope so.'

'You—'

'Come on inside,' I said. 'Relax. Everything's all right.'

She took a few steps inside, got a good look at the apartment, and let go of her jaw. It fell three inches. 'Okay,' she said. 'What happened?'

'I dropped my watch.'

'A cyclone hit it. Now open up, Ed. All of it.'

I didn't tell her the difference between Billy and Ralph and a cyclone. She would have missed the point. It was easier to sit her down and explain the whole thing as quickly as I could, from Armin through Billy and Ralph. I left out the names and the descriptions but that was all I left out. By the time I was done she had a face the color of ashes.

She said: 'Oh, Holy Christ. They could have killed you.'

'Not in a million years.'

'But—'

'Look at me,' I said. 'I didn't even get a bloody nose. Not even a sprained thumb. And right this minute I'm so full of cognac I can't feel a damned thing. I'll sit around aching tomorrow, maybe. And the day after that it'll hurt once in a while. And nothing the day after that one. Nothing resembling a permanent injury. Those two are professionals, Maddy.'

'They're animals.'

'Then they're professional animals. An amateur could have killed me by accident, would have cracked a rib or two, anyway. But they were perfect. They knew just what to do and they did it.'

She shuddered. I put an arm around her and she turned to me and hugged me. I saw a drop of wet saltiness running down one cheek, wiped it up with a finger.

'Hell, you were right.' She looked at me. 'When you said you could cry on cue,' I explained.

She looked away. 'Just shut up,' she said. 'Or I'll hit you in the stomach. At least I get a chance to play nurse. You're going to bed now, Ed.'

'Like hell I am.'

'Ed—'

'I couldn't fall asleep if I wanted to. And I don't want to. Things are coming to a head, Maddy. A whole slew of two-legged bombs are running around waiting to go off.'

'And you want to be blown up?'

'I want to be there. I want to watch the explosion, set off a bomb or two of my own.'

'You should go right to sleep.'

I shook my head, which was a mistake. It ached. 'I wouldn't stay here anyway. I was letting them come to me, Maddy. It made sense before. Now I'd rather be a moving target. I have to start things on my own.'

'Then go to a hotel. In the morning—'

'The morning's too late.'

She sighed. It was a long and very female sigh. She really wanted to put me to bed and tuck me in and listen to my prayers. The mother instinct dies hard.

'All right,' she said sadly. 'Where are you going to start?'

'Probably with Armin.'

'Armin?'

'The little man who was waiting for me last night. Mr Neatness and Light. His name's Peter Armin and he's staying at a midtown hotel. I think he'll be glad to see me.'

'Why him?'

'Because I know where he is. Because I know who he is, as far as that goes. And because I think he'll help me.'

'Why should he?'

I stood up. 'Because I may be able to help him,' I said. 'Say, you didn't come up with anything, did you? About Clay?'

She looked stunned. She made a small fist out of one hand and used it to tap herself on the jaw. Then she sat there shaking her head from side to side at me.

'I completely forgot,' she said. 'God, I'm stupid. How can I be so stupid? I was so busy listening to you and all that I forgot all about it.'

'All about what?'

'It's probably nothing,' she said. 'I chased all over town looking for that director, Ed, and I couldn't find him. Nobody knew just where he was. He's a periodic drunk or something and he was missing his period. Or having it.'

I waited for her to get to the point. If I knew who Clay was, I didn't necessarily have to bother with Armin. Because Clay was the boy I needed, the missing factor in the equation.

He had the briefcase.

'So I couldn't find him,' she was saying. 'But I got hold of another guy, one who collects lists of angels so hard-up producers can hunt up soft touches. He had the list for *Hungry Wedding*!'

'And Clay was on it?'

'I don't know.'

'Huh?'

'There was no Mr Clay,' she said. 'But then I got the bright idea that Clay could be a first name instead of a last name. So I went through the list again and found a man named Clayton. That's his first name. They didn't have his address.'

I let out a lot of breath. 'That has to be him. What was his last name?'

'Just a minute. It's on the tip of my tongue, Ed. It was something like Rail but that wasn't it. Kale? Crail? Oh, damn it to hell—'

'Maddy—'

'Oh, it's nothing to worry about. I wrote it down, for Pete's sake. I'm just so darn mad that I couldn't remember it. Just a minute – it's somewhere in my purse.'

I waited while she rummaged through a purse and kept saying darn it. Then she managed to find her wallet, took it out and managed to find a slip of paper. She looked at it and smiled proudly at me.

'This is the one,' she said, very positively. 'No address, just the name.'

I told her to read it.

'Clayton Bannister,' she read calmly. 'Does that mean anything?'

8

The human equation picked itself up, dusted itself off and crawled furtively into the woodwork. I wanted to get down on all fours and crawl after it. Everything had worked out so neatly, so flawlessly. Bannister and Armin wanted the briefcase and Clay had the briefcase and—

Sure they did, London.

I told Maddy all about it and watched her eyes bulge.

Two suspects had turned into one, with Clay and Bannister the two sides of the same damn coin.

'Then,' she wanted to know, 'who has the briefcase?'

Briefcase, briefcase, who's got the briefcase. 'It's a good question,' I told her. 'We'll have to find out. Now.'

I grabbed a jacket and a hat and we got out of the apartment. I locked the door and pitched a key under the mat for Cora. Then we left the building.

She wanted me to buy her dinner but I managed to talk her out of the idea of a real meal. Instead we found a deli with a pair of formica-topped tables in the rear. A moon-faced man with bushy eyebrows brought us pastrami sandwiches on fresh rye and two bottles of cold Dutch beer. The apron covering his beer belly was spotless, probably because he didn't wipe his dirty hands on it

Every once in a while an indefatigable cockroach scurried across the floor at our feet. Even this couldn't spoil our appetites. We wolfed down the sandwiches and swilled beer and got out of there.

'Now I put you in a cab and send you home,' I said optimistically.

She wasn't having any. 'I'm going with you, Ed.'

'Don't be—'

'Silly? I'm not being silly.'

'I wasn't going to say that.'

'Oh? What were you going to say?'

'I was going to say: "Don't be ridiculous".'

'Darn it, Ed—'

'One of two things could happen or both,' I told her. 'You could get hurt or you could get in the way. I don't want either one. Therefore—'

'There's another alternative, Ed. I could be of help. To tell the truth, I don't see how you get along without me. You may be a brilliant detective but you forget the elementary things.'

'Like what?'

'Like Clayton Bannister,' she said. 'God, you didn't even look him up in the phone book. You know his full name and you leave it alone.'

'He won't be listed.'

'Are you sure? So sure you won't take the trouble to look?'

Arguing with Maddy was like swimming in a vat of mercury. There was no future in it. We ducked into a drugstore and I went through the Manhattan and Bronx books, the only ones on hand. There were twenty-one Bannisters in Manhattan and nine in the Bronx and none of them was named Clayton. One guy was listed as C Bannister and Maddy wanted me to call him. I told her he lived on Essex Street and our boy wasn't going to turn up in a Lower East Side slum.

So she made me call Information and check on the possibility of a Clayton Bannister in Brooklyn or Queens. The operator was a good sport. She checked. No Clayton Bannister in Brooklyn, none in Queens. Not even one on Staten Island.

So I won the battle and lost the war. I couldn't get rid of Maddy. She had to come along, had to help me find Armin.

We used the drugstore's back door in case one of Bannister's little men was doing a shadow job. We wound up in an alley, followed it to the nearest street and caught the first cab that came by. We hopped into the back seat and I felt like the all-American folk hero, with an arm around Maddy, a hand on the Beretta in my pocket. All I needed was a hip flask.

I had an insane urge to shout *follow that car!* at our driver. But there was no car in front of us. So that killed that.

The Ruskin was a throwback to better times. It stood twelve stories tall at the corner of Eighth Avenue and Forty-fourth Street and remembered the days when the West Side was the best side, which was a long time ago. Now Broadway was fast-buck alley and Eighth Avenue was Whore Row.

The Ruskin stared across early-evening Eighth Avenue, watching whores bloom in doorways like pretty weeds in a dying garden. The lobby was filled with overstaffed Edwardian chairs. The ceiling was high and dripped with chandeliers. We walked to the front desk while thirty or forty years seem to slip away and disappear.

I watched expressions play across the face of the middle-aged desk clerk. Maddy and I weren't married – she wasn't wearing a ring. And we weren't toting luggage. But it was damned early for adultery, wasn't it? And we didn't look like whore and customer.

He just about had his mind made up to take a chance on us when we disappointed him. I told him I wanted to talk to Room 1104 on the house phone. He did a very sad double take, then pointed to a phone on the desk and scuttled for the switchboard. Midway through the first ring Peter Armin picked up the phone and said hello to me.

'Ed London,' I said. 'Can I come up?'

A small and brief sigh came over the wire. 'I am delighted,' he said. 'I'll be most happy to see you. Where are you?'

'In the lobby.'

He chuckled appreciatively. 'Magnificent,' he said. 'You give little advance warning, Mr London. Would you wait five minutes or so, then come straight up?'

I told him that was fine, put the phone down. I asked the clerk at the desk if the hotel had a bar. He pointed through a wide doorway and I took Maddy by the arm and led her toward it.

'I don't want a drink,' she said. 'Why don't we stay in the lobby?'

'Because Bannister may have the place watched. Maybe his man missed us on the way in. If we sit around the lobby he's sure to spot us.'

'That makes sense.'

'No, it doesn't,' I told her. 'But I need a drink.'

The bar matched the lobby. It was more along the lines of an old-style taproom than a hotel bar. I asked for Courvoisier and while the barman poured my drink Maddy changed her mind and ordered a Daiquiri.

'I thought you weren't having any.'

'I wasn't,' she said. 'Ed, I'm worried.'

'I told you to go home.'

She shook her head impatiently. 'I'd worry even more if you were here without me. Look, how do you know what we're walking into? He could have a trap for us.'

'Trap? Hell, all he'll do is sit there with a gun in his hand. He'll do that just as a matter of course to make sure I'm not here with Bannister at my heels. But he won't try to trap me. He trapped me before in my own apartment, for God's sake. He doesn't want me. He wants the briefcase.'

'So does Bannister. And look what his men did to you.'

I told her Bannister and Armin were different men. Their minds worked differently.

She picked up her glass, finished most of it in one swallow. 'What are you going to say to him?'

'That we should cooperate.'

'Huh?'

'He wants a briefcase,' I said. 'I want a killer. That doesn't mean we have to fight each other. I've got a hunch he's in a spot like mine. I think he must be working alone. He could probably use somebody on his side.'

'And you'll be on his side?'

I couldn't tell whether she approved or disapproved. She read the line perfectly straight.

I sipped cognac. I said: 'I'm not sure. I'll have to see how it goes upstairs.

If nothing else, we can probably pool information. He must know the answers to a hell of a lot of questions.'

'Like what?'

'Like what's in the briefcase and what's so important about it. Like why the girl was killed and where she fits into the picture. I'm in the middle of everything and I don't know what it's all about, Maddy. Armin can be of help.'

'If he wants to.'

'Well, sure,' I said. 'If he wants to.'

We left the elevator and found Room 1104 without a hell of a lot of trouble. I knocked on the door and Armin's voice told us to come in.

He was sitting in a chair with a gun in his hand. Every time I saw him he was sitting with a gun in his hand. This one was a Beretta like the first. It was the mate to the one in my pocket.

'This is getting monotonous,' I said. He lowered the gun and Maddy relaxed her grip on my arm.

'I'm terribly sorry,' Peter Armin said. 'You understand, of course. I didn't know for certain that you'd be alone. But that's impolite, isn't it? You're not alone. I don't believe I've met the young lady.'

'My secretary.'

He nodded with majestic understanding. He was dressed well, almost too well. He wore a pair of light-gray flannel slacks and a lime-green Paisley shirt with a button-down collar. The shirt was open at the neck. He wasn't wearing a tie. His shoes and socks were black.

'This room is really too small,' he said. 'Only the one chair. If you'd care to sit on the bed—'

We sat on the bed.

'I'm glad you came in person,' he went on. 'I was afraid you might wish to talk on the phone. I really cannot do business over the telephone. The personal element is lost.'

He killed a little time finding his pack of cigarettes and offering them around. We thanked him and passed them up. He lit a cigarette for himself, smoked thoughtfully.

'You've decided to sell me the briefcase, Mr London?'

I killed time on my own by filling a pipe and lighting it. Maddy got a cigarette and I lit it for her. The three of us sat and smoked.

Finally I said: 'You're a reasonable man, Armin.'

'I try to be.'

'Then let me set up a logical argument. Will you hear me out?'

'With pleasure.'

'Good,' I said. 'Now let's postulate that I don't have the briefcase, don't know much about it. Can you accept that?'

'As a postulate.'

'Good. Bannister's men paid me a visit this afternoon. They came to my apartment. There were two of them. A talker named Ralph and a gorilla named Billy.'

'I was afraid that would happen,' he said ruefully. 'I tried to warn you, Mr London.'

'Sure, but I didn't have the briefcase. Don't forget that postulate we're working on.'

'I see.'

I drew on my pipe and blew out smoke. 'The way I see it, you and Bannister are on opposite sides of the fence.'

'Precisely. And it's a high fence, Mr London.'

'You and I are reasonable men. Bannister is not. If I have to take sides, your side is the natural one to pick.'

He nodded with obvious approval. 'That only stands to reason,' he said. 'As you may remember, it was my whole point in our ... conference last evening. A choice of mind over muscle, one might almost say.'

'Uh-huh.' I looked at him. 'So where are we? You and I are natural allies. Bannister's our natural enemy. You want to get hold of a briefcase. I want to get Bannister for murder – Alicia Arden's murder.'

He nodded.

'The briefcase is worth ten grand to you—'

'More, really. But I can only pay ten thousand.'

'So call it ten thousand. And nailing Bannister to an electric chair is worth a lot of time and effort to me.'

'A worthy aim, Mr London.'

I smiled. It was easy to like Armin. You can't hate a man who speaks your own language, can't despise a guy whose mind works the way your own mind works. Every time he opened his mouth I liked him a little bit more.

'What I'm proposing,' I said, 'is a sort of holy alliance.'

'Against Bannister?'

'Uh-huh.'

'Go on,' he said. 'Your proposition sounds appealing.'

'We work together,' I said. 'We pool information – you've probably got more to contribute than I do – and we join forces. You help me pin down Bannister and I help you get the briefcase. If I get my hands on it I give it to you for five thousand dollars – half of what it's worth to you. If you get it alone, it's yours free and clear.'

He stubbed out his cigarette very elaborately in a small glass ashtray. 'I'd pay you the five thousand in any event,' he said slowly. 'I really would prefer it that way. Otherwise you'd have reason to work at cross-purposes with me under certain circumstances. If either of us recovers the briefcase, you'll still get five thousand dollars.'

I said that was fine.

He thought some more. 'One thing disturbs me, Mr London. How can you be certain that I won't run off and leave you to chase Mr Bannister alone once I've got the briefcase? Or that I'll pay you for it?'

'I can't.'

He turned both palms upward. His gun was tucked into the arm of the chair. 'Then—'

'By the same token,' I said, 'how can you be sure I won't let you go to hell once I get Bannister? We're both taking a chance, Armin. I don't mind trusting you. I think you're trustworthy.'

He laughed, delighted. 'Perhaps I am,' he admitted. 'Up to a point. Do you know something? I really believe now that you don't have that briefcase, Mr London. And that you never did have it at all.'

'I told you that before.'

'But I didn't believe you before.'

'And you believe me now?'

He produced his pack of Turkish cigarettes again, offered them around again, lit one again for himself. 'Do you know anything about confidence men, Mr London?'

'A little.'

'I've had some experience in that area,' he said confidentially. 'One does so many things in order to survive. Are you familiar with the First Law of Con?'

I wasn't.

'Very simply: if the mark does not see your point of profit, you may sell him real estate on the planet Jupiter. If, so far as he can see, there's no reason for you to be swindling him, you can steal him blind.'

'Uh-huh.'

He smiled pleasantly. 'So,' he said. 'For a moment let's take a different postulate. Let us assume that you do indeed possess the briefcase. If so, what possible advantage could you hope to gain by this meeting tonight? You want to get five thousand for the case when I've already offered you ten. I have to assume you're telling the truth, Mr London. Otherwise I can't see your point of profit.'

Maddy was grinning. She had come to Armin's room determined to hate the little man. Now she liked him. He was a charming son of a bitch.

'I accept your terms,' he said. 'One hand shall wash the other, as it were. It is a bargain.'

I hesitated.

'Isn't it a bargain?'

'Just one thing,' I said. 'About the briefcase.'

'Go on.'

'If it contains espionage material, it's no bargain. Papers relating to the security of the United States of America . . . Hell, you know the cliché, I'm sure.'

He smiled.

'I'm an American,' I went on. 'I don't wave the flag, don't sit around telling everybody what a goddam patriot I am. But I don't play traitor either.'

He puffed on his cigarette. 'I understand,' he said. 'I was not born in this country myself, as you must have guessed. My native land doesn't exist at the present time. It was a small state in the Balkans. The patchwork quilt of Europe – that's what they once called it. Now the patchwork quilt has turned into a red carpet. But that doesn't matter.

'I've travelled all over the world, Mr London. You might call me a picaresque character. I've lived by my wits, really. Now I live in the United States. I married an American girl, and a number of years ago became a naturalized citizen.'

He smiled at the memory. 'I prefer this country,' he said. 'However, I don't think it's paradise on earth, or that all other countries are perforce wretched and abominable. I've been to them and I know better. The fact that you elect your officials and that these elections, except in certain urban localities, are honest ones, doesn't intrigue me much. I'm a selfish man, Mr London. In the pure sense of the word. My comfort is more important to me than abstract justice.'

'That's not so uncommon.'

'Probably not. But what I'm really trying to say is that I find it easier and more pleasant to live in America. The police may not be honest, but they are a little less blatant in their thievery. They may slap a person around but rarely beat him to death. A person's more free to live his own life here.'

He sighed. 'I won't go so far as to say that I wouldn't sell out the United States of America. I know myself too well. I probably would. But the price would be extremely high.'

The room stayed silent for several seconds then. I glanced at Maddy. She'd been listening very carefully to Armin and her face was thoughtful. I looked back at Armin. He was putting out his cigarette. I wondered if he had meant to say all that he said, if maybe his words had carried him away.

He looked up, his eyes bright. 'I become intolerably long-winded at times,' he said apologetically. 'You asked a most simple question and I delivered myself of a long sermon which didn't even supply the answer to your question. Set your mind at rest, Mr London. I'm no spy. The briefcase contains no State secrets.'

'That's good.'

'Thus,' he said, 'there are no problems, no barriers between us. Unless you have another question?'

'That's all.'

'Then we work together? It's a bargain?'

'It's a bargain,' I said.

9

He shook out a cigarette and held it loose and limp between the thumb and forefinger of his right hand. He didn't light it. Instead he turned it over and over, staring thoughtfully at it. Suddenly he shrugged and stuck it back in the pack.

'I smoke too much,' he said. 'I also have a tendency to waste a great deal of time. But it is difficult to know where to begin. I want to give you as much information as I possibly can, yet I also want to take up a minimum of your time. Your time and mine as well. Time is precious. We will profit more through action than through words. Yet words are essential, too.'

In turn he studied the floor and the ceiling and his neatly manicured fingernails. He looked up at me. 'Let me begin somewhere in the neighborhood of the beginning, Mr London. You are a detective. Your profession must bring you in line with crime and criminals to a greater or lesser degree. Perhaps you've heard of the Wallstein jewels?'

A soft bell rang somewhere in the back of my mind. I told him I never heard of the jewels.

He said: 'Franz Wallstein was the second son of a Prussian industrialist. He was born shortly after the turn of the century. His father was a typical member of the Junker caste – a second or third-rate Krupp or Thiessen. The older son – I believe his name was Reinhardt, not that it matters – followed the father into the firm. Franz, the younger son, struck out on his own. In the early thirties he entered the service of a particularly noxious Austrian corporal.'

'Hitler.'

'Or Schicklgruber, as you prefer it. Franz Wallstein was neither well-mannered nor intelligent. Followers of fascist movements rarely are. His sole virtue was his dedication to this questionable cause. While never becoming particularly important, he rose to his own level quickly and enjoyed a certain amount of security. He possessed the qualifications of height, blond hair, blue eyes. He was assigned to a troop of Himmler's Elite Guards in the SS. Later, during the war, he was placed second in command at one of the larger concentration camps. I think it was Belsen; I'm not entirely sure. In that capacity his dedication did not prove entirely flawless. He stole.'

I lit my pipe. 'You were talking about jewels.'

'That's correct,' he said, but went on as though he hadn't been interrupted. 'It was standard operating procedure to confiscate any and all possessions of concentration camp prisoners, up to and including the gold from their teeth after they had been gassed. This property, in theory, became the property of the German Reich, but the facts did not always follow theory. Goering, for example, looted Europe to augment his private art collection. Minor guards would take wrist watches for themselves, a bracelet for a wife or mistress. Franz Wallstein followed along these lines. He seemed to have an interest in precious stones. If a prisoner managed to retain possession of valuable jewelry until he reached Wallstein's camp, the jewels generally wound up in Wallstein's foot-locker.'

He stood up, paused for breath. 'Things went smoothly for Wallstein,' he went on. 'They did not go smoothly for Nazi Germany. The war moved to an end. Wallstein was at once a hunted man, no longer a trusted servant of a secure government. He was not pursued as avidly as Bormann or Eichmann or Himmler himself. But he was on the wanted lists, as they say. His wife was pregnant at the time and must have seemed like excess baggage to him. He left her in Germany, bundled up his jewels and fled the country.

'He went first to Mexico. The political climate there soon turned out to be less than ideal and within several months it was time for him to make his move again. This time he picked a nation where he felt he would be more welcome. He chose Argentina.'

I shook out my pipe, glanced briefly at Maddy. She was listening closely. So was I, but I wished he would get to the point already. Bannister and the briefcase were more important to me than a crooked Nazi and stolen jewels.

'Argentina was a natural home for him,' Armin went on. 'It is certain that he found countrymen there. German is supposed to be the second language of Buenos Aires. Wallstein made himself comfortable, bought an attractive house in a fashionable suburb and married a local girl without bothering to divorce the wife he'd left in Germany. He changed his name to Heinz Linder and opened an importing concern in Buenos Aires. Strong rumor has it that he engaged in smuggling of one sort or another, probably of narcotics. But this remains to be proved. Q.E.D. Whatever his actual means of support, Wallstein-Linder added to his collection of jewels. They reposed in a wall safe on the second floor of his home.'

'And somebody hit the safe?'

He sighed. 'Not exactly, Mr London. The situation is a bit more complex than that. Wallstein was not entirely forgotten. A group of Israeli agents similar to the ones who caught Eichmann were looking for former SS men, Wallstein among them. Two agents followed his trail to Mexico City and lost him there. A few years later they extended the trail to Buenos Aires.'

The bell went off again, louder this time. 'I remember now,' I said. 'About a year ago. He was found dead in Argentina and identified as Wallstein. There was a short article in the *Times*.'

Armin was nodding, smiling. 'The same man,' he said. 'There wasn't much of a story at the time. The Israelis didn't bother to drag him off for a trial as they did with Eichmann. Franz Wallstein was not that important. They only wished to even the score with him: they tracked him down, broke into his home, shot him dead and left him to rot. The news value was small. The Argentine officials denied that he was Wallstein, not wanting to be accused of harboring a fugitive. The Israelis leaked the story but it still got little publicity.'

'They shot him and took the jewels?'

'No, of course not. They were assassins, not thieves. They did their work and left him there. But the small amount of publicity attendant upon the killing was enough to attract the attention of that sort of professional criminal who specializes in precious stones. A ring of Canadian jewel thieves flew down to Buenos Aires and stole the jewels. I don't know the precise details of the crime but it was done well, it seems. They broke into Wallstein's home, tied up his widow, tied up her maid, cracked the safe, grabbed up the jewels and took the first plane out of the country. As I heard it, they were in and out of Argentina in less than twenty-four hours. That may be an exaggeration. At any rate, they worked quickly and left no traces.'

'Any insurance?'

He chuckled. 'On stolen jewels? Hardly. He was just a small-scale importer with not too much money – on the surface. He couldn't attract attention by insuring his collection. It was too great a risk.'

I nodded. 'Go on,' I said.

He shook a cigarette from his pack again and rolled it around some more between his fingers. This time he put it to his lips and lighted it. He drew in smoke.

'Sorry,' I said. 'I didn't mean to change the subject.'

'But you didn't, Mr London.'

'No?'

'Not at all. The fact that the jewels were not insured is really most relevant. Do you know much about jewel thieves?'

I didn't know a hell of a lot. 'They're supposed to be an elite criminal class,' I said. 'They steal jewels and sell them to a fence. That's about all I know.'

'They're elite,' he said. 'The rest is inaccurate.'

He smiled when my eyebrows went up. 'For a good group of jewel thieves, a fence is a last resort. Their first contact is with the insurance company.'

I didn't get it.

'Let us suppose that a collection of gems is insured for half a million dollars, Mr London. Once the theft is a *fait accompli* the company is legally obligated to pay out the face value of the policy to the policyholder. Now let's suppose further that an agent for the thieves approaches an agent of the insurance company and offers to sell the jewels back for, say, two hundred thousand dollars. The company invariably pays. It's a clear saving to them of three hundred thousand. And a top thief always prefers to deal with an insurance company, you see. He gets a better price and runs less risk of a double cross.'

'Why?'

'Because the company has to preserve its good name in criminal circles. I'm not joking, Mr London. It sounds ludicrous at first but it follows the laws of logic. Perhaps, insurance companies only encourage criminal behavior by this practice. They don't seem to care. The figures on their own balance sheets are of greater concern to them.'

'That's ... that's unfair!'

That was Maddy talking and we both turned to look at her. Armin grinned at her. He said: 'Unfair? To whom, my dear? Not to the policyholder, certainly – he gets his – possibly – irreplaceable jewelry returned. And not to the insurance company, which saves money. And not to the thieves, unfair to whom?'

'To the public—'

'Oh, but the public gains, too,' Armin told her. 'Any loss the company sustains is passed on to the public in the form of higher premiums, therefore, it's to the public's advantage for the company to save money.'

'But—'

She stopped after the one word and looked around vacantly. She was very unhappy. She's slick and smooth and big-city, but she was lost now. I rescued her.

'Okay,' I said. 'The jewels weren't insured and the Canadians had troubles.'

'Correct,' he said. 'They had troubles. They flew from Buenos Aires to New York, then from New York to Toronto. That was their base of operations. They cached the spoils and took up residence, for a time, in some hotels on Yonge Street.'

'How many were there?'

'Four men.'

'And how much were the jewels worth?'

'That's hard to say. Prices of stolen goods are almost incalculable, Mr London. There are so many factors involved. The Hope Diamond is priceless, for example, but worthless to a thief. He couldn't sell it.'

I wanted facts and he kept giving me background. 'That doesn't apply here,' I told him. 'The original owners are nameless, probably dead.'

'Precisely. The Wallstein jewels are as readily convertible into cash as valuable jewels could be. Still, an appraisal is difficult. The figures I've heard quoted place the total worth at somewhere around four hundred thousand dollars. Retail, that is.'

I whistled. Maddy took a deep breath. And Peter Armin smiled.

I said: 'That's a lot of money.'

'And that's an understatement. At any rate, the thieves had to find a fence, a receiver for the jewels. Two of them were in debt and strapped for cash. They couldn't unload a little at a time. They needed a big buyer to take the lot off their hands right away. They were willing to settle for one hundred thousand.'

The picture was shaping up but the edges were still fuzzy. I wanted to hurry him up but it didn't seem possible. He was giving me plenty of theory and plenty of background with an occasional fact for flavor. He sat in his chair and smoked his Turkish cigarettes and I listened to him.

'The thieves knew several reliable fences. All of them were financially incapable of handling a transaction of such proportion. They might have arranged to split the deal between a few of them but they wanted to get it all over with in a hurry. They wanted one fence for the works.' He paused for breath. 'They couldn't find such a man in Toronto. There was one in New York, but they knew him solely by reputation.'

'Bannister?'

'Of course. Mr Clayton Bannister. What do you know about him, Mr London?'

I knew that he played rough and talked ugly. I knew I didn't like him at all.

'Not much,' I said.

'A most impressive man in his own way. He began during World War II with two partners named Ferber and Marti. The three of them grew fat with a number of black market operations. Gasoline stamps, unobtainable items, that sort of thing. They made a good thing of the war, Mr London. Of the three, Mr Bannister alone remains. Mr Ferber and Mr Marti are dead. Murdered.'

'By Bannister?'

'Undoubtedly, but no one ever managed to prove it. Since then he's made an enormous amount of money in extra-legal activities while retaining a veneer of respectability. He has close ties with the local syndicate and remains independent at the same time. I've already said that he acts as a receiver of stolen goods. He does other things. He probably imports heroin, probably exports gold, probably receives smuggled diamonds and similar contraband. He heads a small but strong organization and his men are surprisingly loyal to him. He rewards the faithful and kills traitors. A good policy.'

'What does he look like?'

'Like a gorilla. But I can do better than that. I have one of the few photographs in existence of him. A rare item, that. Here – have a look at it.'

He took a snapshot from the pigskin pocket secretary and passed it to me. I looked at a head-and-shoulders shot of a man about forty with a massive and almost hairless head, a wide dome with fringe around the edges. He had a bulldog jaw and beady pig eyes set wide in a slab of a forehead. The mouth was a firm thin line, the nose regular, a little thick at the bridge.

I studied it, passed it to Maddy. 'This the man at the party?'

She looked at it.

'Add five years,' Armin told her. 'Add twenty or thirty pounds. Add the foul-smelling cigar he habitually smokes. And you'll have Mr Bannister.'

She said: 'I think it's him.'

'But you're not sure?'

'Almost sure, Ed. He had a hat on when I saw him and he never took it off. And that bald head is the most distinctive feature in the picture. I'm trying to imagine him with a hat on. I didn't get a good look at him and it was months ago and there wasn't any point in remembering him, not at the time. But I'm pretty sure it's him.'

'It has to be,' I told her. I turned to Armin. 'Okay – how did the thieves get in touch with him?'

'They didn't.'

'No?'

'Not exactly,' he said. He lit another cigarette and looked at me through a cloud of hazy smoke. 'Mr Bannister seemed to be the right man for them. But they didn't really trust him. None of them knew him. Honor among thieves is largely a romantic invention and they had no cause to believe that Mr Bannister was an honorable man. They wanted to deal with him without getting close.'

'Sure. They couldn't stop him from taking the jewels and telling them to go to hell.'

'Precisely. They could hardly take him to court. They had skill and wits while he had muscle. They picked an intermediary, a go-between.'

'And that's where you fit in?'

He laughed. 'No, not I. Not at all. One of the thieves was sleeping with an American girl at the time. They sent her to New York with a message for Mr Bannister.'

Maddy said: 'Sheila Kane.'

'If you wish. They knew her as Alicia Arden. A young girl, young and strangely innocent. A lost soul, to be maudlin and poetic about it. Previously she had associated with elements of what they seem to call the Beat Generation. That was in San Francisco. In Los Angeles her friends were petty mobsters. By this time she was living with a jewel thief in Toronto. He briefed her, sent her to New York.'

I tried to picture the girl. 'Young and strangely innocent.' A girl who ran with thieves and who found Jack Enright exciting, awe-inspiring. She made a funny picture. Every time I learned something new about her, the picture went out of focus and came back different.

'Now the plot thickens,' Armin was saying. 'A cliché. But an apt one. Alicia came to New York with a few sample jewels and hunted for Mr Bannister. He tries to pass himself off as a country squire. Has a large estate in Avalon on the tip of Long Island. He's a minor patron of the arts – supports a poor painter or two, donates regularly and substantially to several museums, occasionally backs a theatrical production. Alicia got his ear on one pretext or another, then told him her business.'

'And he liked it?'

He sighed. 'The details grow difficult now. Hazy. Mr Bannister must have suggested a double cross – she would help him and they would leave the thieves out in the cold. Maybe he offered her twenty or thirty thousand outright. That must have looked better than whatever crumbs her boyfriend was tossing her. At any rate, she cooperated with Mr Bannister.

'She told the thieves to come to New York with the jewels. They let her know where they were staying and she relayed the information to Mr Bannister. Then she went to their hiding place with one hundred thousand dollars. She paid them. They were supposed to give her the jewels in return. They didn't.'

'You mean they were rigging a double cross of their own?'

He shook his head. 'Not at all. Really, they were honest in their way. They feared Mr Banniser and wanted to be out of the city before he could get to them. Instead of the jewels they gave Alicia the briefcase.'

I said: 'I thought we'd get to that sooner or later. Now what in hell is in the briefcase?'

'Directions. A set of directions and a pair of keys which would permit the holder of the case to claim the jewels. They thought this would save them from a cross, since Mr Bannister couldn't chance killing them before he had the jewels. They were wrong.'

'How?'

'Alicia traded the money for the briefcase and left. Minutes later Bannister's thugs broke in on the thieves and took back the money. The thieves disappeared.'

'They skipped town?'

'I rather doubt it,' he said. 'I believe a cement overcoat is the American term. You could probably find the four of them on the river bottom.'

Maddy shuddered. I put an arm around her and Armin looked on with fatherly approval.

'It all grows jumbled after that point,' he said. 'I believe Alicia carried her double cross to its logical conclusion. She had the briefcase. It could make her richer than cooperation with Mr Bannister could. So she stopped being Alicia Arden and turned into Sheila Kane. She must have been planning this all along. Her alias was established in advance.'

'Maybe she was afraid of winding up in the river. Or maybe she wanted the twenty grand in her hands before she gave him the case.'

Armin conceded that was possible. 'She disappeared,' he said. 'Several weeks passed. Then everybody found the poor girl at once. Mr Bannister found her and had her murdered. But he didn't recover the briefcase. You found her, but you didn't find the case either. I was certain you had, but I was wrong. And I was able to find the girl but not the briefcase myself.'

I looked at him. 'It's about time we got around to you,' I said. 'You know all about it without fitting in anywhere. Just how did you get into the act?'

'I didn't.' I stared at him and he smiled back at me. 'Let me put it this way, Mr London. I learned of the situation. My livelihood hinges upon my ability to hear of situations where a profit is in the offing. I heard of this one, worked very carefully, found the girl out, and arrived too late on the scene. I'm still searching for the briefcase. I intend to make a spectacular profit when I get hold of it.' His smile spread. 'Does that answer your question?'

'I guess it has to.'

He held out both hands. 'My contribution,' he said. 'Now you must keep your part of the bargain. What do you know?'

'Not much.'

'It may help. Will you tell me?'

I gave him most of it. I left out Jack Enright's name, kept some of the details purposely vague. He listened to all of it.

'That helps,' he said. 'It explains things.'

'It does?'

'Of course. I now understand several points which made no sense before. Your presence, for example. I had to think you were after the briefcase since there was no other explanation for your interest in Alicia. I also understand how she found an alias so easily. It was waiting for her because of her double life with your friend. Yes, it makes sense now.'

There was silence for a few seconds. Maddy broke it. 'You said you went to the apartment,' she said to Armin. 'Was that after Sheila ... Alicia ... was killed?'

'That's correct. After Mr London's friend and before Mr London. Say ten o'clock.'

'And the apartment? What did it look like?'

He shrugged. 'As Mr London found it. The apartment neat, the girl garbed in stockings and garter belt. That's all.'

'Just like that,' I said.

'Just like that. I searched thoroughly, of course, but I left everything as I found it. A bizarre tableau. But I left it as it was.'

'Then somebody was there after my friend and before you.'

'Possibly.'

'But—'

He said: 'Not necessarily, though. Your friend, Mr London, is neither criminal nor detective. He entered, reacted, left. He may have seen what you and I saw without it registering on his mind. You and I were emotionally stable, saw the scene as it was. But your friend must have been distraught—'

'He was a wreck.'

'And consequently may have seen his mistress dead without seeing anything else. The death alone stayed in his memory. He arranged the rest unconsciously to conform with his vision of what should be, not what was.'

'That's pretty far out, isn't it?'

'I'm not stating it as fact, Mr London. Purely as a supposition. It makes a certain amount of sense, doesn't it?'

'Maybe.'

'Think it through,' he suggested. 'The apartment was neat all along. Alicia was at home. Bannister or his men came in, searched the apartment, found nothing, killed her. Perhaps they molested her sexually. He employs that type of thug—'

I reminded him that there was no evidence.

'There doesn't have to be,' he said. 'She was hardly a virgin. Or suppose they stripped her to search her, if you prefer it that way. They killed her and left. Your friend came, saw, and ran screaming, his mind unhinged. I came, searched, and left. You came, removed the body, and went away with it.'

His analysis was logical enough. I let it lie there. Something was a little out of whack but I could worry about it later.

I stood up, turned to Maddy. 'Let's go,' I said.

'Leaving?' He looked disappointed.

'Might as well,' I said. 'I'm going to see where I can get with Bannister. In the meantime you can work from the angle of the briefcase. With both of us handling opposite sides of the street we should double our chances of getting somewhere.'

'We should.'

'We've made progress already,' I told him. 'There's just one thing more.'

I took out his Beretta, let him look at it. I think there was a second or two when he thought I was going to shoot him with it.

'This is yours,' I said. 'You might as well have it.'

He did one hell of a take. He stared hard at me, then burst out laughing. He was a little guy but he laughed like a dynamo. It took him a few minutes before he could talk again.

'Oh, that's funny,' he said. 'That's really funny. But I still have the mate to that gun, Mr London. And since we're working together I'd like you to keep that one for your own protection. You might need it.'

He started laughing again. 'But that's funny,' he said. 'That's really very funny.'

10

We left him laughing and rode the elevator down to the lobby. I stopped there to relight my pipe. I'm glad I did. Otherwise I probably would have missed him.

He was the kind of guy it's easy to miss. He sat in a big armchair and disappeared in it. He had his nose buried in a copy of the *Morning Telegraph* but his eyes showed over the top of it and they were looking at us.

We had a tail.

I finished lighting the pipe, took Maddy by the arm and steered her toward the door. I heard a rustle behind us as he started to fold up his paper. 'Don't look around,' I said, 'but we've got a shadow. A little man who isn't there.'

'How do we get rid of him?'

It's not hard to duck a shadow if you know he's there. You can tell your cabby to do some tricks with his hack, or you can walk in one entrance of a building and out another, or you can play games on the subway, getting off the car just before the doors close and letting your tail ride to Canarsie alone. But I didn't feel like just ducking the little bastard. He was Bannister's present to me and I wanted to send him home looking ugly. I was sick of Bannister and his presents.

'Could you stand a screen test?'

She didn't understand.

'You're an actress,' I told her. 'I've got a little acting for you to do. Game?'

I told her about it and she was game. We walked out of the Ruskin and down the block to Forty-third Street. We cornered at Forty-third and idled in a doorway, waiting for our friend to catch up with us. He was lousy. He took the corner and breezed past us without spotting us.

Now we were tailing him.

He must have thought we were shuffling along ahead of him in the crowd. He kept on going, taking life easy, and we stayed with him all the way to Broadway.

Then Maddy went into her act.

We picked up a little speed and moved even with him, Maddy on the inside. Just as we moved into the mainstream of pedestrian traffic Maddy brushed up against him and let out a yell they could have heard in Secaucus. Everybody within three blocks turned and stared at her. The little guy stared, too, and his eyes popped halfway out of his pudgy head.

So it was my turn. I yelled: 'You rotten son of a bitch!' Then I grabbed him with one hand and hit him with another. He bounced off the side of the building and looked at me with the sickest expression anybody ever had.

'Horrible,' Maddy kept telling the world. 'Dirty little pervert. Put his hands all over . . . oh, horrible!'

The jerk looked the part. He had runny eyes and a weak mouth and glasses half an inch thick. When I hit him the second time he lost the glasses. They landed on the sidewalk and somebody ground them into the pavement.

I was still hitting him when a cop turned up. He was big and rosily Irish and he wanted to know what the hell I was doing. I didn't have to tell him. The crowd – a big one, and all rooting for me, defender of chastity and feminine virtue – let him know just what was happening and why. He gave our shadow a very unhappy look.

'I could take him in,' he said. 'But it's a heap of trouble. You'd have to swear out a complaint and make an appearance in court. And I'd have to come in and testify. Work for everybody.'

I commiserated with him.

'I'll tell you,' the cop said. 'Why don't you just belt him a few times and forget him? He won't pull a stunt like that again, I'll tell the world. And my eyes will be open for him from now on.'

That sounded like a good idea. I stood the shadow up against the wall and hit him in the face. He lost a few teeth and his nose started to bleed.

'Tell Bannister to go to hell,' I told him.

I hit him again. Then I piled Maddy into a cab and we left him there.

'I wish you'd put that thing away,' Maddy was saying. 'It scares me stiff.'

I'd been checking the Beretta to make sure it was loaded. It was. I put it back together and gave it a pat, then dropped it back in my jacket pocket.

'Take off your jacket,' she said. 'Relax.'

I hung my jacket on a doorknob and sank down again on the couch. We were in Maddy's apartment where the cab had dropped us. It was late.

'Poor Ed,' she said. 'How do you feel now?'

'Don't remind me.'

'Bad?'

I nodded. 'The cognac wore off,' I said. 'I can feel my stomach again. I should have stopped for a bottle.'

'Look in the kitchen.'

I gave her a long look, then stood up and went into the little kitchen. Red and white linoleum covered the floor. A gas stove sat in one corner and looked dangerous. An antique refrigerator sat in another corner and looked undependable. There was a rickety table between them, painted to match the linoleum, and on top of it there was a bottle of Courvoisier. A pint, unopened.

I picked it up gently and carried it back to the living room. Maddy had a smile on her face and a gleam in her eyes. 'This,' I said, 'was not here yesterday.'

'The great detective is right.'

'And you're not much of a brandy drinker. You didn't buy this for your own consumption, Madeleine.'

She blushed beautifully. 'The detective is right again,' she said. 'I bought it this afternoon before I went detecting for you. I sort of hoped you'd be up here soon. Now pour yourself a drink while I sit here and feel wanton.'

I opened the bottle and poured drinks for both of us. I gave her about an ounce and filled my glass to the brim. I drank off some of the brandy and told my stomach it could relax now. Then I gave Maddy her glass and sat on the couch with her, sipping and smoking, while the world got better again.

She said: 'You're not going home tonight.'

I started to say something but she didn't give me a chance. 'Don't flatter yourself, Ed. I don't have any designs on your virtue. Not in your condition. It would probably kill you.'

'Sounds like—'

'—a good way to go. I know all about it. Don't hand me a hard time, Ed. You're staying here tonight. You can't go back to your apartment. You'd be a sitting duck and God knows how many people want to shoot you.'

'Not too many,' I told her. 'I could always take a hotel room.'

She said *no* very emphatically. 'It'll take you hours to find one and hours to fall asleep. And this is the best hotel in New York, Ed. Here you get congenial companionship, room and board, and the use of an untapped phone. What more could you ask for?'

'That's plenty. You make it sound sensible.'

'It is sensible,' she insisted. 'And you're staying. Agreed?'

I agreed. I slipped an arm around her and took a sip of the cognac. I was getting tired but I didn't feel like sleep. I was too comfortable to think about moving.

'I've got a feeling,' she said suddenly. 'I don't think you should be on that Peter Armin's side.'

'Oh? I thought you liked him.'

She bit her lip. 'I do, kind of. But he's a crook, Ed. He wants to make an illegal profit on stolen jewels. If you get the briefcase back are you going to give it to him?'

'Uh-huh.'

'Even though it's illegal?'

I took a sip of the cognac. 'We made a bargain,' I told her. 'Besides, I'm looking for a killer. Not a batch of jewels. A murderer.'

'But—'

'And the murderer's all I give a damn about,' I went on. 'Why in hell should I care what happens to the jewels? Armin's as much entitled to them as anybody else. Who do they belong to? Wallstein's dead and buried. His widow shouldn't get them – they weren't his to give her and she wasn't married to him legally, anyway. The original owners are either dead or lost. Who's next in line? The government of Argentina, as a reward for harboring a Nazi?'

I took a breath. 'I don't care about them. Armin may be as crooked as a corkscrew. As far as I'm concerned he's welcome to the briefcase and the jewels and whatever he can get out of this mess. All I care about is a killer.'

'Then why did you ask for five thousand dollars?'

'Because otherwise he would have thought I was insane. And because Bannister's boys ruined my home and my appetite. I've been shot at and followed and slugged. Hell, I don't have a client – I might as well get a little compensation one way or the other. I can use five grand.'

She nodded, digesting this. I couldn't tell whether she approved or not. Hell, I'm not a plaster saint. Single men in barracks don't grow into them.

'What I wonder now,' I said, 'is how much of Armin's story is true.'

'You think he lied?'

'I'm sure he lied. It's a question of degree.' I shrugged. 'I can't swallow that routine of his about being a clever operator waiting in the wings to make a neat profit. It's too damned cute. I'd like to know where he fits in.'

'Any ideas, Mr London, sir?'

'A couple,' I said. 'Notice how formal he is? You're not the only one who calls me "Mr London." He's never called me anything else. He even refers to our boy Clay as "Mr Bannister".'

'It's a common affectation, Ed.'

'Sure. But Sheila-Alicia was always just plain "Alicia" to him. I've got a hunch he knew her when. Think back a minute. He talked about her almost reminiscently. Remember?'

'I didn't notice. But now that you mention it . . .'

I grinned. 'Now that I mention it, I think he's one of the jewel thieves. Or Alicia's buddy from the past, hooking up with her again to pull a quick one.'

We sat there thinking that one over. I got my pipe going again, worked on the cognac. 'One thing comes first,' I told her. 'The briefcase. Nobody's got it and it's in the middle of everything. I think I'll ring up Jack Enright tomorrow.'

'Why?'

'Because I think I can pry a little more out of him. The girl must have been nervous as all hell just after she pulled the rug out from under Bannister. She may have dropped a hint or two about the briefcase.'

'But he said—'

'I know what he said. Memory's a tricky proposition. I'm going to try him on Armin's theory about the apartment, then on the briefcase. He may be able to remember a little more now. His big concern now is keeping himself in the clear and preserving the harmony of his happy home. His memory might work better now that he's had a day or two to cool off.'

She took my pipe from my mouth and placed it in an ashtray. 'Speaking of which,' she cooed, 'it's time for you to cool yourself off. You've been through the wringer today, Ed. Drink up your brandy and we'll go to bed.'

I leered lecherously.

'To sleep,' she said. 'Not to bed. To sleep.'

I finished the brandy.

Her bed was soft and welcome, the sheets cool and clean. I let my head sink into the pillow and opened my eyes to look at darkness. Water was running in the bathroom. I pictured her washing her face, brushing her teeth, drying herself with a towel.

Pretty pictures.

The bedroom door opened inward. The light was behind her and I saw her slender body silhouetted in the door frame. She touched a switch and the light died. She came into the room, closed the door behind her. I could barely see her in the darkness.

'Ed?'

I didn't answer her.

I heard a nightgown rustle. She lifted the covers on her side of the bed and slid under them. 'Goodnight, Ed,' she whispered. 'Sleep well. I'll make breakfast for you in the morning, Ed.'

I still didn't say anything. I heard her breathing beside me, sensed the sweet warmth of her body. I remembered that body, remembered the night before.

I reached for her.

For an instant she gasped, surprised. Then my mouth found hers and we kissed. I took her shoulders in my hands and felt her body begin to tremble.

'Oh,' she said. 'Oh, Ed. Ed, we can't, not tonight, Ed. You're all tired and all hurt and we can't. Ed—'

I ran a hand over her body, all clean and soft and warm through the sheer nightgown.

'We can't, Ed. Ed, darling, we can't, I want to, I want to but we can't.'

I put my face to her cheek and breathed the fragrance of her hair. I kissed her again and heard her sigh.

'We can't,' she said. 'We can't we can't we can't we can't—'

I drew her body very close to mine. I whispered softly into her ear.

'We can,' I said. 'And we will.'

We did.

She amazed me in the morning. She scrambled eggs and fried bacon and toasted rye bread, and she didn't even try to talk to me until I was working on my second cup of strong black coffee. I had never known a woman could behave so magnificently in the morning, or look so lovely. I told her this and she beamed at me.

'The phone,' she said. 'You were going to call Enright.'

I picked up the receiver and dialed his number. A female voice found out who I was and told me to hold the line. I did. Then Jack picked up the phone.

'Ed, Jack. I've got to talk to you. Important.'

He said: 'Oh, Christ.' Then he didn't say anything for a minute or two. A juvenile voice wailed unhappily in the background. 'I'm busy as all hell right now, Ed. You at home? I'll call you as soon as I get a free moment.'

I told him where I was and he took down the number. 'Stay there,' he said. 'I may be a while. Bye, Ed.'

I told Maddy he'd be calling back. We cleared off the table. She washed the dishes and I dried them. Then we sat around waiting for the phone to ring, with the whole scene so damned domestic that I couldn't stand it. Finally the phone came through for me and I stood up to answer it.

'It might be for me,' she said. 'I'll take it.'

I was already at the phone.

'Please,' she said. 'You'll compromise me.'

'You've already been compromised. And after the way you kept saying we couldn't. You were wrong.'

'So you're Superman. Now . . . hey, let go of me, you oaf! It's the middle of the murky morning and the phone's ringing. Let go!'

I got out of the way. She answered the phone while I stood by, waiting for her to hand it to me when Jack identified himself. This didn't happen.

The phone was for her and I listened while she talked to somebody named Maury. She spent most of her time listening, tossing in an occasional uh-huh. Then she made scribbling motions in the air until I brought her a scrap of paper and a pencil. She took them and began jotting down mysterious information. This went on for a few minutes, until finally she said: "Thanks, sweetie" at least four times and kissed the telephone mouthpiece twice. Then she hung up and turned to me, her eyes bright.

'It was Maury,' she said.

'Thanks. Who's Maury?'

'My agent. And Lon Kaspar's auditioning for the lead in *The House of Bernardo Alba*, it's the Lorca play and they're doing a revival over on Second Avenue and it's this afternoon and Maury thinks I've got a great chance and—'

She ran out of breath before she ran out of words. I asked her when she had to be at the theater.

'Eleven-thirty, if I can. What time is it?'

'Quarter to eleven.'

'What!'

'We slept late and ate slowly and graciously. You better hurry, Maddy. But don't you get to study the part?'

'It's just a reading today. Oh, God, I've got to rush. God, I have to hurry. It's all the way across town, dammit. You wait here for your phone call, Ed. The door locks by itself when you close it. I have to rush.'

I kissed her. She held onto me for a minute, then pulled away. 'Dammit to hell,' she said. 'I wanted to stay with you today. I thought we could hunt the killer together. Then this came up.'

'I wouldn't have let you come along.'

'You couldn't have stopped me. But one little call from Maury . . . damn.'

I grinned. 'Is it a good part?'

'It's a beautiful part,' she said. 'Simply beautiful. And Maury thinks I can get it. He says Kaspar knows me and likes my work. I've got to run, Ed. One call on the old phone and away goes Maddy. I'll be home sometime this afternoon, I think. Call me.'

She was still talking on her way out the door, still bubbling and babbling as she went down the stairs. From the front window I watched her hail a cab. My smile followed her down the street.

A sweet kid.

I poured a third cup of coffee and sweetened it with a taste of cognac. I lit a cigarette to go with it.

A hell of a sweet kid.

I thought about Jack Enright. I thought about Kaye, his wife and my sister. Evenings at their place, the three of us plus whatever girl Kaye was tying to fix me up with at the time. 'You ought to get married, Ed London. It's no life for a man, being a bachelor. You should meet a nice girl and settle down.'

And I thought about Maddy, and how sweet she was in the morning, and how sweet she was at night. And Kaye's words made more sense than they ever had before.

Which scared me.

The phone rang half an hour after Maddy left. I answered it. It was Jack.

'Sorry I had to hang up on you,' he said. 'I was up to my neck in work and I didn't want to talk on that phone of mine. I'm on a pay phone now. Is your line safe?'

I told him it was.

'Did you see the paper. Ed? They had a bit about Sheila. That she was involved with some gangsters and they killed her.'

I wondered where they got that. 'They're right,' I said.

'Then why not let it go? You know how those men operate. Fly a killer in from the other side of the country, then fly him away when he's done. You can't solve a crime like that. Why knock yourself out trying? Why waste time?'

'You all worried about my time, Jack?'

A sigh. 'All right,' he said. 'Okay, I'm scared. If you come up with anything you'll have to give it all to the police. Then everything's out in the open. I'm scared, Ed. I've got a lot of things to be scared about. A family and a practice. I don't want them to blow up in my face.'

'I can keep you out of it.'

'Can you?'

'Uh-huh. And I couldn't let go even if I wanted to, Jack. Two heavies handed me a beating yesterday. Another guy was tailing me. Somebody else missed me with a bullet a while back. I've been on one end or the other of enough handguns to win the West ten times over. So I can't leave it alone.'

'God,' he said. 'They're trying to scare you?'

'They're trying to get a briefcase from me. I don't have it.'

'Who does?'

'I don't know. Jack, didn't Sheila ever mention anything about a briefcase? Anything about jewels or criminals?'

'No. Never. Let me think.' I let him think. 'Never,' he said flatly. 'I told you what she talked about. There was never anything about a briefcase or jewels or crooks.'

I let go of it. 'About the apartment,' I said, shifting. 'When you found Sheila. Maybe you were mistaken, maybe the apartment was neat and Sheila was naked and your mind did a little dance with itself. You were under a strain, Jack. You might not have seen things the way they were. Hell, you're a doctor. You know how the human mind can react to shock.'

I listened to heavy breathing. Then: 'You think you and I saw the apartment the same way.'

'That's right.'

He hesitated. 'That's been bothering me,' he said finally. 'I almost called you last night. I wanted to tell you about it.'

'Want to tell me now?'

'It's just a feeling I had.'

'Go on.'

He said: 'I was thinking about the murder. The way I found the body. I went over it in my mind and it didn't seem to mesh together properly. Do you know what I mean? I had a certain distinct memory – a dead girl, Sheila, and a messed-up apartment, and all that. But somewhere in the back of my mind was the idea that it wasn't that way at all. There was a conflicting picture that hadn't been there before. A picture of Sheila nude and dead in the middle of a neat apartment. I don't know if the second picture is real or if it stuck in my mind when you described it to me. It could be either way.'

'I see.'

'I'm not sold on it one way or the other,' he went on. 'But if you've got a hunch I was seeing things, well, I'll go along with you. It makes sense to me.'

I said something innocuous. He told me again that he hoped I'd keep him out of it and I said I'd do my best. We spent a few seconds looking around for something to say to each other, then settled on 'So long' and ended the conversation. I held onto the receiver and studied it, trying to think clearly. Then I put it down and poured the last of Maddy's coffee into my cup.

The conversation with Jack hadn't proved anything one way or the other. He was too busy trying to forget for ever the fact that he had managed to commit adultery and get mixed up in a murder. Now all he cared about was staying in the clear and smelling like a rose. Anything he said or did was going to be colored by that desire. He'd go along with any theory I came up with just to keep things simple.

I finished the coffee, washed out my cup and put it away. I found a broom and gave the apartment a quick sweeping. I wrote Maddy a note, then read it over and decided it was painfully cute. I tore it up and wrote her a blander one, put it on the rickety kitchen table and set the brandy bottle on top of it.

At the door I turned to take a last look at the apartment and think pleasant thoughts about the girl who lived in it. Then I went down two flights, passing Madame Sindra and the machine shop, and out onto the street.

The sun was high in the sky and the air was hot. I managed to snag a cab on Eight Avenue. I sat back and gave my home address to the driver, letting him fight the traffic.

A few points bothered me. Both Armin and Bannister knew I went to the girl's apartment. They sure as hell didn't pool information between them. Which meant both of them had seen me.

How?

They couldn't both have kept the apartment under surveillance at the same time. They both knew I went there, but neither one knew I didn't come out with the briefcase.

Why?

I tossed it around and didn't get anywhere with it. I lit my pipe while the cab clawed its way through the beginnings of the noon rush hour. My cabby inched his way north on Eighth Avenue, jockeying for position with Puerto Rican boys pushing hand trucks of ladies' dresses. I sat and smoked.

The city was getting hotter as the day rolled along. Maddy was reading for a good part; I was chasing a briefcase and a killer. A good day.

When we hit Forty-second Street I started wondering about my own apartment. I lost the thought when we passed the Ruskin and Peter Armin came back to mind. I got back to it a few blocks along the line and wondered what sort of a job Cora Johnson had been able to do. And how much of the damage was permanent.

And how well five grand would compensate for it.

My stomach-ache wasn't bothering me. Ralph and Billy still were, though. I sat there and remembered. And hated them.

I reached into my pocket. The Beretta was still there, small and sleek and deadly. I stroked cool metal and thought about Ralph and Billy.

I climbed stairs to my apartment, lifted a corner of my Welcome mat – which says Go Away, incidentally – and picked up my key. This was one of Cora's less logical habits; she couldn't believe I had two keys to my own apartment and always left the damned key precisely where I had left it for her. This always gave me a bad moment. I couldn't be sure whether she'd been there or not until I opened the door.

I bent over again, scooped up the *Times*. I straightened up, stuck key in lock, held my breath, and pushed. She had been there.

I thanked her silently. The place looked livable again. Hell, it looked great – each book was back in the book-case, the rugs were clean, the furniture polished. I closed the door and tossed my newspaper on a chair. There would be time to read it later on. Now it was more fun to look around.

Some of the books were still ruined, of course. A bookmaker could patch up most of them as soon as I had time to run them in. And the chair cushions were still slit open. But Cora had done one beautiful hell of a job. I took a deep breath, feeling very pleased with the world in general and with Cora Johnson in particular.

Only one thing was out of whack. I looked at it and the room started to spin around. I stood there with my mouth wide open and my stupid face hanging out.

There was a tan cowhide briefcase on the coffee table and it had never been there before.

11

I went to the shelf and poured a little cognac in one of the glasses. I drank it off and turned around.

The briefcase was still there.

One of the slick mags had a feature running a few years back under the title 'What's Wrong With This Picture?' The pitch was quietly mindless – a Mona Lisa frowning on a wall, a man with two left hands, a face without eyebrows. The reader was supposed to puzzle it out, figure out what was wrong.

Hell, it was easy. The briefcase was wrong. It wasn't supposed to be there at all, and there it was.

It should have been funny as hell. By the time I finally managed to sell Armin on the idea that I never had the case to begin with, wham – there it was. For a crazy second or two I wondered if it had been there all along, if Cora had unearthed it for me while she straightened up. That little piece of insanity didn't last long. Somebody had brought the briefcase there while I was out. Somebody had given me a present.

Why?

I wasn't going to worry about whys just then. I went to the door, locked it and slid the bolt home. I took the briefcase from the coffee table and sat down in a chair to examine it. I turned it over and over in my hands like a little kid with a Christmas present trying to guess what was inside. I shook it to see if it would rattle. It didn't.

It was well-made and it was expensive. The leather was top-grain quality, the stitching neat and precise. It looked like an English job, which fit Armin's little story about Canadian jewel thieves. But since most of the better briefcases sold in the States are English ones, it really didn't mean too much one way or the other. So there was nothing to do but open the thing. So I opened it.

The inside had more things going for it. There was a long and detailed letter typed flawlessly on plain white bond. It bore no date, no return address, no signature. It led off with a simple 'Dear Sir' and went on from there.

The instructions were complicated. Two keys were supposed to be in the briefcase. One, according to the letter, would fit a small locker in Central

Terminal in Buffalo, New York. There was a strongbox in that locker, and the second key would open the strongbox. The box itself contained still another key, this one fitting a locker located in a station of the Toronto subway system. That locker, finally, held the Wallstein jewels.

The nameless person who wrote the letter apologized very carefully for the complexity of the directions. He was sure, he said, that the reader would appreciate them. By use of two lockers plus a strongbox, a man with keys but without instructions would be lost. So would any outsider who happened to break into the Buffalo locker – he'd find a meaningless key. If somebody was lucky enough to break into the Toronto locker he'd get the jewels, but nobody would know which Toronto locker to open unless he had the instructions in the first place and the key in the second – the key from the Buffalo locker.

I had to read the damned thing three times through before I could figure out which key was which and what the hell it was all about. By the time it made sense I had to admire whoever figured it all out. Nothing was left to chance. And there was another advantage – in the time it took to follow all the directions, the thieves would be out of town. And safe.

It was cute. But for all the good it had done the thieves they could have filled the briefcase with jewels and let it go at that. Bannister had managed to put them all in the river – except for Armin, possibly – and to get his dough back at the same time. Proving, maybe, that the best laid plans of jewel thieves gang aft aglay. They're in the same boat with the mice and the men. And it leaked like a sieve.

So now I had the briefcase. The next step, according to the book, was to turn it over to Peter Armin and collect a quick five thousand dollars for my troubles. Somehow I couldn't quite see myself doing this. Not just yet. I had told Maddy the truth – my main interest was catching a killer and I didn't care who Armin was or what he did with the jewels. But the briefcase might be useful to me. Maybe I could catch a murderer with it. Armin could wait a day or two for his briefcase and I could wait a day or two for my money. The killer came first.

I looked at the briefcase with respect. It was a bomb that could go off any minute, a nitro bomb that would behave unpredictably. I decided to dismantle it.

I staggered through the directions again. It was the fourth time around for me and this time I memorized them. There wasn't all that much to remember. Just a pair of locker numbers. When they were tucked away in my mind I found a sheet of typing paper and hauled out my old portable. I copied the letter word for word, substituting new and meaningless numbers for the original ones. Then I tore the original letter into little strips of paper and flushed them down the toilet. I felt like a character in a bad Mitchum movie.

I found the pair of keys in a pocket in the briefcase. Their numbers had been filed off and they looked innocent as vestal virgins. I replaced them with two keys of my own. One of them would open the door to a place in Greenwich Village where I'd lived years ago. Another would open the door to an apartment where a girl I once knew once lived. She was married now, and she didn't live there any more. So I didn't need the key.

I filed the sides of both keys, put them in the pocket of the briefcase, zipped it shut. I added the new set of phony instructions and closed the briefcase.

My bomb was a dud now.

I remembered telling Maddy something about bombs, saying they were going to start going off, that I wanted to set off a few of my own. I wondered if you could set off a dead bomb, a dud.

It was worth a try.

The kid with all the pimples was scratching himself. He looked up at me and gave me something that was almost a smile. Then he found my car and turned it over to me.

'I thought you just worked nights.'

'Usually,' he said. 'Like today I'm working days. Win a few; lose a few. Today's a good day for a convertible. You can roll down the top and look at the sunshine.'

'Uh-huh. Want to fill the tank?'

He studied the gauge. 'Not worth the sweat,' he said. 'She's almost full now, see? You got to do a lot of driving to empty her, a whole lot. I can fill her when you bring her in.'

'I'll be doing a lot of driving.'

'Well—'

'Fill the tank,' I said.

He filled the tank but he didn't have his heart in it. I told him to put it on the tab, pulled out of the garage and left him scratching and mumbling. I felt better with a full tank of gas. It's one of two prerequisites for a trip to the end of Long Island. The second is courage.

I took Second Avenue south, found the Queens Midtown Tunnel and left the relative sanity of Manhattan for the hinterlands of Queens. I followed a variety of confusing expressway – which is where the courage came into the picture – until I managed to pass through Queens, rush through Nassau County and wind up in Suffolk County.

If you've got enough money, and if you don't like New York, and if Westchester and Connecticut are either too arty or too Madison Avenue for you, you stand a good chance of winding up in Suffolk County. The towns were smaller there, the buildings lower and further apart. I had the top down and the fresh air was choking me. My lungs weren't used to it.

I drove through the countryside and tried to pretend that it wasn't really there. I remembered a line out of Sydney Smith to the effect that the country is sort of a healthy grave. Sydney Smith was right.

Bannister, according to Armin, lived in something called Avalon. I had copied down his address on the back of the snapshot Armin gave me, and when I hit Avalon I pulled over to the curb and fumbled through my wallet until I found it. I looked at it, remembered what Bannister was supposed to look like, then turned the photo over and checked the address. He lived on Emory Hill Road.

There was gas still left in the tank but there was room for more. A gas-pump jockey loaded me up without an argument, polished my windshield, checked my oil and water, and tried to sell me a new fuel pump. He also told me how to get to Emory Hill Road. It ran along the outskirts of Avalon. Living on the outskirts of Avalon is like living in a suburb of New Jersey, or a satellite of the moon. It's ridiculous.

I followed his directions, found Emory Hill Road. I nosed the Chevy past a batch of estates that would have embarrassed Veblen. They were all the last word on the subject of conspicuous consumption. I passed them all by until I found one which made the rest look like Tobacco Road set to music. It had to belong to Clayton Bannister. Nobody else would want it.

First there was the house itself. The manor house, that is – I'm sure that's what he called it. It was a cockeyed cross between Christopher Wren and Le Corbusier, a mixed marriage of the seventeenth and twentieth centuries with the assets of neither and the liabilities of both. I had never seen anything like it before; twentieth-century baroque was a brand-new concept. Flying buttresses do not go with picture windows.

The architect must have shot himself.

There were two other small houses. One must have been the guest house. The other was the garage but it looked more like a stable. A futuristic stable, of course, but still a stable. I saw a Rolls Silver Ghost and a Mercedes 300 and tried to imagine Bannister at the wheel riding to hounds, with Ralph and Billy bellowing 'Tallyho!' at the tops of their impure lungs. An arresting picture.

I parked the Chevy in front of the estate and looked around for a chrome-and-steel hitching post. There should have been one, but there wasn't. I yanked the emergency brake, killed the ignition and got out of the car. I looked at carefully landscaped grounds covered with too many different kinds of shrubs and flowers. He'd have done better cultivating one small garden.

I filled a pipe and got it going. I dropped the match onto the lawn and hoped it would start a fire. Then, briefcase tucked under arm, I started up the road to hell. It was paved with flagstones instead of good intentions.

When I was about thirty yards from the manor house its carved oak door burst open and a gorilla exploded out of it, gun in hand. It was Billy. He ran quickly and awkwardly and stopped a yard away from me.

'Whatcha want?'

I said: 'Take me to your leader.'

'Huh?'

'The boss,' I said patiently. 'I want to see the boss.'

When he looked as though he understood, I held up the briefcase. 'For the boss,' I said. 'A present.' He reached out a paw to snatch it away but I pulled it back and smiled sadly. 'Not for you, Billy Boy. For the boss. Mr Bannister. The king.'

He was still mulling that one over when the other half of the goon squad appeared. Ralph. He walked up quickly, his face a mask, took the gun away from Billy and listened to my speech.

'Go tell the boss who's here and what he wants,' he told Billy. 'I'll stay here and watch him.'

He stayed there and watched me while Billy hurried home with the message to Garcia. We had nothing to say to each other so we stood and glared away. He kept the gun on me and looked as though he wanted me to move so he could put a hole in my stomach. I didn't and it made him unhappy.

He broke the silence.

'What I figure,' he said, 'is the boss'll tell Billy to tell me to take the briefcase away from you and send you home.'

I didn't answer him.

'What I figure,' he went on, 'is you want him to pay you for it. It's stupid, you ask me. He woulda paid you before, when he asked you. You weren't selling. You were so smart and you had to get beat up, now you come to sell to him? He can kick you out on your ear. You could of saved yourself a drive, you could of put it in the mail or called up and said come and get it. You don't make sense.'

I didn't answer him. A bird sang songs in a nearby tree. The wind rustled leaves in other trees. The big carved oak door opened and Billy's big head appeared.

He called: 'The boss says bring him in.'

Ralph managed to register surprise without changing expression. A neat trick. He nodded slowly, then stepped aside and motioned with the gun. I looked at the gun. It was bigger than the Beretta in my pocket.

'You go inside,' he said. 'I walk behind you; I keep this pointed at you. Don't get fancy.'

I didn't get fancy. There were three marble steps at the head of the flagstone path. I climbed them and walked through the open door into the room. Billy pointed through another doorway and led me through to the living room. I followed with Ralph right behind and felt like meat in a sandwich.

The living room had thick wall-to-wall carpeting and a beamed ceiling. The beams were huge. They almost gave the room the air of a cathedral, but misfired slightly. The furniture was large and heavy and ugly. There were books in a bookcase, all expensively bound, mostly in sets, all, undoubtedly, unread.

I looked at the room. I looked at Ralph and Billy, both standing in front of me now. I looked at Ralph's gun.

And I looked at Clayton Bannister.

He didn't look like his picture now. His baldness didn't show because he was the world's first country squire to wear his hat in his house. He also wore light gray flannel slacks, a red plaid hunting shirt open at the throat and expensive shoes. He had a large cigar in his mouth and he talked around it.

'You're tough to figure,' he said. 'You're supposed to be tough and you're supposed to be smart and I don't think you're either one. What's the bit, London?'

'I brought you a present.'

'And you think you'll get paid for it? You had your chance, dumbhead. You know what I woulda paid for that briefcase. Twenty grand. Maybe thirty. Now I get it for nothing, dumbhead.'

I fingered the briefcase. 'You'd pay me twenty grand,' I said. 'Then you'd send some boys around to take the money back and blow my brains out. That's smart?'

His face darkened. 'A cutie,' he said. 'Don't get cute. I don't like it. You gonna give me that thing?'

I tossed it to him. He caught it with surprising grace for a man of his bulk. He opened it with his eyes on me, then lowered his gaze to study the contents. He read the letter quickly, nodding from time to time to prove he could read. Then he looked up.

'Where's the keys?'

'In the pouch with the zipper.'

'They better be,' he said darkly. He opened the zippered compartment and took out the keys. He studied them, smiled with obvious pleasure, put them back in the pouch, zipped it shut, put the letter back, zipped the briefcase and tossed the whole thing onto an overstuffed sofa.

'You know what it's all about, London?'

'Jewels,' I said.

'Smart boy. Just jewels?'

'The Wallstein jewels.'

'Very smart boy.' He took the cigar from his mouth and pointed at me with it, looking at Ralph and Billy as he did so. They stood on either side of him, Ralph with his gun drawn, Billy with his apey arms at his sides.

'This is a smart boy,' he told them. 'You look at this boy; you listen to him; he's smart. You hear how he talks? He talks better than you two put together. He talks better than me and I'm not so damn stupid. He's what you call cultured.'

He sighed. 'But he's still a dumbhead. You see?'

They both nodded dutifully.

'You,' he said. 'London. You take a good look at this place? The house and the grounds? You check out the trees and furniture and all?'

'I saw them.'

'Whattaya think?'

'Impressive,' I said.

'Impressive,' he echoed. He thought it was a compliment. 'You think I know a goddam thing about architecture? I know what I like, anybody knows that, but that's all. You see that picture on the wall? It's by Matisse. What I know about art you can put in your ear. What I know about Matisse you can put in the same ear and have room left. I bet you know a hell of a lot about architecture. And about art. I bet you know about Matisse. Right?'

'Some.'

'I also bet you don't have a house like this one,' he said. 'I also bet you don't have a Matisse hanging on the wall. I don't mean a goddam copy. I mean what they call an original. Right?'

I told him he was right. I didn't bother telling him I wouldn't live in his house on a bet or that I didn't like Matisse. This would have annoyed him.

'I got and you don't, London. You know why?'

'Money, probably.'

'Part right. Money and power. I want a house, I go hire an architect and tell him what I want. I want a good picture, I call a dealer and tell him I want the best. That's why I got this briefcase.'

He walked over to a heavy mahogany drum table with ugly claw feet. He ground his cigar to a pulp in an ashtray. He came back and pointed at me, this time with his finger.

'You got to get the point of this, London. You had the briefcase and I wanted it. I offered to pay you off. You, you had to be smart. Too smart. You didn't want to play. Money wasn't enough, so power came in. I sent a little muscle to show you I wasn't playing games. The muscle knocked the crap out of you. The muscle told you you could get your head knocked-in playing cute. So now I got the briefcase and you got nothing.'

I looked at him.

'Muscle,' he said reverently. 'How long you think you'd have a President without an army? Or a business. You take when they started labor unions. The workers, the slobs, went out on strike. They wouldn't work. So the boss, he got some muscle going for him. He hired some slobs and told them to break a few heads. All of a sudden there wasn't a strike any more. Everybody was working.'

I told him the unions were still around. He looked at me scornfully. 'You know why? They got smart. They got muscle of their own and they broke heads on their own. You see?'

I nodded. I looked at Billy, the muscle we were batting back and forth. He looked muscle-bound and stupid. I looked at Ralph. He was more of a right arm than a muscle. He looked useful and his gun looked dangerous. More dangerous than my Beretta. I wondered if it was the same gun he killed the blonde with.

'And you're the smart one,' he was saying. 'So I got the briefcase and you got crap. I don't have to pay you a penny, London. You know what I can do now? I can tell Ralph to shoot a hole in your head. Not in here – why mess up the place, get the rug bloody?'

'You got the girl's rug bloody.'

He gave me an odd look. 'We take you outside,' he went on. 'Billy tells you to go outside and you go because he tells you and you don't want another beating. Then Ralph shoots a hole in you and Billy digs a deep hole and buries you. The gardner plants flowers.'

He laughed, his heavy body shaking. 'Better,' he said. 'We take you outside and we hand you a shovel and tell you to dig. We tell you you're digging your own grave and you dig it, anyhow. You think you wouldn't dig it? You think you can't make a man do any damn thing in the world?'

He was probably right.

'We tell you to dig and you dig. We tell you to lie down and you lie down. And then we shoot you and cover you up and plant the flowers and you disappear. Nobody ever knows what happened to you; you're gone. You never were in the first place.'

I nodded slowly. 'All because of power.'

'You got it, London.'

'Muscle,' I said. 'There's only one thing wrong with having muscle working for you.'

'What's that?'

'The kind of person you have to have around.'

'You mean Billy?'

'I mean Billy.' I took a deep breath and wondered if they would really make me dig my own grave, and if I was really weak enough to do it.

'I mean Billy,' I repeated, looking at the gorilla. 'You know about him?'

He looked puzzled.

I looked at Billy and remembered the kind of punch he threw. I thought about what Ralph had said before, remembered how Billy had reacted. And wondered if it still worked that way.

'About him and his mother,' I said, loud. 'He sleeps with his mother, Bannister. He does things with her. Bad things.'

And that was Billy's cue.

He came in high and he came in hard and he came in fast. I saw him coming, saw Ralph raise his gun behind him and take aim. Ralph wasn't going to shoot. He didn't figure it would be necessary. He was waiting.

So was I.

It happened quickly. Billy was hunting for my head and he threw a big fist at it. I ducked and let the punch go over my shoulder, then came up underneath him and pivoted. That lifted him up and spun him around. His own tremendous forward motion did all the rest of it.

And I threw him at Ralph.

He had come in high and hard and fast and he went out the same way, flying straight for Ralph. The little man – the right arm – went overbackwards with the big man on top of him. Maybe Ralph was trying to shoot me. Maybe the gun went off by accident, a pure reflex action.

It didn't matter. Either way it went off, a loud noise only slightly muffled by Billy's bulk. Either way Billy's T shirt turned red with his blood. Then the two of them hit the floor with an impact as loud as the gun shot. They did not move.

I looked from them to Bannister. He had a gun in his hand. It was a big gun and it was pointed at me.

12

It was so quiet I could hear the country noises outside. Birds singing, crickets chirping, the wind in the trees. A scene of pastoral bliss. I looked at him, then at the gun and then at him again.

'That's the trouble with muscle,' I said. 'It can work both ways. Billy's muscle just got him killed.'

The gun didn't waver. The mouth smiled but the eyes were colder than Death.

'Cute,' he said. 'Very cute. What was that? Judo?'

'Something like that.'

'Using his own muscle against him,' he said slowly. 'Yeah, I get it. I had a Jap working for me once, little guy skinny as a bird. He could get cute like that, toss a guy my size clear across the room and off the wall. You know what you just did?'

I let him tell me.

'Same thing as Billy,' he said. 'You used your brains against you. You got so cute that in a minute or so I shoot you and you're dead. Your brains get blown out. What good are they then?'

I put my hands in my jacket pockets and tried to look casual about it. The Beretta was right where it was supposed to be. I tried not to think what would have happened if Ralph or Billy had taken it away from me. It was better not to think about things like that.

'You'd kill me anyway,' I told him. 'What's the difference?'

'Maybe. Maybe not.'

'Sure you would. You've got enough killings under your belt. One more wouldn't hurt you.'

He laughed like a clown. 'Dumbhead,' he said. 'I haven't killed anybody all by myself in fourteen years. You'll be the first. Unless Ralphie wakes up to save me the trouble.'

I looked at Ralph and decided he wouldn't wake up for a while. 'So you don't pull the trigger yourself,' I said. 'You order the hits instead. It's the same thing.'

He didn't answer.

'You're just a killer, Bannister. You killed a batch of jewel thieves to save yourself a hundred grand. You killed a girl when she crossed you. Now I'm next. Congratulations.'

He looked amused. I kept my hands in my pockets. My right hand closed around the Beretta and my index finger looked around for the trigger and found it. I was glad now that it was such a small gun. It made a neat bulge in the pocket, small enough so that he didn't even notice it.

'You're a pig,' I said. 'With all your money and all your power you're still fresh from the gutter. And the gutter smell clings to you. It won't wash off. You'll go on killing like an animal and living like an animal until somebody blows your brains out. Or until they strap you in the chair and throw the switch.'

He wasn't Billy and he didn't get angry. His voice came out low and flat. It rasped like chalk on a blackboard.

He said: 'Dumbhead. You know what you got for brains? You got crap for brains. Every time you try to get smart you get dumber and dumber.'

'Really?'

'Yeah, really, you stupid bastard. You think I order a hit for the hell of it? Anybody kills for nothing is stupid. Those snatch-and-grab boys got hit because they crossed me. Somebody crosses you, you have to hit him. They came to me and asked a hundred grand for a batch of jewels. I paid their price and they tried to cut and run. No jewels for me. So they got hit and the dough came back where it belonged.'

'What about the girl?'

He looked at me. 'Alicia?'

I nodded.

He laughed and his big shoulders shook. 'Dumber and dumber,' he said. 'We never hit the girl. Why hit her?'

'Because she double-crossed you.'

'That broad crossed everybody,' he said. 'She was in line for a hit. But why cool her before I got the briefcase from her? The hell, I didn't even know where she was hiding out. She disappeared fast.'

'Then how did you know I had the briefcase? If you didn't know where she lived, you didn't see me coming out of her apartment. So how did you spot me?'

'I didn't.'

'You had a tail on me last night,' I said. 'I sent him home with his head in a sling. How did he pick me up?'

'You're in the wrong world, London. I didn't have you tailed.'

I remembered a little mousy man with glasses. 'A little guy. He picked me up at the Ruskin, where Armin is staying. And then—'

His smile spread around some more. 'Is that where he's staying?'

'You already knew that, Bannister.'

'I guess I know it now. Thanks.'

I shifted gears again. It was cuter than hell – the more I knew, the more things got jumbled up all over again. 'You didn't spot me with Alicia's body,' I said. 'But you figured I had the briefcase. Right?'

'Right.'

'Then—'

My ignorance had him so happy I thought he was going to start giggling any minute. 'So goddamn dumb,' he said. 'I got a phone call. You learn a lot of things over a phone. I learned you had the briefcase. And you did. So?'

'Who called you?'

'A little bird. You ask a lot of questions, you know that? What do you care about answers? I shoot you and you're dead. You believe there's a thing like heaven?'

'No.'

He nodded swiftly. 'Good. Neither do I. So you're dead, and when you're dead it's all over. In an hour or so you get stiff. Your hands and feet turn white. Powder white, fishbelly white. A couple days after that you start to rot. And whatever you got going for you in your head, whatever your brains are loaded with, it rots too. The questions and the answers – they rot. Why ask?'

'Curiosity.'

'It killed a lot of cats, London.'

I took very careful aim with the Beretta. He was right but his reasons were all wrong. I didn't need any more questions and answers. I had all the answers that mattered. There were a few questions left here and there but Bannister wasn't going to be able to answer them.

Everything was coming into focus now. Everything was taking shape and working itself out.

I didn't need Clay Bannister any more.

'Dead,' he was saying now. 'Didn't have to kill you before. No point. Hell, you did me a favor. I take the briefcase and toss you out. What can you do to me? Nothing. You don't have a story to take to the cops and you're too small to give me a hard time on your own. I brush you away like a horse brushes flies.'

'You can still do that.'

He shook his big head. 'Uh-uh,' he grunted. 'You killed one of my boys.'

'Ralph killed him.'

'Uh-uh. You killed him. So now it's your turn for some of the same. You still sure you don't believe in heaven? You want to squeeze in a round of last-minute praying?'

He could have gone on that way for another half hour. His voice was ugly but he liked the sound of it, liked the way his neo-Nietzschean crap rolled off his tongue. He might still be talking now. But I was sick of listening to him, sick of staring into the muzzle of his gun.

I steadied the Beretta and squeezed the trigger.

For a little gun it made one hell of a noise. Bannister's face started to change expression from satisfaction to horror. He got halfway there and wound up wearing a silly half-smile. I wondered how long it would take the undertaker to wipe it off his face.

I was aiming for his face but the bullet came in low. It took him in the neck, right in the center of the throat, and he fell in slow motion, the gun in his hand all the way to the floor. When he was on his knees he squeezed the trigger in a death grip and a bullet plowed a furrow in the thick carpet.

He fell the rest of the way, then stopped moving. A river of blood flowed from the hole in his throat. The thick carpet sopped up most but not all of it.

I felt a little like Lady Macbeth. 'Yet who would have thought the old man to have had so much blood in him?' But the little lady was swimming in guilt, and I couldn't feel anything but numb satisfaction no matter how hard I tried. Nobody ever deserved death more thoroughly. Nobody's death ever came in a more appropriate manner.

Just for the record I took his pulse. He turned out to be just as dead as he looked. Then I walked over to Billy, grabbed hold of his wrist, and found out he was as dead as his boss. I glanced at Ralph – he didn't seem to be breathing, and when I looked for a pulse I couldn't find one. Maybe he had a heart attack. Maybe I scared him to death.

Then I saw beads of blood in both his ears and figured out what happened. The fall with Billy on top of him had been a healthy one. He fractured his skull and he was dead.

Which meant there were three of them. Three dead men on a thick carpet in an ugly living room. Three bodies cooling off under a beamed ceiling in a Long Island manor house. Three gunshots in ten minutes.

And one worn-out detective who needed a drink. Badly.

And all at once I remembered another picture. A picture of an apartment where a dead and nearly nude blonde lay still and silent in the center of an immaculate room. The scene I was in now was just as surrealistic. Maybe it was Death itself that was surrealistic. Maybe the rest was just the frame for the picture.

I got out of there in a hurry. I wiped off everything I could have touched in one way or another – a doorknob here, a chair there. I wiped off three hands and wrists while I tried to remember whether it was possible to get a print from a dead man's skin. I took a final look at the three of them and remembered they had been alive just a few minutes ago, all three of them, and that I was responsible for their deaths.

I wasn't sorry.

I remembered the beating they had handed me and the search they had given my apartment. I thought about all the people they had managed to mess up in one way or another in the course of their lives. So I wasn't sorry at all. They had it coming.

I picked up the briefcase. It was beginning to feel like an old friend. I carried it out of the house, wiped the brass doorknob and closed the carved oak door. The bullet in Bannister's throat was my only souvenir. And ballistics wouldn't be able to do a thing with it. Peter Armin wouldn't own a traceable gun.

From the front seat of the Chevy I looked out at the house again. Bannister's house, his estate. The sun was still shining and I blinked at it. I'd been expecting dark clouds and gloomy weather. But the real world doesn't have the artistic balance of a Gothic novel. Bannister's lawn was still neat, still blindingly green. Birds went on singing in his trees.

They didn't seem to miss him at all.

I pushed the accelerator to the floor and let the Chevy have her head. The top was still down and the rush of very fresh air shook me out of my mood. A few miles down the road I pulled over to the curb to fill a pipe and get it going. There was a small hole in my right-hand jacket pocket, the one the bullet went through. It was black around the edges. The gun in that pocket felt heavier now than before. Actually it was lighter by a bullet. It still felt heavier.

I goosed the Chevy and we got going again.

There was one little headache – I'd beaten the brains out of a little guy with glasses, and unless Bannister was lying for the sheer hell of it the guy hadn't been tailing me at all. But that was something to worry about later. For the time being I had plenty to do. I had answers to all the questions now, values for all the unknowns in my human equation. X and Y and Z had names and shapes and faces. I knew all I had to know.

I left Suffolk County behind, hurried through Nassau, got done with Queens as quickly as I could. I rode under the East River, felt trapped in the tunnel, then came out in Manhattan again. It felt good. I'm a city boy – I was born here and I like it here, and it's the only spot that feels like home. Boroughs like Brooklyn and Queens are a waste of time and space, and the rest of Long Island is the country.

'And the country is a healthy grave.'

There was a parking space down the block from my building. It was a tight squeeze but the Chevy fit in it. I slipped the briefcase out of sight under the front seat, walked to my door with my right arm draped over the bullethole in my pocket. In my own apartment I got out of the jacket, emptied its pockets and heaved it down the incinerator. It was a shame, because it was kind of a nice jacket, but it had to go. I put on a fresh jacket, put wallet and handkerchief and gun in the right pockets, and poured out a slug of cognac. I sat down in a chair and worked on the cognac while I flipped through the *Times* at long last.

I wasn't exactly killing time. In the first place, I needed the drink. In the second, there was a chance that the Alicia bit was still getting an occasional few lines of printer's ink, and I wanted to know about it if it was. So I sipped and flipped, in approximately that order. There was nothing about the late Alicia Arden. There was something else.

I almost missed it. It was on one of those catchall back pages, a short bit most of the way down the fifth column. I noticed it because they had happened to run a picture with it and pictures on the inside back pages are rare. This was a good news photo – a clear and infinitely sad shot of a dead little man propped up against a brick warehouse wall.

So I read the article. Nothing sensational, nothing spectacularly newsworthy. The sad little man in the photograph had been found in the very small hours of the morning after having been shot twice in the center of his chest. Police found him in the very West Thirties, the warehouse district on the wrong side of Eleventh Avenue. He had been killed elsewhere and dumped where he was found. In addition to the bullets, he'd been beaten around the face.

There had been no identification yet. He'd had no wallet, no papers. His fingerprints were not on file. He had one identifying mark, a six-digit number tattooed on his right forearm.

Nothing much at all. But it made me look at the picture again, and it actually took a second look to recognize him. His face had never been the memorable sort and it was less so in a news photo. But I had seen him before.

He was the tail I'd pounded on Times Square the night before.

I went back to the car. The briefcase was still on the floor under the seat, right where I had left it. I put it next to me and started the engine. I had a little more trouble getting out of the space than getting in, but the Chevy was in a good mood and we made it.

It was time to deliver the briefcase and collect my reward.

13

The air was gray, the sun smothered by clouds. Eighth Avenue swam with the human debris of late afternoon. A pair of well-dressed Negro pimps stood like cigar store Indians in front of the Greek movie theater across the street. A Madison Avenue type, his attaché case at his feet, leafed dispassionately and sadly through a bin of pornographic pictures in a bookstore. Taxi drivers honked their horns and pedestrians dodged rush-hour traffic. All over neon signs winked in electric seduction.

The Chevy was parked on Forty-fifth Street. I left it there and went into the Ruskin with the briefcase tucked under one arm. I found the taproom and had a double cognac. It went down smoothly and made a warm spot in my stomach.

In the lobby I picked up the house phone and called Peter Armin. He picked up the phone right off the bat.

'London,' I said. 'Busy?'

He wasn't.

'I've got a present for you,' I told him. 'Okay to bring it right up?'

A low chuckle came over the phone. 'You're an amazing man, Mr London. Come right up. I'll be anxious to see you.'

I rang off, stuffed tobacco into a pipe and lit it. I walked to the elevator. The operator was a sleepy-eyed kid with a very short brushcut and a wad of gum in his mouth. He chewed it all the way to the eleventh floor, telling me at the same time who was going to win the fight at St. Nick's that night. I yeahed him along, got out of the car and found Armin's door. I knocked on it and he opened it.

'Mr London,' he said. 'Come in. Please come in.'

We went inside. He closed the door, then turned to me again. I looked at him while he looked at the briefcase I was holding. He was very pleased to see it. His clothes were different again – chocolate slacks, a dark brown silk shirt, a tan cashmere cardigan. I wondered how many changes of clothes he carried around in that suitcase of his.

'An amazing man,' he said softly. 'You and I make a pact. Within twenty-four hours you produce the briefcase. One might almost be tempted to presume you'd had it all along. But I'm sure that's not the truth.'

'It isn't.'

'May I ask how you took possession of it?'

I shrugged. 'Somebody dropped it in my lap.'

'Just like that?'

'Just like that.'

'Amazing, truly amazing. And Mr Bannister? Have you any news of Mr Bannister?'

'He's dead.'

'You killed him?'

'I think he had a heart attack.'

He chuckled again. 'Marvellous, Mr London. *De mortuis*, of course. *De mortuis nil nisi bonum.* Yet I cannot avoid thinking that few men have merited a heart attack more whole-heartedly, if you'll excuse the play on words. You're a man of action, Mr London, and a man of economy as well. You waste neither time nor words. A rare and enviable combination in these perilous times.'

He stopped, reached into a pocket of the cardigan and dragged out his Turkish cigarettes. He offered me one, as usual. I passed it up, as usual. He took one himself and lit it.

'Now,' he said. 'If I might have the briefcase?'

'One thing first.'

'Oh?'

'A matter of money,' I said. 'Something like five thousand.'

He was all apologies. He scurried over to the dresser, opened the bottom drawer, drew out a small gray steel lockbox with a combination lock. He spun dials mysteriously and the box opened. There was an envelope inside it. He took it out and presented it solemnly to me.

'Five thousand,' he said. 'The bills are perfectly good and perfectly untraceable. If you'd like to count them—'

'I'll trust you,' I said. I stuffed the envelope in my inside jacket pocket.

'Now the briefcase?'

I said: 'Of course.' I handed it to him and he took it from me, his small hands trembling slightly. He accepted the case the way a man takes into his arms a woman he has lusted after without success for a long period of time. I stood and watched him as he sat down in his chair and opened it.

He reacted just the way he was supposed to. He unzipped the briefcase quickly, ignored the letter and opened the pouch with the keys in it. He took them out, looked them over.

His face changed expression.

For a moment or two he sat still as Death and did not say a word. Then, his eyes still on the keys, he said: 'There seems to be some sort of mistake, Mr London.'

I didn't say anything.

'Something's gone wrong,' he said. 'Somewhere along the line there's been a slip. These are not the right keys.'

'Of course not,' I said. 'I know that, Mr Wallstein.'

The words sank in slowly. He stayed where he was, not moving at all for a minute or two. Then his eyes left the keys and climbed an inch at a time until they were looking at me.

They widened when they were focussed on the Beretta in my hand.

He said nothing at first. His face changed expression several times and I could see his mind working, looking for avenues of escape, seeing each in turn sealed off in front of him. When he got around to speaking his voice was a thousand years old. He sounded like a man who had been running very hard and very fast for a very long time. And who was now discovering that he had been running in the wrong direction.

'A most amazing man,' he said. 'And just how much do you know, Mr London?'

'Most of it.'

He sighed. 'Tell me,' he said. 'I'd like to see how much you know and how you determined it. I don't suppose it will be much in the way of consolation. But it's important for a man to know just where he cut his own throat.'

'Keep your hands where I can see them.'

'Certainly,' he said. He placed them palms-down on his knees. 'And if you could point that gun elsewhere—'

He had shown me the same courtesy before, in my own apartment. I could hardly refuse him. I lowered the gun slightly.

I said: 'Your name is Franz Wallstein. You occupied a fairly important position in Nazi Germany. You stole a small fortune in jewels and managed to make a clean break when the roof fell in in 1945. You ran for Mexico, then skipped to Buenos Aires. You set yourself up as an importer under the name Heinz Linder and you were doing pretty well. Then the Israelis found your trail again.'

'They are relentless,' he said.

'But you had advance warning. Not much warning – it didn't leave you time to cash in your home or your business. But you did have enough time to make sure your trail would end forever in Buenos Aires. You found someone who looked enough like you to pass for you. He didn't have to be a perfect double – you'd been under wraps for fifteen years. You took him home with you and shot him dead.'

He listened with no trace of expression on his face. I got the impression that he was discovering himself now in the words I spoke. His eyes were deep, his features relaxed.

'Maybe you bought cooperation from the government,' I went on. 'That's supposed to be pretty easy in Argentina. At any rate, you left your double dead in your home and let the Israelis take credit for the kill. Then you staged a robbery – filled your suitcase with jewels and caught the first plane to Canada. It was an easier country to enter than the United States. But it wasn't as easy to set up shop there as it was in Argentina. You've got expensive tastes. The money must have gone pretty quickly. You needed more money and you needed it in a hurry.'

'Debts pile up,' he said softly. 'And a hunted man must keep his credit good.' There was the ghost of a smile on his lips.

'You still had the jewels. They were negotiable, especially if you sold them off a few at a time. But that wasn't good enough for you. You wanted to latch onto the money without letting go of the jewels. You're a man who likes beautiful things and you wanted to keep them.'

I paused. 'Am I right so far?'

'More or less. I could never have received a shadow of their worth. And they're very beautiful stones, Mr London.'

'They must be. Let's take it a little further. You met Alicia Arden. She knew about a fence – Bannister. That was fine, but you still wanted to sell the jewels without letting go. So the two of you cooked up a swindle. You managed to hook up with three or four professional thieves and you sold them on the notion of acting as agents for the sale of the jewels. According to what you told them, they would go to New York to handle the transfer of the gems for the money.'

'It's common enough,' he said. 'They took their chances in return for a cut of the proceeds.'

'That was the setup, sure. You even let them cache the jewels and make up only one set of keys. That was to keep you from stealing the stuff back and leaving Bannister holding the briefcase. They were honest thieves, as you said. But they weren't careful enough. You and Alicia fixed things so that both Bannister and the thieves would be out in the cold.'

'You know the details, Mr London?'

I looked at him. I wondered where Maddy was, what she was doing. I glanced out the window and watched the sky turn darker. I looked back at him.

'I can guess,' I said. 'Alicia was supposed to come to New York to negotiate with Bannister. Then she told Bannister he could pull a switch and save himself a hundred grand – this kept him from haggling over the price. When the time came, he gave her the money and sent her where the thieves were staying. She was supposed to trade the money for the briefcase, but instead of turning the case over to Bannister she held onto it.

'Then you came into the picture. You would get the money from the thieves and leave them for Bannister, who would get rid of them by killing them. It was neat – the thieves wouldn't be looking for you because they'd be dead. And Bannister didn't even know you were alive. You and Alicia would have the money and the jewels. Free and clear.'

I drew a breath. 'But she didn't play it that way, did she?'

'No,' he said quietly. 'She did not.'

'She must have made a fresh switch of her own. She set up the deal without telling you about it.'

He managed a smile. 'She was supposed to make the switch on a

Wednesday. It took place a day early. I did not know about it until it was over.'

'She made the switch,' I said. 'She turned over the money to the thieves and took the briefcase in exchange. Then she called Bannister and told him they wouldn't play ball. He killed them and took his dough back. She lost the money that way – but she had the jewels all to herself now. And they were worth a hell of a lot more than a hundred grand.'

He nodded, agreeing.

'So you found out about the cross. And you went hunting for Alicia Arden. You knew her very well. You knew what to look for and where to look. You didn't have Bannister's organization but you had something more valuable in your knowledge. He never found her. You did.'

My pipe had been out for a while. I put it in a pocket. 'So you broke in on her and killed her,' I went on. 'You didn't use a Beretta then. You had another gun and you used it to put a hole in her face. You killed her before you did anything else. She had crossed you and you were furious. Bannister was after her more as a matter of profit-and-loss than anything else. He might have killed her, but not unless he found the briefcase first. But you wanted her dead. That was more important than the briefcase.'

His face darkened. 'For each man kills the thing he loves,' he quoted. 'I was in love with her, Mr London. A human fault. A reasonable man is a man who never loves. Reason goes only so far. I loved her. When she betrayed that love I killed her. Another common pattern.'

He took out another cigarette and lit it. I watched him smoke. I wondered what he was thinking now.

I said: 'You had to be the killer. If Bannister had killed her he would have turned the place upside-down. But you're a neat man. You wouldn't confuse a search with a sacking. You must have cleaned as you searched.'

'It was easier that way.'

'And you left her there,' I said. 'You couldn't find the briefcase so you kept the apartment under as close surveillance as you could. There was a limit – you were alone, and you couldn't be there all the time. You didn't see my friend visit the apartment. But you saw me and thought I took the briefcase.'

He shook his head. 'I thought you had it all along. I thought you were working with her.'

'Same thing.' I shrugged. 'That's what I got so far. Also that you were the one who took a potshot at me when I was heading up the stairs to my apartment. Just a warning, I guess. So I'd be in a mood to team up with you.'

'I wasn't trying to kill you.'

'Of course not. When you really tried to kill someone, you didn't miss. I was a sitting duck there, wasn't I? But that was just a warning. Last night you didn't miss.'

'Last night?'

'I know about it,' I said. 'I ran into the guy outside. He was in the lobby and he followed us when we left here. Maybe he thought I was a buddy of yours. Maybe he wanted to talk to me. I'll never know.'

He shrugged.

'He was an old friend of yours,' I went on. 'I never got to know his name. Did you know it?'

'No.'

'Just a little man with a harmless face. One of the little men who spent some time in that camp of yours across the ocean. A concentration camp victim looking for you. He found you, too. How long was he on your trail?'

'He wasn't.'

'No?'

'He lived in New York, Mr London. And he saw me, here in New York. And recognized me.'

'And got killed for it.'

'He'd have killed me, Mr London.' His shoulders heaved in another shrug. 'He was willing to risk death. He cared only for revenge.'

'And he got his revenge. I might have had trouble making the final connection without him. But the forearm tattoo gave it away. You had to be Wallstein then. Everything fit into place.'

'You were lucky.'

'I know that,' I said. 'Well, that's what I got. Did I come close?'

His lips curled into a smile. His chuckle sounded happy. 'Too close,' he said. 'Far too close. There are points here and there where you're wrong. But they are really immaterial, Mr London. They do not matter.' He heaved a sigh. 'I never thought you would guess this much. How did you figure it out?'

I watched him put out his cigarette. He didn't seem nervous at all. He was more interested in seeing where he missed the boat than in finding a way out. There was no reason not to tell him. It wouldn't do him any good to know.

'A magician would say you made too much use of misdirection,' I told him. 'An actress friend of mine would say you over-acted. From the start I had to figure out where you belonged in the overall scheme of things. Your routine about making a living by being in the right place at the right time was a little far-fetched. You knew too much. You had to belong somewhere in the middle of things. At first I guessed you were one of the thieves.'

'That's what I wished you to think.'

I nodded. 'But you sold that too hard. You made a point of telling me what Wallstein was like, being careful to describe someone wholly unlike yourself. You made him tall and blond, a typical SS type, while you yourself are short and dark. You pictured him as a thoroughly unattractive character, one of whom you disapproved highly. Franz Wallstein, obviously, was not the kind of man you like.'

A slight smile. 'And perhaps that was not wholly untrue.'

'Maybe not. But I wondered how you would know so much about Wallstein, even if you were one of the thieves. It seemed unlikely. And it was just as funny for you to waste so much time telling me about him. I had to guess you were selling me a bill of goods.'

'Was that all?'

I shook my head. 'There was more. You gave me a lot of surface detail on the profession of larceny. But you never got around to describing the very brilliant crime in which the jewels were stolen. From that I guessed that there hadn't been any crime. You were Wallstein and you stole your own jewels.'

He was nodding, digesting all of it. 'More,' I said. 'I tied you to Alicia Arden from the start. Not from what you said about her – you were properly vague. But you always called her Alicia, never used anything but the first name. I was Mr London to you every time. Bannister was Mr Bannister. Once I realized you weren't one of the thieves, the rest came easily.'

He looked away. 'I didn't even realize it,' he said. 'I guess she was always Alicia to me and nothing else. Of course.'

He looked up at me again, his jaw set, his eyes steady. 'I could offer you a great deal of money,' he said. 'But you have the keys as it stands. You can get the jewels without my help. Besides, I suspect a bribe would have no effect on you.'

I told him it wouldn't.

He sighed. 'What next, Mr London? Where do we proceed from here?'

'That's up to you,' I said.

'May I smoke, Mr London?'

I told him to go ahead. I raised the gun to cover him but he didn't make any false movements. He shook out a cigarette, put it to his lips, set the end on fire with his lighter. The cigarette didn't flare up and blind me. The lighter wasn't a cleverly camouflaged gun. He lit his cigarette and he smoked it.

I lowered the gun.

'If you turn me in,' he said, 'you'll be faced with problems.'

'I know.'

'The police will want to know about your part. You broke a law or two yourself. You moved a body. You were an accessory after the fact of murder.'

'I know.'

'Withholding information – another crime. Not to mention Mr Bannister's heart attack.'

'That was self-defense.'

'You might have difficulty proving that to the police. They might call it murder. You might go to jail.'

I shrugged. 'Not if I handed you to them,' I said. 'I think they'd make allowances.'

He pursed his lips. 'Perhaps,' he said. 'You're licensed as a private detective, aren't you? Couldn't they revoke your license?'

'If they wanted to.'

'So much trouble,' he said. 'And they probably wouldn't even hang me. They might, but I doubt it. It would be hard to prove murder, harder still to prove premeditation. I might get life imprisonment. But not death.'

'You quoted *The Ballad of Reading Gaol* a while back,' I reminded him. 'Know the rest of it?'

He nodded. 'I'm fond of Oscar Wilde.'

'Then you remember his description of prison. And of course you had something to do with a prison yourself, didn't you?'

'Our prisons were worse, Mr London. Much worse. The Austrian corporal had unhappy ideas. American prisons are not like that.'

'They're no bed of roses,' I said. 'And if they do electrocute you, it won't be nice. It's worse than being murdered. All the anticipation beforehand. It's not nice.'

We sat and looked at each other for minute or two. The verbal fencing wasn't a hell of a lot of fun. I wanted to be out of there, to get away from him.

'So the situation is unhappy for us both,' he said. 'Wouldn't it be simpler to let me go free?'

'It would.'

'But you won't?'

'No,' I said. 'I won't.'

'Because of what I am? Because I'm Franz Wallstein?'

'Because you killed the girl.'

A long sigh. 'You would have to be a moral man, Mr London. It's unfortunate.'

I shook my head. I said: 'It's not a matter of morality. It's tough enough living with myself the way things stand. It would be tougher if I let you go. I'm practical, not moral.'

'And you find it more practical to turn me in than to let me go?'

'Yes.'

'No matter how much trouble it causes you?'

'Yes.'

We killed a few more seconds. The sky was almost black now. In a few minutes it was going to start raining. I wondered how Maddy's audition went. I wondered where she was and what she was doing. I wanted to be with her.

'Mr London—'

I waited.

'I've said this before in quite another context. We are both reasonable men.'

'To a point.'

'Of course, to a point. But there is a way for you to achieve your objective without trouble. It would simplify your problems and mine as well. It would be easier for us both.'

I nodded.

'Do you know what I mean?'

'I think so.'

'Justice will be served,' he said. 'Whatever precisely justice may be. Expedience, quite another goddess, will be served as well. And I think you shall find it no more difficult to live with yourself as a result. Do you follow me?'

'Yes,' I said. 'I follow you.'

He got to his feet. 'Now follow me literally,' he said. 'Keep your gun on me. Because I'll kill you if given the chance. You shouldn't give me that chance.'

I didn't. I stayed behind him and I kept the Beretta centered on his back. He led the way to the bathroom, opened the door of the medicine cabinet. He took out a small phial of pills, held it up and studied the contents thoughtfully.

'I've carried them for so long a time,' he said. 'When the Reich fell we all supplied ourselves with them. I've had them ever since. Some of us carried them in our mouths, ready to bite down on the capsule when it became necessary. Himmler managed that. He cheated his captors, died before their eyes.'

I didn't say anything.

'I've had them with me ever since,' he went on. 'Even when I felt most secure they were always within reach. Habit, perhaps. I almost took them once. It was in Mexico City. I was in the air terminal waiting for a plane and two Jewish agents passed within arm's reach of me. I had a pill in my mouth. I was ready to use it the minute I was recognized. But they did not recognize me.'

He uncapped the phial and tilted it. A large brown capsule rolled into the palm of his hand. He studied it.

'I threw that pill away,' he said. 'Not then. Not until I was in Buenos Aires. I took it from my mouth when I stepped onto the plane, and I sat in my seat in the plane with the pill clutched in my hand. I expected agents to meet the plane. They did not. I took an apartment in Buenos Aires and threw the pill away. But I kept the others. And now I have occasion to use them.'

There was a glass on the shelf over the sink. It was still in its cellophane wrapper. He set the pill on the shelf and unwrapped the glass. He let the water run for a minute or two, then filled the glass to the brim.

'I'm not sure about this,' he said. 'Do I swallow the pill or crush it in my teeth? Swallowing would be simpler. But the capsule might not dissolve. It didn't dissolve when I had it in my mouth.'

He went on talking in the same gentle tone of voice. 'I could have thrown the water in your face,' he said. 'It would have been a chance, if a slim one.

But I think you would have shot me. And the shot might not have killed me, and then we would have had the unpleasantness of police and a trial and the rest. It's really not worth the chance. But how do you measure worth here? Is it worth any risk to save one's life? All the logic in the world won't answer that question.'

He poured the water into the sink, put the glass back on the shelf. He picked up the pill and held it between thumb and forefinger.

'They're supposed to be painless,' he said. 'Almost instantaneous. I wonder if that's so or not. I really hope so. I'm a physical coward, Mr London.'

'You're a brave man.'

'That's not true,' he said. 'Bravery and resignation are not synonymous, not by any means. I'm simply a resigned coward.'

He put the pill in his mouth. Then he changed his mind and took it out again.

'There's one point,' he said. 'You might as well know this. I lied to you about one thing. I did it more to simplify procedures than anything else. Alicia wasn't nude when I left her. After I killed her, that is.'

'I know.'

'Do you know what she was wearing?'

'Yes.'

A smile. 'You know so many things, Mr London. There are things I wish I knew. I wish I knew just what will happen after I put this little pill to use. Will it end there? The religious myths are really a little hard to take, yet I wish I could accept them. Even Hell would be preferable to simple nonexistence. The churches make a mistake, you know. Simple nothingness is more terrible than any Hell they have managed to devise. Sulphur and brimstone cannot compare.'

'Maybe it's like going to sleep.'

He shook his head. 'Sleep implies an eventual awakening. But I'm afraid it's a moot point. A semantic game. And why puzzle over it when I can find out the answer in an instant?'

I wanted to tell him to put down the pill, to run, to catch a plane and disappear. But I thought of the dead blonde and the dead thieves and the corpse in Argentina. I thought of a little man found leaning against a Hell's Kitchen warehouse, and I thought of six million of his relatives in German ovens.

I still wanted to let him go.

He smiled at me. Then he popped the pill into his mouth and closed his eyes. His jaws twitched once as he bit into the pill. His eyes opened, and for a tiny speck of time he looked at me. Then he fell to the floor and died.

14

I gave my car back to the garage. The same kid was still on duty and he had something suitably inane to say. But I didn't hear it. I wasn't listening.

The air smelled of a storm on the way. It had begun that way and it was ending the same way, with the city crouching under rain clouds. I walked home with the briefcase under my arm. I climbed the stairs and nobody shot at me from behind. I unlocked my door and went inside. There were no surprises – no dark little men with guns, no briefcases, no disorder. Just my apartment, just as I had left it.

I filled a glass with cognac and worked on it. I thought about love and death. I thought about Alicia Arden, about the kind of girl she must have been, about the girl she had been to the men who had known her. I thought about a girl of my own and found myself smiling. I picked up the phone and dialed Maddy's number.

'Hi,' I said. 'How was the audition?'

'Ed,' she chirped. 'Oh, it was fine, it was great, I'll tell you about it later. But what happened? Are you all right?'

'I'm fine.'

'How ... how did everything go?'

'All right. Lots of things happened.'

'Tell me. You didn't get hurt, did you? You're all right?'

'I'm fine,' I said again. 'I'll tell you when I see you.'

'Can you come right down? Or should I come up?'

'Neither,' I said. 'I'll be down in an hour or so. We can grab a late dinner. I'll take you out and feed you.'

'I'll cook, Ed. I feel like cooking tonight. Why don't you come down right away? I thought you were all finished.'

'Almost,' I said. 'I'll see you in two hours at the outside. And cook a big dinner. I'll need it.'

I stood there a moment, thought about her, remembered how her voice sounded. I wondered what was coming up next for us, what she would be to me and what I would be to her. I thought about love, about its effect on some people I knew. It was either the most essential single thing in the world or the one thing a man had to learn to get by without, and I couldn't make up my mind which way it worked. You could argue either side.

I lit a pipe, poured more cognac. And made another phone call.

Kaye answered. When she recognized my voice she started talking very fast and very shakily.

'Oh, Ed,' she said. 'Ed, I've been worrying about you. What's the matter?'

'Nothing's the matter,' I told her. 'What do you mean?'

She hesitated. 'Oh, I don't know. But you've been calling Jack and seeing Jack and I was all worried.'

'What about?'

'About you.'

'Me?'

A pause. 'Ed, if you're . . . sick . . . you can tell me, Ed. I have a right to know. I—'

I laughed, as much out of relief as anything else. 'It's not for me,' I improvised. 'It's for Jack. He needed a detective and wanted to keep the business in the family. A few clients did a skip and he wanted me to run a tracer on them, get them to pay their bills. I don't think you should worry yourself sick over it.'

She sounded very happy. 'But I worry,' she said. 'I mean, you're all alone in the world, Ed.'

'I've got a pretty sweet sister—'

'You know what I mean. If you had a wife to take care of you I wouldn't worry.'

I laughed again. 'Maybe I will,' I said. 'Soon.'

'You've got a girl?'

'Dozens of them. But there's one who's been getting important. I'll tell you all about it one of these days. Look, put your husband on, will you?'

She said something sweet, and I said something sweet, and then she put her husband on.

And I talked to him.

After that I took a fast shower and a faster shave. The shave was a little too fast – I wound up slicing off part of my face. I couldn't stop the bleeding with a styptic pencil so I slapped a Band-Aid on the gash and grinned at myself in the mirror. Just everybody in New York had swung at me or shoved a gun in my face in the past few days, and the only way I could get hurt was by cutting myself with my own razor. Hell, maybe it would leave an interesting scar.

I went back to the living room. Then I sat down in one of the leather chairs and waited for him.

He knocked at the door. When I told him it was open he came in, a little out of breath, his hair poorly combed and his face redder than usual. His tie was loose and his face was weak with the same fear I'd seen there before.

'I got here as soon as I could,' he said. 'Hope I didn't keep you waiting, Ed. Something the matter?'

I took a step toward him. I threw the briefcase at him and he raised his hands instinctively to block it. It bounced off his hands and landed on the floor.

'This is yours,' I said. 'You forgot it last time you were here.'

'For God's sake, Ed!'

'You son of a bitch,' I said. 'You rotten bastard.'

I hit him in the face. He backed off, his hands up to cover his face, and I belted him in the middle. When he folded up I hit him in the face and he went to the floor. He started to get up.

I said: 'Stay there, Jack. If you get up I'll knock the crap out of you.'

He stayed there.

'I never suspected you,' I told him. 'Never. Hell, I didn't want to suspect you. You were Kaye's husband, I was doing you a favor to begin with. And you played me for a sucker from the word go. You're a rotten son of a bitch, Jack.'

He opened his mouth. I waited for him to say something but he changed his mind. He bit his lip, closed his mouth. He looked away from me.

'How did you meet Alicia?'

'I told you. She came to my office.'

'Was that part true?'

He nodded.

'Then that's where the truth stopped. You met her and the two of you wound up in the hay. You were mannered and polished and socially acceptable and she was warm and blonde and good in bed. So the two of you hit it off fine.

'She was also talkative. She told you all about Wallstein and Bannister and a half-million bucks worth of stolen jewels.'

'Ed—'

'Shut up. This didn't happen on East Fifty-first Street. It happened in her apartment in the Village. Because the apartment and the alias came later. She never thought of them. They were your ideas. The whole double-cross gimmick was your idea all the way, wasn't it?'

'It just happened,' he said.

'Happened?'

'You know what I mean. We were talking about . . . the jewels. And we both thought—'

'I think it was your idea, Jack.'

He didn't say anything.

I said: 'She was a floater all the way, took things as they came. Her life wasn't easy but she knew how to get by. She was Wallstein's mistress and he idolized her. And he was going to have enough money to keep her happy as soon as his deal went through. No, I don't think she could have thought of the double cross. That had to be your idea.'

I looked at him and saw how weak and gutless he was. I was hoping he would get up so I could knock him down again. I remembered Wallstein telling me I wasn't a violent man. But now I felt violent.

'So you rented an apartment for her,' I went on. 'And gave her a phony name. And just to be safe you took the briefcase away from her. Why? Didn't you trust her?'

'Of course I did. Damn it, I loved her!'

'Then why did you take the briefcase? Why not let her hold onto it? Because you had the case all along, Jack. That's why Wallstein didn't find it when he killed her. It wasn't there. Why take it if you trusted her?'

'I thought it would be safer with me.'

'Safer from whom?'

'Wallstein, Bannister. Everybody.'

'Then you didn't think she was very safe, did you?' He looked up, puzzled. 'Even with the new apartment and the alias, you knew somebody might get to her. And if they did, you wanted to make sure you had the briefcase. She wasn't so important. But the jewels were.'

'That's a lie!'

'Is it?'

He looked at the floor again. 'She was all that mattered,' he said brokenly. 'I didn't care about the jewels. I didn't give a damn about them. I was in love with her.'

I let it go. 'You had it all set up with her,' I said. 'You doped out a way to cross Wallstein and Bannister both at once. Then you and Alicia would lie low for a while. I suppose after that you were going to skip the country. Where were you going to go?'

'Brazil. I don't know.'

'And live happily ever after. But Wallstein got to her first. He loved her, too – everybody loved that girl, Jack. He loved her enough to kill her after she crossed him up. And Wallstein wasn't the sort of man who killed if he could avoid it.'

'He was a crook.' His eyes flared. 'He was a rotten Nazi.'

'He was also a better man than you are. He killed her and he went through that apartment from floor to ceiling looking for a briefcase that wasn't there. Because you had it.

'She was already dead when you got there. And you fell apart, Jack. Suddenly the whole world was falling in on you. Hell, you were scared green. That's when you stripped her.'

His mouth fell open.

'Yeah, you stripped her. That's the only way it adds up. She was wearing something that could be traced to you. Or you thought it could. I can even guess what it was. You told me once how she liked to sit around the house in that man's bathrobe you bought her. Was that what she was wearing?'

He nodded slowly.

'Maybe the stockings and garter belt were underneath the robe. Maybe she was nude and you started to dress her, got as far as the belt and the stockings and panicked. It doesn't make a hell of a lot of difference. Either way, this girl you loved so much was dead as a lox and you were busy staying in the clear. You were noble as hell, Jack.'

He closed his eyes. 'I couldn't think straight,' he mumbled. 'I didn't know what I was doing.'

'That's an understatement. You were blundering around like a kid in a cathouse. By the time you got out of there you realized that you could burn all the bathrobes in the world without getting clear. You had to get the body out of that apartment or it would be traced to you. But you didn't have the guts to do your own dirty work. You came running to me with a scrambled story, confessed to cheating on Kaye in order to cover up all the rest of it. And you fooled me, damn it. I moved the girl's body and got you out of it.'

I lit my pipe. 'Remember what you told me a few minutes ago? The briefcase wasn't important to you. The girl was all that mattered. You said so, right?'

He nodded.

'And you lied. You had that briefcase and you weren't going to give it up no matter how dead Alicia was. You never thought of telling me about it.'

'I didn't want to . . . complicate things.'

'You didn't want to pass up a fortune. That's more like it. By the time I moved the body you were making a deal of your own with Bannister. You called him up, ready to sell him the briefcase and make a quick profit for yourself. With Alicia dead there wasn't any point to running for Brazil. But you could still use a hundred grand tax free. You called Bannister and tried to work a deal. He wanted to know who you were. And you got scared.'

'I thought he would kill me.'

'So you threw him a bone,' I said. 'You gave him my name.'

'I wasn't thinking.'

'That's a good excuse, isn't it? You use it every other sentence. It's a little worn out now. Anyway, Bannister wasn't as stupid as you were. The minute he had me on the phone he knew I wasn't the guy who called him in the first place. But you gave him a place to start. I was the only name he knew and he decided to work me over for all I was worth. He put a pair of thugs on my neck and they gave me a hard time. And that was your fault.'

'I didn't know—'

'You never knew anything.' I was disgusted with him. 'You loused up everything you touched. You were the clumsiest clod in history. Your lies were so clumsy I believed them and your actions were so stupid they were impossible to analyze. First you were going to skip the country with Alicia and the jewels. Then she was dead and you were set to sell the jewels on your own. Finally things got so shaky you were scared to breathe. The money didn't look so big any more. My phone call this morning had you jumping out of your skin, didn't it?'

'Yes. I was afraid.'

I nodded. 'So you wanted to get rid of the briefcase. It was simple once you found out I wasn't home. While I waited for your call, you came over here. Maybe you were going to stick the briefcase under my mat, then found the key and came inside. You dropped the case on the coffee table and called me from my own phone. That was a cute touch. So you must have figured you were lucky to be out of it. You still had Kaye and the kids, even if you didn't care about them—'

'I—'

'Don't tell me how much you love them,' I said. 'I'm sick of all your passionate attachments. You had your wife and your daughters and your position and your practice. The romantic life just wasn't worth it any more; you were happy to be in the clear. That's why you were so glad to switch that line of yours about how Alicia and the apartment looked when you found her. Anything to let yourself off the hook.'

He was silent now. I turned my back on him and poured a drink, half-hoping he'd make a break for it so I could have an excuse to take him apart again. But hitting him wouldn't be much of a kick now. The hatred and anger were slipping away and contempt was taking their place. He wasn't worth hitting.

'Get up,' I said.

He looked worried. 'Go on,' I said. 'Get up. I'm not going to hit you. I'm sick of looking at you – you look pretty damned silly on the floor.'

He stood up shakily. His eyes were wary.

'Jack, why?'

I watched him while he thought about it. He took his time getting his answers ready, and when he got going I had the feeling that he was talking as much to himself as to me.

'I'm not sure,' he said. 'I . . . Kaye and I haven't loved each other in years. A marriage can get very stale without going completely dead. We went stale.'

'Just like that?'

'A little at a time. I don't know. I sat around in a rut and didn't know it. Maybe I made a mistake going into medicine. I was never that crazy to be a doctor. Money and respect and security – they motivated me more than any real interest in medicine. And then I met Alicia.'

He paused for breath. 'Each of us was just right for the other, Ed. It was almost chemical. A chemical reaction. She was a footloose thing who never knew what was going to happen next to her. She'd been a prostitute and a marijuana smoker and a con-man's partner and everything else under the sun. She told me stories that made my hair curl. She was excitement for me; I wasn't in a rut any more.'

'Go on.'

'I don't know. I had to make one big break, one stab in the right direction. With the money from the jewels we could make a whole new life for ourselves. It looked too good to be true.'

'How long before the new life turned into a rut?'

'It wouldn't have happened,' he said doggedly.

'Sure.'

'Ed, we loved each other.'

'Sure. You loved Kaye once, didn't you?'

He sighed. 'That was different. I was a different man, a younger man. It was a different sort of love. I loved Alicia very much.'

'So you killed her.'

He stared at me. He started to say something but I didn't give him a chance. I held up a hand to shut him up.

I said: 'You killed her. You and Wallstein both loved her and both of you killed her. You set her up for him. If you weren't in the picture, she and Wallstein would have pulled off their swindle. They'd have wound up safe in Canada. You made her cross him and he killed her. He was a braver man than you, Jack. He killed her with a sword. You killed her with a kiss.'

After a very long moment he gave me a slow nod. I waited for him to say something.

'You ought to kill me,' he said finally.

'Probably.'

'You should.'

I shook my head. 'I've killed too many men today,' I told him. 'Four of them. Can you believe it? Four men, and you're worse than any of them. But I'm sick of killing and sicker of playing God. I couldn't kill you.'

'What ... what are you going to do with me?'

'I can't turn you over to the cops,' I said. 'And it would be silly as hell even if I could. I'd be hurting Kaye and the girls more than you. And I can't even beat you up – I haven't got the stomach for it. You're a rotten son of a bitch and I can't do a thing to you.'

He stood there and didn't say a word.

I said: 'Get out of here. Get out, get away from me, stay away from me. I don't want to see you again or speak to you again. Go home to Kaye and pretend you're a husband. She needs you. I don't know how in hell anybody could need somebody like you, but she needs you. She can have you.'

He didn't move.

'Damn you, get out!'

He turned and walked to the door. He opened it and left, closed it behind him. I heard him go down the stairs and leave the building.

I went over to the window. It was raining now, big heavy drops that soaked the pavement. I opened the window to let some fresh air into the place.

15

She sat across from me with one elbow on the table and her forehead resting in the palm of her hand. With her other hand she held a spoon and stirred a cup of black coffee. Her eyes were focussed on the coffee. She wore a pale green sweater over a simple white blouse and she looked beautiful.

I wondered what it would be like to sit across a table from her two or three times a day. I could think of worse ways to spend a day. Or a week, or a lifetime.

She said: 'Curiouser and curiouser, said Alice.'

'You don't get it?'

She shook her head. 'No, that's not it. I understand what happened and everything. But the people are confusing.'

'I know.'

'That Peter Armin. I suppose I should call him Wallstein, shouldn't I? But I can't think of him that way. He . . . didn't seem like a Nazi. I just can't picture him sticking out his hand and screaming "Heil Hitler." It's not consistent.'

'He wasn't exactly a storm trooper, Maddy.'

'Hardly. He was more like . . . oh, who was the one? The propaganda one. You know who I mean.'

'Goebbels,' I said. 'Joseph Goebbels, Minister of Propaganda. Hitler's brain. I think you're right. Wallstein was that kind of guy.'

She screwed up her face. 'I liked Armin, Ed. Isn't that silly? I actually liked the man.'

'I liked him myself.'

'And Enright turned out to be such a bastard. And he doesn't get punished.'

'You're wrong.'

'I am?'

I nodded. 'There's a balance here. It's pretty neat. Death was the worst punishment for Bannister and his boys. And for Wallstein. And life is the worst punishment for Jack Enright.'

She sat back and thought it over. 'Uh-huh,' she said finally. 'Yes, I suppose you're right. I see what you mean.'

She got up to get the pot and pour us each another cup of coffee. I took a sip. It was a little too hot and I set it down to cool. I liked the way she made coffee. I liked the way she cooked.

'She must have been quite a girl,' she said suddenly.

'Alicia?'

'Uh-huh. Or Sheila. Everybody has two names. Did you notice that? It makes it hard to talk straight. Oh, you know what I mean. She must have been . . . interesting.'

'Because of what she did?'

'Not that so much. Because of the effect she had on men. Wallstein and Enright both fell in love with her. And the two of them were so completely different.'

'Maybe they each saw a different girl.'

'Maybe.'

I tried the coffee again. 'They were different men,' I said. 'That's what had me spinning around all the time. Wallstein was a pro and Enright was a total amateur. Each of them acted differently and lied differently. As soon as I caught onto that much everything got a hell of a lot simpler.

'Wallstein used misdirection. He was a pro and he lied like a pro. Enright didn't know how to lie. Hell, he couldn't tell me a thing about Alicia without tipping his hand. In his place Wallstein would have invented a whole background for the gal to throw me off the trail. All Jack did was play it dumb and tell me he didn't know anything about her.'

'He said she was in the theater—'

'Uh-huh. He picked that one out of the air. She must have mentioned the party she went to with Bannister back when she was setting up the deal. He tossed me that one to make me happy, handed it to me for the hell of it.'

She was nodding. 'And the same goes for the apartment and everything about it.'

'Right. He had his way of lying and so did Wallstein. They must have had separate ways to love her. And to kill her.'

I took her hand and rubbed my fingers across the back of it. I looked down at the top of her head. Her hair was clean and fresh. I listened to the rain outside, smelled fresh coffee, thought about things.

'Ed? I just thought of something. The police will investigate, won't they?'

'Hell, they ought to. They'll find three corpses in Avalon and a fourth in the Ruskin. If they don't investigate they've got rocks in their heads.'

'Won't they tie you in?'

'Not a chance,' I said. 'Wallstein will go as an obvious suicide. They won't even dust for prints and they won't turn mine up even if they do. I left his Beretta there – if they run a ballistics check on it they can award him posthumously with Bannister's murder, call it triple murder and suicide. It's nutty that way but it closes their file for them.'

She nodded. 'How about the money?'

I looked at her.

'The five thousand dollars you took from Armin.'

'I'm keeping it.'

'But—'

'Hell,' I said, 'there's nothing else to do with it. He doesn't have any heirs. And I can use five grand, Maddy. I've got as much right to it as anybody else.'

She thought it over. 'You're right,' she said. 'I guess. What about the jewels.'

'Those I don't keep. I can rationalize five thousand bucks but not half a million. And I wouldn't know what to do with that kind of money. One way or another it would make a slave out of me.'

'So what do you do with them?'

'I already did it,' I said. 'I put the right keys in an envelope along with an anonymous covering letter with all the details. I sent them to the Israeli embassy. Hell, the original owners are probably dead. And they'd probably have wanted the jewels to go to Israel. They've got more right to them than anybody else I can think of.'

'I see.'

'Oh, to hell with it,' I said. 'It's just a way to get rid of them, to tell you the truth. I don't care what they do with those jewels. They can irrigate the goddam Negev or buy guns to shoot poor barefoot Arabs with. I don't give a damn what happens to the jewels. Just so I'm rid of them.'

She didn't answer. We drifted off into one of those long silences that come over you when you run out of the subject of a conversation. I looked at her and tried to figure out whether she agreed with the decisions I had made, and then I started wondering why in hell I should care what she thought about it.

I thought that maybe I loved her – whatever that meant – and I thought about two other men in love and what love had done to them, what it had made them do.

It was still raining outside. I had taken a cab to her apartment, leaving the Chevy in the garage, and I knew what was going to happen next. The two of us would manage to decide that it was raining pitchforks out there, by God, that I'd have a hell of a time catching a cab, that I might as well stay the night. And we would sit quietly together and listen to quiet music, both of us trying to be properly nonchalant until it was a decent time to crawl into bed.

I knew this was going to happen and I wasn't ready to complain about it. What I didn't know was what was going to happen next. In another day or another week or another month.

I broke the silence. 'The audition,' I said. 'You were going to tell me.'

She clapped her hands like a happy child. 'Oh, God! I forgot completely. Your news upstaged mine. Ed, I read that part and he loved me. He positively loved me.'

'You got the part?'

'He wants me to read again, or at least he said so. But while I was waiting for you I got a call from Maury and he said it's in the bag. Kaspar thought I was the greatest thing since vaudeville and I couldn't miss. The reading's some kind of formality.'

I told her it sounded great.

'More than great,' she said. 'It's marvellous and magnificent and delerious and delovely and everything.' Her face went serious again. 'This could be that break we were talking about, Ed. Kaspar has a hell of a reputation and the play is beautiful. Really beautiful. And the critics will eat it up. They always go nuts over Lorca revivals – there was one a year and a half ago, just a short run, and I saw it and it was the most amateurish mess with a terrible cast and rotten direction. And they got rave reviews.'

She paused and breathed again. 'It could be a tremendous break,' she said.

'When do you go into rehearsal?'

'Maury wasn't sure. Kaspar didn't say a word on the subject, of course. He never says anything. But Maury said Kaspar was talking about rehearsing upstate and opening out of town first. He's done that before. We'll probably leave New York around the middle of the month and spend the summer in some hole upstate, then open in New Haven or Boston at the start of the season. That's a guess, anyhow.'

She smiled at me. 'Will you miss me, Ed?'

'Sure,' I said.

'Will you?'

'Uh-huh. Especially at night.'

And then, while we talked about other things, all in preparation for the inevitable trip to the bedroom which we both wanted and needed very much, I thought about some other things that had been going through my mind. Thoughts about how she looked in the morning, how she would be to come home to. How the name Maddy London sounded.

That kind of thing.

Those thoughts seemed sort of silly now. Adolescent. In a week or two she'd be clearing out of town for a few months. She'd go without a thought, and by that time I'd watch her go without a thought myself. Maybe something would happen with us when she came back in the fall.

And maybe not.

We carried our cups of coffee into the living room. She put soft music on the record player and we sat on the couch and listened to it. I had a little brandy. She relaxed against the arm I put around her.

'Nice place,' I said.

'You like it here?'

'Uh-huh. It's easy to unwind here.'

She smiled softly, and when she spoke there was a little extra emotion behind the words. 'You should like it,' she said. 'After all, you've been here before.'

Grifter's Game

This is for Loretta

1

The lobby was air-conditioned and the rug was the kind you sink down into and disappear in without leaving a trace. The bellhops moved silently and instantly and efficiently. The elevators started silently and stopped as silently, and the pretty girls who jockeyed them up and down did not chew gum until they were through working for the day. The ceilings were high and the chandeliers that drooped from them were ornate.

And the manager's voice was pitched very low, his tone apologetic. But this didn't change what he had to say. He wanted the same thing they want in every stinking dive from Hackensack to Hong Kong. He wanted money.

'I don't want to bother you, Mr. Gavilan,' he was saying. 'But it is the policy of the hotel to request payment once every two weeks. And, since you've been here slightly in excess of three weeks—'

He left that one hanging in the middle of the air, smiling and extending his hands palms-up to show me that he didn't like to talk about money. He liked to receive it, but he didn't like to talk about it.

I matched his smile with one of my own. 'Wish you'd told me sooner,' I said. 'Time flies so fast a man can't keep up with it. Look, I want to get upstairs and change now. Suppose you have the bill ready for me when I come back downstairs. I have to go to the bank anyway. Might as well kill two birds with one stone, so to speak. Pick up some money and settle my tab for the moment.'

His smile was wider than mine. 'Of course, we'll be happy to take your check, Mr. Gavilan. That is—'

'No point to it,' I said. 'My account's with a Denver bank. It'd take weeks before the check would clear. But I've got a draft on a bank in town. So just have the bill ready when I get downstairs and I'll pay you in cash later this afternoon. Good enough?'

It was definitely good enough. I walked over to the elevator and settled myself in it without calling out my floor. When you stay at the Benjamin Franklin for a day or two, the operator remembers where you live.

I got off at the seventh floor and found my room. The chambermaid hadn't gotten around to it yet and it was the same mess I had left behind me when I went down for breakfast. I sat on the unmade bed for a minute or two, wondering just how much the tab was going to come to at

Philadelphia's finest hotel. One hell of a lot, no matter how I figured it. Better than three weeks at ten dollars a day. And better than three weeks of signing for meals, signing for the liquor room service sent up, signing for laundry service and dry cleaning and every other service Philadelphia's leading hotel had to offer. An impressive sum.

Maybe five hundred dollars. Maybe less, maybe more.

One hell of an impressive sum.

I reached into my pocket and found my wallet. I took out my money and counted it. It came to a little over a hundred bucks. And, needless to say, there was no draft on a Philly bank, no account with a Denver bank, no stocks, no bonds, no nothing. There was a hundred bucks plus, and that was all there was in the world.

I found a cigarette and lighted it, thinking how lucky I was that they'd carried me for almost a month without hinting for money. Most people get picked up on less than that. Fortunately, I was cagy and I had been playing it cool. I didn't just come on like a deadbeat. That's important.

For instance, I never signed for tips. Two reasons for that. For one thing, I didn't see any percentage in conning bellhops and waitresses who were probably as broke as I was. And when people sign for tips they get watched closely. Everybody watched them.

So I tipped in cash and I tipped heavy – a buck to a bellhop, a straight twenty per cent to a waitress. It was expensive, but it was worth it. It had paid off.

I got out of my clothes and went into the can for a shower. I took the hot spray first, then the cold. I like showers. They make me feel human.

White I toweled off I looked at myself in the mirror. The front was still there – the hard body, the sloping shoulders, the suntan, the narrow waist, the muscle. I looked solid and I looked prosperous. My luggage was top-grain cowhide and my shoes were expensive. So were my suits.

I was going to miss them.

I got dressed in a hurry and I put everything on my back that I could. I wore plaid bathing trunks under my slacks and a knit shirt under the silk one. I stuck cashmere socks – two pairs of them – between my feet and my shoes. I wore my best tie and stuck my second best tie in my pocket. I used all four tie clips on it – the jacket covered them up.

And that did it. Anything else would have made me bulge like a potato sack, and I did not want to bulge. I stuck the wallet in my pocket, left the room a little messier than it had been, and rang for the elevator.

The manager had my tab ready for me when I hit the lobby again. It was a big one. It came to a resounding total of six hundred and seventeen dollars and forty-three cents, a little more than I had figured. I smiled at him and thanked him and left, mulling over the bill as I walked.

The bill, of course, was made out to David Gavilan.

David Gavilan, of course, is not my name.

I needed two things – money to spend and a new town to spend it in. Philly had been kicks, but things just hadn't panned out for me there. I'd spent a week looking for the right angle, another week working it, and the third week finding out that it was a mistake to begin with.

There was a girl in it, naturally. There always is.

Her name was Linda Jamison and she smelled like money. She had short black hair and wild eyes and pretty breasts. Her speech sounded like finishing school. She looked well and dressed well and talked well, and I figured her for Main Line or something damned close to it.

But she wasn't Main Line. She was just sniffing around.

It was a panic, in its own quiet way. I picked her up in a good bar on Sansom Street where the upper crust hobnob. We drank gibsons together and ate dinner together and caught a show together, and we used her car, which was an expensive one.

Things looked fine.

I dated her three days straight before I even kissed her. I was setting this one up slowly, building it right. I am twenty-eight already, too old to be fooling around. If I was going to score I wanted to do it up brown. Maybe even marry her. What the hell – she wasn't bad to look at and she looked as though she might even be fun in the rack. And she smelled like money. I liked money; you can buy nice things with it.

So I kissed her a little on the fourth date, and kissed her a little more on the fifth date, and got her damned bra off on the sixth date and played games with her breasts. They were nice breasts. Firm, sweet, big. I stroked them and fondled them and she seemed to enjoy it as much as I did.

Between the sixth date and the seventh date I used my head for something more than a hatrack. I ran a Dun & Bradstreet on her at a cost of ten whole dollars, and I discovered that the Main Line routine was as queer as a square grape. She was a gold-digger, and the silly little bitch was wasting her time digging me. Clever little moron that I am, I was wasting time and money digging *her*. It would have been funny except that it wasn't.

So the seventh date was the payoff all across the board. I took her out again, and in her car, and I managed to drive around for three hours without spending a penny on her. Then I drove the car to her apartment – a sharp little pad that was evidently her investment in the future, just as the room at the Franklin was mine. We went into her apartment and wound up in the bedroom after not too long.

This time I was not playing games. I got the dress off, and I got the bra off, and I buried my face in bosom-flesh. I got the slip off and I got the garter belt off and I rolled down the stockings. I got the panties off and there was nothing on the bed but little Linda Jamison, the girl of my dreams.

The battle was won, but I was still damned determined to play it to the hilt. I ran a hand over her, starting at the neck and winding up at the

Promised Land. She moaned happily, and I don't think that moan was an act. She was hot as a sunburn.

'Linda,' I said softly, 'I love you. Will you marry me?'

Which made her ecstatic.

From there on in, it was heaven and a half. I came at her like a bull at a matador and wrapped myself up in velvety skin. She made love with the freshness of an impatient virgin and the ingenuity of a sex-scarred whore. Her nails poked holes in my back and her thighs almost choked me.

It took a long time. There was the first time, wild and free, and it was very good. There was in-between, with two heads sharing a pillow and wild sweet talk in whispers. The sour note was the fact that we were both lying like rugs. But it was fun just the same. Don't misunderstand me.

And then there was the second time – controlled now, but still more passionate. If that is possible. It was, underneath it all, a very strange sort of lovemaking. We were playing games, and I knew what the score was and she only knew half of it. It was hysterical.

Maybe it would have been worth it to string her along for a little while. She was good, damned good, in case I haven't managed to make that point yet. I could have gone on dating her, gone on sleeping with her for a week or so. But the game had already been won and the sport was losing its excitement. I decided to get it over with.

We were lying on the bed. I had one hand on her breast. It felt nice.

'Linda,' I said, 'I . . . I lied to you.'

'What do you mean?'

'I know it won't matter to you,' I said. 'If I didn't know you so well, I probably wouldn't be able to risk telling you. But I do know you, my darling, and there's no room for secrets between us. I have to tell you.'

Now she was getting interested.

'Linda,' I said, 'I am not rich.'

She tried not to do a take, God bless her. But I had a handful of breast and I could feel her stiffen when the words reached her. I almost felt sorry for her.

'I put on an act,' I said. 'I met you, you see, and I fell for you right off the bat. But there was such a gulf between us. You were rich and I was churchmouse-poor. I didn't figure I had a chance with you. Of course, that was before I knew you. Now I realize that money doesn't matter to you. You love me and I love you and nothing else is the least bit important. Right?'

'Right.' She did not sound very convincing.

'But now,' I said, 'I had to tell you. You see, I had no idea things would progress that fast. I mean, here we are, and we're going to be married. So I had to let you know that I had . . . well, misrepresented myself, so to speak. I know it won't make any difference to you, but I wanted to tell you.'

And from that point on it was no contest. When I called her the next day, nobody answered her phone. I went to her building, checked with the landlord. She had moved out, bag and baggage, and she had left no forwarding address. She was two months behind rentwise.

It was hysterical.

So now it wasn't quite as funny as it had been. Now I was on the street myself, close to broke, with no discernible prospects. It was summer and it was hot and I was bored. I needed a change of scene, a new place to operate. It had to be a town close by but out of the state, a town I knew and a town that wouldn't remember me. Too many towns remembered me. The list grew every few months.

Then I had a thought. Atlantic City. Three years ago, a Mrs Ida Lister, pushing forty but still shapely, still hungry, still a tiger in the hay. She had reimbursed me quite amply for two weeks' worth of stud services. She had picked up all the tabs, popped for a new wardrobe, and hit me with around five hundred bucks in cash.

The jewels I stole from her set me up for another three thousand bucks. Atlantic City.

A cruddy little town. A three-way combination of Times Square, Coney Island and Miami Beach. It was hardly the most exciting place in the world.

But it was a dollar or so away from Philly by train and on the right side of the Jersey line. It was a resort town, a town filled with floaters and a properly neutral shade of gray. It was a new place to connect. Properly, this time. No more fooling around. No more winning the battles and losing the war. No more games with chesty chickens like Linda Jamison.

I got in a cab and told him to take me to the railway station. He hurried along on Market Street and I wondered when the flunkies at the Franklin would realize I had skipped.

It was a slow train but it didn't have very far to go. It passed through Haddonfield and Egg Harbor and a few more towns I didn't bother to remember. Then we were pulling into Atlantic City and the passengers were standing up and ready to roll.

The sun was hot as hell and I couldn't see a cloud in the sky. I was glad I'd worn my bathing suit. It would be good to get out of my suit and into the water. I've always liked to swim. And I look good on the beach. It's one of my strong points.

I was out of the railway station before I realized something. I needed to stay at a hotel, and I couldn't stay at a hotel without baggage. Oh, I *could* – but not very well. Without luggage it's strictly a pay-as-you-go proposition, and at the type of place I had in mind the tab was going to come to fifteen dollars a day without meals, twenty with. Rates are high in resort towns in the tourist season. Sure, there are rattraps anywhere, holes where a room is two bucks a day with no questions asked. But that wasn't for me. If you go anywhere, you go first-class. Otherwise there's no point in going, to begin with.

Luggage. I could pick up a second-hand cardboard suitcase in a hockshop, fill it with old clothes and a phone book or two. But that wouldn't do me a hell of a lot of good. The big hotels frown when a guest checks in with cheap luggage. The chambermaids don't go wild over a suitcase filled with phone books.

I had no choice.

I walked back into the railway station, walked in slow. There was a line at the luggage counter and I joined it. I looked over the merchandise set on display and tried to pick the best. It wasn't hard. Two matching suitcases, monogrammed L. K. B., nestled on the top of the counter. They were top-grade stuff, almost new. I liked the looks of them.

I took a quick look around. Mr. L. K. B. was taking a leak or something; nobody seemed to be interested in his luggage, including the attendant.

I took both bags.

It was that simple. No baggage check, nothing. I picked up the bags, tossed the attendant a buck, and strolled off. Nobody questions a buck tipper. Not an attendant who gets crapped on five times a day for forty bucks a week. The attendant wouldn't even remember what luggage I had taken, and I'd be long gone before L. K. B. realized just what had happened. People take their time putting two and two together, and even so they generally come up with five.

A cab took me to the Shelburne. A doorman opened the door and took my bags. A bellhop took them from the doorman and walked me over to the desk. I gave the desk clerk a quick smile and asked for the best available single. I got it. He asked me how long I'd be staying and I told him I didn't know – a week, two weeks.

He liked that.

My room was on the top floor, a pleasant palace big enough for six full-sized people. The furniture was modern, the carpet thick. I was happy.

I took off my clothes, took another shower to get rid of the train smell. I stretched out on the double bed and thought happy thoughts. I was Leonard K. Blake now. A good name, as good as David Gavilan, as good as my own.

I got up, walked over to the window, stared out. There was the boardwalk, and on the other side of the boardwalk there was the beach, and on the beach there were people. Not too many people on this stretch of beach, because it was private – reserved for guests of the Shelburne. No rubbing elbows with the garbage. Not for Leonard K. Blake. He went first class.

There were men on the beach, and there were girls on the beach, and there were children on the beach. I decided that it was about time there was *me* on the beach. It was too hot a day to sit around the hotel, air conditioning notwithstanding. I needed a swim and I needed some sun. Philly has a way of turning a tan complexion to a sallow pallor.

I put the swim trunks back on, hung up the suit in the closet, put the rest of the stuff I'd brought with me in the dresser drawer. I stuffed L. K. B.'s bags in the closet. I could unpack later and find out what little goodies I had inherited from him. From the looks of the luggage, his clothes would be good enough to wear. I hoped he was my size.

I took the bathers' elevator to the beach level and accepted a towel from another faceless attendant. The Shelburne had a private pathway from the hotel under the Boardwalk to the beach, which was handy. I found a clear spot, spread out my towel, and played run-do-not-walk into the water.

It was a good day for swimming. I let the waves knock me over for a while, then got up the strength to fight back and give them a run for their money. I gave that up, stretched out on my back and floated. I managed to stay awake, though. An uncle of mine once tried floating on his back at Jones Beach and fell asleep. The Coast Guard picked him up fifteen miles off-shore. So I stayed awake.

After awhile, staying awake got to be a bit of a chore. I got out of the water and clambered up on the beach like a walrus with leaden arms. Or forelegs. Whatever it is that walruses have. And I found my towel and stretched out on my stomach.

And fell blissfully asleep.

Her touch woke me. Not her voice, although much later I remember having heard it while I slept, about the same way you can remember the ringing of an alarm clock that you never got up to turn off.

But her hands woke me. Soft hands on the back of my neck. Fingers drumming out not-too-complex rhythms.

I rolled over and opened my eyes.

'You shouldn't sleep like that,' she was saying. 'Not in this sun. You'll get a bad burn on your back.'

I smiled. 'Thanks.'

'You don't have to thank me. I wanted to wake you up. I was lonely.'

I looked at her. I looked at the very good body in the one-piece red suit. The suit was wet and it hugged her like an old friend. I looked at the blonde hair that was blonde all the way to the roots. I looked at the mouth. It was red and wet. It looked ravenously hungry.

And, out of habit, I looked at the fourth finger of her left hand. There was a mark there from a ring, but she wasn't wearing the ring now. I wondered whether she had taken it off before coming to the beach, or when she spotted me.

'Where's the husband?'

'Away,' she said, her eyes laughing at me. 'Away from me. Not here. I'm lonely.'

'He's not in Atlantic City?'

She reached out a finger and chucked me under the chin. She was just a little too good-looking. That bothered me. When a woman's beauty blinds you, your work suffers. A certain part of your anatomy leads you around. That can gum things up.

'He's in Atlantic City,' she said. 'But he's not *here*.'

'Where's here?'

'The beach,' she said. 'Where *we* are.'

Where half a hundred other people also were.

'Want to go swimming?'

She made a face. 'I already did,' she said. 'It's cold. And my bathing cap is too tight. It gives me a headache.'

'So go without one.'

'I don't like to. I hate to get my hair wet. Especially with the salt water. You have to wash forever to get it out and it ruins the hair. I have very fine hair. I mean the hairs are thin, that is. I'm not complimenting myself.'

'You don't have to,' I said. 'Everybody else must do that for you.'

That one got the smile it had to get. A little experience and you learn the language. You have to.

'You're sweet,' she said. 'Very sweet.'

'Isn't your husband sweet?'

'Forget him.'

'How can I? He's married to the most beautiful girl in the world.'

Another smile.

'Well?'

'He's not sweet. He's old and he's fat and he's ugly. Also stupid. Also revolting.'

It was quite a list.

'So why did you marry him?'

'He's also rich,' she said. 'Very rich. Very very very rich.'

We forgot her husband. She did, anyway. I didn't, because he was an important part of the picture. The fat, ugly, old husband, who was also rich. The pretty wife, who wanted more than the old husband was giving her. It was almost standard.

The deviations from the norm were small ones – they only bothered me a little. For one thing, she was too young. Not too young to marry a rich old goat, because you can do that at any age. But too young to chase.

She was twenty-four – or twenty-five or twenty-six or twenty-seven. It was perfectly logical for her to be married to the old goat, perfectly logical for her to be interested in getting into the sack with somebody else.

But at her age, and with her looks, she shouldn't be the one to do the pursuing. She didn't have to be chaste, but she should at least be chased, to coin a phrase.

Later on, when the years went to work on the high breasts and the clear skin, then she could get into the act a little more. She could do the chasing, and she could do the paying. But at this stage of the game there were plenty of guys who would chase her without any encouragement whatsoever, plenty of guys who would bed down with her without expecting to be paid for their labors.

Of course, we hadn't talked about payment yet. We hadn't even talked about bedding down.

We were swimming.

Anyway, we were in the water. Her bathing cap was trying to save her fine blonde hair from the horrors of the salt water; and the two of us were busy letting the waves knock us over. Then, of course, she wanted to learn how to swim, and I wanted to teach her.

I held out my hands and she stretched across them, learning to float on her stomach. She managed to lie with her breasts on one of my arms and her thighs across the other. I could feel the sweet animal warmth of her even in the cold water.

'Like this?'

I told her she had it down pat.

'Now what do I do?'

'Move your arms.'

She moved more than her arms. She moved them in an overhand crawl so that her breasts bounced around on my arm. She kicked gently with her long legs and her thighs worked on the other arm.

I wondered who was getting a lesson.

We clowned around some more. She told me her name was Mona and I told her my name was Lennie. She was a lot of fun, besides being a sex symbol. From time to time I even managed to forget that she was somebody else's wife, a potential meal ticket. I thought we were just two nice people having fun on a beach.

Then I would remember who she was and who I was and the pleasant illusion would fade and die.

'Lennie—'

We were on the sand again and I was drying her back with a big striped towel.

'I have to get back to the room, Lennie. I think he's waiting for me. It's been a while.'

I knew who *he* was.

'When can I see you again, Mona?'

'Tonight.'

'Can you get away?'

'Of course.'

'Where and when?'

She thought for all of three seconds. 'Right here,' she said. 'At midnight.'

'Isn't the beach closed at night?'

She smiled at me. 'You're a clever man,' she said. 'I'm sure you can find a way to get out here all by yourself. Don't you think so?'

I thought so.

'Midnight,' she said. 'I hope there's a moon tonight. I like it when there's a moon.'

She turned and left. I watched her go – she had a good walk, just a step on the right side of whorishness, as much provocation as a woman could get away with without looking like a slut. I wondered how long it had taken her to learn to walk like that. Or if it was natural.

The sun dried me. I walked back over hot sand to the passageway, through the passageway to the bathers' entrance. I tossed my towel back to the attendant and smiled at him. I rode up in the elevator to the top floor and walked to my room. I had buttoned the room key into the pocket of my swim shorts. I brought it out, wet, and opened the door.

I took another shower, this one to get rid of the salt water. It took longer than it should have, because the hotel had a cute set-up whereby you could take a salt water shower or a fresh water shower, depending upon how you felt about life in general. I goofed the first time around. It was a nice shower, but it left me as salty as ever. Then I figured out the system and rinsed with fresh water.

By the time I was done it was time for dinner. The idea of wearing the same damn clothes I'd worn on the train didn't particularly appeal, and I decided to have a look at L. K. B.'s donation. With luck, his clothes might fit. With more luck, he might have packed some cash in his suitcase. Some people do, believe it or not.

The bags were locked. But suitcase locks, like trunk locks, are all the same. I found a key that fit the little bag and opened it.

Whoever the hell he was, he was the wrong size. His pants were too short and too big in the waist and the behind. His underwear fell off me. But his feet, God bless him, were the right size. There were two pairs of expensive shoes in the little bag and they both fit me. There were also ten pairs of socks which I didn't bother to try on. If the shoes fit, the socks would fit. Unless the guy had very unusual feet.

That took care of the little bag. I put his junk in my drawers and stuck the bag back in the closet. I got the big bag and propped it up on my bed, then opened it with the key.

I hung up the jackets in the closet without looking at them. I was pretty sure they wouldn't fit anyway, and I didn't want to chance running into the bum with his jackets on. Shoes and socks he wouldn't notice, whoever he was. A suit he might.

I got lucky again with his shirts. We were built differently, he and I, but his arms were the same length as mine and his neck the same circumference. His shirts fit me, and he had a lot of shirts. I put them in the drawers.

There was the usual junk – tie pins, cuff links, shirt studs, miscellaneous junk. I went through everything and put everything away. His clothes were from New York and I wondered if he was, too, or if he simply went shopping there.

Then I came to the box.

I thought of money, first of all. It was a small wooden box made of teak or mahogany and it was about the same size and shape as a dollar bill. I took a deep breath and prayed that it held a stack of hundreds. Maybe the bastard was a doctor and he wasn't depositing his receipts, working some kind of a tax dodge. Maybe a hundred different things.

The box gave me trouble. It was locked and none of my keys fit it. I gave up fooling around after awhile and set it on the dresser. It was hinged at the back. I had a little file that went right through those hinges.

I started to open the box. Then I stopped, found a cigarette, and lighted it. I was playing a little game with myself. The box was a present, and I had to try to guess what the present was. Money? Pipe tobacco? Fertilizer?

It could be anything.

I took off the lid. There was a piece of tissue paper on top and I removed that right away.

There was nothing under the paper but white powder.

I was completely destroyed. There is nothing quite so compelling as a sealed box. I had the contents turned into a mental fortune, and now old L. K. B.'s box turned out to be a bust. Powder!

Maybe there was something underneath the powder. I got ready to blow it away, and then all of a sudden some little bell rang deep inside my head and I changed my mind.

I stared at the powder.

It stared back.

I managed to finish my cigarette and butt it in an ashtray thoughtfully provided by the management of the Hotel Shelburne. Then I turned back to the box. I put one finger to my lips and licked it, then dipped it gingerly into the powdery substance.

I licked the finger.

It was absolutely astonishing. I blinked rapidly, several times, and then licked my finger again, dipping it once more into the box.

I licked it another time.

There was no mistaking the taste, not now, not after many years. When you work in a racket, even briefly, you learn what you can about the racket. You learn the product, first of all. No matter how small your connection with the racket or how little time you spend with it, this much you learn. I had played the game for two months, if that, in a very small capacity, but I knew what I had on my dresser.

I had approximately sixty cubic inches of raw heroin.

2

For a few minutes I just stood there and felt foolish. I'd picked up more than a wardrobe at the railway station. I'd picked up a fortune. How much was the heroin worth? I couldn't even begin to guess. A hundred grand, a quarter of a million, maybe more, maybe less. I had no idea and I didn't even want to think about it.

I couldn't keep it and I couldn't sell it and I couldn't give it back. If L. K. B. ever found me with it he would kill me as sure as men make little green virgins. If the government ever found me with it they would lock me up and drop the key in the middle of the China Sea.

I could throw it away. Did you ever try throwing away a hundred grand, or a quarter of a million?

I put the lid back on the box and tried to figure out what to do with it. I couldn't hide it. People who carry around large quantities of heroin are not amateurs. If they search a room, they find what they are looking for. And if L. K. B. and his buddy boys realized I was their pigeon, no hiding place in the room would keep the heroin away from them. And I had to hold onto the stuff. It could be my trump card, the only thing that would keep me alive if they ever caught on. I could use it to work a deal.

I needed a hiding place for the time being, though. I rejected the standard ones, the cute places where a real pro always looked first. The toilet tank, the bed, the outer window sill. I stuck it on the floor under the dresser and tried to forget about it.

I got dressed in a hurry and left the hotel. The store I was looking for was two long blocks off the Boardwalk on Atlantic Avenue near Tennessee. I went in and bought a good attache case for twenty dollars and change. It was a nice case – I didn't know you could get them that good so far from Madison Avenue.

I lugged the case back to the hotel, bought a pair of Philly papers at the newsstand in the lobby, then went back to my room. The little box with the hinges filed through was right where I'd left it under the dresser. I took it out, wrapped it up tight in paper so it wouldn't come open, and put it in the attache case. Then I crumpled up paper and packed it in tight so that nothing would rattle around. I used all of the paper, closed the case and locked it up. I made a mental note to get rid of the key. When the time came, I could always break the thing open. But I didn't want to have the key on my person.

I hefted the case a few times experimentally. It was neither too heavy nor too light. It could have been almost anything.

Then I took it back down to the lobby and hauled it over to the front desk. The room clerk waited obligingly while I picked up my case and put it on the desk between us.

'Wonder if you'd do me a favor,' I said. 'I've got a commercial presentation here that I'm in the middle of. Not valuable to anybody but me, but there's always the chance that somebody might walk off with it not knowing what was in the case. The company would raise hell if that happened. Could you stick it in the safe for me?'

He could and did. He started to write out a claim check for me but I shook my head.

'I'd only lose it,' I told him. 'I'm not worried about it. I'll pick it up before I go.'

I gave him a dollar and left him with a safeful of heroin.

I had time to kill and thinking to do. I left the hotel again and took a walk on the Boardwalk. If anything, it was worse than when I'd been in town three years back. There were more hotdog and fruit juice stands, more penny arcades, more bingo games and carney booths and flashy souvenir shops. Sex was also present. The professionals stuck to the bars on the side street, but the amateur competition cluttered every board on the Boardwalk. Young girls walking in twos and threes and fours; blondes who got their hair from bottles; fifteen and sixteen and seventeen-year-olds with their blouses too sheer and their blue jeans too tight, their makeup too thick and their strut too obvious. Victory girls who didn't know the war had been over for fifteen years.

The boys were there because the girls were there. They played a game as old as the world, the boys trying to score, the girls trying to be scored upon without looking cheap about it, as though there was a way in the world for them to look otherwise. The boys were clumsy and the girls were clumsier, but somehow they would manage to get together, manage to find a place to neck and pet and make sloppy love. The girls would get pregnant and the boys would get gonorrhea.

One hotel had a terrace facing on the Boardwalk with umbrella-topped tables and tall drinks. I found an empty table and sat under the shade of the umbrella until a waiter found me, took my order, left me and returned with a tall cool vodka collins. It came with a colored straw and I sipped it like a kid sipping a malted. I lighted a cigarette and settled back in my chair. I tried to put everything together and make it add up right.

If I had a tighter connection with a branch of the narcotics trade it would have been easier. A while back I'd done a few jobs for a man named Marcus. It was strictly messenger-boy stuff – pick up this, take it there, give it to so-and-so. I hadn't seen Marcus in years and I didn't know where he was. He probably wouldn't even remember me.

That made selling the stuff impossible.

My other connection was L. K. B. I didn't know who he was, but I had an idea that it wouldn't be too hard to find out. He had arrived just that day, and he had probably checked into a hotel already. All I had to do was run down the list of recent arrivals at the six best hotels in town. Somebody would have those initials, and he would be my boy. I could get in touch with him from a distance, try to work a deal with him and sell his own stuff back to him.

It might work. It also might get me killed. The best I could hope for was a few thousand, a slim fraction of the value of the stuff. And I would spend the rest of my life waiting for a knife in the back.

I didn't like that.

I sipped more of the drink. A man walked by with a girl on his arm. Two old ladies rolled by in a rolling chair pushed by a bored Negro. Victory girls passed, looked at me, decided I was too old, and hurried on with their tails twitching.

I decided to sit tight. For the time being I was in the clear. The way things stood, the worst that could happen was that I skipped the hotel and left them with a box of heroin. If everything broke right, I could get out with a box in tow, hold it for a few years until everybody forgot about it, then find a way to sell it off a little at a time without raising anybody's eyebrows.

In the meantime there was Mona. I thought about her and remembered that she would be on the beach at midnight, waiting for me. I almost forgot the heroin, just thinking about her.

I dropped a buck for the drink and some change for the waiter on the table, and I left. Two blocks further along the Boardwalk I found a good restaurant where they served me a blood-rare steak and very black coffee.

The movie was lousy, a historical epic called *A Sound of Distant Drums*, a technicolor cinemascope package with pretty girls and flashing swords and people getting themselves killed flamboyantly. I dozed through most of it. It was a little after ten when I finally got out and headed for the hotel.

I doubled around behind the hotel, found the passageway to the beach and walked through it. There was a pier that ran from the Boardwalk to the ocean and I stayed close to it so that nobody would see me from the Boardwalk and remind me that I wasn't supposed to be on the beach. It was a silly rule to begin with, but Atlantic City was that kind of a town, built with the aid of a stopwatch. The beach closed at a certain hour, the pools in the hotels closed at a certain hour, the world folded up and disappeared at a certain hour. An insomniac could lose his mind in Atlantic City. Even the television shows went off the air at one o'clock.

The beach was empty. I walked down to where the water met the land and watched the waves come in. The sea is hypnotic, like the flames in a fireplace. I don't know how long I stood there, watching the waves without moving a muscle or thinking a thought. I remember that the wind was cold, but that I didn't mind it.

I gave up the game finally, walked back a few steps onto the beach, took off my jacket and made a pillow out of it. I was early – she wasn't due until midnight. If she was coming at all. I wondered about that.

I stretched out on sand and propped up my head on my jacket. I let my eyes close and let my body relax, but I did not fall asleep. I dozed a little.

I barely heard her coming because my mind was on something else. When I did hear the feet on the sand I knew it had to be her. I lay there without moving and listened to her moving.

'You're always sleeping,' she said. 'Sleeping all the time. And now you're ruining your clothes. That's not very intelligent of you.'

I opened my eyes. She wore a very simple red dress and no shoes at all. The moonlight played on her and showed me how stunning she was.

'We can lie on this. You can ruin your suit all you want, but I'd hate to get this dress all sandy.'

For the first time I noticed the blanket she was carrying. I grinned.

'Aren't you even going to get up?'

I stood up and looked at her. She started to say something but stopped with her mouth hanging open. I could understand it. There was something electric in the air, something neither of us could have put into words. Small talk was suddenly impossible. I knew it and she knew it.

I took a step toward her. She held out the blanket and I took hold of two corners and walked backwards. We spread the blanket on the sand and straightened up and looked at each other some more. The electricity was still there.

I wanted to say something but I couldn't. I am certain that it was the same for her. It would have been like talking through a wall. First we had to tear down the wall. Then there would be a time for talking.

I pulled my shirt out from my pants. I started unbuttoning it. I got it off and let it fall to the sand. I turned to her and she came close, reaching out a hand and touching my chest.

Then she turned around and asked me to unhook her.

I had trouble with the hook-and-eye at the top of the dress. My hands weren't working properly. Finally I managed it. I unzipped the dress all the way down past her waist but I didn't touch her skin at all.

She shrugged and the dress fell from her shoulders.

'The bra, Lennie.'

I took off the bra for her. It was black. I remember liking the contrast of the black bra and the pale skin. Then I turned away and took off the rest of my clothes.

When I turned to her once again we were both naked. I looked at her, all of her. I started at the face and looked all the way down past breasts and waist and hips to bare feet. Then I came back up again and my eyes locked with hers.

No words.

We walked toward each other until our bodies touched. I wrapped her up in my arms and held the sweetness of her against me. The silly voices of a thousand people drifted down from the Boardwalk like words from a brainless dream. The waves pounded behind us.

She kissed me.

And then we sank together to the blanket on the beach and forgot the world.

I was lying on my side looking over the beach to the sea. Above the water the moon was almost full. Her panties were a wisp of black silk on the sand beside me. I watched the waves and listened to her breathing.

I felt very strange, very weak and very strong at once. I remembered why I had come to Atlantic City in the first place, and I remembered all the things I had done for so many years, and everything seemed foolish, silly. I remembered, incongruously, Mrs Ida Lister. I had slept with her, too, in Atlantic City. Not on the beach, but in a plush, air-conditioned hotel room. Not because I wanted to, but because she was picking up the tab.

It had all been so stupid. Not wrong, not immoral. Merely stupid. And so had the years of skipping hotel bills, and living on the edge of the law, and looking for the one big connection that would make everything all right.

Now, somehow, the connection had been made. I could see clearly for the first time. Things looked different now.

'Lennie—'

'I know,' I said.

'It was—'

'I know, Mona. For me, too.'

I rolled over to look at her. Her body was not the same. Before it had been something to desire, something to break down into its component parts of breasts and hips and thighs and belly and behind, something to assess. Now it was *her* body. Now it was a body I had known. It was her.

'I can't stay much longer.'

'Why not?'

'Keith. He'll wonder where I am. He won't care, but he'll wonder.' Her voice was very bitter.

'Is that his name? Keith?'

She nodded.

'How long have you been married?'

'Almost two years. I'm twenty-five. We were married two years ago this September. I was twenty-three then.'

She said it as though she was thinking that she would never be twenty-three again.

'Why did you marry him?'

Her smile was not a happy one. 'Money,' she said. 'And boredom, and because twenty-three isn't eighteen any more, and all the other reasons. Why do pretty girls marry rich old men? You know the answer as well as I do.'

I found a pack of cigarettes in my jacket pocket. They were crumpled. I took one out and straightened it out, then offered it to her. She shook her head. I lighted it and smoked for a moment or so in silence.

'Now you go back to him?'

'I have to.'

'And then what?'

'I don't know.'

'Then we meet here every midnight for a week or two,' I said. 'And each night you go back to him. And then the two of you go away and you forget me.'

She didn't say anything.

'Is that how it goes?'

'I don't know.'

I dragged on the cigarette. It didn't taste right and I buried it in the sand.

'This hasn't happened before, Lennie.'

'This?'

'Us.'

'So we let it go?'

'I don't know, Lennie. I don't know anything any more. I used to know all the answers. Now somebody changed the questions.'

I knew what she meant.

Her voice was very distant now. 'We have a house in Cheshire Point,' she said. 'On a two-acre lot with big old trees and expensive furniture. My clothes cost money. I have a sable coat and an ermine coat and a chinchilla stole. We didn't even bother with mink. That's the kind of money Keith has.'

'How did he make it?'

She shrugged. 'He's a businessman. An office downtown on Chambers Street. I don't even know what he does. He goes downtown a few times a week. He never talks about the business, never gets mail at the house or brings work home. He says he buys things and he sells them. That's all he says.'

'What do the two of you do for kicks?'

'I don't know.'

'You have a lot of friends? Congenial companionship? Bridge parties on Saturday nights and steaks in the back yard?'

'Stop it, Lennie.'

'Are you going back to Cheshire Point with him? To share his bed and have his kids and spend his money? Are you—'

'Stop it!'

I stopped it. I wanted to reach for her, to roll her up in my arms and tell her that everything was going to be all right. But I didn't believe it myself.

'I'll have one of those cigarettes now, Lennie.'

I took out two, straightened them out, gave her one and kept one for myself. I scratched a match for her and cupped it in my hands. She came over to accept the light and I looked down at the top of her head and thought how beautiful she was. I envied Keith and realized that he would envy me. It always works that way.

'It probably doesn't mean anything anyway,' she said. She was talking to herself now, not to me. 'It was just once. It happened, we were both ready for it, it was good. But it didn't mean anything. I can forget you and you can forget me. In a week we would forget each other. It doesn't mean a thing.'

'Do you really believe that?'

Silence for a moment.

Then, bitterly, 'No, of course not. No, I don't believe it.'

'Would you leave him?'

She smiled. 'I'd leave him in a minute,' she said. 'But that isn't what you mean. You mean will I leave his money.'

I didn't say anything.

'Do you have any money, Lennie?'

'Fifty dollars. A hundred, maybe.'

She laughed. 'He spends that much on a whore.'

'What does he need one for? He's got you for a wife.'

I didn't realize how that sounded until I heard it. I watched her face fall. 'I suppose you're right,' she said. 'He doesn't need a whore. He's married to one.'

'I didn't mean that. I—'

'But it's true.' She took a deep breath, then let it out. She stuck her cigarette in the sand and straightened up. 'I can't leave him, Lennie. I've got all that money and I can't let go of it. It wouldn't work.'

I didn't say anything.

'Two years,' she said. 'Why didn't I meet you two years ago? Why?'

'Would it have made a difference?'

'A big difference,' she said. 'Money is funny. That rhymes, doesn't it? But it's true. I wasn't born this way, Lennie. I could have lived without money. People manage. If I had met you before I met Keith—'

'If this blanket had wings we could fly it.'

'Or if it was a magic carpet,' she said. 'But don't you see what I mean? Now I'm used to money. I know what it's like to have it. I know what it's like to be able to do anything I want and buy anything I want. I couldn't go back to the way it was before.'

'How was it before?'

'It wasn't that bad,' she said. 'I wasn't deprived. We didn't starve. We owned our own home, never worried about eating regularly. But we didn't have money left over. You know what I mean.'

I knew what she meant. And I wondered what I was doing, trying to convince her to throw it up and marry me. So we could starve hand in hand? So we could raise children and live in a frame house in Yahooville? So I could carry a lunch pail to work and owe the bank and the finance company and everybody else in the world? For what? For a girl who didn't even know my real name?

But I heard myself say, 'It could work. We could make it work, Mona.'

She looked at me, her eyes very bright. She was about to say something that never got said. I wondered what it was.

Instead she got to her feet and began to put clothes on. I watched her while she dressed.

'I'll leave the blanket here,' she said. 'The hotel won't miss it. It would look funny if I came in carrying a blanket.'

She was looking at me now. 'I have to go,' she said. 'I really have to go.'

'Do I get to see you again?'

'Do you want to?'

I wanted to.

'I'll . . . I'll get in touch with you. Somehow. But I have to go back now.'

'To Keith.'

'To Keith,' she echoed. 'To being his wife. To being Mrs L. Keith Brassard.'

I barely heard her. I watched her go, watched that perfect, half-whore, half-lady walk of hers carry her up the beach alongside the pier. I watched her and thought about her and thought about myself, and I wondered what had happened to the two of us, and what was going to happen from here on in.

She was almost to the Boardwalk before I remembered her final words and realized hysterically just who her husband was.

L. Keith Brassard.

3

I folded the blanket very methodically until it was a little cushion two feet square. I planted my rump on it and sat at the edge of the shore looking out on the water. I wanted to run out into the water and swim like a maniac until I wound up in some place that was not Atlantic City.

He's a businessman. An office downtown on Chambers Street. I don't even know what he does.

She would be back by now, taking the elevator up to her room. I wondered where her room was. Maybe it was on the same floor as mine.

He goes downtown a few times a week. He never talks about the business, never gets mail at the house or brings work home. He says he buys things and he sells them. That's all he says.

I wondered whether or not he had told her about the missing suitcases. It was pretty obvious she didn't know anything about the heroin. If his suitcases were stolen, that wouldn't mean a thing to her. A man who bought her a sable coat, an ermine coat and a chinchilla stole undoubtedly could replace the contents of two suitcases without taxing his budget. A man who lived in Cheshire Point luxury could afford to buy himself a few more suits and a new batch of underwear.

I thought about him and I thought about her and I thought about me. We were each pretty special. L. Keith Brassard – an import-export man with a new slant on life, a tall man in narcotics with a pretty wife and a perfect front. Mona Brassard – a dryness in the throat and a moistness in the palm of the hand, a sweetness that caught at you and strangled you. She wanted me and she wanted money and I don't know how in hell she could have us both.

And Joe Marlin. That was my name, before it was David Gavilan, before it was Leonard K. Blake, before a lot of names. Do names matter? They never did.

But for some damned reason I wanted her to call me Joe.

We were cuties, Dave and Lennie and I. We had the white powder and we had the warm woman. We were riding free and loose. We had everything but a future.

I smoked a cigarette all the way down and threw the butt in the ocean.

Then I stuffed the hotel's blanket under the pier and walked back to the Boardwalk.

I picked up the phone in my room and asked room service for a bottle of Jack Daniels and a pail of ice and a glass. I sat down in a chair then and waited for something to happen. The air conditioning was turned all the way up and the room was well on its way to becoming a refrigerator.

There was a knock at the door. The bellhop was there, a wiry kid with quick eyes. He put the bottle of bourbon and the bucket of ice on the dresser, then gave me the tab. I signed for it and handed him a dollar.

Except for the eyes he was a college boy on summer vacation. The eyes knew too much.

'Thanks,' he said. Then, 'Anything you want, I can get it for you. The name is Ralph.'

He left and I settled down with the Jack Daniels.

I put a pair of ice cubes in a water tumbler and poured three ounces of bourbon over them. While the ice cooled the liquor I sat back in a chair and thought about things. Then I started my drink. The liquor was smooth as silk. The label on the bottle said they filtered it through charcoal or something. Whatever they did to it, it worked.

I drank some more and smoked a little. The liquor loosened me up until my mind started working again, fishing around for answers, finding new questions to ask.

I should pack up, get out, forget her. But I knew that if I left, I would never find her or anyone like her again. Before, I had managed to live without her. But now I had had her. How had she put it?

Don't you see what I mean? Now I'm used to money. I know what it's like to have it. I know what it's like to be able to do anything I want and to buy anything I want. I couldn't go back to the way it was before.

I had had her – once – and I was used to her. I knew what it was like to have her, to love her and be loved by her. Love? A weird and shifty word. It made me feel like the hero of a popular song.

But I couldn't go back to the way it was before.

She was right and I was right; only the world was wrong. We needed each other and we needed that money, and if there was a way to get both I didn't know where to find it. I tried looking for it at the bottom of the glass but it wasn't there. I filled the glass again, skipping the ice this time around. The liquor was smooth enough without it.

I had the heroin. I could take it to New York and sniff around in the wrong streets until I made a connection, then unload for all I could get. It might work. The money might be enough, enough to take us away from L. Keith Brassard. Enough to get out of the country – South America, or Spain, or the Italian Riviera. We could live a long time on the money. We could buy a boat and live on it. Once, I learned how to sail. There is nothing like it. And you can take a boat and lose yourself in a million little islands all over the world, islands where it's always warm and the air is clear and clean. We could go anywhere.

And we could never look behind us.

Because we would never get away. He was not an ordinary husband, not a straight Westchester burgher with a lawful mind and lawful friends. Anybody carrying that much horse was very well connected indeed. The word would go far and wide, and there would be an unofficial but firm price on a certain man and a certain woman. Some day somebody somewhere would look twice at us. We could run but we could not hide.

We wouldn't last long that way. We'd start off loving each other very hard, and then every day we would do a little more private thinking about the men who were going to catch us. It wouldn't happen all at once – we'd forget those men, and then something would happen that would force the memory of them upon us, and we would run again.

And then it would begin to happen. She would remember being Mrs L. Keith Brassard and living in Cheshire Point with her ermine coat and her sable coat and her chinchilla wrap, with a big solid house and heavy furniture and charge accounts. She would remember how it felt not to be afraid, and she would realize that she had never been afraid before she met me; that she was always afraid now, a little bit more afraid with every passing day. Then she would begin to hate me.

And I would remember an uncomplicated life, where you left one town when things became overly difficult, where the biggest threat was a watchful hotel manager, and the biggest problem the next meal. I would look at the soft sweetness of her and I would think about death – a slow and unpleasant death, because the men he would send would be experts at that sort of thing. And, inevitably, I would begin to hate her.

I couldn't have her and I couldn't have the money, not that way. I drank more bourbon and thought about it and drew blanks. There had to be a way, but there wasn't.

The bottle was half-gone when I thought of the way, the only way. Another person might have thought of it at once, but my mind has certain established channels in which it runs and this was out of known waters. So it took a bottle of Jack Daniels before I got around to it.

Brassard could die.

That scared the hell out of me, and I had two more quick drinks, got out of my clothes and into bed. I fell asleep almost at once. Maybe the liquor was responsible for that. I don't know. Maybe I slept because I was afraid to stay awake.

I was dreaming, but it was one of those dreams you forget the minute you come awake. The knocking at the door woke me up and the dream slipped away from me. I opened my eye very tentatively. I wasn't hungover and I felt fine. At least I would have, given a few hours more sleep.

The knocking began again.

'Who is it?'

'Chambermaid.'

'Go away.' Great hotel, when the chambermaids wake you up in the middle of the morning. 'Come back next year.'

'Open the door, Mr Blake—'

'Go play in traffic. I'm tired.'

The voice changed to a coo. 'Lennie,' it said, '*please* open the door.'

For a minute I thought the dream was back again. Then I jumped out of bed and wrapped up in a sheet. She looked cool and fresh in a white cotton blouse and a pair of sea-green clamdiggers. She came right on in and I closed the door.

'You're nuts,' I said. 'For coming here. But of course you know that.'

'I know.'

'He could have seen you. He'll wonder where you went. It wasn't too brilliant of you.'

She was smiling. 'You look silly,' she said. 'Wrapped up in that sheet like an Arabian sheik. Were you sleeping?'

'Of course. It's the middle of the night.'

'Middle of the day, you mean.'

'What time is it?'

'Almost noon,' she said. 'And he couldn't have seen me, anyway. He was out of the hotel at the crack of dawn. Business, he said, something unexpected. Even in Atlantic City he has business. Business before pleasure. Always.'

I knew what business he had. A whole boxful of business that had neatly disappeared.

She pouted. 'Aren't you glad to see me?'

'You know the answer to that one.'

'You don't seem glad. You didn't even kiss me hello.'

I kissed her. And then it all came back, all the way back, and it was the night on the beach all over again. One kiss did that. She was that kind of woman.

'That's better.'

'Much better.'

Very deliberately she removed the blouse and the clamdiggers, kicked her shoes under my bed. She wasn't wearing anything else. I couldn't stop looking at her.

Her eyes were laughing. 'You silly man,' she said. 'You don't need that silly sheet, do you?'

I didn't.

Much later I opened my eyes. She was curled up like a sleeping kitten with her blonde hair all disorganized on the pillow. I reached out a hand and ran it over her body from shoulder to hip. She didn't stir.

I reached over for the pack of cigarettes on the table at the side of the bed. I found a match and lighted a cigarette. When I turned back to her she had her eyes open.

She smiled for an answer.

'You're pretty great, you know.'

Her smile widened.

'I'm going to miss you.'

She bit her lip. 'Lennie—'

I waited.

'Remember what I told you on the beach? That I couldn't give up the money?'

I remembered.

'I found out something today. Here. With you.'

I waited some more.

'I . . . still can't give up the money.'

The cigarette didn't taste right. I took another drag and coughed on it.

'But I can't give you up either, Lennie. I . . . don't know where we go from here. I want the money and I want you and I can't have both. I'm a spoiled little girl. I can't *do* anything. All I can do is want.'

I knew what the answer was and I knew that I was scared to hand it to her. But the die was cast. I couldn't see the spots, couldn't tell whether we had come up with seven or whether we had crapped out royally. Either way, the pattern was there already. It couldn't be changed from here on in.

'How old is Keith?'

She shrugged. 'Fifty,' she said. 'Fifty-five. I don't know. I never asked him. That's silly, isn't it? Not knowing how old you own husband is. Fifty or fifty-five or something around there. I don't know. Why?'

'I was just thinking.'

She looked at me.

'I mean . . . he's not a young man, Mona. Men his age don't live forever.'

I left it like that, hanging in the middle of the air, and I watched her face try not to change expression. She didn't quite make it. It was terrifying, in a way. We were a little too much alike. We had both been thinking of the same thing. I guess it had to be that way.

'Maybe his heart isn't too good,' I went on, talking around the whole thing. 'Maybe some day he'll fall on his face and it'll be all over. It happens every day, you know. It could happen to him.'

She fed my own words back to me. 'If this bed had wings we could fly it, Lennie. Or if it were a magic carpet. His heart's in perfect shape. He goes to the doctor for a physical three times a year. Maybe he's afraid of dying. I don't know. Three times a year he goes to the doctor, spends the whole day there getting the most complete physical examination money can buy. He went less than a month ago. He's in perfect physical shape. He was bragging to me about it.'

'He could still get a coronary. Even when you're in perfect shape—'

'Lennie.'

I stopped and looked at her.

'You don't mean he could have a heart attack. You mean something else.'

I didn't say anything.

'You mean he could have an accident. That's what you mean, isn't it?'

I drew on the cigarette. I looked hard at her and tried to figure out a way to fit all the pieces together. If there was a way to do it, I couldn't find it. The pieces had jagged edges and they didn't mesh at all.

'I wish we weren't us,' she was saying now. 'I wish we were other people. Other people wouldn't think rotten things. This is rotten.'

I left it alone.

'I don't love him, Lennie. Maybe I love you. I don't know. All I know is I want to be with you and I don't want to be with him. But he's . . . a good man, Lennie. He's good to me. He isn't mean or cruel or vicious or—'

He was a dope peddler on a grand scale, an import-export cookie who imported the wrong thing. He was a top link in a cutie-pie game that sent high-school kids out doing armed robbery to pacify the monkey he put on their shoulders, a game that had caused more human agony than all other cutie-pie games combined.

But she didn't know this, and I didn't know how to tell her about it. And therefore he was a good man, not mean or cruel or vicious.

'What do you want to do now?'

What she wanted to do was change the subject. She had a good way to do it. She put out her arms for me and forced a smile.

'We've got a few more hours,' she said. 'Let's spend them in bed.'

It seemed like a pretty good idea at the time. But after awhile I dropped off to sleep and she didn't. I shouldn't have done that, I guess. It was a mistake. But I wasn't in any condition to do too much deep thinking at the time, and that was a shame.

Because when I did wake up she was shaking me by one shoulder and looking at me all wide-eyed and frightened. I didn't catch on to it right away. I had to hear it before it soaked in.

'Lennie—'

I sat up on the edge of the bed and took her hand off my shoulder. Her nails had been digging into me. I don't think she realized it at the time.

'The bags—'

I don't think too cleverly when I wake up. I was still lost.

'Lennie, what are you doing with Keith's bags in your closet?'

It was a hell of a good question.

She was so confused she couldn't think straight. She stood there bubbling and babbling. I had to slap her twice across the face to calm her down. I didn't hit her very hard, but each time I slapped her it hurt me. Finally I got her to sit down in a chair and keep her ears open and her mouth shut.

There were a lot of things I didn't want to tell her just yet and a few more

I'd have preferred never to tell her. But I didn't have any choice. She had seen the L. K. B. bags in the closet. God alone knew what had prompted her to rummage through my closet, but this was beside the point. The point, simply enough, was that the cat was halfway out of the bag and it couldn't hurt to bring it out the rest of the way.

'Don't interrupt me at all,' I told her. 'This is a long story. It won't make sense to you until you've heard all of it.'

I started with getting off the train from Philly and needing luggage. It went back farther than that, went years back, but the rest of it wasn't important. Not for the time being, anyway. If things broke right I would have a whole lifetime to tell her the story of my life. If they didn't, then nothing much mattered.

I told her that I took his luggage at random, checked into the hotel under a phony name, met her, opened his bags, and found the heroin. She didn't believe that part of it at first but I went over it again and again until it made sense. There was a hysterical expression on her face when the news soaked in. She was seeing old Keith in a new light now. He was a dope peddler, not a nice guy. She had managed to live with him for two years without tumbling to this juicy little fact, and she couldn't have been more surprised if I had told her he was a woman.

I ran it from alpha to omega and then I stopped because there was no more to tell. Her hubby was a crook and I had his supply in the hotel safe. We were together in my room and the world was taking us for a joy ride.

'This changes things, Lennie. Joe, I mean. I guess I have to call you Joe now, don't I?'

'I guess so.'

'Joe Marlin instead of Lennie Blake. All right. I like it better. But this changes things, Joe. Doesn't it?'

'How?'

'Now I don't want his money,' she said. 'I couldn't stand living with him any more. Now all I want is you. We can forget him and just run away and be together forever.'

It sounded good but it didn't work that way. She wasn't seeing the whole picture yet. He was still old Keith. Now he made his money in a dirty business and it sickened her. But she didn't see that the man himself was different.

'We'd be killed, Mona.'

'She stared at me.

'We'd run and we'd be caught. He's a gangster, Mona. You know what a gangster is?'

Her eyes went very wide.

'You're his woman,' I went on. 'He bought you and he's been paying heavily for you. Ermine coat, sable coat, chinchilla stole. Those things run into money.'

'But—'

'So now he owns you. You can't run away. He'll catch you and he'll have you killed. Do you want us to die, Mona?'

I saw the look in her eyes and I remembered the slight contempt in her voice when she talked about Brassard's physical exams. She had said that maybe he was afraid of death. He wasn't the only one. She was afraid of dying herself. That made two of us.

'We can't run,' I said. 'We wouldn't get away.'

'It's a big world.'

'The mob is a big mob. Bigger than the world. Where do you want to run?'

She didn't have an answer.

'Well?'

She bit her lower lip. 'The accident,' she said. 'Before you said he could have an accident. Didn't you?'

'I worded it a little differently.'

'But that's what you meant. I suppose he could still have an accident, couldn't he?'

'I thought you didn't want to think about things like that.'

'It's different now, Joe. I didn't know what kind of a man he was. Now it's different.'

It wasn't the least bit different. Before he was kind and generous and now he was mean and vicious. This was the wrapper. It was a game to make murder a little bit easier to swallow. Sugar on a pill. But the pill was the same no matter how goddamned sweet it tasted. The pill was still murder.

'Joe?'

I was starting to sweat. Atlantic City was getting too warm for us and the air conditioning in the room could never change that. I cupped her chin in my hand and tilted her head up so that she was looking at me.

'When are you and Keith going back to Cheshire Point?'

'Joe, I don't want to go with him. I can't go with him, Joe. I have to stay with you.'

'When are you going back to Cheshire Point? Just answer the questions, dammit.'

'A week. Six days, I don't know.'

I played mental arithmetic. 'Okay,' I said. 'First off, you don't see me any more. If we pass on the Boardwalk you don't even look at me. No matter where Keith is, understand? Because he has friends here. I don't want any connection between the two of us. Nobody can see us together or the game is over.'

'I don't understand. Joe—'

'If you kept your mouth shut you might have a better chance of understanding.'

Her eyes were hurt. But she shut up.

'I'm leaving here the day after tomorrow,' I said. 'I'm checking out bag and baggage and I'm going to New York. I'll find a place to stay under another name.'

'What name?'

'I don't know yet. It doesn't matter. You won't have to get in touch with me. I'll get in touch with you. Just stay put. As far as you're concerned, nothing has happened. Keith is good old Keith and you never met me. Got that?'

She nodded solemnly.

'Don't forget. You have to keep saying it over and over to yourself so that you don't slip out of character. You're Keith's wife. I never happened to you. You're going to go back with him and you're going to be the same woman he took with him to Atlantic City. The same all across the board. You don't know a thing. You got that? You understand the part you're going to have to play?'

'I understand.'

Now came the harder part. Hard to tell her, hard to think about. 'You'll have to sleep with him,' I said. 'I . . . wish you didn't. I don't like it.'

'Neither do I.'

'Maybe you can tell him you're sick,' I said. 'It might work. But just remember that if this breaks for us you'll never have to sleep with him or look at him or think about him again for the rest of your life. That might make it a little easier.'

She nodded.

I hesitated, then looked around for the pack of cigarettes. She wanted one too, which was understandable. I gave her one and took one for myself and lighted them both. We smoked for a few minutes in relative silence.

'Mona,' I said, 'I'll need money.'

'Money?'

'To pay the hotel bill,' I said. 'I can't afford a skiptracer on my tail. And I have to get the package of heroin back from the desk.'

'How much will it cost?'

'I don't know. And I'll need money to operate on in New York. Not much, but as much as I can get. I hate to ask you for it—'

'Don't be silly.'

I grinned. 'How much can you spare?'

She thought for a moment. 'I have a few hundred in cash. I can let you have it.'

'How will you explain it?'

'If he asks I'll tell him I saw some jewelry and wanted it. I don't think he'll ask. He's not that way. He doesn't care what I spend or how I spend it. If I told him I lost it at the track he wouldn't mind.'

'You're sure it's safe?'

'Positive.'

'Put as much as you can spare in an envelope,' I said. 'One of the hotel's envelopes. Don't write anything on it. Sometime this evening pass my room. The door will be closed, but not locked. Open it, drop the envelope inside, then beat it. Don't stop to say anything to me.'

She smiled. 'It sounds like a spy movie. Cloak and dagger. Bob Mitchum in a trenchcoat.'

'It's safer that way.'

'I'll do it. After dinner?'

'Whenever you get a chance. I'll be here until I get the envelope. I'll leave for New York the day after tomorrow. I don't want to rush things. Good enough?'

'I guess so.'

'Get dressed,' I said. 'I'll see you in New York.'

We both got dressed in a hurry. Then I motioned her back, walked to the door and opened it. A chambermaid was strolling down the hall, taking her time. I waited until the maid got out of the way.

Before I sent Mona out I grabbed her and kissed her very quickly. It was a strange kiss – passionless, and surprisingly intense at the same time. Then she was out in the hall heading for the elevator and I was closing the door and walking back toward the bed.

There was a drink or two or three in the bottle of Jack Daniels. I finished off the bourbon and felt a little better.

4

I got the money a few minutes after six. It was a very strange feeling – I was lying on the bed with the light out, riding along on the slight edge the bourbon had been able to give me. The air conditioner was whirring gently in the background. Then the door opened less than six inches, an envelope flopped to the floor, and the door closed.

I hadn't even seen her hand. And this made the entire affair so impersonal it was startling. The door had opened by itself, the envelope had come from nowhere, and the door had closed. There were no living creatures involved in the process.

I picked up the envelope, shook the contents down to one end and ripped open the other end. Tens and twenties and fifties. I counted them twice and got a total of $370 each time.

They went in my wallet and the envelope went in the wastebasket.

It hit me all at once and I fell on the bed trying not to laugh. It was funny, and at the same time it was anything but funny, and I muffled my face with a pillow and howled like a hyena.

If it was anyone but Mona, it would be so simple. I would smile a happy smile, walk out of the hotel, and catch a train for Nowheresville with three hundred and seventy hard-earned dollars in my kick. When you looked at it that way it was the simplest and deftest con I had ever pulled in my life. Sweet and easy, without a problem in the world.

Except that I wasn't pulling a con. Now, with the money handed to me on a solid gold platter, I was going to pay my hotel bill, play my cards properly, and wind up going to New York and waiting for her. I don't know whether it is funny or not, but I was laughing my fool head off.

When I ran out of laughs I grabbed a shower and shave and went to the hotel next door for dinner. Nobody goes to the hotel next door for dinner. You either eat in your own hotel or you go to a restaurant. That was what I was bargaining on. I didn't want to run into Mona and I didn't want to run into Keith. Not until I was ready for them.

The dinner was probably good. Big hotels cook dependably if not imaginatively. They don't ruin steaks, which was what I ordered. But I didn't taste my dinner. I thought about him and I thought about her and I tasted murder instead of meat. I kept a cigarette going throughout the meal and paid more attention to it than to my steak. I sat staring into my coffee for a long time. Then when I started to drink it, it was room-temperature and horrible. I left it there and went to a movie.

The movie made about as much sense to me as if the actors had been speaking Persian and the subtitles were done in Chinese. I remember nothing about the story, not even the title. The show was there to kill time and that is all it did. I looked at the screen but I didn't see it. I thought. I planned. I schemed. Call it what you want.

I would have liked to get out of Atlantic City then and there. Staying around was a risk that grew greater every minute that I spent in the miserable town. And, now that I had decided to pay for my room, every extra day was an expense that I couldn't quite afford. Mona's contribution to my welfare, combined with the little money of my own that was left, gave me a drop over four hundred dollars. It was going too fast to suit me.

But I couldn't leave yet. I needed a look at my man, my L. Keith Brassard. I needed to know the enemy before I would decide how and when and where to kill him.

The movie ended and I went back to the hotel. The Boardwalk was a little less heavily populated than usual but as raucous as ever. I stood for a moment or two watching a pitchman explain how you could live an extra ten years if you squashed vegetables in a patented liquifier and drank the crap you wound up with. I watched him put a cabbage through the machine. It started out as a head of cabbage. Then the machine went to work on it. The pitchman flipped the pulpy remains into a garbage pail and proudly lifted a glass of noxious-looking pap to his lips. He drained it in a swallow and smiled broadly.

I wondered if you could do the same thing to a human being. Put him in a patented liquifier and squeeze the juice out of him. Flip the pulp in a garbage pail. Close the lid tight.

I walked on and drank a glass of pina colada at a fruit juice stand. I wondered how they made it and got a frightening mental picture of a pineapple and a coconut waltzing hand in hand into a patented liquifier in a sort of vegetarian suicide pact. I finished the pina colada and headed for the hotel.

A man walked out as I walked in. I caught only the quickest of looks at him but there was something familiar about him. I had seen him before, somewhere. I had no idea where or when, or who he might be.

He was short and dark and thin. He had all his hair and it was combed neatly and worn fairly long. His black moustache was neatly trimmed. He dressed well and he walked quickly.

For some reason I hoped to God he hadn't recognized me.

I saw him the next day.

I woke up around ten, got dressed in slacks and an open shirt and went down to the coffee shop for breakfast. I was starving, strangely enough, and

I wolfed down waffles and sausages and two cups of black coffee in no time at all. Then I lit the morning's first cigarette and went out to wait for him.

I went to the hotel terrace where I'd had a drink the first night. I found a table under an umbrella. It was close enough to the Boardwalk to give me a good view and far enough away so that nobody would notice me unless they worked at it. The waiter came over and I ordered black coffee. It was a little too early for drinking, although the rest of the customers didn't seem to think so. A garment-district type and a broken-down brunette were knocking off daiquiris and whooping it up. Getting an early start, I thought. Or still going from the night before. I forgot all about them and watched the Boardwalk.

And almost missed them.

After your first day in Atlantic City you stop watching the rolling chairs that plod back and forth along the Boardwalk. They're part of the scenery, and it is out of the question that anybody you know might ride in one of them. I had forgotten the chairs, concentrating on the people who were walking, and I barely saw them. Then I got an eyeful of yellow hair and took a second look, and there they were.

He was short and he was fat and he was old. He was also every inch the good burgher from Westchester, and it was no longer hard to see how he had fooled Mona. Some honest men look like crooks; some crooks look like honest men. He was one of the second kind.

He had a firm, honest chin and a thin-lipped, honest mouth. His eyes were water-blue – I could see that even from where I was sitting. His hair was white. Not gray but white. There is something very regal about white hair.

I watched that nice-looking honest old man until the chair stopped in front of the Shelburne and they got out of it. Then I drank my coffee and wondered how we were going to kill him.

'More coffee, sir?'

I looked up at the waiter. I didn't feel like moving and I didn't feel like more coffee.

'Not just yet.'

'Certainly, sir. Would you care for something to eat, perhaps? I have a menu.'

When they want you to defecate or abandon the toilet they make no bones about it. I didn't want food and I didn't want coffee. Therefore I should pay the man and go away. They had fifty empty tables on that terrace and they wanted fifty-one.

'Martini,' I said, tired. 'Extra dry, twist of lemon.'

He bowed and vanished. He reappeared shortly thereafter with martini in tow. There were two olives instead of one and he had remembered the twist of lemon, which most of them don't. Maybe he wanted to be friends.

I don't know why I ordered the drink. Ordinarily I would have left about then. I didn't want a drink, didn't want a meal, didn't want more coffee and

I had already seen Brassard. These factors, combined with my thorough lack of love for both terrace and waiter, should have sent me on my way.

They didn't. And I got another look – a longer and closer one – at L. Keith Brassard.

I don't know how he got there. I looked up and there he was, three tables down, with a waiter at his elbow. My waiter. He was giving me the profile and he looked as solidly respectable as ever.

I sat there feeling obvious as all hell and wished I had a newspaper to hide behind. I didn't want to look at the man. There's an old trick – you stare hard and long at somebody and they fidget for a minute or two, then turn and look at you. It's not extrasensory perception or anything like that. They catch a glimpse of you out of the corner of an eye, something like that.

I was positive that if I stared at him he would turn around and look at me. I didn't want that to happen. Whatever way we played it in New York, I was coming on with one great advantage. I knew him and he didn't know me. It was a trump card and I hated like hell to lose it in Atlantic City.

So I nursed the drink and watched him part-time. The more I watched him the harder he looked at me. You have to be very hard inside if you can get away with looking soft. It's much easier to be a success as a gangster if you look like a gangster. The closer you are to the Hollywood stereotype, the quicker acceptance comes to you. If you look more like Wall Street than Mulberry Street, Mulberry Street doesn't want to see you.

He was going to be a hard man to kill.

I was chewing the first olive when he got company. There had to be a reason more pronounced than thirst for him to be biding his time on the terrace, and the reason appeared in short order. The reason was short and thin, well-dressed with long hair neatly combed and black moustache properly trimmed. The reason was the man I had half-recognized the night before walking out of the Shelburne. Now I remembered him.

And almost choked on the olive.

His name was Reggie Cole. He worked for a man named Max Treger, and so did half of New Jersey. Treger was a wise old man who occupied a secure and nebulous position at the top of everything that happened in the state of New Jersey on the uncouth side of the law. Treger I knew solely by reputation. Reggie Cole I had met once, years ago, at a party. Reggie was smaller then, but the years and Max Treger had been kind to him. Reggie had risen – he sat at the right hand of God, according to rumor.

Now he sat at the right hand of L. Keith Brassard. I got him full-face that way and I was worried. It had been a long time since that brief meeting, but I recognized him. There was all the reason in the world for him to remember me. I had taken a girl away from him. The girl was a pig and I'm sure he hadn't cared much at the time, but it wasn't something he would forget.

I waited for him to look up and see me. But he and Brassard were busy – they were talking quickly and earnestly and I wished I could hear what they were saying. It wasn't hard to guess the topic of conversation. Brassard was supposed to be delivering enough heroin to keep all of New Jersey stoned for a long time. The horse had miraculously disappeared. Which was sure as hell something to talk about.

I swallowed the second olive whole. I put enough money on the table to cover the martini and the coffee and the waiter, tucking the bill under the empty glass so that it wouldn't blow away.

Just as I was starting to get up, a head came up and small eyes looked at me. A short, puzzled look – probably exactly the same as the one I had given him the night before. A look of vague and distant recognition. He remembered me but he didn't know who I was.

The next time around he would know. I hoped the conversation with Brassard was serious to take his mind off me.

I got up and tried not to run. I walked away with my back to the two of them and hoped to God they weren't looking at it. The sweat had my shirt plastered to my back by the time I reached the Shelburne. And it wasn't even a particularly warm day.

There was no point in staying around any longer. I had already gotten more than I'd bargained for – a look at him and a hint of who his buddies were. As well as I could figure it, Brassard had come running to Atlantic City with a cargo of heroin. He wasn't a delivery boy – it was *his* heroin, bought and paid for and ready for resale. Nobody was going to accuse him of welching or anything of the sort. His only headaches were financial ones.

If anything, Max Treger was the man who looked bad. From Brassard's point of view, the only man who could have picked him so neatly was the man who knew what he was carrying. Treger had a solid reputation for honesty-among-thieves and all that, but with that big a bundle hanging fire Brassard was undoubtedly suspicious. I hoped he would raise enough hell so that somebody would get mad and shoot holes in his head. It would save me a lot of work.

But I didn't think it would happen. In a few days Brassard would convince Treger that he wasn't playing heroin hopscotch and Treger in turn would convince Brassard that he had better rackets under his thumb than petty larceny. The two clowns would put their crooked heads together and come up with an unknown quantity. They would start looking for this unknown quantity, at which time it would be very unhealthy to be me.

I wanted to run but it was too early. The big headache was the goddamned luggage. The bags were ordinary enough but they could be recognized especially when the Red Alert went out on them. I didn't give a damn if somebody remembered them in a week or so – by that time I'd be snug in New York with my trail as well-covered as it was ever going to be. But I didn't want anybody to tip until I was as far as possible from Atlantic City.

I gave the railway station a buzz from my room and found out that there was a train to Philly every morning at 7:30. There was another every afternoon, but the morning train was a hell of a lot safer. Everybody is properly asleep at that hour, and at the same time there's nothing suspicious about checking out then, as there would be for a train leaving at, say, four in the morning. The less people who saw my bags on the way out, the better I would feel about it. The less chance of Brassard being around, the happier I was.

I called the desk in the middle of the afternoon to leave a call for six the following morning, which must have puzzled the hell out of them. Then I phoned room service for more Jack Daniels and let the afternoon and evening spend themselves in a mildly alcoholic fog. It was gentle drinking. I had nothing better to do, and at the same time I had no overwhelming compulsion to get stoned to the earlobes. I paced myself properly and kept a comfortable edge on until I felt tired enough to sleep. Then I threw down a few extra shots and slipped over the edge so that sleep would come a little more quickly. Which it did.

My eyes opened the second the phone rang and I came thoroughly awake at once. I took a salt water shower, this time on purpose, and then chased away the salt with cold fresh water. I used up three little towels before I managed to get dry.

I dressed and went downstairs. There was a different monkey behind the desk but he was just as obliging as the first. He gave me no trouble at all. He handed over the attaché case and I gave him my nicest smile in return.

All the way back through the lobby to the elevator and up too many flights to my room I felt as though half the English-speaking world was staring at the attaché case.

I actually tried to open it, then remembered locking it and consigning the key to limbo. It was a shame. I couldn't very well leave either of Brassard's bags lying around. If the case were open I could transfer the heroin to one of his bags and let the case lose itself. This way I had three bags to carry. It would be no problem at first, but it might be trouble when I switched trains.

I packed all of my stuff and all of Brassard's stuff into his two suitcases. Since I had come with next to nothing, this wasn't the hardest thing in the world. Then I went back down to the lobby, let a bellboy carry my bags to the inevitable waiting taxi, and wandered over to the desk.

The monkey hoped I had enjoyed my stay.

'Wonderful town,' I told him, lying in my teeth. 'I needed the rest. Feel like a new man.'

That much was true.

'Going back home now?'

'Back to Philly,' I told him. I'd used a good address off Rittenhouse Square when I checked in.

'Come back and see us.'

I nodded. He should sit on a hot stove until I came back. He should hold his breath.

I went out the side entrance. The cab was there with my bags nestled together in the trunk. I gave the bellhop a buck and hoped he would forget all about the luggage.

At the railway station I bought a ticket straight through to Philadelphia. I carried my baggage on the train. It was tough to lug three pieces without looking awkward but I managed it somehow. The conductor came by, took my train ticket and gave me a seat check good to Philadelphia. I settled back and let the train chug its way past Egg Harbor and Haddonfield. Then we were in North Philly and I was leaving the train. Me and my three little suitcases. I remembered the story of Benjamin Franklin as a young man running through the streets of Philadelphia with a loaf of bread under each arm and another one in his mouth. I knew precisely what he looked like. And I hoped Philly was used to the sight by now.

I tried to get excited but I couldn't raise the necessary enthusiasm. There was no problem, no sweat, no headache. Who was going to remember another proper young man with three suitcases? Who would Brassard's men question – commuters? Conductors?

No problem.

If some cutie-pie figured out the orthographic relationship between L. Keith Brassard and Leonard K. Blake, he might trace me through to the railway station, might find a clerk who knew I'd bought a ticket to Philly. But nobody in the world was going to figure that I'd gone to New York.

No problem.

In less than three minutes I was off the train, down the stairwell, through the tunnel, and on the opposite platform. I waited there for less than five minutes before a train for New York pulled up and I got on. I put my suitcases up on the luggage rack and relaxed in my seat. When the conductor came by I let him sell me a ticket straight through to Boston. It wasn't necessary, not in the least, but I wanted to play everything to the hilt.

It sounds like a spy movie. Cloak and dagger. Bob Mitchum in a trenchcoat.

I thought about Mona and wondered how long it would be before I saw her again. I thought about the first time on the beach, and the times in my hotel room. I thought about the way she moved and the tricks her eyes played.

She was right as rain with the Bob-Mitchum line. I was overplaying things. We had nothing at all to worry about. I was on my way to New York without leaving a trace of a trail. Brassard was out looking for wrong trees to bark up. We had it aced.

All we had to do now was get away with murder.

5

I checked into the Collingwood Hotel as Howard Shaw. The Collingwood was a good second-class hotel on Thirty-fifth Street just west of Fifth. My room was thirty-two dollars a week; it was clean and comfortable. I had a central location without being in the middle of things the way I would have been in a Times Square hotel. I stood that much less chance of running into old familiar faces.

The door clicked shut behind me and I dropped my three suitcases on the floor. I shoved the attaché case under the bed and decided to hope for the best.

The Collingwood was a residential hotel and there were no bellboys to scoop up your bags. Nobody saw the L. K. B. monogram on the luggage on the way up, which was fine with me. Getting rid of the luggage was the next step, of course. It might have been simpler to check them in a subway locker and throw the key away, but they were too good and I was too broke. I ripped the labels out of all of Brassard's clothing except for what fit me, stuffed the clothes into the suitcases, and went downtown to where Third Avenue turns into the Bowery.

I sold better than three hundred dollars' worth of clothing to a round-shouldered, beetle-eyed man for thirty dollars. I pawned two suitcases worth over a hundred bucks for twenty-five. I left Brassard's stuff to be bought by bottle babies, and I went back to my hotel and slept.

It was Thursday. Sunday or Monday they would be coming back to New York. Now they were together at the Shelburne. Probably in bed.

I dreamed about them and woke up sweating.

Friday I looked him up in the phone book. There was a single entry, not even in bold-faced type. It said *Brassard, L. K. 117 Chmbrs . . . WOrth 4–6363*. I left the hotel and found a pay phone in a drugstore around the corner. I dialed WOrth 4–6363 and let it ring eight times without getting an answer. I walked over to Sixth and caught the D train to Chambers, then wandered around until I found 117.

It was the right building for him. The bricks had been red once; now they were colorless. All the windows needed washing. The names of the tenants were painted on the windows – *Comet Enterprises, Inc. . . . Cut-Rate Auto*

Insurance ... Passport Fotos While-U-Wait ... Zenith Employment ... Kallett Confidential Investigations ... Rafael Messero, Mexican Attorney, Divorce Information. Nine stories of cubbyholes, nine stories of very free enterprise. I wondered why he didn't have a better office. I wondered if he ever came to the one he had.

His name was on the directory. The elevator was self-service and I rode it to the fifth floor. I got out and walked past the employment agency to the door marked L. K. Brassard. The window glass was frosted and I couldn't see a thing.

I tried the door and wasn't particularly surprised to find out that it was locked. The lock was the standard spring lock that catches automatically when you close the door, and there was a good eighth of an inch between the door and the jamb. I looked around at Zenith Employment. Their door was closed. I wondered what the penalty was for breaking and entering.

The blade of my penknife took the lock in less than twenty seconds. It's a simple operation – you fit the knife blade in between the door and the jamb and pry the locking mechanism back. Good doors have the jamb recessed so that this cannot be done. This one was a bad door. I opened it about an inch and looked around again. Then I shoved it open, walked in and locked it behind me.

The office looked like what it was supposed to be. One of the oldest remaining roll-top desks in America stood in one corner. There was an inkstand on it. I looked around hysterically for a quill pen and was almost surprised not to find one.

There were half a dozen large ledgers on the desk and I went over them fairly carefully. I don't know what I expected to find. Whether the entries were coded or merely blinds I couldn't tell. It was a waste of time studying them.

The drawers and pigeonholes of the desk yielded a lot more of nothing in particular. There were bills and canceled checks and bank statements. Evidently he had a certain amount of legitimate business in addition to the main event. From what I could make out, he imported a lot of Japanese garbage – cigarette lighters, toys, junk jewelry, that sort of stuff. That fit into the picture. It was easy to see heroin coming through Japan by way of China or Hong Kong or Macao.

I sat in his leather chair in front of his desk and tried to put myself in his place. What hit me the hardest was the very double life he was leading. He was not a crook in the same sense as, say, Reggie Cole or Max Treger. Everybody who knew Treger knew just what sort of a man he was. He managed to stay out of jail because nobody managed to collect the evidence that would put him where he belonged. But if Treger had a wife, Mrs T. knew just how her husband kept mink on her back. Some of Treger's neighbors snubbed him while others pretended he was just one of the boys – but they all knew he was a gangster. The people in Cheshire Point didn't know that about good old L. Keith Brassard.

I tapped out a drum solo on the top of that very respectable desk and wondered why the hell I had come to his office in the first place. I didn't know what I'd expected to find, or hoped to find. I wasn't a federal narcotics agent trying to crack a dope ring. I was a wise guy who wanted to kill Brassard and wind up with his wife. So what was I doing there?

I wiped off everything I remembered touching. It probably would never matter, but I didn't want to leave my prints in his office in case they ever tied me to him. There was one scrap of paper I'd found with four phone numbers on it and nothing to tell what the numbers were. I copied them down.

He could tell the office had been entered. I did what I could, but I knew there would be some items out of place. I hoped there was a maid with a key – then he might not suspect a search.

On the way back to the hotel I picked up a few pairs of slacks and some underwear. I found a suit and an extra sport jacket and arranged to have them delivered to me at the Collingwood by Monday. All together the clothes came to over a hundred, and left me with not much money. It hurt to spend that much on clothes, but I couldn't see any way to avoid it. I needed the clothes. And they couldn't be too cheap or it wouldn't look right. Then I picked up a fairly respectable looking suitcase for twenty-five bucks. That hurt too.

By the time I got back to the hotel I felt pretty rotten. I was tired and bored and perspiring. The shower took care of the perspiration but the boredom remained. I had nothing to do and no place to go and I did not like myself very much. And I missed her so much I could taste it.

I had a good dinner with a drink before and a brandy after. Then I went out and bought a bottle and took it to bed.

Saturday came and went without my accomplishing very much. I went to a barber and got a crew cut, something I hadn't done in one hell of a long time. When I got back to my room I gave myself a long look in the bathroom mirror. The haircut had changed me more than anything else could have. It made my face rounder, my forehead higher, my whole appearance a good two years younger.

I went down to the drugstore, picked up a handful of paperback novels, went back to the hotel and spent the rest of the day reading, and sipping what remained in the bottle. I had time to kill and I wanted to get it out of the way as quickly as possible. If I could have spent two days in a coma I would have been glad of it. I didn't want to think and I didn't want to plan and I didn't want to do much of anything. I just waited for the time to go by.

Sunday afternoon I walked over to Penn Station and looked her up in the Westchester phonebook. She lived on something called Roscommon Drive. I memorized the number and left.

I called her that evening.

It was a warm night and the fan in the phone booth did not work. I put in a dime and dialed her number and got an operator who sent back my dime and told me to deposit twenty cents. I dropped in the original dime and another one and the phone rang. A man's voice said hello to me.

'Is Jerry there?'

'I'm afraid you have the wrong number.'

'Isn't this Jerry Hillman's residence?'

'No,' he said. 'I'm sorry.'

He hung up on me and I sat there in the hot booth hearing his voice again in my mind. It was a cultured voice. He spaced his words and talked pleasantly.

I left the booth and walked around the block. They were home. I took out a cigarette and smoked it in a hurry. I had to get in touch with her and I wasn't sure how to do it. I wondered if his phone was tapped. Most likely it was. I figured he probably tapped it himself. It wouldn't be the first time.

I called again from the same booth and this time she answered it. When she said hello I saw her in my mind and felt her in my arms. I started to shake.

'Is Jerry Hillman there?'

'No,' she said. 'You must have the wrong number.'

She recognized my voice. I could tell.

'Isn't this AL 5–2504?'

'No,' she said.

I sat in the phone booth for over fifteen minutes. I held the phone to my ear with one hand to make it look good while I held the hook down with the other. Then the phone rang and I lifted the hook and said hello.

'Joe,' she said. 'Hello, Joe.'

'How has it been?'

'All right,' she said. 'I suppose. I missed you, Joe.'

'I've been going crazy waiting for you. I was afraid you wouldn't catch the number. Where are you calling from?'

'A drugstore,' she said. 'I . . . I was ready for your call. Keith answered the first time and said it was a wrong number. But I knew it was you.'

I took a breath. 'I have to see you,' I said. 'Can you get into Manhattan tomorrow?'

'I think so. He's going to the office. I'll ride in with him and tell him I have to do some shopping. I can get in sometime between nine and ten. Is that all right?'

'Perfect.'

'Where are you staying?'

'A hotel,' I said. 'The Collingwood. Just east of Herald Square.'

'Should I meet you there?'

I thought about it for a minute. 'Better not,' I said. 'There's an Automat on Thirty-fourth between Sixth and Seventh. Meet me there.'

'Thirty-fourth between Six and Seventh. I'll be there. I love you, Joe.'

I told her I loved her. I told her how much I wanted her.

'I have to get off now,' she said. 'I came down to the drugstore to buy Tampax. He'll wonder what's taking me so long.'

'Tampax?'

I must have sounded disappointed because she giggled at me with a very sexy giggle. 'Don't worry,' she said. 'It was two birds with one stone, Joe. It was an excuse to go to the drugstore and an excuse to keep Keith away from me tonight. I don't want him touching me tonight, Joe. Not when you're this close to me. I couldn't stand it.'

She hung up and I stood there with a receiver in my hand. I walked out of there and tried not to shake visibly. I stopped at a little bar on the way home and tossed down a double shot of bourbon, then sipped the beer chaser very slowly.

The bartender was a big man with a wide forehead. He was listening to hillbilly music on a portable radio that blared away on top of the back bar. The song was something about a real grade-A bitch who was causing the singer untold heartache. The bartender polished glasses in time to the not-very-subtle rhythms of the song. Two or three guys were doing solo drinking. A man and a woman were drinking and playing footsie in a back booth.

How long since I'd seen her? Less than a week. Five or six days. But you can forget a lot in that amount of time. I remembered what she looked like and what she sounded like and how it felt to hold onto her. But I had forgotten, in part, just how much I needed her.

The sound of her voice had brought all of it back to me. Brought it back forcibly.

I wondered how I would kill him. I would have to be the killer, of course. And I would have to do it alone. She'd be the prime suspect, the first one the cops would get to, and I'd have to make sure she had a perfect alibi.

I could kill him at home or at his office. At home might be better – Manhattan homicide cops are too damned thorough. Westchester homicide would be a little less likely to know what was doing.

How? A gun or a knife? The proverbial blunt instrument? Or would I ring his neck with my hands? I tried to remember whether or not you could get fingerprints on a human being's neck. I didn't think you could.

I started to shake some more. Then I had another double bourbon and another beer and went back to the hotel.

6

I got to the Automat at nine. The girl in the cashier's cage dealt me a stack of nickels and I wandered around playing New York's favorite slot machines. I filled a tray with a glass of orange juice, a dangerous-looking bowl of oatmeal, a pair of crullers and a cup of black coffee. Then I found a table that gave me a good view of the entrance and started in on my breakfast.

I was working on a second cup of coffee when she showed. I looked at her and my head started spinning. She was wearing a very simple blue-gray summer dress that buttoned up the front. She looked sweet and virginal and lovely, and I waited for her to rush over to my table and wrap herself around my neck.

But she was so cool it almost scared me. She looked right at me and the shadow of a smile crossed her face. Then she swept on past me, broke a quarter into nickels and invested the nickels in coffee and a glazed doughnut. Then she stood with the tray in her hands, looking around for a place to sit. Finally she walked over to my table, unloaded the tray and sat down.

'This is fun,' she said. 'The cloak and dagger stuff, I mean. I'm getting a little carried away with it.'

I had too much to say and there was no convenient place to begin. I started a cigarette to go with the coffee and plunged in somewhere in the middle. 'Have any trouble getting here?'

'None at all. I rode in with Keith on the train. I told him I had to do some shopping. Remind me to do some shopping later. I'll buy a pair of shoes or something. Anything.'

'It must be nice to have money.'

I just threw the line out; maybe it was a mistake. She turned her eyes on me and her eyes said a great many things that cannot be translated too easily into English. Sure, it was nice to have money. It was nice to be in love, too. Many things were nice.

'Joe—'

'What?'

'I was thinking that maybe we don't have to kill him.'

'Not so loud!'

'No one's paying any attention to me. Look, there's another way that I've been thinking about. We won't have to kill him if it works out.'

'Getting soft?'

'Not soft,' she said.

'What then?'

'Maybe scared. I understand they electrocute murderers in New York. I . . . don't want to be electrocuted.'

'You have to be convicted first.'

Her eyes flared. 'You sound as though you hate him,' she said. 'You sound as though killing is more important than getting away with it.'

'And you sound as though you're trying to back out. Maybe that's what you want. Maybe we should forget the whole thing. You go your way and I'll go mine. Buy yourself all the shoes you want. And a few more furs. And—'

And a man sat down at our table. An old man, broken by time, with a frayed collar on his clean white shirt, with spots on a wide polka-dot tie. He very solemnly poured milk over a bowlful of corn flakes and sprinkled two tablespoons of sugar on top of the mess while we watched him with our mouths open.

'Let's go,' I said. 'Come on.'

No matter where you are in Manhattan there is a bar around the corner. There was a bar around the corner now and we went to it. We found the most remote of the three empty booths and filled it. I hadn't wanted a drink; now I needed one. I had bourbon and water and she had a screwdriver.

'Well?'

'You've got everything wrong,' she said. 'I'm not trying to get out of anything. You can be pretty saintly about this, can't you? You don't have to live with him. You don't—'

'Get to the point.'

She took a sip of her drink and followed it with a deep breath. 'The heroin,' she said. 'Do you still have it?'

I nodded.

'We can use it,' she said.

'Sell it and run?' I got ready to tell her all over again why that wouldn't work. But she didn't give me a chance.

'Plant it,' she said. 'Put it in his car or around the house or something. Then you or I would call the police anonymously and tip them off. They would search and find the heroin and arrest him.'

A bell rang somewhere but I ignored it. 'Just like that?' I said. 'Plant it, tip the fuzz, and send hubby off to jail?'

'Why not?'

'Because it wouldn't work.'

She looked at me.

'Let's see just what would happen, Mona. The police would run the tip down and find the heroin. Then they'd ask him how it got there, and he'd say he didn't have the vaguest idea. Right?'

She nodded.

'So they'd take him in and book him,' I went on. 'The charge would be possession with intent to sell. In ten minutes a very expensive lawyer would have him out on bail. Ten months later his case would come up. He'd plead not guilty. His lawyer would tell the court that here was a man with no criminal record, no illicit connections, a respectable businessman who had been framed by person or persons unknown. They would find him not guilty.'

'But the dope would be right there!'

'So what?' I took a sip of the bourbon. 'The jury would acquit him forty-nine chances out of fifty. The fiftieth – and that's a hell of a long shot – they'd find him guilty and his lawyer would file an appeal. And he'd win on the appeal unless an even longer long shot came in. Even if both long shots broke right – and I'm damned if I ever want to buck odds like that – it would still be two to three years before he saw the inside of a jail for more than five consecutive hours. That's a long time to wait, honey. And there's a damn good chance that sometime during those two or three years he would figure out who tipped the cops. At which time he would find a very capable gunman who would shoot a large hole in your pretty head.'

She shuddered.

'So we have to kill him.'

'I didn't want to.' Her voice was very small.

'You know another way?'

'I thought – But you're right. There isn't any other way. We have to . . . kill him.'

I drank to that. I ordered another round and the bartender brought the drinks, bourbon and water for me, another screwdriver for her. I paid for them.

'How?'

I didn't answer her.

'How will we—'

'Hang on,' I said. 'I'm trying to think.' I put my elbow on the table and rested my forehead in the palm of my hand. I closed my eyes and tried like hell to think straight. It wasn't particularly easy. Brassard and money and Mona and heroin were chasing one another around a beanpole with my face. There had to be a way to fit all the pieces together and come out with a plan. But I couldn't find it.

'Well?'

I lighted a cigarette, then studied her face through a cloud of smoke. I rested the cigarette in a small glass ashtray and took her hands in mine. All of a sudden whatever plan I might have thought of became quite unimportant. It was like the first time. And the second time, and every time. I guess *electric* is the right word for it. It was exactly that effect.

Electric. One time I saw a man pick up a lamp cord that had frayed right through to the bare wire. The current glued him and the cord together. He couldn't let go. The voltage was a little too low to kill him, but he remained stuck to that wire until some young genius cut the power.

That's how it was.

'Joe—'

'Let's get out of here.'

'Where are we going?'

'My hotel.'

'Is that safe?'

I stared at her.

'Someone might see us,' she said. 'It would mean taking a chance. And we can't afford to take chances.'

She knew how much I needed her. And now she was teasing, playing games. I looked at her and watched her turn into a sex symbol in front of my eyes. She did not look sweet and virginal and lovely any more. I looked at the very simple summer dress and saw breasts and belly and hips. I looked at her eyes and saw lust as naked as my own.

'I'll go shopping now,' she said. 'I'll buy a pair of shoes so that Keith won't wonder why I came to the city. Meanwhile you go back to the hotel and think up a jim-dandy plan. Then you call me and tell me all about it and we'll see what we can work out. That's the safe way.'

'To hell with the safe way.'

'But we can't afford to take chances. We've got to do it the safe way, Joe. *You* know that.'

They were just words and she didn't mean them at all. I stood up without letting go of her hand, crossed over to her side of the booth and sat down next to her. Our eyes locked.

'Joe—'

I put my hand on the very soft skin of her throat. I ran it down slowly over her breasts to her thighs. I pressed her.

'Now,' I said. 'Now tell me about the safe way.'

We caught a cab right outside the bar. It was less than three blocks to the Collingwood but we were in too much of a hurry to walk.

It was almost too good.

Maybe the tension was responsible for it, the tremendous mutual need for something that would push the fear away and postpone the immediacy of what we were planning to do. Maybe some grain of morality imbedded within us both made our adultery as amazingly gratifying as it was.

Whatever it was, I was all in favor of it.

I lighted cigarettes for both of us and gave one of them to her. We lay side by side and smoked them all the way down without saying a word. I finished mine first and stubbed it. It took her a few seconds more. Then she flipped the butt out the open window.

'Maybe I'll set fire to New York,' she said. 'Maybe the whole city will burn.'

'Maybe.'

'Or maybe it landed on somebody's head.'

'I doubt it. The window opens out on an airshaft. Nobody walks around down there.'

'That's good,' she said. 'I wouldn't want to set anybody on fire.'

'Not even me?'

'That's different.'

I kissed her face and her throat. She stretched out on her back with her eyes closed and purred like a fat cat in front of a hot fire. I stroked her and she purred some more.

'How, Joe?'

And we were back where we started from. Back to murder. Now, for some reason, it was easier to talk about it. Maybe our lovemaking was responsible for that; maybe strong proof of our mutual need was a means of justifying our actions.

'Joe?'

'Let's talk about Keith,' I said. 'Has he been acting any different lately?'

'Like how?'

'Because the heroin is missing.'

'Oh,' she said. 'At first he seemed worried about something. He still acts a little . . . well, irritated, I guess.'

'That figures.'

She nodded slowly. 'But he's not doing anything different,' she said. Not running around or anything. He's his usual self.'

'That figures too. He's not an errand boy. He's an executive. All he can do is pass the word and see what happens.'

'I guess so.' She yawned and stretched. 'So life goes on. He gets up in the morning and reads the paper. Then he does the crossword puzzle. Did I ever tell you about that? He's sort of a crossword puzzle nut. I can't even talk to him when he's working on one of them. Every morning the *Times* comes and every morning it's the same ritual. First the financial page and then the crossword puzzle. And if he's stuck on the puzzle it doesn't matter. He doesn't throw the damned thing out like a sensible person would. He keeps plowing away at it until it's done. He even uses a dictionary. Did you ever hear of doing crossword puzzles with a dictionary? That's the way he does them.'

I pictured him at the breakfast table, pencil in hand, dictionary at his side. I could see him working very steadily, filling in all the blank squares with neat letters. Of course he would use his dictionary, and of course he wouldn't quit until he was finished. It was all in character.

'Then he goes to the office,' she went on. 'Monday, Wednesday, and Friday. He goes to the office.'

I looked up. 'I thought he didn't have a regular schedule?'

'He doesn't, exactly. Sometimes he works on a Tuesday or Thursday, if he's busy. But almost every Monday and Wednesday and Friday, off he goes to the office. Then he comes home, and we eat, and it's another dull evening with Mr and Mrs L. Keith Brassard. Then it's morning, and another dull day.'

She grinned. She reached out a hand and touched me, a gentle touch. I reached for her.

'Not now, Joe. You were going to tell me the plan. How you're going to kill him.'

How *you're* going to kill him. Not *we're* going to kill him. But at the time I hardly heard the difference.

'I'm not going to tell you, Mona.'

'No?'

I shook my head.

'Don't you trust me?'

I had to laugh. 'Trust you? If I didn't trust you there would be no point in the whole thing. Of course I trust you.'

'Then tell me.'

'I can't.'

'Why not?'

Part of the reason was that I didn't know myself. But I didn't want to toss that one at her. There was another reason, and I decided it would have to do for the time being. 'The police are going to question you,' I told her. 'Up and down and back and forth. You're money and class, respectable as all hell, so they won't use the bright lights and the rubber hoses. Not the class-conscious Westchester police. But at the same time he's a rich old man and you're a pretty wife, so they'll suspect you.'

'I'll have an alibi.'

'No kidding.' I went looking for another cigarette and set fire to the end of it. 'Of course you'll have an alibi. That's what the cops will figure in the first place. They'll read it for a standard wife's-boyfriend-slays-rich-hubby gambit. Page three in the *Daily News* four days out of five. They'll be quiet, and they'll be polite as Emily Post's little boy, but they will be sharp. The more questions you can say *I don't know* to, the better off we'll both be. The less you know, the easier it'll be to give that answer. So I'm telling you as little as possible.'

She didn't say anything. She wasn't looking at me now. She was staring across the room, looking at the far wall. At least it looked that way, but I got the feeling that she didn't see that wall at all. I got the feeling that she was looking right through it, way out into space.

I wondered what she saw.

'Joe,' she said.

I waited.

'I'm worried,' she said. 'I tried not to think about it before. But you're right. Page three in the *Daily News* four days out of five. They'll question me.'

'Of course they will.'

'Maybe I'll crack.'

'Don't be silly.'

'Maybe—'

I looked at her. She was trembling. It wasn't a good old-fashioned case of the shakes, but I could see it. I took her in my arms and rubbed the back of her neck. I held her close and stroked her until I could feel the tension drain out of her, and then I kissed her once and let her go.

'Don't worry, Mona.'

'I'm all right now. I just—'

'I know. But don't worry. They won't work you that hard. You won't know anything, remember? You'll tell them the same things you told me the first time you met me. You don't know exactly what Keith does for a living. He doesn't have any enemies that you know about. You don't know why anybody would want to kill him. It doesn't make any sense to you. He was your husband and you loved him. Don't overwork the grief bit, but let yourself react naturally. You'll probably be a little sorry once it's done, you know. The normal human reaction. Let it show, but don't milk it.'

She nodded.

'Keep calm,' I said. 'That's the important thing.'

'When?'

I looked at her.

'When are you going to do it?'

'I don't know.'

'You don't know or you're not telling me?'

I shrugged. 'A little of both. Probably this week, probably on one of the days when he goes to work.'

'At his office?'

'Maybe. Maybe not. Don't leave the house until he's off to work. Understand?' She nodded.

'Is there a maid or something around there?'

'Two maids. Why?'

'I just wondered. Be in the house with them when he leaves for work. Got that?'

A nod.

'And don't worry. That's the important thing. If you just take it easy there won't be a thing in the world to worry about.'

I squashed my cigarette like a bug and started thinking. My mind was working now. Things were beginning to take shape. I was turning into a machine, and that made everything just that much simpler. Machines don't sweat. You throw a switch or turn a crank and the machine does what it's supposed to do. The machine named Joe Marlin was thinking now. I thought like clocks tick.

'Afterward,' I said. 'That's the big thing. If the hit goes properly, they won't sweat you too much. But they'll remember you. They'll list the crime as unsolved and they'll leave the file open. I can't come and move in with you the day he's in the ground. It wouldn't be too safe.'

She seemed to shiver.

'The scandal will bother you,' I said. 'You'll stay at home awhile and then you'll go to a real estate agent. You don't want to live in Cheshire Point any more. It bothers you. You're not comfortable there any more. You just want to get away by yourself for a good long time. You can think about another house later.'

'It's a nice house—'

'Just listen to me, will you? You tell him to sell the house furnished and all. Don't act hungry for money. There will be plenty of money. Tell him to list the house and take whatever he thinks is the most it'll bring. Tell him there's no rush, he should use his own judgment with the price. Then go to a travel agency and book a flight to Miami.'

'Miami?'

'Right. You fly to Miami about a week after the hit. Maybe ten days at the outside. You'll have plenty of dough – insurance, loose cash. You'll go first-class, stay at the Eden Roc. You're a widow whose husband met a rather scandalous death. You want to forget about it.'

'I see.'

I got another cigarette going. I looked at her and I could see wheels turning inside her head. She was not a stupid woman. She would remember everything I was telling her. That was good. If she forgot, we were in trouble.

'I'll be in Miami Beach myself,' I said. 'I'll get a room at the Eden Roc. You see, right after the hit, I'll get the hell out of New York. Go to Cleveland, Chicago, some place like that. A week or so later I'll head for Miami. We'll be two strangers winding up at the same hotel. We won't know each other, won't arrive at the same time, won't even come from the same town. We'll meet cold and warm up. A nice relationship developing and blooming in a fast-moving resort town where relationships like that are no cause for comment. We'll talk, date, fall in love. Nothing will connect us with Keith or New York or anything before Miami Beach.'

'A fresh start.'

'You got it. From there on we do what we want. Travel, maybe. A trip around the world. Europe, the Riviera, the works. We'll have each other and we'll have a worldful of money and two lifetimes to spend it in.'

'It sounds good.'

'It's as good as it sounds,' the machine said. 'Now repeat back to me exactly what I've told you.'

No tape recorder could have done it better. I heard her through, reviewed a detail or two with her, and told her she better get going. We got up from the bed and started dressing. I watched her put that virginal dress on that sensual body and felt like tearing it off again. But there would be time. Plenty of time.

I was straightening my tie in the mirror when I heard her laughing. I turned around and looked at her. She was fully dressed and she was standing close to me. I looked at the top of her head – her hair was neatly combed.

She was looking at my feet.

'What's so funny?'

She went right on laughing. I looked down and didn't get the joke. My socks matched. My shoes were good brown cordovans and I'd had a shine just a day or so ago.

She looked up and she was trying to control the laughter. I asked her once again what was so funny and she giggled.

'The shoes,' she said. 'You're wearing his shoes. He's still alive and already you're wearing his shoes.'

I looked at the shoes, at her. She was right, of course. They were his shoes, from his suitcase. They fit perfectly and I had seen no reason to chuck them out. I stood there, a little uncertain, trying to decide how to react. Then I started to laugh, too. It was funny. We laughed until it wasn't funny any more and then I walked with her to the door.

'You'll need money,' she said.

'I suppose so.'

'I've been watching money since we were in Atlantic City,' she said. 'And I had some set aside around the house. I brought it today, almost forgot to give it to you. I don't know how long it'll last but it should be some help.'

She gave me an envelope. It had his name and address in the upper left-hand corner. I made a mental note to destroy it.

'You won't call me again?'

I shook my head.

'And we won't see each other?'

'Not until it's done.'

'Suppose something happens? How do I get in touch with you?'

'What could happen?'

'An emergency.'

I thought about it. 'No emergencies,' I said. 'None where getting in touch with me will do any good.'

'You're afraid I'll put the police on you?'

'Don't be silly.'

'Then—'

'I don't know where I'll be,' I said. 'And nothing could come up, nothing where it would help to have us in contact with one another. Just do what I told you. That's all.'

She shifted her weight from one foot to the other. It was an awkward moment.

'Well,' she said, 'I'll see you in Miami.'

I nodded, awkwardly, and then I reached for her. She half-fell against me and my arms folded around her. I don't know whether the kiss was a sign of love or a bargain sealed in lipstick instead of blood. I let go of her and we stared at each other.

'Today was good,' she said. 'It'll be hard. Waiting a month for you.'

Then she was gone. I watched her for a few seconds, then closed the door. I sat on the bed and tore the envelope open. I burned it in an ashtray, feeling slightly melodramatic, and flushed the ashes down the toilet, feeling still more melodramatic. Then I counted the money.

There was a lot of it. Over seven hundred dollars. It wasn't that much when you stopped to consider train fare to Chicago or Cleveland, then a plane to Miami. It wasn't much balanced against all the expenses I was going to run up in the next month. But it was still seven hundred dollars. It would be more than useful.

Then a thought sailed home. This was the second time Mona had given me an envelope filled with money. Both times it was shortly after we had finished making love.

That bothered me.

7

Monday night was monotonous. I ate dinner, sat around my room at the Collingwood, and waited for time to go by. I thought about her and I thought about him and I thought about myself, and I wondered how I was going to do it. I'd made it look good for her. I'd let her think I was the boy genius with the whole routine down pat. Maybe the act set her mind to rest, but I wasn't fooling myself. I was a novice at murder.

I kept putting it together and it kept coming out wrong. My thoughts went in the usual places. I wanted to kill a man and get away with it. There are a few standard ways of doing this, and I ran them all through my head and looked for one that would fit. None of them did.

I could make it look like an accident. But the trouble with that is that there is no margin for error. When you fake an accident, or a suicide, you make one mistake and the ball game is over. One mistake and it's no longer an accident or a suicide. It's a murder, and you're it.

Cops are too good. Crime labs are too good. I could slug that fat bastard behind the ear, load him into his car and drive him over the nearest convenient cliff. Then the snoops would begin snooping. I'd leave a fingerprint somewhere, or some little punk would figure out that he'd been hit over the head before he went over the cliff, or any one of another thousand things.

Or I could get a gun, and I could stick the barrel in his fat mouth, and I could wrap his lousy hand around it and pull the trigger for him and blow his brains all over the nearest wall. And something would be wrong, something somewhere, and somebody would know it wasn't suicide.

Then they would take Mona and they would lean on her. She'd do fine at the beginning. She'd throw it back as hard as they threw it at her.

For a while.

But they wouldn't be able to let go, because it would be murder and she would be their only suspect. They would push it as hard as they could, and she would crack before they did. Maybe she wouldn't confess, but they'd get my name out of her and pick me up, and then they would play both sides against the middle. They would scare us and make us mad, and they would break us.

They have capital punishment in New York State. They use an electric chair. In first degree murder, the chair is mandatory unless the jury recommends mercy.

They wouldn't. Not for us.

I added it up again, and each time it came out death. I worked it around again and again, over and over, and it wouldn't break properly. It wasn't fair – he had her, and he had all that money, and I wanted both of them.

There had to be a way.

I slept on it and dreamed about it. The bad dreams took up most of the night. There was an aggravating sameness about them – dreams of running, with or without Mona, running madly away and not getting away at all. We were running through a coal-black tunnel most of the time, with something very frightening chasing us and gaining on us. We would be reaching the end of the tunnel, with the darkness opening onto a pool and green grass and a picnic table, and the evilness behind us would snatch us up just as we approached the mouth of the tunnel. I never found out what the pursuer was planning to do to us, because each time, I awoke sweating at the moment of capture.

At 8:30 I got out of bed with a new angle. It was taking shape, and I sat on the edge of the bed with the day's first cigarette turning to ashes between my fingers while I let the idea play itself out. It was an intriguing idea, and it took into consideration the one salient point I hadn't stopped to consider the day before.

Brassard was a criminal.

I remembered what Mona had said. *Let's not kill him, Joe. Let's frame him and have him sent to jail.*

But that wouldn't work. I'd handed her a bucket full of all the arguments against that one. It didn't stand a chance.

Something else did. Brassard, alive, could not be framed. Not in a million years.

Brassard, dead, was another story.

I sat there and thought it through. Every once in a while something would get tangled up and I had to start in at the beginning all over again. But all the tangles smoothed themselves out. The more I thought about it, the better it looked. When it was just about perfect I got up from the bed and went into the bathroom to shower and brush my teeth.

I sang in the shower.

I dressed in suit and tie and clean white shirt. I went downstairs and had two scrambled eggs and two cups of black coffee at the lunch counter down the street. Then I walked over to Thirty-fourth street and caught a crosstown bus to Third Avenue. The bus was crowded and I had to stand all the way. I didn't mind.

The pawnshop I was looking for wasn't the one I'd picked to hock my suitcases at. It was on Thirty-second and Third, a hole in the wall behind the inevitable three golden balls. The owner was a small, unassuming man with wire-rimmed glasses and frown lines in his forehead. His name was Moe Rader and he was a fence.

There was a kid in his shop when I walked in. The kid was trying to sell Moe a watch. I pretended to look at a saxophone while they dickered over the price. The kid settled for ten bucks, and I waited for him to take his money and go home while I wondered who the watch had belonged to, and how much it was really worth.

Then the kid was gone.

'I want a gun,' I told Moe.

'Rifle or handgun or shotgun?'

'Revolver. A .38 or thereabouts.'

'You have a permit, of course?'

I shook my head. He smiled sadly, showing teeth filled with gold. 'If you do not have a permit, I cannot sell you a gun.' He used the tone of someone explaining an obvious fact to a very small child.

I didn't say anything.

'It's the law,' he said.

I still didn't say anything. I took out my wallet and found a pair of fifties. I took them out and put them on the counter. He looked at me, at the money, at me again. He was trying to figure out who I was.

'People,' I said. 'Augie Manners, Bunny DiFacio, Ruby Crane. People.'

'You know these people?'

I nodded sagely.

'Tell me something about them.'

I gave him the names of two night clubs that August Manners owned unofficially. I told him when Bunny DiFacio went to Dannemorra and why. I started to tell him something about Ruby Crane but he held up a hand.

'Enough,' he said. 'The back of the store, please.'

I walked past him and into the back room. He went to the door, turned the lock, pulled down the window shade. Then he came after me, searched a shelf, produced a gun. It was a .38 revolver, Smith and Wesson. Just what I'd ordered.

'This have a history?'

He smiled the same sad smile. 'Perhaps,' he said. 'A young boy found it in somebody's glove compartment. He brought it to me for sale. The original owner has not seen fit to report the theft to the police. We get a listing of stolen goods, you know, and I checked it carefully. I have a suspicion that this gun is not registered at all. Is that what you want to know?'

That was what I wanted to know. The gun was clean. It couldn't be traced to Moe, much less to me.

'I'll need ammunition,' I said.

'A box?'

'Enough to fill the gun. Six bullets.'

'You only intend to use it once?'

I didn't answer that one. He didn't really expect me to. He put half a dozen shells in a small cloth bag like the ones Bull Durham comes in. He put the bag in a little box and gave it to me.

I left the store without saying good-bye. I had a gun and six bullets and he had two fifty-dollar bills. It was that simple.

I was sitting on the edge of the bed again. The gun and the bullets nested snugly in one of my drawers in between several shirts. I was thinking again. It was getting to be a habit.

If we faked an accident, we were dead. If we faked a suicide, we were dead.

We had to fake a murder.

Respectable Westchester burghers don't get killed often. When they do, if they are old men with young wives, it is not hard to figure out why they were killed or by whom.

But crooks are different. Crooks get killed all the time, for any number of reasons. And crooks get killed professionally. They get killed by gunmen from out of town, flown in for the job and flown out when the job is over. Gangland hits don't get solved. Gangland hits are perfect crimes. The cops don't kill themselves trying to find the killer. It would be a waste of their time.

In a sense, L. Keith Brassard was a respectable burgher. In another sense, he was a crook.

I had to kill the crook. I had to make it look like a mob hit, professionally planned and professionally carried out. I had an untraceable gun, and that was the first step.

There were other steps. But when they were done, it would be simple. It wouldn't make page three in the *Daily News*. It would be on the front page, and it would say that a Westchester gangster with a solid-gold front had been bumped by the boys. The world would leave the widow alone. They'd feel sorry for her.

They'd leave her for me.

I opened my drawer, took another look at the gun, and smiled. I closed the drawer, left the hotel, grabbed lunch. Around three that afternoon I decided to call Brassard's office and see if he was in. I looked through my wallet for his number, trying to remember whether or not I had jotted it down. I hadn't, but I had four other numbers which I stared at for several minutes. Then I remembered copying them from a slip of paper in Brassard's office.

I called them in turn from a pay phone.

The first two didn't answer. The third was a bar on the East Side in the sixties, the fourth a Greek night club in the Chelsea district. I rang off on both of them.

I guessed that the numbers were drops, contacts for Brassard's heroin business. This didn't do much for me one way or the other. It made it a little more certain Brassard was in the business, but I already knew that. I started to tear up the slip of paper, then changed my mind and returned it to my wallet.

A phone book gave me his number. I dialed WOrth 4–6363 and let it ring itself hoarse. Then I hung up and went back to my room. I used a knife blade on the lock of the attaché case and it popped open in less than a minute.

The package was still there.

I looked at it, shook a little, put it back in the case and locked it up again. I dropped my penknife into my pocket and hefted the attaché case.

I felt very shaky carrying all that heroin on the subway. But I managed it.

I got off the elevator at the fifth floor, looking very much the picture of the aspiring young businessman. My suit was pressed and my tie was straight and my attaché case was held as casually as all hell. The door was open over at Zenith Employment but nobody was looking out of it.

I let myself into Brassard's office. I closed the door behind me and looked around. The office was unchanged. I browsed around carefully. The only thing missing was the slip of paper with the four phone numbers. I thought about that one for a minute and decided to do it up brown. I found a pencil in a drawer, then got the slip from my wallet and copied the numbers on his desk pad. I came as close to his handwriting as I could remember.

Then I opened the attaché case again. I took out the small box of heroin lovingly and put it on top of the desk. Then I opened a desk drawer and took out four plain white envelopes.

I filled each of them in turn about a third of the way with heroin. I sealed them, put three in the top center drawer and wedged one into the space between the desk blotter and the leather desk set that kept the blotter in place. I let the envelope stick out a bit. Then I opened one of the bottom drawers and put the big box of heroin in the back.

That way, I figured, they'd have to look for it a little, and at the same time they couldn't help spotting it. It was sort of like a treasure hunt for little kids. The first envelope was hanging there in plain sight. No detective could possibly miss it. The other three were in the center drawer, the first place they would look. After that, of course, they would turn the office upside-down and inside-out. Then they'd find the main box and the ball game would be over.

Then the telephone started to ring.

I turned green. I backed away from the desk as though it was wired for electricity. I flattened out against the wall for no imaginable reason and counted rings.

It rang twelve times.

Somebody was trying to reach him. Somebody who was fairly sure he was there. Unless, of course, it was a wrong number. There was always that possibility. It could be a wrong number.

Then it started to ring again.

I got a quick mental picture – Brassard coming into his office any minute, finding the heroin. I got that picture and my knees started to shake. The envelopes were a nice gimmick but I couldn't risk them. I snatched the one from the desk blotter, then grabbed three more from the desk drawer. I crammed them into my pockets and prayed that he wouldn't look in the bottom drawer.

And that the cops would.

I took a look around and prayed again for salvation. Then I got out of that office and rang for the elevator.

There was a fruit juice stand across the street. I found a free stool, ordered a hot dog and a glass of pina colada, and watched the doorway to his office building. It was almost five, and I started regretting the moment of panic. I should have left the envelopes there. He wouldn't head for the office, not at this hour.

I looked down at my attaché case. No heroin, not any more. Now I had heroin in my pockets instead. A lot of it.

I worked on the hot dog and sipped the pina colada through a narrow straw. I watched the entrance, watched office girls head home from work, watched cleaning women get set for haphazard mop-up operations.

Then a cab stopped and he got out of it. He paid the driver and the cab went away. My eyes stayed on him while he vanished into the building.

He was there for fifteen minutes.

It was a nerve-wracking, stomach-knotting quarter of an hour. On top of everything else, I had to justify my presence at the fruit juice stand by consuming two more hot dogs and two more pina coladas. Food had a tendency to stick in my throat, and it was hard.

Waiting was harder. Waiting, and wondering what he was finding, and what he was thinking, and what mistakes I had made. Waiting, and wondering where in the world to go from here. Waiting.

He came out, looking the same. I wondered if he was worried, or if I should be worried. I wondered how I was going to do it if he had discovered the boxful. There would be no way then. If my pigeon had tipped, there was only one thing to do. I had to throw up the whole thing, leave New York, forget Mona. It ought to be easy enough. I'd left many cities, forgotten many women. You just got up and went.

I remembered her, and what she was like, and what it was like to be with her. And I knew that I couldn't leave, couldn't give it up. We were in it no matter what happened.

I watched him get in a cab and go away. I finished slurping my pina colada and took a very deep breath of stale air. I walked across the street, walked into the building, rode the elevator to the fifth floor.

I jimmied the door again. It was getting tiresome. I opened the desk drawer and checked. He hadn't found the heroin. It was still there, the contents of that bottom drawer undisturbed.

A world of tension drained out of me. I reached into my pocket, rescued the four envelopes, returned them to their places. I glanced at the desk pad — the numbers weren't there any more. He'd torn up my slip of paper.

I sighed. It was a weird little game all right. I hauled out my wallet, found the slip of paper again, copied the numbers back onto the desk pad.

I played the let's-wipe-away-our-fingerprints game again, then slipped out of the office and left the building. I was beginning to think of it as my office and my building. Hell, I spent more time in it than he did.

I walked a few blocks, pitching my attaché case in a convenient trash can. I didn't need it any more. I wasn't lugging heroin around town now. It was planted properly.

A fortune in heroin. An amusing plant, I decided. An expensive investment.

I was too tired for the subway. I hailed a cab and sank back into the seat, suddenly exhausted. It had been a busy day. Too busy, maybe. I wondered how busy the next few days were going to be. Very busy, probably.

Then I thought some more about those four phone numbers. The son-of-a-bitch probably knew his own handwriting. He probably remembered tearing up those numbers once already, and he probably knew damn well that he hadn't written them the second time around. He was probably suspicious, and that was fine.

Maybe he'd push the panic button. Maybe he'd call people and let them know something was funny. That was fine, too. It would make everything else seem that more plausible.

Because no matter what happened, he wouldn't be going back to the office that night. He'd be going home to Mona. And those four little phone numbers would be around the next day.

I had to make sure that he wouldn't.

8

After dinner I packed my suitcase and checked out of the Collingwood. I found a locker at Grand Central and shoved the suitcase into it. The gun, loaded, stayed in my inside jacket pocket. It bulged ridiculously and jiggled up and down when I walked. In the washroom of the train to Scarsdale I switched it from the jacket pocket to the waistband of my trousers. That felt a hell of a lot more professional, but it worried me. I was afraid the thing would go off spontaneously, in which case I wouldn't be much good to Mona. I tried to think about other more pleasant things.

By the time we hit Scarsdale I was beginning to shake inside. There was too much time to kill and no convenient way to kill it. I wondered whether I had taken the wrong turn. Maybe it would have been better to stay overnight at the Collingwood, then grab an early train up. That would have given me a sleepless night's sleep. But it left too much to chance. I had to pick up a car, which meant I had to hit Westchester while it was still dark out. And it was safer if I came in on a crowded train, which ruled out 4 A.M. trains. So I had picked the best way, but I still wasn't feeling too good about it.

I found a movie house a block from the train station, paid my half a buck and went in to be hypnotized. I took a seat in the back and tried to get used to the feeling of the gun in my pants. The metal wasn't cold any more. It was body temperature, or close enough, and I'd been wearing it so long it felt as though it was a part of me. I stared at the screen and let time pass.

I saw the complete show at least twice. This was not difficult. My mind couldn't stick with the picture but rambled all over the place. Even the second time through, the movie's plot sailed far over my head into the stratosphere. The movie was a thoroughly anonymous and relatively painless time-killer. It was after midnight when the last show let out and I followed the crowd out onto the empty streets of Scarsdale.

It started to get easier. The movie had turned me into the machine I had to be. Gears shifted. Buttons were pushed and switches were thrown. I found a bar – bars stay open later than movies, maybe because eyes are weaker than livers. I took a stool in the back all by myself and nursed beers until closing. Nobody talked to me. I was a loner and they were people who drank every night in the same bar. That might have been dangerous, except that they could not possibly remember me. They never noticed me in the first place.

The bar closed at four, which was fine. I went into an all-night grill for a hamburger and a few cups of coffee. It was four-thirty almost to the minute when I left the grill, and that was just about right.

It was good weather, just beginning to turn from night to day. The air was fresh and clean, a good change from New York, with just enough of a trace of bad smells mixed with the good to keep you from forgetting that you were in the suburbs, not the country. The sky was turning light, anticipating the sun which would rise in an hour or less. There were no clouds. It was going to be one hell of a nice day.

I walked off the main street to a side street, off the side street to another side street. The neighborhood was not bad at all. It wasn't rich Scarsdale but middle Scarsdale – fairly ordinary one-family homes that cost in the mid-twenties solely because they were in Scarsdale, trees in front, hedges, the white-collar works. I had a long walk because too many people kept their cars in their garages. Then I found what I was looking for.

On the left-hand side of the street a green Mercury was parked snug against the curb. On the right-hand side there was a black Ford a year or so old. The Ford was the car I wanted. I wanted it for the same reason that the hired killer I was pretending to be would want it. It was ordinary, inconspicuous. If you are going to steal a car for a murder, you steal a black Ford. It's one of the rules of the game.

There was only one problem. The Ford's owner might wake up early. If he drove into New York every morning, he'd probably get up around seven. If he saw the car gone, and if he called the cops, the alarm for that Ford would go out before I wanted it to.

That's where the Merc came in.

I worked fast. I took the plates off the Merc, carried them to the Ford, took the plates off the Ford and put the Merc plates in their place, then crossed the street once more and put the Ford plates on the Merc. That sounds complicated – all I did, of course, was switch plates. But it would make a big difference. While the Ford owner would report his *car* missing, the Merc owner wouldn't report his *plates* missing. The chances were that he wouldn't even notice, not for a good long while. How often do you check your license plates before you get into your car?

So, even if the Ford owner reported the car stolen and some hot-shot cop checked my car, it would have different plates. Which might make a difference. Then again, it might not. But I was taking enough chances as it was. Whenever there was a chance to minimize the risk, that was fine with me.

I wiped off both sets of plates with my handkerchief, then slipped on a pair of ordinary rubber gloves, the kind they sell in drugstores. I'd bought them before I left New York, and now I was going to need them. They were good gloves – not surgical quality, but sheer enough so that my hands didn't feel like catcher's mitts. I took a good look around, prayed in silence, and opened the door of the Ford. I settled myself behind the wheel and set about jumping the ignition. It wasn't hard. It never is. I was fourteen years old when I learned how easy it was to start a car without a key. It's not the sort of thing you forget.

The car purred kittenishly. I let it scurry along to the corner. Then we took a turn and another turn and still another turn, and then we were on the main road north in the general direction of Cheshire Point. I left Scarsdale with no regrets. It was a nice place for auto theft but I would hate to live there.

The Ford was fine for murder but strictly garbage on the open road. The engine knocked gently from time to time and the pickup was several seconds behind the accelerator. The car moved like a retarded child. It was further encumbered with automatic transmission, which keeps you from shifting gears at the proper time, and power steering, which is an invention designed to drive anybody out of his mind.

I pushed the Ford along and thought about the car Mona and I would have once the whole mess was cleaned up. A Jaguar, maybe. A big sleek beast with a dynamo under the hood and an intelligent over-all approach to Newtonian mechanics, automatic division. I wondered if anybody had ever made love to her in the back seat of a Jag. I didn't think so.

Cheshire Point made Scarsdale look like Levittown. I drove around and looked at one-acre plots with half-acre mansions and smelled money. The streets were very wide and very silent. The trees lining them were very tall and very somber. It was a suburb created by expatriate New Yorkers who had fled with only their money intact, and because it was such an artificial town at the surface it was hard finding my way around. The place had very little sense to it. Streets wandered here and there, evidently intent solely on having a good time, and directions became meaningless.

I found Roscommon Drive after a struggle. It was wider than most of the streets and a parkway ran down the middle of it, a five-yard strip of shrubs and grass and greenery. I looked for house numbers, figured out where I was, and drove until I found Brassard's house. It was what I think they call Georgian Colonial. Mostly stone with white wood trim. A rolling lawn kept short and green. A large elm in the middle of the lawn. Very impressive.

I had pictured the home before. But I had never seen it, and seeing it did something to me. I gently brushed away the picture of L. Keith Brassard, Lord Of the Dope Trade, and replaced it with the illusion of complete respectability. I looked at rolling lawn and the big old elm and I saw that nice old man rolling along the Boardwalk in a rolling chair with his pretty young bride beside him. It would be fiendish to kill that man. It would be a foul, despicable crime to murder L. Keith Brassard, Pillar Of Cheshire Point.

I had to shake myself to get rid of the illusion. I had to work hard to remind myself that he wasn't a nice old man, that the fine old house was held together with needle marks and rubbery veins, that his pretty young bride was the woman I loved. I had to remind myself that he was a rotten old bastard and that I was going to murder him, and I told myself again what I had told myself a countless number of times – that the fact that he was a rotten old bastard made murdering him altogether fitting and proper.

But it was hard to believe when I looked at that house. Not the splendor of it – successful crooks live more like kings than most kings do. But the utter respectability . . .

I shook myself, more violently this time. The next step was to find the railroad station. According to Mona, he walked to the station every morning and left the car for her. That meant it was close by, and I had to figure out just how close by, and I had to know how to get there in a hurry. It would be important.

The Ford found the station; I really can't take any credit for it. The Ford nosed around until it turned up at the standard brown shed with rails running past it. Then the Ford, demonstrating a wonderful memory, found its way back to Roscommon Drive, put two and two together, and doped out the precise amount of time required to drive from the house to the station along the shortest possible route. It took about seven minutes.

It was still too early. I thought about parking in front of Brassard's house and waiting for him. I thought about Brassard looking out the window, seeing me, and coming out with a gun of his own. Then I looked around for a diner.

I found one. It had a parking lot and I nestled the Ford in it, then stripped off the gloves and pocketed them. The coffee was hot and black and strong.

I needed it.

I put the gloves back on later, then opened the door and slid in behind the wheel once again. If anybody had seen me I would have looked very strange to them. How often do you see a guy put on a pair of rubber gloves before he gets into his car? But nobody did, and I started the car and headed back to Roscommon Drive. It was around 8:30. He'd be working his crossword puzzle now, sitting at the breakfast table with pencil in hand and newspaper before him and cup of coffee at right elbow. I wondered if he was using the dictionary this time around, if the puzzle was hard or easy for him.

Three doors from his house I braked to a stop, plopped the Ford into neutral and pulled up the hand brake. I left the motor running. From where I sat I could see his house – the heavy oak door, the flagstone path. And, hopefully, he couldn't see me.

I wanted a cigarette. And, while I knew there was no reason in the world for me to go without that cigarette, I remembered what crime labs did with cigarette ashes. I knew it didn't matter, they could know everything there was to know about me including what brand of cigarettes I smoked and what toothpaste I used to keep my mouth kissing-sweet and whether I wore boxer shorts or briefs, and they still wouldn't be anywhere close to knowing who I was. There was nothing to link me to Brassard, nothing to make the cops think of me in the first place or second place or third place. They could have a full description of me and still get nowhere.

But I didn't smoke that cigarette.

Instead I straightened my tie, which was straight to begin with, and studied my reflection very thoughtfully in the rear-view mirror. The mirror image was cool and calm, a study in poise. It was a lie.

I waited. And wished he would hurry up with his puzzle. And waited.

I rolled down the window on the right-hand side of the car. I opened my jacket, took out the gun. I wrapped my hand around it, curled my finger around the trigger. It was a very strange feeling, holding the gun with a glove on my hand. I could feel it perfectly, but the presence of the glove, a thin layer between flesh and metal, seemed to remove me a little from the picture of violence. The glove rather than my hand was holding the gun. The glove rather than my finger would pull that trigger.

I understood why generals didn't feel guilty when their pilots bombed civilians. And I was glad I was wearing the gloves.

8:45.

The oak door swung open and I saw him, dressed for work, briefcase tucked neatly under arm. She was seeing him to the door, looking domestic as all hell with her hair in curlers. He turned and they kissed briefly. For some reason I couldn't begrudge him that last kiss. I was almost glad he was getting the chance to kiss her good-bye. I wondered if they had made love the night before. A few days ago the thought would have sickened me. Now I didn't mind it at all. It was his last chance. He was welcome to all he could get.

She turned from him. The door closed. I released the emergency brake and threw the car into gear.

I did not breathe while he walked down that flagstone path to the sidewalk. She would be in another room now, maybe with one of the maids. Or she would be expecting it, maybe at the window to watch in morbid fascination. I hoped she wasn't at the window. I didn't want her to watch.

He reached the sidewalk and turned away from me, heading for the railroad station. I drove up behind him. Slowly.

He walked well for a man his age. If he heard the Ford he didn't show it. One arm held the briefcase, the other swung at his side. The gun felt cold now, even with the rubber glove.

I drew up even with him, braked quickly, leaned across the seat toward him. Now he turned at the sound – not hurriedly, not scared, but wondering what was coming off.

I pointed the gun at him and squeezed the trigger.

Before there had been the total silence of a very quiet street. The noise of the gunshot erupted in the middle of all that silence, much louder than I had expected. I felt as though everybody in the world was listening.

I think the first bullet was enough. It hit him in the chest a few inches below the heart and he sank to his knees with a very puzzled, almost hurt expression on his face. The briefcase skidded along the sidewalk. I did not want to shoot him again. Once was enough. Once would kill him.

But the professionals don't work that way. The professionals do not take chances.

Neither did I.

I emptied the gun into him. The second bullet went into his stomach and he folded up. The third bullet was wide; the fourth took half his head off. The fifth and sixth went into him but I do not remember where.

I heaved the gun at him. Then I put the accelerator on the floor, for the benefit of any curious onlookers, and the Ford took off in spite of itself. I drove straight for two blocks with the gas pedal all the way down, then took a corner on two wheels and relaxed a little, slowing the Ford to a conservative twenty-five miles an hour.

I was sweating freely and my hands itched inside the gloves. I had to struggle to keep from speeding. But I managed it, and the ride to the station took the estimated seven minutes.

I parked the car near the station. I cut the motor, pulled up the handbrake. I stepped out of the car, closed the door, peeled off the rubber gloves and tossed them into the back seat. I wiped my hands on my pants and tried to keep calm.

Then I walked to the station. There was a newsstand on the platform and I traded a nickel for a copy of the *Times* and waited for the train to come. I had to force myself to read the headlines. Castro had confiscated more property in Cuba. There was an earthquake in Chile. No murders. Not yet.

The train came. I got on, found a seat. The car was a smoker and I got a cigarette going, needing it badly. I opened the paper to the financial pages and studied row upon row of thoroughly meaningless numbers.

I glanced around. Nobody was looking at me. Dozens of men in suits sat reading the *Times*, and none of them looked at me. Why should they?

I looked exactly the same as they did.

9

In all of life it is the little things that stay with you. I first made love to a woman several months after my seventeenth birthday. The woman has disappeared completely from my memory. I do not know what she looked like, what her name was, only that she must have been close to thirty. Nor do I remember anything about the act. It was probably pleasurable, but I can't specifically recall pleasure and I don't think pleasure had anything to do with it. It was a barrier to be crossed, and the pleasure or lack of pleasure in the crossing was, at the time, immaterial.

But I remember something she said afterward. We were lying together – on her bed, I think – and I was telling myself silently that I was a man now. 'God,' she said, 'that was a good one.' Not *That was good* but *That was a good one.*

I must have mumbled something in the affirmative, something stupid, because I remember her laugh, a curious mixture of amusement and bitterness.

'You don't know how good it was,' she said. 'You're too damn young to know the difference. Young enough to do a good job and too young to know what you're doing.'

I don't know what that proves, if anything. Except that the mind is a strangely selective sort of thing. The act itself should have been significant, memorable. But the act, once finished, left no impression that I can still remember. The conversation remains.

It was the same way with murder. I'm talking now about impact, not memory, but it comes out pretty much the same. I had killed a man. Killing, I understand, is a pretty traumatic thing. Soldiers and hired gunsels get used to it, sometimes, but it takes a while. I had never killed before. Now, after careful planning and deliberate execution, I had pointed a gun at a man and emptied it into him. True, he was socially worthless – a parasite, a leech – but the character of the man himself did not alter the fact that I had murdered him, that he was dead and I was his killer.

But the mind is funny. I had planned his death, I had killed him, and now it was over. Period. The simple fact of murder seemed to be something I could live with. I would not be plagued by guilt. As a result either of strength or weakness of character, I was a killer with a reasonably clear conscience.

And now the rest of it. Three things stayed with me, stuck in the forefront of my mind. The very weird expression on his face the instant before I shot him, first of all. A total disbelief, as if he had suddenly wandered into a different time-continuum where he did not fit at all.

Then there was the noise of the first gunshot. It rang so loud in my ears that the other four senses, smell and sight and taste and touch, disappeared entirely into the portion of time when the shot dominated the morning. All that sound in the middle of all that sensory silence – it was impressive.

The third thing was the utter stupidity of putting all those bullets into that very dead body. I think shooting a dead man may well be more emotionally offensive than shooting a live one. There's a concentrated brutality about it, which may explain why the newspapers and the public go wild when a murderer hacks up a corpse and stuffs it piece by piece into subway lockers, or whatever. Murder, at least, is rational. But the ridiculous mental picture of a killer emptying a gun into a man with a hole in his head is senseless, stupid, and much more terrible.

The look in a man's face. The sound of a gunshot. The waste of three or four or five bullets.

These were significant, important.

More so than murder.

The commuter train unloaded us at Grand Central. I folded the *Times* and tucked it under my arm, then followed the fold out to the lower level of the station. I was confused for a few seconds; then I got my bearings and headed for the locker where I had left my suitcase. I found it, fished out the key, unlocked the thing and picked up my bag. I carried it to the ticket office where a stoop-shouldered old man with shaggy gray hair and thick, almost opaque eyeglasses sold me a one-way coach ticket to Cleveland. The human robot at the Information Desk informed me that the next train to Cleveland left in thirty-eight minutes from Track 41. I found Track 41 without too much trouble and sat down on a bench with my suitcase between my knees.

The train was a comfortable one. It called itself the Ohio State Limited, passed through Albany and Utica and Syracuse and Rochester and Erie and Buffalo, and was due at Cleveland at 9:04 in the evening. I added thirty mental minutes to the time of arrival and settled down with my newspaper. In due course the conductor appeared, snatched my ticket and replaced it with a narrow red cardboard affair with numbers on it. He punched one of the numbers and tucked the cardboard slab into the slot on the seat in front of me. Shortly thereafter another kind gentleman made his appearance. He sold me two pieces of bread with a sliver of American cheese between them and a paper cup of orange juice to wash the sandwich down with. I handed him a dollar and he returned a nickel to me. There's nothing quite like the railroads. No other mode of transportation since the covered wagon has been able to cover such a short distance in so long a time at such a high cost. It's an accomplishment.

We hit Albany on time. We were five minutes late getting into Utica and seven more minutes behind by the time we got to Syracuse. We lost eight minutes on the road to Rochester and an additional five getting to Buffalo. Then we waited for some obscure reason in the Buffalo terminal. Maybe there was a cow on the tracks. Something like that.

It was a quarter to ten when we made Cleveland. The train was supposed to swing south next, heading for Cinci by way of such unlikely places as Springfield and Columbus and Dayton and similar silliness, and I didn't want to think how far behind it would be when it finally made port in Cincinnati. I got off in Cleveland, suitcase in hand, and looked for a hotel and a restaurant in that order.

The hotel was at the corner of Thirteenth and Paine, rundown but respectable, reasonable but not cheap. The room had a stall shower, which helped, and a big bed which looked inviting. I changed to slightly less Madison-Avenue clothing and went out for dinner.

The restaurant was one of those let's-pretend-it's-1910 places – imitation gaslamps, sawdust on the floor, waiters with white coats and broad-brimmed straw hats. The food made up for it. I had a steak, a baked potato, a dish of creamed spinach. I drank bourbon and water before dinner, black coffee after. The coffee came in a little pewter pot with a wooden handle. What do murderers eat? What do they drink?

The *Cleveland Press* didn't have the story. It was a veritable storehouse of information about Cleveland, starting with fires and municipal corruption and finishing off with a little Conning-Towerish column of sloppy homespun-yet-sophisticated verse that almost made me throw up the steak. Here and there a reader could discover that there was a world outside of Cleveland, by George, with things happening there. There was a rocket doing something at Cape Canaveral, a revolution in Laos, an election in Italy. There was a murder in New York but the *Cleveland Press* didn't know it.

I found a trashcan to stuff the *Press* into and looked around for a newsstand that stooped to carrying New York papers. Most of them didn't. One of them did and I let him sell me the *Telly*. I took it back to the hotel, opened it up and plowed through it.

It took a lot of plowing. I started with the front page and worked toward the back, and suddenly I was on page 22 and so was the story. It filled six paragraphs in the third column and was topped neatly by a two-deck eighteen point head that read like so:

MAN SHOT DEAD OUTSIDE
HOME IN WESTCHESTER

Gunfire shattered the early-morning calm today in residential Chesh-ire Point when five bullets fired from a moving car felled a prominent importer steps from his own door.

The victim was Lester Keith Brassard of 341 Roscommon Drive, 52-year-old importer with offices in lower Manhattan. He was killed as he left his home for his office. Local police recovered a stolen car, believed to be the murder vehicle, several blocks from the scene of the crime.

Mona Brassard, the victim's wife, was unable to advance any information as to a possible motive for the slaying, conducted in typical gangland fashion. 'Keith didn't have an enemy in the world,' she told police and reporters. She admitted that he had seemed nervous lately. 'But it was something about business,' she said. 'He didn't have any personal problems. None that I knew about.'

Arnold Schwerner, detective on the Cheshire Point police force, agreed that the slaying seemed pointless. 'He could have been hit by mistake,' he theorized. 'It looks like a pro job.'

Schwerner's statement was in reference to the method of murder – several shots from a stolen car. This method has been in vogue among gangsters for years.

Cheshire Point police are working on the killing in close cooperation with detectives attached to Manhattan's Homicide West.

The last paragraph was the kicker. If Homicide West was tied in already, that meant the cops were looking for a business motive for the murder. That, in turn, meant that the office would get some sort of going-over. I couldn't be positive they'd hit the heroin, but the odds were long that they would. Homicide West is by no means a lousy outfit.

I re-read the part where they quoted Mona and I couldn't help grinning like a ghoul. She had carried it off perfectly, hitting just the right tone. *Keith didn't have an enemy in the world* – except for his lovely wife and her boyfriend. *He seemed a little nervous lately. But it was something about business. He didn't have any personal problems. None that I knew about.*

The right tone. She hadn't tried to explain things for them, but had given them a few hints and let them reconstruct it for themselves. I'd staged the job right – a slaying conducted in typical gangland style. Now she had reacted properly, and the heroin was the next link in the chain. When they found that, the ball game was over. That made it a gangland slaying, all right. What the hell else could it be?

I folded the newspaper and put it in the wastebasket. Then I set a cigarette on fire and found a chair to sit in. I wanted to get some plans made, but it wasn't easy. I kept seeing that look of total disbelief on the face of Lester Keith Brassard. I hadn't known his name was Lester. It explained why he preferred Keith. So would anybody in his right mind.

I would see the face, and I would hear the shot. Then I would see myself stretched across the front seat of that black Ford pumping bullets into a corpse. According to the papers, the police thought the car was moving at the time. That was fine with me. That meant two killers, one firing the gun and the other handling the driving. The crime lab could probably figure out that it hadn't happened that way, but by that time it would be a moot point. For the time being, let them figure on two killers. Or five. Or a damned platoon.

The face, and the shot, and the exercise in studied stupidity. They paraded in front of me, and I wondered if maybe this was what they meant by guilt. Not sorrow for the act, not a feeling that the act was wrong, not even a fear of punishment – but a profound distaste for certain memories of the act, certain sensory impulses that lingered persistently.

I don't think Brutus was sorry that he knifed Caesar. I don't think he thought it was wrong.

But I am positive the line *Et tu, Brute* haunted him until he ran upon the sword that Strato held for him. That line would do it for him, just as the blood did it for Macbeth and his good wife.

I lighted another cigarette and tried to think straight. It was not easy.

According to plan, she would leave for Miami a week to ten days after the murder. It was Wednesday now, Wednesday evening, and by the Saturday after next she would be at the Eden Roc. I had told her I would be there before her. I could leave any time.

The funny part of it was that I didn't entirely want to. I had been a machine, oiled and primed for the murder, and now that it was over and done with I felt functionless. I was through. The easy part remained, but I didn't even want a hand in the easy part of it. A weird thought nagged at me. I had better than five hundred bucks left. I could pack up and go – find a new town, use the dough for a fresh start. I could forget all that woman and all that money.

And the face and the noise and the five useless bullets.

It was an emotional reaction to murder, not sensible, not logically considered. It wasn't logical because then I would have killed L. Keith Brassard for nothing at all. The spoils belonged to the victor. I had won, and now Brassard's wife and Brassard's money were mine to keep. Both were desirable. It would be idiotic to turn down either of them.

It came out the same way if you looked at the emotional set-up piece by piece. I still loved Mona, still wanted her, still needed her. Even if I had the money, I was nowhere without her. She made the difference. She was the New Life, the Higher Purpose, all of that crap.

I had to laugh. A face and a noise and five extra bullets sat on one side. Mona and money were perched on the other. The choice was so simple, so obvious, that there really was no choice. I'd be in Miami by Saturday and she'd be there four or five days after that.

I ground out my cigarette, glad that all that nonsense was settled. The air outside was heavy with industrial smoke and human perspiration. I forced myself through it, found a bar, had a drink. A whore sat there waiting for me to pick her up. The impulse was suddenly strong; the desire for a magical release from all that tension was tough to resist. I looked at her and she smiled, showing at least fifty-three teeth, none of them hers to start with.

She was the kind of woman who looks fine if you don't get too close. A hard, tough body built for action. A face camouflaged with too much of every cosmetic known to modern woman. Cheap clothes cheaply worn. And I remembered the line from Kipling: *I've a neater, sweeter maiden in a cleaner, greener land.*

I turned away from her and paid attention to my drink. I finished it, scooped up my change and walked away from Mandalay. I thought about a movie and decided I really didn't have the strength to sit through one. They were good time-killers, but enough is enough. Maybe someday I would be able to go to a movie because I wanted to go to a movie. Maybe someday I would be able to go to a movie and watch the damn thing.

But not for a while.

I walked around for a few more minutes, maybe half an hour altogether. I passed movie theaters, passed bars that I didn't bother entering. I wandered past the Greyhound station and again the impulse came, the urge to get on the first bus and go wherever it went. With my luck it would have gone to New York.

More walking. Then it occurred to me that, for one thing, I was dog-tired, and, for another, I had absolutely nothing to do. The obvious course of action involved going back to my hotel and hitting the sack. But I knew instinctively that I wouldn't be able to fall asleep for hours. After all, I had recently finished committing a murder. You do any of several things after committing a murder, and falling asleep with ease is not one of them. It only stood to reason that, this being my first homicide to date, it would be sunrise before I could start thinking seriously about something like sleep.

I decided not to be logical. The sleepy clerk tossed me my key and the sleepy elevator operator ran me up to my floor. I felt a kinship for both of them. I got out of my clothes, washed up, and crawled under the covers.

I got all ready to count sheep. The sheep were little naked Monas and they did not look like sheep at all. They were only woolly here and there, and they were not built much like sheep. Nor were they jumping over a fence. Instead they leaped gaily over a corpse. You know who *he* was.

By the time the fourth Mona got over the corpse, I had gotten over my insomnia. I slept like a corpse, and nobody jumped over me.

10

I made the front page of the *Times*. Not the lead story, which was devoted to the names somebody called somebody else in the Security Council of the United Nations. Not even the second lead, which was devoted to some new invention in the realm of municipal corruption. But, by *Times* standards, I got a big play – ten inches of copy set double-column in the left-hand corner of page one. That's the equivalent of the front-page banner in the *News* or *Mirror*, which, I found out later, I also made.

The headline on the Times story read: NARCOTICS CONNECTION SEEN LIKELY IN CHESHIRE POINT MURDER. As is generally the case with *New York Times* headlines, that turned out to be the understatement of the year. The story, with ten inches of copy on the front page and fifteen more on page 34, made everything very nice indeed. I couldn't have asked for anything more.

Homicide West had located the heroin after what the *Times* graciously referred to as 'a meticulous scrutiny of Brassard's offices at 117 Chambers Street.' I didn't see any need for meticulous scrutiny – not with an envelope of heroin sticking out from under a desk blotter and three more in the top drawer. But I didn't want to quarrel with the *Times*.

The cache of heroin, according to the *Times*, had a retail value in excess of a million dollars. What in the world that meant was anybody's guess. By the time the stuff was retailed it would have passed through the hands of fifteen middlemen and would have been cut as many times. The retail value was pretty much irrelevant, and there was no way of figuring out what the wholesale value of the stuff might have been. Nor did it matter much, when you stopped to think about it.

From there on, naturally, they had put two and two together. And, naturally, had come up with four. The phone numbers, said the *Times*, were those of several well-known narcotics drops. Why they were still open if they were known as narcotics drops was neither asked nor answered. What with the dope and the numbers, and a meticulous scrutiny of Brassard's books, Homicide had managed to figure out that Lester Keith Brassard was an importer of more than cigarette lighters.

This fact, coupled with the mode of murder employed, made the final conclusion inevitable. Brassard had been bumped by racket boys, either because he had crossed them or because they wanted to move in on his operation. The *Times* reporter, who had obviously seen a few too many movies about the Mafia, thought this might be an aftermath of the Appalachian meeting, with the mob moving out of the drug trade. According to this interpretation, poor Lester Keith was a high-ranking mobster who refused to go along with the shift in policy and had suffered the consequences of 'bucking the syndicate.' It was a pretty fascinating theory and a marvelous example of interpretative journalism in action. I hoped the kid would cop himself a Pulitzer for it.

There were three or four paragraphs about Mona in the story and they all said just what I wanted them to say. The distraught widow was completely taken aback by the new developments in the case. Any intimation that her husband was less than a solid citizen shocked the marrow from her bones. Of course she had never been quite clear on what he did for a living. He wasn't the sort of man who brought his business home from the office. He made a good living, and that was as much as she knew. But she just couldn't *believe* that he would be mixed up in something ... something actually *criminal*. Why, it just wasn't like Keith at all!

She should have been an actress.

I liked that article. What it left out was as important from my point of view as what it included. The Cheshire Point side of the case had disappeared almost completely. A few witnesses had popped out with the usual mutually-conflicting stories. One insisted the three killers had called out *This is for Al, you bastard* before shooting. The rest came a little closer to reality, but not a hell of a lot. The important part was that nobody seemed to give a damn about the shooting itself any more. Brassard, unmasked as a scoundrel, would not be mourned. The police, busy chasing down narcotics leads, wouldn't care about the killing as such. Mona would be left alone, except for the sob-sister reporters whom she'd quite justifiably refused to speak to. Nobody would be especially surprised when she put the house up for sale and headed for Florida to get away from it all. Nor would anybody take much notice when she married me four or five months later, on the rebound, so to speak. It would be perfectly consistent, and that was the important thing. Consistency. You can build a whole world of lies, as long as each lie reinforces every other lie. You can create a masterful structure of sheer logic if you begin with one false postulate. All it takes is consistency.

That night I saw a movie. The whole day up to that point had been unreal. It was a waiting time and nothing was happening. I felt only partially alive, hibernating without being able to sleep. The total lack of eventfulness was overpowering, especially after a time of planning and a time of acting and a time of running. So this time the movie was not a time-killer but a vicarious experience, an attempt to replace my own passiveness with the activity of the celluloid images.

Perhaps this is why I watched the movie more closely than I would have normally. It was a Hitchcock film, an old one, and it was gripping. The switches from tension to comedy, from the terrifying to the ridiculous, were amazingly effective. But for a change I saw past the surface to the plot itself, and I saw that the plot was ludicrous – a web of preposterous coincidences held together by superior writing and acting and directing.

Later, lying in bed and trying to sleep, I realized something. I tried to imagine a movie in which the hero steals two pieces of luggage, one of which is loaded with a fortune in raw heroin. Then the same hero happens to pick up or get picked up by a girl who subsequently turns out to be the wife of the guy who owns the luggage and the heroin.

Coincidental?

More than that. Almost incredible. At least as farfetched as the picture – and yet I had been able to accept coincidence in life simply because it had happened to me. The fictional coincidences in the Hitchcock film were different. They had not happened in life, but only on the screen.

It was something to think about. I had never looked at it quite that way before, and I spent a little time running it through my mind.

'Would you care for a magazine, sir?'

I shook my head.

'Coffee, tea, or milk?'

I shook my head again. The stewardess, as pretty and as faceless as Miss Rheingold, wandered off to bother somebody else. I looked out the window at the ground and saw clouds instead. They look very different from above. When you fly over them they are not white puffballs of cotton at all, just shapeless, moderately dense fog. I stared at them for a few more seconds, but they didn't do a hell of a lot to hold my interest. I looked away.

It was Saturday morning. The plane was a jet, flying direct to Miami, and we would be landing a few minutes past noon. The night before, I had phoned the Eden Roc and reserved a single; it would be waiting for me. That was a piece of luck. There was a time when Miami Beach was empty in the summer. Now the summer season is as busy as the winter one, although the prices are a good deal lower.

'Attention, please.'

I listened to the male voice come over the loudspeaker and wondered what was wrong. I remembered that I was on a plane, and that periodically planes crashed for the sheer hell of it. I wondered, quite calmly, whether we were going to crash.

Then the same voice – the pilot's – went on to tell me that we were cruising at an altitude of so many feet, that the temperature in Miami was such-and-such, that landing conditions were ideal and that we were destined to arrive on time. The pilot closed with a message advising me to select his airline for future flights and I thought what an idiot I was. We were not going to crash. All was well.

We landed on time, happily. I got off – the stewardess called it *deplaning*, a cunning word – and wandered away to wait for my luggage in the terminal. The sun was hot and the sky was cloudless. Good Florida weather, good beach weather. Mona and I could lie on the beach and soak up the sun. We could lie on the beach at night and soak up the moonlight, too. I remembered Atlantic City, the first time, on the beach at midnight. Life is a circle.

The luggage got there after ten minutes or so and I traded my baggage check for it, then carried it to the waiting limousine which would cruise northward to Miami Beach. The tall, rangy driver was a native of the state. There were two ways to tell – his speech, which sounded more like Kentucky or Tennessee than Deep South. Dade County natives have that hill inflection nine times out of ten. The other tip-off was his total lack of a suntan. The people who live in Miami know enough to stay out of the sun. Only the Yankee tourists are sun-worshippers.

He was also a good driver. He made fine time, dropping me at my hotel sooner than I'd expected. A bellhop snatched my bags and I followed him to the front desk. Yes, they had my reservation. Yes, my room was ready for me. And welcome to the Eden Roc, Mr Marlin. Right this way, sir.

I was on the fifth floor, a big single with a huge bathroom and a view of the ocean. I looked out the window and saw browned bodies dotting a golden beach. The sea was very calm – no surf at all, gently rippling waves. I watched a gull swoop for a fish, watched one little kid chase another little kid along the edge of the shore, watched two college-boy-types burying a college-girl-type with sand. Miami Beach.

The beach was pleasant that afternoon, the sun warm, the water refreshing. I stayed out until it was time for dinner. The crowd thinned out as the day wore away. Fat middle-aged men from New York rubbed sunburn cream on themselves, changed into loud sportclothes and went to play gin rummy on the terrace. Mothers herded children back to their rooms. The sun went away.

After dinner I caught the floorshow. The headliner was a busty female singer who was even worse in person than she was on records. But the comic was amusing and the band passable. Drinks were expensive. I wasn't worried. When the time came to settle the tab, Mona would be on hand with half the money in the world. No sweat in that department.

That was Saturday. Sunday was about the same, and Monday and Tuesday. My tan deepened and my muscles loosened up from all the swimming. Monday afternoon I spent awhile in the gym, working out gingerly. Then I went to the steamroom and sweated. A big Pole without a hair on his head massaged me for fifteen minutes and left me feeling like a new man. I had never been in better physical shape.

I drank the nights away, always getting slightly high and never taking on too much of an edge. I kept turning down chances to sleep with the wives of other men. The need for a woman was strong, and the women were startlingly available, but one trick never failed me. I would look at them and compare them with Mona. They never came close.

Wednesday I started to expect her. I spent most of the afternoon in the lobby, my eyes flashing to the desk every ten minutes or so. It was a full week since the murder and she would be around any time from then on. There were no complications. The murder was getting very little play in the New York papers – a few inches in a back page of the *Times* now and then, nothing much else. I waited for her.

When she didn't show on Thursday I got impatient. After all, I had told her a week, ten days tops. And with everything running so smoothly she didn't have to waste any time. All was clear. To hell with cloaks and daggers, Mitchum in a trenchcoat. I wanted my woman.

She didn't show Friday, either.

I drank too much Friday night. I sat in front of the bar and poured too many shots of straight bourbon down my throat. It could have been dangerous, but I became a silent drunk instead of a noisy one, which was fortunate. A bellhop poured me into bed and I woke up early with a brand-new hangover. There was a wire running through my head from one ear to the other. It was red hot and somebody was strumming it. A Bloody Mary made things a little better. Only a little.

Saturday morning. A full week of Miami Beach, which is plenty. And no Mona. I waited all day long in the lobby and she did not show up.

I started to sweat. I almost walked over to the desk to ask if she had a reservation, which would have been a new experiment in stupidity. Instead I went outside and walked down Collins to the first bar. It had a pay phone and I used it to call the Eden Roc. I asked for Mrs Brassard.

'One moment,' the clerk said. I waited more than a moment and he came back again.

'I'm sorry,' he said. 'But we have no one staying here under that name.'

'Could you check the reservations?'

He could, and he did. There were no reservations for Mrs Brassard, either.

I went to the bar and had a drink. Then I went back and tried to straighten myself out. Maybe she forgot which hotel to stay at, or maybe the Eden Roc was full, or something. I made half a dozen calls. I checked the Fontainebleau and the Americana and the Sherry Frontenac and the Martinique and two other places I no longer remember. Each time I asked first for Mrs Brassard, then asked if she had a reservation there.

Each time I drew a blank.

There was an answer, somewhere. There had to be. But whatever it was, I couldn't figure it out. I was looking at things wrong, or things were happening wrong, and I felt like a rat in a maze. They have a cute little ploy at the psychology laboratories. They take a rat that's been taught to solve mazes and they put him in a maze with no way out. The rat tries everything and nothing works. Then, inevitably, the rat reacts to all this frustration by sitting in a corner and chewing off his feet.

I didn't chew off my feet. I went back to the Eden Roc and took a cold shower and thought about the bill that was going to fall due any day. I wondered if I'd be able to cover it. And I wondered how long it would take her to show up. The only answer was that she hadn't bothered with a reservation. Maybe she had had to stay in New York until the estate was settled. You read about things like that. Legal problems that can tie you up for a while. Little things.

I told myself that story until I believed it. And the night came and went, and the next morning I hit the beach and let the sun bake a lot of bitterness and anxiety out of me. I swam and slept and ate and drank and that was Sunday.

I was up late Monday morning. I went to breakfast, which they serve at the Eden Roc until three P.M., and then I headed for the elevator.

The clerk was too quick for me.

'Mr Marlin—'

I could have pretended not to hear him. But the bill was going to get to me sooner or later and there was no particular point in dodging it for a day or so. I could probably cover it anyway. So I went over to the desk and he smiled at me.

'Your statement,' he said, handing me a folded hunk of yellow paper. I showed him I could be just as polite as he was and put it in my pocket without looking at it.

'And a letter,' he added. He gave it to me. It must have been a reflex, because I put that one in my pocket without looking at it, and this was not easy.

'Thanks,' I said.

'Do you know how long you'll be staying with us, Mr Marlin?'

I shook my head. 'Hard to say,' I said. 'Nice place you've got here. Enjoyable.'

He beamed.

'Few more days,' I said. 'Maybe a week. Might even be two weeks. Then again, I might have to leave on a moment's notice. Hard to say.'

The smile remained. It seemed rude to walk away in the middle of such a nice smile but he held it so firmly that he left me no choice. I let him smile across the lobby while I rode upstairs in the elevator.

First the statement. It was a honey, and it scared me. It came to an impressive $443.25. More than I'd figured. Too many days, too much good food, too much liquor. I didn't *have* $443.25.

I folded the yellow paper back on the original folds and made a place for it in my wallet. Then I took out the envelope and turned it over and over in my hands like a child trying to guess the contents of a birthday present. It was thick. No return address.

I opened it.

There was a sheet of plain white paper. It was the wrapper. It held money.
Money.

Hundred-dollar bills.

I counted them, thinking how immaterial the hotel bill had suddenly become. There were thirty of them, each crisp and fresh and new, each a hundred. Thirty hundred-dollar bills. Thirty hundred dollars. Three thousand dollars.

A lot of money.

And all the worry drained out of me, because I knew that there was no longer anything to worry about. Mona had not forgotten I was alive. The estate was not tied up – not if she could ship me three grand in cash.

There were no problems.

I hefted the money. It was more than cash – it was a symbol. It meant very definitely that everything was all right now, no worry, no sweat. God was in His heaven and all was right with the world. It was her way of telling me this – an apology for her tardiness and a promise that she would be around soon. I felt myself growing warm at the thought of her. Soon, I thought. Very soon. Very, very soon.

She had gotten tied up. Well, that sort of thing could happen. And she couldn't chance a letter or a phone call or a wire. She had trusted me to wait for her, and now she was making sure that I knew all was well. I felt guilty suddenly for worrying. It had been rotten of me.

But I would make it up to her.

She was in New York now. But soon – any day now – she would be on her way to Miami.

Any day.

First things first. I put on swim trunks, threw a towel over my shoulders and picked the top six bills off the roll. I put the rest in the wallet and popped the wallet into the dresser drawer. I looked around for the wastebasket, then changed my mind and flipped the envelope in the drawer too.

In Miami Beach you can take an elevator to the lobby in your bathing suit. The only formal part of the place is the financial end of things. And I was taking care of that now.

The clerk had the same smile on his face.

'Might as well get this out of the way,' I told him. And I pushed five hundred dollars across the desk.

'You hang onto the change,' I went on, feeling richer than God. 'Put it on my account. Just one pocket in these trunks and it's too damn small to be much good.'

I walked across the lobby to the beach entrance and felt seven feet tall and eight feet wide. It was Chamber of Commerce weather again and I was in the right mood for it. I found a spot to dump my towel, then ran straight into the ocean. The waves were higher than they had been and I dived right into the middle of one. It felt great.

A funny-faced man with a very deep tan and a very large stomach was teaching his little daughter how to swim. He held his hand out, palm up, and she had her stomach on it while she flailed the water madly with her arms and kicked furiously with two small pink feet. I grinned at her and at him and felt happy.

I swam around some more. I went over to the terrace and had a vodka collins. I stretched out on my towel and let the sun bake the vodka out again.

It was a good thing I already had a pretty deep tan, because I fell asleep there with the sun going full blast. It was a nice way to fall asleep. There was all that warmth, and there was my head dancing with memories of Mona and thoughts about Mona and nice things like that. There was a cool breeze off the ocean and the pleasant babble of kids and an occasional skywriting plane droning away over the ocean.

So I slept.

The sun was gone when I woke up. So was the heat – the beach was cold and I was chilly. I wrapped up in the towel and headed for my room.

The funny part of it was that a lot of the pleasant glow of well-being had set with the sun. Now, oddly, something seemed to be wrong, which was ridiculous. I shook myself angrily, not even amused this time around. What the hell – I'd drifted off to sleep dreaming happy dreams, and I'd gotten up feeling troubled again.

What was it? The face and the noise and the five bullets? I still thought about them, once in a while, whenever I drank a little too much.

But that wasn't it.

Something else.

I let myself into my room, found a fresh pack of cigarettes and got one going. The smoke didn't taste good but I smoked anyway, nervously, and ground the cigarette out with half of it still to go. What was wrong?

I walked over to the dresser, opened the drawer. I took out my wallet and looked at all that wonderful green paper that had come all the way from New York. I looked at the plain envelope it had come in.

Maybe I saw it before. You can do that – see things and not notice them consciously. They stick with you, deep in your mind, and they nag at you.

Or maybe I was psychic.

Or maybe something just smelled wrong. Maybe something didn't add up no matter how nice I made it sound. Maybe a few hours in the sun made up for the rationalization and let the bad smell reveal itself.

I looked at that plain envelope from New York. I looked at it until my eyes bulged.

It was postmarked Las Vegas.

11

We made love in my room at the Shelburne. Then, while I was lying on my bed in the dark smelling the last traces of her perfume, the door had opened less than six inches. An envelope fell to the floor and the door closed at once.

That envelope had contained three hundred seventy dollars.

We made love in my room at the Collingwood. Just before she left she gave me an envelope. That one had contained somewhat better than seven hundred dollars. Maybe my performance was better that time, or maybe stud service gets increasingly more profitable as you go along.

This time the pay was three grand and I hadn't even made love to her.

Now I remembered the bad feeling at the Collingwood after she gave me the money. The weird feeling that the money was a payment for services rendered. That was obviously what the three grand constituted – payment, probably in full, for the removal of her husband. I wondered what the market price was for husband bandicide. Or was there a set price? Maybe it varied, because there were plenty of variables that deserved consideration. The net worth of the husband, for example, and the comparative misery of living with him. Those were important factors. It ought to cost more to kill an obnoxious millionaire than to bump a good-natured and uninsured pauper. It only stood to reason.

Three thousand dollars for murder.

Three thousand dollars.

Three thousand dollars and not even a note that said *good-bye*. Three thousand dollars and not a word, not a return address, nothing. Three thousand dollars as a kiss-off, with a plain envelope plainly saying *It's over, you're being paid for everything, go away and forget me and to hell with you.* Three thousand dollars' worth of very cold shoulder.

With three thousand dollars you can buy two hundred thousand cigarettes. I smoke two packs of cigarettes a day. Three thousand dollars would keep me in cigarettes, then, for almost fourteen years. With three thousand dollars you can buy four hundred fifths of good bourbon, or one fairly good new car, or three hundred acres of very cheap land. With three thousand dollars you can buy thirty good suits, or one hundred pairs of good shoes, or three thousand neckties. You can shoot pool for six thousand consecutive hours if you want.

Three thousand dollars for murder.

It was not nearly enough.

What surprised me was the strange calm that had come over me, probably because the full impact hadn't reached me yet. I was seeing everything in a different light – Mona, myself, the whole picture of the curious little game we had played. I was her pigeon all the way down the line. I killed for her, more for her than for the money. I ran to Miami and waited for her, and she ran to Vegas and forgot me.

But why pay me at all?

Not as a sop to her conscience, because I knew full well she didn't have one. Not to even things out, because three thousand dollars was hardly a fair share.

Why?

I thought about it, and I came up with two answers that seemed to fit. One of them was sensible enough. Without some kind of word from her, I'd panic. I'd wonder where she was and I'd try to get in touch with her. Eventually I'd find some way to bollix things up. She didn't want that to happen, so she had to let me know I was being brushed off. Her way was perfect – no note, no call, no wire. Just properly anonymous money.

The other answer could make sense only to Mona. She was a girl who was used to having things break right with her. Maybe, if she gave me a little piece of change, I would go away and disappear. Maybe I'd be happy with my tiny cut and leave her alone. Maybe I'd take the dough, given to me out of the goodness of her heart, and skip with it. Wishful thinking. But Mona was a wishful person.

Three thousand dollars. I could forget all about her with three thousand dollars. I could use the money to cruise Miami Beach good and hard until I found myself a rich divorcée and parlayed her into a life-long meal-ticket. I could buy a fresh start with three grand, and that was what she was counting on me to do.

She didn't know me at all.

Somehow the thought of sea and surf had lost its charm for me. So had the thought of food. But the bar was open, and liquor was far from unattractive. I drank but did not get drunk. I was too busy listening to small voices located somewhere deep inside my brain. They did not stop talking.

I think I would have been able to forget her if the money had been the main thing. But it hadn't. I shot holes in Keith Brassard because I wanted his wife, not his money. And I had been double-crossed not by a temporary partner in crime but by the potential reward of the crime itself. Two things – I couldn't let her get away with it. And I couldn't let her get away from me.

I drank bourbon and thought about murder. I thought of ways to kill her. I thought of guns and knives. I looked at my hand, fingers wrapped tight around an old-fashioned glass, and I thought of barehanded murder. Strangling the life out of her, beating the life out of her. I drank some more bourbon and remembered a face and a noise and five bullets, and I knew that I was not going to kill her.

For one thing, I was certain I could never kill anybody again. The thought came to me, and I accepted it at once as gospel, and then I began to wonder why it was so. Not because killing Brassard had been difficult, or frightening, or even dangerous. But because I did not like killing. I didn't know whether or not that made sense and I didn't care. I knew it was true. That's all that really mattered.

I was not going to kill her. Because I did not want to kill, and also because that would not solve anything. There would be a risk for no reward but revenge. I would get vengeance, but I would not get that money and I would not get Mona.

I still wanted the money. And I still wanted the woman. Don't ask me why.

'Do you have a match?'

I had a match. I turned and looked at the girl who wanted a match. Brunette, mid-twenties, chic black dress and good figure. Dark lipstick on her mouth, a cigarette drooping from her lips, waiting for a light. She didn't want a match.

I lighted her cigarette. She was poised and cool but not at all subtle. She leaned forward to take the light and to give me a look at large breasts harnessed by a lacy black bra. Eve learned that one the day they got dressed and moved out of Eden. It has been just as effective ever since.

I remembered the whore in Cleveland and the snatch of song from Mandalay. I paraphrased it now in my mind: *I've a richer, bitchier maiden in a funny money land.* Mona was rich and a bitch and in Vegas. Bad verse but accurate.

The *neater sweeter* routine was an empty dream. The girl on the stool beside me was pretty. I didn't have to pretend I was a priest any more.

I returned her smile. I caught the bartender's eye and pointed meaningfully at her empty glass. He filled it.

'Thank you,' she said.

The conversation was easy because she did all of it. Her name was Nan Hickman. She played jockey to a typewriter for a New York insurance company. She had two weeks' vacation. The rest of the stenos used their two weeks to hunt a husband in the Catskills. She didn't like the Catskills and she didn't want a husband. She wanted to have fun but she wasn't having any.

She was sweet and warm and honest. She was not cheap. She wanted to have fun. In two weeks she would go back to the Bronx and turn into a pumpkin. Her mother would know who she went out with and when she came in. Her aunts would try to find husbands for her. She only had two weeks.

I put my hand on her arm. I looked at her and she didn't look away. 'Let's go upstairs,' I said. 'Let's make love.'

I left change on the bar. We went upstairs, to her room, and we made love. We made love very slowly, very gently, and very well. She'd been drinking something with rum in it and her mouth tasted warm and sweet.

She had a good body. I liked the way her body was pale white from her breasts to her thighs and tan on arms and legs and face. I liked to look at her and I liked to touch her, and I liked to move with her and against her. And afterward it was good to lie next to her, hot and sweaty and magnificently exhausted, while the earth shifted slowly back into place.

For a while there was no need to talk. Then there was, and she said little things about herself and about her job and about her family. She had an older brother, married and Long Islanded, and younger sister.

She didn't tell me that she was the closest thing in the world to a certified virgin. She didn't apologize for picking me up and sleeping with me. She wanted to have fun.

And she didn't talk about tomorrow, or the day after tomorrow, or the days after that. She didn't talk about home or family or marriage or little white houses with green shutters. Nor did she ask me any questions.

I looked at her pretty face, at her breasts and belly. I thought what a good thing it would be to fall in love with her and marry her. I wished I could do just that and knew that I couldn't.

I've a richer, bitchier maiden . . .

I waited until she was sleeping. Then I slipped out from under the sheet and got dressed. I didn't put on my shoes. I did not want to wake her.

I looked down at her. Some day somebody would marry her. I hoped he would be good enough for her, and that they would be happy. I hoped their children would look like her.

I walked out, holding my shoes in one hand, and went back to my room.

After breakfast the next morning I checked out of the Eden Roc. The desk clerk was sorry to see me go. Sorry or not, the smile never left his face.

He checked my account. 'You have a refund coming, Mr Marlin. A little over thirty dollars.'

'Tell you what,' I said. 'Didn't have a chance to leave anything for the chambermaid. Why don't you hang onto the money, spread it around here and there?'

He was surprised and pleased. I wondered how much of the money would stick to his fingers. I didn't care. I didn't need the thirty-odd dollars and it didn't make any difference to me who got it.

Surprisingly few things made any difference to me.

I found a phone booth at a bar – not the same one I had used before but pretty much the same. It was a complex proposition. I called Cheshire Point

Information and asked for the largest realtor. I got through to his office and asked if 341 Roscommon Drive was on his list. It wasn't. Could he find out who had it? He could, and would call me back collect. I waited.

I had never before had the experience of accepting a collect call in a pay phone. The operator ascertained that it was really me on the line, then told me to throw money into the machine. I did.

'Lou Pierce has the property on the board,' he told me. 'Pierce and Pierce.' He gave me their number and I jotted it down.

'High asking price,' he said. 'Too high, if you ask me. I can give you the same sort of property, same neighborhood, maybe five thousand dollars cheaper. Good terms, too. You interested?'

I told him I didn't think so but I'd let him know. I thanked him and told him he'd been a big help. Then I rang off, threw another dime in the hole and got the operator. I put through a call to Pierce and Pierce and got somebody named Lou Pierce on the phone almost immediately.

'Fred Ziegler called me,' he said. 'Told me you've got your eyes on the 341 Roscommon Drive place. Believe me, you couldn't do better. Beautiful home, lovely grounds. A bargain.'

I almost told him Ziegler had said different but checked the impulse. 'I've seen the property,' I said. 'I'm not interested in buying. I'd like some information.'

'Oh?'

'About Mrs Brassard.'

'Go ahead,' he said. Part of the warmth was gone and his voice sounded guarded.

'Her address.'

There was a pause, a brief one. 'I'm sorry,' he said, not sounding all that sorry at all. 'Mrs Brassard left strict instructions to keep her address confidential. I can't give it out. Not to anybody.'

That figured.

I was prepared for it. 'Oh,' I said, 'you don't understand. She wrote to me herself, told me where she was staying. But I lost her Nevada address.'

He was waiting for me to say more. I let him wait.

'She wrote you, huh? Told you where she was staying, but you lost the letter?'

'That's right.'

'Well,' he said. 'Well. Look, I'm not saying I don't believe you. Seems to me if somebody wrote me the name of a hotel in Tahoe it wouldn't go out of my head, but I got a better memory than a lot of people. But all I can do is what she told me. I can't go giving out confidential information.'

He already had.

I put up a minor bitch to preserve appearances. Then I acknowledged his position, thanked him anyway, and hung up on him. I hoped the conscientious objectionable didn't realize how many beans he had spilled.

I picked up my bags, left the bar and found a cab to dump them into. I climbed in after them and sat down, heavily.

But I lost her Nevada address.

It must have been luck, saying Nevada instead of Vegas. I'd been angling for the address itself, not the name of the town. Somehow the possibility that she might mail the letter out-of-town hadn't occurred to me. I'd been hunting the address, and I hadn't gotten it. Now I didn't need it any more.

Tahoe. Not Vegas. Good old Lake Tahoe, where I had never been in my life. But I knew a little about Tahoe. I knew it was small enough so that I could find her with ease whether I knew the name of her hotel or not.

Tahoe.

And I got another part of the picture, a picture of Mona Brassard throwing dice in a posh club in Tahoe and laughing her head off about the poor clod searching all over Vegas for her. It made a funny picture.

She would be surprised to see me.

They didn't have a direct flight to Lake Tahoe. TWA had one to Vegas with one touchdown in Kansas City en route. That was good enough for me. I didn't want to get to Tahoe before I was ready, anyhow. There was plenty of time.

The flight was a bad one. The weather was fine but the pilot hit every air pocket between Miami and Kansas City. There were a lot of them. The flying didn't do anything to me other than annihilate my appetite. It had a stronger effect on a few passengers; most of them managed to hit the little paper bags that TWA thoughtfully provided, but one got the floor by mistake. It kept the trip from getting too dull.

I was very calm, considering. Again, it was that weird calm that I seem to get possessed by when I ought to be tense, by all the standard rules. The machine bit was coming on again. I had a function, a purpose. I didn't have to worry over what I might do next because I knew full well what I was going to do. I was going to wind up with Mona and the money. It was that simple.

Why on earth did I want either of them? A good question. I wasn't sure, but I was entirely sure that I did, and that was the only relevant question. So I stopped worrying about the whys.

The pilot surprised everybody with a smooth landing in K.C. I spent the twenty-five minutes between landing and takeoff in the Kansas City airport. It was a pretty new building that smelled of paint and plastic. There was a pinball machine that I took a shine to. I used to be good on pinball machines and this was an easy one. I had seven free games coming to me, and then suddenly it was time to get on the damn plane again. I found a bored little kid and told him he could play my games off for me. He stared at me in amazement and I left him there.

The rest of the ride was better. They had either changed pilots or found a brand-new atmosphere for us to fly through because the trip to Vegas was smooth as silk. I let the waitress serve me a good dinner and permitted her to refill my coffee cup two or three times. The food went down easily and stayed there. Maybe air travel was coming into its own.

I laughed, remembering the airline slogan. You know the one. *Breakfast in London, lunch in New York, dinner in Los Angeles, luggage in Buenos Aires.* That one.

It didn't work that way. My luggage and I both wound up in Las Vegas in time to watch the sun set. We got together, my luggage and I, and we took a cab to the Dunes. I'd phoned ahead for a room and it was ready for me. They don't play games in Vegas. The luxury is incredible, the price fair. The gambling brings in the money.

I took a hot shower, dried off, dressed, unpacked. I went downstairs and found the casino. The action was heavy – no town in the world has as many bored people as Vegas. Bitter little girls sitting out a divorce action, mob types looking for relaxation and not finding it, nice people like that.

Red came up six times straight on the roulette wheel, in case you care. A man with buck teeth put a twenty-five-dollar chip down at the crap table, made seven straight passes, dragged off all but the original twenty-five, and crapped out. A stout matronly type with a silver fox stole hit the nickel jackpot on the slot machine, cashed the nickels in for half-dollars, and put every one of them back into the box.

Vegas.

I watched men win and I watched them lose. They were playing a straight house. Nothing was loaded. The house took its own little percentage and got rich. Money made in bootlegging and gunrunning and dope smuggling and whoremongering was invested quite properly in an entire town that stood as a monument to human stupidity, a boomtown in the state with the sparsest population and the densest people in the country.

Vegas.

I watched them for three hours. I had half a dozen drinks in the course of those three hours and none of them got close to me. Then I went upstairs to bed.

It was a cheap evening. I didn't risk a penny. I'm not a gambler.

12

Las Vegas is a funny town in the morning. It's strictly a night-time town, but one where night goes on all day long. The game rooms never close. The slots, of course, are installed next to every last cash register in the city. Breakfast was difficult. I sat at a lunch counter, drinking the first cup of coffee and smoking the first cigarette. A few feet away somebody's grandmother was making her change disappear in a chromed-up slot machine. It bothered me. Gambling before noon looks about as proper to me as laying your own sister in the front pew on Sunday morning. Call me a Puritan – that's how my mind works.

I finished the coffee and the cigarette and left the hotel. It was a short walk to the Greyhound station where a chinless clerk told me that buses left for Tahoe every two hours on the half hour. I managed to figure out without pencil or paper that one would set out at 3:30. That would be time enough.

First I had something to do.

I had to find the man. So I went looking for him, and it could have been easier and it could have been harder.

I was searching for a man I did not know. I walked around the parts of Vegas that the tourists never see – the run-down parts, the hidden parts, the parts where the neon signs are missing a letter here and there, the parts where the legal vice of gambling gives way to wilder sport.

It took three hours. For three hours I wandered and for three hours I looked very conscientiously through another pair of eyes. But after three hours I found him. Hell, he wasn't hiding. It was his business to be found. And you can always find men like him, find them in any town in the country. Waiting. Always waiting.

He was a big man. He was sitting down when I found him, sitting in a small dark café on the north side of town. His shoulders were slumped, his tie loose around his neck. He looked big anyway. He drank coffee while everybody else in the place drank beer or hard liquor. The coffee cup sat there in front of him while he ignored it and read the paper. Every once in a while when the stuff in the cup was room-temperature he would remember it was there and drain it. Seconds later a frowzy blonde would bring him a fresh one.

I picked up a bottle of beer at the bar, waved away the proffered glass and took a drink from the bottle. I carried it to his table, put it on the table and sat down opposite him.

He ignored me for a few seconds. I didn't say anything, waiting for him, and finally the newspaper went down and the eyes came up, studying me.

He said: 'I don't know you.'

'You don't have to.'

He thought it over. He shrugged. 'Talk,' he said. 'It's your nickel.'

'I could use some nickels,' I said. 'A whole yardful of them.'

'Yeah?'

I nodded.

'What's your scene?'

'I buy. I sell.'

'Around here?'

I shook my head.

'What the hell,' he said, slowly. 'If this was a bust I would have heard about it by now. A yard?'

A nod from me.

'Now?'

'Fine.'

He remembered his coffee and took a sip. 'It's a distance,' he said. 'You got a short?'

I didn't.

'So we'll take mine. Ride together. The dealer and the customer in the same car. It's nice when the right people run a town. No sweat. No headaches.'

I followed him out of the café. Nobody looked at us on the way out. I guess they knew better. His car was parked around the corner, a new, powder-blue Olds with power everything. He drove easily and well. The Olds moved through the main section of town, along a freeway, around to the outskirts of the south side.

'Nice neighborhood,' he said.

I said something appropriate. He pulled to a stop in front of a five-room ranch house with a picture window. He told me he lived there alone. We went inside and I looked at the house. It was well furnished in modern stuff that wasn't too extreme. Expensive, not flashy. I wondered whether he'd picked it himself or found an interior decorator.

'Have a seat,' he said. 'Relax a little.'

I sat down in a chair that was far more comfortable than it looked while he disappeared. The transaction was going almost too smoothly. My man was right – it was very nice when the right people ran a town. No headaches at all.

I looked at the walls and waited for him to come back. He did, holding a little paper sack neatly rolled. 'Thirty nickels for a dollar,' he said. 'Bargain day at the zoo. You picked a good time. The store is overstocked so we have a sale. You want to count 'em?'

I shook my head. If he wanted to cheat me, a count wouldn't make any difference. I was reaching for my wallet when I remembered something else that I needed.

'A kit,' I said. 'I could use a kit.'

He looked amused. 'For you?'

'For anybody.'

He shrugged. 'That's a dime more.'

I told him that was okay. He went away again and came back with a flat leather box that looked as though it ought to contain a set of draftsman's tools. I took the box and the sack and gave him one hundred and ten dollars – a dollar and a dime in his language. He folded them twice and stuck them into his shirt pocket. For small change, maybe.

On the way back to the center of town he became almost talkative. He asked me what I was doing in Vegas and I told him I was just passing through, which was true enough.

'I travel a lot,' I said. 'Wherever there are people. Places get warm if you stay too long.'

'Depends how well connected you are.'

I shrugged.

'See me when you hit Vegas next,' he said. 'I'm always in the same place. Or ask and they'll take a message for me. Sometimes the price gets better than it was today. We can always deal.'

'Sure.'

Just before he let me out of the car he started to laugh. I asked him what was so funny.

'Nothing,' he said. 'I was just thinking. It's such a groovy business. Depressions don't even touch us. Isn't that a gas?'

I left my bags in my room at the Dunes. I wasn't ready to check out, not for the time being. And at 3:30 I caught the bus to Tahoe. It was not crowded. Neither were the roads and we made good time. It was a good trip – hot sun, clear air. I sat by myself and looked out the window and smoked cigarettes. The bus was air-conditioned and the smoke from the end of my cigarette trailed up along the window pane and disappeared.

We hit Lake Tahoe in time for dinner. And I was hungry. I found the washroom in the bus station first, tossed a quarter in a slot and let myself into a private cubicle with fresh towels and a big wash basin. I washed up, straightened my tie and felt almost human.

I ate a big dinner in a hurry. But I barely tasted the food. Then I left the restaurant and made the rounds.

It was too early at first but I was looking anyway. If she was in Tahoe she would be gambling. And there just weren't that many casinos. Sooner or later we were going to run into each other.

In the first casino I went over to the crap table and made dollar bets against the shooter. When my turn came up I passed the dice and left. I was a few dollars ahead and could not have cared less.

In the second casino I put the crap table profits into a slot machine. I kept looking around for her but didn't find her. So I left.

Then I passed a men's shop, saw a hat in the window, and remembered that it might be better all across the board if I saw her before she saw me. A hat was supposed to be a good prop, altering the shape of your head or something. There are places where a man with a hat on stands out. The owners themselves don't know enough to take their hats off inside.

I went inside and bought the hat. It was an Italian import, a Borsalino, and it was priced at twenty bucks. It seemed sort of silly, shelling out twenty bucks for a hat I was going to wear once and throw away. But I reminded myself that it no longer mattered what anything cost. A five-dollar hat might do as well, but I was not in a store that sold five-dollar hats. I bought the Borsalino and wore it out of the store.

It didn't look bad. It had a high crown and a narrow brim. It was black, very soft.

I studied my reflection in the store window. I experimented until the hat looked good and did its job well. Then I went to the next casino.

I picked them up a few minutes past nine in the Charlton Room. I was nursing a bourbon sour and watching the roulette wheel when I saw them. They were at the crap table just a few yards away. I took my drink with me and moved off.

I had known he would be with her. I could even have told you what he looked like. Black hair – black, not dark brown – and broad shoulders and expensive clothes. Hair combed too neatly, hairs always perfectly in place. Clothes worn too well, too casual to be true. And an easy laugh. The looks and effect of two types only, gigolos and fags. He wasn't a fag.

I knew the rules of the game. She would give him a certain amount of money to play with and he would keep it, win or lose. Of course he would tell her that he'd lost, and she could believe it or not, depending upon her own state of mind.

What she probably didn't know was that he also got a cut of her net losses. This was the house's idea, so that he would keep her playing as long as possible. She couldn't have known this, but she wouldn't have cared anyway. The money didn't matter to her, not if she was getting all that she was paying for.

I tried to hate the gigolo and couldn't. He wasn't hurting me, for one thing. For another, the reason I knew so much about his particular method of earning a living was that I had played the same record myself from time to time. It's tough feeling superior to yourself.

She had the dice now. But she wasn't conforming to the stereotype of the woman with the kept man in her pocket. Usually a woman in that position is trying her damnedest to have all the fun in the world. A perpetual smile, wild gesturing and brittle laughter. And underneath it all a profound uneasiness. The last shows up in the hand clutching too tightly at an elbow, the laugh at something not at all funny, the general impression of being a semi-competent actress at a very important audition. Auditioning for what? The world? Or for herself?

But Mona wasn't like that. She seemed so desperately bored it was astounding. The guy next to her was pretty as a picture and she hardly seemed to know he was there. The action at the crap table was as fast as it ever gets and it bored her stiff. She threw the dice, not as if she hated them, but as if she was trying to get rid of them.

I couldn't keep my eyes off her. I kept looking at her face and trying to reconcile the beauty and, yes, innocence, with the person I knew she was. I looked at her, stared at her, and once again took all the pieces of the puzzle and glued them together with library paste. I tried to imagine living with her, and then I tried to imagine living without her, and I realized that either alternative was equally impossible.

Looking at Mona made me remember the other girl, the girl at the Eden Roc. I had forgotten her name, but I remembered that she lived in the Bronx and worked for an insurance company and wanted to have fun on her vacation. I remembered the love we had made, and I remembered how she looked when she dropped off to sleep. I remembered thinking how good it would be to fall in love with her, and marry her, and live with her.

But I had forgotten more than her name. I tried to picture her face and failed. I tried to recall her voice and missed. The only picture I got was an abstract one composed of the qualities of the girl herself. They were fine qualities. Mona lacked almost all of them but beauty.

Yet everything about Mona stayed in my mind.

I found a slot machine that took nickels and gave it one of mine. I pulled the lever very slowly and watched the dials to see what would happen. I got a bell, a cherry and a lemon. The nickel slots, I discovered, were more fun than the dollar slots. I couldn't win anything and I couldn't lose anything. I could only waste time and watch the dials spin.

I tried again. This time I lucked out with three of something or other. Twelve nickels galloped back at me.

I could not live with her and I could not live without her. An interesting problem. I had imagined, earlier, what it would be like to have Mona for a wife. I knew how her mind worked. Keith was dead, not because she had hated him, not because she had wanted me, but because she no longer needed him. He was excess baggage. And, because he was excess baggage, he had been jettisoned in flight. It would make no tremendous difference if I took his place. Not that she would kill me, but that she would leave me, or do her damnedest to make me leave her. It would not be any good at all.

And I knew damn well what would happen if I tried living without her. Every night, no matter where I was or who I was with, I would think about her. Every night I would picture her face, and remember her body, and wonder where she was and who she was sleeping with and what she was wearing and—

One of the most common murder patterns in the world is that of a man who murders a woman, proclaiming *If I can't have her, nobody can.* It had never made any sense to me whatsoever. Now I was beginning to understand.

But I had decided that I could not kill her.

I could not live with her or without her. I could not kill her. And I certainly did not intend to kill myself. It looked insoluble.

I dropped another nickel in the slot machine and thought that I was very clever to have hit the answer all by myself. I pulled the lever and watched the dials.

They hit one more casino after that one. It was midnight when they left the second one, midnight or a little after. They'd had a few drinks and they both seemed a little bit high. They walked and I followed them to the Roycroft. It was the best hotel in Tahoe and I had more or less figured all along that they'd be staying there.

I waited outside, then hit the lobby after they were already in the elevator. I looked around the lobby but this time I didn't even notice the money-smell in the air. Hell, the Eden Roc was just as plush. And I'd paid the tab there all by myself. Well, almost. At any rate, I was getting tougher to impress.

I saw the bell captain and walked over to him. He looked me over carefully from the new Borsalino to Keith's shoes on my feet. Then his eyes and mine got together.

'That couple that just came in,' I said. 'Did you notice them?'

'I may have.'

Straight from Hollywood, this one. I smiled gently. 'Mighty fine-looking couple,' I said. 'You know, I bet you aren't too observant. Here they are, staying here, and you don't notice them at all.'

He didn't say anything.

'What I mean,' I said, 'is that I'll bet you twenty dollars you don't even know what room they're staying in.'

He thought about it. 'Awright,' he said. 'Eight-oh-four.'

I gave him the twenty. 'That was very good,' I said. 'But it doesn't move me. I'll bet you a hundred you don't have a key that would open their door.'

He almost smiled. 'No trouble,' he said.

'Not for the world.'

He vanished. He returned. He traded me a key for a hundred-dollar bill.

'If there's trouble,' he said, 'you don't know where you got that key.'

'I found it under a flat stone.'

'You got it,' he said. 'Keep it quiet, huh?'

'Sure.'

He looked me over, very carefully. 'I don't think I get it,' he said.

'For a hundred and twenty you don't have to.'

He shrugged elaborately. 'Curiosity,' he said. 'The human comedy.'

'It killed the cat.'

Another profound shrug. 'You her husband?'

I shook my head.

'I didn't think so. But—'

'That guy upstairs with her,' I said. 'You've seen him? The one with the shoulders and the hair?'

The expression on his face told me just how much regard he had for the boy upstairs.

'*He's* her husband,' I explained. 'I'm her jealous lover. The bitch is two-timing me.'

He sighed. It was better than a shrug. 'You don't want to talk straight,' he said, 'maybe I'll watch television. They're funnier on television.'

He had a right to his opinion. I found a chair in the lobby and sat in it, giving them time to get started at whatever they were going to do. The ceiling was sound-proofed and I tried to count the link holes in it. I'm not enough of an idiot to count the holes themselves, of course. I count the holes in one of the squares, and then I see how many squares there are on the whole ceiling. And then I multiply it out.

What the hell. It's something to do.

I finished a cigarette, then got up and put another one in my mouth. I set it on fire and dragged hard on it. I took the smoke way down deep in my lungs and held onto it. Then I let it out, slowly, in a single thin column that held together for a long while. You can get slightly dizzy that way, but the dizziness can make you feel more confident. I felt very confident.

I walked over to the elevator. The op was reading the morning paper. He was studying the morning line. It is a hell of a thing when you live in Nevada and still have to play the horses. I shook my head sadly and he looked up at me.

'Eight,' I said.

He didn't say anything. He piloted the car to the eighth floor and I got out. The door closed and he sailed down to the main floor again to study the racing form. I hoped he would lose every race. I felt very mean.

I walked one way, came to a room number, and found out that I was headed the wrong way. I turned around and worked my way to 804. There was a *Do Not Disturb* sign on it which somehow seemed very funny. I thought that it would be fun to knock so that they could tell me to go away.

I didn't.

Instead I finished the cigarette. I walked all the way back to the elevator to dunk it in an urn filled with sand instead of grinding it into the thick carpet. Then I walked all the way back and stood in front of the door some more.

A sliver of light came through the door at the bottom. Not much. As if one little lamp were turned on.

Which meant the stage was set.

I took the key out of my pocket. I stuck it into the lock. It went in soundlessly and turned soundlessly. I said a silent prayer of thanks to the mercenary bell captain. A penknife is effective, but it is not subtle. I felt very much like being subtle.

It was a very nice hotel. The door did not even squeak. I opened it all the way and there they were.

The main light was off but they had left the closet light on, which was very coy of them. It let me see without squinting. There was quite a bit to see.

She was on the bed. Her head was back on the pillow and her eyes were closed. Her legs were bent and parted.

He was between them. He was earning his keep and working very hard at it. He seemed to be enjoying it. So did she. But there was no way of telling with either of them.

I stepped inside, very thankful that Keith's shoes didn't squeak. I turned and closed the door. They did not hear me or notice me in any way.

They were too busy.

For several very long seconds I watched them. Once, long ago, when I had been too young to know what it was all about, I happened to watch my mother and father making love. I didn't really know what they were doing. But I knew what Mona and her friend were doing and there was something almost hypnotic about the performance. Maybe it was the rhythm. I'm not sure.

Then it was time. I really wanted to come on with something extremely clever but my brain refused to supply anything really appropriate. It was a shame. You don't get too many opportunities like that one.

But nothing clever came to mind. And I didn't have all night. So what I said, finally, was about as trite as you can get. Concise and to the point, but not very original.

I said: 'Hello, Mona.'

13

They didn't even finish what they were doing. They stopped at once. He rolled away from her and came up on the balls of his feet while she lay there trying to cover herself with her hands. A silly gesture.

He could have dressed, tied his shoes, and walked right past me. I had no quarrel with him. I wasn't ready to run around proclaiming my undying love for him, but I wasn't ready to kick his face in, either. He was out of his element. A bedroom bouncing-bee had turned into more than that and it was time for him to pick up his pants and go home.

That wasn't his style. He could read it only one way – I had intruded on his privacy, interrupted his sport, made him look foolish. That was the only diagnosis those beautiful blue eyes could report to that muscle-bound brain, and there was only one way that body could react to that sort of information.

He rushed me.

He must have played football once. He came with his head way down and his arms outstretched. Anybody looks silly enough like that but he looked sillier. He was nude, and *all* men look ridiculous nude. But there was something else. He rushed me, and I stared at the top of his head, and I saw that every last strand of hair remained magically in place.

I kicked him in the face.

He did a little back-flip and wound up sitting on his can. The point of the shoe had come into pleasant contact with his jaw and he was dizzy – unhurt, unmarked, but dizzy.

He tried to get up.

The funny thing is that I still wasn't mad at him at all. But I knew that I had to show him just where he stood in the overall scheme of things. I did not want him in my hair. I had more important things on my mind than the stupid son-of-a-bitch.

I did not bother playing fair. That would have been stupid. I waited until he got halfway up and then I kicked his face in again. It was a better kick this time. It split his lip and took out a tooth. He wouldn't be pretty for the next month or so.

He wouldn't be able to earn a living, either. Because I put the next kick between his legs. He made a little-girl sound way in the back of his throat that turned into a strangled moan before he was done with it.

Then he blacked out.

I turned to Mona. She was all wrapped up in a robe now. I could tell that she was frightened but she managed to hide most of the fear. I had to give her credit.

I waited her out. Finally she tried a smile, gave it up, and sighed. 'I'm supposed to say something,' she said. 'I suppose. But where do I start?'

I lighted a cigarette.

'I would have come to Miami,' she said. 'Except I was afraid if we made contact too quickly—'

'Shut up.'

She looked as though she had been slapped.

'You don't have to talk,' I said. 'I'll talk. But first we get rid of your friend.'

'He wasn't my friend.'

'You looked pretty friendly there for a few seconds.'

She swallowed. 'He wasn't like you, Joe. Nobody was. You were always the best. You—'

'Save it,' I said. I was annoyed at her for trying that. She should have been able to do better. 'We're getting rid of your friend,' I said again. 'Then we talk.'

I walked over to the phone, picked it up and asked for the bell captain. He was there in no time.

'Upstairs,' I said, 'in eight-oh-four. A little job I'd like you to do for me. A favor.'

'This is the jealous lover?'

'The same.'

'Still feeling generous?'

'Very. Still greedy?'

A low chuckle. 'Be right up,' he said, and rang off.

I checked Hair-and-Shoulders. He was still out. 'Dress him,' I told her. 'In a hurry. Get his clothes on. You don't have to make him look beautiful but get him dressed.'

She went to work.

'The bell captain'll be here in a minute,' I went on. 'Don't get cute. You won't be able to carry it off. I'll take us both to the chair if I have to.'

'You wouldn't.'

'You sure of that?'

No answer. She went on dressing him and I waited for the bell captain. A few minutes later there was a knock on the door, quite discreet, and I let him in.

I gave him another hundred. 'Our friend had an accident,' I said. 'Too much to drink. Then he fell down and hurt himself. Somebody ought to take him home.'

He looked at Shoulders, then at me. 'A lovely accident,' he said. 'It couldn't happen to a more deserving fellow. Not stiff, is he?'

I shook my head. 'But tired,' I said. 'I'm tired, too. I'd carry him back to his apartment but I really need my sleep. I thought maybe you'd take care of him for me.'

He smiled.

'One more thing,' I said. 'The lady and I would like a certain amount of privacy. For quite awhile. No phone calls, no knocks at the door. Can you take care of that?'

He looked at Mona, then back at me. 'A cinch.'

I waited there while he picked up Shoulders. He draped him over his own shoulder and smiled sadly at me. Then he carried him out of the room like a sack of wet laundry and I closed the door after him and slid the bolt home.

She turned to look at me. This time her eyes were very wide with the fear showing through them. Breathing wasn't easy for her.

'Are you going to kill me, Joe?'

I shook my head.

'Then what do you want? Money? You can have half of it, Joe. There's so much. More than I need, more than you need. You can have half. Is that fair enough? I'll give you half, I was going to give you half anyway, and—'

'Don't lie to me.'

'It's the truth, Joe. I—'

'Don't lie.'

She stopped talking and looked at me. Her eyes were hurt. She was telling me with her eyes that I shouldn't call her a liar, it wasn't nice. I should be nice to a pretty girl like her.

'No lies,' I said. 'We're going to play a brand new game. It's called *To Tell the Truth*. Like on television.'

She looked very nervous. I lighted a cigarette and handed it to her. She needed it.

'You were damned good,' I told her. 'You were so good that you didn't even have to cover all the loopholes. You let me see the holes in your story and I wrote them off as coincidences. That was very good.'

I remembered the Hitchcock movie I saw in Cleveland. You can get away with coincidences if your direction is tight enough. And Mona was a fine director.

'Let's start at the beginning,' I said. 'Keith was supposed to be a heroin importer. That was his business. And you weren't supposed to know a thing about it. That should have sounded fishy right at the beginning. How in the hell would he run a game like that without you knowing? And why would he take you along to Atlantic City while he was working a deal? He wasn't on vacation – he was hauling a load for Max Treger and you knew the score right from the start. That was a cute bit.'

She looked unhappy.

'Here's the way I figure it,' I went on. 'You were at the station. You saw me pick up Keith's bags. He didn't, but you did. You could have stopped me right then and there but that was too easy. Your mind was starting to buzz, wheels were turning. There might be an angle in it for you. So you didn't say a word.

'So I picked up the luggage, and then you picked me up. You took your time, maybe, but you sure as hell didn't sit on your hands. You found me on the beach, made a date with me, and met me on the beach that night. And you let me figure out who you were by inches. L. Keith Brassard's pretty little wife. You let me take two and two and put them together until they came up five.'

'I liked you.'

'You were nuts about me. You were right on hand the next morning with the chambermaid routine. You knew I had the heroin but that was all you knew. Somewhere there had to be something for you. You were sniffing around. Hell, even the way you woke me up was beautiful. You shook me and blabbered about finding Keith's bags in my closet. It was lovely. You didn't even have to fake being confused. You were confused, all right. You couldn't find the horse and that confused the daylights out of you.'

I stopped and shook my head. Saying it aloud was somehow different from running it through my mind. Everything fit perfectly into place and there was no room left for doubt. It all added up with nothing out of place.

'If the horse had been there you probably would have disappeared with it. God knows what you would have done with it – maybe tried to swing a deal on your own, maybe tried to sell it back to Keith or something. God knows. But you saw that you couldn't get it back. And your mind went on working. Maybe you could use me, get me to kill Keith for you. That was a good idea, wasn't it?

'And you played it perfectly, made me suggest it, let me act as though it was my idea from the beginning. You were tired of him. He was beginning to get in the way and you wanted out. But you wanted the money and maybe I could get it for you. You were cool about it, Mona. You were perfect.'

'It wasn't like that, Joe—'

'The hell it wasn't. It was that simple. So simple it never occurred to me. You faked everything beautifully. Even the bed part. You pretended to fall in love with me. You acted so perfectly I fell on my face.'

Her face was funny. Very sad, mournful. I looked into her eyes and tried to probe. They were opaque.

So I let go of it. I sat there and looked at her and she looked back at me. I smoked another cigarette. When she talked, finally, her voice was just a little bit more than a whisper. There was no pretense left. I knew that she would tell me the truth now because there was no longer any reason for her to lie. I knew, I understood. And, as a result, I could no longer be lied to. The lies would only bounce at her.

She said: 'There's more, Joe.'

'There is?'

A slow nod.

'Then tell me about it. I'm a good listener.'

'You'd like to believe it was just the money,' she said. 'It wasn't. Oh, in the beginning the money was most of it. I'll admit that. But then ... then we were together and it was ... more ... than just the money. It was us, too. I thought about what it would be like, you and me together, and I thought about it and—'

She broke off. The room was noisy with silence. I drew on my cigarette.

'And somewhere along the line it turned into just the money again. Because you didn't need me any more.'

'Maybe.'

'What else?'

She thought it over for a moment or two before answering. 'Because you killed him,' she said.

'Huh?'

'You killed him,' she repeated. 'Oh, we were both guilty. Legally, that is. I know all that. But ... inside, when I thought about it, you were the one who killed him. And if I went to you I killed him, too. But if I was alone by myself it didn't work out that way. I could pretend he just ... died. That somebody killed him but that I myself had nothing to do with it.'

'Did it work?'

She sighed. 'Maybe. I don't know. It was starting to work. Then I thought about you and I knew you were waiting for me in Miami and wondering what was wrong. And I thought that you had to get something for ... what you did. That's when I sent you the money. The three thousand dollars.'

'I didn't know you had a conscience.'

She managed a smile. 'I'm not that bad.'

'No?'

'Not that bad. Bad, but not rotten. Not really.'

She was right. And I realized, somehow, that I had known this all along. A strange sensation.

'What now, Joe?'

Her words shattered silence. I knew what was coming next but it didn't seem right to tell her. I wanted to stretch the moment out for half of eternity. I didn't want *what now* to come up just yet. Neither of us was ready for it.

'Joe?'

I didn't answer.

'You said you weren't going to kill me. Did you change your mind, Joe?'

I told her I wasn't going to kill her.

'Then what do you want?'

I put out my cigarette. I took a breath. The air in the room was very thick, or seemed to be. Breathing was difficult.

'To marry me?'

I nodded.

'You want to marry me,' she said. Her voice had a light, almost airy quality to it. She was talking as much to herself as to me, testing the words. 'Well, all right. I . . . it's not very romantic. But if that's what you want, it's all right with me. I won't argue.'

I heard her words and listened past them. I tried once more for a picture of marital bliss and once more it wouldn't come into focus. The only image I got was the one I'd visualized earlier. It wouldn't work the way she wanted it.

I wished to heaven it would. But it wouldn't, not without my little solution. My method was the only way, much as I was beginning to dislike it.

So I sat next to her, close to her, and I smiled gently at her. She returned the smile, hesitantly. Her world was beginning to return to focus now. There we were, smiling at each other, and pretty soon everything was going to be all right. A slight change in plans, of course, but nothing drastic.

I said: 'I'm sorry, Mona.'

Then I hit her. I got the right spot, just over the bridge of the nose, and I did not hit too hard. A hard blow there breaks off parts of the frontal bone and sends it into the brain. But I was gentle. All I did was knock her out – she lost consciousness at once and fell very limp into my arms.

When she came to a few minutes later there was a gag in her mouth. Strips of bedsheet tied her feet together and other strips held her hands behind her back.

She stared at me and the expression on her face was one of sheer and unadulterated terror.

'Someday you'll adjust to this,' I told her. 'Someday you'll understand. I don't expect you to understand now. But you will, in time.'

I took the two packages from my jacket pocket. The paper sack, tightly rolled, and the neat leather kit. I unrolled the paper sack and took out one of the little black capsules. I opened the leather kit and let her see what was inside.

She gasped.

'Funny,' I said. 'The way we always come back to this. Keith sold it, I bought it. You know the funniest part of it? I had to pay good money for this stuff. I threw away a boxful of it to frame Keith, left a fortune's worth to make things look groovy for the New York cops. And here we are again. Full circle.'

I took the small spoon from the leather kit. It was the kind of spoon you stir your coffee with in a café espresso in Greenwich Village. I settled the capsule on the spoon, then got out my cigarette lighter and flicked it. I held the spoon over the flame and watched the heroin melt. My hand was surprisingly steady.

I looked at Mona. Her eyes on the flame from the lighter were the eyes of a cat in front of a fire. Hot ice.

'You're just too independent,' I said. 'You live inside yourself. And when people take too much from you, too much *of* you, you run away and hide. That's no good.'

She didn't answer, of course. Hell, there was a gag in her mouth. But I wondered what she was thinking.

'So you're going to be a little less independent. You're going to have something to depend on.'

I picked up the hypodermic needle. I pushed the plunger all the way in, stuck the tip of the needle into the melted heroin on the spoon. When I let the plunger out again the needle filled with liquid heroin.

The needle looked very large. Very dangerous. Mona's eyes were round and I could hear the wheels turning in her head. She didn't want to believe it but she had to.

'Don't be frightened,' I said, stupidly. 'It isn't that bad, not when you have money. You take so many shots a day and you function almost as well as a normal person. You know what group has the largest percentage of addicts in the country? Doctors. Because they have access to the stuff. They're morphine addicts, generally, but it's about the same thing. And they get all they need. If you never have withdrawal symptoms it's not so bad. Not as rough on your system as alcohol, for example.'

She didn't even hear me. And I was being cruel, taking too much time to do what I had to do. I stopped talking.

I found a good spot in the fleshy part of her thigh. Later I could graduate her to the main line, the big vein that led straight to the heart. But skin-popping was fine for the time being. I didn't want to get her sick from an overdose.

I held up the needle. I stuck it into her and rammed the plunger all the way in. She tried to scream when it hit but the gag was in her way and the only sound that came out was a small snort through her nose.

Then the heroin hit and she went off to Dreamland.

14

It took her an hour to come out of it. She was still slightly drugged so I took the gag off. There wasn't much chance of her giving out with a yell. I asked her how she felt.

'All right,' she said. 'I suppose.'

We talked for a few minutes about very little. I put the gag back on and went downstairs. There was a newstand in the lobby and I picked up a few paperback books. I went back to the room and sat around reading until it was time for her next shot.

She didn't fight the second quite as much as the first.

That set the pattern. We stayed there for three days, with me going down intermittently for food. Every four or five hours she got her shot. The rest of the time we stayed in the room. Once or twice I untied her completely and we made love, but it was not very good at all. It would get better.

'I'm sick of Tahoe,' I told her one morning. 'I want a few grand. I'll buy a car and we'll go to Vegas.'

'Use your own money.'

'I haven't got enough.'

'Then go to hell.'

I could have hit her, or threatened her, or merely ordered her to give me the money. But this was as good a time as any for the test. Instead I shrugged and waited.

I waited until her shot was half an hour overdue. Then she called my name.

'What's the matter?'

'I . . . want a shot.'

'That's nice. I want four grand. Where are you keeping it?'

She shrugged as if it didn't matter. But I could see the need beginning to build in her, the nervousness behind those eyes, the tension buried in those muscles. She told me where the money was. I found it, then got out the kit and cooked her up another fix. This time she was visibly grateful when the heroin took hold. It was a mainline shot this time and it reached her faster than the others.

I paid cash for the car, a nice new Buick with a lot under the hood and so much chrome outside that it looked like a twenty-fifth-century cathouse on wheels. I loaded her into the car and we drove back to Vegas. She was very docile on the trip. We got to Vegas, reclaimed my room at the Dunes, and it was time for her shot.

I do not know how long it takes to turn a person into an addict. I do not know how long it took with Mona. Addiction is a gradual process. I merely pushed the process along, let the addiction pile up. She became a little more nearly hooked with every passing shot. Hooked physically and emotionally. It's a double-barreled thing.

'I'm leaving,' she said.

I looked at her. It was two in the afternoon, a Friday afternoon. We were still at the Dunes. Two hours ago she had had a shot. In two hours she'd be due for another.

She was wearing a red jersey dress with a simple string of pearls around her neck. Her shoes were black suede with high heels. And she was telling me that she was leaving.

I asked her what she meant.

'Leaving,' she said. 'Leaving you. Walking out, Joe. You don't tie me up any more. It's very sweet of you. So I'm walking out on you.'

'And not coming back?'

'And not coming back.'

'You're hooked,' I told her. 'You're a junkie. Try walking out and you'll wind up crawling back. Who do you think you're kidding?'

'I'm not hooked.'

'You really believe that?'

'I know it.'

'Then I know who you're kidding,' I said. 'You're kidding yourself. So long.'

She left. And I waited for her to come back, waited past the time when the shot was due.

And she came back.

She did not look like the same girl. Her face was a dead fishbelly white and her hands couldn't stay still. She was twitching uncontrollably. She hurried into the room and threw herself into a chair.

'You walked out,' I said. 'Don't tell me you're back already. That's a pretty quick trip.'

'Please,' she said. Just that – please.

'Something wrong?'

'I need it,' she said. 'I need it, damn you. You're right, I was wrong. Now give me a shot.'

I laughed at her. Not out of cruelty, not because I was pleased. I laughed at her so that she would get the full picture. She had to know, inside and out, that she was hooked. The sooner she knew it, the more deeply the addiction would ran.

I watched her twitch with pain and sheer need. I listened to her beg for the shot and I pretended not to hear her. I watched her scramble around on her hands and knees looking for the hypo. I'd hidden it. She couldn't find it.

Then she stood up and tore that fine red dress all the way down. She removed her bra, her underclothing. She cupped her breasts in her hands and offered them to me.

'Anything,' she said. 'Anything—'

I brought out the needle and fixed her. I watched the pain drain from her features and I stroked her body until she stopped shivering. Then I held her very gently in my arms while she cried.

After that it was all downhill. I didn't even have to threaten her in order to get her to agree. Whatever I said, went. It was that simple.

A justice of the peace married us in Vegas. He asked us the time-honored questions. I said I did and she said she did, and he pronounced us man and wife. We moved out of the Dunes and into three rooms and a kitchen on the North side of town. She transferred her money to a Vegas bank and opened an account with a Vegas broker.

And I built up a close relationship with the big man who hangs out in the café and drinks cold coffee. Every five days he sells me one hundred dollars' worth of capsules. Every four hours Mona takes a shot. Six capsules a day. A thirty-pound monkey, in junkie argot. A twenty-pound monkey for us, because I get wholesale prices. The quantity buyer always has the edge, even when the commodity is an illegal one.

As if it made a difference. As if ten dollars a day or twenty or thirty or forty dollars a day could have the slightest effect on us. My wife has an alarming amount of money. And it looks as though it's going to last forever, too, because the broker took good care of us. He put part of the dough in bonds, part in common stocks, the rest in high-yield real estate. We can live big on income and never look at the principal. There is a point where you stop counting money; it is wealth then, not just money. Ten dollars, twenty dollars, thirty dollars – it couldn't matter less.

The habit doesn't bite. Mona is not one of the junkies I see from time to time in the café, hollow-eyed and shivering, haggling with the big man. For a drug addict, Mona is sitting pretty.

But there are times when I look at her, at this very beautiful and very wealthy woman who happens to be my wife and who also happens to be an addict. I look at her and I remember the woman she used to be, the free and independent one. I remember the first night on the beach, and I remember other nights and other places, and I know that something is gone forever. She is not so much alive now. The face is the same and the body is the same but something has changed. The eyes, maybe. Or the deep darkness behind them.

The bird in your cage is not the same bird as the wild thing you caught in the forest. There is a difference.

So many things could happen. Some fine day the big man could disappear forever from the café. She'd be a deep-sea diver with her air-hose cut, and we'd burrow through Vegas turning over flat stones to find a connection, and I would have the rare privilege of watching Mona die inside. By inches.

Or a raid, and cold turkey behind bars, banging her head against the walls and screaming sandpaper curses at the guards. Or an overdose because some idiot somewhere in the long powdery chain forgot to cut the heroin when it was his turn. An overdose, with her veins blue and her eyes bulging and death there before she gets the needle out of her arm.

So many things—

I think she's happy now. Once she got used to being addicted – how do you get used to addiction? A good question – once she got used to it, she began to enjoy it. Strange but true. When you have an itch you enjoy scratching it. Now she looks forward to her shots, takes pleasure in them. A certain amount of reality is lost, of course. But she seems to think that what she gets in its place more than compensates for reality. She may be right. The real world is often vastly overrated.

Strange.

'You should try it,' she'll say now and then. 'I wish I could tell you what it's like. It's really something. Like a bomb going off, you dig?'

She retreats into hip talk when she gets high.

'You should make it, Joe. Just one little joy-bomb to get you moving. So you can see what it's like.'

A strange life in a strange world.

A funny thing happened yesterday.

I was giving her her four P.M. fix. I cooked the heroin, sucked it up in the hypo, picked up her leg and hunted around for the vein. She was just at the point where she needed the shot and in another five or ten minutes she would have started to shake. I found the vein and fixed her and watched the graceful smile spread on her face before she went under.

Then I was washing the spoon, getting ready to put the kit away. Some junkies don't take good care of their equipment. They die of infection that way. I'm always careful.

I was washing the spoon, as I said, and then I was putting it away. I stopped – maybe I should say I slowed down – and then I was picking up another little capsule filled with funny white powder, putting it on the spoon.

I wanted to take a shot myself.

Silly. Her words hadn't done it, her invitations to find out what it was all about. I wasn't a kid looking for kicks.

So naturally I put the cap away. And I put the spoon away and put the syringe away. I locked up the kit and the bag of capsules. Even in Vegas you never know when some cop is going to decide his arrest quota is off for the month. I never leave things lying around.

I put everything away.

For the time being.

And I've been thinking about it ever since. I have a damned good idea what is going to happen. It may be the next time I give her a shot, or a week from then, or a month. She'll slip away from me, with the same grateful smile fading slowly on the same sad and lovely face, and I will begin to wash the works.

Then I'll take a shot of my own.

Not for kicks or thrills or joy. Not for pleasure or escape, not as a reward and not as penance. Not because I crave the life of a junkie. I don't.

Something else. To share with her, maybe. Or maybe the nagging knowledge that every time the heroin takes hold of her she slips that much further away from me. Something like that, I don't know. But one of these days or weeks or months I'll take that shot for myself.

I think we're going to be very something together. Whatever it is, at least it will be together. And that's what I wanted, isn't it?

You Could
Call It Murder

This is for Amy Jo, who was born yesterday.

1

It started at the Tafts, at dinner. All through the meal I had the distinct impression that something more than food was in the offing. The food itself was certainly excellent enough – a fine rare rib roast flanked with roasted potatoes, an excellent red Bordeaux to complement the roast, broccoli au gratin, chef salad with roquefort dressing, all followed up by berry pie, rich strong coffee and snifters of Drambuie. When casual acquaintances invite one in for that sort of meal there's little cause for complaint, but I couldn't help thinking that something was a little out of line.

Perhaps it was the conversation – carefully casual, almost elaborately inoffensive. Perhaps it was the air of repressed urgency that permeated the large dining room. Whatever it was, I was not at all surprised when Edgar Taft called me aside.

'Roy,' he said. 'Could I talk to you for a minute or two?'

I followed him through the living room to his study, a heavily masculine room with pine-panelled walls and a hunting motif. We sat down in large brown leather chairs. He offered me a cigar. I passed it up and lit a cigarette.

'There's something I wanted to discuss with you, Roy,' he said. 'I've got a problem. I need your help.'

'I thought the dinner was too much to waste merely for the pleasure of my company—'

'Cut it out,' he said. 'You know I like getting together with you. So does Marianne. But—'

'But you've a problem.'

He nodded. He stood up abruptly, then began to pace the floor of the study, his eyes troubled. He was a large man, with strong features and firm gray eyes. His hair was iron-gray, his shoulders broad. He was a few years past fifty, but good looks and an almost military carriage took years off his appearance.

He wasn't the sort of man you'd expect to have a problem. Or, if he had one, you'd expect him to solve it himself. He had a great deal of money and he'd made it all by himself. He made his first small fortune years ago as a wildcat well-driller in Texas, doubled that speculating in the stock market, and pyramided those profits by buying control of an unknown electronics corporation, speeding up research and making profits hand over fist. Now, officially, he was retired – but I was relatively certain he had his hands in pies here and there. He was too dynamic to put himself out to pasture.

He turned to me suddenly. 'You know my daughter?'

'I met her once,' I said. 'A tall girl, blonde. I don't remember her name.'

'It's Barb. Barbara.'

I nodded. 'It must have been four years ago when I saw her last,' I said. 'She was in that awkward stage between girl and young woman, very careful not to trip over her own feet or say the wrong word. But very pretty.'

'She's older now,' he said grimly. 'But still in that awkward stage. And much more beautiful.'

'And a problem?'

'And a problem.' He ducked the ashes from his cigar, then turned again to face me. 'To hell with it, Roy. I might as well come right out and say it. She's missing.'

'Missing?'

He nodded. 'A missing person,' he said. 'Whatever that means, exactly. A week ago I got a letter from some old bitch who's the dean of women up at Radbourne. That's a little college in New Hampshire, the place where Barb was going. Letter said Barb had been missing from school for a few days. They wanted to check, find out if she was home, let us know she wasn't there.'

'But she wasn't here?'

'Of course not. I got worried as hell, thought somebody might have snatched her, thought she could have gotten smacked by a car or God knows what. I made a few phone calls to the college and had them check things out. She cashed three big checks the day before she took off, cleaned out her checking account. From there it wasn't too hard to figure.'

'I see,' I said. 'You assume she left on her own?'

'Sure. Hell, she must have. Cleared out with her money and a suitcase full of her clothes. Those checks added up to a little over a thousand dollars, Roy. Not enough to retire on, maybe. But enough to go about as far as she would want to go. You can go around the world on a thousand bucks.'

I put out my cigarette. 'Why would she want to go?'

'Damned if I know. Hell, maybe she had reasons. She wasn't doing too well in school, according to what they told me. Barb was always a smart kid but she's never been much of a student. She was failing a course or two and not breaking any records in the others. Or it might be some guy – some sharp little bastard who figures on marrying her and cutting himself in on my money. That's why I've been sitting on my hands, figuring I'd hear from her, get a call or a wire saying she's married.'

'But that hasn't happened.'

He shook his head.

'How old is she, Edgar?'

'Twenty. Twenty-one in March'

'That makes marriage less likely,' I told him. 'It's December now. You'd think she'd wait until she's twenty-one to marry without consent, especially with only three month to wait.'

'I thought of that. But she's impulsive. Hard to figure.'

I nodded briefly. 'Is the school investigating?'

'Not their job. They checked around town but that's all.'

'And you haven't called the police?'

'No.'

'Why not?'

He looked at me. 'A batch of reasons,' he said. 'First off, what cops do I call? Radbourne's in some town called Cliff End. I think it's a ghost town when the college closes shop for the summer. They've got a three-man Mickey Mouse police force straight out of the Keystone Cops. They can't do a hell of a lot. Neither can the New York cops – she isn't here in New York, or if she is there's no way to know about it. The FBI? Hell, it's not a kidnapping. Or if it is, it's a hell of a funny one.'

He was right.

'That's not all,' he went on. 'I'm rich, Roy. Every time I spit one of the tabloids finds room for it. I don't want this in the papers. Maybe it's perfectly innocent, maybe Barb just took off for a week or so and nothing's wrong. But as soon as I yell for the police, Barb's got herself an ugly reputation for a long time. I don't want that.'

He paused. 'That's why I called you,' he said. 'I'm scared to pick out an ordinary private detective. I've used plenty of them in my business and I know which ones you can trust. Even the big agencies have operatives who talk too damned much. And you never know when one of their boys is going to hit a situation with blackmail potential and open up shop for himself. I need a friend, somebody I can trust all the way.'

'And you want me to find her?'

'That's it.'

I thought about it. It's no easy matter to turn up a missing person, harder still when that person could be almost any place in the country, not to say the world. The needle in the haystack analogy had never fit more perfectly.

'I don't know what I can accomplish, Edgar. But I'll be glad to do what I can.'

'That's all I want,' he said. He sat down at his desk and opened a drawer, took out a checkbook. He uncapped a pen, filled out a check in a hurry, tore it from the book and handed it to me. 'This is a retainer, Roy. Any time you want more dough, all you have to do is ask for it. I don't care what this costs me. The money doesn't make a hell of a difference. I just want to have Barb back, to know that nothing's wrong with her.'

I took the check, glanced at it. It was made payable to Roy Markham in the amount of ten thousand dollars. It was signed Edgar Taft. I folded it twice and gave it a temporary home in my billfold.

'That enough?'

'More than enough,' I said honestly. 'I—'

'You need more, just yell. Don't worry how high your expenses go. I'm not going to worry about them. Just do what you can.'

'I'll need information.'

'I'll give you what I can, Roy.'

'Pictures would help,' I said. 'For a starter. It's been awhile since I saw Barbara.'

He was nodding. He opened the same desk drawer again and took out a plain white envelope. He passed it to me. 'These are the recent ones,' he said. 'All within the past two or three years. She doesn't take a good picture but they're not too bad.'

I opened the envelope, took out a handful of snapshots. The girl in the photographs was a prettier one than I remembered. She was becoming a very beautiful woman. Her forehead was broad and intelligent, her mouth full, her hair long and light and lovely.

'These will help,' I said.

'What next?'

The next question was harder. 'How do you get along with her, Edgar? Are you . . . close? Friendly?'

'She's my daughter.'

'I know that. Are you on good terms?'

He frowned, then looked away. 'Not good terms,' he said. 'Not bad terms either. I've spent a lot of time making money, Roy. Almost all my time. It's the only thing I know. I'm not highly educated, don't read books, can't stand high society and fancy parties. I'm a businessman and it's all I know. I suppose I should have learned to be a family man somewhere along the line. I didn't.'

I waited.

'I never spent much time with Barb. God knows she had everything she ever wanted – clothes, money, a trip to Europe last year, expensive schooling, the works. But not too much closeness, damn it. And it shows.'

'How?'

'We don't get along,' he said. 'Oh, we don't throw rocks at each other or anything. But we don't get along. She thinks I'm a dull old man who pays the bills. Period. She's a hell of a lot closer with Marianne than with me. But she doesn't take Marianne into her confidence either. She keeps a lot to herself.'

He paused. 'Maybe that's why I don't have any idea where she is now. Or what she's up to. Maybe that's why I'm a lot more scared about this business than I should be. Hell, I don't know. She's a funny kid, Roy.'

'Has she ever been in trouble?'

'Not . . . not really.'

'What does that mean?'

He thought it over. 'It means what I said,' he said finally. 'She's never been in any real trouble. But she travels with a pretty fast crowd, Roy. A bunch of kids like her, kids with more money than they should have. You know, when I was a kid my old man had a pot and a window and that was all. A pot to crap in and a window to throw it out of. That's supposed to turn a kid into a criminal, right?'

'Sometimes.'

'With me it worked the other way. I looked around and I told myself that, dammit to hell, I was going to have better than this for myself. I never got through high school. I dropped out and took a job working twelve hours a day six days a week. I banked my money so I'd something to work with, some capital to play around with. Then I looked for the right long shots and backed them all the way. I started with nothing and I came out of it with a pile.'

'And it's the other way with Barbara?'

'Maybe. Hell, I don't know exactly what I'm trying to say. Her crowd has too much dough. She gets a big allowance and spends every penny of it, wouldn't dream of saving a nickel. She knows there's more waiting for her. She drives her car too damn fast. She goes out with guys who drink too damn much. She stays out too late. Maybe she sleeps around. They say all college girls sleep around. You know anything about it?'

'They're too young for me.'

He didn't smile. 'Sometimes I worry,' he said. 'Maybe I don't worry enough. I can't talk to her about it, can't talk to her about a damn thing. Whenever I try talking to her she goes off the handle and we have a little fireworks. We yell at each other for awhile. Oh, to hell with it. I want you to find Barb, Roy. I want you to bring her back here. That's all I can say.'

I asked several more questions but his answers weren't of much help. He didn't know the names of any of her friends at Radbourne, didn't know of any man or boy she had been seeing on a steady basis. I suggested that his wife might be able to help.

'Uh-uh,' he said. 'I've been over this with Marianne a dozen times already. I know everything she knows.'

'That's not too much.'

'I know it,' he said. 'Hell, I know it. Will you do what you can?'

'Of course.'

We shook hands on it, more or less to seal the bargain that had already been made the moment I took his check. The interview was over. He led me out of his study into the living room. Marianne was waiting for us.

She was a sweet, frail woman with quiet gray hair and trusting puppy-eyes. She was the sort of person whom no one swore in front of. I had always had the impression that she was much stronger inside than anyone suspected.

'Roy's going to help us,' Taft said.

Marianne smiled. 'I'm glad,' she said softly. 'You'll find Barb, won't you, Roy?'

I said I would try.

'Of course you'll find her,' she said, blandly dismissing the possibility of failure. 'I'm so glad you'll be helping us. Call us as soon as you find Barb, won't you?'

I told her I would. I thanked her for dinner and told her very truthfully that it had been a marvellous meal. Then Edgar Taft walked me out of the house and down the long sloping driveway. His car was parked in front.

'No car,' he said. 'How come? You don't like to drive in New York?'

'I had a car for awhile,' I told him. 'I got rid of it.'

He looked at me. 'It would be in New York and I would be in San Francisco,' I explained. 'Or it would be in San Francisco and I would be in London. It never quite managed to catch up with me. So I decided I would get along without it.'

'You still do that much travelling?'

I nodded. 'I like to keep on the move,' I said. 'I still maintain my brownstone in the east sixties but I'm hardly ever there. Right now I'm staying at the Commodore.'

'I called your office—'

'You called my answering service,' I said. 'My office is my suitcase. I've only been in New York a week. And I guess I won't be here much longer.'

'Well,' he said. 'Hop in. I'll run you down to the station.'

The Taft home was in Bedford Hills, a wealthy estate section in upper Westchester County. The house was a huge Dutch colonial with a view of the Hudson. Ancient trees shaded the rolling lawn. I got into the front seat of his Lincoln and we drove off.

We talked about odds and ends for part of the trip. Then, as we were nearing the railroad station, he asked me where I was going to start.

'There only seems to be one place,' I said. 'I'll have to begin at the college. Radbourne. What did you say the name of the town was?'

'Cliff's End. Cliff's End, New Hampshire.'

It sounded desolate enough. I asked him if any trains went there. He said he didn't know, that Barbara always drove up. She had a red MG sports roadster. The license number was written on the back of one of the snapshots he had given me.

'Keep in touch with me,' he said at the station. 'Call me collect once a day. After dinner's the best time to catch me. Hell, Barb might turn up any minute. I wouldn't want you wasting your time.'

'I'll call you.'

'Fine,' he said. 'Do your best, Roy.' He checked his watch. 'The next New York train should be through in fifteen minutes or so. Luck.'

I shook hands with him. His grip was firm. Then I walked to the railway platform and looked back, watching the Lincoln drive off. I lighted a cigarette and waited for the train to come.

The platform was empty of others. I stood smoking and thought about Edgar Taft and his errant daughter. Something refused to jibe, something was inconsistent. I couldn't pin it down offhand – I could only realize for certain that things were not entirely as they seemed to be.

Which, in American terminology, was the way the ball bounced, the way the tootsie rolled. *Sic friat crustulum*, as they might put it in Rome. Thus crumbles the cookie.

The train came and I boarded it. It was a rolling antique but its seats were comfortable. I sat in one of them, took a paperbound book from my back pocket, and read some verses of Catullus until the poor old train managed to haul itself into Grand Central.

I closed the book, left the train. I walked upstairs and into the Commodore lobby, then took an elevator to the fourteenth floor. It would have been the thirteenth floor, but for a rather bizarre American custom of eliminating that floor from the overall scheme of things.

The bellhop brought me a pint of scotch and a bottle of white soda. I put some of each into a glass and worked on the mixture, with a half dozen pictures of Barbara Taft spread out in front of me. I looked at the pictures and tried to figure out a way to find the girl.

It would not be easy.

She had a car and she had a sizeable bankroll, and with either of the two she could put a great distance between herself and the town of Cliff's End. I wondered if she was simply taking a week or two off. Edgar Taft had said she was a girl who ran with a wild crowd; if that were so, it didn't seem unlikely that she might decide to run off from school on a lark.

And, if that were so, why was he so worried?

There were more questions than there were answers. I took a hot bath and let muscles loosen up and tension float away. I dried off, combined a little more scotch with a little more soda, and got into bed. The bellhop had also brought ice cubes, for no good reason. I prefer the British custom of taking liquor at room temperature, a source of never-ending amusement to Americans. Ice kills the taste.

It had been a long day. I put the snapshots of Barbara Taft in my wallet, took out Edgar's check, looked at it reverently. I endorsed it over to my bank, stuck it in a bank-by-mail envelope, and dropped it in the mail chute in the hall. Then I went back to my room and finished my drink and got into bed.

Sleep came quickly.

2

Cliff's End is an elusive destination. First you ride the New York Central to Boston. You wait there for an hour or so, then change to a railroad called, strangely, the Massachusetts Northern. This leaves you in a hamlet known as Byington, New Hampshire. There, after a wait of another pair of hours, you board a bus which eventually drops you in Cliff's End.

I did this. The ride – or rides, really – was at least as bad as it sounds. Perhaps worse. It was late afternoon when I left the bus in Cliff's End, deposited without ceremony at the main intersection of the town in knee-deep snow. I lit a cigarette and started looking for the college.

It wasn't difficult to find, since there wasn't much more to the town. Girls with pony tails and boys with crew cuts hurried in all directions. Boys threw snowballs at girls. Girls ducked and giggled, or giggled and ducked. I asked one where the Administration Building was. She pointed vaguely to my left. It was a tactical error, because a callow youth promptly beaned her with a snowball. She giggled anyway.

I left her giggling and found the Administration Building more or less on my own. It was a large brick Gothic affair with huge and apparently pointless towers rising at either end into the blue sky. I went inside and had someone show me where the dean of women had her office. Her name, it turned out, was Helen MacIlhenny. I introduced myself and she beamed at me.

'Sit down, Mr Markham,' she said. 'Mr Taft called me this morning. He said you'd be up sometime today and asked me to help you as much as possible. I'll be glad to.'

She was nearly sixty and still growing old gracefully. Her black hair was only slightly salted with gray and her eyes were chunks of flint in a taut, keen face. She had a wedding ring on her ring finger and a fragile gold brooch on the front of her suit jacket. She smiled nicely.

'Now I'm not too sure what help I can give you,' she said. 'I told Mr Taft as much as I knew. I don't know that much, Mr Markham. Barbara simply disappeared. One day she was here and the next day she was not.'

'When was she last seen?'

'Let me see . . . today is Thursday, isn't it? Barbara missed all her classes a week ago Tuesday. She attended an eleven o'clock French class Monday morning. No one has seen her since then.'

'Then she could have left any time after noon on Monday?'

'That's right.'

'Was she sharing a room with another girl?'

Helen MacIlhenny nodded. 'The girl's name is Gwen Davison. Her room is in Lockesley Hall – Room 304. I'm sure she'll cooperate to the best of her ability.'

'Was she a close friend of Barbara's?'

'No – that's why she'll cooperate.' The dean's eyes twinkled at me. 'I can't imagine a less likely pair than Barbara and Gwen, Mr Markham. Gwen is the perfect student, in a sense. She's not brilliant, never the shining star, but she does her work thoroughly and has maintained a B-plus average for three years now. Never in trouble, never emotionally upset.'

'And Barbara's not like that?'

'Hardly. Do you know her?'

I shook my head.

'Barbara,' she said, 'is not the perfect student.'

'I gathered as much.'

'Yet in a sense she's a more rewarding individual, Mr Markham. She's a very deep person, a profound person. She's subject to fits of depression that seem almost psychotic in their intensity. She will throw herself into a subject which interests her to the exclusion of all other subjects. She feels things deeply and reacts very dramatically. She falls in and out of love frequently. Is a picture beginning to emerge?'

'I think so.'

She leaned forward and fixed her eyes upon me. 'It's hard for me to find words for this. The girl's dynamic – you have to know her to understand her. She's not an easy girl to handle. But I have the feeling that she's worth the effort, if you follow me. There's a great deal of potential there, a lot of personality. She could turn into a spectacular person.'

I switched the subject. 'Where do you think she is?'

'I have no idea.'

'Do you think she went to get married?'

She pursed her lips and considered it. 'It's possible, Mr Markham. The runaway marriage is always a possibility on any college campus. If it's the case, she's not marrying a Radbourne boy.'

'None missing?'

'None. But she could have married someone else, of course. Someone from another college. Someone from New York.'

'What do you think?'

'I doubt it.'

'Why?'

Her eyes narrowed. 'I didn't tell this to Mr Taft,' she said. 'I didn't want to set him on edge. According to what I've learned so far, Barbara was in some kind of trouble.'

'How do you mean?'

'I wish I knew. She may have been pregnant but I somehow doubt it. A few girls have mentioned that she was acting nervous lately, just before she disappeared. Nervous and withdrawn and tense. Worried about something and not saying what.'

I said, 'Pregnant—'

'It happens in the best of families, Mr Markham. And in the best colleges.'

'But you don't think it happened to Barbara?'

'I don't. Frankly, I don't think it would have worried her that much. That seems odd, doesn't it? But I suspect Barbara would simply have found herself a good abortionist and had an abortion. And would have returned without missing a single class that she didn't want to miss.'

I switched the subject again. 'Was she going with any boys in particular?'

'With several. Lately she was dating a boy named Alan Marsten. I've talked to him and he says he knows nothing about Barbara's disappearance. You might want to talk to him.'

I wrote the name down. 'That's all I can think of,' she said, rising. 'If there are any other questions—'

I told her I couldn't think of any myself.

'I have an appointment, then, which I might as well keep. You have the run of the campus, of course. And if there's anything more, please call me. Will you be staying in Cliff's End overnight?'

'I might be.'

'You'll probably have to,' she told me. 'The last bus passes through in an hour and a half and you'll be here longer than that, won't you?' She didn't wait for an answer. 'Mrs Lipton rents rooms by the day and keeps a nice home. The address is 504 Phillips Street. I understand the rates are reasonable enough. For meals you might try either the school cafeteria or the tavern in town. I recommend the tavern. It's been a pleasure, Mr Markham.'

I followed her out of her office, waited while she locked the door with a small brass key. Together we walked out the front entrance of the big building.

'It must be interesting to be a detective,' she said idly. 'Do you enjoy it?'

'I enjoy it.'

'I suspect it's a little like being a dean,' she said thoughtfully. 'You'll want to see Gwen Davison now, no doubt. Lockesley Hall is that way – the three-story brick building along that path. Yes, that's the one. Good luck, Mr Markham.'

I stood for a moment and stared after her. Her stride was firm and she moved along with surprising speed for a woman her age. Her mind was even faster.

I turned and trudged off through the snow.

I had the wrong mental picture of Gwen Davison. I went to Room 304 of Lockesley Hall expecting to meet up with a round-faced and sexless creature wearing tortoise-shell glasses and a frozen stare. She was not like that at all.

In the first place, she was pretty. Her hair was jet black, curling in little ringlets. Her complexion had sprung full-blown from a soap advertisement and her figure from a bra advertisement. Young breasts strained against the front of a pale blue cashmere sweater. Warm brown eyes measured me and held approval in abeyance for the time being.

I revised my estimate of her. I'd expected a frigid student and she was not that at all. She was, instead, the perfect American coed. She was the girl who played everything by one book or another, who would play sex by the marriage manual and life by Norman Vincent Peale, who would marry a company man and have two-point-seven children.

'I don't know where Barb is,' she said. 'I don't know what happened to her. I bet she deserved it, whatever it is.'

'You don't like her?'

She shrugged. 'I don't like her or dislike her. We had nothing in common but this room.' She gestured around. The room they had in common was nothing to go into ecstasies over. There were four walls and a ceiling and a floor, with the usual amount of dormitory furniture. It did not look like the sort of place somebody would want to live in.

'And she was no bargain to room with,' she went on. 'She was a pill. She would come at five in the morning, turning on lights and banging doors and raising hell. She'd drink too much and heave it up in the sink. She was a real pleasure, believe me.'

'When did you see her last?'

'Monday morning.'

'Not since then?'

'No. Somebody said she went to her eleven o'clock class. I don't know for sure. But she didn't stay here Monday night.'

'Did you report it?'

'Of course not.' She gave me an odd look. 'Listen, I didn't like Barb. I told you, she's a pill. I can live without her. But if she wants to spend a night somewhere that's her business.'

'Has she done that before?'

She let that one pass. 'When I didn't see her for two nights I called the dean. I thought something might have have happened to her. That's all.'

I asked her if she cared if I smoked. She didn't. I lighted a cigarette and blew a cloud of smoke at the ceiling. I tried to concentrate. It didn't work.

I wasn't getting anywhere. I wasn't even getting pointed in the right direction. All I knew was that Barbara wasn't on campus, which was something I managed to guess a long while back. The dean of women liked her but disapproved of her, her roommate neither liked nor approved of her, and I didn't know where in God's good name she was.

A puzzle.

'Did she take her car?'

'Naturally,' Gwen Davison said. 'Anybody with a car like that one would take it along.'

'And her clothes?'

'Just a suitcase full. She left more clothes than I own. Wouldn't you know she's two sizes bigger than I am?'

I looked at the dark-haired girl, glanced at the front of her sweater. I was willing to bet that a certain portion of Barbara's anatomy was not two sizes larger than Gwen's. It was simply a biological impossibility.

'I'd like to look through Barbara's clothes,' I said. 'And her desk and books. If it's all right with you.'

'I don't care,' she said. 'Just leave everything like you find it. That's all.'

She took that as a signal to ignore me. She picked up a book – a sociology textbook – and buried her face in it. I went over to Barbara's desk and started to open drawers and look through papers. It was a waste of time.

There were letters and papers. The letters were all from home, all from Marianne, and they were all bright and cheerful and insipid. The papers were mostly notes of one sort or another, scraps of poetry that Barbara had been working on, random lecture notes. They were arranged in no particular order.

I looked through her dresser, feeling rather like a Peeping Tom as I went through mounds of undergarments. I checked her closet and came up with nothing. I learned a few things, but they all seemed to be things I had already known.

'Gwen—'

She turned to look at me.

'She left in a hurry,' I said. 'She threw a few articles of clothing into a suitcase and hurried off. And that's puzzling. Dean MacIlhenny said that Barbara has been nervous lately. I'd expect that she would have been planning to leave, would have taken the time to pack everything. But she left almost all her clothing behind. It's as though she ran off on an impulse.'

'She's an impulsive girl.'

'What do you think happened?'

She thought it over. 'I think something was worrying her. She gets depressed every once in a while and sits around the room moping. She was doing that. And she got a little hysterical, if you know what I mean. You know – laughing very shrill and short over nothing at all, pacing the floor like a caged lion. It was getting tough to live with her.'

'And you think she just left on the spur of the moment?'

'I told you before,' she said. 'I don't know what she did and I don't care. But if I had to guess, that's what I would say. I think she grabbed a suitcase and hopped in that hot little car of hers and took off for awhile. Then she got involved in something and forgot to come back. You know what's going to happen next?'

'What?'

'She'll come back,' she said positively. 'She'll come back in her flashy car with her suitcase in her hand and a smile on her face and she'll expect everyone to hug her and kiss her and welcome her with open arms. She's in for a shock, I'm afraid.'

'Why?'

'Because this is a little too much,' Gwen Davison told me. 'You can't disappear for a week and a half without a word. They'll throw her out of Radbourne for this one.' She frowned. 'Not that it should matter to Barb. What does she need with a college degree? With her father's money she can buy herself an honorary degree if she wants. She's fixed for life with or without college. So why should she care?'

We talked for a few more minutes but I didn't get anything more from the girl. The only boyfriend of Barbara's she knew of was the one Helen MacIlhenny had mentioned, Alan Marsten. She didn't care for him either.

'One of the Bohemian element,' she said. 'You know the kind. He never wears anything but paint-spattered dungarees and a dirty sweatshirt. Gets his hair cut once every six months. Sits around looking romantic and artistic. You can usually find him hanging around at the little coffee shop in town. It's called Grape Leaves. God knows why.'

I thanked her and left. It was colder outside now and the sky was darker. Now it was snowing again, the flakes drifting down slowly through crisp air. I pulled up my coat collar, lit a cigarette, and headed toward town.

The streets of Cliffs End were cold and uninviting. Without the college, the town would have been a typical tiny New England village, a cluster of low buildings grouped around the inevitable village square with its inevitable colonial courthouse. The college changed this, and while it may have greatly enhanced the prosperity of the region, that was about all it did on the plus side. The stores aimed their displays at the student trade. The villagers sat on their stoops, locking endlessly and mumbling mean things about the collegians. It was a cold little town, and the snow was only partially responsible for the coldness.

I found Grape Leaves across the street from the tavern. It was closed; a hand-lettered sign in the window announced that it would open in an hour or so. I crossed the street to the tavern, remembering all at once that I hadn't had anything resembling a meal since breakfast. The sandwiches I wolfed down in various bus and train stations had been little but a hedge against starvation. Now I was ravenous.

The tavern was English in decor and had me momentarily homesick for London. I sat on a hard wooden chair at an old wooden table and ordered a mug of ale as a starter. An aproned student brought me the ale in a pewter mug with a thick glass bottom. It was full-bodied and delicious.

The food didn't quite match the ale but it was better than I had expected. I had a small steak with onions and a baked potato with another mug of ale to keep them company. The two ales had my head a little fuzzy and I cleared things up with a pot of black coffee.

By the time I left the tavern, lights were on in the coffee house across the street I went over, swung open a door and went inside. The place was furnished in imitation Greenwich Village, which may be a redundant description. Candles dripped over chianti bottles on the small tables. A handful of students, most of them the worse for wear, were draped over tables, lost either in conversation or thought or whatever esoteric reveries were provided by the paperbound books they were reading. A waiter asked me what I wanted. When I told him I was looking for Alan Marsten he pointed to a boy about twenty slouching over a small cup of coffee at a table set against one wall. Then he turned away and ignored me.

I went over, sat opposite Alan Marsten. He looked up, stared blankly at me, then went back to his coffee. Moments later he looked up again.

'You're still here,' he said slowly. 'I thought maybe you'd go away.'

'You're Alan Marsten?'

'Why?'

He was wearing the uniform Gwen Davison had described – blue denim trousers spattered with various hues of paint, a sweatshirt similarly decorated, a pair of dirty chukka boots. His hair was long and needed combing. He could have used a shave.

'I want to talk with you,' I said. 'About Barbara Taft.'

'Go to hell.'

The words were venomous. He fixed watery blue eyes on me and hated me with them. His fists were clenched on the table top.

'Who are you, man?'

'Roy Markham,' I said.

'It's a name, I guess. Who sent you?'

'Edgar Taft. Barbara's father.'

He snorted at me. 'So the old man is starting to sweat. Well, he's got it coming. You tell him he can go to hell for himself, will you? What does he want?'

I looked at him and tried to guess what Barbara could have seen in him. His features were good except for a weak mouth and chin. I wondered what he thought he was – hipster or beatnik or angry young man. I decided he was just a slovenly kid.

'Barbara's missing,' I said. 'He's worried about her. He wants to know where she is.'

'So do I.'

'You don't know?'

He looked at me carefully. 'I don't,' he said. 'If I did, I wouldn't tell you. I wouldn't tell anybody.'

'Why not?'

'Because it's Barb's business what she does. She's a big girl now, man. She can take care of herself.'

'Maybe she's in trouble.'

'Maybe.'

'Is she?'

His eyes mocked me. 'I told you,' he said. Barb's a big girl. She can take care of herself. What's your bit, anyway? You some kind of a cop?'

'I'm a private investigator.'

'I'll be a son of a bitch. The old man's got private eyes looking for her. Somebody oughta shoot him.'

He was getting on my nerves. 'You take quite an interest in all this, don't you?'

'Maybe.'

'Why? Was she paying your bills for you?'

'Don't let the clothes fool you,' he snapped. 'My old man's just as loaded as Barb's. And just as much of a bastard.'

I wasn't getting very far. I lighted a cigarette and smoked, waiting for him to say something else. A girl with long black hair and too much lipstick asked me what I wanted to order. I asked for coffee and she brought me a demitasse cup of it. It was black and bitter and it cost me a quarter.

'What the hell,' he said finally. 'I couldn't tell you anything even if I wanted to. I don't know where she went.'

'She left without telling you?'

He nodded. 'I wasn't surprised. Something's been bugging her. She's in trouble, bad trouble.'

'What kind of trouble?'

He shrugged. 'There's all kinds. Money trouble, man trouble, pregnant trouble, school trouble, sadness trouble. I don't think it was money – her old man gives her enough bread, even if he doesn't show her anything else. I don't think she was pregnant—'

'Were you sleeping with her?'

'None of your business,' he said, angry now. 'What I do is my business. What Barb does is her business.'

Which could mean anything, I decided. 'You love her?'

His eyes clouded. 'Maybe. Big word, love. She's gone, maybe she's coming back, maybe she isn't. I don't know.'

I asked him a few more questions and he didn't have answers for them. He said he didn't know why she had left or where she might have gone, didn't know anyone likely to be able or willing to supply any of the answers. I wasn't sure whether or not he was telling the truth. I had a hunch he knew more than he was ready to tell me, but there wasn't much I could do about it.

I finished my cigarette. There were no ashtrays; I dropped the butt to the bare wooden floor and squashed it with my foot. I left the coffee there. The management was welcome to reheat it and collect another quarter for it.

And I left Grape Leaves.

It was close to eight. I found a drugstore, changed a pair of dollars for the telephone booth. The pharmacist had heavily lidded eyes and dirty hands. I wondered how many contraceptives he sold to Radbourne students.

I shut myself up in the phone booth, put a dime in the slot and managed to convince the operator that I wished to call Bedford Hills, New York. I didn't bother trying to get her to make the call collect as Edgar Taft had suggested. It would have been too much trouble.

Instead I poured nickels and dimes and quarters into the telephone until the woman was satisfied. After an annoying delay a phone started to ring. Someone picked it up midway through the first ring and barked hello at me.

I asked for Taft.

'Who's this?'

'Roy Markham,' I said.

'Markham,' the voice said. 'You the private eye that Taft sent to look for his daughter?'

'That's right.'

'You can quit looking.'

'Who's this?'

'Hanovan,' the voice said. 'Homicide. We found the girl in the Hudson, Markham. It looks like suicide.'

I said: 'God.'

'Yeah. It was messy. It's always messy. She spent a few days floating and they don't look too beautiful after a few days in the river. They never look beautiful dead.'

I didn't say anything.

'I guess that's it,' he said. 'But you don't have to look for her any more.'

'Can I speak with Mr Taft?'

'I don't know, Markham. He's pretty broken up. We had a doc come over and give his wife a sedative, put her to sleep for awhile. But Taft—'

I heard noises in the background. Then Taft's voice, loud, came over the wire.

'Is that Roy Markham? Gimme the phone, damn it. Let me talk to him.'

Somebody must have given him the phone. He said: 'It's terrible, Roy. God, it's awful.'

I didn't know what to say or whether I was supposed to say anything at all. He didn't give me time to worry about it. 'Get right back to New York,' he said. 'Come up here right away. These cops think she killed herself. I don't believe it, Roy. Barb wouldn't do a thing like that.'

'Well—'

'You get here as soon as you can,' he went on. 'Somebody murdered my daughter, Roy. I want that killer. I want you to find him and I want to see him go to the chair. I want to watch him die, Roy.'

I didn't say anything. I looked through the phone booth's glass door. The pharmacist was busy counting pills. A pair of students near the front of the store were leafing through a display of magazines.

'Roy? You're coming?'

I let out my breath and realized that I had been holding it for a long while.

'I'm coming,' I said. 'I'll be there as soon as I can.'

3

I found a mercenary student with an ancient Packard and bribed a ride to Byington. The buses weren't running and I can't say I blamed them. Snow carpetted the roads while wind blew more snow across the road at us. But the old car was tough as nails, built for rough weather and bad roads, and the boy knew how to drive. He got me to Byington in far less time than the bus would have taken, pocketed his bribe with a huge smile, turned the Packard around and aimed it at Cliff's End once again. Less than twenty minutes passed before the Massachusetts Northern came to take me to Boston. I picked up the Central there and rode it to New York, then got off it and onto another which carried me back up the Hudson Valley as far as Bedford Hills. I called the Taft home from a pay-phone in the station – it was late and no cabs were handy. The policeman who said his name was Hanovan answered and told me he'd send a car around for me. I waited until an unmarked black Ford pulled up and a hand waved at me.

I went over to the car, got into it. The man behind the wheel was wearing a rumpled gray business suit. His hair was black, his nose broad, his eyes tired. I asked him if Hanovan had sent him.

'I'm Hanovan,' he said. 'So you're Markham. I was talking to Bill Runyon about you. He said you're all right.'

'I worked with him once.'

'He told me.' He took out a cigarette and lighted one without offering me the pack. I lighted one of my own and drew smoke into my lungs. The car's motor was running but we were still at the curb. I wondered what we were waiting for.

'I wanted to talk to you,' he said. 'Without Taft listening. That's why I stayed around his place. There's nothing to do there but I wanted to talk to you.'

I said nothing.

'The kid killed herself,' he said. 'No question about it. We fished her out of the Hudson around Pier Eighty-one – that's the Hudson Day Line slot near Forty-second Street. Death was by drowning – no bumps on the head, no bullet holes, nothing. She took a jump in the drink and drowned.'

I swallowed. 'How long had she been dead?'

'That's hard to say, Markham. You leave somebody in the water more than two days, you can't tell too much. The doc says she was in for three days minimum. Maybe as many as five.' He shrugged heroically. 'That's as close as he would make it. Look, let me tell you what we got. The way we figure it, she hit the water from one of the piers between Fifty-ninth Street and Forty-second. Her car turned up in a garage on West Fifty-third between Eighth and Ninth. It's been there since late Monday night and the guy we talked to didn't remember anything about who parked it. That fits the time, Markham. It's Thursday night now. That would be four days in the water, which checks with what the medical examiner guessed.'

I nodded.

'We figured she garaged the car and went for a walk. The docks are empty that time of night. She walked out on a pier, took off her clothes—'

'She was naked when you found her?'

He nodded emphatically. 'Suicides usually work that way. The ones who go for a swim, anyways. They take everything off and fold it up neat and then go and jump.'

'Did you find her clothes?'

'Nope. Which is no surprise, if you stop and think about it. You leave something on a pier and you're not going to find it three days later. She was a rich kid, wore expensive clothes. Somewhere a longshoreman's got a wife or girlfriend with a pretty new dress.'

'Go on.'

He turned his hands palms-up. 'Go where? That does it, Markham. Look, she went and she jumped. Period. She was a moody kid and she wasn't doing well in school. So she took what looked like an easy out, turned herself into a floater. It happens all the time. It's not nice, it doesn't look pretty or smell sweet. But it happens all the time.'

'Was she pregnant?'

He shook his head. 'We checked, of course. She wasn't. That's why a lot of 'em go swimming. Not this one.'

I dragged on the cigarette and watched him out of the corner of an eye. He seemed perfectly at ease, a rational man explaining a situation in a straightforward manner. I rolled down the side window and dropped my cigarette to the ground. I turned around and looked at him again.

'Why?'

He looked back at me. 'Why did she kill herself? Hell, I don't know. She probably—'

'That's not what I mean. Why give me such an elaborate build-up? I'm not your superior. You don't owe me a report or a favor. Why tell me all this?'

He colored. 'I was just trying to help you out.'

'I'm sure you were. Why?'

He studied his own cigarette. It had burned almost to his fingertips. 'Look,' he said. 'This girl – Taft's daughter – killed herself. I know it. You know it. Even Taft's wife knows it.'

'But Taft doesn't?'

'You guessed it.' He sighed heavily. 'Now ordinarily if a suicide's old man wants to make noise, I just nod and gentle him and then leave him alone. I don't sit and hold his hand all night long. The hell, I'm a New York City cop and this is Westchester. Why worry about him?'

I didn't say anything.

'This is different, Markham. Taft is rich. He knows a lot of people, throws a lot of weight. I can't tell him he's full of crap, can't brush him off. I have to be nice.'

'And you want me to tell him she killed herself?'

'Wrong.' He put out the cigarette. 'He wants you to investigate,' he said. 'I told him we'd follow it up but he doesn't have any faith in us, mainly because I already told him how sure I am that it's suicide all the way. What I want is for you to tell him you'll work on it, you're not too sold on the suicide bit yourself. Then you move into the case.'

'And look for a mythical killer?'

'I don't give a damn if you sit on your hands, Markham. I want you to make like you're working like a Turk. Gradually you can't find anything. Gradually he wakes up and realizes what I been trying to tell him all along. Gradually he sees it's suicide. And in the meantime he stays off my back.'

I didn't say anything. He asked me if I got it, and I told him that I got it, all right. I didn't like it.

I didn't enjoy the notion of wasting my time and Edgar Taft's money just to do the New York police a favor. I didn't enjoy the 'gradual' routine – a gradual let-down of Edgar Taft, a gradual change in tone.

'You'll do it, Markham?' I didn't answer him. 'Look at it this way. You'll be doing the old man a favor. Right now he's all broken up. He can't stand believing any daughter of his knocked herself off. It's a big thing with him. Okay – so you got to let him believe somebody killed her. And he wants action. So you give him what he thinks is action until his mind gets used to the idea of what really happened. It makes things a lot easier for a lot of people, Markham. I'm one of them. I admit it. But it makes it easier for Taft, too.'

'All right,' I said.

'You'll go along with it?'

'I said I would,' I told him, my voice tired now. 'Now why don't you try shutting your mouth and driving?'

He looked at me and thought it over. Then he put the car in gear and stepped down heavily on the gas pedal. Neither of us said a word on the way to Taft's house.

Edgar Taft was crushed but strong, broken but surprisingly firm. He didn't rant, didn't rave, didn't foam at the mouth. Instead he talked in a painfully placid voice, explaining very earnestly to me that the police were a bunch of fools, that deep down inside he knew Barbara as he knew himself, that she couldn't kill herself any more than he could.

'A batch of damn fools, Roy. They couldn't find crap in a latrine, not even if you took them and stuck their heads down the holes. I'm giving you full authority and all expenses. I'm telling them to cooperate with you. That's one nice thing about money, Roy. If I tell them to cooperate with you they'll let you do any damn thing you want. Roy—'

There was more. But it was all in the same vein, all stamped from the same mold. What it boiled down to was that he wanted me to find his daughter's murderer. That was all there was to it. I let him know that it was a tall order, agreed that the police were being far too quick to write the case off as suicide, and told him I'd do what I could.

Marianne was different, though.

She was as well-mannered as ever, as neat and sweet and soft-spoken as she had always been. She was the gracious lady, accepting reality and greeting it with decorum, maintaining her position and being what she was supposed to be.

'Roy,' she said. 'I'm . . . I'm very glad to see you, Roy. This is all very hard for me. My daughter committed suicide, Roy. Barb killed herself, jumped into the water and drowned herself. This is hard for me.'

It was hard but she was handling it nicely. I had always thought of her as a person with internal strength and now she was proving me correct. I took her arm. We found a sofa and sat side-by-side on it. I lighted cigarettes for us both.

'Poor Edgar,' she said. 'He can't believe it, you know. He'll scream at imaginary killers forever.'

'And you?'

Her eyes clouded. 'Maybe I'm more realistic,' she said. 'I . . . I was afraid this had happened . . . or would happen . . . from the moment we found out she had left school. I think I got my tenses scrambled in that sentence, Roy.'

'I wouldn't worry about it. Edgar says Barbara wasn't the type of girl to commit suicide.'

'Edgar is wrong.'

'He is?'

She nodded. 'He's wrong,' she said again. 'He has never understood her, not really.'

'He says he knows her as he knows himself.'

That brought a smile. A joyless one. 'Perhaps he does,' she half whispered. 'Or did. Because there's very little left to know now, is there?'

'Marianne—'

'I'm all right, Roy. Really, I'm all right. To get back to what I was saying – Edgar and Barbara were very much alike. She was the same sort of person. Maybe that's why they fought so much. I used to think so.'

I looked at her. 'He wouldn't choose suicide, Marianne.'

'You think not?' Her eyes were amazingly firm. 'He's never failed, Roy.

He's never had any reason to kill himself. Barb evidently failed, or thought she did. I suppose it amounts to the same thing, doesn't it?'

Hanovan drove me back to New York. He turned on the radio and we listened to some sort of teenage craze playing a guitar and groaning horribly. I suppose it served its purpose – at least Hanovan and I were relieved of the necessity of speaking to one another, which was fortunate.

Actually, I had no reason to dislike him. In a sense he was advising a course of action which was probably the best thing all around for the people involved. Naturally it made his life a great deal simpler, but it also made for a psychological solution to Edgar Taft's traumas.

I managed to ignore both Hanovan and the ersatz music until he let me out of the car at Times Square. I was exhausted without being sleepy. I was as hungry as I was tired – the small steak at the tavern in Cliff's End had been far too small, and far too long ago. I found an all-night restaurant, went in and sat down. A waitress brought me a mushroom omelet with home fries and a cup of black coffee. I ate the omelet and the potatoes and tried not to listen to a juke box which gave forth with the same sort of pseudo music I'd tried not to listen to in Hanovan's car. I drank the coffee, smoked a cigarette.

Outside on 42nd Street it was cold. Not so cold as the humble hamlet of Cliff's End, but cold enough to make me give up the idea of walking across town to the Commodore. The wind had a snap to it and my breath smoked in the cold air. I stepped to the curb and flagged down a taxi.

He pulled over. I opened the door, stepped inside. I muttered 'Commodore' at the husky driver and started to close the door. Then all at once somebody was yanking it open again and piling into the cab with me.

'You've got to help me!'

The somebody was a girl. Her hair was black and short, her eyes large and frightened. She was struggling to catch her breath and it seemed to be a lost cause.

I asked her what the matter was. She tried to tell me, opened her mouth without getting any words out, then whirled in her seat and pointed. I followed the direction of the point. Two grim characters, short and dark and ugly, were grabbing a cab of their own.

'After me,' she stammered. 'Trying to kill me. Oh, help me, for God's sake!'

The driver was staring at us and wondering what in God's name was happening. I couldn't say I blamed him. I was wondering pretty much the same thing myself.

'Just drive,' I told him.

'You still want the Commodore?'

'No,' I said. 'Just drive around. We'll see what happens.'

He drove around while I saw what happened. He turned downtown on Broadway, held Broadway to 36th Street, headed east on 36th as far as Madison, then swung north again. I kept one eye on the girl and the other gazing out through the rear window. The girl stayed in her seat and the cab with the two grim ones in it stayed on our tail. Whoever they were, they were following us.

'They still got us,' the driver said.

'I know.'

'Where next?'

I leaned forward in the seat. 'I'll wager ten dollars you can't lose them,' I said.

He grinned happily. 'You lose, buddy.'

'I'd love to lose.'

The grin widened, then disappeared entirely. He had no time for grinning now. He instead devoted himself wholeheartedly to the task of losing our tail. He was a professional and he gave me my money's worth.

He gunned the car north along Madison Avenue, slowed down a little, then shot through 42nd Street on the yellow light. The light was red for the boys behind us. This didn't bother them. They ran the signal, narrowly missed a light pickup truck, and stayed with us.

The cab driver swore softly. He took a corner on two wheels or less, put the pedal to the floor for the length of the block, ran a red light on his own and went the wrong way on a one-way street. Then he ripped around another corner, shot along an alleyway between two warehouses, drove three blocks normally, and let out a long sigh.

'Ten bucks,' he said. 'Pay the man.'

Our tail was gone, if not forgotten. I put a crisp ten dollar bill into his outstretched palm and watched it disappear. I turned to the girl, who was as wide-eyed as ever, if not so frightened. I noticed for the first time that she was quite beautiful, which was fine with me. If one is going to make a practice of rescuing maidens in distress, one might as well select lovely maidens.

'Oh,' she said. 'Oh, thank you.'

I asked her where she wanted to go next. She was flustered. 'I really don't know,' she said. 'I . . . I was so frightened. They were going to kill me.'

'Why?'

She looked away. 'It's a long story,' she said.

'Then suggest a place where you can tell me all about it.'

'I don't know where. They have my address so we can't go to my apartment. I—'

The cab was still cruising in traffic and the meter had an impressive total upon it already. I thought quickly. There was a girl I knew rather well named Carole Miranda. She had an apartment on the western edge of Greenwich Village, and she was in Florida for a month or so. Which meant that her apartment was vacant.

I had a key to it. Never mind why.

'Horatio Street,' I told the driver. 'Number Forty-nine, near the corner of Hudson.'

He nodded and headed the car in that direction. I had a few dozen questions to ask the girl but they would all keep until we got to Carole's apartment. In the meanwhile we both sat back and enjoyed the ride. She fell back in her seat in an attitude of total collapse, which was her way of enjoying the ride. I looked at her, which was my way.

A beautiful girl. Her hair was short and jet black and it framed a pale oval face. Her skin was cameo white. Her small hands rested in her lap. She had thin fingers. Her nails were not polished.

It was hard to tell much about her figure. Her body was wrapped up in a heavy black cloth coat that left everything to the imagination. My imagination was working overtime.

'We're here,' the driver told me.

'We're here,' I told her. She opened the door on her side and I followed her out of the cab. The numbers on the meter were high enough for me to give him a five dollar bill and tell him to keep the change.

We stood on the sidewalk in front of a remodelled brownstone with a vaguely cheerful air about it. The windows had windowboxes which held flowering plants in better weather. The building's wooden trim was freshly painted in bright reds and blues. A wreath of holly decorated the blue front door.

'Where are we?'

'A friend's apartment,' I told her. 'The friend is out of town. You'll be perfectly safe here.'

This satisfied her. On the way to the door she held my arm and relaxed a little against me. I opened the front door, unlocked the inner door in the vestibule with one of the keys Carole had given me. We walked through a hallway lit with shaded blue bulbs and up two flights of stairs. The stairs squeaked in protest.

'This is exciting,' she said.

'It is?'

'Like an illicit affair,' she said. 'Where is this place? The top floor?'

I told her it was.

'God,' she said. 'Then it's not so exciting. Nobody would be able to carry on an illicit affair after a climb like this. Besides, my nose bleeds at heights.'

We managed the remaining two staircases. I found the door to Carole's apartment, hoped that she was really out of town, stuck a key in the lock and opened the door. I fumbled for a lightswitch, found it, and brightened the room.

'Now you can tell me all about it,' I said.

'I—'

'But first I'll build some drinks. Wait a moment.'

She waited a moment while I remembered where Carole kept her liquor supply. I found a bottle of good scotch and a pair of glasses. I put the scotch in the glasses, kept one for myself and gave her the other. We clinked them together ceremoniously and drank.

'My name's Roy Markham,' I told her.

She said: 'Oh.'

'Now it's your turn. But you've got to tell me a great deal more than your name. You've got to tell me who you are and who those men were and why they were chasing you.'

'They wanted to kill me.'

'Start at the beginning,' I said. 'And let's have all of it.'

She asked for a cigarette and I gave her one, lighted it for her. I took one for myself, then sipped more of the scotch. We sat together in silence on Carole's big blue Victorian sofa for a few moments. Then she started.

'My name is Linda,' she said. 'Linda Jeffers. I live here in New York. On East End Avenue near Ninety-fourth Street. Do you know where that is?'

I nodded.

'I'm a secretary. Well, just a typist, really. I work at Midtown Life in the typing pool. It's just a job but I like it, sort of.'

I waited for her to get to the point. While she was on her way there she told me that she was twenty-four, that she'd come to New York after going to college in southern Illinois, where her family lived, that she wasn't married or engaged or going with anyone, that she lived alone. This was all interesting, but it hardly explained why a pair of thugs wanted to murder her.

'You see?' she said suddenly. 'I'm just an ordinary person, really. Just like everybody else.'

I could have told her that was not true. She had taken her coat off, and she was wearing a mannish paisley shirt and a black wool skirt, and the body that filled them was not at all like everybody else. It was a superior body.

Her waist was slim, her bust full-blown and good to look at. She had very long legs for a short girl, and when she crossed them I could see that they were as good as they were long, with trim ankles and gently rounded calves. It was a fine body and it went nicely with her fine face.

'Just like everybody else,' she repeated oddly. 'Except that they want to kill me.'

'Who are they?'

'A man named Dautch. I don't know his first name.'

'Was he one of the ones following us?'

She nodded. 'The shorter one.'

'And why is he after you?'

'It's very simple,' she said. 'I saw him kill a man.'

4

'It was the most horrible thing that ever happened,' she told me, her eyes wide and her voice trembling. 'I was home at the time. It was three days ago. Monday evening. I live in a building kind of like this one. Except I live in a room, not an apartment. Just a furnished room. It's a nice neighborhood and the rent's cheap enough for me to afford and—'

'You saw a murder,' I reminded her.

'Yes. It was at night, around nine. I was in the hallway on the way back to my room. There's no bathroom in my room, I just have this furnished room, and—'

She actually blushed. I didn't know American girls still knew how to accomplish it. I told her to go on.

She did, in a rush. 'A man named Mr Keller had the room at the end of the hallway. His door was open. There were two men in there with Mr Keller. They were arguing, shouting at each other. I heard Mr Keller call one of them *Dautch*. That's how I know his name.'

'What were they arguing about?'

'I'm not sure. Money, I think. Mr Keller kept saying he didn't have it and the two men kept on arguing with him. Then the other man – not Dautch – hit Mr Keller in the stomach. Mr Keller let out a moan and started to fall forward. Then he straightened up and went straight for Dautch.'

'And then?'

She closed her eyes for a second. She opened them and looked at me, her face a mask of fear. 'It happened very quickly. I heard a *click*. Then Mr Keller stepped back with a horrible look on his face. He put his hands to his chest. There was blood coming through the front of his shirt. He started to say something. But before he could say a word he fell over onto the floor.'

'What did you do?'

'I'm afraid I must have screamed or something. Because all of a sudden Dautch and the other man were turning and looking at me. Dautch had a bloody knife in one hand. I don't know what would have happened next. But I ran into my room and locked the door. I even pushed the bed in front of it. I was scared they were going to kill me the way they killed Mr Keller.'

'But they left you alone?'

She nodded. 'One of them wanted to break down my door and take care of me. That's the way he said it. But the other told him they couldn't waste time. I just stayed where I was and prayed. I was sitting on the edge of the bed to make it harder for them to open the door. Then I heard them going down the stairs. It sounded as though they were dragging something heavy.'

'Keller's body?'

She shuddered. 'It must have been. I . . . I stayed right where I was for about half an hour. I was scared stiff, too scared to move. Then I moved the bed out of the way and unlocked my door and went back to see if Mr Keller was still there. I thought I could help him if he was still alive. But I knew he was dead, I was sure of it. Anyway, I thought I could call the police.'

'The body was gone.'

'That's right,' she said. 'There . . . there wasn't even any blood on the rug, nothing to show that anything had happened. I even started to think it was my imagination or something. I knew I couldn't call the police. They would tell me I was crazy. I kept reading the newspapers to see if they found Mr Keller anywhere. But they didn't.'

'So you never got in touch with the police,' I said. I thought it over. 'Well, I can do one thing for you. I can find out if Keller turned up.'

'How?'

'By calling the police and asking them. That's simple enough, wouldn't you say? Could you give me a full description of the man?'

She stared at me for a moment or two, then described Keller for me. I went over to the phone and dialed Police Headquarters. I asked for Hanovan at Homicide. He answered the phone gruffly.

'Roy Markham,' I told him. I'm looking for an unidentified corpse, male, around thirty-five, dark brown hair, sallow complexion, going bald in front, about five-eight, medium build. You turn up anything like that since Monday night?'

'Why?'

'I just wondered.'

'To hell with you,' Hanovan snapped. 'Listen—'

'You listen,' I said sweetly. 'I'm supposed to receive full cooperation from all police officers. Don't you remember? Now give me a little of that cooperation, damn you.'

He was silent for a long moment. Then he said he would check. I held the line while he disappeared for a few minutes, 'Nothing,' he said finally. 'Nothing even close on the unidentified list. Nothing even close on the identified list. You gonna tell me what this is all supposed to be about or should I guess?'

'You may guess,' I told him. 'And thanks very much for your cooperation.'

I hung up and turned to Linda. 'Your Mr Keller hasn't put in an official appearance yet,' I said. 'So evidently there's little point in your contacting the police.'

'How come they told you that?'

'Well get to that later,' I said briskly. 'Let's get back to this fellow Dautch. He was after you tonight. Is that the first you've heard of him since the murder?'

'No. He . . . he called me the next day. At least I think it was him. I picked up the phone and a voice told me to forget everything I saw last night or I would get hurt. Dautch rang off before I could say a word.' She paused. 'I've had a few more calls like that since then. Always the same voice. Sometimes he's been very . . . explicit. About what would happen if I didn't forget Keller. He said filthy things, things he would do to me.'

'And then you saw him tonight?'

She hesitated. 'I ate a late dinner downtown tonight. I had the feeling that somebody was following me but I didn't see anybody. But I didn't want to go home. I went to a movie by myself on Broadway. And even in the theater I felt that there was somebody watching me. It's a terrible feeling. The picture was lousy but I stayed for the whole double feature. I was afraid to go home. And then finally I had to leave.'

'And you saw Dautch?'

'That's right. That's how I . . . landed in your lap, I guess. That's what happened, isn't it?'

'Worse things have happened.'

She smiled. 'You're sweet,' she said. 'Anyway, I was on Forty-second Street and I saw him, him and the other man. They were behind me and I looked at them and they looked at me. I don't think they were going to try anything. I think they were just following me waiting for a chance to get me alone. I ran for the nearest cab. It happened to be the one you were getting into but I didn't let that stop me.' She grinned. 'I just hauled open the door and hopped inside. I don't think it was too ladylike but I wasn't worried about it then.'

I thought it over. There had to be something I could do for the girl but I was damned if I could put my finger on it. A man was trying to kill her and all she knew was his last name. I could try to find out who he was, could try to discourage him from bothering her any more. I could find out more about Keller and try to solve things completely – by sending Dautch to the chair.

But all that would have to wait until morning.

'Now it's your turn,' she said. 'Roy, all you did was call the police and they told you everything you wanted to know. Are you a policeman?'

'Not exactly.' She looked at me questioningly. 'I'm a private detective,' I explained.

'That sounds exciting.'

'Sometimes,' I said.

'What are you working on? Can you help me? Or are you busy? Or do you just do divorce snooping and things like that?'

So I told her about it, because there was nothing much else to do and because I felt like talking. I ran through my initial discussion with Edgar

Taft a night earlier, told her about my pursuit of wild geese in New Hampshire, told her about the phone conversation with Taft, the return to New York, the game we were playing with the man in Bedford Hills.

'Then you're not doing anything,' she said slowly. 'You're just pretending to look for a killer.'

'Not exactly.'

She looked at me.

'I'm not entirely convinced of this suicide,' I said.

'But if the police—'

'The police are occasionally wrong. You've got to consider their position. There's an enormous temptation to write off a homicide as a suicide whenever possible. It makes their work a good bit easier.'

'That's terrible!'

I shrugged. 'I'm sure they believe it's a suicide,' I said. 'It certainly follows an established pattern. But I don't think they've investigated as diligently as they might.'

'Then you're going to waste your time looking for a killer who doesn't exist?'

'You could call it that.' I smiled. 'To be truthful, I suspect the suicide verdict is the right and proper one. I suspect my hesitation to accept it stems more from a personal distaste for getting paid for work without performing it. Edgar Taft has hired me. He's paid me a sizeable retainer and will pay me more. I can't abandon the case, much as I'd like to. So I might just as well give value in return, if it's possible.'

She was silent. I looked at her and saw how pretty she was. I wondered where Dautch and his friend were, and what they were doing. I wondered why Keller had been murdered.

'Besides,' I said, 'there are a few points here and there that bother me. People in Cliff's End seemed reluctant to talk to me about Barbara Taft. There was a secret somewhere that no one was saying anything about. God alone knows what it might be. Probably just my imagination. But I want to take a closer look.'

'You're not going back up there?'

'Not yet. Not until we straighten out this Dautch-Keller business, anyway. But I'll probably get back there in time. I'd dearly like to delay my trip until the spring, though. It's cold in New Hampshire.'

We sat there and finished our drinks. It took me that long to remember what time it was. It was very late.

I stood up.

'Where are you going, Roy?'

'Back to my hotel. It's late. We both need our sleep.'

'Don't go, Roy.'

'No?'

'No.'

'Why not?'

'Because I don't want you to.'

Maybe it was too late for me. I was thick-headed, more so than usually. I stood looking at her while she stood up and moved closer to me.

'I don't want to stay here alone,' she said.

'Frightened?'

She nodded.

'I suppose I could sleep on the couch,' I suggested, idiotically. 'I'd be right here then. In case you wanted me for anything.'

She laughed, a sweet girlish laugh. She came close to me and was all at once in my arms, her face pressed against my chest. My arms went around her at once and I held her close. I may have been an idiot, but there are limits.

I tilted her face up and found her mouth with my own. I kissed her. Her lips were sweet. Her own arms went around my neck and her soft young body was tight against me.

'You silly man,' she was whispering. 'You're not going to sleep on the couch. You're going to sleep in the bed, you silly old thing, and so am I. And that way you'll be right there when I need you. And I'll need you.'

And then she kissed me again.

We moved softly through the apartment, turning off lights and discarding articles of clothing. We found Carole's bedroom in the darkness, and we found her bed in the darkness, and, finally, we found each other in the darkness.

There were violins and muted trumpets and crashing cymbals and all the other orchestral paraphernalia one reads about in cheap novels. There were her breasts, firm and full and sweet, offering their young freshness to me. There was her soft and wonderful body, and there was her small animal voice at my ear making small animal noises. Then, afterward, there was sleep.

When I awoke I was the only one in the bed. It was bitterly disappointing. I called her name once or twice, fumbled my way out of the bed and into my clothing. Then I found her note. It was pinned to her pillow, and I should have seen it in the first place.

Roy darling, it read. *A working girl must work. I'm off to the typing pool at Midtown Life. I hope I don't drown in it. I get finished with work at five and I'll come right back here. Please be here when I get here. You have the only key, and I'd feel silly as sin cooling my heels in the hallway.*

By the way, your 'friend' who lives here has funny taste in clothes. I borrowed one of her dresses. By the way, I think I'm jealous . . .

There was more, but it was a little too personal to repeat. It was also too personal to leave lying around. I read it, smiled a silly smile, and shredded it. I threw the pieces into the toilet and flushed them away.

My watch told me that it was ten-thirty. I found a small restaurant on Hudson Street which was open. Most restaurants in the Village begin serving breakfast at noon – which, when you stop to think about it, makes a considerable amount of sense. Ten-thirty is altogether too early an hour for a civilized man to be awake. I went into the restaurant and ate orange juice, toast, and coffee. It wasn't much but it appeased the inner man.

It was then time to begin annoying the police.

I went to the Homicide division. My boon companion Hanovan wasn't around but he had left word to the effect that I was an abominable nuisance who had to be tolerated. They tolerated me. Someone brought me a copy of the medical examiner's report on Barbara Taft.

I read it carefully, which was only a waste of time. It said essentially what Hanovan had told me a night ago – death had occurred roughly three to five days ago, death had been caused by drowning, and no supplementary injuries were described. There were contusions here and there upon the body of the corpse but they were interpreted as having been caused while the body was in the water. None were on the head, which seemed to kill the notion that she'd been knocked unconscious before being dumped into the river.

I put the report back and asked to see the criminal records of everybody named Dautch. This jarred them a little. They asked why and I told them it was none of their business, which may have been stretching things a bit. But the orders to humor this British idiot had evidently been firm ones indeed. A uniformed policeman brought me a tray filled with cards. There were fourteen of them in all. Who would have suspected that that many persons named Dautch had criminal records in New York City?

I looked through the cards. Four of the men were obviously out of the picture. They were all over fifty, white-haired and feeble. Five more were currently serving sentences in one prison or another. Of the five who remained, one was nineteen years old, two were tall and blond, one was a Negro. The final 'suspect,' if you want to call him that, just didn't seem to fit the mold. He was a former bank teller who had been convicted once of minor embezzlement and who was now working as a shoe salesman in Washington Heights. I couldn't picture him as the heavy type who'd been giving Linda such a bad time.

I sighed. I lighted a cigarette and returned the tray of cards to the long-suffering policeman. There seemed to be no additional way to bother him, so I left the station.

There was a public telephone booth on the street corner. I went into it and called my answering service. There had been half a dozen calls since I spoke to them last. I jotted down names and numbers on a slip of paper, thanked the properly honey-voiced girl on the other end of the line, and caught a cab back to the Commodore.

It is hard to say which I needed more, the shower or the shave. I had both and felt human again. I put on clean clothes, went to the phone and began calling the names and numbers on the piece of paper.

Dean Helen MacIlhenny came first. She'd had a roundabout report of what had happened and wanted to check it with me. I confirmed what she had heard.

'A terrible thing,' she said. 'I feared this, of course. It's a dreadful thing when a student ends his or her life.'

'You were afraid it would happen?'

'Of course,' she said. 'Weren't you, Mr Markham? Neither of us suggested the possibility, of course. One never does. But one always fears suicide when a moody youngster is missing. It's one of the less pleasant facts of life. Or of death.'

I agreed that it was unpleasant.

'And it happens once or twice a year,' she went on. 'Even at a small college like Radbourne. You can count on it – one, two suicides each year. It's awful that it had to happen to someone like Barbara. I thought a great deal of the girl. Difficult to handle but worth the handling.'

We talked some more, then ended it. I told her I might be coming up to Cliff's End soon to round out the case. She assured me that I should always be welcome there and that she'd do anything she could to assist me.

I made three more calls, none of them having anything to do with Barbara Taft. One was to a tailor who had a suit ready for a preliminary fitting. I told him I was damnably busy and made an appointment for a week later. My bank had a check of mine that I'd written standing up. The signature was different from normal and they wanted to check with me before honoring it. I told them to go ahead. Another number turned out to belong to a man who wanted to sell me some life insurance. When I found out what he wanted I told him that it was sneaky of him to leave a number with no explanation. Then I told him to go to the devil and rang off on him.

That left two calls to make. One was to a tabloid newspaper. A reporter with gravel in his throat asked me if I had any statement to make in regard to my role in 'the Taft case.' I told him I'd been retained by Edgar Taft. He asked me what else I had to say. I said that was all and rang off.

Then I called Edgar Taft himself.

'Just wanted to check with you,' he said. 'Got anything yet?'

'Not yet.'

'I've been thinking,' he said. 'Listen, they think she killed herself. They think she drove all the way from New Hampshire to New York just to throw herself into the Hudson. That make any goddamned sense to you?'

'How do you mean?'

'Hell,' he said. 'Think about it, Roy. Now let's forget about the kind of girl Barb was. I say she wouldn't have killed herself in a million years, but let's forget that for a minute. Suppose she wanted to do it, she was depressed, maybe she was a little sick in the head. Okay?'

'All right. But—'

'Let me finish,' he said. 'Now, wouldn't she just go ahead and kill herself there in Radbourne? Or maybe race her car and crack it up on the road? Hell, why should she drive all the way into New York, go straight into the city without even stopping at home, then park the car neat as you please and take a jump in the river? It doesn't add up.'

'Unless she wanted to see somebody here first.'

'You mean some guy?'

'A man or a woman. Anyone.'

He didn't say anything for a moment. 'Maybe,' he said. 'I guess it could have been that way. But I can't see it, Roy. I know somebody killed her.'

He paused. 'You'll really work on it, won't you? That cop sounded so goddamned sure of himself I think he was measuring me for a padded cell of my own. Don't just play along with me, Roy. Don't just humor me. If you don't want to work for me, tell me. I can get somebody else.'

'I want to work for you, Edgar.' I wasn't lying. There *were* too many loose ends for me to accept the suicide pitch that easily. 'I think there's a lot in what you've just said. I don't know what I can accomplish, but I want to work on it.'

'That's all I wanted you to say.' He laughed mirthlessly. 'I'm a pest,' he went on. 'I'll probably call you once a day. Ignore me, Roy. I'm used to yelling at people until I get results. Just do what you have to do and ignore me.'

I wanted to tell him it would be as easy to ignore a tornado. Instead I repeated that I'd do what I could. Then I replaced the receiver and left the hotel.

That afternoon was a painful process of calling people and checking leads that didn't even begin to develop. All I succeeded in obtaining were some negative results. A friend in the newspaper morgue at the *Times* brought me what copy had appeared concerning Barbara Taft. There was next to nothing, and none of it helped.

I ran through other sources and drew other blanks. I managed, in short, to kill a batch of hours until all at once it was five o'clock. That made it time to go back to Horatio Street. I had to be there when Linda arrived. After all, I didn't want her to cool her heels in the hallway, as she had put it.

I caught a cab and let my driver worry about the rush hour traffic. He sweated and cursed his way to Horatio Street. I got out of his taxi, paid him, tipped him, and went into the building.

I walked into the vestibule, stuck my key in the door. I opened it and started inside.

Some sixth sense warned me. It warned me just in time, and I stepped back quickly.

The sap whistled past my ear.

I caught the hand that held it, twisted quickly and moved forward. My man spun around. I let go of him and sank a fist into his middle. He folded up and I hit him in the face.

But there was another one. He had a sap, too, and he hit me on the head with it. The world spun around and I got a glimpse or two of celestial bodies. I recognized Mars and Saturn. And a boatload of miscellaneous stars.

I went down to one knee. The first one – the one I had belted, the one who had missed me with *his* blackjack – was standing against one wall, doubled up in pain and looking unhappy. The other one was ready to hit me over the head again.

I rolled out of the way. He missed me – evidently neither of them could do much against a moving target. I picked myself up and threw myself at him and we both went down to the floor with me on top. I took one hand and hit him in the face with it. The room was still rocky and my head hurt horribly, so I took my hand and hit him again.

It was a mistake.

Because, while I was busy lying there and pounding one clown in the face, the other clown had time to make a partial recovery. I remembered him a little too late. I started to get out of the way but this time, by God, he knew how to nail a moving target.

The sap crashed over the back of my head and I flopped onto the floor as a fish flops into the bottom of a boat. The whole bloody galaxy paraded itself in front of my eyes this time. I even saw Uranus.

Then all the stars and planets winked and were gone. The world turned black and grew quiet.

And that was that.

5

First I heard voices.

The voices were high and soft and gentle, and for an unhappy moment or two I thought I had died and gone to heaven. Then reality returned; no angels possessed such thick accents, such ear-bending overtones of native New York. Angels, of course, speak the Queen's English – or what's a heaven for?

'He must be dead, Bernie,' one of the angels was saying. 'Lookit the guy. He ain't moving.'

'He ain't dead,' Bernie said.

'Yeah?'

'Yeah.'

'Who says?'

A superior snort from Bernie. 'You're a stupid lug, Arnie. You ain't looked at him, you lug. He's breathin'.'

'Yeah?'

'Yeah.'

Silence for a moment. The one named Bernie seemed to be right. I *was* alive. I could tell because I could feel my head. I didn't really want to but I couldn't help it. It felt as though someone had dropped a pneumatic hammer upon it. I began to remember the pair of clowns who had waited for me, the sap that had put me out of the picture.

'You're full of it, Bernie. He's dead.'

'Wanta bet?'

'How much?'

Difficult as it was, I rolled over a bit and opened an eye or two. The light was a shaft of yellow pain that burned straight through my brain. 'Hello,' I said pleasantly. 'Hello, Bernard. Hello, Arnold. You'd better save your money, Arnold. I'm not dead yet. Almost, but not quite.'

'Jeez!'

'Precisely,' I said. 'That's it exactly.' I made the mistake of trying to stand up. It didn't seem to work. My legs tried their best but proved unequal to their task. The room rocked and I sat down again. I was still in the hallway of Carole's building on Horatio Street and it was beginning to look as though I'd be there until the end of time.

'Bernard,' I said. He stepped forward. I reached into my jacket pocket and found that they'd left me with my wallet. I took it out and found a dollar bill in it. I folded the dollar crisply and passed it to Bernard.

'What's that for, Mister?'

'For being a good boy,' I said. 'For running to the nearest drugstore and bringing Uncle Roy a triple Bromo Seltzer.'

'Who's Uncle Roy?'

'I am,' I said. 'Now get that Bromo, will you?'

He gave me an uncertain nod. He punched Arnie in the arm and they took off, heading out of the building and down the street. I wondered if I would ever see them again. Probably not, I decided. When you're fool enough to give a twelve-year-old child a dollar, you shouldn't expect to see him again.

I tried to get up again. This time it worked, even though it felt miserable. I stumbled through the vestibule and sat down outside on the stoop in front of the building with my head in my hand. A passing couple stared at me oddly. I didn't blame them in the least. I shook a cigarette free from the crumpled pack in my pocket and managed to get it lighted. I sucked harsh smoke into my lungs, coughed, then took another drag from the cigarette. The world swam around for a few seconds and came back into focus. My head still ached.

It would probably be doing that for awhile.

I didn't remember Linda until I glanced at my watch. It was six-thirty. I had been unconscious for about an hour, and during that time Linda must have returned from work. I thought about the welcome the pair of thugs must have given her and my stomach started to turn over.

They had her now. And I had a headache and a bad conscience. I wondered where they had taken her, what they had done or were going to do with her.

Dautch had her, of course. But how the hell he managed to pick her up was beyond me. I was fairly certain they hadn't managed to follow us the night before. Our cab driver had been a master, and he had lost them neatly. They could have picked up her trail at her office, of course. If they knew she worked for Midtown Life, they could have watched the building and followed her home.

But they were there before she arrived. Before I arrived, for that matter.

Which meant they must have recognized me. They must have seen me in the cab with Linda, must have known who I was. Then they picked me up at the Commodore during the day and followed me and—

Fine.

But how did the bloody bastards manage to get back to Carole's apartment building before I did?

'Hey, Mister—'

I looked up, and my faith in America's youth was restored. Bernie and Arnie stood before me. Bernie was holding out two large paper cups, one filled with water, the other with Bromo powder. I took them from him, poured the water into the Bromo, and watched it fizz the way it does in the television commercials. Then I drank it down, and it tasted horrible.

But it helped. I took a deep breath, dragged once more on my cigarette, and got to my feet.

'Here's your change, Mister.'

'Oh, no,' I said. 'That's yours.'

'Yeah?'

'A birthday present from your Uncle Roy,' I said.

'It ain't our birthday.'

'A Christmas present,' I said. 'Christmas comes soon, you know.'

'We know,' Arnie said. 'Mister, listen. Bernie and me hang around here almost all the time. You ever want a favor, you just ask us. We'll help you out.'

I patted them on the head and told them that was fine. I walked away, wondering what possible help two twelve-year-olds could possibly be to me. Perhaps they could fetch me another bromo the next time I walked into a cosh. That was something.

A cab was heading uptown on Hudson Street. I hailed it and sank gratefully into the seat. This time no sweet young brunette tugged open the door and climbed in after me. I rode by myself, and I was lonely.

The hard part was finding a place to begin.

Linda Jeffers was gone, if not forgotten. As far as I could determine, she stood a fairly good chance of getting her brains shot out of her head. I couldn't quite understand Dautch's motives; the girl obviously wasn't going to run for the police, and even if she did he remained pretty much in the clear.

But the fact remained that Dautch and his bully boys were chasing her and had caught her. Maybe she had been feeding me a story – maybe she was running from Dautch for another reason entirely, and no man named Keller had been murdered at all. Whatever had happened, I had to do something. I had to find a girl.

I thought of going to the police. The idea made a certain amount of good sense. There were approximately twenty thousand policemen in the city of New York, and there was only one of me. They could do a better job of manhunting – or womanhunting, as the case may be – than I could, if only by sheer weight of numbers.

But what was I supposed to give them? I had a name – Dautch – and I'd already determined earlier that they couldn't match that name to a record in police files. I had another name – Linda Jeffers – but that wouldn't do them much good either. And I had a farfetched tale of accidentally seen murder which I was beginning to lose faith in on my own.

They would laugh their heads off at me.

I decided to find out a little bit more about Linda Jeffers. She had said that she lived on East End Avenue near 94th Street. Maybe I could find out something about her where she lived. Maybe, for that matter, she had changed her mind and had gone home from work first.

I bid goodbye to my taxi at the corner of East End and 93rd. There were four residential brownstones on the block between 93rd and 94th, in addition to the headquarters of the Peruvian embassy and a home for unwed mothers. I passed up the embassy and the foaling pen and made inquiries at the four brownstones. None of them had a tenant named Linda Jeffers, nor had any had a male tenant named Keller.

There were a few more buildings that I tried on the next block, between 94th and 95th Streets. Again I got the same answers. No one knew anything about Linda, or about Keller. Out of sheer desperation I tried a few buildings on 94th itself, thinking I'd mixed things up. I had no luck.

Maybe I'd got things all wrong. Maybe she said West End Avenue. Maybe she said 84th Street. Maybe.

And maybe not.

I grabbed another taxi and returned to the Commodore. Someone was playing games with me and I didn't understand it at all. I had been handy and Linda had tossed me a convenient line of patter designed to keep me from getting in the way. For one reason or another she'd been chased by somebody – and there was no reason to assume his name was really Dautch, since everything else had been a lie. My cab was nearby and I was a pleasant host. I'd been lied to, utilized, and paid off in bed.

And that was that.

I didn't like it. I didn't like getting coshed in a hallway by a pair of thugs simply because some girl was playing me for a sucker. I didn't like chasing wild geese all over metropolitan New York.

I didn't like being used.

And the hellish fact remained that the girl was still in trouble. Somehow or other she had managed to louse herself up. Somehow or other Dautch – or whatever in hell his name was – had gotten hold of her again. I didn't know whether he wanted to kill her or what, but after the chase they'd given us last night he obviously wanted her and she just as obviously wanted to stay away from him.

Well, the devil with her. I had more important things to worry about than a girl who was playing me for a bloody fool to begin with. I stopped at the desk at the Commodore and picked up a few scraps of paper, plus a pair of letters. I stuck them into a pocket without bothering to look them over and told the chap behind the desk to send up a boy with a bottle of scotch when he had the chance. Then I rode the elevator to my floor and went to my room. The elevator ride set my poor head spinning again and I stretched out on the bed for a second or two to get my bearings again.

The doorbell woke me ten minutes later. I had dozed off with amazing ease. I got to my feet, opened the door, and signed for a bottle of scotch. I opened it in a hurry and poured a great deal of it into a water tumbler. It helped. It did an even better job than the bromo seltzer which Bernie and Arnie had brought me.

Then I looked at the papers from the desk. The two letters were bills. I wrote checks to cover them and dropped them into the mail chute in the hall. Next I checked the messages.

One was from Edgar Taft. It said that he had remembered I was without a car and thought I might appreciate the use of one. Besides, he went on, he had no further use for Barb's MG and didn't want to have it around. Accordingly it was parked in the Commodore's garage waiting for me to put it to use.

Which was pleasant. If one is going to have a car, one might as well have a good car. And if I was going to make any additional trips to Cliff's End, it would be a great joy to avoid the nefarious combination of buses and trains I'd been forced to take the first time around.

The other scrap turned out to be the bill from the Commodore. It was the end of the week, and there was my bill, and wasn't that nice of them? I scrawled out a check and made a note to drop it off at the desk on my way out.

My glass was empty. I poured more scotch into it, took a small sip, and all at once the silly thing was empty again.

Strange.

Then it was full again.

And then it was empty again.

Strange, I thought. Fool glass must have a hole in it. Scotch disappears the instant it's poured.

Strange.

Then I was stretched out on the bed, too tired and too drunk to bother removing my shoes. My eyes closed themselves and the world crept away on little cat feet, leaving me floating in the middle of the air.

I dreamed about Linda Jeffers and Barbara Taft. I dreamed about getting hit over the head, about racing through dark streets in a fast taxi that turned into an MG. I dreamed ridiculous dreams and I slept the sleep of the just.

Which may or may not have been fitting.

The phone wailed like a V-2 over London. The blitz had been a long while back, but I still felt like diving under the bed and waiting for the All Clear to sound. Instead I picked up the receiver and mumbled a groggy 'Hello' into it.

American telephone operators invariably possess metallic voices. This girl sounded like a robot. 'Mr Roy Markham? I have a long distance call for you. Is this Mr Markham?'

I admitted that it was.

'One moment, please.'

I waited the moment, as she had requested. Then a voice came over the line.

'Mr Markham?'

'Who is this?'

'Helen MacIlhenny,' the voice said. 'The Dean of Women at Radbourne.'

'Oh,' I said. 'What is it?'

'I'm sorry to bother you,' she said. 'Were you sleeping?'

I grunted. I wondered what time it was. My watch was still on my wrist; I hadn't remembered to take it off before passing out. It said 3:48 but I refused to believe it.

'What time is it?'

'Time?' She sounded stupefied. 'Time?'

'Time.'

'Oh,' she said. 'A quarter to four. Mr Markham, something terrible has happened.'

She didn't have to tell me that. Something perfectly dreadful had happened, by God. Someone had called me in the middle of the bloody night.

'Mr Markham? Are you there?'

'I'm here.'

'I hate to call you at this hour,' she went on. 'But I just heard, it was just discovered, and I thought you would want to know right away. Because it fits in with what you're doing, of course. It's horrible, but it fits in.'

'What does?'

'Do you remember Gwen Davison?'

I remembered a large-breasted girl, a girl who had roomed with Barbara Taft, a girl who hadn't been much help to me.

'Yes,' I said. 'I remember her. Why?'

She searched for the right words. 'She . . . she was found, Mr Markham.'

'I didn't know she was missing.'

'No, that's not what I mean. She was found . . . dead. She was murdered.'

My face fell.

'Murdered,' Helen MacIlhenny went on. 'She was stabbed to death on the campus. A pair of students found her. And do you remember a boy named Alan Marsten?'

The beatnik type, the one in Grape Leaves. 'I remember him.'

'The police are holding him. They've accused him of the murder. They think he killed her.'

Things were happening much too quickly for me.

'I thought you might want to know,' she went on briskly. 'I felt this might . . . fit in . . . with your investigation of Barbara's death. Don't you think?'

'You were right.'

'And while it's a bad time to call—'

'I'm glad you called,' I told her, honestly enough. 'This puts everything in a new light. How long does it take to drive from New York to Cliff's End?'

The question caught her by surprise. 'Why . . . five or six hours, I believe. Why?'

'I'm coming right up,' I said. 'I'll be there as soon as I can. Will you be awake?'

Her voice was grim. 'I shall be awake, Mr Markham. I doubt that I'll get much sleep for the next several days. I couldn't sleep even if I had the time. And I don't have the time.'

'Then I'll see you shortly,' I said. 'And thanks again for the call.'

My clothes felt as though I had slept in them, probably because I had. I stripped, took a fast shower, and dressed again. The slight pain of a hangover had taken the place of the thunderous throb that the blackjack had given me. I took a quick nip of scotch from the bottle, a hair of the dog, as it were. Then I went down to the lobby.

'There's a car for me,' I told the doorman. 'An MG that a man left for me. Will you get it?'

He nodded and ran off to get it. He had it pulled up in front a few moments later, a fire-engine red affair that was sleek and low and lovely.

'Hell of a car,' the doorman assured me. 'Bet you can really travel in a wagon like that one.'

I told him I hoped so. I gave him a dollar and got into the bucket seat behind the wheel. I hadn't driven a sports car in a long while but it all came back quickly enough. I wrapped myself up in the safety belt, got the car going, put it into low and started up.

A gas station attendant filled the small tank and gave me enough road maps to get me to Cliff's End. I studied them for a few minutes, figured out the right route and marked it on the various maps with a pencil. Then I put the maps on the seat beside me and aimed the car at the East Side Drive. That was the fastest way out of the city.

The car was a demon on wheels. Traffic was light at that hour, since not everyone was as much of a fool as I was. I kept the accelerator pedal close to the floor and the car moved along speedily.

I was in Connecticut long before daybreak. There was one long lovely stretch of road that ran right through Connecticut, and the traffic was heavy on that road, but all the cars were heading toward New York – batches of early-morning commuters on the way to Madison Avenue. No one seemed to be heading north and I had the whole road to myself.

The MG sang to me and we moved across Connecticut and into Massachusetts. It was a clear day once it got started with the sun hot and heavy in the sky. There was a slight breeze but nothing strong. There was no snow falling and hardly any left on the roads, which was a blessing.

When the car and I neared the New Hampshire border the weather remained the same but the road conditions were worse. Snow was piled up on the sides of each road I took, and here and there the paved surface was slippery. With a less sure-footed car I would have had to take it easy, but the

MG knew how to hold onto the road. The pedal stayed near the floor and the car went on speeding madly.

Gwen Davison was dead. Alan Marsten was supposed to have killed her. And Barbara Taft's suicide was looking a little less like a suicide every minute.

Confusing.

Dean Macllhenny had guessed it would take five or six hours to get to Cliffs End. I could understand why – it was a hellish trip from the New Hampshire line on, with winding roads and rotten weather. Five or six hours would have been good time.

But Barbara Taft's car was hell on wheels. I made the trip in four hours flat.

6

I drove straight to Helen Macllhenny's home, a small house on a tree-lined street. The porch light was on and other lights burned in what seemed to be the living room. I left the MG at the curb, walked up a snow-covered path to the door. I rang the bell and she opened the door for me.

'You've gotten here so quickly,' she said. 'Oh, is that Barbara's car? Or have you one like it?'

'It's Barbara's. Or was. Her father is letting me use it.'

'It's quite a car,' she said. 'I've always wanted to ride in one of those little things. Men used to take me riding, but that was in the rumble seat days, I'm afraid. No more.' Her eyes brightened. 'But I'm letting you freeze yourself. Come right inside, Mr Markham.'

She poured coffee into cups and we sat sipping it. 'I was just ready to go to my office,' she said. 'I'm due there in half an hour, at nine o'clock. But I thought perhaps I'd go early in case you arrived at an early hour. You got here sooner than I expected.'

'It's a fast car.'

'It must be. Mr Markham, this is a terrible situation. It's . . . it's dreadful.'

I did not say anything.

'Gwen Davison murdered. Murder is an exceedingly ugly word, Mr Markham. Bone-chilling.'

'Where was she found?'

'In her own room, the room she shared with Barbara. She was killed with a knife, slashed in the stomach and across the breasts and—'

She broke off and turned away.

'I think you told me they're holding the Marsten boy,' I said. 'How did they come to suspect him?'

'It was his knife. One of the students recognized it and the police picked him up. He admitted it was his knife when they showed it to him.'

'Did he confess?'

'No.'

I lighted a cigarette. 'Did he come up with an explanation?'

'He's a strange young man,' she said. 'His defense is a passive one, Mr Markham. He has said that someone must have stolen the knife from him.

He refuses to say where he was when Gwen was killed. He must have killed her.'

'But no one saw him?'

'No.'

'When was she killed?'

'Around midnight.'

I thought it over. 'In her dormitory room?'

'That's right,' she said. 'Male students are not allowed in the women's dormitories at that hour, needless to say. But I've hardly so much as thought about that.' She managed a tiny smile. 'It's a relatively minor infraction of the rules. In comparison to murder, that is.'

Gwen Davison was dead and Alan Marsten seemed to be her killer. And somewhere there had to be a connection between this new death and the death of Barbara Taft.

Finding it was something else.

'Where's Alan now?'

'In jail,' she told me. 'The jail in Cliff's End isn't really much of a prison, Mr Markham. It's just a room in the little police station with a few bars across the door. There's rarely anything resembling a serious crime here. Once in a while a student becomes intoxicated and spends the night in the cell. We've never had a . . . a murder before. Not to my memory, and I've been here a good many years.'

I didn't bother mumbling that there was a first time for everything. I put out my cigarette in a small crystal ashtray, finished my coffee and got to my feet. 'I'll want to see Marsten,' I said. 'Do you think you could fix that up for me with the police force?'

She smiled. 'It's already arranged. I anticipated your wishes. They're expecting you.'

I told her I'd drop her off at her office on the way. She was pleased by this, since it would give her a chance to ride in the MG.

'It's been a long time,' she said. 'Do I have to fasten this safety belt thing?'

'We won't be going that fast.'

'That's good,' she said. 'It's like an airplane. If any of the students see their good dean breezing along in this little thing I'll never live it down.'

I grinned at her. 'I'll bet you've had lots of men take you for a spin.'

'But then the cars were all Marmons and Stutz Bearcats, Mr Markham. This is quite different.'

I dropped her off at her office. She told me the ride was much better than a Marmon or a Stutz. Then she told me how to find the police station. 'It's not much,' she explained. 'If you don't look closely you won't even see it.'

I found out what she meant. A small white frame building, one story high and less than twenty feet wide, crouched at the end of a dead-end street. It was the police station. A uniformed sergeant sat behind an old oak desk. He was the only man in the station house.

I told him who I was and what I wanted.

'Ayeh,' he said. 'Ayeh.' His voice was resolutely New England. 'You're the Englishman the dean was talking about. Come for a look at our killer, did you?'

'That's right.'

'Hear ye want him for something else. A killing he did in New York.'

'Well,' I said. 'I'm not so sure about that.'

'Shouldn't be hard to extradite him,' the man said. 'Though I reckon we can try him here about as well. You want to see him now, do you?'

'Yes.'

'This way.'

He led me to the back of the building. There was a heavy wooden door there. Its single window was barred with rusty slabs of iron. I looked between the bars. Alan Marsten was sitting on the edge of an ancient army cot, his head in his hands. He did not look up.

The police officer fitted a key into a lock and turned it. The door swung open, its rusted hinges creaking in metallic protest at this invasion of privacy.

'There he be,' the policeman said. 'You say what you want with him. I'll pay no mind.' He winked a rheumy eye. 'I know how you big-city detectives work,' he added confidentially. 'I'll be aways up in the front there. I won't hear a thing. You knock that killer around a mite, I won't know about it.'

I stepped into the cell. The door creaked shut and a key turned in the lock again. I listened to his receding footsteps as he left me alone with the boy.

I said: 'Alan.'

He looked up, blinked, recognized me. 'You,' he said. 'The private fuzz. What do you want?'

'To talk.'

'Yeah,' he said. 'Talk. Solid. You got any straights? They lifted mine.'

'Straights?'

'Cigarettes,' he said. 'It's slang. You know – the picturesque language the American peasants speak.'

I gave him a cigarette, scratched a match and presented him with a light. He took a very deep drag, coughed, blew out a lungful of smoke. 'Thanks,' he said. 'I go nuts without a cigarette every few minutes. I smoke too much, I'll get cancer, I don't care. It's a laugh, huh? I won't live long enough to get cancer. They'll hang me. Or what is it they do in New Hampshire? Hang you or gas you or electrocute you or what?'

I told him I didn't know.

'Maybe they abolished the death penalty. Probably not – you can't expect much from a backwards hole like New Hampshire. And even if they did, then I'd stand trial in New York. You want me for Barb's murder, huh?'

I didn't say anything.

'Hell with it,' he said. 'Barb's dead. They can do whatever they want to do. I don't give a damn.'

'Did you kill Gwen Davison?'

He looked at me, surprised. 'Now that's a fresh angle,' he said. 'Everybody else asks why I killed her. They don't even think I might be innocent. You're a breath of fresh air, man.'

'Did you?'

He looked away again. 'No,' he said. 'I didn't. Do you believe me?'

'I don't know.'

'Well, that's something,' he said. 'That's the closest yet. At least you didn't come right out and say no, man. You're way in front of second place.'

'She was killed at midnight,' I said.

'I'm hip.'

'Where were you at the time?'

He shrugged.

'Where were you, Marsten? Listen, you bloody fool – you're neck deep in this affair, whether you know it or not. The cop at the desk gave me permission to beat the truth out of you if I feel like it. He says he doesn't much care whether you hang in New Hampshire or New York. Why don't you try talking?'

His eyes were defiant. 'I was all alone,' he said. 'How's that for an alibi? I was all alone and nobody saw me. I wandered around, here and there. That all right?'

'You're lying.'

Another shrug. The little fool didn't seem to give a damn whether I believed him or not.

'How did your knife wind up in Gwen's body?'

'I don't know.'

'Someone take it from you? And what were you doing with a knife in the first place?'

He looked thoroughly bored. 'Maybe someone took it,' he said. 'Maybe it grew wings and flew away. I keep it in a drawer in my room. I never missed it until they told me it was used to kill Gwen. Hell, they didn't even tell me. They stuck a bloody knife in front of me and asked me if I saw it before. So I told them. What the hell, they woulda found out anyway.'

'And why did you have the knife?'

'I used it to cut my fingernails.'

I didn't want to hit him. I knew that the insolence came from fear, that the withdrawal and generally obnoxiousness of his personality was more a defense mechanism than anything else. But a little knocking around wouldn't hurt him. If he was innocent, it might jar him out of his reveries. If he was the killer, then I felt he had it coming.

I said: 'Get up.'

'Why, man?'

He didn't move. I bunched a hand in his shirt front and dragged him to his feet. I slapped him across the face, hard, and held him with the other hand. He looked startled.

I closed my hand into a fist and hit him in the stomach. I let go of him and he sat down heavily on the bed. His eyes were angry.

'So you're a big man,' he said. 'Congratulations.'

'You want more?'

'No,' he said.

'Then you're ready to talk?'

'Yeah,' he said. 'Sure.'

I said: 'Barbara Taft was mixed up in something that got her killed. Gwen Davison was in the same thing, in one way or the other. And you're tied in. All I want to know is what it's all about.'

He looked at me.

'Well?'

'Oh, to hell with it,' he said. 'Everybody wants to give it to me in the neck. I thought you were going to be different but you had to come on like a heavy. Edward G. Robinson with an English accent yet.'

I didn't say anything.

'You don't get anything from me, man. You're just another bastard like the rest of them. You want to hit me, go ahead and hit me. Maybe it'll make you feel like a big man. Take out all your aggressions.'

'I'm not going to hit you.'

'No?'

'No.'

'Solid,' he said. 'Then get lost, huh? You're a bigger drag than Gwen was.'

'Is that why you killed her?'

He frowned. 'Jesus Christ,' he said. 'Here we go again. That was one straight out of television. Why don't you hire a decent writer?'

'I'd like to, but this is a low-budget show. You're not too popular around Cliff's End, Marsten. You might need a friend. If you decide you do, you might call me. The chap on duty will get in touch with me.'

'Sure. But don't hold your breath.'

I took out my pack of cigarettes, lighted one for myself, then tossed him the pack and a book of matches. 'You might want these,' I said.

He looked at me, eyebrows raised, for a second or two. I saw wheels turning in his mind. Then he shrugged and stuffed the pack into a pocket.

I went to the door and called for the jailer to come let me out of the cage. Prisons do not exactly have an uplifting effect upon my spirit. I wanted to walk outside and breathe fresh air again. This was a one-room small-town jail, if you could call it a jail at all. But the air was the air of all prisons everywhere and I didn't care for it.

'Man—'

I turned around. Alan Marsten had a thoughtful expression on his face.

'My old man is rich,' he said. 'He'll send up one of his expensive lawyers.

One of those city cats who can make these hicks look like idiots. He'll get me off, won't he?'

I listened to the measured steps of the jailer. He was not setting any speed records.

'Won't he, man?'

'Maybe,' I told him. 'It may be interesting to see whether he can or not. Whether they hang you or not.'

The jailer opened the door and gave me another conspiratorial wink. He slapped me on the back and I had a strange urge to wipe myself off. I left Alan Marsten wondering whether or not he was going to hang, left the jailer hawking and spitting into a green metal wastebasket at the side of his desk, left the grayness of the police station for the blinding whiteness of sunlight reflected from the snow. The MG was waiting where I had left it, a low-slung kitten with blood-red fur. I drove away very fast.

Mrs Grace Lipton lived in a large old house on Phillips Street. She rented out rooms to tourists and to a few students who had somehow arranged for permission to live off-campus. Helen MacIlhenny had recommended the boarding house on my first visit to Cliff's End. Now it looked as though I was actually going to have to remain in the town overnight. I paid the old woman three dollars for a night's lodging, lugged my overnight case in from the MG, and took a quick shower.

Dean MacIlhenny was in conference somewhere when I returned to the Radbourne Administration Building. I waited in her office and killed time by putting through a call to Hanovan in New York. I made the call collect, just to see what would happen, and he surprised me by accepting the charges.

'I'm a son of a bitch,' he said, with surprising accuracy. 'You're actually working on the case.'

'Of course.'

'Find anything?'

'Enough to cast doubt on your suicide verdict,' I told him.

'Yeah?'

I gave him a quick run-through on what had happened at Radbourne, explaining that Barbara Taft's roommate had been murdered by her erstwhile companion, according to the police. He digested this in silence.

Then, 'You think he did it?'

'No.'

'Any reason?'

'Just a feeling.'

I could almost hear him shrugging. 'Hick cops,' he said. 'I figure you know more about it than they do. This is okay, Markham. This is good.'

'It is?'

'Yeah. For us, anyway. Look, the Taft kid was mixed up in something, right? We gotta figure it that way. It's no coincidence – whether she knocked herself off or whether she had help, there's still a tie-in between her and the killing up where you are. Right?'

'It would seem that way.'

He ignored the sarcasm. 'Which ties it to the college,' he went on. 'It's not a New York case any more. We can't do a thing with it except cooperate with New Hampshire.'

I wanted to compliment him on his fearless and tireless dedication to duty. I saved myself the trouble. 'Speaking of cooperation,' I said.

'Yeah?'

'I can use some assistance,' I said. 'I had a run-in with a young woman a day or so ago. She gave me a story about witnessing a murder and being in trouble. The name she palmed off on me was a false one and I think her story was just as false as her name. But she's in trouble.'

'How do you know?'

'There were a pair of thugs after her. They followed us but we got clear of them. Then the next morning I was waiting to meet her and they were waiting for me.'

Hanovan snorted. 'You got cold-decked?' The amusement danced through his words.

'There were thirty of them,' I said. 'And they all had atomic ray guns. I think they made off with the girl and I think they may have killed her.'

'Gimme a description.'

I gave him a very full description. I even told him she had an appendectomy scare, plus a mole high on the inside of her right thigh.

He whistled happily. 'Just a casual acquaintance,' he said.

'That's right.'

'You got a good life,' he said. 'This got anything to do with the Taft run-around?'

'No,' I said. 'It's just a favor you're going to do me. Let me know if she turns up anywhere, or if you get a line on the name Linda Jeffers.'

I gave him Dean MacIlhenny's number, plus the number of Grace Lipton's phone. Then I rang off and lighted a cigarette.

Another conversation with Helen MacIlhenny gave me no more in the way of pertinent information. It yielded two things only – a renewed appreciation for the woman, and permission to go through Gwen Davison's room. According to her, the police of Cliff's End hadn't gotten around to searching the room. Evidently the concept of discovering a motive for the murder was out of their ken. Hanovan may have been wrong about a good many things, but I couldn't argue with his opinion of small-town police.

The room in Lockesley Hall was silent and cheerless. The neatness and precision of the dead girl still characterized the room. Everything was clean and in its place, and this made the bloodstained floor just that much more incongruous.

I closed my eyes and saw her standing there, saw a faceless assailant moving toward her with a knife. I wondered why no one had heard her scream, or at least heard the sounds of a scuffle. No girl, however precise and orderly, stands stock-still and permits herself to be stabbed to death.

I guess that she knew her killer. Whoever he or she may have been, Gwen had admitted the killer to her room, had permitted the killer to get close enough to her to stick a knife into her before she could shout for help.

It was something to think about.

So, for that matter, was the idea of a man or boy entering a dormitory at midnight and leaving it after midnight without being seen.

I lighted a cigarette and started to look through her desk. I found piles of school notes from all the years she had been in Radbourne, all classified by subject matter and secured with paper fasteners. Her penmanship was perfect Palmer method, her typing painfully flawless.

All her clothes were folded neatly in the drawers of her dresser. I went through them more as a matter of form than because I expected to find anything. She had a great many sweaters; I guessed she must have been proud of the way she filled them.

Now all she would ever fill was a shroud. And a hole in the earth somewhere.

Something kept me in the room even after I had decided that I was wasting my time, even when I began to feel ghoulish about going through stacks of clothing which she would never wear again. Something kept me hunting methodically for a scrap of a clue, a gram of evidence pointing in one direction or another.

Perhaps it was the total lack of motive for her murder. As even an oaf like Hanovan had been acute enough to realize, there was an obvious connection between Barbara Taft and Gwen Davison. They had lived together and they had died almost simultaneously. Which meant that Gwen's killing had a motive, a reason.

Which I could not seem to locate.

So I went on with my silly search. Maybe it was my detective's sense of smell that kept me going, maybe some sixth sense, maybe some form of intuition.

Whatever it may have been, it was valuable.

It worked.

It worked, as it happened, on the top shelf of Gwen Davison's closet. It worked when I hauled down a hatbox, its sides securely sealed with masking tape. I wondered momentarily why anyone would take the trouble to fasten a hatbox with masking tape. Then I stripped off the tape and had a look.

There was a single manilla envelope in the box. It was eight inches wide by ten inches long and it was fastened by a metal clasp. The clasp looked as though it had been opened and closed many times.

I opened it.

I took out a sheaf of photographs. They were all glossy prints, all just slightly smaller than the dimensions of the manilla envelope which had contained them.

I looked at them.

To be honest, I stared at them. I stared hard at each in turn, and there were six all told. They were not the best existing examples of the art of photography. In some the backgrounds were out of focus. In others the shots were slightly under-exposed.

This did not lessen my interest.

They were the sort of pictures which may be purchased in back rooms of small stores in Soho, or around the Times Square area, or in the tenderloin district of almost any large city. In each picture there was a man and a girl on a bed. In each picture the man and girl were participating in one or another form of sexual intercourse.

Pornographic photographs.

Which in itself was not all that remarkable. Gwen Davison would not have been the first college girl with an interest in vicarious sexual excitement.

But there was more. The faces of the men, in all six photographs, were either turned from the camera or deliberately blocked out from sight. The faces of the girls were plainly visible in each picture. The faces, in two instances, were familiar.

I took one photograph and studied it. The girl in the picture was tall and blonde. She was engaging in sexual relations with a man in a rather bizarre manner and her expression indicated considerable pleasure.

I put the picture away hastily. There is something extraordinarily revolting in the notion of looking at pornographic pictures of a corpse. And this girl was a corpse now.

It was Barbara Taft.

And then I looked once more at the other picture I had recognized. I saw the bright eyes, the full breasts, the pretty face. I saw the dark hair, the trim waist.

I saw the appendectomy scar. I saw – just faintly visible, but unmistakably present – the mole high on the inside of her right thigh.

I saw the face. The face of a girl I had known before, but under a name which was probably false.

Linda Jeffers.

7

By the time I returned to the police station, a younger man had replaced the older one behind the desk. He was tall enough to make me feel short and young enough to make me feel old. He had a forest ranger's build and a boy scout's face. His eyes were blue and very frank.

'Roy Markham,' I said. 'I'd like to see the Marsten boy.'

He motioned for me to sit down. 'Pete told me about you,' he said. 'I'm Bill Piersall. The kid's lawyer is in with him now. Have a seat.'

I had a seat. 'He's got an honest-to-God Philadelphia lawyer in there,' Piersall said. 'The Marstens live in Philadelphia. Main Line family. So the lawyer's a Philadelphia lawyer. Isn't that one for the books?'

'It certainly is,' I said, to make him happy. It seemed to make him happy at that. 'What time did he get here?'

'The lawyer?'

I nodded.

'About an hour ago. Been with him all this time. Wonder what he's got to talk about.'

'Did you hear any of it?'

He shook his yellow-topped head. 'Not a word,' he said. 'Well, I did hear a word at that. More than a word. That lawyer said a few things before I left the cell. But I'm damned if he used a word of less than four syllables. Every other one out of his mouth was a regular jawbreaker.'

'Have you any idea how long they'll be?'

'No idea,' he said. 'I guess we just wait for 'em.'

We waited for them. It would have been easier to take the picture to Helen MacIlhenny for identification, but I couldn't quite see myself showing pornographic pictures to the Dean of Women. Some men may be able to carry off a play like that. I would have had trouble.

I reasoned that Alan Marsten would be able to tell me who Linda Jeffers was as well as Mrs MacIlhenny. And there was more to it than that. Unless I was a good distance from the trail, Marsten knew a lot more than he was telling me. The picture might be a chink in his conversational armor, so to speak. Once I put that single card on the table, he might be willing to come out of his shell.

At least it was a possibility. But first of all I had to identify the girl. I'd made a big mistake in telling Hanovan of New York Homicide that my little pigeon with the mole on her thigh didn't have anything to do with Barbara Taft. She was in it up to the top of her pretty head. She and Barbara were part of a bloody set, for that matter – a set of dirty pictures in a straight-laced girl's closet.

Which was interesting.

Things were taking their own sort of shape now, and some of the pieces of a giant jigsaw puzzle were starting to wind up on the table. But I still had far too few pieces to put them together and come up with anything vaguely resembling reality. I needed more, and I hoped Alan could give me some of it.

Right now it looked like blackmail, of course. But it was a blackmail game with six girls caught in the middle, not just one or two. It seemed to have the dimension of a full-scale blackmail ring with a lot of planning back of it and a great deal of potential profits in the offing.

It looked like a great many things. But I was still up six different trees at once. I couldn't begin to know who was doing the blackmailing, much less guess who had done the killing.

I was half finished with a third cigarette by the time Marsten's lawyer put in an appearance. He called commandingly from the cell and Piersall and I walked there. Piersall opened the door and the lawyer stepped out. He was tall and sandy, his bearing stiffly erect, his eyes sharp.

I begged his pardon and stepped past him into the cell.

'And who are you, sir?'

'I'm Roy Markham,' I said. 'I'm going to have a word with your client, counsellor.'

He didn't like that at all. He didn't like the idea of my talking with Alan in private, and I didn't want him around when I started showing dirty pictures. Alan settled the argument simply enough by telling the fellow to get lost. He didn't like it one bit, but he got lost.

Piersall locked us up in the cell again.

'So that's your lawyer.'

'That's my lawyer,' he said. 'He's not much to look at, is he? But he's sharp as blue blades. He's a whip. Nothing but the best for Mr Marsten's boy Alan.'

He was still sitting on the edge of his cot. He was smoking one of the cigarettes I had left with him. He didn't sound as happy as his words indicated. He looked even worse – there were worried lines in his forehead and around the corners of his mouth, and I could see nothing but tension in his eyes.

I didn't waste time. I took the picture with Linda in it from the manilla envelope, glanced at it myself, then passed it to him. I asked him if he knew the girl.

He didn't have to answer; his eyes did that for him. There was instant recognition combined with a great amount of shock. His jaw fell and he gaped at me like a goldfish in a bowl.

'There are more pictures in the envelope,' I said.

He nodded dully.

'And you've got a few things to tell me,' I went on. 'This time you're going to talk. You know a bloody bit more than you've said so far and I want to hear it.'

He nodded again. 'Yeah,' he said. 'Solid. Where'd you get these?'

'What do you care?'

'Hell,' he said. He looked at the picture, then gave it back to me. 'I can talk to you now,' he said. 'You got the picture of Barb, huh?'

'In the envelope.'

'That's what I was afraid of. I didn't want to open up about . . . things . . . unless somebody already knew about the pics. I don't know. Silly, I guess. I figured if Barb was dead the pictures at least could stay a secret. You know what I'm talking about?'

'No.'

'Oh. What do you know, man?'

I said: 'I can guess. Someone took pornographic photographs of six girls, maybe more. Barbara was one of them. She was being blackmailed, being taken for heavy money.'

'Right so far.'

'That's as far as I've taken it,' I said. 'Now it's your turn.'

He dropped his cigarette to the floor of the cell, covered it with a foot and ground it out slowly and deliberately. He looked up at me finally.

'What do you want to know?'

'You could start with the girl in the picture. Who is she?'

'Name's Jill Lincoln. She was sort of a friend of Barb's. Part of the same crowd.'

'Did you know she was being blackmailed?'

He shook his head. 'I only knew about Barb. And I didn't know all of it. Only what she told me.'

'Go on.'

'A couple weeks ago,' he said. 'I was with her and she was so nervous I thought she was going to turn green any minute. She kept losing track of the conversation, kept wandering off and getting lost in her own words. I asked her what was the matter, what was bugging her.'

'And?'

'She wouldn't say. She kept saying everything was all right, she was just worried about an exam she had, some jazz like that. I could tell it was something else. She didn't worry like that about her classes. She just didn't care that much. So I kept hitting her with questions, telling her she should tell me all about it.'

He looked away. 'We were very close,' he said. 'Not that I knew everything on her mind, nothing like that. She had her life and I had mine, you know. We weren't even going together as a steady thing. But we were close. We could talk to each other. She had something bugging her, she generally would tell me about it.'

'Go on.'

He shrugged. 'So she told me. We were sitting in her car and she flipped open the glove compartment and took out a picture. She handed it to me. It was like the one you showed me. Except with Barb in it. Barb and some cat.'

'She showed it to you?'

'Yeah. I almost folded. She didn't even blush or anything, just handed it to me and said "Here – isn't this cute?" I asked her where the hell it came from.'

'What did she say?'

'She didn't exactly say,' he told me. 'She said somebody was blackmailing her, threatening to send the picture around if she didn't play ball.'

I said: 'Why should that worry her so much? She's supposed to have run with a fairly fast crowd. Her parents knew that. I'm sure they didn't suspect she was a virgin.'

He looked at me. 'Use your head, man. There's a difference between knowing your daughter sleeps around a little and seeing a picture of it. And the bastard was going to do more than send a print to Barb's old man. A few prints were going to some school officials. Other prints were going to other people. And then the negative was going to be sold to one of those outfits that sells pictures like that around the country. You know – cut-rate kicks for kiddies. They'd be selling Barb's picture at every high school in America. Get the picture?'

I got the picture. It was an ugly one.

'It meant getting kicked out of school,' Alan Marsten went on. 'It meant a rotten reputation for a hell of a long time. It meant trouble in spades. Barb didn't like the idea.'

'Did she say when the picture was taken?'

'She told me a little of it. There was this party – her and some of her friends and a batch of people from out of the college. Some of the dead-end kids around town, I figure. She got stoned, said she thinks there was something in the drinks besides alcohol. After that she didn't remember. Maybe she didn't want to remember. I don't know.'

'And she didn't say who the blackmailer was?'

'Not a word. She wouldn't tell me how much he wanted from her, either. I figured if it was such a big bite I could help her out with it, get some extra dough from my old man. But she didn't want to talk. So we didn't talk.'

'And that was all?'

'That was all.' He fished in his pocket for cigarettes, selected one. It was bent. He straightened it out with his fingers, put it between his lips, scratched a match and lighted it. He took a deep drag of smoke and blew a cloud of it at the ceiling.

'Then Barb cut out.' he said. 'I figured she couldn't take it any more, wanted to run away some place and try starting over. Maybe she figured if she left town she could call the bastard's bluff, wait him out or something.'

'Then she died.'

'Yeah,' he said heavily. 'You came up here looking for her, came on to me at Grape Leaves with a hatful of questions. I told you to get lost. I figured the way I said. Then I heard she was dead and a whole lot of things didn't matter any more.'

'And now you're in jail.'

He laughed. 'Solid – I'm in jail. And you're asking all the questions and I'm coming through with all the answers. You mind a question, man?'

I told him to go ahead.

'Where'd you find the pictures?'

'In Gwen Davison's closet.'

His jaw fell again and his eyes bulged. 'You kidding?'

'No.'

'I don't get it,' he said. 'She was the blackmailer? And one of the other girls killed her?'

'Do you think so?'

'What else, man?'

I drew a breath. 'She didn't have the negatives,' I said. 'Just a set of prints.'

'Maybe she kept the negatives somewhere safe.'

'There's more,' I told him. 'I can hardly picture a girl like her engineering something like this. It's too complex. There are too many sides to it.'

I didn't bother adding that whoever had set everything up obviously had connections with New York – hoods to hire, strings to pull. It was none of his business. It was purely a private headache of mine.

He said: 'I guess I don't get it.'

'Neither do I. You didn't kill Gwen, did you?'

'Why would I?'

'Maybe you discovered she was in on the blackmail circuit,' I suggested. 'You were in love with Barbara. You blamed Gwen for Barbara's death. So you murdered her with your knife.'

'You don't believe that, do you?'

I didn't. He'd been too surprised by the picture, too surprised that I'd found it in Gwen's room. But it was something to toss at him, whether I believed it myself or not.

'It keeps coming back to the damn knife,' he said. 'You know what happened with that knife? Hell, you won't believe it.'

'Try it out.'

'I gave it to Barb,' he said. 'A few days before I left, I gave it to her. She asked to borrow it. God knows what she wanted it for. I didn't ask. I let her take it.' He managed a grin. 'Now, who in hell would believe a story like that?'

'I might.'

'Yeah?'

'But I don't know if a jury would,' I said.

After I left him I found a telephone and put in a call to Jill Lincoln's dormitory. A girl answered the phone almost at once and told me she'd check to determine whether or not Jill was in her room. She checked and determined that she wasn't. I told her there was no message and put the receiver back on the hook where it belonged.

Then I went down the street to the tavern. The next step was to get hold of Jill Lincoln, preferably by the throat. I had a good many questions to ask her and she was going to supply the answers if I had to hold her upside down and shake them out of her. But she would keep – I couldn't find her at the moment, and it was late enough in the day for my stomach to be growling bearishly. Lunch had somehow been left out of the picture that day. Breakfast had been ages ago.

I was starving.

I remembered the small steak and decided it was too small. I told the waiter to bring me the biggest sirloin they could find in the kitchen, with the biggest baked Idaho beside it. In the meanwhile, I added, he should try to find me a mug or two of ale. He brought the ale in a hurry and it went down easily.

Jill Lincoln.

She was quite a girl, I decided. She had switched her initials around, provided herself with a fresh name, concocted a far-fetched story and made me believe it. She set me up for a rap on the head, then disappeared neatly and left me to chase around the city trying to rescue her.

But why?

It made no more sense than anything else. And no less – because nothing at all seemed to make sense. The most alarming single fact about the entire affair was that the more I learned, the less logical everything became. I kept getting more and more pieces of the jigsaw puzzle, and none of them fit with any of the others. It was incredible.

According to Alan, the blackmail routine was an explanation for Barbara's suicide. I couldn't see it that way myself. She had a great deal of money at her disposal and her father was more than generous. She'd drawn over a thousand dollars before she left Radbourne. So the blackmailer, whoever he was, could hardly have had her with her back to the wall.

So why should she kill herself?

And, further, why run to New York to do it? That still didn't add up. If she were going to commit suicide, she still might as well have done it in New Hampshire.

Which brought it around to murder again. But why would a blackmailer murder a victim? There are simpler ways than that to grow rich. It would be the classic example of killing the goose that lays golden eggs.

The waiter saved me by bringing my steak. I pushed Barbara and Gwen and Jill from my mind forcibly, picked up knife and fork and attacked a hunk of thick red meat. I had two more ales to wash it down and left the table, finally, feeling several pounds heavier and several degrees more at peace with the world. I used the telephone on the wall in the tavern to try Jill Lincoln again. A different female voice answered this time, but the information was the same. Jill was out. I passed up another opportunity to leave a message, returned to my table and paid my check. I went outside and took a deep breath of cold air.

What next? I could run around like a headless chicken if I wanted, but I couldn't see how that would do me much good. Jill was the person I had to see. Until I saw her I was too much in the dark to get anywhere.

The thought crossed my mind that something could have happened to her, that maybe she was in danger in New York. That seemed unlikely, but in this case everything that was unlikely was as apt to happen as everything else. Or maybe she was still in New York – it seemed as though students could be absent from Radbourne for an incredible length of time before anybody noticed or reported their absence.

I gave up, got into Barbara's MG and drove back to Mrs Lipton's home for wayward detectives. I would have to assume that Jill was somewhere around, that eventually she would go to her dormitory and I could contact her there. In the meanwhile I could sit in a comfortable room, shave the stubble from my face and otherwise take things easy.

I found my way back to the old house and parked in front of it. I killed the engine and pocketed the key. I was halfway to the door before I heard my name called in an urgent whisper.

I turned and saw her.

'Roy,' she said. 'Come here.'

She was by a clump of bushes at the side of the house. I walked to her, not sure whether I was supposed to chuckle appreciatively or to belt the bloody life out of her.

'Hello, Jill.'

'Oh,' she said. 'You found out my name.'

'Uh-huh. I saw your picture.'

'Roy, I've got to talk to you.'

'That's the understatement of the century,' I said. 'You've got a great deal of talking to do.'

'Not here,' she said. 'Oh, Christ. It's not safe here. Look, can we go to your room?'

'My room?'

'Upstairs,' she said.

'That's crazy. I'm relatively certain Mrs Lipton would object to my entertaining college girls in my room. And—'

'Roy.'

I looked at her. She knew how to fake fear – I remembered her magnificent act in the taxi when we first met. But I couldn't believe she was faking now. There were beads of perspiration on her upper lip and she had developed a nervous tic under her left eye. Even Actors Studio has trouble teaching one tricks of that order.

'I took a chance coming here, Roy.'

'You take a good many chances.'

'This was a big one. Let's go to your room. If they see us together they'll kill me.'

'If we go to my room, do I get hit over the head again?'

She bit her lip. 'I'm sorry about that. Honest, I'm sorry. I didn't know that was going to happen. I'm sorry about a lot of things.' She frowned. 'Can't we go to your room?'

'Oh, hell,' I said. 'Sure, we can go to my room. Come on.'

8

The simple course seemed by all odds the best one to pursue. I did not attempt to spirit Jill into Mrs Lipton's house via a rear window, or send her scuttling up a ladder, or otherwise get her to my room by stealthy methods. No doubt Grace Lipton was already familiar with such methods, since student boarders rented her rooms. Nonchalance appeared a better gambit. I took Jill by the hand and led her through the doorway, into the house, down the hall, past the living room where Mrs Lipton sat immersing herself in television, up a flight of stairs and into my room. Nobody questioned us, looked askance at us, or otherwise interfered with us.

I closed the door, turned the latch. She tossed her coat over a straight-backed chair while I hung mine on a hook in the small closet. Then she sat down on the bed while I stood lighting a cigarette and watching her through the smoke. She stared back at me in silence while I shook out the match and found an ashtray to drop it into. The fear was still present in her eyes.

'This had better be good,' I said.

'It will be.'

'And it had better be true. You're quite an effective little liar, Jill.'

'You believed all of it?'

'I even went looking for you on East End Avenue. If that's any satisfaction to you.'

Evidently it was. A smile turned up the corners of her mouth, then died there as her face took on a serious cast once more. 'I'm awfully sorry about that, Roy. I didn't want to feed you a story like that. I kept wanting to break down and tell you the truth. But I couldn't.'

'Start at the beginning.'

She sighed. 'Could I have a cigarette? Thanks. You said something about seeing a picture of me before. When we were out in the cold, I mean. Did you see it?'

I nodded.

'There were six of us, Roy. Me and five other girls. Barb Taft was one of us and—'

'I saw the whole set.'

'The six?'

286

'Yes.'

She dragged on the cigarette. 'Well,' she said. 'Well, it's quite a display of artistic photography, isn't it? You probably can figure out most of it, then. We were at a party, Roy. A party in Fort McNair – that's the next town along Route Sixty-eight and it's even smaller and duller than Cliff's End.'

'Whose party was it?'

'Some guys in Cliff's End. One of the girls – I think it was Barb but I'm not sure – managed to get herself picked up by one of the guys. His name is Hank, Hank Sutton. He's the leader.'

'Of the blackmail mob?'

'That's right, Roy. He's a . . . a gangster. I didn't think they had gangsters in little hick towns like this one. But he's in charge of numbers and bookmaking and God-knows-what-else in this half of New Hampshire. Even when I found out about him, I thought he must be small-time. But he has connections with New York gangsters. I found that out.'

I put out my cigarette. 'Let's return to the party.'

'Sure. Well, it was . . . quite a party. The six of us aren't a bunch of vestal virgins. I guess you figured that out for yourself, didn't you? Well, we're not. But we didn't think it would be that kind of a party. I mean, we figured on some heavy necking, and maybe going the limit if we felt like it.'

'You didn't feel like it?'

'We didn't have any choice. I don't know what that bastard Hank put in the drinks, but it worked. God, did it work! I remember the way the party started but that's about all I remember. The rest is a big blank. Then I remember coming out of the fog when they let us out of their cars back on campus. We sat around for two hours drinking coffee and trying to wake up and trying to figure out what happened.' She paused dramatically. 'Well, in a few days we found out.'

I said: 'They showed you the pictures?'

She shook her head. 'They mailed 'em to us. Each of us got a set of prints in the mail, six pretty little prints in a manilla envelope. No note, no letter, nothing. You can imagine what it was like opening the envelope.'

'I know what it was like.' I decided to toss her a curve. 'I found one of those envelopes. It was in Gwen Davison's closet.'

I waited for a monumental reaction. Jill disappointed me. She didn't bat so much as an eyelash, just nodded as if that was perfectly natural.

'Must have been Barb's set,' she said. 'Don't . . . uh . . . lose them, will you? I wouldn't want them floating around campus. It might be a little embarrassing.'

'It might,' I agreed. 'Let's get back to the pictures. Did this Hank Sutton get in touch with you?'

'On the phone. He told me what he was going to do with the pictures if I didn't "play ball." I asked him what playing ball meant. It meant two hundred dollars from each of us. That was a starter. He wanted more money again not too long ago. Just a day or two before Barb disappeared, as a matter of fact.'

'How did you pay him?'

'I got together with the rest of the girls. We decided that we had to pay off, at least for the time being. Until we figured out something we could do. Each of us kicked in the two hundred bucks and I carried the loot to Hank.'

'You were the messenger?'

She nodded soberly. 'Little old me. It was bad enough paying him a cool twelve hundred dollars. That wasn't enough. He decided he liked me. He . . . he made me stay there with him. It wasn't very much fun, Roy.'

I could imagine. I looked at her, still nervous but beginning to pull herself together. I was getting plenty of pictures now, including the pornographic ones in the manilla envelope, but outside of that we weren't getting anywhere in particular. I still hadn't the vaguest notion whether Barbara had killed herself or whether she had had help. I still didn't know who had slashed the young life out of Gwen Davison.

I said: 'How come you picked me up?'

'In New York? That was on orders, Roy. Orders from Hank Sutton.'

'Tell me about it.'

She nodded. 'Well, Barb took off. You know about that. I thought she was going for money or something, or just trying to run fast and hard to stay away from Hank and Radbourne and the whole rotten mess.

'But instead she killed herself. Hank learned about it almost as soon as the police fished her out of the Hudson. Then he heard you were on the case – I don't know how. So he sent me to New York to work on you.'

She paused and narrowed her eyes. 'I didn't have any choice, Roy. He told me to go and I went. I was blackmailed into it – he still had the pictures, and as long as he had them I had to do whatever he wanted.'

'Go on.'

'I went to New York. Hank had men there checking on you. They must have followed you all over the place. I'm surprised you didn't notice them.'

'I wasn't looking for them.'

'I guess not. Of course, you couldn't know anybody would want to follow you, could you?'

I agreed that I couldn't. She finished her cigarette and managed a smile. It wasn't a very firm one. 'So that was that, Roy. I picked you up coming out of the restaurant on Times Square. I ran for your cab and hopped into it. Then those two men – they were some of Hank's New York friends – pretended to be chasing me. They weren't supposed to chase too hard. Even with an ordinary cabby we would have gotten away. The driver we had lost them so nicely it didn't look like a set-up at all.'

'That's true enough. What were you supposed to do next?'

'Just what I did – give you a phony story, find out what you knew about Barb and whether or not you were going to investigate. Hank figured that if you stayed on the case you'd find out about the pictures, and it would be messy. He thought I could find out whether you were interested in it or if you were going to let it die a natural death.'

'And I was interested.'

'Uh-huh. So then I was supposed to try and divert your interest. Jesus Christ, it was like a spy movie or something. You know – Mata Hari and all that jazz.'

I said: 'Divert my attention. And that accounts for your performance in bed, I imagine.'

'You rotten bastard!'

'Well—'

'I was supposed to pump you, dammit. That's all. Then I was supposed to arrange a meeting with you for sometime the next day and stand you up. That way you would think I ran into trouble. It was supposed to make you forget all about Barb.'

She was standing up now, her eyes fierce, her hands on her hips and her nostrils flaring. I told her to cool herself off. She thought it over, then sat down again,

'I slept with you because I wanted to,' she said finally. 'Take that and feed your ego with it if you want. I'm not a tramp. I've been around, I lead a full life for myself. I'm not a tramp. Don't call me one.'

I looked at her. 'Why did you come here tonight?'

'To talk to you.'

'Why?'

'Because I think you can help me. Because I think we can help each other. I've already told you a few things, haven't I?'

'Nothing I hadn't guessed,' I said. 'Why did your playmates give me a blackjack message?'

Her face darkened. 'I'm sorry about that. I didn't know they were going to.'

'How did the plans go?'

'They weren't too exact.' She crossed one leg over the other, gave me a quick flash of thigh and a secret smile to accompany it. 'I was supposed to stand you up last night. Then this morning or afternoon you'd get a phone call or a visit or something. A call from me or a visit from some of the boys. That would get you all wound up and you'd forget about Barb.'

'Then the plans changed.'

'Uh-huh. Hank called me this morning, Roy. He told me that Barb's roommate was knifed by that Al Marsten kook. That made it pretty obvious that you were going to get interested in Barb all over again. So I hurried back here.'

I found my suitcase in my closet, opened it, took out what was left of the pint bottle of scotch the bellhop had brought me. I looked around for glasses and found none. There was probably a glass or two in the lavatory down the hall but I did not feel like going on an expedition. I opened the bottle and took a long drink straight from it.

'Don't I get any, Roy?'

'No,' I said.

I took another drink, longer, and recapped the bottle. I unpacked my suitcase – since it looked as though I'd be around Cliff's End for a good time – and buried the bottle in a dresser drawer between a pair of white shirts. I turned to face her again, the scotch doing inexplicably magnificent things to my bloodstream.

I said: 'It's a bloody shame.'

'It is?'

'Yes.'

'What is?'

'That you're not younger, or that I'm not older. You deserve a spanking, old girl. You should be turned over someone's knee and beaten to the point of tears.'

'Me?'

'You. Did you happen to realize that you're up to your neck in at least one and probably two murders? Or didn't that occur to you?'

'What are you talking about?'

'I'm talking about murder. Barbara, for example. The suicide notion was foggy from the start. Now it's turning to pea soup, and thin soup at that. Dishwater, perhaps.'

'You think she was killed?'

'Probably.' I studied her. 'And then there's Miss Davison, for that matter.'

'But Alan—'

'—is sitting in a cell,' I finished for her. 'Accused of her murder. I don't think he's guilty.'

'Then who is?'

'I don't know, I'm afraid. How does Hank Sutton look for the role? He's got a finger in all the other pies.'

She thought it over elaborately. She tapped me for another cigarette, then managed to convince me that she deserved some of the scotch herself. I liberated the bottle from the dresser and passed it to her, watching her take it straight from the bottle without coughing or wrinkling up her pretty nose.

'That was a help,' she said, returning the bottle. 'I'd like to think Hank did it, Roy. I'd like to find a good reason to send him to the electric chair. Or watch somebody else send him. God, I hate that man!'

'But—?'

'But I can't believe it. Roy, when I talked to him on the phone this morning he was shocked. He couldn't believe it about Gwen, how it would have you back here on his neck and all. Why would he kill her? He was trying to let things cool down and that only stirred them up again.'

She was right.

'Anyway, let's forget him for a minute,' she said suddenly. 'Don't you want to know why I came to see you?'

'I already know.'

'You do?'

'Certainly,' I said wryly. 'You recently witnessed a murder. A man named Dautch—'

'Damn you, Roy!'

I laughed at her. 'Now we're almost even,' I said. 'So you can tell me now.'

'It's like this,' she said. 'Hank Sutton has those pictures. The negatives, anyway. And God knows how many prints he has of each of the pictures.'

'Go on.'

She went on. 'I've been to his house, Roy. To deliver the money, of course. And before that ... at the party.'

'The photography session?'

She colored. 'The photography session,' she repeated. 'Yes, I suppose you could call it that. Oh, you could call it a lot of things, Roy. But to hell with it. Listen – I've been to his house. It's a big old place on the outskirts of Fort McNair and he lives there all by himself. He has ... company, sometimes. I was his company once or twice, so I know. I told you about that, how he thought I was a lot of fun. An extra dividend in the blackmail game.'

I nodded and wished she would come to whatever sort of point she was attempting to make. Hank Sutton lived alone in a large old house. But what did that have to do with anything?

'Those pictures are making everything a hell of a mess, Roy. If they were out of the way you might be able to get somewhere with your investigating. And the rest of the girls and I could take things easy, relax a little. It's horrible, knowing that there are pictures like that in existence. Sort of a photographic Sword of Damocles.'

I was beginning to understand.

'It would be so simple, Roy. We would go there late after he was asleep. And we'd get inside the house and take the pictures away from him.' Her eyes drilled into mine, radiating sweetness and warmth and innocence.

'You'll help me,' she said. 'We'll get them. Won't we, Roy?'

9

The road was a ribbon of moonlight and the red MG was a lunar rocket. And, while that particular imagery might have worried Alfred Noyes, it didn't bother me in the least. I had other far weightier considerations on my mind.

'Bear right,' Jill was saying. 'Then take the next left turn past the stoplight.'

I nodded and went on driving. It was late – well after midnight, and I'd been up since four in the morning. It was almost late enough for me to behave like a bloody fool, and I was doing just that. We were on our way to the house where Hank Sutton lived. We were going to steal some dirty pictures from him.

The wisdom of this move was still lost on me, as it had been when Jill first suggested it. She'd had a properly difficult time selling the notion to me. But she was evidently a good saleswoman. We were headed for Sutton's house, ready to do or die, hearts set on securing the photographs once and for all.

It wasn't completely aimless, as I saw it. Jill herself was about as hard to figure out as a four-year-old's riddle, as transparent as a broken window. She wanted the photos back because she was tired of being blackmailed, tired of taking orders from New Hampshire's version of Al Capone. Her childish chatter about getting hold of the photographs in order to clear the air was a lot of bloody nonsense designed to make me think she was taking her stance on the side of the angels.

Still in all, she happened to be right – if for the wrong reasons. The damned pictures cropped up no matter which way I turned around. In a sense they were the focal point of the entire case. As long as this Sutton individual had them in his possession, he would be tossing body blocks at me every step of the way.

But if we had them he might be out of the picture altogether. Perhaps that was too much to hope for, but at the least he would be subdued, with one major weapon taken away from him. It was vaguely analogous to nuclear disarmament; he might still start a war, but he couldn't do nearly so much damage.

And we were on our way.

'Turn right,' she said. 'Uh-huh. Now keep going straight ahead for three or four blocks. You're in Fort McNair now. Isn't it an exciting town?'

'Not particularly,' I told her. It wasn't – very few tiny towns are especially exciting after midnight. This one was no exception, with its tree-shaded lanes and green-shuttered houses. It might be a fine place to live, but I'd hate to visit there.

'You're now almost out of Fort McNair, Roy.'

'That was quick.'

'Wasn't it? There's his house, on the other side of that open field. See it?'

I nodded.

'Open fields on every side. He likes peace and quiet. It should make everything easier for us, don't you think?'

I nodded again. I had slowed the car down and we were coasting in now. I pulled to a stop in front of the field she had mentioned and looked beyond it to Sutton's house. All the lights were out. There was a car in the driveway, a late-model Lincoln.

'He's home,' she said. 'That's his car, the only one he's got. So he's home.'

'Asleep?'

'He must be. Or in bed, anyway. He might have a girl with him, Roy.'

'Not with the lights out,' I said.

'Why not?'

'Because you can't take pictures in the dark.'

That made her blush a little. She turned off the blush, took out a cigarette and let me light it for her. 'The front door's probably locked,' she said. 'How good are you with locks?'

'Fairly good.'

'You're a talented guy, Roy. Okay, you go in the front door. The stairs are straight ahead, one flight of stairs up to the second floor. His bedroom's right at the landing.'

'Bedroom?'

'That's where he keeps the pictures. He has them in this metal lockbox that he keeps under the bed. You can just take the whole box. You don't have to open it.'

She was an amazing girl. I took another long look at the house and the car, then a shorter look at Jill. She was waiting for me to say something.

'That's all I have to do,' I said. 'Merely pick the lock, head up the stairs, sneak into the bedroom where he's either sleeping or making love to someone, crawl under the bed, grab the lockbox, and leave.'

'Uh-huh.'

I said: 'You must be out of your mind.'

'Can you think of a better way?'

I thought of a great many superior methods, such as turning the car around on the instant and driving directly back to Cliff's End. I suggested a few methods of this nature and she frowned at me. She looked extremely unhappy.

'You can do it,' she said. 'I told you he's all alone. Or he has a girl there, but she won't be any trouble. He's probably alone. He'll be asleep and you'll be awake. Why should you have a hard time with him?'

I asked her where she would be during all this fun and games. 'I'll wait here for you,' she said. 'In the car. If anybody comes or anything I'll hit the horn and warn you. And when you come out of the house I'll scoot up in front with the car so you can just hop in. I know how to drive this buggy. Barb used to let me take it for a spin. I'm a good driver.'

I told her that was reassuring. I got out of the car, leaving the keys with Jill. She slid easily behind the wheel and grinned at me. I went around to the trunk, opened it. There was a tool kit there, and in the tool kit I managed to locate a tire-iron. It seemed ideal for slamming Hank Sutton over the head, so I dropped it into a pocket and went around to Jill's window.

'Up the stairs and into the bedroom,' she said. 'The bedroom door's on the right of the landing. Don't forget.'

'I won't.'

'My hero,' she said, only partially sarcastic. 'My hero in baggy tweeds. Give me a kiss at parting.'

I gave her a kiss at parting and she turned it into Penelope saying so-long to Ulysses. Her arms wound themselves around me neck and her tongue leaped halfway down my throat. When she let go of me there were stars in her eyes.

'Be careful,' she said. 'Be careful, Roy.'

I was careful.

Very carefully I walked up the path to the house. I made my way up a trio of wooden steps that only creaked slightly. There was a door bell at the side of the door frame, and there was a knocker on the door itself, and I repressed a psychotic urge to ring bell and bang knocker and shout *Halloo!* at the top of my lungs.

I did not do this. Instead I fished in my pocket for my knife, a clever instrument made in Germany and equipped to perform every task from removing the hairs in one's nose to dissecting laboratory animals. It wouldn't cut a damned thing – the cutting blade wouldn't hold an edge to save itself. But it was excellent for opening locked doors.

The glass-paned storm door had a hook which dropped into an eye attachment screwed into the door-jamb. I slid the long cutting blade of the knife between the door and the jamb to lift the hook. This took care of the storm door.

The real door was heavy oak. It had two locks – a pintumbler type of spring lock and a supplementary bolt turned manually. I used the screwdriver blade of the knife to ease back the bolt, then sprang the spring lock with the cutting blade. I turned a brass knob and eased the door open slowly and gently. It opened without making a sound.

I looked into the darkness and listened carefully. The old house was silent as the grave and dark as a blackout in a Welsh coal mine. I stepped inside and drew the door shut behind me. A clock was ticking in one of the other rooms. I stood and listened to it, waiting for my eyes to grow accustomed to the darkness.

They did this a bit at a time. Gradually I became aware of the fact that the darkened interior of the house was not entirely black, that there were shapes and shades and shadows. A staircase loomed in front of me. I approached it, counted fourteen steps, and wondered how much the stairs would creak when I walked up them. Jill hadn't mentioned that point.

But they barely creaked at all. I walked up them like a man who had been riding horseback for several days without a pause, keeping my feet on the outward edges of the steps and being careful never to step in the middle of a plank. I stood without moving at the top of the stairs and wished for a cigarette, a long drink of scotch, and a seat in the parlor car of a fast train bound for New York. I dipped a hand into my pocket and drew forth the tire-iron. I hefted it in my hand. It was heavy.

I held onto the tire-iron with one hand, reached for the doorknob with the other. I turned it and heard the beginnings of metallic protest. It whined like a mosquito zeroing in for the kill. I took a deep breath and threw the door open. It made enough noise to wake the dead, and Hank Sutton was not even dead. He was very much alive.

He came out of sleep in a hurry. I saw the shadowy outline of his big body moving in the equally big bed. He swung both legs over the side of the bed and started to his feet.

'Who the hell—'

The room was completely dark, the shades all drawn. I moved from the doorway to one wall and pressed my back against it. He didn't know who I was or where I was and he couldn't see a thing. He hadn't moved.

'Okay,' he snapped. 'You're here, whoever you are. Why not turn on a light if we're gonna play games?'

I didn't answer. I heard the sound of a drawer opening, saw his hand move around by the tiny night table at the side of the bed. The hand came out of the drawer holding something that could only be a gun.

'To hell with you,' he said. 'You start talking fast or I blow a hole in your damned head.'

But he was pointing the gun away from me, at the doorway. I took a deep breath and hoped he didn't hear me sucking air into my lungs. He had the gun and I had a tire-iron, and a gun can be a far more effective weapon than a tire-iron.

But I knew where he was. Which was even more of an advantage. I didn't have all the time in the world. At any moment his eyes would become aware of the fact that he was awake again, at which time he would be able to see.

And once he could see, the fact that he couldn't hear me wouldn't make a world of difference. He would shoot a hole in my head just as he had promised.

'Come on, damn it! Who in—'

I rushed him.

I ran straight at him at top speed, with the tire-iron going up and coming down. The gun went off, rocking the room and filling it with the subtle stench of burning gunpowder. But the gun went off in the direction he had been aiming it, and that was not the direction I was coming from.

Then the tire-iron was curving down in a lovely arc, smashing all hell out of his wrist. The gun clattered from his hand and bounced around on the floor. I caromed into him while he roared like a gelded camel and held onto his wrist with his other hand. I bounced away from him – every action having an equal and opposite reaction – and wound up on the floor. Somewhere in the course of it all the tire-iron managed to lose itself.

'Son of a bitch,' he howled. 'What are you trying to do – kill me? You son of a bitch—'

I wasn't trying to kill him. I was trying to knock him colder than his pair of thugs had done for me in New York. I got to my feet and went for him. This time he saw me coming and threw a right at me.

It was a mistake. The punch landed but it hurt him more than it hurt me. He swung at me before he remembered what had happened to his wrist, and when his hand ran into my chest he howled again and fell backwards.

It was my turn. I hit him in the stomach with all my weight in back of the punch and he doubled up neatly. I crossed a right to his jaw and he straightened out again. He went back against a wall, then lowered his head and charged me as a wounded bull charges a matador.

He ran into a knee and fell flat on his face.

He wasn't moving. I picked up his head once or twice and banged it against the floor purely for sport. Then I went back to the doorway and rubbed one hand around the wall until my fingers found the lightswitch. I turned on lights and blinked – my eyes had grown completely accustomed to the darkness by then. I found a now-crumpled pack of cigarettes in my pocket, extracted a now-crumpled cigarette, and lighted it.

Hank Sutton was a big man. He had more hair on his chest than he had on his head. His nose must have been broken once and set poorly, and his wrist had been broken just recently by my tire-iron. He was stretched out on the floor and sleeping like a baby. I didn't even have to be careful not to wake him.

I looked under the bed and spotted the strong box. It was an ordinary gray steel affair about a foot long, six inches deep and four inches high. I reached under the bed and dragged it out. It had three circular tumblers with numbers on them from one to ten which constituted a sort of combination lock that wouldn't really keep a determined individual out of the box. I could have opened it in a moment or two but I didn't want to waste the time.

So I left him there. I picked up my tire-iron, tucked his .38 into the waistband of my trousers and his strongbox under one arm, and went down the flight of stairs in a hurry. This time I didn't bother stepping carefully, and this time each board that I hit squealed like a frightened mouse.

It was lovely – I had gone in there, smashed his wrist with a tire-iron, stolen a box of dirty pictures and taken his gun in the bargain. And the bloody fool didn't even know who I was! He hadn't so much as seen my face or heard my voice.

He was going to be unhappy. He was going to wake up with a quietly magnificent headache, with his blackmail material out the window and his gun along with it. I knew about the headache – his friends had given me one of my own in New York, and he had it coming. But the finest part of all was he wouldn't know who on earth had done it all to him.

Which was cute.

I got downstairs, tossed the front door open and went out through it. I saw the MG still parked in front of the field, and as I headed down the walk I heard her start the motor and head toward me. She slowed down long enough for me to get into my seat, then put the accelerator on the floor.

'Hey! Take it easy, girl.'

She looked at me. 'He'll be after us, Roy. He'll want to get that box back. He'll—'

'He's sleeping like a corpse.'

'You didn't wake him?'

'I awakened him. Then I put him to sleep again.'

'You ... you killed him? Roy—'

The conversation was rapidly getting inane. So I told her to shut up for a moment, and then I told her what had happened, and then all at once the car was parked at the curb and the motor was off and she was in my arms, hugging me fiercely and telling me how wonderful I was.

It got involved.

Finally I said: 'Hurry up and drive, Jill. It's late and we both have to get to bed.'

'To bed? Why?'

'Because there's not enough room in an MG.' I kissed her nose, her eyelids. 'And you and I need a great deal of room.'

'I know,' she said softly. 'I remember.'

'Then start driving.'

She shook her head stubbornly. 'You're wrong,' she said.

'About what?'

'About there's no room in an MG. There's plenty of room. You never knew Barb Taft very well, did you?'

'Not very well.'

She grinned. 'Barb would never have owned a car if there wasn't enough room. See?'

I saw.

'Besides,' she went on, 'if I started driving now it would break the mood, and this is much too nice a mood to break. Don't you think so?'

'It's a fine mood.'

'Uh-huh. And besides, I don't want to wait. All the way back to Cliff's End, for God's sake. And then trying to sneak into your moldy old room. I don't want to wait.'

Her mouth nuzzled against my throat. Her body pressed hard against mine and her voice was a whisper of warmth.

'We can stay right here,' she said. 'And we can have a very enjoyable evening. I think.'

And, as it turned out, she was correct.

10

I dropped her off at her dormitory despite her protests. She wanted to come with me, wanted to be on hand when I opened Sutton's strongbox, but I wouldn't listen to her. I explained that it was too damned late as it was, that I wanted to open the box in the privacy of my own room, and that sneaking her up Mrs Lipton's stairs once in an evening was quite enough. She argued a bit and pouted a bit and finally accepted the state of affairs. She kissed me goodbye almost passionately enough to change my mind, then scampered off to her dormitory.

I drove back to Mrs Lipton's, parked the car outside and carried the strongbox up to my room. It was the middle of the night, almost the middle of the morning, and soon false dawn would be painting boredom upon the face of the sky. I was exhausted and the bed beckoned.

So did the strongbox. I sat down on the edge of the bed with it and looked it over thoughtfully. The combination lock was a simple affair – three dials of numbers running from zero to nine, with a consequent nine hundred ninety-nine possibilities, the same as the odds in the policy slip racket.

I started spinning the dials aimlessly, trying to hit the right combination, then gave that up as fundamentally insane. Instead I took Hank Sutton's gun, hefted it by the barrel, and slammed the butt against the box.

It made a hellish noise. I sat still for a moment and felt guilty. I wondered how many boarders I had managed to awaken. Then I decided that one might as well wake them all and slammed the strongbox again with the gun.

This time it opened. I put the gun away in a drawer and opened the box. Its contents were no phenomenal surprise. First of all there were twelve negatives – two each of the six poses. I guessed that he was getting ready to pull the old gambit of selling the negatives for a high price, then resume the blackmail dodge. There were prints, too. Eighteen of them, three sets in all. All of them equally glossy, equally detailed, and equally pornographic.

I didn't waste time looking at them. I put them back in the box, adding the set I'd found in Gwen Davison's closet. Tomorrow I would have something to burn in a convenient field; for the time being only sleep interested me.

The strongbox – and the gun as well – went into a dresser drawer. While putting them away I came across what little remained of my bottle of scotch, and this could not have worked out more neatly if I had planned it. I finished the bottle and put myself, at very long last, to bed.

I was awake suddenly. It was noon and I was still tired but I'd had the magnificent luck to wake up tired or not. I sat on the edge of the bed and looked around for cigarettes. There didn't seem to be any.

It was that sort of day. There are days when one bounces out of bed filled with life and easy of spirit. There are other days when one wakes up coated with a fine layer of foul sweat, and on those days that sweat seems to have seeped into one's brain. And it was that sort of day. My brain felt sweaty.

I shook my head to clear it, then shuffled down the hall to the community bathroom. Someone was in it. I went back to my room and shifted uncomfortably until someone got out, then took his or her place. The shower was either too hot or too cold all the while I was under it, the spray either too hard or too soft. I struggled with the controls only for a small while. On days like that, you cannot fight with fate. You do not stand a solitary chance of success.

The towel provided might have blotted a small puddle of ink. It wouldn't do for a full-sized human being. I did as much as I could with it, then trundled back to my room and waited for the water to evaporate. I had a strong urge to roll around in the rug but managed to control myself.

One of *those* days.

I got dressed and dragged myself out of the house. The cold spell had broken, which should have been a pleasant turn, but it was the wrong day to expect pleasant turns. Rain had come with the warm air, rain that mingled with the fallen snow and made slush out of it. In New York you learn to accept slush as part of the winter wonderland environment. In New Hampshire you expect a little better in the way of weather.

I squished through the slush to the MG and wondered if it would refuse to start. But the gods smiled and the engine turned over. I drove over to the main street of town and parked the car.

The drugstore didn't have any of my brand of cigarettes left. I should have expected as much. I settled for a pack of something else, then went next door and smoked a cigarette while a waitress brought me orange juice and toast and coffee. There was nothing wrong with the orange juice, but the toast was burnt and the girl put cream in the coffee.

Which was par for the course.

I ate the toast without complaining, had her trade the cup of dishwater for a cup of black coffee, and smoked my way through the day's second cigarette. Then I sat there for a few moments wondering what was going to happen next. Something, no doubt. Something abominable.

So I left the lunch counter and went to the police station. And it happened.

I asked the old policeman if I could talk to Alan Marsten. He stared at me. 'You mean you ain't heard?'

'Heard what?'

'About the kid,' he said. 'About what he did, the Marsten kid.'

'I didn't hear anything,' I said mildly.

'No?'

'I was sleeping,' I said patiently. 'I just awoke.'

'Ayeh,' he said. 'Sleeping till noon, eh? You private police have the right deal, by God. Sleeping till noon!'

We had the right deal, by God. I wondered if they would throw me in jail for hitting the old fool in his fat stomach. I decided they probably would.

'The Marsten boy,' I reminded him.

'Escaped.'

'What!'

He smiled with relish. 'Escaped, I said. Run off, took to the woods, disappeared.'

'When? How? What—'

'Hang on,' he said. 'One at a time. First the *when* part. Happened about three hours ago, just after I come on duty. Then the *how* – that lawyer of his came in to see him. I opened the door and the kid gave me a hit over the head that was enough to put me out on the floor. When I came to he was gone. They say he ran out, jumped in a car that some damn fool left the keys in. And off he went like a bat out of hell.'

I must have had a magnificently foolish expression on my face because he was smiling patronizingly at me. 'The lawyer,' I managed to say. 'What about the lawyer?'

'Kid hit him. Hit him same as he hit me, with one of the legs he busted off that little chair in his cell. The lawyer was still out cold by the time I got up.'

There was probably little enough that was even mildly humorous about it, but it came at the right time, on top of no cigarettes and burnt toast and coffee with cream in it, on top of an occupied shower and a feeling of ill-being and everything else that went along with it. The mental picture of that fine Philadelphia lawyer tapped on the head with a chair leg was too much for me.

I laughed. I howled like a hyena, clutching my belly with one hand and pawing the air with the other. I roared and whooped hysterically while the excuse for a policeman watched me as if I had lost my mind. Maybe I had.

The laughter stopped almost as suddenly as it had started. I straightened up and tried to get my dignity back. 'No one knows where he was headed?'

'Nope.'

'Or why he ran off?'

'Hell,' he said. 'Guess that's easy enough. He figgered he better run away before we hang him. He's guilty as hell and he wants to save his neck.'

I didn't believe it. The more the situation developed, the more little puzzle-pieces started to come into view, the less likely it seemed for Alan Marsten to have killed Gwen Davison. After what I'd learned in the past day he was bloody well coming into the clear. I was all ready to suggest releasing the boy, when the little fool decided to set himself free.

'We'll get him,' the cop assured me. 'You know what they say – he can run but he can't hide. Dumbest thing a man could do, running away like a rabbit the way he did. That way not a soul in the world's going to believe he didn't cut that girl to pieces.'

He dropped me a sly wink. 'More'n that, I don't figger his lawyer's going to love him. Not going to work too hard to get him off. The boy really let him have it with that chair leg, let me tell you. By God, that fancy talker had a lump on his head the size of a turkey egg!'

He had a lump on his own head. It was more the size of a duck egg, as it happened, but I decided against mentioning it to him. He probably already knew.

Instead I thanked him, for nothing in particular, and left him there. I went out into the slush again and used the butt of one cigarette to get a fresh one started.

On the way to where the MG was parked I ran into Bill Piersall, the younger and somewhat more competent Cliff's End police officer. He told me what the other one either hadn't known or hadn't thought worth mentioning. The car Alan Marsten picked was a dark blue Pontiac, three years old, with New Hampshire plates. The state troopers already had word of the jailbreak plus descriptions of boy and car, and they were in the process of throwing a roadblock around the area.

Which, according to Piersall, was not a difficult procedure. 'Just a few roads out of here,' he explained. 'They can seal 'em all off in no time at all. That boy's caught in a net, Mr Markham. He can't get far.'

'What if he stays in town?'

He looked at me blankly. 'Why'd he do that? He's a dead duck if he stays around. Why, he just about admitted his guilt by taking off like that. He stays around and he doesn't have the chance of a fish in the desert.'

'Perhaps,' I said. 'But he might be safer trying to hide out. Especially with the roads sealed.'

He nodded thoughtfully. 'We'll check,' he assured me. 'We'll give the town a good going-over, see if we can't turn him out. But I think he'll be off and running, Mr Markham. I think they'll pick him up on Route Seventeen heading south, as a matter of fact. He's running scared, you see. Might be safer for him, trying to hide, but he won't stop to think on that. He busted out of that cell because he was scared and he'll run for the same reason.'

He was on his way to the station house. I let him go and got into the red MG, fitted the key into the ignition and started the motor running. Piersall's analysis was intelligent enough, I thought, but it was probably wrong.

If I was right, Alan hadn't killed Gwen Davison. And, in that case, he wasn't running away out of fear. He was running in an attempt to accomplish something, to find somebody, to perform one task or another. And if that were so, he wouldn't be leaving Cliff's End. He'd either go straight for whomever it was he wanted to see, or he'd hide out and wait for things to clear up.

That was the way it appeared to me. Which, taking into consideration the way the day had gone thus far, indicated that Piersall was probably right. Alan was a killer on the run and they'd pick him up at the roadblock on Route 17.

It was that kind of a day. But it has to be a hellishly bad day before I'll stop playing out my own hunches. And things weren't quite that bad yet.

Not quite.

I drove back to my home away from home first of all. Those photographs were still around, and as long as they remained in existence they were a potential weapon for anybody who had his hands on them. As far as that went, I didn't know whether or not Mrs Lipton made it a practice of going through her guest's drawers simply out of curiosity. I didn't want her to get an eyeful.

I parked the car and went into the large tourist home. Mrs Lipton met me with a smile and asked me if I would be staying another night. I smiled back at her, told her I probably would, and paid her for another evening. She held the smile while she pocketed the bills, then stepped out of my way and let me go up the stairs, taking them two at a time. I went into my room and closed the door after me.

The strongbox was in the drawer and the pictures and negatives were in the strongbox. I carried the box to the lavatory, locked myself in, and tore each of the eighteen photos into tiny and innocuous shreds. I did the same for one strip of six negatives, but I changed my mind and folded the other strip, putting it into my wallet. There was always the chance that the photos might come in handy at a later date. Even if they didn't, I could always make prints and sell them to high school children if the going got rough.

I flushed the shredded prints and negatives down the bowl, unlocked the door and left the bathroom for whoever might want it. I put the broken strongbox back in my drawer because there wasn't much else to do with it, tucked the gun back into the waistband of my trousers. God knew what use I might have for it, but it could conceivably come in handy.

Back in the MG again, I sat for a moment feeling like a yo-yo top on a string, bouncing back and forth all over the town of Cliff's End and accomplishing nothing at all. Thoughts like that can only depress one. I got the car going again and drove off.

Jill wasn't in her dormitory. A hallmate told me she had classes from one to three that afternoon, then usually dropped over to the college coffee shop for a bite to eat. I left a note on her desk to the effect that I would meet her at the coffee shop after three on the chance that she returned directly to her room. I looked at my watch – it was one-thirty, which gave me an hour and a half to kill before I could see her. I looked for a way to kill it.

Helen MacIlhenny was one way. I found the dean in her office, evidently not too busy to see me. I sat down in a chair and looked across her desk at the woman. She asked me if I was getting anywhere and I told her the truth.

'A few dozen things are happening,' I said. 'But no pattern's developed yet. Maybe I've accomplished nothing. It's hard to say.'

'Are you piling up clues?'

I smiled sadly. 'It doesn't work that way in real life,' I said. 'Only in the comic books. You pick up a piece here and a piece there and you never know which are clues and which are trivia. Then the final piece drops into place and everything works itself out. It's fun when it's over, but a headache while it's going on.' I turned the sad smile into a grin. 'A headache some of the time, anyway.'

'Meaning now, I suppose?'

'Meaning now.'

She nodded. 'Is there anything I can do for you, Mr Markham? Anything I can tell you?'

'Maybe. Is there anything on the order of a curfew for the students here? A bed check or something of the sort?'

'Freshmen have to be in their dormitories by midnight, two o'clock on weekends. It's strictly enforced.'

'And the older girls?'

'No curfew,' she said. 'We have a rather liberal philosophy of education at Radbourne, Mr Markham. We believe that you have to give a student responsibility in order to teach him to handle it. A bed check or curfew would be rather inconsistent with that way of thinking.'

'It would. Is attendance required at classes?'

'Only the first and last class of each session. If a student is going to acquire knowledge, he or she will do so out of motivation, not compulsion. Class attendance is not required. Some students learn the material as well on their own. And, to be painfully frank, some of our lecturers aren't worth getting up at eight in the morning to listen to. As the students are well enough aware, Mr Markham.'

I nodded. 'Then it would be possible for a student to leave campus for a day or two without anyone realizing it.'

'Oh,' she said. 'You mean Barbara—'

'Not specifically.'

'Oh,' she said again. 'Yes, I would be inclined to say that it's possible enough, Mr Markham. A student could go away and return without it coming to my attention, or to the attention of anyone in authority. Of course, a prolonged absence would not go unrecognized. Barbara's case is a case in point. Some students worried about her and called the matter to my attention.'

She thought for a moment. 'And a prolonged absence would not be disregarded,' she went on. 'There's no hard and fast rule against it, you understand. But it would be discouraged.'

I didn't say anything. I was not thinking about Barbara Taft at the moment. As a matter of fact, I was clearing up Jill Lincoln's trip to New York, among other things. I looked at Helen MacIlhenny. She had a thoughtful expression on her face.

'Mr Markham,' she said, 'I have the feeling that you know something which I don't know.'

'That's not likely, is it?'

Her sharp eyes twinkled. 'Oh, I'm afraid it's highly likely. You ought to tell me. I'm supposed to have my finger on the pulse of Radbourne, so to speak. The dean must know all that goes on around this little campus.'

'So must the detective,' I said.

'Then you don't have anything to tell me? I've a feeling something has been going on behind my back, something serious. And that it's linked with the murder.'

I admitted that it was possible. 'When I have something,' I said, 'I'll let you know about it.'

'Will you?'

'Of course.'

'I wonder if you will, Mr Markham.'

There was a pregnant pause. It was my turn to ask her something so I picked up my cue.

'What do you know about a girl named Jill Lincoln?'

'Jill Lincoln? Why?'

I tried to be nonchalant. 'Someone mentioned her as a close friend of Barbara's,' I said. 'I may be having a talk with her soon to find out if she knows anything. I like to know something about a person before a conference.'

'Is that all?'

'Certainly.'

She looked quizzically at me. 'Oh, well,' she said. 'I suspect you'll tell me what you want to and when you want to, and I suspect that's your privilege. What do you want to know about her?'

'Whatever you feel is pertinent.'

'I see. Well, there's not much to say, I'm afraid. I've never had much contact with the girl, Mr Markham. She's a reasonably competent student and she's never been in any serious trouble, the sort that has to be brought to a dean's attention.'

'From a wealthy family?'

'Why do you think that?'

'I don't know.' I shrugged. 'Barbara seems to have had friends from the upper circle, so to speak.'

Helen MacIlhenny frowned at me. 'Radbourne's liberalism is a social affair as well, Mr Markham. There's remarkably little grouping along dollar lines. As a matter of fact, Jill's family is not too well off at all, hardly in a class with Barbara's. Her father owns two or three dry-goods stores, as I understand it. He's no candidate for the poorhouse, not by any stretch of the imagination. Devoutly middle-class – that might be a good way to put it. No, Jill doesn't come from wealthy parents.'

On the way to the police station I stopped in the drugstore, took up temporary residence in the telephone booth and put through a call to the Taft home in Bedford Hills, Edgar Taft wasn't in but Marianne was.

She took the call.

'Roy,' she said, 'I was hoping you would call. Now, while Edgar was out.'

'Something happen?'

'No,' she said. 'Nothing's happened, not really. But I wanted to tell you that . . . that you don't have to waste any more time up in Cliff's End. You can come back to New York now any time you feel like it.'

'Really? Is that Edgar's idea?'

She hesitated. 'Not . . . exactly. Roy. I appreciate what you've done. He was very upset emotionally by Barb's death; you know that. You've been a settling influence. Otherwise he would have sat around feeling that nothing was being done, and he's a man who cannot live with that feeling.'

She stopped, probably for breath. I waited for her to get back on the track.

'But now I think he has accepted the fact that Barb committed suicide, Roy. I've . . . I've tried to help him reach that conclusion. His attitude has been a common one. He thinks of suicide as a cowardly act, the act of a worthless person. But I've been making him . . . I should say helping him . . . to realize that Barb was a very sick girl, an extremely disturbed girl. And that can make a difference. He sees that now.'

I let her wait for an answer until I had a fresh cigarette going. Then I said: 'So now he's cooled off and I'm supposed to drop everything. Is that the idea?'

'More or less.'

'I see. Marianne—'

'You could come to New York, Roy. Come up to our place this evening, talk to Edgar, tell him you've been working like a dog and nothing's turned up to indicate anything but suicide. Then tell him that as far as the reason for her depression goes, it seems as though it'll be impossible to determine it for sure. Tell him it was just one of those unfortunate things, that—'

'Marianne.'

She stopped.

'I can write my own dialogue, Marianne. I don't need a script, you know.'

'I'm sorry,' she said.

'I'm afraid I'll be in Cliff's End another day or so at the least. Not solely because of your daughter's death. I'm involved in another matter as well.'

'In Cliff's End?'

'That's right.'

A significant pause. 'I see, Roy. Well, all right. I just thought that the sooner he could be reassured once and for all that Barbara wasn't murdered. Well, you'll be back soon enough, I suppose.'

'I suppose so.'

'Yes,' she said. 'Roy, I want you to know how much I appreciate everything you've done so far. It means a great deal both to Edgar and to myself.'

I didn't answer.

'When Edgar comes home, should I give him any message? Or I could call his office if it's anything important. He doesn't like it when I disturb him during office hours—'

'I thought he was retired.'

A slight laugh. 'Oh, you know Edgar. He'd lose his mind without an office. Roy, is there anything you want me to tell him? Any message?'

'No,' I said. 'There's no message.'

I put the phone on the hook and wondered why something bothered me. I should have felt relaxed enough. I did not.

Alan Marsten. I had to get to the police station and find out what, if anything, had happened. Piersall had his theory, that the boy would be caught at a roadblock, and if it were true he had probably been caught already.

If not, I wanted to find him.

Because if Piersall was wrong and I was right, then Alan Marsten was on his way somewhere, looking for somebody, ready to do something. Somebody might get hurt – either Alan or the person he was looking for.

Who would he be after? Why had he run – like a rabbit or like a lion, depending upon your point of view – and what in the name of the Lord was he planning?

Good questions.

Then I thought of an answer . . .

11

Bill Piersall had lost most of the forest-ranger look. He sat behind his desk now, a cup of black coffee at his elbow, the receiver of a phone pressed to one ear and gripped tightly in one hand, a cigarette burning itself out between the second and third fingers of the other hand. As far as the phone conversation went, he seemed to be doing more listening than talking. I stood in front of his desk, ignoring his waving signals to sit down and relax. Instead I shifted impatiently from one foot to the other and waited for him to finish up.

He did, finally. He cursed somewhat boyishly and set the receiver in its cradle, then fastened weary eyes on me.

'Nothing so far,' he said. 'Not a damn thing.'

'No action with the roadblocks?'

'Oh, we've had action in spades,' he said bitterly. 'Three suspects hauled in so far and none of 'em looked any more like that Al Marsten than you or me. One of 'em was thirty-six – can you imagine that? Thirty-six years old and madder than hell to be pulled in like a crook, and ready to sue the whole damn state of New Hampshire for false arrest.'

He picked up the coffee cup and drank most of what was in it. He put the cup down and made a face. 'Cold,' he explained. 'Even the coffee's cold in this godforsaken state.'

'You've had nothing then?'

'Nothing.' He finished his cold coffee and screwed up his face once more in disgust. 'Looks like you're right,' he said, not too grudgingly. 'Must be he's hiding out in town. Not even a native could get through those roadblocks, and he's no native. He doesn't know the country at all.'

'Where are the blocks?'

'One's down on Seventeen between here and Jamison Falls. That's where I thought we'd get him. And there's a few—'

'How about Sixty-eight? Is the road blocked?'

'Sure.'

'This side of Fort McNair?'

He was shaking his head. 'Other side,' he said. 'Sixty-Eight's the only road through McNair so they might as well close it further down to make sure he didn't get there before 'em. What's happening in McNair?'

'I'm not sure,' I said. 'But I think we'll find Alan Marsten there.'

'You know something?'

'I might. Want to help me take a look?'

'Right!'

He was up and around the desk like a shot. He dropped the cigarette to the floor and covered it with his foot. Then the two of us were out of the building.

'My car's by the corner—'

'We'll take mine,' I said. 'It moves faster.'

We piled ourselves into the MG. I noticed the gun on his hip on the way and remembered that I had a gun of my own, on my own hip. His was in a holster while mine was tucked under my belt.

I wondered if we'd be using them.

I got the MG going and gave the engine its head. The car picked up quickly and scooted over the road.

'Some car,' Piersall said.

'It's a good one.'

He was laughing and I looked at him. 'Just thinking,' he said. 'Just struck me. Wouldn't it be hell if some dumb son of a bitch of a trooper stopped us for speeding? Wouldn't it be the thing?'

'Don't worry,' I said. 'They couldn't catch us.'

I put the accelerator pedal all the way to the floor and left it there.

'Hank Sutton,' I said. 'Know anything about him?'

We were hitting the outskirts of McNair and I let the MG slow down a bit. The weather was beginning to clear up. I remembered how the weather had matched the miserable mood of the early part of the day. I wondered if the improvement was supposed to be an omen.

'I know he's a son of a bitch.'

'Is that all?'

'Nope,' he said. 'I know he runs everything crooked in this part of the state. And that a lot of people would like to see him in a cell. Or with a rope around his neck. He lives in McNair, doesn't he?'

'Yes.'

'That where we're going?'

'Yes.'

'I'll be a son of a bitch,' Bill Piersall said. 'I'll be a ring-tailed son of a bitch.'

There was something totally disarming about the way he swore. It was almost embarrassing, as it is when you overhear a maiden aunt use a dirty word. It seemed improper, a betrayal of the Scout Law or something of the sort.

'We going up against Sutton?'

'Probably. He's in this up to his ears.'

'In what?'

'This Marsten mess.'

'Didn't Marsten kill the gal?'

'No.'

'Son of a bitch,' he said. 'Who did? Sutton?'

I said: 'I don't know who killed her. But now Sutton's going to kill Marsten. Maybe.'

'I don't get it,' he said, puzzled. I told him that I really didn't get it myself, not entirely, and that we'd both know a lot more about it in a short enough span of time. This didn't really satisfy him but it left him without any questions to ask. So he stopped asking questions.

Either I remembered the route Jill and I had taken the night before or the car knew the way all by itself. Whichever was the case, I made the right turns and did the right sort of driving until, all at once, we hit the other side of McNair and Sutton's large and ancient house came into view. There it was on the other side of the field in front of which Jill had waited just the night before.

We didn't wait by the field. I pulled the car right into the driveway and hit the brakes hard. We stopped dead just a few feet from the rear of Sutton's big Lincoln. It was still where it had been the night before.

And a blue Pontiac was parked in front of the house.

'He's here! I'll be a son of a—'

But we were in motion before he could get the word 'bitch' spoken. We got out of the car and started moving automatically. He was heading for the house's side door while I went around in front.

'I'd like to get that bastard,' he said. 'That Sutton bastard. He's big but he's not too big to take down a peg.'

'Well, he's inside.'

'Yep,' he said. 'Maybe he'll come out.'

He shouted: 'Open up, Sutton! Police!'

There was no answer. I tried the door; it was locked. I didn't bother playing childish games with my German knife this time. I aimed Sutton's gun at Sutton's lock and squeezed the trigger. There was an appropriately impressive noise and the smell of burning wood. Then I kicked the door and it swung open.

Piersall was at my side suddenly. Evidently he'd decided to give up the side door approach and join me at the front. He shouted at Sutton again. There was no answer.

We went inside to the vestibule, guns still drawn. I looked up at the flight of stairs that I'd gone up so slowly and silently the night before.

Then I saw motion. I grabbed Piersall and gave him a shove and dove myself for the floor.

A gun went off and a bullet went over our heads.

We crouched on either side of the vestibule archway. Sutton was in the bedroom at the head of the stairs, the room where I had halfway knocked his head in just twelve or thirteen hours ago. He couldn't come down and we couldn't go up.

'Must be another staircase,' Piersall was saying. 'I'll go around, see what I can do.'

I shook my head. 'No other stairs,' I said. 'Not in a house like this one. There's this staircase and that's all. He's stuck up there and we're stuck down here.'

'We can wait him out. Call back for help, starve him out.' He scratched his head. 'Maybe have them drag up some tear gas. That gets 'em every time.'

'On television?' He looked sheepish and I felt ashamed of myself. 'Anyway, he's got the boy. Alan Marsten. He may still be alive but he won't be unless we get him in a hurry.'

'How?'

It was a bloody good question. On the surface it looked as much like a stalemate situation as anything had ever looked. But there had to be an answer. There were two of us and there was only one of Sutton.

And that should make some sort of difference, a difference in our favor. Two to one is fine odds.

I peered carefully through the archway. His gun went off again and I jerked back. The bullet was a foot off and it still seemed too close.

'He's got us shut up tight,' Piersall said. 'And we got him shut up just as tight.'

I tried to remember back to the night before. Something about his room—

'There's a porch in back,' I said. 'An upstairs porch off the bedroom, a sort of small balcony.'

'There is, huh? You sure?'

'You can see it from the road,' I lied.

'Didn't notice it,' he said. 'What do you figure?'

'You stay here,' I told him. 'Don't let him get out of that bedroom. Take a shot at him every few minutes to keep him sitting up there. I'll see what I can do.'

'You going up on that porch?'

'I may.'

He whistled soundlessly. 'That's a neat trick,' he whispered. 'If he sees you coming—'

'Then I'm dead.'

'You said it. Sure you don't want to wait him out?'

'We'd wait all day. I'd rather take the chance.'

I took a pot shot at Hank Sutton's doorway and let the noise of the gunfire cover me while I scurried out of the house like a frightened rabbit. Then I went through the driveway and alongside the house to the back yard. There was a porch off the bedroom. Incredibly enough, you *could* see it from the road.

The garage contained everything on God's good earth, with the singular exception of a ladder. I looked around for a ladder until I was convinced it wasn't there, then backtracked to the house itself again. The garbage cans were arranged in a neat row by the side of the cellar door. If I could haul one close to the porch without Sutton hearing me, and if I could stand on it and reach the porch—

And if wishes were horses.

I hadn't seen many beggars riding recently. None but Alan Marsten, and he had come riding in someone else's car. If wishes were Pontiacs—

I found one of the garbage cans, the only one not filled with garbage of one sort or another. I picked it up, first setting the lid in the snow, and carried it over close to the porch. Then I inverted it so that I'd have a surface to stand on and set it down.

It made noise. But at that precise moment one of the men inside the house shot at the other man, and that covered the comparatively small sound of the garbage can. I managed to climb up on top of it, again making a small amount of noise that no one seemed to notice.

Now I could reach the porch.

I found a convenient pocket and dropped Sutton's gun into it, hoping it wouldn't go off while I was climbing and shoot a hole in my leg. I reached up and took hold of the edge of the porch floor with both hands, then got one hand onto a bar in the wooden railing. I hoisted myself up partway and saw that I'd gauged things badly. I was climbing up directly in front of the door that opened out onto the porch. If he looked around he would see me. And if he saw me, he would be looking at the world's most beautiful target since the invention of the bull's-eye. I had both hands on the damned railing, and if I let go I'd fall on my face.

But there were compensations. This way at least I had the ability to see inside of the bedroom. I took a good look.

Sutton had his back to me. I saw the gun in one of his big hands. He was by the door, ready to squeeze off another shot at Piersall.

Then I saw Alan.

He was not much to look at. He was crumpled up by the foot of the bed and it was impossible to tell whether he was alive or dead. I saw bloodstains – or what looked like them – on the rug. It seemed logical to assume the blood was Alan's.

I pulled hard with both hands and raised myself a few more feet. I reached for the top of the railing, took hold of it and wondered how strong it was. It was evidently strong enough. I placed both feet on the outer edge of the porch floor and prepared to step over the railing.

A gun went off and I almost fell down again. Sutton jerked his head back – evidently Piersall had squeezed off another shot at him.

I drew a breath. Then I drew my gun, taking it from my pocket and letting my index finger curl around the trigger. I wanted him alive, but it might be hard that way.

I looked at Sutton. He still hadn't turned toward me, which was ideal. I hoped he wouldn't.

I succeeded in getting one foot over the rail. I started to bring the other one over to keep it company, then stopped in the middle of the act and poised there like a ballet dancer in the fifth position.

Because Alan Marsten moaned.

The sound was barely audible through the porch door, but it must have been clear enough to Hank Sutton. I stood there posing prettily while he turned around in the direction of the moan. I brought up the gun to cover him.

But he didn't see me. He was looking at Alan.

Then he turned the gun on Alan. And I realized at once that he was going to eliminate this moaning nuisance, that he was going to shoot Alan dead.

I yelled: 'Sutton!'

He whirled at the noise and his gun came up fast, away from the boy and pointed straight at me. I must have fired at about the same time he did, because I heard only one noise. A bullet snapped through the glass door and whined over my shoulder. Another bullet – one of mine – snapped through the door and took him in the center of his big barrel chest.

He grunted. He took one reluctant step backward, and then a big ham of a hand came up to grope around that hole in his chest. It did not do him any good. He backed up again – just a half-step this time – and then reversed his direction, pitching forward onto his face.

And there I was, with one foot on either side of the railing. I reacted very slowly now, almost numb. I picked up the retarded foot and promoted it, lifting it ever-so-gently and leading it over the railing. The porch door was locked so I shot the lock off for the sheer joy of it. The bloody gun was a toy now and I was a child playing games.

I went to the head of the stairs and called for Piersall.

Sutton was stone cold dead. We rolled him over and checked his pulse. We put a shard of broken glass from the porch door first to his nose and then to his mouth. There was no pulse, no heartbeat, and no breath frosted the shard of glass. We let go of him and he fell back down again, staring at the ceiling through empty eyes.

'Pretty shooting,' Piersall said admiringly. 'He was going to shoot you, eh?'

'He tried. He was getting ready to put a bullet in the boy. To get him out of the way, I'd guess.'

That reminded us that there was a third person in the room. We turned to Alan. He was conscious, after a fashion. But he had obviously taken a rugged beating. One eye had been hammered shut and his face was caked with blood from nose and mouth. He was missing an occasional tooth and it was an odds-on wager that a few of his ribs were dented.

He said: '—had the pictures.'

I listened to him. We had to get him to a hospital in a hurry, but first I wanted to get everything he had to tell me.

'Thought . . . thought I took them. I didn't. Came after him to get them. But—'

He stopped, tried to catch his breath by sucking huge mouthfuls of air into his lungs. His good eye closed for a moment, then managed to open.

He said: 'Bastard.'

And that was the extent of his conversation. He closed his good eye again and quietly passed out. I decided it was his privilege. I didn't blame him a bit.

'This kid's got to go to a hospital,' Piersall said. 'He took a beating.'

'I know. Is there one nearby?'

'Five miles down the road. Want to give me a hand with him? We better be careful – he'll have broken ribs and God alone knows what else. We don't want to make him any worse than he is already, the poor son of a bitch.'

We each took an arm and managed to get Alan to his feet. We walked him over to the stairway, then got him downstairs a slow step at a time.

'Be a son of a bitch,' Piersall said again. The swearing was beginning to sound somewhat more natural now. He was growing into it.

'Got to give that kid credit,' he said. 'He went up against a bastard, all right. Sutton can take most anybody. Could, that is. Guess he can't take anybody now, can he?'

'I guess not.'

'That was pretty shooting,' he told me again. 'I was just a damn fifth wheel, wasn't I? Sitting safe and cozy while you went and climbed right up after him.'

'One of us had to stay there.'

'Yeah,' he said. 'I guess.' He bit his lip. 'But that was sure nice shooting.'

We carried Alan out of the house and down the walk. He was still unconscious and I hoped he would stay that way until he was in the hospital where a needle of morphine would make things easier for him. Sutton was a professional, and nobody can hand out a beating the way a professional can.

'Hell,' Piersall said. 'How we gonna do it?'

'Do what?'

'Take him there,' he said. 'Only room for one in that damn MG. One plus a driver, I mean. We can't stick him in the trunk, can we?'

We rather obviously couldn't.

'Suppose we could take him in the Pontiac,' he said doubtfully. 'But it's going to be cute enough at the roadblock as she stands. Some of those troopers don't know me. They'll give us a hard time if they see the Pontiac.'

'Take the MG.'

'Just me and him?'

'That's the idea,' I said. 'It moves faster, for one thing. For another, you don't need me along. And you can strap him in with the safety belt. That will keep him in place.'

'I never drove one of these,' he said. Then he grinned hugely. 'It'll be fun trying, I guess. She got a regular H shift or what?'

I explained that there were three forward speeds and showed him where each gear was. Then we loaded the still-unconscious form of Alan Marsten into the right-hand seat and strapped him securely in place.

Piersall settled himself behind the wheel. He played around with the gearshift lever until he figured it out for himself, then turned to look at me.

'How'll you get back to town?'

'In the Pontiac or the Lincoln. One or the other.'

'Good luck,' he said. 'That was sure some action we had, wasn't it?'

'It was.'

'We don't get much of that around here,' he said. 'It's mostly a quiet town, quiet part of the country. I hardly ever shot a gun before in what they call the course of duty. Warning shots now and then, that kind of thing. But never shooting to kill.'

'A little excitement never hurts,' I said.

'Yeah. Well, I'm glad somebody finally got to Sutton. He was a son of a bitch, a real live son of a bitch. And now he's a dead one.'

He started the MG, put her in low and drove away. I watched him until he was out of sight, then walked over to the Pontiac. The keys were not in the ignition.

I swore softly, then checked the Lincoln. No keys.

I went back into Hank Sutton's house, tugged a lamp loose from the wall socket and cut off a length of wire. I stripped the ends with my knife, carried the wire to the Lincoln and pretended I was an all-American juvenile delinquent running a hot-wire on a car for a joy ride around the block.

If I had to hot-wire a car, it might as well be the Lincoln. Not only was it more fun to drive, but the Pontiac was a car the police would be looking for. I didn't want to be stopped.

I remembered what to do and did it. Amazingly enough it worked. The engine turned over and I put the Lincoln in reverse and backed out of the driveway. After the MG, the Lincoln was bulky and awkward, an oversize and overweight bundle of metallic nerves.

But on the highway it loosened up and showed me what a nice clean motor it had. I pointed the car toward Cliff's End and glanced at my watch. It was only a quarter to three, and it didn't seem possible.

I was going to be on time for our date.

12

The Radbourne coffee shop was a cold gray room in the basement of the student lounge. A cluster of tables – round ones seating eight and square ones seating four – gleamed of formica here and there around the room. Students drank coffee, sipped unidentifiable beverages through straws, munched cheeseburgers and talked noisily, and incessantly.

I looked around for Jill and didn't find her. I went to the counter, bought a cup of coffee, and carried it to an empty table. I sat down and lighted a cigarette while I waited for the coffee to cool. And for Jill to arrive.

At a table not far from mine a young man and a girl sat eating ice cream. The boy was the all-American type – crew cut, broad forehead, boat-neck sweater, khaki trousers, an intelligent-but-unimaginative expression on his face. The girl was quietly pretty, with light brown hair and rosy-apple cheeks. There was something naggingly familiar about her, and yet I was certain we had never met.

Then I realized just what it was that was so naggingly familiar, and I looked away guiltily. She was familiar, certainly. I had seen her picture.

And in that picture she had not looked nearly so wholesome.

I tried the coffee. It was still too hot and I sat the cup back in its saucer and took another deeper drag on my cigarette. I looked at my watch. It was after three, and Jill was due any minute.

I wondered how Alan Marsten was. He'd taken a hell of a beating, a professional job of punishment quite professionally administered. But he was a game lad. Game enough to knock out a pair of men in order to escape from his jail cell. Game enough to go up against a heavyweight type like Hank Sutton. All of which made him very game indeed.

I hoped he'd be all right.

Now Alan was in a hospital, mending, and Sutton was in his own house, lying dead and growing cold and stiff. And I was waiting for a pretty girl to come and drink a cup of coffee with me, and wondering when in God's name she'd arrive.

She arrived, ultimately. It was almost three-thirty when she walked in the door, her hair neatly combed, her expression alert. She was carrying a leather notebook under one arm and was wearing a loose gabardine coat over a heavy sweater and a pair of plaid slacks.

I saw her before she saw me. She stood up straight and surveyed the room with sharp eyes, looking everywhere but at me. Then finally she saw me and headed over to my table. She dropped herself heavily into the chair directly across from me and slammed her briefcase quite dramatically upon the table. Her cheeks were pink from the cold and her eyes were bright.

'Hi, Roy.'

'Hi.'

'I got your note,' she said. 'You wanted to see me.'

'That's right.'

'How come?'

'To talk.'

A heavy mock sigh. 'That's disappointing,' she said. 'That's disappointing as hell.'

'It is?'

'Uh-huh.'

'Why?'

'Because,' she whispered, 'I thought maybe you wanted to make love to me. But all you want to do is talk. And that, kind sir, is disappointing.'

She stood up again. 'Not that I'm unwilling to talk,' she said. 'But first my system demands coffee. Wait here, Roy. I'll be back as soon as I convince the idiot behind the counter to sell me a mug of mud.'

I watched her walk to the counter, her full hips swaying ever so slightly under the coat. I tried my coffee again, and this time it was drinkable. Jill came back, her coffee cooled and polluted by cream and sugar. She sat down again and asked me for a cigarette. I gave her one. As she leaned forward to take the light I held for her I could smell the perfume of her hair. I looked at her, and I remembered the night before, and another night not too long before that.

She said: 'Hello, you.'

I didn't say anything.

'Hey! Did you hear about Alan?'

'What about him?'

'He broke out of jail,' she said. 'Isn't that just one for the books?'

'I heard.'

'One for the books,' she repeated. 'I don't know exactly what happened – I heard it fourth or fifth or maybe tenth-hand. But he hit his own lawyer and slugged a cop and stole a car and ran out of town.'

I told her that was substantially what had happened. Her eyes narrowed.

'Then that cinches it,' she said. 'Sort of kills your theory, too.'

'My theory?'

'That he was innocent He wouldn't bust out of jail if he was innocent, would he?'

I didn't answer.

'He must have killed Gwen,' she said. 'It probably broke him up when Barb killed herself – I guess he was more deeply involved with her than anybody realized. And he knew Barb and Gwen never got along very well. So that probably set him off. Made him want to get revenge, if you see what I mean. As if Gwen had anything to do with what happened to Barb.'

I nodded thoughtfully.

'It's kind of nutty,' she said. 'But he's kind of a nut. He always has been – you know, a little weird. Something like Barb's death could set him off and make him go nuts all the way.'

I picked up my cup of coffee and drained it, then set down the empty cup in the saucer. I looked up at the clock on the wall, looked over at the lunch counter. I was very tired now, tired of murders, tired of violence, tired of the college of Radbourne and the town of Cliff's End and the whole bloody state of New Hampshire. I wanted to go someplace far more civilized and get disgustingly drunk.

I said: 'Marsten has been found.'

She stared. 'You're kidding!'

'I'm serious.'

'But . . . oh, that's impossible! Roy, you let me babble on and on about him and he's already been found. You're terrible, did you know that? But tell me about it, Roy. Where was he? Who found him? What happened?'

I drew a breath. 'I stopped by the police station on the way over here,' I told her. 'They couldn't tell me too much. They'd just received a phone call a moment or two ago from the state troopers. They found Marsten in a town a few miles north of here. They didn't tell me which town, but I don't suppose it matters.'

I watched her face very carefully. 'He seems to have gone berserk,' I went on. 'They found a man there whom Marsten had murdered. Then the boy put a gun in his mouth and blew his brains out. Murder followed by suicide.'

She tried to keep the relief from showing in her face. She was a rather accomplished actress but she was not quite good enough. Her mouth frowned but her eyes could not help dancing happily.

She said: 'What on earth—'

'Some neighbors called the police,' I said. 'When they heard the gunshots. It seems that Marsten broke into this man's home in order to use his place to hide out. Evidently the man resisted in one way or the other and our boy didn't like that. Alan had a gun – God alone knows where he found it – and he shot the man.

'Then I suppose he suddenly realized just what he had done. He'd killed Gwen Davison and had murdered an innocent man, and the two acts were too much for him. So he killed himself, and that's the end of it.'

Now the relief was obvious. She was one happy little girl now. She drank more coffee, finishing her cup, and flicked ashes into it from her cigarette.

'Then I was right,' she said.

'Evidently.'

'Well,' she said. 'That clears up your job, doesn't it? You can tell Barb's folks she committed suicide, but don't tell them about the picture – it would only make them feel bad. And Gwen's murder is all solved now.' She smiled. 'And I'm off Hank Sutton's blackmail hook, thanks to you. You did me quite a favor last night, Roy. Quite a favor.'

I didn't say anything.

'Poor Barb,' Jill Lincoln said. 'Poor kid – if she had just kept a good grip on herself everything would have been all right. I tried to tell her just to hang on, to keep paying off Sutton until we found a way to stop him once and for all. But she was a pretty mixed-up kid, Roy. And that was enough to push her over the edge.'

'It's a shame, isn't it?'

She nodded sadly. 'Poor Barb,' she said again. 'And poor Gwen, getting killed almost by accident. And poor Alan and that poor man who got in his way. It must have been terrible for Alan, Roy. That one horrible moment when the curtain lifted and he realized what he had done. And then killing himself.'

She lowered her eyes and studied the table-top. I reached across the table and covered her hand with my own.

'Come on,' I said. 'Let's get out of here.'

'Where do you want to go?'

'Some private place. Any suggestions?'

She though it over. 'I guess my room's okay.'

'In your dormitory?'

'Uh-huh.'

'Am I allowed in there?'

'During the day you are. Let's go.'

We got up from our chairs and walked out of the coffee shop. She tucked her leather notebook under one arm and buttoned up her gabardine coat. As we left the building she took my arm.

'Where's your car, Roy?'

'I left it downtown. We can walk to your dorm, can't we? It's not far.'

We walked to her dormitory. I'd left Sutton's Lincoln parked a short way down the block, but her dormitory was in the other direction and we did not pass the big car. I was glad of that. It was an uncommon sort of car, and I suspect she might have recognized it.

We went into her building, climbed stairs to her floor, walked down the hall and into her room. Her roommate was not in. Jill tossed her notebook onto a bed, then turned to close the door of the room.

'Now watch this part closely,' she said. I watched closely. She rummaged around on the top of her dresser until she managed to locate a hair pin. Then she returned to the door and did something with the hair pin. She turned to me triumphantly and beamed.

'See?'

I didn't see.

'Come here,' she said. 'I'll show you.'

I came and she pointed. I looked while she explained. 'I drilled a little hole through the gizmo that keeps the door shut,' she said, 'and when you stick a pin in, it locks the door. You aren't allowed to padlock the doors or anything, but this works perfectly. Now nobody can get in, not while the pin is in place. It's perfect.'

I told her it was amazing to what lengths college students would go to secure privacy. I told her the mechanism she had devised was ingenious. Then she threw her arms around my neck and kissed me. It was the typical Jill Lincoln kiss, the sort that tickles one's tonsils.

'Privacy,' she said. 'You Tarzan. Me Jane. That—' pointing '—bed.'

I managed to smile.

'Oh, damn it,' she said.

'Damn what?'

'Just it. You'll be going back to New York now, won't you? I mean, the case is all bottled up or bundled up or whatever it is a detective does with cases. You won't be able to stay here and dally with me much more.'

'That's true.'

'Am I fun to dally with, Roy?'

'Great fun.'

She grinned. 'You don't dally so badly yourself, kind sir. Maybe I can get down to New York every so often. Maybe we can do a little more dallying.'

'Maybe.'

She stepped forward again, ready to be kissed, and even now I wanted to take her in my arms and kiss her, hold her, make lovely love to her. The personal magnetism of the girl was extraordinary. Even now, knowing what I knew, with all the puzzle fragments securely locked in place and the whole ugly picture revealed, the girl managed to be charming and exciting.

But I stepped back. Her eyes studied mine and, perhaps, saw something there. She waited for me to say something.

'You're very pretty, Jill.'

'Why, thank you—'

'You're very pretty,' I repeated. 'Have your lawyer get a great preponderance of men upon the jury, dear. That way you won't hang. You'll go to prison for a very long time, but you won't hang.'

She stared at me. She had grown very secure now, and was perfectly happy about everything, and my words were coming out of left field.

'Because you killed Owen.'

Her jaw fell.

'That's right,' I said. 'You killed her. Alan Marsten let Barb borrow his knife. She must have given it to you. And you killed Gwen with it.'

'Is this supposed to be a joke, Roy? Because it's not very funny.'

'It's no joke.'

'You really think I—'

'Yes. I really think you killed her.'

She stood stock still for a moment, nodding her head slowly to herself. Then she turned around, walked to the bed sat down on it. She picked up her leather notebook and toyed with the zipper, her eyes on me.

She said: 'You're out of your mind, you know.'

'I don't think so.'

'Really?'

'Really.'

'Then pull up a chair,' she said, her voice acid. 'Sit down and tell me all about it. This ought to be interesting. Did I have any particular reason for killing Gwen?'

'Yes. She was fouling your blackmail operation and you were afraid you'd find yourself in trouble.'

Her eyes went as wide as tea-cups. 'My blackmail . . . oh, you're kidding.'

I pulled up a chair near the bed and sat down. 'It was a very pretty set-up,' I said. 'I have to grant you that. I guessed that someone was on the inside, that Sutton couldn't have worked it out all by himself. You gave me a quick story about Sutton being a pick-up of Barb's, told me the rest of you went along to the party for the lark. But that didn't add up.

'An operation like this one needed preparation,' I went on. 'Someone had to pick the right girls, had to have enough of their confidence to get them to the party in Fort McNair. The girls had to have money, for one thing. No one would be fool enough to blackmail the average college girl for anything more than her maidenhead. The average college girl gets a few dollars a week and no more. But the girls in your little group were good subjects for blackmail, weren't they?'

She did not answer. She was still playing with the zipper on the notebook, running it back and forth, avoiding my eyes with her own eyes.

I went on. 'At first I thought Gwen was the inside girl. It seemed logical enough at the time – she resented Barbara Taft's wealth, and when I found the photographs in her closet I thought she was in on the operation. That notion had me wandering around in circles. I couldn't get anywhere with it.

'It was much more logical to figure it the way it actually happened, Jill. One of the girls being blackmailed wasn't really being blackmailed at all. She was on the inside, setting things up and taking her cut of the profits. And she was always above suspicion as far as the blackmail victims were concerned. They thought she was in the same boat they were in. They never realized she had set them up for Hank Sutton.'

'And I'm the girl?'

'Yes.'

'Why? Why me?'

'Several reasons,' I told her. 'First of all, you were the pauper of the group. Barb certainly wouldn't have been a blackmailer, not with the funds at her disposal. I thought of that possibility, as a matter of fact, but it didn't make much sense. Dean MacIlhenny told me this afternoon that you don't have much money at all, Jill. You act rich and you dress expensively, but your father hasn't much money. It had to come from somewhere.'

She didn't say anything.

'And you were the girl Sutton used to run his errands; you admitted that much on your own. You came to New York to set me off the trail. You collected the blackmail money for him. You knew where his house was and had been there often enough to have the layout committed to memory. My God, you even knew where he stashed the negatives! He wouldn't tell you that if you were on his hook – it wouldn't do him any good. But as his partner, you had a certain right to know.'

She was gnawing at her lower lip. I could see her trying to figure out a way into the clear. She hadn't been able to find one yet.

'Let me tell you what happened, Jill. You arranged things and they were working splendidly. Then Barbara Taft disappeared and you started to worry. I came to Cliff's End looking for her and you worried a little bit more, enough to tell Sutton all about it. He wasn't even around campus; he never would have known I was investigating. But you were here and you found out.'

'Then what happened, Roy?'

'Then you followed me back to New York,' I said. 'You had Sutton phone friends of his in New York and arrange for a pair of parties. His friends chased us in the cab so that you could pump me for information. Then they let us get away and I stashed you in an apartment in the Village.'

'Where we made love.'

I ignored that. 'You left early in the morning,' I went on. 'You caught the first train back to Radbourne and left me to get my head knocked in by more of Sutton's friends. You told me the other day that you came back here when Gwen was killed. That was a lie, Jill. You came back right away, figuring I was confused enough for the time being. Then you killed Gwen.'

'Why would I kill her?' She was smiling now but the smile didn't quite bring itself off. 'I was trying to throw you off the trail, remember? Why do something to increase your suspicion and bring you up here again?'

'Because you couldn't help it.'

'Why not?'

'Because Gwen found Barb's set of photographs,' I told her. 'She recognized your picture and called you up.'

'So I killed her because she was going to blackmail me? Don't talk like a moron, Roy. I was a blackmailer myself, remember? And I didn't have any money, so she couldn't blackmail me, of course. So that knocks your theory—'

'She wasn't blackmailing you.'

'No?'

'She wasn't a blackmailer,' I went on. 'She was the sort of girl who believed in playing everything by the book. She came across the photographs, had enough sense to realize that somebody was being blackmailed with them, and decided to go to the authorities. But first she wanted to find out what she could about it. She called you over, told you what she was going to do, and probably asked you if you would go to the police with her.'

I lighted a cigarette. I blew a cloud of smoke at the ceiling and sighed.

'And you got panicky, Jill. You had the knife with you and you used it. Or you told her not to do anything until you had a chance to talk with her at length, then returned that night and knifed her with Alan Marsten's knife. That sounds more likely, come to think of it.

'You see, Alan couldn't have slipped in and out of a girl's dormitory at that hour without attracting attention. He couldn't have gotten close enough to kill her without her screaming. But you could, Jill. And you did. She was expecting you and she was hardly afraid of you. You killed her and left her there and walked out with no one giving you a second glance.'

'Roy—'

'Hold on,' I said. 'And sit still, dear. You're getting a little nervous just about now, aren't you? Let's not make any sudden moves. I want you to listen to this all the way through.'

She stopped fidgeting and looked at me levelly. Even now it was more than a bit difficult for me to believe that everything I was saying was true. She looked like a sweet and demure college girl.

Not like a blackmailer.

Or a murderess.

'Then I came along again,' I said. 'You hated like hell to let me know who you were, but you couldn't help yourself. For two reasons – I would probably find out anyway if I poked around long enough. And more important, you needed a little help. As long as Sutton had those photographs, you were in trouble. He could work the blackmail game and it could backfire, with you getting hurt. Or he could start blackmailing you, as far as that went.

'But with Sutton out of the picture one way or another, he couldn't do much of anything. So you sent me after him to get the pictures, figuring that one of three things could happen. He could kill me, in which case at least I was out of your hair. Or I could kill him, in which case everything was every bit as perfect. Even better.

'Or I could get the pictures – which is what happened, of course. That helped. There was still more.'

She looked at me. 'Oh, tell me,' she said, the sarcasm a bitter edge to her words. 'Tell me everything, dear Roy. Don't make me guess.'

I said: 'I dropped you at your dorm last night. Then I went home to sleep and you came outside again. Do you want me to tell you where you went?'

'Of course.'

'You went to the police station. Oh, you didn't go inside, because that would have been senseless. You went around the rear and banged on Alan's window. You awoke him and fed him a story, a long story about how a man named Hank Sutton had been responsible for Barbara's death in one way or the other. I don't know what you said – maybe that he was blackmailing her and she killed herself, maybe that he actually murdered her. It doesn't really matter. Whatever it was, it was enough to set him off like a bomb. He broke jail and went after Sutton.'

'Why did I do that?'

'Because you thought it could only help you. If Sutton killed Alan, then Alan would be forever tagged with Gwen's murder. Everyone would reason that an innocent boy wouldn't escape from a jail cell.

'And if Alan killed Sutton, that was just as good as far as you were concerned. Alan would hang, certainly, and Sutton would be out of the way.'

'Really?'

'Really.'

'Well,' she said. 'Well, they're both dead, aren't they? So it worked out perfectly. And with them both dead you'll have a hard time convincing anybody that there's any truth in this little fantasy of yours, won't you?'

I just smiled.

'Well? Won't you?'

I said: 'Alan Marsten might help me out.'

'But he's dead!' Her eyes were wide again. 'God damn it, you said he was dead!'

'So I lied,' I said. 'You can sue me.'

She lowered her eyes again and we sat there in silence. She unzipped the leather notebook all the way a little at a time, her fingers nervous.

I told her what had happened, how Bill Piersall and I had managed to get to Sutton's house, how I had shot Sutton dead, how Alan was already at the hospital recovering.

'Then I'll tell the police about you,' I said. 'And if they don't believe me, he can help out with an appropriate word here and there. And then do you know what will happen?'

'What?'

'Then you'll go to jail,' I said. 'And you'll stand trial for murder. You'll be found guilty. But I don't think you'll hang, not with enough men on the jury. You'll wind up in prison for life. With good behavior you'll be out in twenty or thirty years or so.'

'Roy—'

'What?'

She decided not to answer. I wondered why she kept fooling around with the leather notebook. She was dipping one hand into it when I caught on.

I dove for her. By the time I got to her there was a gun in her hand but she just was not fast enough. I hit the gun with one hand and her jaw with the other. The gun flew against a wall and went off aimlessly, a bullet plowing into the ceiling. Plaster showered down on us.

I stood up shakily. She sat up even more shakily, rubbing her jaw where I had hit her with one hand. The game was up now and she recognized the fact. Her eyes held a beaten look. She was giving up.

And then all Hades was breaking loose. The gunshot attracted a certain amount of attention, with half the female population of Radbourne banging on our door and wondering what was wrong. And the door, of course, was locked. Her hair pin held it securely in place.

I walked over to pick up the gun. I kept it trained on her and back to the door, pulling out and discarding the hair pin. I opened the door and turned to the first girl I saw.

Then Jill was yelling. 'He tried to rape me! Call the police; he tried to rape me!'

The girl looked at me.

'Call the police,' I told her. 'By all means. I want them to arrest Jill for murder.'

'Murder?'

'Gwen Davison's murder. Hurry, will you!'

The girl looked at me, at Jill, at me again. Jill went on shouting something foolish about rape while I ignored her manfully. The girl nodded to me, then went off to find a policeman.

I walked toward Jill again. Her eyes were dull now. She'd made one last-ditch attempt, a final round of desperation, and it had not worked.

'You didn't have a chance,' I said.

'No?'

'No. Nobody could rape you, Jill.'

'Why not?'

'Because you'd never resist,' I said,

Then I sat down in the chair again and kept the gun pointed at her while we waited for the police to come.

13

It Ended at the Tafts', at dinner.

Dinner was sandwiches and beer this time, and none of us were very hungry. Jill Lincoln was in jail in New Hampshire, charged with the murder of Gwen Davison. Alan Marsten was in a hospital recuperating. Hank Sutton was in a morgue, decomposing. Barbara Taft was dead and buried.

During dinner I did the talking and Edgar and Marianne listened in silence. Painful silence. I said the things I had to say and they listened, because they had to listen, certainly not because they wanted to.

Edgar Taft stood up, finally.

'Then she really did kill herself, Roy.'

I'm afraid she did,' I said.

'It doesn't play any other way, does it?'

'No.'

He nodded heavily. 'You'll excuse me,' he said. 'I'd like to be alone for a few moments.'

Marianne and I sat there awkwardly while he left the room and went to his study. She looked at me and I looked back at her. I waited.

'I'm sorry you had to tell him,' she said.

'That it was suicide?'

'The rest of it, Roy. Those ... those pictures. That filth. All of it.'

'It would come out in Jill's trial anyway.'

'I know. But it seems so—'

She let the sentence trail off unfinished. I took a cigarette from my pack, lighted it, offered her one. She shook her head and I blew out the match and dropped it into an ashtray.

'You didn't want me to tell him about the pictures,' I said. 'Is that it?'

'It's just that—'

'But you knew about them all along,' I said, interrupting her. 'Didn't you, Marianne?'

Her hands shook. 'You knew,' she said. 'You *knew*—'

'Yes,' I said. 'I knew. I knew that you knew, if that's what you mean. There was a reason for Barbara coming to New York to commit suicide, Marianne. Because that's not why she came here. She came to see her mother.'

She had closed her eyes. Her face was very pale.

'Blackmail bothered her,' I continued. 'She didn't like being bleeded even if she could afford the money. She didn't like letting some filthy crook hold a filthy picture over her head like a sword. They say you cannot blackmail a truly brave person, Marianne. I suspect there's quite a good deal of truth in that statement. And I suspect that Barbara was a very brave girl.'

'Brave but foolish, Roy.'

'Maybe.' I sighed. 'She was brave enough to want to call a blackmailer's bluff. She was confused as hell – she left school, dropped out of sight for awhile, then came home. She came to you, Marianne. Didn't she.'

She said: 'Yes.' The word was barely audible. It was more a breath than a word.

'She wanted support,' I went on. 'She told you about the pictures and the blackmail. She told you she was going to tell the man to go to hell, then tell the police what he was doing. She knew there was going to be publicity, and that it would be the worst kind – she would be asked to leave school, perhaps, and there would be nasty rumors.'

'It would have been bad for her, Roy. A reputation around her neck for life. It—'

'So you told her to go on paying. You probably were harsh with her, although that hardly matters. What mattered to Barbara was that her mother wouldn't back her up, that her mother seemed to be more interested in appearances than in reality. That ruined her, Marianne. Her own mother wouldn't support her. Her own mother let her down.'

'I never thought she would kill herself, Roy.'

'I know that.'

'I never thought ... I was horrible with her, Roy. But it seemed more sensible to pay the money than to risk the publicity. I didn't take anything else into consideration. I—'

She broke off. We sat there, awkward again. I finished my cigarette.

'That's why you didn't want me to work too hard on the case,' I said. 'That's why you told me on the phone to drop it as quickly as I could. You thought I might turn up the pictures, and you didn't want that.'

'It would have hurt Edgar.'

'It's hurting him now,' I said. 'But Barbara's death hurt him a great deal more.'

She said nothing.

'I'm sorry, Marianne.'

'Roy—'

I looked at her.

'You won't ... tell Edgar, will you?'

Appearances were everything. She still lived in a little world of What Other People Think, and reality was not rearing its ugly head, not if she could help it. She was poised and polished as a figurine. And as substantial.

'No,' I said. 'Of course not.'

The train transported me to Grand Central Station. I walked to the Commodore, reclaimed my key from the clerk, picked up bills and messages. I took an elevator to my room and put the bills and messages into a drawer without looking at them.

I took off my coat, my jacket, my tie. I could hear Christmas carols coming from somewhere. I wished they would stop. Christmas was coming any day now and I didn't care.

I picked up the telephone, called Room Service. I asked the answering voice to send up some scotch. I told him to forget about the ice and the soda, and to make it a fifth, not a pint.

I sat down to wait for the liquor. The Christmas carols were still going on and I tried not to listen to them.

It was the wrong night for them.

The Girl with the
Long Green Heart

For Betsy and Po

1

When the phone rang I was shaving. I put my razor down and walked across the room to pick up the phone on the bedside table.

A woman's voice said, 'It's eight-thirty, Mr Hayden.'

I thanked her and went back to finish shaving. I put on a plain white shirt and the good blue suit I had bought in Toronto. I picked out a dark blue tie with an unobtrusive below-the-knot design and tied it three times before I got the knot as small as I wanted it. I gave my shoes a brief rub-down with one of the hotel's hand towels, got the day's first cigarette going, and went over to my window to have a look at the city.

It was my first real look at Olean. I had gotten into town the night before on a puddle-jump flight from Toronto to Buffalo to Olean. My cab ride in from the airport had been less than a scenic tour. At that hour the city looked like any small town with everything closed. There were two movie houses, the Olean and the Palace, and one had already turned off its marquee. A few bars were open. I had gone straight to the Olean House and straight to bed.

Now, in daylight, the town still had little to set it apart. My room was on the third of four floors, and my window looked out across North Union Street. The Olean Trust Company was directly across the street, flanked by a chain five-and-dime and a small drugstore. The street ran to eight lanes, with cars parked at angles to the curb on both sides of the street. Most of the parking spaces were taken.

On the extreme right, I could just see the Exchange National Bank building. It was eight stories tall, twice as high as any of the buildings near it. Wallace J. Gunderman had an office in it, on the sixth floor.

I went downstairs. There were no messages for me. The gray-haired woman at the desk asked me if I would be staying another night. I said that I would. I picked up the local paper at the newsstand in the lobby and carried it into the hotel coffee shop. Businessmen and secretaries sat around drinking morning coffee. I took a table in front, near a group of lawyers who were discussing a hearing on a zoning ordinance. I ate scrambled eggs and bacon and drank black coffee and read everything of interest in the Olean *Times-Herald.* Gunderman's name kept cropping up. He was on a committee of the City Club, he was heading up the Men's Division of the United Fund campaign – that sort of thing.

I had a second cup of coffee and signed the check. Outside, the air was warm and clear. I walked the length of the block, turned and came back to the hotel. It was nine-thirty when I got back to my room. I looked up Gunderman's number in the phone book and gave it to the hotel operator.

A girl said, 'Mr Gunderman's office, good morning.'

'Mr Gunderman, please.'

'May I ask who's calling?'

'John Hayden. I represent the Barnstable Corporation.'

There was a very brief pause, a short intake of breath. 'One moment, please,' she said. 'I'll see if Mr Gunderman is in.'

I lit a cigarette while she saw if Mr Gunderman was in. When he came on the line he sounded younger than I had pictured him. His voice was deep and resonant.

'Mr Hayden? Wallace Gunderman. I don't believe I know you, do I?'

'No,' I said. 'I'm representing the Barnstable Corporation, Mr Gunderman, and I wondered if I could drop by and see you sometime this afternoon.'

'You're here in Olean?'

'That's right.'

'Could you tell me what you want to see me about?'

'Of course. It's our understanding, sir, that you own a fairly sizable tract of land in northern Alberta. Our corporation is a Toronto-based outfit interested in—'

'Oh, so that's it.'

'Mr Gunderman—'

'Now you wait a minute, sir.' He was a few decibels short of a full-fledged roar. 'You must think I'm an awfully stupid man, Mr Hayden. You must think that just because a man's been played for a sucker once he can be raked over the same coals forever. I took a neat beating on that Canadian land. I made the mistake of listening to one of you smooth-talking Canuck salesmen and I fell for his line like a ton of bricks. I shelled out one hell of a lot of money for some of the most useless land in the world.'

I let him go on. He was doing nicely.

'That was five years ago, Hayden. It took me awhile to quit being ashamed of myself. I'm not ashamed any more. I was a damn fool. I've been a damn fool before, and I'll probably be one again before I die, but I've never been enough of a damn fool to make the same mistake twice. You people took me once. You taught me a lesson, and goddamn it, I learned that lesson. I'm not in the market for another patch of moose pasture, thank you.'

'Mr Gunderman—'

'For Christ's sake, don't you get the message? I'm not interested.'

'Just let me say one thing, Mr Gunderman.'

'You're just wasting your time. And my time as well.'

'There's just one point of misunderstanding, Mr Gunderman, and as soon as we clear the air on that I think you'll see my point.'

'I already see your point.'

I took a breath. I said, 'Mr Gunderman, you seem to think that I'm interested in selling you land at inflated prices. That's not my intention. I'm here in Olean to make a firm offer on behalf of the Barnstable Corporation to *buy* your land *from* you.'

There was a fairly long pause. I put my cigarette out in the ashtray.

'Did I hear you right, Mr Hayden?'

'I said I'm here to make you an offer for your land in Alberta,' I said. 'We wrote to you not long ago but never received an answer.'

'I never got that letter.'

'I'm sure it was sent. In any case—'

'Just a minute. Maybe my girl can dig up that letter. That's the Barnstable Corporation?'

'Yes.'

I held on while he sent his secretary on a search of the files. I had a fresh cigarette working by the time he was back on the line. His voice was pitched a lot lower now. He sounded almost apologetic.

'I have that letter after all,' he said. 'It's from someone named Rance.'

'Douglas Rance. That's our company president.'

'And you are—'

'Just a hired hand, Mr Gunderman.'

'I see.' He thought that over. 'According to this letter, you people want to purchase my Canadian holdings for a combination preserve and hunting lodge. Is that right?'

'That's right.'

'Well, I can't understand how I overlooked this letter, Mr Hayden. I must have thought it was a solicitation of one sort or another and just tossed it aside, and then it wound up in the files. I'm sorry for the attitude I took before.'

'Oh, I can understand that.'

'You could if you'd ever been taken by those swindlers. No reflection on your country, Mr Hayden, but there are a lot of smooth operators based on your side of the border. You say you want my land for a hunting lodge?'

'Yes, that's right.'

'Well, I'd like to give this some thought before I see you. You said you're here in town. Where can I reach you?'

'I'm at the Olean House. Room 309.'

'You'll be there for the next hour or so?'

'Yes.'

'Then I'll call you within the hour.'

He called at ten. I picked up the phone on the third ring. This time around he was slicker than oil. Was I free for lunch? I said I was. Could I drop over to his office around noon? I could. He was at the Exchange Bank building, and did I know where that was? I did. Well, good. He would see me then.

I got to his office a few minutes after twelve. His name was listed on the building directory downstairs, just his name and the number of his office. I rode an outmoded elevator to the sixth floor and found my way around the corridors to a door with his name on it. It opened into an anteroom. There were bookshelves and a magazine rack to the left. On the right side was a steel desk with a girl behind it.

Quite a girl. Her hair was a deep chestnut brown and there was a lot of it. Her eyes were large, and just a shade lighter than her hair. She looked up from her typewriter and gave me a smile filled with sugar and spice and everything nice. Could she help me?

'I'm John Hayden,' I said. 'I've an appointment with Mr Gunderman.'

The eyes brightened and the smile spread. She looked as though she wanted to say something. Her tongue flicked over her lips and she got to her feet.

'Just one moment,' she said. 'I'll tell Mr Gunderman that you're here.'

She walked through a door marked *Wallace Gunderman Private*. I watched her go. She was worth watching. She was a tall girl, almost my height, and she had a shape to carry the height. Slender enough to be called willowy, but a little too full in bust and hips for that tag. She wore a skirt and sweater. Both were probably too tight. I wasn't about to complain.

The door closed after her. When it opened a second time she led Wallace J. Gunderman out of it. She stepped aside and he came across the room to shake my hand.

'Mr Hayden? I'm Wally Gunderman. Hope I didn't keep you waiting.'

'Not at all.'

'Good,' he said. He was a tall, thick-set man with iron-gray hair and bushy eyebrows and a sunlamp tan. He could have posed for Calvert ads. 'Have you met my secretary, Mr Hayden? Mr Hayden, this is Evelyn Stone. Evvie's the girl who managed to bury your Mr Rance's letter in the files.'

'I was *sure* you'd seen that letter, Mr Gunderman—'

'And maybe I did, dear. At least you didn't throw it away.' He laughed. 'But we can forget that now. I'm just glad you people didn't let the matter drop after one letter. Do you like Italian food, Mr Hayden? Because there's a pretty good Italian place around the block.'

'Sounds fine to me.'

'Good,' he said.

His car was parked in front of the building in a spot reserved for him. It was a Lincoln Continental, a convertible, dove-gray with lighter gray leather upholstery. He had the top down.

'Beautiful weather these past few weeks,' he said. 'We usually get a lot of rain in September, but so far it's held off. How's the weather in Toronto?'

'Cooler than this, but nice.'

'And I suppose the winters are equally bad here and there. You have it colder, but we get a little more in the way of snow. You don't have a Canadian accent. Are you originally from Canada?'

'Not even close. I was born in New Mexico, near the Colorado border.'

'Been in Canada long?'

'Not very long.'

We made exciting talk like that while he drove the few blocks to the restaurant. It was called Piccioli's. There was a small bar, and the tables were covered with red checkered cloths.

'Not fancy,' Gunderman said, 'but clean, and the food's good.'

They had a fairly good crowd for lunch. Gunderman had a booth reserved and we went to it. A slim dark-eyed waitress brought us drinks, Scotch with water for him and a martini for me. Gunderman said the Italian specialties were very good, but that I could get a decent steak if I wanted one. I ordered lasagna. He had one of the veal dishes with spaghetti.

The lunch conversation was small talk that avoided the main issue very purposefully. I followed his lead. We talked about Canada, about his one trip to the American Far West. He asked me if I'd been to Olean before, and I said I hadn't.

'It's not a bad little town,' he said. 'A good place to live. We're a little off the beaten track here. Up along the Mohawk Valley, the Erie Canal route, it's one town after another. You've got a lot of growth there but you've got all the problems of that kind of growth, the slums, everything. We don't have that kind of growth but at the same time we're not stagnant, not by a long shot. And there are a few stagnant areas in this state, John. I don't know if you've ever been in the central part of New York State, but you take a county like Schoharie County, for example – why, they've got less population today than they did during the Civil War. We've had steady growth, not tremendous growth but just healthy growth.'

We were John and Wally now. He added cream to his coffee and settled back in his chair.

'I certainly can't complain,' he said. 'This town has been good to me.'

'You've lived here all your life?'

'All my life. Oil made this town, you know. You could figure that from the name of the city. Olean, like oleaginous or oleomargarine. Oil. The oil fields here and in northern Pennsylvania were producing around the time that Oklahoma was just a place to dump Indians. And the wells still pump oil. Secondary and tertiary extractions, and not as important as they were once, but that oil still comes up.'

'Is that where you got started?'

'That's where the money first came from.' He grinned. 'My father was a wildcat driller, bought up oil leases and sank holes in the ground. He was in the right spot at the right time and he made his pile and it was a good-sized pile, believe me. I still see income from wells that he drilled.'

'I see.'

'But I never did much with oil myself. My dad died, oh, it's about thirty years now. I wasn't thirty myself then and there I was, his sole heir, with a guaranteed income from the wells and a pretty large amount of principal, and this with the country right in the middle of the Depression. Everybody figured me to move to New York or some place like that and just live on income. I surprised them. Know what I did?'

'What?'

'I started buying land like a crazy man. Scrap land and wasteland and farm land that wasn't paying its way and timber land with the hardwood growth all cut and gone. Land nobody wanted, and this was in the thirties when land was so cheap you could have had an option on the whole state of Nebraska for maybe a dollar and fifty cents. That's an exaggeration, but you know what I mean. Land was cheap, and the craziest damned fool in creation was the man interested in buying it. At least that was what people thought. Hell, there would be a piece of land where the oil rights had already been sold, and where there was no oil there anyway, nothing but rocky soil, and I would go and buy it, and you can't blame the people for thinking I was out of my mind.'

'But I guess you made out all right, Wally.'

He laughed like a volcano erupting. He was enjoying himself now. 'Well, I guess they found out who was crazy,' he said. 'One thing about land, there's only so much of it in the world, and there won't ever be more. Every year there's more people in this country, and every year there's more industry and more housing and more of everything else, and there's always the same amount of land. And the best thing to buy for the long pull is the land nobody wants. You buy it and hang onto it and sooner or later somebody wants it, and then he has to pay your price for it. When they were looking to put up a shopping plaza east of the city, it was my land they picked for it. When they decided to cut Route 17 as a four-lane divided highway from Jamestown to New York, I was sitting with the land on either side of the old two-lane road. And when some smart boys figured out the money they could make growing Christmas trees on scrub land, and they wanted to buy in this area, I had a hell of a lot of land for them to pick from what I'd bought awful damned cheap. So you can say I made out all right, John. There's some chunks of land around here that I bought twenty years ago and couldn't get my money out of today, but there aren't many like that. And I'm happy to keep them anyway. They'll pay off, sooner or later.'

I made the appropriate comment and started on my coffee. He lit up a cigar and chewed the end of it for a few minutes.

Then he said, 'That's what burned me the most about that tract of moose pasture up in Canada. Here those sharp-shooters took me at my own game. Here I am in the land business, buying land cheap all over the Southern Tier, and they sell me useless land at such a high price I still can't believe I went for it. You know about that promotion?'

'Just how much land you hold, and that you're supposed to have paid a pretty stiff price for it.'

'Stiff.' He finished his coffee. 'You don't know the half of it. I got a fast-talking sharpie who called me on the phone and went on about uranium strikes in the area and how his real estate brokerage house wanted to turn over a lot of land in a hurry, and how the uranium rights were sure to sell on a terrific royalty arrangement, and he sent along just enough in the way of promotional material to make me convinced I was getting in on the ground floor of the greatest bargain since the Dutch bought Manhattan Island. I went for it like a fish for a worm. Except it wasn't even a worm on that hook, it was a lure, and when I bit on it I was hooked through the gills and back out again. All that money for some acreage I could graze reindeer on, if I had some reindeer.'

'Didn't you have any legal recourse?'

'Not a bit. That was the hell of it. Everything they did was legal. They were contracting to sell me land, and they sold it, and I bought it, and it was mine and my money was theirs and that was that. I don't think they could have pulled it off in the States. But Canada's a little more lenient when it comes to government regulation. They get away with murder up there.'

He shook his head. 'But I'm running off at the mouth. Anyway, I guess we're back to the subject that got us here in the first place. We're talking about my stretch of land. You want to buy it, is that right?'

'That's right.'

'Well, I won't say it's not for sale. What kind of an opening offer did you have in mind?'

'I believe there was a figure mentioned in Mr Rance's letter,' I said carefully.

'There was, yes, but I thought it was just a feeler. There was an offer of five hundred dollars.'

'Well that's what I'm prepared to offer, Wally.'

He grinned. 'As an opening offer?'

'As a firm price.'

The grin faded. 'That's a hell of a figure,' he said. 'If you had any idea what that hunk of property cost me—'

'Yes, but of course you paid an inflated price for it.'

'Still in all, I sank all of twenty thousand dollars into that land. There's an even seventy-five hundred acres of it, most of it in Alberta but a little chunk edging into Saskatchewan. That's better than eleven square miles. Closer to twelve square miles, and you want to steal it for five hundred dollars.'

'I wouldn't call it stealing, exactly.'

'Well, what would you call it?' He ducked the ash from his cigar and rolled the cigar between his thumb and forefinger. His hands were very large, the fingers blunt. 'That's about thirty dollars for a square mile of land. Well, more than that. Let me figure a minute—'

He used a pencil and paper, calculated quickly, looked up in triumph.

'Just a shade over forty dollars a square mile,' he said. 'That's pretty cheap, John. Now I wouldn't call that a high price.'

'Neither would I.'

'So?'

I took a breath. 'But Barnstable's not looking to pay a high price,' I said. I looked at him very sincerely. 'We want to buy land cheaply, Wally. We can use this land – we have a client who's interested in a hunting preserve in that area, but we have to get that land at our price.'

'When you figure my cost—'

'But at least this enables you to get out of it once and for all, and to cut your loss. Then too, once you've sold the land you can take your capital loss on it for tax purposes.'

He thought that over. 'I had an argument with my tax man on that a few years ago,' he said slowly. 'You know what the guy wanted me to do? Wanted me to sell the works to someone for a dollar. Just get rid of it for nothing so that I'd be transferring title and I could list a twenty-thousand-dollar loss. I couldn't see giving something away like that, not something like land. I'd rather keep the land and pay the damn taxes.'

'Well, we would be paying you more than a dollar.'

'Five hundred dollars, you mean.'

'That's right.'

He called the waitress over and ordered another Scotch and water. I joined him. He remained silent until the girl brought the drinks. It was past one now, and the lunch crowd had thinned down considerably. He sipped his drink and put it down on the table and looked at me.

'I'll tell you something,' he said. 'At that price I just wouldn't be interested.'

'I'm sorry to hear that.'

'But I think you'll have trouble finding anyone who'll be inclined to take the kind of offer you've made me.'

'There's a lot of land up in that neck of the woods,' I said.

'Yes, I know that.'

'And we've had little difficulty buying it at our price so far,' I went on, and then stopped abruptly and studied the tablecloth in front of me.

'You're interested in more than just my land, then.'

'Well, that's not what I meant to say. Of course we've bought occasional parcels of this type of property before, but—'

'For hunting lodges.'

'Actually, no. But we've had occasion to purchase unimproved land in the past, and in cases like this, we're usually able to get the land at a low price. When you're dealing with worthless land—'

'No land is useless.'

'Well, of course not.'

His eyes probed mine. I met his glance for a moment, then averted my eyes. When I looked back he was still scanning my face.

'This is beginning to interest me,' he said finally.

'I had hoped it would.'

'And one thing that interests me is that you haven't upped your offer. I figured from the beginning that if you would open with an offer of five hundred you'd be prepared to go to double that. But you haven't given me any of the usual run-around, about calling the home office and trying to get them to raise the ante. None of that. You've just about got me convinced that five hundred is as high as you intend to go.'

'It is.'

'Uh-huh. Anything important happening in Canada that I don't know about?'

'I don't understand.'

'I mean that it would be quite a joke if it turned out that there really was uranium on that land, wouldn't it?'

'I assure you—'

'Oh, I'm sure there isn't.' I was obviously uncomfortable, and he was enjoying this. 'I'm sure the land is just as rotten and deserted as it always was. But I am interested, and not so much in your offer as in what lies beneath it. That's something that I find very interesting.'

'Well,' I said.

He finished his drink and put the glass down. 'This whole situation is something I'd like to give a certain amount of thought to. Five hundred dollars is an almost immaterial factor here as far as I'm concerned. The question is what I want to do with the land, whether or not I want to own it. You can appreciate that.'

'Then you might consider selling?'

'Oh, yes,' he said. He was not very convincing. 'But the thing is, I want to think it over. Were you planning to stay overnight in Olean?'

'I was going to fly back this evening.'

'You ought to stay,' he said. 'I'll tell you, I'd like to have dinner with you tonight. I have to get moving now, I'm late for an appointment as it is, but I'd like to go over this with you and perhaps get a fuller picture. It might be worth your while if you spent an extra day here.'

'Well—'

'And there's a really fine restaurant out on Route 17. Marvelous food. Could you stay?'

He talked me into it. He signaled the waiter and took the check. I didn't fight him for it.

I divided the rest of the afternoon between a barbershop down the street from the hotel and a tavern next door to the barbershop where I nursed a Würzburger and watched a ball game on television. When I got back to the hotel there was a message for me to call Mr Gunderman. I went to my room and called him.

'Glad I reached you, John. Listen. I'm in a bind as far as tonight is concerned. There's a fund-raising dinner that I'm involved in and it slipped my mind completely this afternoon. Then I thought I could get out of it but it turns out that I can't. They've decided that I'm the indispensable man or something.'

'That's too bad,' I said. 'I was looking forward to it.'

'So was I.' He paused, then swung into gear. 'I'll tell you – I really did want to see you, and now I've gone and gotten you to stay over and all. How would it be if I sent my secretary to sub for me? I don't know if you noticed, but she's easy on the eyes.'

'I noticed.'

He chuckled. 'I can imagine. Now look – you don't have a car, do you?'

'No, I flew in and then took a cab. I could have rented a car there, I suppose, but I didn't bother.'

'Well, Evvie drives. She'll pick you up at your hotel at six, is that all right? And then you and I can get together in the morning.'

'That sounds fine,' I said.

I spruced up for my date. I remembered the dark brown hair and the brown eyes and the shape of that long tall body, and I combed my newly-trimmed hair very carefully and splashed a little after-shave gunk on my face. I took off the blue tie and put on one with a little more authority to it.

There was a Western Union office down the block, sandwiched in between the Southern Tier Realty Corp. and a small loan company. I got a message blank and sent a wire collect to Mr Douglas Rance at the Barnstable Corporation, 3119 Yonge Street, Toronto, Ontario, Canada.

I wired: ALL GOES WELL. PROSPECT DUBIOUS AT FIRST BUT HAVE HOPES OF SUCCESSFUL TRANSACTION. STAYING OLEAN OVERNIGHT. JOHN HAYDEN.

Then I went back to the Olean House to wait for Evvie.

2

It was the tail end of July when Doug Rance dropped around to see me. I didn't even recognize him at first. It had been a good eight or nine years since we had seen each other, and we were never close, never worked together. Now he was about thirty-three to my forty-two. Before, when I'd known him, he was just a raw kid and I was an old hand.

It was a Wednesday night, around twelve-thirty. I was working the four-to-midnight swing at the Boulder Bowl, and the night had been a slow one. The bowling leagues ease off during the summer months and open bowling only gets a heavy play on the weekends. By eleven-thirty the place was just about empty. I rolled a pair of unimpressive games, helped the kid with the mop-up, and made a note for Harry to call AMF in the morning and tell them one of their automatic pin-spotters had died on us. I locked up a few minutes after twelve, had a short beer around the corner, and walked the rest of the way to my room on Merrimac.

When I got there, Rance was waiting for me. He was sitting on a chair with his legs crossed, smoking a cigarette. He got up when I walked in and gave me a large grin.

'The door was open,' he said.

'I don't lock it.'

I was trying to place him. He was about my height with a lot of curly black hair and a smile that came easy. A very good-looking guy. Ladies'-man looks. He crossed the room and stuck out his hand and I took it.

'You don't make me, do you? It's been a while.'

And then I did. The first image that jumped into my mind was of a young, good-looking guy standing up straight and listening pop-eyed while Ray Warren and Pappy Lee bragged about a sweet chickie-bladder con they had pulled off in Spokane. He wasn't that young now, or that fresh. Well, neither was I.

'You're looking good,' he said.

'Well, thanks.'

We stood around looking at each other for a few seconds. Then he said, 'Say, I picked up a bottle around the corner. I didn't know what you're drinking these days but I got Scotch. Is that okay?'

'It's fine.'

'If you've got a couple glasses—'

I found two water glasses and went down the hall to the john and rinsed them out. He poured a few fingers of Cutty Sark into them and we sat down. He took the chair, I stretched out on the bed and put my feet up. It was good Scotch.

I asked him how he'd found me.

'Well, I was in Vegas, Johnny. I asked around, and somebody said you were here in Boulder. Something about your working at a bowling alley. I went over to the place but I didn't want to bother you. One of the kids told me where you were living and I came on over.'

'Why did you come?'

'To see you.'

'Just to talk over old times?'

He laughed. 'Is that a bad idea?'

'It's a funny reason to come this far.'

'I guess it is. No, I've got business with you, Johnny, but let's let it wait for now. I was surprised as hell when they told me you were here. I've never been to Colorado before. You like it here?'

'Very much.'

'How'd you happen to pick it?'

I told him I'd grown up not far from here, just across the border in New Mexico, a smallish town called Springer. 'Like elephants, I guess. Going home to die.'

'Nothing wrong with you, is there?'

'No, I was just talking.' I worked on the Scotch. 'I would have gone to New Mexico, maybe, but I've got a record there and it didn't seem like a good idea. This is about the same kind of country.'

'A hell of a lot of mountains. I flew to Denver and drove up in a Hertz car. Mountains and open spaces.'

'You can get pretty hungry for open spaces.'

'Yes, I guess you can. Was it very bad, Johnny?'

'Yes, it was very bad.' He offered me a cigarette. I took it and lit it. 'It was very bad,' I said.

'I can imagine.'

'Have you ever been inside?'

'Three times. Twice for thirty days, once for ninety.'

'Then you can't imagine,' I said. 'Then you can't have the vaguest goddamned idea about it.'

He didn't say anything. I reached for the bottle and he gave it to me. I poured a lot of Scotch in my glass and looked at it for a few seconds before drinking it. I felt like talking now. I'd been out for eight months, and ever since I got out of California I hadn't run across anybody who was with it. Conversation with straight people is limited – you can't talk about the library at San Quentin, or about the first long con you worked, or about any of the things that made up your life for so many years. You can drink with them and gab with them, but you have to keep a lid on the major portion of yourself.

'I was in Q,' I said. 'I did seven years. You couldn't know what it was like. I didn't know, not until I was in. San Quentin's a model prison, you know. Recreational facilities, a good library, and the guards don't beat you up at night. There's only one thing wrong with the place. There's this cell, and there are these iron bars, and they lock that door and you have to stay inside. That's all. You have to stay inside.

'I drew ten-to-twenty. It was a sort of variation on the badger game and there was long green in it. The girl fakes a pregnancy and then there's a fake abortion and a fake death, and the mooch winds up with the hook in him all the way up to his liver. Only this time the whole play turned sour and we bought it, but good. I drew ten-to-twenty for grand larceny and extortion and a half a dozen other counts I don't remember.'

'And got out in seven.'

I finished the Scotch. 'Seven years and three months. I could have made it a year earlier if I'd put in for parole.'

'You didn't?'

'I didn't want it. Parole is a leash – you get out a little sooner but you have to stay on that leash, you have to report to some son of a bitch once a month, you have to stay in the state, you have to live like a mouse. I stayed very straight inside. I made every day's worth of good time I could make. I never got in trouble. But I didn't want parole. I didn't want any leash on me that could yank me back any time somebody decided I belonged inside again. I'm out now and I'm staying out. Nothing gets me back in again.'

He didn't say anything. He filled our glasses. I put out my cigarette and got up from the bed and walked over to the window. There were a lot of stars out. I watched them and said, 'I guess you made a trip for nothing, Doug.'

'How's that?'

'Because I'm not interested.'

He got up and came over and stood beside me. 'You didn't even wait for the pitch.'

'That's because I know I'm not swinging.'

'It's a beautiful set-up, Johnny.'

'They always are.'

'This one's gilt-edged. All triple-A, front to back. The least you ought to do is hear about it'

'I don't think I want to.'

He didn't say anything for a few minutes. We both worked on our drinks. He sat down on the chair again and I got back on the bed. When he started in again he came through from a new direction.

'You're some kind of manager at the bowling alley, Johnny?'

'Assistant manager.'

'Sounds pretty good.'

'Not really.'

'The pay pretty decent?'

'Eighty-five a week. I should get raised to a hundred by the end of the year, and then it levels off.'

'Well, that's not too bad.'

I didn't say anything. He looked around at the room, which was not very impressive. I paid eight a week for it and the price fit the accommodation. I said, 'But there's no bars on the windows, and nobody locks me in at night.'

He grinned. 'Sorry,' he said. 'Listen, I didn't mean to pry, but I couldn't help catching the stuff on your dresser. What's doing, some kind of a course?'

'I'm taking a correspondence course in hotel management.'

'Yeah?' He looked genuinely interested. He was pretty good at it. 'Are those things any good?'

'This one isn't. I did a little studying at Q, hotel management and restaurant operation. I figured I'd follow it up now. The gaff on this deal is only fifty bucks, so I can't really get burned too badly.'

'You're interested in that, huh?'

I nodded. 'It's a good life, with the right set-up.'

'You got any plans?'

'Nothing definite. There's a place west of the city that I like. A roadhouse with rooms upstairs and a couple of cabins in back. The location is perfect, it's right on a road that gets a lot of traffic and there's not much competition around. The owner doesn't know what to do with the place. He's a lush and he just knows how to sell drinks and how to build himself a case of cirrhosis. With the right kind of operation the place would be a gold mine.'

'You sound as though you've thought about it. What would you want to do, manage the place?'

'I'd want to own it.'

'Is it for sale?'

'It would be, if anybody wanted it. Right now it looks like a losing proposition, because it's not being run the way it should be. A person could swing the deal with ten thou in cash and good terms for the rest. Then you would need another ten to put into the place, and a contingency fund of at least five more. Say twenty-five thousand, thirty at the outside, and a man could have a place that would go like a rocket.'

'Is this place far from here?'

'A few miles. Why?'

'I'd like to have a look at it.'

I looked at him and started to laugh. 'Now what the hell,' I said. 'You're hustling me pretty hard, aren't you, fella?'

'Maybe. Is the place open now? We could take a run over there and grab a drink. My car's right outside.'

'Why?'

'Why not?'

He had a rented Corvair parked two doors down the block on the other side of the street. Bannion's was about three miles south and west of the town. There were half a dozen cars in the lot when we got there, eight or ten customers inside, all but two of them at the bar. Bannion didn't have a waitress working. We got our drinks at the bar and took them to a table in the back. We stayed there for about fifteen or twenty minutes. Three of the customers left while we were there. Nobody else came in.

I did most of the talking. The place had tremendous possibilities. Bannion had completely ignored the tourist business, and the only people who rented his rooms were couples looking for a quick roll in the hay. Hot pillow trade was always worthwhile for a place like that, but tourist trade was good, too, especially with all the skiers in the winter and all the vacationers in the summer.

The food potential was good, too. The place needed extensive renovation and remodeling, but the physical plant itself was ideal. I talked a blue streak. Rance couldn't have cared less, but he knew enough to seem interested and I was interested enough myself to go on talking whether he gave a damn or not.

On the way back to my place he said, 'Well, you sold me. You could make a go of it there.'

'More than a go. I could do damned well.'

'And you need how much bread? Twenty-five thousand?'

'Thirty would be better. I could probably do it on twenty-five, but that's squeezing.'

'Got anything saved?'

'Not much.' I lit a cigarette. 'I'm saving money. You saw the room I live in. I make eighty-five a week and take home a little better than seventy after deductions. I live cheap. No car, low rent. I can save half my pay with no trouble at all.'

'And you need twenty-five or thirty.'

'Uh-huh.'

I let it go at that. If I saved twenty-five hundred a year, it would take me almost nine years, counting interest, to save twenty-five thousand dollars. He could manage that kind of arithmetic as well as I could, and I didn't like to spend too much time thinking about those figures. They didn't do much for my enthusiasm. They transformed all the plans to the approximate level of prison dreams. *When I'm outside I'm going to own eight liquor stores and ten whore-houses and sleep all day.* That kind of scene.

He parked the car and came back up to the room with me. He said, 'I'd like to outline this grift for you.'

'But I'm not on the grift any more. Why draw me pretty pictures?'

'I looked at your dream. Why not listen to mine?'

'We'd be wasting time. You won't even tempt me.'

'Can't I try?'

'I hate like hell to be hustled, Doug.'

'Who doesn't?' His face relaxed in that easy smile again. 'Look at it this way – I made a trip for nothing. That was the chance I took, right? I came unannounced because I wanted to see you. I have this thing hanging fire and I wanted you in it with me.'

'Why me?'

'Because you'd be only perfect for it. But the hell with that for the time being. The point is that I'm here, I made the trip, and if I can't get you in it with me I could at least get you to give the thing a listen and tell me how you think it would play. You've been a lot of years on the long con, Johnny.'

'Too many years.'

'Well, a long time. You were an old hand when I was still heating up zircons and selling them as diamonds to jewelers who didn't know better. I'm just getting into the big play.'

'Who've you worked with?'

'I was up in Oregon. Portland. I was with Red Jamison and Phil Fayre and some other guys. I don't know if you know them.' I knew Red and Phil. 'We had this wire, it was the first job I worked with an elaborate store arrangement. The first one where I had a big piece of the action.'

'What did you do?'

'I was inside. Red did the roping, Phil and I and half the people on the Coast were inside the store. We took this wholesale druggist for seventy-five thou and a few other mooches for ten or twenty apiece. It was beautiful the way it worked. The whole thing, the bit about a man at the track with a transistor set-up that got the results before the store did. It all worked like a beautiful piece of machinery. It was sweet.'

He told me all about it. The wire con is one of the three standard long cons, and as old as you can get. You keep being surprised when it still works after all those years. He told me all the cute little details and I could tell just how much of a kick it was for him, a kick to pull it off, a kick to remember it and talk about it. In a lot of ways he was the same kid I'd known before, in love with the whole pattern of the life, in love with the whole idea of being with it. I tried to remember if I had been like that once, all enthusiasm and excitement. It didn't seem possible.

'But that's history,' he said. 'Let me tell you what I've got on the stove now. You know the Canadian moose pasture bit, don't you?'

'I worked it once.'

'That's what I heard. How did you work it? Stock?'

'Uranium stocks.'

'You've heard it worked with land?'

'I know somebody was doing it that way somewhere in the East. It's the same thing, isn't it?'

'Just about,' he said. 'It's also just about played out, although there are still a few boiler rooms going in Toronto. I was inside of one with half a dozen phones going full-time.'

'Is that what you want to set up?'

He laughed. 'No, this is nothing like that. This is quicker and neater and easier and the score is a lot bigger. This is a fresh wrinkle on the whole thing. I'll tell you, Johnny, this is one I dreamed up all by myself. I heard this girl's story—'

'What girl?'

'A girl I met in Vegas. I'll get to that. I heard her story, and I got a picture of this mooch in my mind, and I just let it lay around there. I wasn't in Vegas to line up a con and I wasn't there for a woman, either. I never pull a job in Vegas, or anywhere else in the state. That place is strictly for gambling for me.'

'You gamble a lot?'

'I'm a high roller when I'm not working. Everybody has a weakness, Johnny. On the con or off it, everybody has one thing that gets to him. Women or liquor or gambling or something. The trouble is when you've got more than one vice. You know, I'm getting way off the track here. Let me just give you a fast picture. It's getting late and all, and you must be pretty beat, and I'm not so bright-eyed and bushy-tailed myself. I'll just sketch it in for you.'

He gave me just the outline. He ran through it very quickly, very sketchily. He knew what he was doing. He was working me the same way you work a mark at the beginning, the same way a fisherman works a trout. Just teasing, poking the bait around, giving a flash of it and then jerking it away before you can even make up your mind whether or not to bite. I knew I was being hustled. It didn't bother me.

For one thing, it was impossible to dislike Doug Rance. He was too genuinely charming. A confidence man has to have one of two things going for him. He can be so tremendously charming that the mark likes him at first meeting, or he can be so obviously honest and sincere that the mark trusts him from the opening whistle. If the mooch likes you, or if he trusts you, you are halfway home; the rest is just mechanics.

Doug made it on charm. I was the other way, I was a man people were likely to trust. I don't know why this is so, but it is. I've always played things that way, pushing the honest-and-sincere bit, but you can't make it on acting talent alone.

Charm and sincerity. The best two-handed cons feature a pair of men who compliment one another in this respect, one of them charming and one of them sincere. Doug wanted me in this one, and he probably knew what he was doing in picking me. The odds were that we would work well together.

I let him get all the way through the pitch and I listened to him all the way. He skipped most of the details, so it was hard to tell if the thing was as good as it sounded right off the bat. There could be snags he hadn't thought of, rough spots he'd glossed over. On the surface, though, the thing looked beautiful.

'It's a new one,' I told him.

'I thought it was.'

'Of course, I've been out of circulation for seven years. But I think you found something new.'

'Do you like it?'

'Yes,' I said. And lit a cigarette and added, 'But I'm afraid it's not for me. I'm just not buying.'

'Oh, I know,' he said easily. 'I just wanted your opinion. I wish I could have you in on it, but you can't win them all.' He got to his feet. 'I'm going to split, Johnny. I'm halfway dead. I've got a room over at the Mountain Lodge.'

'Where do you go from here?'

'I'm not sure. I figure I'll be in town until tomorrow night, anyway. Maybe we'll get together, huh?'

What a sweet soft hustler he was. I stood up. 'Drop around. We'll have lunch.'

'Fine.'

When he had his hand on the knob I gave him the first nibble. The words just came out by themselves. What I said was, 'Just for curiosity, how big do you think you'd score on this one?'

He pretended to think. 'Hard to say. I know what I figured your end at.'

'Oh?'

'About thirty thou,' he said.

3

I tried not to think about it. I listened as his car pulled away, and I blocked out the echo of his parting line, and I got undressed and crawled into bed and found out in no time at all that I wasn't going to drop off to sleep all that easily. I flipped the light back on and killed some time working on my correspondence course homework. Actually I was taking two courses at once, one in hotel and restaurant management and one in basic accounting. I worked out four of the accounting problems before my eyes started backing up on me. I lit a fresh cigarette and sat down on the edge of the bed.

So I thought about some of the things I hadn't wanted to think about. Like how long it would take to save thirty thousand dollars, and how old I would be when I had it. Fifty at the earliest, and probably a lot more like fifty-five. I was forty-two, and forty-two was still young enough for big plans and hard work, but fifty – well, fifty was a lot closer to being old. And fifty-five was closer still.

I thought about spending another ten years in that little room, scrimping and saving to beat hell. Adding up score sheets at the Boulder Bowl, grabbing quick lunches at diners and coffee pots. Dreaming through correspondence courses.

I had liked that life, too. But a man can endure many things day by day that become unthinkable when seen as a larger chunk of time. My life was all right as long as I lived it a day at a time. See it as ten years of the same thing, with Bannion selling his place to somebody else somewhere along the line, with the dream evaporating and the correspondence courses discontinued and nothing left but the habit; work and sleep and save. See it that way and the window grows bars and the door locks itself and the eight-dollar room turns itself into a cell.

Doug had left the bottle of Cutty. I let it alone. Dawn was breaking by the time I managed to get to sleep. I did not sleep well, I did not sleep long. There were dreams I don't remember. Around nine o'clock I woke up, chilled and damp, certain at first that I was not here in my room in Boulder but back in my cell at San Quentin.

I showered, I shaved, I smoked. If only there was something really wrong with his grift, I thought. If only there was a pretty snag I could catch around my finger. If only I could see the flaw. But on the surface it looked too very perfect, with a big payoff for maybe three months of work, and with no chance at all of a foul-up that could lead me back to a cell.

Rance showed up at eleven-thirty. 'I'm catching a four o'clock plane from Denver,' he said. 'I'll have to drive back there. Let's grab lunch now.'

'Come on in and sit down.'

'Oh?'

'I want to hear the whole thing,' I said. 'It sounded too damned good last night. I want to prove that there's something wrong with it.'

'And if there isn't?'

'Well.'

He took it from the top. It went back five years to a time when a few of the New York boys were working a boiler-room operation out of Toronto. It was a standard high-pressure operation with one important difference. Instead of peddling uranium or oil stocks, or mineral rights, the promoters were selling parcels of raw land itself. They bought up the land for thirty to fifty cents an acre and sold it for three or four dollars an acre.

'Goldin and Prince were on top of this one,' he said. 'You've got to remember when this was, just five years ago. The uranium stock con got its first big play right after the war, and then it came back strong during the Korean thing and for about a year after that. By the time it ran its course everybody had a little bell inside his head that rang when you mentioned the words *Canadian uranium stocks*. The newspapers and magazines ran features on the con and Washington circulated lists of bad stocks and everybody got wise, even the thickest marks around. But Goldin and Al Prince had a gimmick working for them. They weren't selling stocks. They were pushing the land itself, and that let the mark see that he was getting something. You tell him he can buy a thousand acres of valuable land for three or four thousand dollars and he doesn't see how he can get taken. The land is real, it's there for him to look at. Half the time he doesn't know what a thousand acres is. All he knows is that it's a lot of land. It's maybe four hundred dollars worth of land that he's paying ten times actual value for, but he doesn't know this.'

I said it was expensive – Goldin and Prince had to buy the land in the first place, and that cost more than printing up stock certificates.

'They didn't care. They were operating on the mooches' money, buying the land after they'd collected, and they didn't mind knocking ten per cent off the top to cover the cost of the land itself. Besides, the whole thing came out perfectly legal. They promised land and they delivered land, and any extra promises were verbal and uncollectable. It worked for them. They sold half of Canada, or close to it. Northern Alberta and Saskatchewan, some tracts in the Yukon and in the Northwest Territories.'

I told him to go on. 'All right,' he said. 'That's the background. Now you've got a bunch of marks around the country who own land they paid maybe ten times too much for. They're stuck with it. Right?'

'Right.'

'Good. Now we skip to this frail I found in Vegas. She's a secretary in her late twenties. For the past six years or so she's been working for this millionaire. For about four of those years she's been sleeping with him. All this time his wife was sick. She thought he was going to marry her when the wife finally died. A year ago the wife died.'

'And he didn't marry her.'

'Didn't and doesn't plan to. She's not too happy about this. She's a good-looking broad; she was married once before and the marriage fell in. Now she's stuck in a hick town working for this guy and she'd like to get the hell away from him and make a good marriage. She figures that she needs front money to do this. She wants to marry rich, and that means going where the money is and living the part. She'd like to pick up a healthy piece of change, and she'd also like to stick it into this guy and break it off, because she figures he has it coming.'

'She really expected him to marry her?'

'Yes. She was bitching about him and I started drawing her out just automatically, and she gave me a good picture of the guy. That started the wheels turning. You can see how it went. I said something about how she'd probably like to see him get taken but good, and she mentioned that he had been taken once before, when she had just started working for him. And of course it was this Canadian deal that had hooked him. He bought a nice stretch of mooseland from Capital Northwestern Development, which was what Goldin and Prince were calling themselves about that time.'

'How deep did he go?'

'Twenty or twenty-five thou.'

'Jesus.'

'Uh-huh. So now we come to the mooch himself. His name is Wallace J. Gunderman. He lives in someplace called Olean, in western New York near the Pennsylvania border. His father got rich in oil. Gunderman got richer in land. If he wasn't so rich you'd laugh all over him, because he'll buy any piece of land he can get at his price. He's a nut on the subject, according to what Evvie said.'

'Evvie?'

'Evelyn Stone, that's her name. But Gunderman. He'll buy any piece of land, no matter how worthless it is. He started doing this about thirty years ago. He made out very well. Part of this was a matter of luck, of being in the right place at the right time and having the cash to operate on. Another part was shrewdness. He's supposed to be a tough man in a trade.'

He went on about Gunderman. Five years ago Gunderman had gone for a minimum of twenty thousand dollars and had wound up with a chunk of scrubland with a fair market value in the neighborhood of two grand. He was rich enough to stand that sort of a loss without any trouble, but the whole thing hit him where he lived. He was proud of himself, of his head for business, and here he'd been taken in his own backyard, on a land swindle. This wasn't easy to live down. He still owned the land and he liked to tell people that he would make out on it eventually, that any land would be valuable if you held it long enough. But he was itching to get the bad taste of that con out of his system. He had been crazy to take that kind of a beating. If he could wind up turning his loss into a profit, if he could make out nicely on that Canadian land, then he would wind up crazy like a fox.

'You can see where he stands, Johnny.'

'Uh-huh.'

'The right type of set-up—'

'And he's there with both hands full.'

'That's the idea. And here's how it works, and this is all mine and I think it's beautiful. Gunderman gets a letter making him an offer for his Canadian land. This gets his head spinning right away. Nobody's ever been interested in this land and he can't understand why anybody would want it. What he probably figures from the go is that there's been a uranium strike in the neighborhood, or something like that, and he wants to find out what's up. He checks, and nothing's up, the land is as worthless as ever.

'Then you go to see him and repeat the offer. You—'

'What am I offering?'

'About five hundred dollars.'

'For something that ran him twenty thou?'

'Right. Of course he doesn't take it. Then he finds out we've been making the same kind of offer to other men who got caught in the Capital Northwestern Development swindle. That stirs him up. It's not just his land, it's a whole lot of land that we're looking to buy. He can't figure out why, but two things are certain. First of all, he's not going to sell that land of his, not for anything. And second, he's going to be hungry to find things out.'

Bit by bit we would let Gunderman figure things out. We wanted to buy his land for five hundred dollars because it was worth in the neighborhood of two thousand dollars, maybe as much as three. We were a group of important Canadians with a lot of legitimate interests who had managed to get hold of a list of men taken in by Capital Northwestern Development. We were attempting to buy their land from them at twenty to twenty-five per cent of its fair market value. For around fifty thousand dollars we would be able to acquire title to a huge block of Canadian real estate worth close to a quarter of a million dollars, and with a tremendous potential for future price appreciation. A potential Gunderman could certainly understand – the investment value of unimproved land was his personal religion. The more he nosed around the more he learned about our operation, and the more he learned about it the more he liked it.

'So he doesn't want to sell us his land, Johnny. He wants to buy our land, the whole package.' He lit a cigarette. 'You like it so far, Johnny?'

I slipped the question. 'If it's such an attractive deal, why would we be willing to sell it to him?'

'That's where it gets pretty. Remember what we're supposed to be. We're a syndicate of highly respectable Canucks who've hit on something a little sneaky. Legal, sure, but sneaky. We're capitalizing on an old con game and buying land surreptitiously for a fraction of its value. We're dealing with people who've been taken to the point where they think of their land as utterly worthless, and we're buying it in very cheap.'

'And?'

'And we don't want to turn this into a long-term deal. We want to get in and get out, to take a quick but sweet profit and go about our business. You'll be working outside, getting tight with Gunderman. He'll figure out what a perfect man he'd be for us to deal with, taking this piece of land that ran us around fifty thousand and selling it to him for maybe double that. I figure we'd try for one-fifty and settle for an even hundred thou.'

'Go on.'

'Right. Now here is where Gunderman has to prove that we can trust him. We would be selling the land damned cheap at a hundred thou. We're willing to do that if we're sure of who we're dealing with. We can't afford the risk of selling to somebody who's going to turn around and dump it for a fast buck. We've got our personal reputations to consider. We've got to sell to the type of man who will sit on that land for a few years, letting it increase in value as far as that goes, and then sell right for a good price later on. That way we don't come out of it with our reputations in a sling.

'And of course this is perfect for Gunderman, because he wants the land for long-term investment, not for a fast deal. He'll sit on it for five years if he has to. We let him convince us of this, and then we sell to him, and that's all she wrote.'

I wondered if Rance knew just how perfect it was. The trickiest part of any con game is the blow-off, when you've got the mooch's money and you want to get him out of the way before he tips to the fact that he's been taken. A blow-off can be very blunt or very subtle or anything in-between. In the short con games you can just blow your mark off against the wall, sending him around the corner while you jump in a cab and get out of the neighborhood. In a long con, you ought to do better than that. The longer it takes him to realize he's been had, the less chance there is that he'll squawk and the less chance that it'll do him any good.

This was tailored for a perfect blow-off. Our Mr Gunderman might die of old age before he found out he didn't really own any land in Canada.

I said, 'We don't sell him land. We sell him our company.'

'Instead of faking deeds?'

'Sure. That way he never gets around to a title search or anything else. He buys a hundred percent of the stock of our corporation. He thinks the corporation owns certain real estate and it doesn't. I'll tell you something. I think the whole deal might even be legal. He'll be buying a corporation and he'll be getting a corporation. If there's nothing on paper—'

'Jesus, I think you're right.'

By then I was hooked. I think I must have known it myself. Once you start improving a scheme, building on it, smoothing it, you are damned well a part of it.

We had lunch at the Cattleman's Grill. Open steak sandwiches and cold bottles of ale. We let the deal alone during lunch. We found other things to talk about. Doug picked up the tab.

Afterward, we drove around in his car. I lit a cigarette and pitched the match out the window.

'About the money arrangement,' I said.

'Uh-huh.'

'How did you figure it?'

'I figured you in for thirty.'

'Out of a hundred? That doesn't sound too wonderful.'

'Well, it won't be a hundred, Johnny. We'll gross a hundred, but there are going to be some expenses that have to come out of the nut, and then there's twenty off the top for the girl. Now—'

'That's too damned much for the girl,' I said.

'It can't be less.'

'The hell it can't. She ought to be in for a finder's fee of five thou and no more. Why twenty?'

'Because she did more than set this up. She's going to be working this from the inside, right there in his office. She'll be in on the whole play, and she'll have to scoot after it's over. Besides, there has to be a big piece in it for her or she won't go. She wants a stake to go hunt a husband with, and if it's not enough of a stake she'll get shaky and pull out.'

I let that ride. 'So how did you figure the split?'

'Twenty off the top, plus maybe ten more off the top for expenses, leaves seventy. I figured forty and thirty.'

'What's wrong with evens?'

The smile stayed. 'Well, it is my job, Johnny.'

I knew it wasn't the five. This was the first con he was working from the top, and he needed the glory as much as the money. If we split it down the middle he didn't get as much of a boost out of it. We tossed it back and forth. I told him to pare the girl's end of it down to seventeen-five and to cut himself down to thirty-seven and a half and give me thirty-five even. He didn't like it that way. He said he'd chop her to seventeen-five and add her end to mine, keeping forty for himself.

'You can swing your deal with thirty easy, Johnny. Ten to buy the place, ten to fix it up, and ten more in reserve. Two and a half more is just gravy.'

So we settled it that way. Forty thousand dollars for him, thirty-two thousand, five hundred for me, seventeen thousand and a half for Evelyn

Stone. The extra twenty-five hundred wasn't really important to me as money. It was a question of face. We agreed that anything over and above the hundred thou would be split down the middle between us, with the girl out of it.

I said, 'We're going to need front money.'

'I've got the bankroll.'

'How much?'

'Close to ten grand.'

'I'd feel better with double that. But ten should do us without much sweat. I've got a few hundred set aside. Living money, eating money.'

'We can do it on ten.'

'It might mean cutting it close. The more you can spend on your front the better off you are. And sometimes it isn't even a question of spending it, it's having it in the bank. Oh, the hell. Where do we kick this off from? Toronto?'

'That's where our store will be. Our company.'

'Then there's no worry. Unless something happened to him. Do you know Terry Moscato?'

He didn't.

'Well, he ought to be all right. He wouldn't be in jail, he's in too good to take a fall. He used to work out on the Coast and then he went East and wound up in Toronto, and he'll loan us front money. It has to be strictly front money, dough that sits in a bank account in our name and that goes straight back to him as soon as we're out of it. We'll have to pay a thousand for the use of ten, but it's worth it.'

'See why I wanted you on this, Johnny?' He took a hand from the wheel and punched me gently on the knee. 'I never would have thought of an angle like that. The extra touches. But I'll learn them, kid.'

I wasn't listening. It was that old familiar feeling, getting into it, getting with it again, feeling your mind start to slip into gear. Funny after so many years. *The extra touches.* A whole batch of them were coming to me now. The hell with it, we could talk about them later.

'I'll need eight days,' I told him.

'For what?'

'One day to decide if I'm in. And a week's notice before I leave my job.'

'I thought you already decided you were in.'

'I want twenty-four hours to make sure.'

He shrugged this off. 'And a week's notice? That's a new one. You're not going to come back and play assistant manager anymore, Johnny. What the hell do you care about giving notice?'

The same reason you don't do any grifting in Nevada. I don't crap where I eat.'

'Oh.'

'I'll be coming back to this town,' I said. 'Not as a flunky, no, but to live here and do business here. I want to leave it right.'

I spent the hour before I started work on the telephone. I sat in a booth at a drugstore and kept pouring change down the slot. I called a lot of people that I couldn't reach and reached a lot of others. I spent my dinner hour at the telephone, and I got back on the phone that night after I left the alleys. I spoke to people who knew Doug Rance vaguely, to some who knew him well, to one or two who had worked with him not long ago.

You damn well have to know who's working with you. When you're all wrapped up in a big one you live a whole slew of lies all at once, and if you have a few people in on it who are lying back and forth and conning each other as much as they're conning the mooch, then you are looking for trouble and fairly certain of finding it. This doesn't mean that good con men are inherently honest in their dealings among themselves. They aren't. If they were honest, they wouldn't have gone on the C to begin with. I expected Doug would lie to me, and I expected to lie to Doug, but not to the point where we'd be fouling each other up. If there were things I ought to know about him, I wanted to know them now.

He checked out pretty well. They knew him in Vegas, all right. He was a high roller, an almost compulsive gambler, but he never gambled while he worked. On a job, he was nothing but business. I had wondered about that.

He was in love with the life, which was another thing I had managed to figure out by myself. He was good and he was smooth. He was attractive to women but he could generally take them or leave them. He'd done a short bit in a county jail in Arizona, and he'd done time twice in California, a vag charge in Los Angeles and a ninety-day stretch at Falsom for petty theft, a short con that hadn't worked right

Everyone I talked to, everyone who knew him, seemed to like him well enough. That much figured. That was his stock in trade.

It was another late night for me, but this time I slept. In the morning I walked over to his hotel and we had a bite together. He asked me if I'd had a chance to run a check on him.

'Sure.'

'How did I make out?'

'You've got good references.'

He laughed. 'I'm glad you asked around,' he said. 'I'd hate to work with anyone who wouldn't take the trouble. You in, Johnny?'

'All the way.'

'You won't regret it. Smooth as silk, all the way, and nothing's going to go sour on us.'

I gave notice that afternoon. I told Harry that I had to leave at the end of next week, that I had a very attractive opportunity waiting on the East Coast and I couldn't afford to pass it up. He was unhappy. He told me he could maybe see his way clear to a ten-a-week raise if I cared to stay. I told him it wasn't that, that this was a real chance for me.

'Maybe you'll come back some day,' he said. 'Not to work here, maybe, but to open up a place of your own. This is a good place to live, John.'

'I'd like to come back.'

'Hope you do. I hate to lose you, I really do.'

4

That was Friday. The following night I finished work at midnight. I had Sunday off, so Doug picked me up after work and we drove to Denver. He gave the Corvair back to the Hertz people. We caught a jet to Chicago, changed planes and flew on to Toronto. We spent Sunday renting apartments. He took a two-room place in a good building, and I booked a sixty-a-month room in a residential hotel on Jarvis near Dundas. I paid a month's rent on the place. We picked out a spot for our offices, rented them Monday morning in Doug's name. Then I flew back to Denver.

By that Thursday Harry had found a man to replace me at the alleys. I spent a few hours that afternoon breaking him in, then went back to my room and threw a few things into a suitcase. I had cleared out my bank account and I had the money in cash, something like eight hundred bucks and change. I threw out some of my clothes along with my correspondence course debris and other odds and ends. Then I was on another plane, headed again for Toronto by way of Chicago.

By this time Doug had set some of the wheels in motion. He found us a Richmond Street lawyer who was handling the incorporation procedures for us. Doug gave him a list of tentative names – Somerset, Stonehenge, and Barnstable, all of them crisply Anglo-Saxon. Our lawyer checked them out and discovered that there was already a Somerset Mining and Smelting, Ltd., and a Stonehenge Development, Ltd. Our third choice was open. The lawyer filled out an application for letters-patent for the Barnstable Corporation, Ltd., and shot it off to the Lieutenant-General of the Province of Ontario.

All of this was routine. We incorporated with two hundred shares of stock of a par value of one dollar. We stated our corporate purpose on our application, listing ourselves as organizing for the purpose of purchasing and developing land in the western provinces. We gave the address of our head offices as 3119 Yonge Street, Toronto. We listed three officers – Douglas Rance, President; Claude P. Whittlief, Vice-President and Treasurer; and Philip T. Liddell, Secretary. Liddell was our lawyer. Whittlief was me – just another hat to wear, another name to sign. We gave our capitalization as fifty thousand dollars, Canadian. You don't have to show your capital, just proclaim it. Fifty seemed like a decent figure.

The charter went through and we were the Barnstable Corporation, Ltd., with a charter from the Province to prove it. We painted that name on the door of the Yonge Street office and had the phone company put in a bank of telephones. A printer on Dundas ran off a ream of stationery on good high rag content bond. Our incorporation was duly listed in the appropriate section of the Ontario *Gazette*.

We opened an account at one of the downtown offices of the Canadian Imperial Bank of Commerce. All checks on our account had to be signed by Rance and countersigned by me as Claude Whittlief. We deposited seventy-five hundred dollars of Doug's capital in the account. It wasn't enough of a balance. I went on the earie and found out that Terry Moscato had moved across the border to Buffalo. I flew down to see him and told him I needed ten thousand dollars for about two months, maybe three.

'For what?'

'Front money,' I said. 'It goes in a bank account and it stays there, Terry.'

'Because I wouldn't want to be financing this at a lousy ten per cent.'

'Strictly front money, Terry.'

Not that he trusted me, but that he knew that I knew better than to play fast with him. People who crossed him had trouble getting insurance, and I was well aware of this, and that was enough collateral as far as he was concerned. I got ten grand from him in cash, bought a cashier's check for that amount at a bank, flew back to Toronto and stuck the money in the Barnstable account.

So we were in business.

A store is a vital element in the operation of a big con. It must look more like what it's pretending to be than the real article itself. The most difficult illusion to maintain is one of furious activity. The store – in our case, the office and the corporation itself – was geared for one thing and one thing only, the act of parting a certain fool from his money with a minimum of risk. But we had to give the appearance of conducting a full-fledged business. Our bank account had to show activity. Our office had to receive a sensible volume of mail.

Doug hired a secretary to answer the phone and type occasional letters. There were a variety of letters that we kept her busy with. Some of them were dictated just so she would have plenty of work. They never wound up in the mailbox. Carbons went in the files, and the letters themselves went in the trash barrel. Others were requests for catalogs and information, and these were duly mailed and brought mail in return.

Finally, we had her dash off a list of letters to men who had been swindled by Capital Northwestern Development. Doug Rance knew a man who knew Al Prince, and Al Prince supplied us with a master list of guppies he and Goldin had taken for a swim in the CND gambit. We picked some names off the list, carefully selecting men who had only lost between five hundred and two thousand dollars. We sent off letters on Barnstable stationery with Doug's signature offering to purchase their land for about three or four cents on the dollar, ostensibly for a hunting preserve, and stressing that their sale to us would enable them to take a tax loss and cut their losses on the deal.

'This doesn't make sense,' Doug said. 'Why in hell buy their land?'

I explained it to him. When we approached Gunderman, he would do a little checking on his own hook, and he would run down some of the men who had sold land to us and confirm that we were actually buying the property.

'The hell,' he said. 'That's no problem. He'll dictate his letters to Evvie and she'll sidetrack them.'

'But she can let these go through,' I told him, 'and Gunderman will get actual confirmation. And we'll have actual deeds to show him along with the phony ones. The cash involved won't be much. A few dollars here and a few dollars there, and we won't sink more than a thousand at the outside into land.'

'Does Gunderman get one of these letters?'

'No. Have the girl send him one, but don't mail it to him, mail it to our girl in his office. Let her sneak it into the files without showing it to him.'

'So he can discover it later?'

'Right,' I said.

What the hell – the girl was in on the play for seventeen-five. She might as well make herself useful.

We let our girl write up about thirty of those letters and we mailed out eight or ten of them. Two men wrote back immediately accepting our offer, and we sent them checks by return mail. Others wrote asking for more information, which we dutifully supplied. One of those later accepted our offer. One man said that he had already disposed of his land at a price slightly higher than our offer in order to take a tax loss. Two men wanted to get us to boost our offer, and we wrote back stating that our original offer had been firm and we couldn't possibly raise it. One of these men accepted, one didn't.

We wound up spending about three hundred dollars on moose pasture and got title to around twenty-nine hundred acres.

Activity in our bank account was even simpler to create. Doug would write checks to various persons. I countersigned the checks as Whittlief, then endorsed them on the back with the name of the nonexistent payee and put them through my own account, an account I'd taken out under the name of P. T. Parker. I cashed each check through the Parker account and redeposited the money in the Barnstable account. With a balance of between twelve and seventeen thousand dollars, we managed to show a turnover of around forty thousand dollars in the first month of operation, and the only cost to us was that of banking fees, which were small enough. Anyone who looked at our bank statement would see a record of steady activity with a lot of money coming in and a lot going out. Anybody looking at our corporate checkbook would see a wide variety of men and companies listed as payees for various checks. No one would uncover the fact that almost every one of those checks had gone through one P. T. Parker's account. Parker's name appeared on the cancelled checks, but we weren't showing those around.

There was a lot of waiting to do. No matter how much activity we feigned, you couldn't get around the fact that we were stuck with leading fundamentally inactive lives until our front had had time to age and ripen a little. Fortunately we weren't trying to live the part of an old established firm. Part of our cover was that we had incorporated only recently, that the Barnstable outfit was an organization of sharpshooters set up on a short-term basis with a specific purpose.

All well and good, but we still had to be two months in operation before I could set about the business of roping Gunderman. This was still a remarkably short time. I've known cons who would set up a store in one city a year in advance, just letting it build up by itself while they made a living at something else or on the short con or working other gigs or whatever. Then the store would be waiting for them when they were ready to use it.

I knew a man named Ready Riley from Philadelphia – dead now, and I miss him – who was facing a sentence of ninety days for some misdemeanor. He got out on bail before sentencing and set up a perfect front for a very pretty swindle. His store was a fake gambling casino. He set all the wheels in motion, then got sentenced and did ninety days standing on his ear, and got out of jail and pulled off the con and left town with a fat wallet. He had already earned his nickname before that job, but he lived up to it then.

Well. We had ourselves two months to burn and I didn't have much to do. My room was a few steps up from the place I'd had in Boulder. I had a private bath, and the furniture was a little less decrepit. I couldn't spend too much time in the room because I was supposed to be working. I couldn't spend much time at the office because I was supposed to be the firm's contact man, meeting prospects and trying to buy their land. I couldn't see too much of Doug because I was supposed to be a hired hand, not someone he'd pick to run around with socially.

I saw a lot of movies. I did some shopping and bought clothes with Toronto labels. I spent enough nights at a jazz club on Yonge called The Friars so that they knew my face and what I liked to drink. I did a lot of reading. I knocked around a lot, got the feel of the city.

It was a good town. Toronto had a feeling of growth and progress to it that reminded me of the West Coast states. There was a lot of money in the city, and a lot of action. The night spots did a good business even in the middle of the week. They closed early, at one o'clock, but they drew well.

There were times when I had to remind myself that I was in a foreign country. The money was different, and it took awhile to get used to two-dollar bills in wide circulation. The people had a slight accent that you could get used to in not much time. The differences were small ones, and mostly on the surface. If you dropped the whole city in the States, it would take you a few minutes before anything seemed out of place.

I did some drinking, but not too much of it. I moved around quite a bit. Now and then I found a girl, but those relationships were strictly short-term, begun at night and over by morning.

Doug had said that everyone was entitled to one weakness, and that his was gambling. He wasn't gambling on the job. If I had a weakness, it was probably women, but I wasn't indulging that weakness on the job either. A mechanical romp, yes. An affair, no. There were enough lies already to live up to, and I didn't want any complications.

And one night I met Doug for dinner and we wound up at a side table at The Friars and nursed Scotch on the rocks and listened to a good hard-bop group. He said, 'I think we're ready. I think tomorrow. I talked to Evvie this afternoon and he's in town, and he doesn't have anything pressing for the next few days to get him sidetracked.'

I didn't say anything. I looked at him, and for a change I saw tension lines in that lover-boy face. They didn't remain there long. A smile wiped them away.

'This is big, Johnny.'

'Uh-huh.'

'If you figure we ought to wait awhile, about another week or two—'

He had managed to pick up elements of a Canadian accent. It showed on certain words. *About* came out *aboat*. I still sounded the same as ever, but then I wasn't posing as a native. I was just a transplanted American.

'Now's as good a time as any.'

'Good,' he said. 'There's a couple ways to get there. You go to Buffalo first, and then south to Olean. There's one plane a day from Buffalo to Olean, or you can do it by bus or train. I think the bus is a better bet than the train.'

'I'd rather fly.'

'That's what I figured, and it makes more sense that you'd fly down for the meeting instead of wasting that time on a bus or a train. You fly American to Buffalo airport and then get a Mohawk flight to Olean. I wrote it out for you.'

He left a few minutes after that. I stayed around for another drink, then walked back to my hotel. I knew I would have trouble getting to sleep. It was more trouble than I'd expected. I kept on thinking of the two bad things that could happen. I could hit a snag at the start, or I could rope him in neatly and then have a wheel come off later in the game.

If it blew up in the beginning, we were out two months time and the money we'd spent so far. This was a tailor-made con. Gunderman might have been the only man on earth we were primed for, and if he tipped right off the bat we could junk the whole operation and forget it. Rance was out his stake, and I could flush away my plans for turning Bannion's roadhouse into a Rocky Mountain Grossinger's.

If it soured later on, we were out more than time and money. If it soured later on, we would go to jail.

I kept dreaming about that. About being locked away, locked up in a cell. I kept waking up in a sweat and sitting around smoking a cigarette and dropping off to sleep again and waking up out of another dream.

The next night I puddle-jumped to Olean. That night I slept well. And woke up, and met my mooch and tossed that lasso around his manly shoulders.

And waited now, in the lobby of the Olean House, for Evvie Stone.

5

She was five or ten minutes late. I waited for her in the lobby. I sat in a red leather chair in front of the empty fireplace and kept glancing over at the doorway. She came through the door and got about a third of the way to the desk, and I stood up and walked across the lobby to meet her.

'Oh, Mr Hayden,' she said.

'Miss Stone.'

'I had to double-park out in front, so if you're ready—'

We left the hotel together. Her car was a white Ford with a small dent in the right front fender. We got in and she spun a very neat U-turn, took a right on State Street and headed the Ford out of town on Route 17. She kept her eyes on the road.

I kept mine on her. She'd changed her clothes for dinner. Now she wore a very simple black dress with a scoop neckline. A green heart hung from a small gold chain around her throat, a very deep green against her white skin. Jade, I guessed. Her arms were bare, her hands very sure on the wheel.

'I'm supposed to be very nice to you,' she said suddenly.

'I think I'll like that.'

We stopped for a light and she turned to look at me. Her eyes were larger than I had remembered them, and deeper in tone. 'You surprised the hell out of me this morning,' she said. 'You don't look like a confidence man.'

'That's an asset.'

'Yes, I'm sure it must be.' The light changed. 'Mr Gunderman doesn't have an important engagement tonight, you know. He just decided that I'd learn more from you than he would.'

'I guessed that. His idea or yours?'

'Well, he probably thinks he thought of it himself. I guess I actually led him into it. He told me he wished he could get more of a line on you, and that he was having dinner with you tonight, but that he didn't think you'd be too keen on opening up to him. I said that a girl could probably draw you out a lot better, and I said something about the way you looked at my legs before. You did look at my legs, you know.'

'I know.'

'I told him this, and he paced around the room and asked me how I'd like to have dinner with you. I let him talk me into it. I'm supposed to give you the full treatment. Dinner at The Castle at a cozy table for two, and then some quiet spot for drinks, and then you'll tell me secrets. You'll let me dig all the information about the Barnstable operation out of you.'

'I might just do that.'

'This is the place,' she said suddenly. 'Isn't it incredible?'

She pulled off the road to the right. There are probably as many restaurants in the country called *The Castle* as there are diners named *Eat*, but this was the first one I'd ever come across that looked the part. It was a sprawling brick-and-stone affair with towers and fortifications and pillars and gun turrets, everything but a moat, and all of this in a one-floor building. A medieval ranch house with delusions of grandeur.

'Wait until you see the inside, John.'

'It can't live up to this.'

'Wait.'

Inside, there was a foyer with a fountain, a Grecian statue type of thing with water streaming from various orifices. The floor was tile, the walls all wood and leather, with rough-hewn beams running the length of the ceiling. The maître d' beamed his way over to us, and Evvie said something about Mr Gunderman's table, and we were passed along to a captain and bowed through a cocktail lounge and a large dining room into something called the Terrace Room. The tables were set far apart, the lighting dim and intimate.

We ordered martinis. 'You might as well order big,' she told me. 'He'll be unhappy if I don't give you the full treatment. This is a quite a place, isn't it? You don't expect it in Olean. But they have people who come from miles away to eat here.'

'They couldn't make out just with local trade.'

'Hardly. The place seats over eight hundred. There are rooms and more rooms. And the food is very good. I think our drinks are coming.'

The martinis were cold and dry and crisp. We had a second round, then ordered dinner. She touted the chateaubriand for two and I rode along with it.

'I get called Evvie,' she said. 'What do I call you?'

'John will do.'

'Doug Rance referred to you as Johnny.'

'That's his style. He'd love it if he could call me the Cheyenne Kid, as far as that goes.'

'Is that where you're from? Cheyenne?'

'Colorado, now. Originally New Mexico.'

'That's what Wally said, but I didn't know whether you'd been telling him the truth or not. You've got him on the hook, John. You really have him all hot and bothered.'

'That's what I thought.'

'What happened at lunch?'

I ran through it for her and she nodded, taking it all in. She was all wrapped up in the play herself. Usually I hate having an amateur in on things too deeply, but she seemed to have a feeling for the game. It wasn't necessary to tell her things twice. She listened very intently with those brown eyes opened very wide and she hung on every word.

'He was hopping when he got back to the office,' she said.

'He was on the phone most of the day, and he dictated a batch of letters to me. Do you want to see them?'

'Not here. I'll have a look at them later. Who did he call?'

'Different people, and he placed a few of the calls himself so I didn't know who he was talking to. I think he made a few calls to Canada. He's sure somebody made a strike up there. Uranium or oil or gold or something, he doesn't know what it is but he's sure it's up there.'

'He'll find out differently.'

'I think he found out a little already. I managed to get him going when he was signing the letters I typed for him. He said he couldn't get any satisfaction, that nobody seemed to know a thing about a mineral strike in the area. And the date on your letter bothers him. He said he could see you coming down as a quick fast-buck operator if you'd heard about a strike, if you had advance information. But that letter is dated six or seven weeks ago, and if you had some information that long ago it would have spread by now. That's what has him hopping, the fact that nobody has heard a word about any developments in that section.'

'That figures. Of course he hinted to me about uranium, and of course I said there was nothing like that, which was what he damn well expected me to say.'

'He's just about ready to believe it now, John. And when I tell him what I managed to learn from you tonight, he'll be sure it's the straight story, or fairly close to it. How much of the play will I give him?'

'Not too much,' I said. I lit a cigarette and drew on it. 'Here's the steak,' I said. 'Let's forget the rest of this until later, all right? I want to give it time to settle.'

We let it alone and worked on the steak. It was black on the outside and red in the middle, a nice match for the red leather and black wood decor of the room. I was hungrier than I'd realized. We made a little small talk, the usual routine about the food and the restaurant and the city itself. She wasn't too crazy about Olean. She didn't give me the chamber of commerce build-up I'd gotten earlier from her boss.

'I want to get out of here,' she said. 'You don't know what this town gets to be like. Like a prison cell.'

I doubted it. I knew what a jail cell was like, and no town on earth was that way.

'You met Doug in Las Vegas?'

'That's right,' she said. 'I had a vacation and I just wanted to get away from all of this, and from Wally. I guess it was June when I went down there, the second or third week. I was supposed to go back, but I didn't plan on going back. His wife had been dead for eight months and he had just gotten around to telling me that he didn't plan on marrying me after all. It wouldn't look too good, he said, and what was the matter with things the way they stood?'

'What was?'

'Everything, as far as I was concerned. I was in a rut, John. A pretty deep one. I should have left this town a long while ago but I didn't have any place to go or anything much to do, and I figured I would stick with Wally and marry him when his wife died. He wasn't that exciting but he wasn't that bad and he does have money and, well, being poor is no pleasure.'

'Agreed.'

She managed a smile. 'So by the time I found out I wasn't going to hear any wedding bells, I took this big long look at little Evelyn Stone and the neat little niche she had cut out for herself. I wasn't too taken with it, John. Here I'd spent a few years with a fairly romantic view of myself, the youngish girl with the wealthy older man, the office wife living a behind-the-scenes life. And then all at once I wasn't so young any more and I was just this girl Wallace J. Gunderman was keeping. And keeping damned cheaply. If you averaged it out, I was costing him less than if he bought it a shot at a time from a cheap streetwalker.'

I didn't say anything. She studied her hands and said, 'I don't like to say it that way, but about that time I started to see it that way, and it didn't set well.'

'Sure.'

'So I went to Vegas for some fun and floor shows and roulette, and maybe a nice rich man would fall in love with me. Except I didn't like the men I met, and then too I couldn't afford the kind of vacation that might have put me in the right places at the right time. And I took a beating at the roulette wheel.'

'And met Doug.'

'Uh-huh.' She smiled again. 'He tried awfully hard to make me, but I just wasn't having any. I liked him, though. Right from the start I liked him.'

'Everybody does.'

'I suppose they must. After awhile he must have decided that he wasn't going to wind up in bed with me, so he started talking to me and listening when I talked. He kept getting me to talk about Wally, and I did because I wanted to tell someone how mad I was at the son of a bitch. I didn't know what he was getting at. Then he came up with the idea and you know the rest of it.'

I nodded. I liked the picture of Doug trying to score with her and striking out. It didn't exactly fit with the way he'd told it to me, but that figured. Nobody likes to paint pictures of himself in a foolish position.

'John? Did he say he slept with me?'

'No.'

'The way you were smiling—'

'It's not that. He said that he didn't try, that he wasn't interested. And when I saw you in the office this morning I didn't get it.'

'What do you mean?'

I met her eyes. 'I couldn't imagine him not being interested. Not when I saw you.'

'Oh,' she said, and colored slightly. Then she said, 'Listen, don't tell him what I said, will you? About him trying and not getting any place?'

'Don't worry.'

'Because he might not like being reminded of it. But anyway, we got along fine once he quit being on the make. And he came up with this idea, and that changed my mind about coming back to Olean. I was back as soon as my vacation was up and went back to work for Wally.'

I didn't ask the obvious question.

'Back to work in every respect,' she said, answering the question I hadn't asked. 'But it was different now. I don't feel like a cheap whore any more.' The brown eyes flashed. 'I feel like an expensive whore, John. A hundred-thousand-dollar call girl.'

A bus boy cleared our table. We passed up dessert and had coffee and cognac. The cognac was very old and very smooth. I broke out a fresh pack of cigarettes. She took one. I gave her a light and she leaned forward to take it. The jade heart fell away from her white skin. The black dress fell forward, too, and there was a momentary flash of the body beneath it, the thrust of breasts.

A hundred-thousand-dollar call girl. Our eyes locked and we smiled foolishly at each other.

The waiter brought the check. She added a tip and signed her name and, below that, Gunderman's. We got up and left.

Outside, it was cooler. She drove and I sat beside her. We didn't seem to be headed anywhere in particular.

She said, 'This town. You'd think I'd be used to it by now, after six years here.'

'Just six years? I thought you were born here.'

'God, no.' She pitched her cigarette out the window. 'Not far from here, actually. I was brought up about twenty miles east of here, a little town called Bolivar. You probably never heard of it.'

'I never even heard of Olean up to now.'

'Then you never heard of Bolivar. It makes Olean look like New York. I got away from there to go to college. I went to Syracuse, to Syracuse University. I was on scholarship. I got married two weeks after graduation and wound up in New York.'

'Doug told me you were married.'

'I told him about it. When I start feeling sorry for myself I get carried away. I probably filled his ear with a lot of that. I married this boy from Long Island that I'd met at school and we went to New York to play house. I was the mommy and he was the man who took the suds out of the automatic washer. I don't know why I should be boring you with all this, John.'

'I'm not bored.'

'You're easy to talk to, aren't you?'

'Uh-huh. I used to be a psychiatrist before I turned crooked.'

'I could almost believe that. What was I talking about?'

'The suds and the automatic washer.'

'That's right. Except that we played it a little different. I was the mommy and he was the baby, that's what it all added up to, really. We never had enough money, either, and his parents hated me, really hated me, and then he started running around.'

'That's hard to believe.'

'You're nice, but he did. I didn't really feel insulted by it, to tell you the truth. I had managed to figure out by then that he was a nice boy, but that I didn't want to spend the rest of my life with a nice boy who needed someone to wipe his nose and help him on with his rubbers. That came out dirty, I didn't mean it that way. You know what I meant.'

'Uh-huh.'

'So I went to Reno and threw my wedding ring in that river there, and came back to Bolivar, and there was a job opening in Olean, the job with Wally, and I took it, and you know the rest. I became a very private secretary. At first it was exciting and then it was secure and then his wife did die, finally, after hovering on the edge for years, and then we weren't going to get married after all and instead of a fiery affair it was a back-door thing with a bad smell to it.'

Her fingers tightened on the steering wheel. When she spoke again her voice was thinner and higher. 'I felt so goddamned good this afternoon. Watching that man, so hot to find a way to make a new fortune for himself, so excited he couldn't sit still. And knowing he's just going to get his nose rubbed in it, and that I'm going to do the rubbing. Oh, that's a sweet feeling.'

For a few minutes neither of us said anything. Her hands relaxed their grip on the wheel and she slowed the Ford and stopped at the curb. 'There are things we ought to go over,' she said. 'You've got to tell me how much I'm supposed to tell him for one thing, and then there are the letters he gave me. I've got them in my purse.'

'Are we supposed to be making a night of it?'

'In a small way, anyway.' Her eyes narrowed. 'He didn't tell me how far to go playing the Mata Hari role. I guess I'm supposed to use my own imagination. There are bars we could go to, but they aren't all that private.'

'My hotel room?'

'I thought of that. I think he might not like that. Everybody knows who I am, that I'm his secretary and that, well, that I'm more than his secretary. He might not like the way it would look if I went to your room.'

'Where, then?'

'My apartment?'

'Fine.'

'But I don't think I've got anything to drink.'

We stopped for a bottle. I paid for it, and she insisted on giving me the money back when we got in the car. This was on Gunderman, she told me. He was footing the bill for the evening.

6

She lived in a newish brick apartment building on Irving Street. Her place was on the second floor. She tucked the Ford into a parking space out in front and we walked up a flight of stairs. She unlocked the door and we went inside. The living room was large and airy, furnished in Danish Modern pieces that looked expensive. The carpet was deep and ran wall-to-wall. It wasn't hard to guess who paid the rent, or who had picked up the tab for the furnishings.

'I'll hunt glasses,' she said. 'How do you like your poison? Water, soda?'

'Just rocks is fine.'

She came back from the kitchen with a pair of drinks. We sat together on a long low couch and touched glasses solemnly. 'Here's to crime,' she said.

'To successful crime.'

'By all means.'

We drank. She tucked her feet under her, opened her purse and pulled out a sheaf of letters. 'He had a list of people who bought some of that Canadian land,' she said. 'Not a complete list, but about twenty names. He wrote letters to all of them asking – well, you can read it yourself.'

I read one of the letters. It was brief and to the point. Mr Gunderman was interested in any dealings or correspondence that Mr So-and-So might have had with the Barnstable Corporation, Ltd., of Toronto. Would Mr So-and-So please let Mr Gunderman know, and would he also notify Mr Gunderman if he had made any disposition of his holdings in north-western Canada, or if he had any intention of so doing?

There were eighteen letters like that. Gunderman's list didn't match ours completely. He was missing a lot of the names we'd gotten from Al Prince, and he had one or two that Prince hadn't given to us. I picked out the letters to the ten men with whom we'd been in correspondence and handed them back to Evvie.

'You can mail these,' I told her. 'They'll tell him just what we want him to know. A few of these pigeons already sold land to us, and the rest have heard from us.'

'What about the others?'

'I'll keep them.'

'Won't he get suspicious if he doesn't hear anything from any of those men?'

'He'll hear from them. What other letters did he dictate?'

I looked through them. There was a letter to the Ontario Board of Trade inquiring in a general way into the commercial purpose and history of Barnstable, and there was a very similar letter addressed to the Lieutenant-General's office. I let those go through. Both of those sources would simply advise Gunderman that we had incorporated at such-and-such a date with so much capital, and that we had organized for the purpose of purchasing and developing land in the western provinces.

This was all a matter of public record, and it was something we wanted Gunderman to know. We could tell him ourselves, but it was much better to let him find out on his own hook from properly official government sources. Let him think he was being shrewd. If you let a man convince himself that he is much cleverer than you are, he will never get around to fearing that you're going to pull a fast one on him.

'And this one here,' she said.

The last letter was addressed to a Toronto detective agency that specialized in industrial and financial investigations. Gunderman asked for a brief report on (a) the Barnstable Corporation, Ltd., (b) Douglas Rance, and (c) John Hayden.

'He asked me to put a call through to these people,' Evvie said. 'I told him I couldn't get through to them and I killed the call, and then he put it all in a letter. I was a little afraid of what might come out. I know he used this agency before, when he got taken the first time.'

'I don't think this letter should go out.'

'That's what I figured. And why I cut off the call. If a detective dug into things too deeply—'

'Uh-huh.'

'But if he doesn't hear from them at all—'

'He'll hear from them,' I said. I swallowed some Scotch, got a cigarette going. She pursed her lips, moistened them with the tip of her tongue. She started to say something, then changed her mind and finished her drink. I went into the kitchen, filled a bowl with ice cubes, brought it and the bottle back into the living room. I put the bowl on the coffee table and added fresh ice and fresh Scotch to our glasses.

'What should we drink to this time, John?'

'*Salud y amor y pesetas*,' I said.

'Health and love and money, I know that one. Isn't there more to it?'

'*Y tiempo para gustarlos.*'

'And time ... what's the rest of it?'

'And time to enjoy them.'

'And time to enjoy them,' she said. 'Yes, that's worth drinking to.'

We touched glasses very solemnly and drank a toast to health and love and money and time to enjoy them. Outside, Olean remained very peaceful by night. The few traffic noises were all blocks away. I looked at her and felt that old urge come on strong from out of nowhere, a fast rush of desire that surprised me. A comfortable couch, a quiet and properly private apartment, a good bottle, a beautiful girl – all of them components in a standard mixture. I put a lid on it and started to tell her just what she should say to Gunderman in the morning.

I ran all the way through it. It was simple enough, no details but a few hints to steer him in the right direction. The hunting lodge story was a blind, of course. I'd been hopping all over the country lately, and I had bought up a great deal of land, and the Barnstable Corporation stood to make a fortune. I was just a hired hand, and I was a little resentful of the fact that I was on straight salary, albeit a healthy salary, while the principals in the deal stood to pick up a bundle without doing much work for it at all. Of course they were very important men and I was just an employee, so I really had no kick coming. Barnstable already owned a vast stretch of Canadian land, and few prospects had given me a hard time the way Gunderman had done, and I didn't care too much whether I bought his land or not, because we already had done so well in the land-purchasing department.

When I got to the end I let her feed it all back to me. She didn't miss a trick, and she added a touch or two all her own. She was very damned good for an amateur. She had the brains for it, and the right attitude. She was a natural girl for the grift. If this fell in, I thought, or even if it didn't, she could probably make a damned fine living as the female half of a badger game combo. She sure as hell had the looks for it.

She filled our glasses again. She said, 'You know, I was very nervous about all of this before tonight, John. I'm not nervous any more.'

'What changed your mind?'

'You did.'

'Mc?'

She nodded. 'Uh-huh. Doug was all fire and enthusiasm and confidence, but I wasn't sure he could bring it all off. But there's something about you, I don't know what it is, maybe just a feeling that you really know what you're doing, that you'll make sure everything runs smoothly from start to finish.' Her eyes narrowed slightly. 'I somehow just trust you, John.'

'Let's hope your boss feels the same way.'

'I think he will. I'm awfully glad Doug was able to get you in on this deal. He told me about you when we were first starting to plan the whole thing, and he said you would be perfect if only you weren't working on something else. That's what I was afraid of, that you would have something else going.'

'I did.'

'Oh?'

'I was assistant manager at a bowling alley in Colorado.'

'Really?'

'Really.'

'I don't—'

I drank some more. 'I got out of prison a little less than a year ago, Evvie. It was the first really hard time I'd ever served, and I decided I wasn't going back, not ever. I took a square job and stuck with it.' I put my glass down. 'Then Doug Rance turned up with a proposition. I said no to him a few times and wound up saying yes.'

'What changed your mind?'

Sometimes you have to share your dreams. It was the Scotch or the girl or a combination of the two, I suppose. I told her about Bannion's dump outside of Boulder and how it would pay off like a broken slot machine with the right sort of operation. And how I couldn't go there for a drink without itching for the money to buy the place and run it the way it ought to be run. And how I was in this deal for the money because there was no other way for me to get that money, and when the deal was done I would be back in Boulder, through with the grift forever and all set to make decent money on the square.

She asked a few questions and I answered them. Then we were both a long time silent. Our glasses were empty. I let them stay that way. I had enough of a load to feel it and I didn't want to get drunk. We smoked a few cigarettes. I kept trying not to look at her, and kept failing in the attempt. This was dangerous. The more I looked at her the more I came up with crazy images. Pictures of the two of us on top of a Colorado mountain, walking hand in hand, as fresh and breathlessly natural as a commercial for mentholated cigarettes. The American Dream, stock footage number 40938.

Well, we all of us had our weaknesses. Doug gambled, I fell in love. It was nothing I wouldn't be able to put a lid on. But I didn't want any more to drink, not now.

'John.'

I turned to her.

'I hope you get what you want, John.'

We looked at each other. She was curled up on that couch beside me like a large cat in front of a fireplace. I knew what I wanted. I wanted to make her purr.

'John—'

I reached for her; she came to me. She smelled as clean and alive as a newly-mowed lawn. I kissed her, and she went rigid and made a weird little sound deep in her throat, and then her arms were tight around me and the tension was gone and we kissed again.

We broke. I lit two cigarettes and gave one of them to her. Her hand was trembling. She dropped the cigarette, and I got down on my hands and knees and chased it. It had bounced under the couch. I picked it up and rubbed the spot where the carpet was lightly scorched. She took it from me and drew on it, coughed, crushed it out in the ashtray. She straightened up and closed her eyes tight. Her hands bunched up into nervous little fists.

'I didn't want this to happen, John.'

I said nothing.

'I don't, I can't, I—'

I waited.

'It has to be real. I don't want another ... I can't ... it has to mean something. It has to—'

I stood up. She hesitated, then got to her feet. I kissed her and held her close. Her body pressed against me all the way. I kissed her again and crushed her closer.

'Yes,' she said.

Afterward she lay on her side with her eyes closed and a lazy grin on her lips. She made a sweet purring sound. I got out of her bed and padded into the living room. The ice had melted. I got fresh ice from the refrigerator and made stiff drinks for both of us. I brought the drinks and our cigarettes back to the bedroom. She had not changed position. She still lay on her side, the same sweet ghost of a smile on her lips. She was still purring.

I put the drinks and the cigarettes on the bedside table and kissed her.

'Mmmmm,' she said. She opened her eyes and yawned luxuriously. 'Oh, God,' she said. 'I really didn't want this to happen.'

'Neither did I.'

'But I'm glad it did. What time is it?'

'Almost one.'

'Is it that late already? I thought it was about ten o'clock.'

'That was three hours ago.'

'Maybe you'd better get dressed.'

'I guess so.'

'I wish you could sleep here, but I think you should probably sleep at your hotel. I don't want Wally to know about this. Actions above and beyond the call of duty. He might even approve, goddamn him. But I don't want him to know about it, or Doug Rance either.'

'Don't worry.'

She had a special beauty nude. Most women look better clothed. Bodies are imperfect. Clothes hide, and also promise, and the promise is too often better than the fulfillment of it. Not so with Evvie.

She still wore the jade heart. I touched it, let my fingers trail down to her breasts. She purred again.

'I'll get dressed and drive you back.'

'Don't be silly.'

'Well, you can't walk, for God's sake.'

'Why not? It's a nice night.'

'It's a long walk.'

'How far?'

'Nine or ten blocks, I think. All the way down to North Union and then over to the hotel. Let me drive you, John.'

'I feel like walking.'

I dressed. I finished my drink and she worked on hers. It was late and the night outside was cold and quiet.

I said, 'He's going to keep you busy tomorrow morning with a million crazy questions. You know what to tell him. Then he may want to see me, or he may try to stall for more time. I don't think I should let him stall too much. I'm going to grab a plane tomorrow afternoon.'

'For Toronto?'

'Yes.' I drew on a cigarette. 'The more I think about it, the more I think I shouldn't see him tomorrow. It would be good if he got tied up with something during the morning that kept him busy until two or three in the afternoon, and then by the time he was ready for me it would be too late and I would have already left for the airport. I think that's the way to do it, to give him the rope so that he can rope himself in a little.'

'What do you have to do in Toronto?'

'A lot of things. I'll dodge around for about a week to give him time to get answers to his letters. Keep a close watch on him in the meantime. If he starts to go off the track, don't keep it a secret. Get on the goddamn phone and call us.'

'Where?'

'You have the Barnstable number. It's on our letterhead. Just call and talk to Doug.'

'Suppose I want to talk to you?'

I told her what hotel I was staying at, and how to reach me. I didn't spend too much time at the hotel. I told her to leave messages if I wasn't there, to give her name as Miss Carmody. If there was a message to the effect that Miss Carmody had called, I would try her first at her apartment and then at the office.

'And when will I see you again, John?'

'In about a week, maybe ten days. I think he'll probably try to get in touch with us, and we'll give him a short stall and then make contact again, probably with me coming down here to Olean again.'

She didn't say anything. I knotted my tie and made the knot properly small and neat. I put a foot on a chair and tied my shoe. I stubbed out my cigarette in the ashtray on the bedside table. It was a copper-enameled ashtray with a red and green geometric design on it, the sort of thing women make in Golden-Ager classes at the YWCA.

She said, 'I'll miss you.'

'Evvie—'

She stood up. I turned to her and kissed her. She was all breathless and shaky. There were deep circles under her eyes.

'I hope I'm not just part of the game, John. Cheat the mooch and sleep with the girl, all of it part of a package deal. I hope—'

'You know better.'

'I hope so,' she said.

The air was cool, the sky clear. There was a nearly full moon and a scattering of stars. Irving Street was wide, with tall shade trees lining the curbs on both sides of the street. The houses were set back a good ways from the curb. They were single homes built forty or fifty years ago. Most of them had upstairs porches. Some had bay windows and other gingerbread. I walked eight blocks down Irving to North Union without meeting anyone. A single car passed me, a cab, empty. He slowed, I shook my head, and he went on.

All but a few of the houses were completely dark inside. Here and there a light would be on upstairs, and in two houses I could see television screens flickering in darkened living rooms.

I turned left at North Union, crossed the street, found my way back to the Olean House. The lobby was deserted except for a sleepy old man at the desk and a very old woman who sat in one of the chairs opposite the fireplace reading a newspaper. I picked up my key at the desk and took the elevator upstairs.

It happens more often than it doesn't. You're caught up in something fast-moving and exciting and secretive, and this sudden common bond masks all of the things that you do not have in common, and moments are infused with a deceptive sort of vitality, and you wind up in the rack. Bells ring, all of that.

I went over to my window. There was nothing in particular to look at. Most of the stores on the main drag didn't even bother keeping their windows lit. I smoked a cigarette.

It happens all the time. You try not to let it get mixed that way, the business and the pleasure. Like not going where you eat, a similar attempt to separate disparate functions. It is rarely as easy as it sounds, and circumstances can make it harder.

I was an old buck gone long in the tooth with an age-old weakness for pretty girls. And she had had four years of Wallace J. Gunderman, and simple biology could make her ready enough for a change of pace, especially when she could so easily talk herself into thinking that it all meant something. So it was all something to take and enjoy and forget soon after. It was just what she had said she hoped it wasn't – part of the fruits of the game, her body along with her boss's money. Take it and enjoy it and kiss it goodbye.

I got undressed and hung everything up neatly. I stood under a too-hot shower. I got out of the shower and sat on the edge of the bed and smoked another cigarette.

I told myself not to think about it. I put out my cigarette and reached for the phone. It took the old man a long time to answer. I gave him my name and my room number and told him to ring me at eleven, and not to put any calls through before then. He asked me to wait a minute. He dug up a pencil and I repeated the instructions to him very slowly while he wrote everything down. Then he read it back to me and I said yes indeed, fine, perfect.

I cradled the phone. I thought about the color of the jade heart against her white skin, and her eyes and hair and the way she smelled and the small sounds she made.

I went to bed and to sleep.

7

I'd been up for an hour and a half when the phone rang at eleven. The woman said, 'It's eleven o'clock, Mr Hayden. You had several phone calls, but I didn't put them through because there was a message that you weren't to be disturbed.'

'Fine. Any messages?'

'The calls were all from Mr Gunderman,' she said. She made the name sound almost holy. 'You're to call him as soon as possible.'

I sat around the hotel room for another half hour. I packed my suitcase, smoked a few cigarettes. I left the suitcase by the side of the bed and went downstairs for breakfast. At noon I called Gunderman's office from a pay phone across the street.

Evvie answered. 'I'm sorry, Mr Hayden,' she said. 'Mr Gunderman is out to lunch.'

'I'm at a pay phone,' I said. 'You can talk.'

'He'll be sorry he missed your call, Mr Hayden. He's been trying to reach you all morning, but he had a luncheon appointment and he was called out.'

'Oh, I get it. There's someone in the office.'

'That's quite correct, Mr Hayden.'

'Who is it? Gunderman?'

'No, I don't believe so.'

'All right, it doesn't matter. I'll give you questions you can answer without any trouble. When do you expect him back?'

'Perhaps an hour, Mr Hayden.'

'How did he take the line you handed him? Was he with it all the way?'

'Yes, that's right.'

'And he's very anxious to see me?'

'I believe so, yes.'

'Then I think it's just as well that he doesn't. There's a plane leaving Ischua Airport at four-thirty this afternoon. When he comes in, tell him I was over to the office. Can you do that?'

'Yes.'

'And that I was sorry we couldn't get together, but I had a few things hanging fire that I had to take care of, and that I'd try to get in touch with him in a week or so. Give him the general impression that I'm sorry I wasted my time here but if he wants to sell and take his tax loss the offer is still open. I'm not pushing, but I'm willing. Have you got that?'

'Yes.'

'I wish I could stay another day. I'll get back as soon as I can, Evvie. There's no chance of you getting up to Toronto for a day, is there?'

'No, I don't believe so.'

'Uh-huh. You might get him to send you on a reconnaissance mission, but that's probably not that good an idea. I'll miss you.'

Silence.

'Bye, baby.'

I cradled the phone. I picked up a paperback and a couple of magazines and went back to the hotel. I sat around in the room for an hour while Gunderman ate his lunch, then checked out of the hotel and caught a cab to the airport. I got there better than three hours before flight time. I checked my bag and walked down the road a little ways to a tavern. I nursed a few drinks and listened to a juke box. The place was very nearly empty.

At four-thirty my plane left, and I was on it.

Doug had to hear all of it twice through. He made a perfect audience. He hung on every word and grinned at every clever turn of phrase and nodded approvingly at every halfway cute gambit. I kept expecting him to burst into spontaneous applause.

'You roped him,' he said admiringly. 'You lassoed that son of a bitch.'

'He's not branded yet.'

'Now we stick it in and break it off, Johnny. Jesus, this is beautiful. How long do you want to leave him hanging? A week?'

'More or less.'

'Won't he try to reach us before then?'

'He won't be able to reach me. If he calls Barnstable, they'll tell him I'm out. The girl will. The girl doesn't even know me, does she?'

'She's met you. I don't know if she remembers the name.'

'She didn't meet me as Claude Whittlief, did she?'

'No.'

'Because if she did, we'd have to get rid of her before the payoff. No, I'm sure she didn't, now that I think about it. So if he tries to reach me he won't get any place, and I don't think he'd want to go over my head and talk with you. If he's as shrewd as I figure him to be, he'll want to work through me, to use me to get the inside dope and to make whatever pitch he might want to make. Remember, he only has a little bit of the picture now, only as much as Evvie's given him.'

'How did you like her, incidentally?'

'She's all right'

'Get anywheres?'

'I didn't try,' I said.

'Not interested?'

'Not on a job.'

His grin spread. 'That's the professional attitude, all right. I could go another cup of coffee. You?'

'Fine.'

We were in a booth at an all-night diner on Dundas about a block or so from my hotel. The food was greasy and so were most of the customers. The coffee wasn't too bad. A bucktoothed waitress with a West Virginia accent brought us more of it. She was a long way from home.

'About those letters,' he said. 'How do you want to handle them?'

I had gone over the letters Gunderman had written to those other pigeons. Of the eighteen, ten had been to people we were already in correspondence with, and those Evvie had mailed. I had the other eight. One man lived in Buffalo, two in Cleveland, one in Toledo, one in a Chicago suburb, two in New York City, and one way the hell up in Seattle.

'We throw out the Seattle one, first of all,' I said. 'It won't hurt him if he doesn't get a reply from everybody, and Seattle is too damn far to run to just to get a postmark.'

'There are remailing services,' he suggested.

I sipped coffee, put the cup down. 'The hell with those. I ran one of those myself about twelve years back. *Letters Remailed – 25¢. Your Secret Address. Mail Forwarded and Received.* I opened every letter and sold the interesting ones to a blackmailer. Somehow I don't think I was the only grifter to run one of those outfits.'

'That's one racket I never heard of.'

'Everything's a racket,' I said. 'The day after tomorrow, I'll have the letters ready. I'll spend tomorrow taking care of the stationery angle. Then I'll fly to Chicago and mail a letter and work my way back on the trains. The cities spread out in a line, Chicago and Toledo and Cleveland and Buffalo, and then a plane down to New York and back again. That's no problem.'

'And the detective agency?'

That was a problem, all right. If we didn't answer that letter at all, Gunderman would get on the phone and call them himself. Evvie couldn't head off the calls forever. If we *did* answer, using a fake sheet of the firm's letterhead (or even a real sheet; it wouldn't be all that hard to run up to their offices and filch a piece of paper and an envelope) we would run into headwinds when Gunderman called to thank them, or sent along a check in payment.

'Let it lie for a day or two,' Doug suggested. 'He won't expect a report from them by return mail, anyway. We'll think of something.'

In the morning I got busy on the handful of letters. There was a printer in town who specialized in doing a little work on the wrong side of the law. He did job-printing for the boys who printed up pornography and trucked it across the bridge into the States, and he was supposed to be fairly good at passports and other documents. I could have had him run off a few different batches of stationery for us, but I didn't want to.

We already had a use for him – he was going to draw up the fake deeds for us, deeds to Canadian land which we did not own. I've never been very tall on the idea of using the same person too many times in a single job. It's not a good idea to let one man get that much of a picture of your operation. He would handle the deeds, and do a good job with that, and that was enough.

I went to a batch of printers and a couple of office supply stores. Each printer made up a batch of a hundred sheets and envelopes, and the stationery stores came through with cheaper standard stuff. I had seven letters to answer, and I wound up with seven hundred sheets and envelopes, each batch with a different name and address and city, each on different paper and in different ink. I got one-day service from everybody, and by six o'clock that evening I had everything I needed.

We typed out four of the responses and wrote out three by hand. We used the office typewriter, cleaning the keys after the first letter, knocking a letter out of alignment before the third one, and otherwise disguising the fact that all four letters were coming out of the same machine. The handwritten letters were no problem at all. I have five very different styles of handwriting, and Doug has about as many. An expert could find enough similarities to guess that any of my five styles was my writing, but the average person would never see a connection. And Gunderman would not be putting our letters under a microscope. The pens were different, the inks different, the envelopes would be zooming in from different cities – he wasn't going to run to a handwriting expert as an extra safeguard.

We varied the text of the letters, too. Five of our seven men wrote Gunderman to tell him that they had sold their land to Barnstable, that Barnstable had paid off promptly and legitimately, and would Gunderman tell them what was the matter with the operation? (I guessed that he wouldn't answer, not wanting to get people curious. If he did, Evvie could simply throw the letters away.) One man replied that he used his land for summer camping and was not interested in selling it to Barnstable, to Gunderman, or to anybody else. The last man, the one in Toledo, wrote that he had turned down Barnstable's first offer in the hope that they might raise it, and that so far they hadn't.

Doug and I both worked on the wording. We kept the letters short and to the point. By the time we were through, the letters were set to do their job. They would convey the impression we were aiming at. Our man Gunderman would be left with the impression that the Barnstable Corporation, Ltd., had managed to buy up half of Canada for a song. Our man Gunderman would be starting to drool.

'The detective agency,' he said. 'Any ideas?'

'None that I'm too crazy about. It would be easy if they had never done any work for Gunderman before. I could go to them, introduce myself as

Gunderman, and give them some very minor piece of work to do for me. Then in the meantime I send Gunderman a faked report on a copy of their letterhead, along with a bill for the same amount as their bill to me. His check would go to them and it would cover the work I'd done, and that would touch all the bases neatly enough.' I shrugged. 'But they've worked for him, and that queers it. They might know him, or at least know enough to know I wasn't Wallace J. Gunderman. And besides, I don't like the idea that much to begin with.'

'It's a little shaky.'

'Uh-huh.'

He looked at me. 'Maybe we should let the letter go through.'

'I don't like that either.'

'What can they find out about us that isn't legit?'

'You'd be surprised.'

He thought that over and decided he agreed with me.

'We'll work it out,' he assured me. 'You get those letters in the mail and I'll see if I can't come up with something.'

'Sure. I might be two or three days.'

'Take your time.'

'Right'

'And don't get hung up on the detective angle. We'll think of something good.'

'Sure.'

I called Evvie's apartment that night. I let the phone ring a dozen times before I gave up, and I called back half an hour later and let it ring another dozen times without getting an answer. It was around midnight by then and she wasn't home, and I knew she must be with Gunderman and I tried not to let it bother me. What the hell, she had warmed his bed for four years already. I couldn't exactly turn jealous because she was playing the same role.

Besides, it was part of the game, wasn't it? It happened all the time. A good percentage of the long cons had a sex angle, with a girl's body helping to tie the mark up tight. The one that put me in San Quentin was one like that. Our mooch started sleeping with a girl who told him she was pregnant. I'd been sleeping with that girl myself, and not in a completely casual way. I hadn't liked it when she spent too much time around other men. But it didn't rub me the wrong way when she played with the mooch. That was part of the game, part of setting him up for the score.

I worked that job as roper. I was the mooch's friend, helping set up the phony abortion. I remembered how I sat with him in the waiting room, how he bit his nails and how his sweat smelled, cold and rancid. And the 'doctor' – Sweet Raymond Conn, dead of a heart attack while awaiting trial – the doctor coming out to the waiting room with horrible eyes to tell us that something had gone wrong, that our little girl was dead as a lox.

Instead of operating, Conn had worked on the girl with makeup. He led the mooch inside, I followed, and Peggy was all spread out on a long white table with waxy cheeks and pale flesh and dead staring eyes. I was terrified that she would blink. She didn't, and not six hours later she scrubbed off the deadish makeup and I took her to bed.

I hadn't seen her since the trial. She drew one-to-five, no previous record and her lawyer did a good job for her, and she was on the street within six months. God knows where she is now, or what she's doing.

So I had no reason to sweat because Evvie was busy earning her keep. Anyway, I didn't own her. One roll in the rack, one sweet time that sealed a bargain and made the gears mesh more perfectly, that was all it was. No burning passion, no eternal flame of love.

I flew to Chicago in the morning with no luggage but a briefcase with a batch of letters in it. The cab from O'Hare Airport to the downtown train station happened to pass through the suburb where Gunderman's unwitting correspondent hung his hat. It was a coincidence worth taking advantage of. I made the hackie stop while I dropped the letter in a mailbox, then rode on to the train station.

The Central had a train that went to New York by way of Toledo, Ashtabula, Cleveland, and Albany. It left around eleven-thirty in the morning. We had enough of a stopover at Toledo for me to duck into the terminal and drop the letter in a mailbox and get back to the train on time. In Cleveland, I left the train and had dinner at a downtown restaurant and mailed another two letters. The next train that went on to Buffalo made too many stops. I passed it up and caught another an hour and a half later, mailed my Buffalo letter and took a ride out to the airport.

There were no more planes that night, by the time I got there. I took a room at a motel across from the airport and left an early morning call. I got up, showered, and called Toronto. Nothing was new, Doug told me. I made my plane and was at La Guardia an hour and twenty minutes later. I took the limousine into Manhattan, mailed the last two letters, rode back to the airport and caught a luncheon flight for Toronto by way of Montreal.

All of this was a lot of travel with not much to do. Detail work, moronically simple, automatic, and fairly expensive. I believe in details. They are almost always worth the trouble.

We had bought seven hundred sheets and envelopes of stationery, used seven of each, and had thrown away the other six hundred ninety-three. All this to keep a crooked printer from figuring out too much of our angle. I had trained and planed around two thousand miles because I didn't believe in remail services, and because there was a bare possibility that Gunderman noticed postmarks on his mail. I didn't regret a dollar of the expense or a minute of the time invested. When you're pulling the string on a big one, you want the whole superstructure to be just right.

I took my time dropping over to the Barnstable office. When I got there it was past five and our secretary was gone for the day. Doug was sitting at his desk looking busy.

'Everything done?'

'Done and done,' I said.

He got a bottle from his desk and made drinks for us. 'Your friend in Olean is starting to get warm,' he told me. 'Three calls for you today, one in the morning and two this afternoon. I had the girl tell him you were out of town the last time he called. Before that she just said you weren't in.'

'Good.'

'You were right on one thing, incidentally. He didn't ask to talk to me. And he didn't really want to give his name to the girl, either. He did, but he was reluctant about it.'

I nodded.

'So everything's moving, Johnny.'

'Except for the detective agency.'

'I've got an angle on that, Johnny.'

'What is it?'

'Watch,' he said. He looked very pleased with himself. He picked up the phone and dialed the operator. He told her he wanted to place a person-to-person call for Mr Wallace J. Gunderman in Olean, New York. He gave her Gunderman's office number.

'You can't talk to him,' I said.

'I can. You can't, because he knows you. He hasn't talked to me yet, and by the time he meets me he'll have forgotten my voice.'

'But—'

He held up a hand. He said, 'Mr Gunderman? This is Gerald Morphy, of Brennan Scientific Investigations. You wrote us about an outfit called the Barnstable Corporation?' A pause. 'Mr Gunderman, I wanted to tell you right away that I don't believe we'll be able to handle this investigation ourselves. Right at the moment we've got almost all of our operatives tied up on an industrial sabotage thing, and we're not accepting any other cases at the moment.'

Another pause. Then, 'I do have a suggestion. If it's satisfactory to you, I'd like to refer the matter to another investigator, a man named Robert Hettinger. He's worked for us in the past. He has his own office now and he's quite reliable and honest. Would that ... yes, certainly. Yes, he'd make his reports directly to you and you could make your own financial arrangements with him. This looks to be a small matter, Mr Gunderman, and while I wish we could serve you directly ... yes, well, I can guarantee the man's work personally. Yes, fine, Mr Gunderman, and it's my pleasure, sir.'

He put the phone down and smiled across the desk at me. He looked as triumphant as a sparring partner who'd just knocked out Liston. 'In two or three days,' he said, 'we send him this.'

He handed me a two-page letter. The letterhead read *Robert M. Hettinger*

... private investigative service ... 404 Richmond West ... Toronto. The report said everything we could have wanted it to say. It invented a fine upstanding background for Rance, who was cast as a scion of an established Toronto family with a background in shipping and land development. It said that I was new in Toronto, an employee of Barnstable, and so on. We couldn't have worked up a cleaner bill of health for ourselves.

There was also a bill for fifty dollars Canadian for services rendered.

I said, 'Who's Hettinger?'

'I am.'

'And the address?'

'You can rent office space at four-o-four Richmond for five dollars a month. I get a desk and mail privileges for that much. I paid them five dollars, and they'll have Gunderman's check for me when he sends it along.' He grinned elaborately. 'Fifty dollars, and when you subtract the cost of the stationery and the phone call and the month's rent on the desk space, we still come out about twenty dollars ahead. I figured we might as well pick up pin money along the way.'

'And if he tries to call you?'

'There's a girl who answers the phone for everybody on the floor there. If he calls, Mr Hettinger is out. But he won't. He'll get the report and send a check, and that's all.'

It was neat and I told him so. He was as hungry for praise as a puppy who had finally succeeded in getting the puddle on the paper. He poured more Scotch for us and as we drank to success, I told him again how neatly he'd fielded the ball, and that was that.

I called Evvie from my hotel. This time she was home. I said. 'John here. You alone, baby?'

'Yes. What is it?'

'Just a progress report. Everything's running smoothly on this end. Your boss is going to start getting letters any day now.'

'Good.'

I told her about the detective agency routine. She thought it was very clever, and I didn't bother mentioning that it was Doug's idea. I asked her how Gunderman was behaving.

'He's falling all the way,' she said.

'I understand he's trying to reach me.'

'Three times today, John. He was upset when you managed to leave town the other day without seeing him. He's positive there's something going on that he could make money on. He doesn't know what the gimmick is but he's sure there is one and he's dying to find it. How much longer do you want to let him dangle?'

I thought about it. 'Maybe I'll take another trip to Olean soon,' I said.

'That would be nice.'

'Let's see. I think maybe the middle of the week, maybe on Wednesday.

He should have enough replies by Monday afternoon so that the whole picture will soak in fast enough. Now here's the bit. Monday, you'll tell him that you got a call from me. I wasn't in Toronto, you're not sure where I was, but I wasn't in Toronto. I called you, and it seems as though I'm anxious to see you, not Gunderman but you. You have the feeling that I'm halfway crazy about you, and—'

'Are you, John?'

'What?'

'Halfway crazy about me?'

I lit a cigarette. 'Anyway, at this point you became the little heroine, doing it up right for the boss. You knew he wanted to see me, so you conned me into coming down to Olean on the excuse of seeing Gunderman. He'll be delighted. And set it up so that I'll come around to his office sometime Wednesday afternoon.'

'You didn't answer my question, John.'

'Did you get what I said?'

'Of course. You still didn't answer my question.'

'I'll give you the answer in person,' I said.

I wound up sitting at the bar at The Friars. They had a piano trio there that wasn't half bad, a West Coast outfit a long way from home. The bass player had worked with Mulligan ages ago. I stayed there until the place closed and walked back to my hotel.

8

'Have a seat, John,' he said. 'Just have a seat and relax. You must have had quite a trip. I hate those little puddle-hopping airlines. You no sooner get your belt fastened than it's time to unhook it because you've landed already; just up and down again. And I guess you've had a belly full of travel lately, haven't you?'

'Well, I've been busy.'

'Now I'm sure you have, John. I'm sure you have at that. I wish I hadn't missed you that morning. Your hotel wouldn't put an early call through to your room, and then you were gone before I could get hold of you. I was sorry about that.'

'I meant to come over in the morning,' I said. 'But it turned out, well, to be quite a late night, and then I went and did more drinking than I usually do, and I felt I ought to sleep a little later than usual. And then when I did wake up—'

I left the sentence hanging. Gunderman nodded slowly and said, 'I suppose you weren't feeling too well, John.'

'No, I guess I wasn't.'

'Probably a little bit of a hangover?'

'Well, I felt a little rocky.'

'I can imagine. I guess Evvie did a good job of showing you the town. I wish I could have come myself. Still, she's better at playing host than I am. And a damn sight better looking than I am, as far as that goes. I think she's taken a shine to you, John.'

I did a good job of trying not to look embarrassed. I took a cigarette and fumbled for matches. He gave me a light and relit his cigar. He could see that I was ill at ease and nothing could have delighted him more. He was enjoying himself tremendously.

'You're a hard man to get hold of, John,' he said. 'I couldn't get your home telephone number, so I had to try you at your office. I'm afraid I made quite a few calls. They didn't tell me that you were out of town at first, just that you weren't in and they didn't know where you could be reached. Then they did tell me you were out of town, but didn't seem to know when you'd be back, so I just went on calling. Your bosses must really keep you hopping.'

'I did a lot of traveling this trip,' I admitted.

'Get much accomplished?'

'Well,' I said vaguely.'

'Buy a lot of land, John?'

I coughed on my cigarette. I looked at him nervously, and he looked back and let his eyebrows climb up a notch. I met his eyes and drew again on my cigarette. I didn't say anything, but then I didn't have to. We had reached a quiet understanding. I was telling him that I knew that he knew that our hunting lodge story was a lot of honey, but that I wasn't too crazy about the idea of discussing it, not for now, anyway.

'Well,' he said easily. 'I ought to tell you, John, that I've had time to think over your proposition, and while the tax-loss features are attractive, certainly, I'm afraid I'm not interested in selling my property. Not for the time being, at least.'

'I see.'

'You don't seem very disappointed.'

I leaned forward in my chair, stubbed out my cigarette in his ashtray, and narrowed my eyes. I said, 'I'm afraid I had more to drink the other night than I usually do. When I was out with Ev – with your secretary. I guess I talked a little more than I wanted to, and I guess she relayed some of what I said to you.'

He just smiled.

'The men who employ me trust me to do my job, Wally, and part of doing my job is keeping certain matters confidential. I . . . if I said anything that I shouldn't have said, and if it got back to you, well, I just wish you'd forget it.'

'Oh? You don't have to worry about my making trouble for you, John.'

'It's not that, but—'

'And if it'll set your mind at rest, you didn't tell me so very much through Evvie. Or if you did tell her everything, then she held out on me.' He chuckled to let me know how plainly impossible it was that she might keep anything from him. 'But I do know a lot more about the operations of the Barnstable outfit than I ever learned from you. After all, I wouldn't keep calling you in Toronto just to tell you that I wasn't interested in your proposition, would I?'

'I didn't think so, no.'

'Hardly. Would you like to know what I've managed to learn?'

I nodded, and he told me. He parroted back just about every fact we had arranged for him to uncover. He gave me dates and figures and names and I let my jaw drop progressively as he built himself up a good head of steam. When he finished I just sat there shaking my head.

'I couldn't have let all of that slip to Evvie.'

'You didn't, John.'

'Why, there are things you know that I don't even know, like exactly when the company was organized. How did you—'

He waved all of this away with one hand. 'When you've been in business as long as I have,' he said, 'you know how to get information. And you'd be surprised how easy it is to find something out once you've made up your mind. When someone comes to offer me money, John, I want to know something about him. When someone wants to buy something from me, I like to know what it is he plans to do with it.' He set the cigar aside and folded his hands on the desk top. 'And that still has me up in the air. You people have bought all of that land, and by God, you've put your hands on a hell of a lot of land. How much acreage would you say you've got, John?'

'I don't honestly know,' I said.

'Oh?'

'I've seen quite a few people, but a large portion of our dealings have been carried on through the mails, or over the telephone. I'm only sent on the road when we don't get anywhere through the mail. So I honestly don't know how large the corporate holdings are, Wally.'

'But Barnstable owns quite a bit of land, wouldn't you say?'

'Oh, of course.'

'Now that's as far as I can go with it,' he said. He sat back and scratched his head. 'I'll tell you the truth, John, I'm damned if I can figure out what you people plan to do with that land. Now I can see that you've been very clever about this. Not you personally, John, but your company, in hitting on this method of purchasing land. By dealing with people who've been cheated on this land in the first place, you're patting yourselves in a position where you can steal it right back.'

'Not steal it,' I said. 'We—'

'Figure of speech, John, but let's not mince words. You folks are picking up that land at a hell of a lot less than it's worth. When you offered me five hundred dollars for land I sank twenty thousand into, all I could see was the difference between five hundred and twenty thousand. Which is a hell of a difference. And I'm damn certain that's all anybody sees when they come up against your offer. When a man overpaid for a piece of property the way I overpaid for that stretch of goddamned moose pasture, all he can see is that he got taken, that he laid out money for something worthless.

'But that land's not worthless because, damn it, no land is worthless, no matter where it is. I ought to know that if anybody should. Hell, the land I've bought that people said wasn't worth a damn, and the money I made on it while those jokers thought I was acting like several kinds of an idiot—'

He launched into a long tirade while I got another cigarette going. He was bragging now, boasting about a deal he had pulled off year ago, and he seemed to like the sound of his own voice so much that I let him listen to it as long as he wanted to. During the war, it seemed, he had bought a ring of property around the perimeter of the city. He bought it cheap, and he was sitting on a whole boatload of it when the postwar housing boom hit at the end of the war. Then he had gone and done the same thing during Korea, with results almost as spectacular.

'I'm getting off the track again. What I mean, John, is that you people are buying up this land for no price at all. Now take my acreage. You offered me five hundred dollars for it, is that right?'

'Yes, and—'

'And do you want to know something? It didn't occur to me for the longest time to stop and figure out what the right market price for that land is. I always knew it was a good sum short of what I had in the property, but I never bothered to pinpoint it Well, I finally did, and do you know what my land actually ought to be worth?'

I didn't answer him.

'Between two thousand and twenty-five hundred dollars,' he said triumphantly. 'And here you were trying to steal all of that for no more than five hundred.'

I drew myself up straight in my chair. 'I don't think you can call that stealing,' I said stiffly. That was a bona fide offer, Wally, and whether or not you happened to like the price—'

'Now hold on.' He got up from his chair, came out from behind the desk. He gripped my shoulder and I let myself relax. 'Just take it easy,' he was saying. 'No one's calling you a thief.'

'That's what it sounded like.'

'Well, then, I apologize. Is that better?'

I let that go. He told me he certainly didn't want to get on the wrong side of me. After all, we were both Americans, weren't we? I might be working for a Canuck outfit, but, damn it, I was a New Mexico boy, and New Mexico and Olean were a lot closer to each other than either was to Toronto, weren't they? They weren't on any map that I knew about, but he was talking and I let him have all the room he needed.

'Here's where it gets funny,' he said. 'See, I know what this Barnstable outfit's been doing. Damned if I don't admire the whole operation, John. If anybody wanted to pick up land at a good price, you couldn't ask for a better way of doing it.'

'And perfectly legal,' I reminded him.

'Oh, perfectly legal.' He smiled momentarily. 'But to get back to what I was getting at. Here I've got the whole thing figured out, what you people are doing and all, and then I run into a snag. Because I'll be damned if I can figure out what you intend to do with the land.'

I didn't say anything.

'Purchase and development of western territory,' he quoted. 'That's the alleged purpose of your incorporation, John.'

'It is?'

He chuckled. 'Didn't know that yourself, did you? But that's the way you boys worded it in your application for a charter. I'm willing to dig a little for information, see? Purchase and development. That might make a little sense, except as far as I can see you folks aren't in any position to do any development, and developing the quantity of land you've bought would be one hell of an expense. You know what the total capitalization of the Barnstable Corporation is?'

'As a matter of fact I don't'

'No reason why you should. It happens to be fifty thousand dollars, which might sound like a good sum of money but which, believe me, is a damned small figure in an operation like this one. Why, John, I'd be willing to bet that you people have spent close to that much just on land.'

'How did you—'

'Why, as I said, John, I have my ways of getting information. Now there are various possibilities involved. You – I don't mean you personally, I mean Barnstable – you might have set up this corporation just for purchase itself, and then you'll do the actual development through another corporation so that you can work out a nice capital gain picture for yourselves. That's one possibility. Or you might augment capitalization once you've got your land purchased, and then you'll float a stock issue or have all the stock holders increase their investment.'

I didn't say anything. He walked over to the window and yawned and stretched and looked at his watch and said that it looked like that time again, and could I use a drink? I thought it over and started to say that I didn't think so.

'Oh, come on,' he said. 'I can use an eye-opener myself, so why not join me?'

He had one drawer of a filing cabinet set up as a makeshift bar. He brought out a bottle of very good Scotch, poured a couple ounces in each of two glasses, and added squirts of seltzer from a siphon.

'British style,' he said. 'No ice. That how they drink up in Canada?'

'Well, I guess most people take ice.'

'That's something,' he said.

We worked on our drinks. He set his down and said, 'You know what bothers me? Even figuring that you'll recapitalize after you've bought as much land as you want, even figuring that, I can't make out why the hell you would want to develop that land now. What the hell can you do with it? You can't build a row of houses out there and expect anybody to buy them. Dammit, I checked what's planned for that area, and there's no prospect of growth there for years and years. It's still wasteland. It may be worth a couple hundred dollars a square mile and you're buying it at forty dollars a square mile, so you're certainly getting it at the right price, but what the hell are you going to do with it?'

I had some more of my Scotch and made circles on his desk top with the glass. I lit a cigarette and shook out the match.

'Wally,' I said, 'why are you so interested in finding out?'

'Can't you guess?'

'I know you got interested because we expressed interest in your land. But it's pretty obvious by now that you're not going to sell to us, and that we wouldn't be interested in raising our offer, so why stay excited about it?'

'You mean why poke my nose in?'

'Well, I wouldn't put it that way—'

'You ought to, John, because that's what I've been doing. I've been poking my nose into something that's not my business. No getting around that.'

'Whatever you want to call it,' I said.

'I suppose I've got a reason.'

'Oh?'

He finished his drink. He pursued his lips and narrowed his eyes and did all those little facial tricks that were supposed to show that he was ready to get down to brass tacks, that he was prepared to talk sincerely about something of prime importance.

'John,' he said, 'I smell money.'

We both paused reverently to let that sink in. He picked up his cigar and put it down again and said, 'John, somebody's setting up to make a pile of money out of a load of moose pasture. I've always been interested in money. And ever since I got raped by those Canadian sharpies you can bet I've been interested in moose pasture. If there's a way to make a nice chunk of dough out of that land, I'd like to know about it. You can appreciate that, can't you?'

'I guess I can.'

'If you've ever been swindled, you know what I mean. It's damn hard for a man to swallow his pride and say the hell with it, he's been taken. A real man wants to get back. Not just to get even, but to come out of the whole thing smelling like a rose. And there's something going on here with Barnstable, and I can't get away from the feeling that there's an opportunity here for Wally Gunderman. You blame me for being interested?'

'I don't know what good it can do you,' I said levelly.

'Don't you?'

'Well, frankly, no. I don't.'

He thought it over for a moment. 'Maybe if you told me a little, John. If you filled in the gaps for me, maybe we'd both know a little more where we stand.'

'Anything I know is confidential,' I reminded him. 'I already told you more than I should have.'

'Now, John, you and I both know you never told me a thing.'

'Well, what I let slip to Evvie, then. Your secretary.' I swallowed. 'If Mr Rance or anybody else in Toronto learned that I had too much to drink and then shot off my mouth—'

'You didn't say a thing I wouldn't have found out anyway, John. And I had already decided to find out what was going on, so I would have done my digging even if you never said a word to the girl.' He winked slyly. 'Besides, John, I'm not about to tell your Mr Rance or Mr Whittlief or anyone else about our conversations. You can trust me, John.'

I brightened a little. He took my glass and freshened both our drinks without asking. I sipped mine and he lit his cigar again and sighed heavily. I looked at him.

'John,' he said, 'I don't mind saying that I'm glad you're the man they sent down here. There are certainly men in the world who might talk more freely than you do, but one thing is sure. When you finally do open up, I'm able to believe what you tell me. If you're not prepared to tell the truth, why, you just don't say anything at all, do you?'

'Uh—'

'The thing is that I feel I can trust you to play straight with me, and that's an important thing.' He lowered his eyes. 'I hope you feel the same way about me, John.'

'Of course I do.'

'Because I'm a man who deals honestly with people. If someone plays fair with me, you can bet that I'll play fair with him. And when somebody does me a favor, or helps me out in any way, you can be damned certain that I'll see he's taken care of and properly. When I have dealings with a man, he has no cause to regret it, and you wouldn't either, John.'

I think I probably looked slightly lost just then. It wasn't all acting. He was approaching the whole question from about five different angles all at once. He had the ball, and he was damn well ready to run with it, but he wasn't too certain where the goal posts were and he was tearing off in several directions without knowing exactly where he was headed. He wanted to win me over, and he wanted to learn what Barnstable was going to do with its land, and he wanted, somehow, to find a way to cut a piece of the pie for himself.

And I wasn't sure how much to give him at once. He was a tricky guy. This was good – the con we had going for us would only work against a shrewd man. There's an old maxim to the effect that you cannot swindle a completely honest man. I'm not sure this is entirely true – it would be hard to test it empirically, because I don't think I have ever met an entirely honest man.

But there is truth to it, and there is a corollary argument: You cannot pull certain cons against stupid men. In the more elaborate long cons, you need to use the mark's native intelligence and shrewdness against him. It's a sort of mental judo.

At any rate, I had to admire Gunderman, at least in certain respects. He was doing a good job of roping me. First he made me feel foolish for blabbing to Evvie, then he let me know that I could trust him, that he wouldn't let Rance know what I'd done. Right away this made us co-conspirators and set the groundwork for future conspiracy. He wasn't as smooth as he could be, and he made his own position a little too obvious, but I had to give him credit; for an amateur, he wasn't that bad a con artist.

Now he said, 'John, you don't mind a personal question, do you?'

'I guess that depends on how personal it is.'

'Well, why beat around the bush? I'll come right out and ask you. How much money do these Barnstable people pay you?'

I hesitated. Then I said, 'Well, around two hundred a week.'

'A little less than that, isn't it?'

'A little.'

'About one-eighty?'

'How did you—'

'Well, I didn't inquire directly, John. It came out in the wash. That's one-eighty Canadian, and with the discount that means you're earning something like a hundred and sixty-five a week. I'll tell you, John, that isn't much for someone doing the work you do. And all the traveling and responsibility.'

'The travel expenses are paid for me.'

'Oh, I know that, naturally. But you still ought to be worth more than that.'

'I manage on my salary.'

'Of course you do. But if you could pick up a piece of change for yourself, why, you wouldn't complain, would you?'

I didn't answer that.

'I'm not saying you ought to work against your employers, John.'

'I couldn't do anything like that.'

'You certainly couldn't, and if I thought you were the kind of man who could, why, I wouldn't want to have any dealings with you. But if you could do me a favor without injuring your employers, that might be something else, don't you think?'

I reached for my drink. He smiled at the gesture, then looked away. Not right now, I thought. Give him a night to think it over some more. Take a little time.

'I'm not sure how much help I could be to you,' I said.

'Why not let me worry about that?'

I lowered my eyes and chewed my lip thoughtfully. 'I ought to think about this,' I said.

'Fair enough. Will you be in town a few days, John?'

I took a breath, then expelled it with the air of someone coming to a minor decision. 'Wally,' I said, 'you must have figured out the main reason I'm here. I don't have to tell you that, do I? That is, I already realized you weren't likely to sell out to Barnstable. That was . . . well, an excuse for the trip.'

'You wanted to see Evvie.'

'That's right.'

'I understand. And why not let the boss pay for the trip, eh?'

I looked very ashamed of myself.

'Perfectly natural,' Gunderman said. He laughed heartily. 'But you will stay in town for a few days, won't you?'

'If I can manage it.'

'Hell, you can manage it, John.' He laughed again. 'Why, with all those phone calls I've made to your office, your boss will be sure I'm the hottest prospect on earth. He won't begrudge you a few days in town, and if the deal falls through for him, well, that's just the breaks of the game. You stay here in town, and you take some time to think things through, because I want you to make your own decision, John. And you drop around here, oh, come by tomorrow afternoon, and maybe the two of us can do some more talking and figure out how things are likely to shape up for us. I think we'll both come out of this okay, John.'

We both finished our drinks. I rallied a little and told him I was glad we were bringing things out in the open, that the one thing I disliked about the Barnstable job was that I hated to misrepresent myself at all. 'The hunting-lodge story,' I said. 'I'd rather tell people the truth right off the bat, that we're prepared to pay so much for their land and that's all. It's a good deal for a lot of them, Wally. They can write off their tax loss and get the bad taste of a bad deal out of their mouths. I'd rather just tell them that and leave it at that, and I know that's how I would handle things if I were a principal in this deal. But I'm just a hired hand.'

He liked the way that sounded. He was very taken with me. I was just the man he wanted me to be. We shook hands and we made arrangements to meet the next afternoon, and I left him there ready to tell Diogenes to put down his lantern and call off his search – Wallace J. Gunderman had just found himself an honest man.

9

When Evvie left the office a little after five I was out in front with the motor idling. She came out of the building and over to the car. I stood holding the door for her. She was smiling hugely.

'Aim a kiss at me,' she said, behind the smile.

I did. She went on smiling and turned just a little in my arms so that the kiss missed her mouth and caught her cheek. Then in a second she was in the car. I walked around it and got behind the wheel, and away we went.

I said, 'You think he was watching?'

'From the front window. That light's red. Why not stop for it and kiss me proper?'

This time there was no audience for the kiss. She made a little choked-up sound and caught at my shoulders with her hands. Our mouths didn't miss this time. She held on, and the wheels went around and came up three bars, jackpot. A horn honked behind us. She slipped away reluctantly and I piloted the rented Impala across the intersection.

'Now that was better,' she said.

She was too damned good to be true. The halfway kiss in front of Gunderman's office building would tell him everything she wanted him to know – that I was hot for her, that she was not interested, but that she would play the game through thick and thin to do the right thing for Poppa Wally. I couldn't have named more than eight women in the country who could have played the scene as well, and those eight were girls who were born to the sport.

I told her how good she was. She glowed a little. I asked her where she felt like going for dinner. Nowhere, she said. She had a pair of filets at the apartment and a hibachi to char them on. How did that sound?

'Home cooking,' I said. 'You'll spoil me.'

'You don't mind? He wanted me to wine you and dine you. He thinks that's the most effective treatment. The big show of money and influence. He knows a few variations, but they're all on the same theme. I told him this would be more intimate.'

'It just might.'

She didn't answer. I turned a corner and found her block, pulled up a few doors from her building. We went up to her apartment and she unlocked the door. She let me make the drinks while she got the charcoal going in the little Japanese stove. I made stiff drinks. We took them back into the living room with us.

'I don't know,' she said.

'About what?'

'Everything. I don't think he's going to fall for it.'

'Why not?'

'I'm not sure.'

'Did he say something?'

She frowned. 'No,' she said finally. 'It wasn't anything he said, nothing like that exactly. Right now he's completely sold. You've got him in your pocket, John.'

'Then what's the problem?'

She thought about it, worked on her drink, looked up at me. 'Maybe I'm just worried,' she said. 'Stage fright.'

'Could be.'

'It just doesn't seem possible that he'll fall for it. He's not a stupid man, you know. He's less of a clod than he seems. He's got a tough streak of sharpness under it all.'

'Then this is tailored for him. A stupid man would never be able to pick up on it.'

'I know, but—' She raised her glass to her lips, lowered it again. 'I'll tell you something, John. I think you're a little too perfect.'

'How do you mean?'

'Too honest and too square. Right now he believes every bit of it. Right now you could probably tell him you're the chief holy man of the Ganges and he wouldn't doubt a word. But he's no believer in the incorruptibility of mankind. If you stay lily-white, he'll start to wonder sooner or later.'

'Go on.'

'Let him see that you wouldn't mind making a buck. Make him draw it out of you a little at a time, but make sure he knows you're glad to look out for number one as long as it's safe.'

I thought it over. 'You're right,' I said.

'It was just an idea—'

'No. You're right. I may have played it a little too angelic. It's an easy role to fall into.' I finished my drink. 'Still worried?'

'Of course.'

'You don't have to be.'

'I'll be worried until this is over. God, if this falls in—' She closed her eyes. 'Doug Rance is sitting safe across the border. You can hop on a plane and disappear far enough so that no one will ever find you. And he wouldn't even try too hard. But me – if he ever finds out, John, I've had it. The viper in his bosom.' She managed a somewhat brave smile. 'He would only kill me,' she said.

A whole batch of lines didn't do the job. *Don't worry, everything'll be all right, it's in the bag* – you don't throw phrases like those at a woman who's telling you how she stands a fair chance of getting killed. You don't say anything at all.

I kissed her. She held back at first, too much involved in dreams of doom to ride it all the way. Then the fear broke and she came to me, and the wheels went around again and the slot machine paid off again. There was nothing casual about it.

I took her on her living room couch with her blouse half off and her skirt bunched up around her waist. The couch was too short, engineered for more sedate pleasures. The lights were all too bright. None of this mattered much.

Afterward, she got up to throw our steaks on the fire. I lit us a couple of cigarettes and made a fresh pair of drinks. We didn't talk much. It wasn't necessary.

'What do I do when this is over, John?'

'Take the money and run.'

'And then?'

I had my arm around her. I drummed my fingers against the curve of her shoulder. 'According to Doug,' I said, 'you've got a program figured. Meet a rich man and marry him.'

She was silent.

'Something wrong?'

'I've already got a rich man. And it wouldn't be very different being married to him. I'd just feel like a whore with a license. I don't know what I'll wind up doing. Right now I can't think very much past a day or two after tomorrow.'

We were listening to an Anita O'Day record. Some song about a nightingale. The mood was as mellow as that girl's voice. We could have used a fireplace with thick logs burning. And some very old cognac.

I said, 'You could always stay with the grift.' I made it light.

'Me?' She laughed softly. 'I'd shake apart into little pieces.'

'Not you.'

'The way I've been?'

'You've been beautiful,' I told her. 'The nervousness doesn't mean a thing. Anyone who knows what he's doing and cares how it turns out gets nervous.'

'Even you?'

'Me more than most.'

'You don't let it show.'

'It's there, though.'

She found a cigarette. I lit it for her. 'Would you work with me again on something like this? I mean if I weren't a part of it to begin with. If I was just another hand in the game. Would you want me in on it?'

'Any time.'

'Then maybe I've got a career after all. We'll be partners.'

'You're forgetting something.'

'Oh?'

'I'm about to retire,' I said. 'Remember?'

'I didn't forget.' She drew on her cigarette, took it from her lips, stared at its tip. 'I wasn't sure whether or not that was the truth. About quitting, buying that roadhouse.'

'Does it sound pipe-dreamish?'

'That's not it. I thought it might be part of a line. It sounded sincere enough at the time, but later, well, you're very good at sounding sincere. Will you really do it, John?'

'Yes.'

'And you're sure you can make a go of it?'

She didn't have to coax me. I was not exactly playing hard to get. I swung into a reading of The Dream, the unabridged version. She kept her head on my shoulder and said the right words at all of the right places. I was long sold on The Dream myself, but now it was coming out rosier than ever.

'Colorado,' she said. 'What's it like out there?'

'You've never been West?'

'Well, Las Vegas and Reno. But that's not the same, is it? All bright lights and no clocks in the casinos and lots of small men with eyes that never show expression. What's Colorado like?'

'Nothing like Vegas.'

'Tell me about it.'

So I talked about air that lifted you up onto your toes when you filled up your lungs with it, and mountains that climbed straight up and dropped off sharp and clean, and the way the trees turned overnight in early October. I probably sounded very chamber of commerce. I'm apt to get that way. I've always loved that kind of country. The grift always kept me in the cities, mostly on the Coast, because that was where the action was. But I never really felt I was breathing in the cities, especially in the smog belt. And in Q there were times, a couple of them, when I found myself gasping like a trout in a net. The prison doctors said it was psychosomatic. They were probably right. It still had felt very damned fine to be back in the mountains.

Anita stopped singing somewhere in the middle of the lecture, and some clown came on the radio with a fast five minutes of news. Evvie switched off the radio and came back and put her head on my shoulder where it belonged and listened some more. When I finally ran out of gas she didn't say anything. I was a little embarrassed. It's hard to talk like a poet without feeling like a jackass.

Then she said, 'You make it sound pretty.'

'It is.'

'You even make it sound . . . possible. Quitting the racket, doing what you said.'

'It's more than possible, Evvie.'

She said, 'I wish—' And let it hang there.

First in Q, and then on the outside, there had been many versions of The Dream. Step by step it focused itself and narrowed itself down. Finding Bannion's had been a final touch. Each version of The Dream had become just a shade more specific than the last.

Each version had had The Girl. Sometimes she was formless, and other times she was remarkably well drawn. Sometimes she was a glorious innocent, and she either accepted my past and forgave it or else she knew not a thing about it. In other versions she was a trifle soiled herself – a grifting girl, or a halfway hooker, or any of a dozen shadow-world types. Part of the past, but with me in the future.

But every version had The Girl.

And I heard myself saying, 'It wouldn't be exciting. But excitement wears thin after awhile. It's good country, Evvie. You'd love it out there—'

She stood up, walked across the room. I sat where I was and listened to my words bouncing off the walls.

She said, 'You're not conning me, are you?'

'I don't think I could.'

'Because that was starting to sound alarmingly like a proposal.'

'Something like that.'

She turned. She looked at me, straight at me, and I drank the depths of her eyes. Then she began to nod, and she said, 'Yes. Oh, yes, yes.'

I saw Gunderman in the morning. I did not much want to see him. I was not in the mood to play a part. The night with Evvie had flattened out the hunger pains, and a hungry man makes a better fisherman.

But the hook was already set, the line already strung halfway across the lake. Even a well-fed angler can reel in a big one, especially when the fish practically jumps into the boat. My heart was not exactly in it, but it did not exactly have to be. Gunderman made it easy.

I followed Evvie's hunch. When I got around to telling him that Barnstable had bought about as much land as was likely to be available at their price, I stopped for a moment and then let on that I would be out of a job before long.

'They'll let you go, John?'

'They won't have anything for me to do.' I looked off to the side for a second, then lowered my eyes. 'Oh, I'll find something else,' I said. 'I generally do.'

'Have money saved?'

'Not a hell of a lot. On my salary—'

'Be handy if you did, though.'

'Well,' I said, 'I'll manage.'

He had Evvie bring us some coffee from around the corner. He stirred sugar into his and got back on the main theme, the opening for one Wallace J. Gunderman. First, of course, he wanted a chance to buy some stock in

Barnstable. I told him he didn't have a chance in a hundred. In the first place, no one would be anxious to sell. In the second, the board would never approve of a stock transfer. Everything was very hushed up, I explained. Even I could figure out that much. They were not looking for publicity. Legal or not, they wanted to keep a lid on things.

'What are they going to do with that land, John? Suppose that they haven't got any development planned. What are they going to do?'

'I've thought about that,' I said.

'So have I. What did you come up with?'

'Just a few ideas.' I stopped long enough to light a cigarette. 'At first I thought they were buying for some corporation. It was so hush-hush I figured they had an important client who didn't want anyone to know what was coming off. But they were buying at random. And there would be one little piece of land in the middle of a few of their tracts, and instead of pushing hard to buy it they would let it go if they didn't get it at their price.'

'I'm with you so far, John.'

'So they have to be buying for themselves. Especially with so many important people involved. And the secrecy, well, they may be doing something legal but they're still playing around in someone else's mess.'

'And so they're wearing gloves.'

'Right.' I drank some of my coffee and made rings on the desk top with the coffee cup. 'I suppose they'll just sit on the land,' I said. 'Just sit and wait until it catches fire pricewise, or until someone wants it enough to give them a pretty profit.'

His eyes narrowed. 'Would they sell some of it now?'

'To you?'

'To me.'

'I don't think so.'

'Why not?'

'I don't think it's what they have in mind. I don't really know too much about that end of the operation, actually. I've spent most of my time here in the States. My only real contact is through Douglas Rance, and he doesn't spend too much time filling me in on the subtleties of company policy.' I let a little more bitterness edge forward. I was still Little Boy Loyal, but I wasn't as important as I would have liked to be.

He said, 'You could probably find out a few things, if you tried. I'd make it worth your while, John.'

I looked at him. Wary, but hungry.

'If it turns out that I can make a deal, I'll cut you in. You wouldn't have to lay out any cash, and you'd be in for a full five percent of any profit I might make.'

'Well—'

'How does that sound?'

'It sounds very generous, but—'

'And that five percent could be a healthy sum, John. I'm not talking nickels and dimes, you know.'

'I know.'

'Will you go to bat for me, then?'

I pursed my lips and took my time. I said, 'But if you don't wind up making a deal—'

He'd thought of that. He wanted me as a sort of partner in the operation, but he knew I would have expenses and he wouldn't want me to take a beating. He passed an envelope across the desk. I hesitated, and I let wariness and greed mingle in my expression, and I took the envelope. After all, Evvie was right. I had to be a little bit on the make or he just would not believe I was real.

'Deal?'

'Deal,' I said.

There was, I found out, an even five hundred dollars in the envelope. If he'd had any class he'd have made it a thou.

I'd told him I was taking an afternoon flight back to Toronto. I had told Doug the same thing. I did not go back to Toronto. That morning a girl with a husky voice and deep circles under her eyes had asked me to spend another night in Olean. She did not have to ask me twice.

I went back to her apartment. She had given me a spare key, and I waited inside, for her to finish work and come home to me. Around four-thirty I called a Chinese restaurant and ordered up some chow mein. I called around until I found a grocery that delivered, and I had a six-pack of beer sent up along with a carton of her brand of cigarettes. We couldn't eat out, and I didn't want to make her cook a meal again.

The table was set when she opened the door. I opened two cans of beer. We ate in the kitchen. The Chinese food tasted as though it had come out of a can. But the beer was cold, and the company was divine.

We didn't talk too much. She wanted to know how much longer it would take, how long it would be before we scored and blew him off once and for all. It was going to take longer than I wanted to think about – not until we scored, necessarily, but until I had a chance to see her again. After the grift was over, she would have to cool it for awhile in Olean before she grabbed a westbound plane. This was all something I didn't want to think about, or talk about.

'I feel better about it today,' she said. 'Not so nervous.'

'It must be love.'

'Maybe that's part of it.'

'It must be.'

I had a second beer. She was still on her first. She went into the living room, switched on the radio. A newscast – someone chattered about some new foreign crisis. She turned the dial and found some music. I left the table and grabbed her and kissed her. She giggled and shook free and scurried over to the front of the room. She paused at the window, and her face went white.

I started toward her. She held out a hand and warned me off.

'His car,' she said. 'Oh, God.'

'So I missed my plane and decided to stay over.'

'No, it's no good. The dishes—'

I moved fast enough for both of us. I scooped up my dishes and my beer and my pack of cigarettes and my lighter and ducked into the bedroom closet with them. I stood there holding onto everything while her clothes blanketed me. They all carried the smell of her. I was dizzy with it.

He knocked. She opened the door. They spent five or ten minutes in the living room. I could hear snatches of their conversation, not enough to add the stray phrases together and come up with something intelligible. I waited in the closet like a refugee from a French bedroom farce. The humor of it was lost on me. I wanted to grab the son of a bitch and push his face in.

Then they came closer, from living room to bedroom, and now that I could follow the conversation I no longer wanted to hear it. Wallace J. Gunderman was in the mood for love.

She said something about a headache. He said something about girls who had convenient headaches all the time. She said it wasn't like that at all. He said, and she said, and he said, and they wound up in the hay and I had to stand there and listen to it.

It is not supposed to bother you. It is, after all, part of the game; a con artist can no more be jealous of his girl's mock-lovers than a pimp can resent his lady's clients. You are not supposed to give a damn. It is, after all, business and nothing more. It is push-button sex, it means nothing, it is, in fact, part-and-parcel of The Game.

I wanted to kill him.

When he was through I heard her saying something about a headache, a really bad headache, and maybe it would be better if he left her alone. He didn't seem to mind. He had gotten what he came for, what he paid for. He was a long time getting dressed, but he left, finally, and I heard his heavy feet on the stairs.

I crept out of my perfumed closet. She was sitting on the bed, her back to me. I went into the kitchen and put the dishes in the sink. When I came back she faced me and shook her head from side to side.

'I could throw up,' she said.

'Easy.'

'I'm awf ... I'm a damn whore.'

'Stop it.'

'I am!'

I slapped her harder than I'd intended. Her head snapped back and she put one hand to her face. 'That hurt,' she said.

'Sorry. But you did what you had to do.'

'I know that.'

'All right, then.'

'But I can't help the way I feel about it. I'm selling myself.'

I took a breath. 'Maybe,' I said. 'But just think what a sweet price you're charging. Because he's going to get hurt. He's going to bleed money.'

She brightened up after a while, but the evening was permanently shot. We struggled through an hour's worth of conversation – or five minutes' worth, stretched to fill an hour. Then I put on my jacket and straightened my tie and left. No woman should have to put out for more than one man in one night.

'It'll be a while,' I told her. 'Call me if anything happens. Or if you get nervous. Or just because you want to.'

I kissed her and left.

10

Doug said, 'We must have crossed a wire or two, Johnny. I was expecting to see you yesterday.'

'I wound up staying an extra day.' I stirred my coffee. 'It looked as though it would play better that way.'

'You should have called. I thought maybe a wheel came off.' He put a match to a cigarette and winked at me. 'You got something going with Evvie?'

'Hardly.'

'No? I didn't figure you to pass up something like that.'

'Not my type,' I said. 'And never when I'm working.'

He laughed. 'Work or play, some kinds of games are always in season. What do you think of her?'

'She's all right.'

'Is she holding up her end of it?'

'Sure, I'll give her that.' Then, grudgingly. 'She's got the talent. She plays the game like somebody who knows the rules.'

'Well, that's good.'

'She's still getting too damned much of the pie,' I told him. 'She's getting about double what she ought to get.'

'We needed her, Johnny.'

I allowed that we probably did, after all, and we let it lie there. We were in a coffeepot around the corner from the Barnstable office. I needed a shave and a shower, but I didn't have to impress anybody just now. I lit a fresh cigarette and finished the coffee and we switched into a rundown on the way the play was heading.

One thing you try hard not to do is lie to your partner. It's not a particularly good policy. You generally have enough lies to keep track of without creating new muddles for yourself.

This was an exception. Evvie didn't want him to know about us, and that would have been reason enough; if he had struck out with the girl, he wouldn't be tickled to hear that I was swinging for the bleachers and connecting. And there was more to it than that.

Evvie and I had suddenly become a team. If he thought of us as a combination, he was going to become very unhappy about the split. It was

406

still the same split, still the same money going into the same pockets, but I knew him well enough to know he wouldn't see it that way. He'd see himself dragging down forty thou while the team of Hayden & Stone walked off with fifty between them.

So I'd let him have the glory. Afterward, when it was all over, it would not matter much any more. Doug would be too busy getting rid of forty thousand dollars over a dice table to worry about his personal prestige. And Evvie and I would be back in Colorado, with Bannion's place in our pockets and the world swinging for us from a yo-yo string. Once it was over, we would have more important things on our minds than Doug Rance.

I signaled our waitress and scouted down two more cups of coffee. Doug wanted to talk and talk and talk; he had to cover every angle of the operation once again to make sure we were rolling free and easy. He didn't have to bother, but he didn't have anything else to do and it's hard to do nothing day after day, putting in your time at the store and waiting for the game to catch up with you.

They always say that the waiting is the hardest time. They always say this on television and in the movies, and they are always wrong; the hardest time, naturally, is when you walk that little tightrope that stretches from just before the score on halfway through the blow-off. That's the hardest time because it's the only time you can get hurt. If things cave in before then, you get the hell out of there. And you stay the hell out of jail.

But the waiting time is when you keep looking for trouble spots, and dreaming of disaster. You can't keep busy because there's nothing for you to do. You have to sit tight and wait, and this is a pain in the neck, and Doug had had enough of it so that he wanted to hash things over more than he had to.

I'd be the same way myself in a few days. We had to let Gunderman hang by his thumbs for a few days, and I could already see where it might begin to get on my nerves.

First I had to wait for Gunderman to call me. He couldn't call me at the office, and I wasn't at my room much, so it took him four days to reach me.

'Not much so far,' I told him. 'Not enough to call you on, anyway. I did find out two things. I couldn't swear to them, they're just hunches so far, but—'

He broke in. Hurry up, hurry up, tell me everything. He wanted to know it all and know it fast.

'Well, they're definitely buying for the purpose we thought, Wally. They won't develop and they aren't buying as anyone's agent. They're picking up land for capital gain.'

'And?'

'And I don't think they want to sit on it very long. I have a feeling that they're looking for a fast turnover.'

'How?'

'I don't know.'

'If I can get in on this, John—'

I let him swim back and forth with it. He stayed on the phone for another ten minutes asking questions while I told him I didn't know the answers. Couldn't I just come out and ask Rance about it? Not yet, I explained. But was there time? And did I feel I was getting anywhere? Oh, he was all full of questions.

'Better hurry up and get those answers,' he said finally, back to his genial old self again. 'Better let us both make a pile of money, John. I think my girl Evvie misses you something terrible.'

Oh, I could have killed him then. I could have reached through space to strangle him long-distance with the phone cord. I tried to keep all of this out of my voice while I got rid of him, and then I went downstairs and around the corner for a pint of Scotch. I came back to the room and called Evvie. A nightly habit of mine. We talked long enough for AT&T to split their stock again, and we said not a word about Gunderman or Rance or Toronto or Olean. We talked about Colorado.

I left Gunderman hanging for the weekend and a day on either side of it. He left messages for me, and I ignored him. I saw every movie in Toronto. I also saw the insides of most of the bars, and looked at the bottoms of a great many glasses. I slept ten to twelve hours out of every twenty-four. There was not much else to do.

I got him at his office at a quarter after two in the afternoon. I said, 'Wally, this is John. I'm afraid you're out of luck.'

He wanted to know what I meant.

'I thought there might be a way to get in on the deal, if they were going to dispose of the land. I didn't understand their whole operation. They're planning on selling, Wally, but they intend to move it all at once. The whole thing in one package.'

'So?'

'That adds up to quite a deal.'

'I'm not interested in nickels and dimes, John.'

'You'd go for the whole parcel?'

'At the right price, I'd grab it.'

'I'm afraid they've already got somebody, Wally. There's a deal hanging on the fire.'

'With who?'

'Someone from the Midwest. A syndicate, as far as I can make out. I don't have every last detail. I've been playing this very close, because I've had to do some detecting from the inside without letting them know what I'm after. It hasn't been that easy.'

'Now you know I appreciate your position, John—'

I cut in on him. 'But I've got most of the picture. I think – God, I hate to go into all of this over the phone. They plan to get completely out from under. They don't intend to sell the land—'

'What the hell—'

'Wait a minute. They're selling the whole corporation, the whole block of Barnstable stock. There are a lot of tax aspects, and there's the matter of publicity. I wish I could get down to Olean and explain this more openly, but I can't possibly get out of town now.'

'Suppose I came up there?'

'That's what I was getting at. Could you come up here?'

'No problem.'

'Because there's a chance ... I'm trying to think on my feet, Wally, because I wouldn't want you to make the trip for nothing. I hadn't realized you might be in the market for the whole thing. It might run six figures, as far as I can tell.'

'I'm good for it. If the value's there, John.'

'And there are other aspects, too. But there's a fair chance that the deal is all arranged with the syndicate, and that you wouldn't even have a chance to outbid them. Not that I think they'd be willing to work it with bidding anyway. I'm ... listen, this is confusing as hell. Can you come up here tomorrow?'

'Why not tonight?'

'Well, I'd want to check out a few angles. I'll tell you what. Make your flight reservations, and I'll figure on meeting you tonight at the Royal York. If anything comes up, I'll call you back before five o'clock. If you don't hear from me, I'll meet you around nine o'clock. Does that sound good?'

He told me it sounded fine.

The element of confusion was not accidental. It was there for a reason. If things were too smooth, he might begin to wonder who had greased the skids for him. But as long as I was a little uncertain as to which end was up, he didn't have anything to be suspicious about.

Getting him to come to Toronto was basic. When you want to win a mooch, you meet him on his home ground. When you want to put him on the defensive, you take him into your own parlor and keep him off balance. Once he got on that plane, Gunderman was committing himself. As long as he stayed in Olean he could tell himself it was just an armchair exercise, one he could back away from whenever the going got rough. Every commitment of time and space and money drew him in a little deeper. The five hundred bucks he'd slipped me was a partial commitment, but he could write off that kind of money easily enough. The trip would tie him up a little tighter.

I went up to the office. Doug had gone for the day. I picked up a phone and called his apartment. 'He's on his way,' I told him.

'When's the meet?'

'Tonight. Nine o'clock.'

'You'll be good, won't you, Johnny?'

'I'll be beautiful. Want to meet him tomorrow?'

'I don't know.' My partner was a little on the nervous side, I decided. 'You think that's rushing things?'

'It's hard to say. I can't be sure how he'll go tonight. How much rope to give him.'

'Enough to tie him up tight, Johnny.' He was silent for a minute. 'You play it by ear,' he said finally. 'If it looks like a good idea, you arrange a meeting tomorrow, a sounding session. You see how he acts, how hungry he seems to you. If he's a little cool about things, then just cool him down some more and send him back to Olean to sit on his money. Invent something about how you wanted him up here to give him the full picture but you can't set up a meeting because the Chicago money is all set to make its pitch. But if he seems ripe, make it that he and I'll get together just so he can let his interest show.' He laughed suddenly. 'Here I am giving orders,' he said. 'I don't have to draw you pictures, Johnny. You know the game.'

'I know the game.'

'If he's ready for it, I suppose tomorrow morning would be the best time. That the way you figure it?'

'Around ten-thirty.'

'Sure. I should fill up the store, don't you think? Bring in a boy or two?'

'Sure.'

'I'll line them up. You do what you can, Johnny, and it'll be ten-thirty at the office. He was good on the phone, huh?'

'Perfect.'

'I think we got him,' he said. 'Jesus, I hope we do.'

I managed to be fifteen minutes late getting to the Royal York. I called his room from the desk. He said he would come right down, and I told him it would be better if we talked in his room. It might not be too good, I said, if anybody happened to notice us together.

He probably thought I was acting a little too much like Herbert Philbrick leading three lives. But he went along with the gag, and I took the elevator to his room.

'Come on in, John,' he said, 'I called room service, and we ought to have a boy coming up with some Johnny Walker Black any minute. Now don't tell me some sharpies from the corn country are going to cut us out of this pie. I'd hate to hear that.'

'Chicago's not exactly the corn country.'

'That where they're from? Not gangsters, are they?'

It's funny how a mooch can give you ideas you might never have thought of on your own. I brushed the question aside and made a note to feed the notion to Doug for future reference. Sooner or later we would need a good reason why the pending deal fell in, and that might be the germ of as good a one as any.

I started in on the main business at hand. I began by going over familiar territory. The men who owned Barnstable were not interested in long term gain. They were all important people who had seen a chance for a fast dollar with a quick turnover. They had bought a parcel of land, and now they wanted to get completely out from under, make themselves a neat hundred per cent profit, and do all of this without getting any dirt on their hands. They cared enough about their reputations to take less for their holdings than they could get otherwise. That didn't matter to them as much as the kind of deal they arranged, and the kind of people they were dealing with.

'You better slow down, John,' he said. 'I think our liquor's here.'

He got the Scotch and ice and glasses from the bellhop, signed the tab and gave the kid a buck. I let him make the drinks. We got back into the swing of things, and I watched the way he worked on his liquor. He was normally a fairly hard drinker, but he wasn't paying the stuff much attention tonight. That meant he was intent on staying on top of things, and that in turn meant that (a) he was hot for the deal and (b) he was no longer supremely confident. I was glad of it on both counts.

'You talk about how they care what kind of people they're dealing with,' he said. 'Isn't one man's money as good as the next?'

'They want more than money. They want it kept quiet.'

'So? If I got a piece of a sweet deal, I wouldn't be anxious to hire a skywriter to spread the word. Anybody who buys in is going to put a lid on things.'

'Not if they want money in a hurry.'

'I don't follow you.'

I laid it out for him. The buyer Barnstable was looking for had to be someone who was willing to sit for a long time before he took his profit. If he started parceling the land and selling it off right away, things would come out into the open and all of this would work to Barnstable's disadvantage. If the buyer held on for a minimum of two years, there was no problem. But it wasn't easy to find someone who would play it that way. Lots of people might say they would keep the property intact, but then they might turn around and do the opposite as soon as the ink was dry.

'That's one thing that occurred to me,' I said. 'You might not want to tie your money up that way. At the price they want, an operator could work things so that he turned a profit in ninety days' time. And that's exactly what they don't want.'

'Well, hell,' he said. 'I don't want it either!'

'You don't?'

I let him show me just how obvious it was. Why, he pointed out, long-term holdings in cheap land were right up his alley. He was no fast-dollar operator. If any man on earth believed in holding on for the big killing, he was that man. Why, if he could buy the right kind of land and get it at the right price, he would sit on it until hell turned cold. That was what made it all so perfect. They had the deal that was perfect for him, and he was just the buyer they were looking for.

'I just don't know,' I said.

'Don't know what?'

'If you were only someone they knew, Wally. So much of this has to be done on trust. If they can't trust the man they're dealing with—'

'Dammit, don't you think they can trust me?'

'*I* do, but they don't know you. Now—'

'I could sell them. This Rance, is he the top dog there?'

'He runs things.'

'Suppose I met him?'

'Well, I don't know.'

'Dammit, what don't you know?' He was upset with me. I was obviously trying to put the brakes on things, and he wasn't having any part of it. I was seeing complexities where everything was as simple as rolling off a girl. I admitted that I might be able to arrange a meeting. It would have to be quick, and I couldn't promise anything. I knew that the deal with the Chicago interests hadn't been finalized yet, but I couldn't guarantee that it wasn't in the bag for them.

'I don't know how well it could work, Wally. The one thing they don't want is someone who's apt to walk in there with a pocketful of lawyers and accountants. They—'

More assurances. His accountant was a glorified book-keeper and that was all, he told me. His accountant kept the taxes down and the books in order, but he wasn't one of these modern morons who didn't put a nickel in a pay toilet without checking it out first with his accountant. And he didn't need legal advice before he took a leak, either.

I more or less knew this side of him already, through Evvie. But it was good to hear him put it into words of his own.

'What kind of money's going to be involved in this, John?'

I told him I wasn't sure, but it looked as though it would run between a hundred and a hundred fifty thou. I made it sound as though I didn't believe that much money existed. That gave him the chance to play the sum down. Nothing was too expensive for the big noise from Olean. The Scrubland King.

'What kind of terms, John?'

'All cash.'

'They won't take any paper at all?'

'Not a chance. It has to be cash. And part of it under the table.'

'Is that right?'

'I think so.'

He thought it over. That's not so bad,' he said. 'Raises the capital gains tax on my end, but that's a long time in the future and there's a thousand ways to dodge that part of it. Thinking up the dodges is the part I leave to the accountants, John. They're a whole lot cuter at that side of the game. But they don't have the imagination for the big decisions. Take away their slide rules and they can't tie their shoes in the morning.'

'You wouldn't mind a cash deal?'

'Why should I mind?'

'It means tying up money.'

'When the profit is there,' he said, 'a man's a fool to worry how he ties up his money. Instead of drawing interest he takes his time and makes a profit ten times the size of interest.'

I was with him until somewhere around midnight. During the tail end of the evening we did a lot less talking and a lot more drinking. He loosened up some and worked harder on the Black Label. He had the right attitude, and as far as I could tell he had taken all the bait without finding a trace of hook so far. He was doing what we wanted. He was pushing hard to sell himself to Rance.

I had already managed to slide a few rough ones past him. I'd dropped the idea in his mind that he might do better playing his own hand instead of bringing his accountants and lawyers too far into the thick of things. This was his style anyway, but it didn't hurt to reinforce it. And I'd set him up for the big hassle of an all-cash deal.

We had considered other possibilities. We had thought about increasing the size of the mythical corporation, inflating our sales price to around a million, taking a hundred thou in cash and paper for the balance. Doug had liked it that way. He thought Gunderman would salivate at the notion of all that profit to be handled with an outlay of a hundred thousand.

I liked it the other way. If the deal was too big, he'd want to look at it a lot harder. To Gunderman, a hundred thousand dollars was a lot less than a million, even if the cash outlay was exactly the same. We wanted to keep him in love with the deal and entranced with the possibilities, but we didn't want him so shaky at the idea of all that money that he would take too long a look at the weak points of our house of cards.

On top of everything, there was something sweet about the notion of the all-cash deal. It fit into the hush-hush aspects of the game. It added, oh, maybe a touch of reality. And by balancing it off against the bit about paying part of the price sub rosa, it all fell right into place. Oh, I liked it fine.

By the time I left his hotel room I knew he'd have to meet Rance in the morning. It made no sense to leave him hanging as much as an extra day. He was set up perfectly now, the timing was ideal, and we couldn't pick a better psychological moment to get this part out of the way. It's tricky when you shift the mooch from the roper to the inside man. You have to handle it just right. Tomorrow was fine.

'I'm their man,' he was still telling me as I left. 'They couldn't find a more logical person to deal with if they looked forever. I've got a batch of arguments to use on Rance. One man's better to deal with than a whole mob, dammit. When you want to keep things on the quiet side you don't negotiate with a whole army. I can tell him a hell of a lot. I can sell myself, John.'

You can sell yourself down the river, I thought. But I just gave him some good sound brotherly advice. Don't push too hard, I told him, and don't rush things. He nodded soberly. He'd be careful, he assured me. He'd do his best.

11

I called Doug that night just to go through the motions with him. I went back to my hotel, figuring I had enough Johnny Black in me to sleep. It turned out I figured wrong. In the morning I would be handing the ball to Doug Rance and it would be my turn to sweat it out on the bench. I got nervous in advance. Sometimes this is good; you get your worrying out of the way and keep cool later on. But I wasn't in the mood for it.

I smoked a few cigarettes and kept reaching for the phone and changing my mind. She'd be sleeping by now. I had no real reason to wake her, nothing to tell her that wouldn't keep. Around two-thirty I gave up, showered, shaved, got dressed and went out. The wind had a sharp cold edge to it. I found an all-night place, had coffee and a ham sandwich. The coffee wasn't bad. I chain smoked and smelled my sweat, the special perspiration of very late hours. A human body too long without sleep, held awake by nerves and little more, is somehow unclean no matter how recent its shower or how close its shave. I had cold feet, and literally so; it was damp down there, with not enough blood circulating.

The greasy spoons draw a greasy crowd at that hour. There were a few night workers, but only a few; Toronto, big and bustling, is still a daylight city. There were drunks either sobering up or waiting for the bars to re-open – it was anybody's guess. There were men and women who had no particular place to go and no pressing reason to go to sleep. There were two or three women who might have been prostitutes and three teenagers who were either faggots or junkies. Sometimes you need a scorecard. Everything looks alike these days.

I lit the last cigarette in the pack and thought about the air in Colorado.

When I was a kid I told stories. People called it lying. It really wasn't; I had a fairly wicked imagination and a tendency to embellish things. I got punished occasionally, but I was not always caught. I became a fairly good liar.

I read some psychology years later in Q. I had remembered something from a college psych course that I wanted to check out, and in the prison library I learned that I had not been what they call a pathological liar. I was always aware that my stories were not true. I was simply good at the game.

So skip a few years. I got fair grades in school – they wrote things like *Could do better with effort* on the margins of the cards. My guidance counselor tried to talk me out of applying to Yale. I had visions – Yale, Yale Law, an apprenticeship with some genius like Geisler or Leibowitz, then back to New Mexico to be the hottest criminal lawyer on the rapidly expanding frontier. Sometimes in the dreams I wound up staying in the big city. Sometimes I went into politics. I always came out Very Important.

Yale turned me down. I wound up at the state university at Santa Fe and coasted for most of three years. I don't remember many of the courses that I took. I was pre-law, but that generally leaves you a lot of room.

Oh, hell. I couldn't stay off probation. During my junior year there was a girl – there is always a girl – and I buckled down and tried harder. We had it figured. I was going to go to Yale Law, she was going to marry me and work to put me through law school, and then segue into the dream for a big finish, hearts and flowers, over and out.

Everything hit the fan at once. Yale Law said no by return mail, the girl missed her period and got scared, and although it turned out to be a false alarm it managed to kill things for us. I went on a too-long drunk and came out of it in time for a mid-term. I wasn't prepared for it, and they caught me with the book open on my lap.

Maybe I could have talked myself out of it. I didn't try, didn't even wait for the news that the Dean wanted to see me. I could have gone home. You always can, they say, but you don't realize this until later. I did not want to go back to Springer. I did not want to make up a fresh story en route and look at their faces and wonder whether or not they believed it. I packed one suitcase and went into town. I started off flat broke, and the few things I hocked – my typewriter, my radio – did not fatten my wallet.

In the Greyhound station men's room I put on my good suit and a clean shirt and a tie. I checked my suitcase and let a yassuh-boss kid shine my shoes. Then I went shopping in the best department store in Santa Fe.

I spent half an hour in the second-floor men's department. I looked at a few suits and some sport jackets. I tried things on but didn't buy much, just a couple of shirts and a five-dollar tie. I paid cash and looked at my watch while the clerk was wrapping the packages. The California bus was due to take off in fifteen minutes.

'Better hurry it,' I said. 'I've got a bus to make.'

He gave me my package and my change. I walked quickly to the escalator, and I took one step, and then I fell down the full flight and landed in a heap on the floor.

It caused quite a stir. I stayed put for the first few seconds and let them make a fuss over me. One woman had screamed tentatively while I was falling, and then a bevy of nervous clerks made properly nervous sounds. I gave them a minute, then shook my head groggily, gulped air, said something unintelligible, started to get up, stopped, got up, slipped, righted myself, and stood there finally looking as out of it as I possibly could.

They hustled me into the manager's office as fast as they could. If anything had been wrong with me this would have been a very bad move, but they were not anxious to have me lying sprawled out at the foot of the escalator; it was rotten public relations. They sat me down and checked me inexpertly for broken bones and asked me how I felt.

'Gee,' I said, 'I don't know. My back's twisted all to hell and gone.'

'It probably shook you up. You should watch your step, son.'

You watch your step-son, I thought. I'll watch my fairy godmother. But what I said was, 'I could swear that stair moved when I stepped on it.'

'Of course it did. It's an escalator.'

'No, the tread slipped sideways. I put one foot square on it and it slipped sideways and I . . . whew, that was some feeling.'

The silence was almost embarrassing. I looked at my watch. It had broken in the fall, and I mentioned this. I asked what time it was. They told me.

'Oh, terrific,' I said. 'I just missed a bus.'

'Where are you going?'

'San Francisco. I live there.'

'You go to school at State?'

'That's right.'

The room cleared a little. Two of them stayed around, and they played the game as though they knew it very well. Their watch department would repair my ticker free of charge, they explained. And they would put me in a cab to the airport so that I could fly to San Francisco.

That was very decent of them, I said.

'Just sign right here, Mr Hayden—'

I got the pen almost to the paper, then stopped. 'Wait a second,' I said. 'Suppose I really racked myself up?'

'Well—'

'Listen, my roommate's old man is a lawyer. He's got this big negligence practice in Albuquerque. The stories Ray told me, say, I'm not signing *anything*.'

They would fix my watch and put me in a cab? Sure they would. I put the pen down and they opened up a little. Nobody wanted to talk about lawyers, I was assured. Nobody wanted to spend weeks or even months in a courtroom. I was all right, and if anything turned up I had his personal guarantee that my medical expenses would be taken care of, but it was very important to him personally that they get the paperwork out of the way. All they needed was my signature.

They sweetened the pot. Just as a token of their concern for my welfare, they would throw in a suit. I could pick any suit in the store, with their compliments.

'Well, I already *looked* at every suit in the store,' I told them, properly baffled. 'I couldn't find anything I even *wanted*, for God's sake. I mean, my Dad buys me all the suits I want.'

I let them make the deal. We closed for a new watch, air passage to S.F., and a flat hundred bucks in cash. I wrote my name on the line and that was that.

It was all very easy. Later on I couldn't believe how easy it had been, how gently I had slipped into the role, how stupid they were. The idiots thought they were being so goddamn smooth about everything. Greasing the skids for me, making me sign myself out of a six-figure nuisance suit for a few bucks and a watch and an airplane ticket. They danced for me like puppets, and they were so busy being cute they never even felt the strings.

The only hard part was at the beginning. Pitching myself down that escalator – that took a little doing. But from there on it was gravy. The first step was a lulu, but the rest of the road was a cinch.

And that, I suppose, was the beginning. I pulled the same dodge a week later in a San Francisco department store and found out I'd had a large dose of beginner's luck. I took a fairly bad fall to start things off, and then I ran up against a floor manager who pegged me for a grifter from the go. As it turned out, I had to spend a week in the hospital. I actually went ahead and got a Market Street lawyer to take the case. This surprised the hell out of the floor manager. I turned out to be one hundred percent clean, a hard-working college dropout with no criminal record and no shady past history whatsoever. They got religion and settled out of court. After I paid the lawyer and the hospital I had almost eighteen hundred dollars to cushion me.

I also had one grift I could never pull again for the rest of my life. Nor was I inclined to. That was one nasty fall on that escalator.

There were other angles.

With eighteen hundred dollars I was in no particular hurry to find a job. Knock around for awhile with time on your hands and the right gleam in your eye and you meet people. Meet the right people and you learn the business. If the life doesn't fit, it's not long before you drop it or it drops you and you look for a calmer way to make a living. If it fits you, then you're home.

I used to think about this in Q. I had worlds of time for thought. I tried to work it back to the beginning, like tracing a river to its source. When I was a kid in geography class I thought rivers had sources that were very dramatic affairs – clear streams of water leaping out of rocks and such. But follow a river back and it spreads into smaller and smaller streams. Trace them one by one and they disappear into acres of dust. The thinking sessions in prison dried up the same way.

If I hadn't busted out of State I'd have screwed things up for myself somewhere else along the line. If I had struck out hard on that first roll down the escalator I'd have found another better angle later on. I was too good at it, and too given to dreams and lies, and far too inept at going through life reading the script.

The crazy things you think of late at night. I never did get to sleep. I drank coffee until it backed up on me and I got a little shaky. I took a long walk in the false dawn and watched the city yawn and wake up. I went back to the hotel, showered again, changed clothes again, and had a respectable breakfast. Before too long it was time to pick up my pigeon and show him the coop.

12

The store was swinging in full-dressed splendor by the time I got Gunderman there. The night before, Doug had called our Manpower secretary and told her to take the day off. Then he made other calls and hired us a batch of day-workers.

With Gunderman actually coming to the office, we had to be able to stand a genuine white-glove inspection. We had to present the illusion of real activity. To do this, we needed people. And, because we were dealing strictly in illusion, we needed people who could play their assigned roles and keep their mouths shut. People who were with it.

We had two men, local grifters who were presently unemployed and who were not averse to picking up half a yard apiece for doing nothing special. One of them wore glasses and sat behind a desk jockeying a rented adding machine. The other leafed through a stack of newspapers and assorted garbage and dictated meaningless memos from time to time into a rented dictaphone.

Our Manpower girl had been temporarily replaced by a pleasant old girl with salt-and-pepper hair and a touch of Scottish burr to her voice. She was an old girlfriend of Winger Tim. She had since married on the square. Her husband was a few years dead. She lived on insurance money, acted in some Toronto amateur theater group, and did per diem work with grifting mobs when she was needed. We got her at bargain rates, just twenty dollars for the day. But she didn't really need the money. She wanted the excitement.

Everything was staged just about right. When I ushered Gunderman into the outer office, one of our men was working the adding machine while the gal – Helen Wyatt – was talking on the telephone to a dead line. She was explaining that Mr Rance was not in. She hung up, and I told her that Mr Gunderman was here to see Mr Rance. She buzzed Doug to tell him this, and while we waited our other hired hand came into the office, said hello to me, hung his coat on a peg and went to work. This was one of my touches. It is better if the scene changes within the store *while* the mark is present. This keeps him from wondering whether things have been set up for his benefit, all waiting for him to come and see.

I turned Wally over to Doug. My partner followed the script, wasting no time on me, hitting Gunderman with a ray of charm while giving the impression that he really had better things to do than spend time with Olean's answer to William Zeckendorf. They wended their pleasant way into the inner office and I walked over to the front desk and chucked Helen under the chin. 'One of these days,' I assured her, 'you and I are going to have a wild affair.'

'Not I. My bones are too brittle.'

'A young chicken like you?'

'Don't tease a poor widow lady, John.' She sighed theatrically. 'I wish I knew what this was all about,' she said. 'Nobody ever lets me read the whole script. Just my own lines.'

I looked her elaborately up and down and assured her that there was nothing wrong with her lines. She told me to go away, and I did. I went to a drugstore around the corner and called the office.

She said, 'Barnstable, good morning.'

I said, 'I had one grunch but the eggplant over there,' and she hung up.

I was not calling just to keep Helen happy in her widowhood. This was more of the illusion. Phones ringing show that an office is in contact with the outside world. All of this helps, not on a conscious level but right back at the base of the mark's mind.

The more elaborately you do this, the better off you are. Cutting corners is always dangerous. When a store is set up perfectly, it gives you so great an edge that you can clean your mark and blow him off and leave him so sold that he simply refuses to believe he's been conned, no matter what. I knew a stock mob that set up a bucket shop that came on stronger than any Wall Street office ever did. They had four marks on the string at once, and they scored with three and let the fourth off because it looked as though he might tip. One of the mooches figured things out a few days later, and the police wound up picking up the other two losers and telling them they had been had.

They had been so well sold that they would not believe it. And when the bulls took one of them by the hand and led him back to the office of that very friendly stockbroker, he wouldn't believe it when the suite of offices turned out to be very empty. He was sure he was on the wrong street. He made the cop check out some other addresses, because he was utterly sold on the legitimacy of that bucket shop.

I kept calling our offices. Not constantly, because we weren't supposed to be all that active. Just often enough so that Gunderman would hear a phone ring every once in a while. He might not take conscious note of it, but it would make an impression.

Once Helen put me through to Doug. I told him the weather was nice and the Yankees were in last place and ontogeny recapitulates phylogeny. He said things like *Mmmmm* and *I don't think so* and *You'd better check it more carefully*. Somewhere in the middle of one of my sentences he told me to call him back, he was busy, and I should go into it in detail. Then he hung up on me and I went and had another cup of coffee.

Then I called again, later on, and Helen told me that our boy was gone. 'I'll put Doug on,' she said.

'That's a sweet friend you've got,' he told me. 'Robbing that clod makes me feel like Robin Hood.'

'You didn't take a shine to him?'

'I hated him. I figured the frail was exaggerating, but he's even worse than she said.'

'How did it go?'

'The right way. Come on up and I'll tell you about it.'

'Do you have to?'

'Huh?'

I told him that I hadn't had any sleep. He laughed. 'Stage fright? An old hand like you?'

'Partly stage fright, I suppose. Mostly some things I wanted to think about. By the time I felt like sleeping I couldn't, because I had to be able to meet him on time. I've been walking around on adrenalin for a couple of hours and I'm just about out of the stuff. I think I'll sack out and catch you later.'

'Good enough. Oh, Johnny—'

'What?'

'Don't go back to your hotel. He told me he has to catch a plane this afternoon. I doubt that he made reservations. You don't want to be asleep at your hotel when he calls. And your desk clerk might screw things up and tell him. Go to a decent hotel and get a good flop.'

'Where?'

'Not the Royal York if he's there. Just a minute. Oh, hell – go to my place. You remember how to get there?'

I'd been to his apartment a few times. I told him I remembered where it was.

'The door's open,' he said.

'You don't lock it?'

He laughed. 'I never lock my door,' he said. 'I trust people, Johnny. I've found most people are basically honest.'

13

I spent the afternoon and most of the night at Doug's apartment. Our respective roles gave him one substantial advantage. As bossman, he was supposed to live it up in a fairly plush apartment. Lackey that I was, I had to make do with a third-rate hotel.

I was back at my third-rate hotel the next day when Gunderman called me. The operator made sure that I was really me, and then I heard Evvie's voice in the distance telling him that she had John Hayden on the phone, and at last his voice boomed in my ear.

'Where the hell were you yesterday? I stuck around waiting for you to call and calling you and not reaching you, John. I wanted to get together with you before I flew back, and then I tried you last night and couldn't get hold of you. Got a girlfriend to keep you busy?'

'I was tied up during the morning,' I told him. 'And then Mr Rance said you'd gone straight back to Olean, so I didn't try you at your hotel.'

'Well, I didn't want him thinking how close we're working on this, John. I'll tell you one thing, though. I like this Doug Rance of yours.'

'He's quite a man.'

'I'll go along with that. I'll bet his background's good. His family. His father had money, didn't he?'

'I believe so.'

'It shows. I understand the English say it takes three generations to come up with a gentleman. I don't know if they're not a little off on their timetable, but they've got the idea. You can always tell whether or not you're dealing with someone who's ... well, call it quality. I'm as democratic as the next person, John, but I'd be a damned fool if I didn't know there's a difference between a man like Rance and a man whose father cleaned out toilets for a living.'

Doug Rance's father didn't clean out toilets for a living. He was an auto mechanic, fairly competent when he was sober, which was not his natural condition. He was generally out of work, and he bought himself a case of cirrhosis of the liver and died of it. I did not pass this data on to Gunderman.

'I think he liked me, John. Talk to him?'

'Not at length.'

'And?'

I hesitated. 'I think you've got a very good chance,' I said finally.

'Just a chance?'

'For one thing, he'll have to talk to some of the other principals. He can't make decisions entirely on his own.'

'If he goes for the deal, the rest of them will follow suit, won't they?'

'I suppose so. But there's that Chicago group. I told you, Wally, I didn't get to talk much with him. I know he liked you and that he was impressed with your approach.'

'I just put my cards on the table.'

'Well, I guess he liked that. The way I see it, you're right on top of the waiting list. You—'

'Waiting list!'

'That's right. What did you expect? The Chicago people have the inside track. If they hang onto it, they're going to swing the deal. If they drop out, you're home free.'

'I don't know if I like that, John.'

'Look—'

'You look, damn it. I sat there in Rance's office and we cleared a lot of air. I'll tell you, he didn't know me from Adam, but by the time I left we had accomplished something. We knew each other and we liked each other, and what's more I made him see just how sensible it was for him to deal with me. Now I've got my proposition hanging there and I'm supposed to wait and find out what happens next.' He paused, and when he spoke again his voice was pitched slower, his words spaced further apart. 'Like proposing to a woman and having her not say yes and not say no, just keeping you waiting until she makes up her mind. A man can tire of that sort of thing.'

I said something sympathetic.

'These Chicago people. I hate this sitting and waiting for them to hit or strike out.'

'I'm trying to sink their ship. What the hell do you expect?'

'You're trying to—'

I let some impatience show in my voice. 'Oh, hell,' I snapped. 'What do you think I was doing until four in the morning? It's going to take some doing, making them look bad to Rance and the others. I've been trying everything I can think of to throw them off the track. Don't you think I want my cut?' I suspect he'd forgotten my cut. 'And don't you think I want to earn it?'

'Well, I'm a son of a bitch,' he said. 'I never even thought about that end of it.'

'I can't think of anything else.'

'My apologies, John. You know I appreciate what you've done, not to mention what you're doing. Have you got something good working?'

'I don't want to talk about it now,' I said. At least that saved improvising a new bit of material. 'Listen, I've got to cut this short. I'll be in touch with you, but don't expect a call every hour on the hour. I'll let you know if anything breaks either way. And don't call me. If there's anything to know, you'll know it.'

Doug thought everything was coming up roses. I wasn't that positive now. The phone call bothered me. He'd gotten fairly belligerent at one point, and this served to point up the thin line we had to walk. We had to keep the carrot just the right distance from the donkey's nose. Too close and he might take a sniff before biting into it. Too far away and he'd get his hackles up and never bite at all.

So Doug was all for coasting along, then rushing into it and pulling it off fast and hard. This could not be. He had to be teased and coaxed, encouraged and yet held back.

Evvie didn't want me to call her any more. It was too risky, she said. She would call me when she got the chance, from some neutral phone so that there would be no record of the call. This didn't make a world of sense but I could figure it out. She was starting to tighten up. We were coming around the far turn and the pace was beginning to get to her. No surprise there. She played the game like one born to it, but talent was never a complete substitute for experience. This was her first time. Everybody's first time is a frightening occasion, especially when you're doing little but wait for the finish. I can still remember the first long con game I ever worked, my role as minor as could be, and the sweat I worked up over it all. And by then I'd already acquired a fair background in the game. For Evvie, entirely new to it and close to the center of things, seeing Gunderman day after day, it had to be hell.

'Maybe you did too good a job,' she said the next night.

'How?'

'He just won't let go of this. He talks about it constantly, John. I don't even understand it. It's not as if this was going to make him suddenly rich. He's rich already. What kind of profit does he think he can turn on this?'

'A handy one. That's not the point.'

'It's not?'

'He got taken once, don't forget. On a moose pasture dodge. This means getting even and then some. You know the man's pride.'

'Of course.'

'That's why he won't let go, kitten.'

'It just worries me,' she said. 'I think what would happen if he ever found out. I get shaky thinking about it. And here I thought I was so level-headed and calm and cool.'

'You're doing fine.'

'Am I? Maybe. I'll tell you something, I don't think I could go through this again. It's not that bad when you know it's one time and one time only. That makes it easier. I couldn't do it again, though. Not ever. You used to do this all the time, didn't you? I don't see how you kept from flying apart.'

'You get used to it.'

'Are you used to it now?'

I didn't answer immediately. Then I said, 'It comes easy. When you know how to do something fairly well and when you've done it for a very long time, it comes easy enough. But no, I don't think I could go back to the life all the way. This is the last one, a final shot at the moon and for a very good reason. I wouldn't want to go through it again.'

'I'm—'

'What?'

'I guess I'm frightened, John.' A pause. 'I wish you could come here. I wish—'

'It won't be long.'

'No,' she said. 'Not long.'

We killed him with phone calls. He was under orders, he was not supposed to call me and he didn't dare call Doug. We goaded him like picadors placing darts in a bull.

'John here, Wally. I can only talk for a minute. I think Rance will call you in a day or two at the outside. I think we've got Chicago hanging on the ropes—'

'They're out?'

'About three-fourths out and going fast. I don't even want to talk about the way I've played it, but I don't think Rance will be in a hurry to deal with them. He may not call you, but I think he will. He'll be anxious to talk price.'

'You mean he'll deal, finally?'

'Now, I don't think he'll be that firm about it, Wally. He may keep it very iffy. What he'll want to do, if he calls, is settle on a price so that he'll have that much out of the way when the deal is in the final stages. Whatever price the two of you reach, it'll be firm as far as he's concerned when the time comes.'

'Do I have room to bargain?'

'I know what he wants.'

'How much?'

'He wants a hundred and a half, a hundred fifty thousand. He wants half of that in cash under the table and the other half showing on paper. Now, I have a pretty good idea what kind of a figure you can arrive at with him. Oh, God. I'll call you back.'

'Wait—'

Click.

'Wally—'

'What the hell happened?'

'Company I hadn't figured on. Where was I?'

He told me where I was.

'That's right. I know it's a bargain at his price, Wally, but I don't think you should have to pay that much. You ought to be able to get in for less than that.'

'I don't want to blow everything for nickels and dimes, John.'

A born mooch. 'Don't worry about that part of it. The thing is, they've got the tax consideration, and that's important to them. That's why part of the money has to be under the table, and that's where you have a big bargaining point.'

'I think I see what you mean.'

'Sure. You offer less money overall but a higher proportion in cold cash. That makes it less like haggling, too. They can accept a lower offer without losing face.'

'I follow you.'

'Start by saying yes to the full price, Wally, But say you'll pay that figure on paper, period. Don't worry about Rance saying yes to it. He won't. He can't.'

'And then?'

'Then you come back with a counter-offer. Tell him you'll go more in cash if he wants, but you want a concession on the price. Offer him fifty each way.'

'And he'll take that?'

'No, but that should open it up. I think he'll settle for seventy cash and fifty on paper. That's a hundred twenty thousand, and that saves you thirty thousand dollars.'

You just have to let them think they're getting a bargain. You have to put them in the driver's seat, and then let them drive over the cliff. When Doug talked to him, he gave Gunderman just a little extra rope. They wound up ten thousand dollars under the figure I'd mentioned. A hundred ten instead of a hundred twenty. I'd supplied good information and Gunderman had showed himself to be a good and proper wheeler-dealer. He'd never dig his way out now. It was piled hip deep all around him, and the fool thought it smelled just fine.

'Wally, I think you should start raising cash.'

'Well, what the hell is this, anyway? Just Wednesday—'

'You don't know how these things move. Or what I've been going through. This isn't a promise, but it would be good if you had the cash on you when the time came. Can you get up the dough without being obvious about it? A little here and a little there?'

'Nothing easier.'

'You're sure?'

'No problem, John.'

No problem at all. Doug called later and told him to raise the money, that he felt the deal was ninety percent firm, that he'd spoken with everyone on the board and every silent partner and all that was needed was the board's formal approval. No problem, none at all. But Barnstable had better make its mind up, he wanted Doug to know. He wasn't handing out an ultimatum, not by any means, but he had another very attractive opportunity open to him and he didn't have the cash to swing them both at once. He'd prefer the Barnstable deal any time, but if they wouldn't close with him soon he might not want to take the chance of losing out entirely.

Not a bad old horse trader, Wallace J. Gunderman. A standard pitch, one you see coming all the way but one you don't want to ignore entirely because it just might be true. A handy way to put on pressure for a closing without seeming to press too hard.

He was good in his element. But we had never been in his element, had never played ball in his league. This was no straight deal. It was a con, and we sat and laughed at shrewd old Wally.

No problem, no problem at all. And on an early-to-bed evening my phone jangled brittly on the nightstand. I cursed Gunderman for waking me and hustled the phone to my ear.

And a kitten's voice said, 'Oh, John. Oh, God—'

'What's wrong?'

'Could you get on a plane right away? Could you come here? Maybe I'm crazy, I don't know. Maybe I am. It's risky, isn't it? We shouldn't see each other now—'

'Evvie, calm down.'

Silence. Then, 'I'm all right.'

'What's the matter?'

'I just better see you,' she said. 'I think he knows. I'm scared to death he knows.'

14

Somehow I beat the sun there. I spilled out of a yawning cabby's hack and dashed up the walk to her door. There was a light on upstairs. I took the stairs two at a time. She met me at the top and collapsed in my arms. She tried to talk and couldn't make it. I got her inside, shut the door. She still couldn't talk. Her eyes were circled in red, her face drawn. She looked like hell. Broken by a life of unquiet desperation. Shredded; wrung out.

I'd done the wrong thing, of course. There are two possible courses of action when things come unglued. If the end is still at all uncertain, you cool it and wait things out from a safe distance. If there is no doubt that the fit and the shan have connected, you fold up your tent and run for cover.

What you do not do, ever, is lead the Light Brigade straight into hell's mouth.

Fine. But my woman had called for help, and the rules were suddenly obsolete. We had been too long apart. She was afraid, and alone. If she was in trouble I had to be with her to get her out. If she was only having nightmares, it was my job to hold her hand.

When she calmed down she said, 'I shouldn't have called you. I guess I'm not as good as I thought I was.'

'Easy.'

'I think I'm all right now. I wanted to call you back and tell you not to come. It doesn't make any sense. I missed you, and I kept getting more nervous all the time and there was nobody handy to lean on. I'm sorry, darling.'

I told her that it was all right. She took the last cigarette from her pack. I gave her a light. She sat close beside me on the couch and smoked.

I said, 'You said you thought he knows.'

'It was probably my nerves.'

'What happened?'

'Partly his attitude. He seems very different. He's a gruff, impulsive man, John, but he's always been even-tempered with me. He blows off steam now and then. Everybody does. But lately he snaps all the time. And the way he looks at me. I catch him looking at me when he doesn't know I can see him. As though he's trying to figure something out, as though he suspects something.'

'You're piling up molehills.'

'Enough of them could make a mountain, couldn't they?' She knocked ashes from her cigarette, put it to her lips, drew on it. 'He needles me about you.'

'How?'

'He refers to you as my boyfriend. In a sarcastic way, but with an undertone that gives me the feeling – I don't know, I guess this must be way off-base—'

'Go on.'

'As though it's a joke but he means it anyway. Do you know what I mean?'

'He's kidding on the square.'

She nodded gratefully. 'As though he has things figured out with almost all of the pieces in place. And he's going along with it, waiting to see what happens, and ready to tear us apart at the end. I'm so *scared* of him. He would kill me. Just like that.'

Her hands were shaking. I took her cigarette and put it out for her. I told her she was adding it up and coming out all wrong.

'Well, what does it mean?'

'It first of all doesn't mean what you think. It's too far out of character. Even if he decided to stick around for the ending once he tipped to the con, he wouldn't play it this way. He'd be poking around everywhere trying to fit all the pieces together. He'd be on the phone with me trying to trap me up. He thinks he's very good at that. He would push it.'

'I didn't think of that.'

'Besides, I know how sold he is. I've been playing him slow for a reason, baby. Slower than Doug would like, all to make sure that nothing will shake him loose. Don't you know why he's acting the way he is?'

'Why?'

'Because he has to have it all. Everything. He can't stand to give a thing away. Not money and not people either. He used you as bait to get me into this thing. Now it bothers him. He can't get rid of the feeling that maybe you gave me a little too much. You belong to him, see? It's all right for him to use you as a teaser, but he doesn't like the idea that maybe you got carried away with yourself and crawled into the rack with me.'

She was nodding slowly. 'He needed you to get me into it on his side, but he's conveniently forgotten that by now. I think he's forgotten that I'm supposed to be cut in for five percent of his action. He never put it on paper, naturally, and I'm damn sure he'd edge out of it if I ever asked for the dough. He's not exactly the last of the big spenders. He sweetened things awhile back with a half a thou for my expenses. Anyone with class would have doubled that figure, minimum. But he's cheap. He picks up dinner checks and he doesn't turn off the lights to save electricity, but he's still a stingy son of a bitch.'

'Well, that's the truth.'

I went on like that, giving her every reason on earth why there was nothing to be afraid of. They weren't all of them logical, but the more I could throw at her the cooler she would be for the rest of the distance. I must have sounded a lot more sure of myself than I actually was. A score is never a sure thing until the cash is in hand and the mooch a thousand miles away. There's never been one yet that didn't have a chance of going to hell on crutches.

But I talked, and she listened, and it seemed to sink in. She asked me if Doug knew I'd come down. I said I hadn't had a chance to tell him, and wouldn't have bothered anyway. She agreed that I shouldn't, and that she'd been foolish to call me and I'd been less than wise to come running.

'But I'm glad you did,' she said. 'How long can you stay?'

'I've got return reservations in two and a half hours.'

'So soon?'

'Uh-huh.'

She sighed. 'I wish you could stay longer. I know you can't. We don't even have time to—' She colored.

'We might have time,' I said.

'I . . . I don't know. I'm not really in the mood, I don't think.'

'It's a bad time for it.'

'And a bad place. But God knows I need you, my darling—'

An invisible violinist played pizzicato on my vertebrae. I turned from her. 'In Colorado,' I said.

'Mmmmm. At Barnstable Lodge.'

We'd taken to calling it that. 'We should find a better name for it,' I said.

'It's a fine name. Do you want coffee? I'll make some.'

She went into the little kitchen to cook water. A fine domestic lady. I did not feel bad about the plane ride. It was nothing, just a little static, and worth a scare to see her, to be with her.

She called in: 'I think I left my cigarettes on the table, John. Bring me one?'

I poked around in the pack. It was empty. I asked her if one of mine would do.

'Not really. I've got a fresh pack in my purse. I think it's in there somewhere. On the television, I think.'

It was. I took it to her, opened the catch, fumbled inside for her cigarettes. She was at the stove spooning instant coffee into a pair of Melmac cups. All at once her eyes went very wide and her mouth shaped a small O. About that time my hand settled on something hard and cold. Some people could have guessed; I had to haul it out and look at it to know what it was.

It looked like a howitzer.

'Why?'

'I . . . oh, I don't even know. I've been dreaming about him, John. He'd kill me if he knew, I know he'd kill me, and I can't even think about it without turning cold inside. I thought it would be good to . . . to have something. In case something happened. I don't know.'

'Where did you get it?'

'It's his.'

'How come you've got it?'

'I took it. He kept it in his desk for years. Then it got switched to one of the filing cabinets. He'll never miss it. I don't think he's looked at it once in the past eight months.'

'Ever shoot it?'

She shook her head.

'Ever handle *any* gun?'

'No.'

'Then you probably couldn't do anything with it if you had to. Nine people out of ten can't hit the side of a garage at twenty feet with a handgun. The only time you might ever shoot this would be if you panicked. You would probably miss and be in deeper than ever. Or else you would kill somebody and get tagged with it.

'But chances are you'd never fire the gun at all. You'd just carry it, and you'd get unlucky and he'd just happen to look in your purse the way I just did. Or someone else would look in your purse, anyone. Or you'd drop the bag and the gun would go off. Or any of a thousand other damn fool things that wouldn't happen if you didn't do a harebrained thing and carry a gun along.'

She stood wordless, and about to cry. The teakettle had been whistling throughout the tail end of my speech. I turned the burner off and the whistle died.

I said, 'I didn't mean to fly at you like that. Guns make me as nervous as a virgin bride on opening night. They scare the hell out of me. I won't even work with anybody who carries one. All they buy you is trouble. A bank robber needs one, a killer needs one, all the thickheaded heavies need them. Nobody with a brain has to have a gun on his hip. Not even you.'

'I feel—' I reached for her arm. She drew away. 'I feel like an idiot,' she said.

'Forget it. I'm just glad I found this thing.'

'I almost wish you hadn't. You must think—'

'I think I'll be glad when this is over. And when you don't have to worry about anything more terrifying than what pattern glassware to buy for our little cabin in the pines. Is this loaded, by the way?'

'I think so.'

I sat down on a kitchen chair, holding the gun gingerly. Guns do bother me. I hunted now and then when I was a kid, but nothing beyond birds and small game. I've never used a handgun. I do not like them at all. This one was a Smith and Wesson, .38-caliber, three-inch barrel, a safety on the grip. I shook my head at the last and thought she would never know to depress the grip safety before firing. The gun was all risk and no reward. I fumbled it open. It was loaded all the way, with a slug waiting there right smack under the hammer, which proved that Wally Gunderman didn't know a hell of a lot more about guns than she did.

I pulled its teeth, set the shells upright on the table top. I put the gun back together again and held it out toward her. She drew away and shook her head.

'I don't even want to touch it,' she said.

'Should I leave it here? I could take it with me and dump it somewhere, but it would be better if you put it back in his files. If you'd rather not—'

'I don't mind. I just . . . put it on the counter, John. I don't want to touch it now. I'll take it with me when I go to work.'

'I'll get rid of the shells for you.'

'How?'

'I'll put them down a sewer. No problem.'

'I'm nothing but problems tonight, aren't I?'

'I'm not complaining.'

'Dragging you all the way here for nothing, and then this—'

'I'm glad I came. And glad I found out about the gun. It's worth the trip just keeping you from toting it around. You don't have to be scared of him, baby. He won't know a thing until you're a million miles away. He may never find out, he may drop dead long before he'd figure out that he's been had.'

'It's this waiting—'

'You won't have to wait much longer.'

We weren't any of us going to wait much longer. I had been laboring on details like Michelangelo on that Roman ceiling. I was so busy getting everything utterly perfect that I'd lost sight of a fairly important fact. Every extra day was just that much more hell for Evvie. I was hard at work on my masterpiece, and she was the one getting all that paint in her eyes. A bad mistake.

Not that day but the next I told Doug we were ready. And the following afternoon he called Gunderman and said yes to the deal, a firm yes, an all-the-way yes. An hour later I called Wally. Everything was set, he told me. In five days time he and Mr Douglas Rance would put it all on paper. The deal was already being set up.

'I'll come in the night before,' he told me. 'You and I, John, we have some celebrating to do. You can show me that town and I'll teach you how to put a coat of paint on it.'

I told him that sounded like a good idea.

So the days crawled by and the nights dawdled but passed, and he came to Toronto like Caesar to Rome. He wanted to hit every bar. We very nearly made it. He drank steadily and steadfastly refused to get bombed enough so that we could call it a day. I drank less than he did but not little enough to stay especially sober.

He did most of the talking. Some of it was about money, some of it was about Evvie. Once be gripped my arm and winked owlishly at me. 'Some woman,' he said. 'Some wonderful woman.'

I looked around to see who he meant 'Not *here*,' he said. 'I mean Evvie. One in a million.'

'One in a million,' I echoed. We were in complete agreement on that point.

He let go of my arm and dumped his face into one hand. He scratched idly at his ear lobe. 'If you only knew,' he muttered secretly.

If *you* only knew, I thought.

And in some other remarkably similar bar he winked conspiratorially at me. I smiled politely and returned the wink, and he threw back his big head and roared.

'Easy,' I said. The waiters were beginning to stare at us. 'Easy, old pal,'

'All mine,' he said.

'Easy.'

'Signed and sealed. All mine.'

'All yours, old buddy. But take it easy.'

He grabbed all the checks, overtipped all the waiters, winked at all the girls, and was the goddamned life of every goddamned party. 'A celebration,' he said, at least four hundred times. 'A celebration.'

I almost told him it was just a shade premature.

15

Maybe I was getting old. When they rang the room in the morning the phone set little devils dancing in my head. I grabbed the phone and said all right, damn it, all right, and put the phone in the cradle and found my way to the john. The demons kept doing the twist inside my skull. I went through the standard wake-up ritual and tossed in a pair of aspirins and a Dexemil. All of this helped me wake up, and this in turn did little more than make me more aware of my headache. Too much Scotch, too little sleep – I was definitely getting too old for the life. The roadhouse in the mountains beckoned.

I put the good white shirt on once again, tied the small knot in the sincere tie, worked my way into the conservative suit. In another couple of hours I could unknot that tie and drop it in a handy wastebasket; in another couple of hours I could wipe the matching sincere look from my face and begin looking like me again. It was about time. The masquerade was beginning to make me ache, the costume was wearing thin on my frame. In another couple of hours—

Outside, the sun was all too bright. I let a couple of cups of coffee pretend to be breakfast and battled the sunlight once again. According to plans, I was supposed to be at the office at ten for the skinning ceremonies. It was time. I stepped to the curb, and a cab glided to me as if by magic. I hopped in and gave the driver the address.

It was funny. In the old days a time like this was always sweetly tense, the precious moment before the kill, the instant frozen in time when the matador stood poised, sword ready, with the great gross bull rushing in to impale himself and die in beauty. On mornings like this my eyes were bright and my head clear, and no quantity of liquor or shortness of sleep could cancel the fresh glory of it all.

It should have been like that now, and it was not. Not at all. Instead the hangover was in full bloom, aided and abetted by little grains of doubt and fear. Something gnawed at me. Something demanded attention. There was the feeling you get when you've left a room and you're dead certain you left a cigarette burning. Or the feeling you're left with after an alcoholic blackout – memory is gone, and you assume at once that you've done something dreadful; there are threads and patches in the back of your mind but not enough to grab onto and pin down, just enough to drive you mad.

'You're flipping,' I said. 'You're falling apart.'

'What's that?'

This last from the cabby. I had been talking aloud and not realizing it, a phenomenon which is always less than comforting.

'Nothing,' I said.

'You talking to me?'

'Just talking to myself.'

'You always do that?'

'Just after a bad night.'

'Oh,' he said.

She'd be in Olean now, waiting. How long? A week for me to clear up everything in Toronto and get back to Colorado. A week was ample; our accounts had to be cleared, our front money had to be paid back, Gunderman's check had to be routed through channels. And it would be a week and more before she could pick up and join me. Call it ten days. In ten days we would be together, in Colorado, with all of his pretty money in our kick.

In ten days I could quit talking to myself.

Doug was already at the office, looking fresh and well-tailored. He looked at me and shuddered.

'Bad?'

'You look like hell,' he said.

'Well, he wanted to celebrate. We did most of the town.'

'I thought you'd bring him with you. No?'

'He wanted to meet me here.'

'At ten?'

'At ten.'

'Fine,' he said. 'He should be here any minute. Everything's set, the papers, everything. That printer does choice work.'

'He's expensive.'

'Well, you get what you pay for, Johnny.'

'That's if you're lucky.'

'Sure.' He walked around behind his desk, sat down, clasped his hands behind his neck, yawned, unclasped his hands and dug a cigarette out of his pack. He lit it and blew smoke at the ceiling. I looked at my watch. It was a few minutes past ten.

'Any minute, Johnny.'

'Uh-huh.'

'So smooth. I'm sorry you were stuck with him last night. He had big eyes to celebrate?'

'Bigger eyes than mine.'

'I hope he didn't drink so much that he forgets to show up. It's been so damned smooth so far. Like silk. Was he holding it pretty well?'

'Better than I was.'

'You didn't let anything out?'

I gave him a look.

'Well, forget I asked.'

I took a cigarette, lit it. The gnawing inside wouldn't go away. I told Doug that Gunderman should be here by now. 'He doesn't get places late,' I said. 'He's always on time. It's one of his virtues.'

'Maybe he wants to play hard to get.'

'Isn't it a little late for that? You don't walk around with your skirt around your waist for a month and then play hard to get when you finally work your way to the bedroom. He should have been here with bells on. He should have been here before I was, for Christ's sake.'

'You're getting a little jumpy, Johnny.'

He was right. I was getting more than a little jumpy, and I liked it less and less. I do not like it when people act out of character. I do not like it when patterns are broken. And I like it least of all toward the end of the game, when it is either in or out and no mending the fences once they break. Things can be shaky in the early stages. You aren't committed, nobody is committed, and you can all feel your way, and back and fill to make things right. But there is no backing or filling as you approach the wire. It has to be perfect, clean and sweet, and any deviations from the norm do not sit well with me.

'Sit down, Johnny.' I hadn't even realized I was pacing. I went on pacing. 'Sit down, damn it, you're making me nervous.' He stubbed out his cigarette. 'You know what's the matter with you?'

'What?'

'You're losing your goddamned nerve. A few years in San Quentin and you get shaky in the clinches. Johnny, you couldn't ask for a smoother job than this. Will you sit down and relax?'

I looked at my watch. 'No,' I said, 'I won't.'

'What are you doing?'

'Calling him,' I said.

I grabbed the phone and rang the Royal York. The desk man was a long time answering. I asked him if Mr Gunderman was in, not to bother him but to see if his key was there. He took his time and then told me no, the key was not in the box.

'Ring his room,' I said.

Doug told me I was crazy. I waved him off. The clerk plugged me in and let the phone ring. He let it ring a long time. Nobody answered that phone.

'Shall I check his room, sir?'

I looked down at my hand. The fingers were trembling slightly all by themselves. 'No, don't do that,' I said steadily. 'He must have left and taken his key with him. It's perfectly all right.'

The clerk didn't pursue the subject. I thanked him, and he rang off.

I said, 'No answer. He didn't leave and he doesn't answer. He always gets places on time and he's not here yet.'

'Johnny—'

'Come on, will you?'

'Where?'

'His hotel.'

He looked at me as if he was measuring me for a strait-jacket. 'He's on his way over here, Johnny,' he said levelly. 'Now calm down, will you? He took his key with him, the way you told it to the clerk, and in one minute he's going to walk through that door, and—'

I took him by the arm and yanked. 'You can wait until hell's six feet deep in snow,' I said. 'He's never coming through that door.'

'Johnny—'

'And we're going over there. And fast.'

'Johnny.' He drew himself up straight. He was trying not to look at all nervous, and he was almost making it. 'This is my set-up,' he said. 'I'm not letting you blow it.'

'It's blown to hell and back,' I told him. 'Move.'

Our cab seemed to crawl. The traffic was thick and the driver less than aggressive. We filled the back of the cab with cigarette smoke and the odor of coolish sweat. All the way there I had the very bad feeling that I had somehow dreamed this entire scene before. Sometime in the depth of sleep I had lived through this episode, and in the morning the memory was gone like smoke. Once I had dreamed this, and I should have remembered the dream. It would have made things much simpler.

When the cab stopped I threw a five at the driver and did not wait for change. On the way into the lobby I told Doug to follow me and not say anything or do anything spectacular. 'We are not stopping at the desk,' I told him. 'We are going straight to his room. I know where it is.'

He didn't answer. He had lost the sense of the play. He knew only that something was very wrong, and that I was probably out of my mind, and that it was easier to go along with me than to make me listen to reason. I got us to the elevator and rode one floor above his. I got us out of the elevator, and we went down the stairs to the right floor and along the corridor to his room.

Doug said, 'I don't get it.'

'You will.'

'He's probably at the office right now. Or he's sleeping; he got bombed last night and he's sleeping it off.'

'If he's at the office he can wait for us,' I said. 'If he's bombed, we'll apologize for interrupting him. We'll say we were worried about him, that we wanted to check.'

'I still say this is stupid.'

'You don't know what stupid is,' I said.

I knocked heavily on Gunderman's door. One thoroughly wishful corner of my mind expected him to lumber to the door and open it. I did not really expect this, and I was not at all surprised when it did not happen. I reached into my hip pocket and got out my wallet. I took out a gas company credit card.

'Johnny—'

'Shut up.'

The corridor was empty. I worked the credit card between the door and the jamb, and Doug nudged me, and I withdrew the card and waited for a man with an attaché case to emerge from a room down the hall and make his way past us to the elevators. When he was gone I wedged the credit card back where it belonged.

Hotel room locks are nothing at all, not in the fleabags, not in the good places either. I popped the bolt back and turned the knob and pushed the door open.

'If he's in there—'

If he was, he hadn't bolted the door. You can't snick back the inside bolt that way. You only get the one that spring-locks the door from the outside.

I pushed the door open. I went inside, and Doug came after me, and I remembered to shut the door after us. We went inside, and there was the bed and the chair and the dresser and some clothes scattered, and there was what I had somehow known we would find. Because I must have dreamed it all one night, dreamed it and forgotten it somewhere in the dark places of the night.

There was Gunderman, sprawled on the floor between the bed and the wall. He was in his pajamas, loud blue cotton pajamas. He had been shot twice at fairly close range. There were two holes in his chest, quite close together, and one of them must have placed itself in his heart because there was not much blood around. Almost all of it was on his pajamas, with just a little soaking into the rug.

Doug was making meaningless sounds beside me. I looked back stupidly to make sure that the door was closed. It was. I looked around the room. The gun was not too far from the body. I went over to all that was left of our pigeon and knelt down beside him. I touched the side of his face. His flesh was cool but not cold, and the bits of blood were drying but not yet dry. Someone with a better background than mine could have said with assurance just how long dead he was. It was out of my line. I never had all that much to do with dead men.

'Oh, Johnny—'

I walked over to where the gun lay. A good manly gun. Guns were not my line either, but I knew the make and model of this one. A .38 Smith and Wesson with a three-inch barrel and a safety on the grip. I knew it well.

'Don't touch it, Johnny.'

I picked up the gun.

'Brilliant,' he was saying. 'Oh, brilliant. Now you've got your prints all over the damned thing, Johnny.'

I knew better. They were already there. I'd put them there long ago in another town in another country. *Get me one of my cigarettes, John* – and that gun in her purse, waiting to be found, waiting to be gripped. She'd never touched it after that. She let me unload it and put it away myself. She never laid a finger on it – until later, alone, with gloves on, once to load it and once this morning to fire it, twice.

I looked down at that dead man and envied him.

16

'She killed him,' I said. I was a little shaky and my eyes weren't focusing properly. 'This . . . I put my prints on this gun a week ago. It was her gun, she conned me into picking it up and playing with it.'

'Where did you see her?'

'Olean. She—'

'You took a trip a week ago? You didn't tell me.'

'She was—' the words came slow, 'nervous, she said. She thought things were falling in. It turned out to be a false alarm, but in the middle of it she set me up to find the gun for her.'

'You never said a thing.' His tone was flat, hard.

'She didn't want me to.'

'She *what*?'

'I was hung on the girl,' I said.

'Give me that again.'

I turned on him. 'I was in love with the bitch,' I said, 'and I was taken. But how the hell did she get here? I talked to her last night. She called me last night, dammit, and she called long-distance. I don't get any of this.'

'Oh, Christ.'

'What?'

'I thought she was calling Gunderman.'

I grabbed his arm. 'Give me that again. From the beginning.'

It was his turn to look worried. 'She flew into town yesterday afternoon,' he said. 'So she would be here after the job was over.'

'After the job—'

'We were going to fly to Vegas. The two of us.' I did not say anything. 'Well, she's a good piece, damn it. She didn't want you to know because she said you tried and struck out.'

'I got the same line.'

'You're kidding.'

'The hell I am. What kind of a damn fool are you, flying her to Toronto? What's the brilliant point of that?'

'Johnny—'

'I talked to her last night. First an operator, person-to-person, and then—'

He was just shaking his head. 'I thought it was Gunderman, Johnny. Oh, Jesus. She said she wanted to call Gunderman and make it seem like a long-distance call. I sat right there in the room with her. I told her how to fake the operator's voice. She held a handkerchief over the phone and talked very distinctly and a little nasally with the phone about six inches from her mouth. And then took the handkerchief off and got close to the phone when she was playing Evvie again. Oh, she is cute.'

'Yeah.'

'And I sat there in the room and thought she was talking to him.'

She was very cute. I thought back to the conversation, trying to remember. 'She asked for me,' I said. 'By name. Were you in the room when she played the operator bit?'

'I must have been.'

'Then—'

'No, she wanted a drink. I went into the kitchen. I thought I heard – oh, damn it.'

I'd admired her timing before. The slipped kiss in front of his office building, the sweet way she had of playing things like a true-blooded professional. And I had thought she was only playing one side. She'd played all three of us, and played us off the wall.

She had never mentioned my name. And she had thrown me a conversation that she could as well have thrown to Gunderman. How she missed me, and how she hoped everything would go all right, and how she couldn't wait to see me again. I remembered now that she had sounded a little less hip than usual. No grifted argot. It wouldn't have done the necessary double duty. She never missed a trick.

'Johnny, if you had *said* something—'

'Me?'

'You said she didn't mean a thing to you. If I knew she did I would have seen her angle. You blew this one, Johnny.'

I forced myself to stay steady. 'You're a pretty one,' I said. 'You're so in love with yourself you can't see straight. You're so damned busy being the hottest puff of smoke since the Yellow Kid. You put this on the screw from the beginning.'

'How?'

'You balled her in Vegas, didn't you?'

He told me so with his eyes.

'You should have said it then. You should have let this thing play straight from the beginning, but you had to be goddamned cute about it. I'd like a chance at you, Rance.'

'Any time.'

I almost swung. I don't know what stopped me, but I almost swung, and that would have torn it for good. It's not a good idea to start a fight and draw a crowd, not when you've got a corpse on the floor and the murder gun carries your prints.

I looked at him and said, 'Later.'

'All right.'

'We've got to dig out from under.'

'Pick up the gun and leave.'

He was full of bright ideas. I told him how far we'd get. We were tied to Gunderman a hundred different ways. There were too many papers in his office with our names on them, too many connections. This had to be staged just as neatly as any blow-off operation. We were blowing off a dead man instead of a live one. That was the only difference. It took just as sure a touch, just as firm a sense of the game.

It took two cigarettes. Then I had it. I said, 'There's a way. You'll need a suitcase. And a wallet with fake identification.'

'I've got both at the apartment.'

'Good. You leave the hotel now. Go out a back entrance, grab a cab, go to your place.' I went over to the window. 'I hope your fake ID sets you up in some far-away place.'

'I've got papers for California. Los Angeles, I think.'

'Good. Throw a few things in a suitcase. California labels, nothing else. You're close enough to his size to do it. Then get in another cab and come back to the hotel. Go to the desk and check in under the phony name. Get a room as close to this one as you can. The same side of the building. Tell them you want to face whatever the hell that street is out there. One floor away is fine. One floor away is better than the same floor, actually. You with me?'

'I guess so.'

'Check in, go to your room, and then get back here. I'll have it set up. We've got a few things going for us. He checked in yesterday afternoon. The kid on the desk now never saw him, not yesterday afternoon and not last night. We've just about got time. Move.'

'Johnny?'

'What?'

'I can't figure the cross. He had the money with him. It might still be around—'

'It won't be. She took it.'

'Even so. She gets seventy thou instead of seventeen-five. She doesn't figure to kill for the difference, does she?'

'I'll tell you later,' I said.

When he left I shut the door and bolted it after him. I did not want any hyperefficient maid stumbling in on me. Then I walked into the john and washed my hands and dried them on a towel and went back to get things in motion. I found his suitcase on the floor of the closet. I packed his clothes in it. I went through the dresser and the pockets of his clothes and picked off everything that gave a clue as to who he was and where he came from. All of this went into the suitcase. I got his money belt – you don't see them much any more, but he'd had one and she would have known about it. I wasn't surprised to find it empty.

There was a cashier's check in his wallet, drawn to the order of the Barnstable Corporation and made out in the amount of forty thousand dollars. I tucked this in my own wallet, then thought a moment and switched his wallet for my own. If I was going to be him I might as well do it right.

When I first started to move him, I thought I might be sick. I got past the first rush of nausea and then things settled down. He wasn't a corpse, he was just a dead weight. I dragged him a few feet away and checked the carpet where he had lain.

It wasn't bad. Not too much blood, really, and the carpet was nylon and not especially absorbent. I wetted some toilet paper and wiped it so that it looked clean. Spectroscopic analysis would show blood for weeks, but if things broke right nobody would come looking, and if things went wrong they wouldn't need bloodstains to hang us.

I tried to keep busy that way. As long as I was doing things, moving and staying active, I didn't have to think so hard about things that were better unexamined. Like the sweet way she'd set it up. Like the reason she worked the cross.

She hadn't killed him for the simple arithmetical difference between seventeen and seventy thousand dollars. She had killed him for the whole bundle. She wanted everything, everything that belonged to Wallace J. Gunderman.

She'd get it, too. Because the bitch had married him.

I lit a cigarette. He'd as much as told me the night before, and I had been too damned stupid to pick it up then and there. All of that coyness – I'd taken it for granted he was acting that way because he thought I was hung on Evvie while he was actually keeping her and using her to keep me on his team. But the words he'd used made more sense now. He had *married* her.

It made more sense that way.

And other parts made sense. The attitude he'd shown all those times pointed out one thing – since his wife died, he had been the one pushing for marriage and she had been busy putting him off. It added up a million times as sensibly that way. She had waited, and she had finally gone and married him just in time to be his widow.

What was he worth? A few million? And to that you could tack on a whole load of extras, like the hate she had for him and the kick she must have felt when the gun went off. It all tallied out to a lot more than the seventeen and a half thousand dollars that she was supposed to get out of the deal. It added up to many miles more than a roadhouse in Colorado and a broken-down grifter for a husband and 'Hearts and Flowers' for a theme song.

We were supposed to get stuck with it. We'd be tied up tight, and she could keep herself in the clear. She had never put anything on paper. We could never drag her into it. We could only tighten the noose around our own necks.

I lit another cigarette and wished to hell Doug would get back. We had a chance, I thought. Getting to his hotel room on time had opened it up for us. And Doug was about his build – that helped. And the timing with the hotel clerks. We did not exactly have the odds on our side, and if we had held those cards in a poker game I would have thrown our hand in and folded. But you can't ever fold when your whole damned life's in the pot. You have to play whatever's dealt.

He knocked on the door and said, 'Doug here,' his voice pitched low and tense. I opened the door. He was wearing a hat and he had a cigar in his mouth. He came inside and drew the door shut.

'He's going to be me,' he said. 'Right?'

'That's the idea.'

'That's why the cigar and the hat, and why I acted middle-aged for the clerk. Gunderman does smoke cigars, doesn't he?'

'Not any more.'

'I guess not. The money was gone?'

'All but the check. That was there. To lead them to us fast, I suppose.'

He shook his head. 'I'd love to kill that girl.'

'You'd have to stand in line. Where's your room?'

It was one flight downstairs. That made it a little easier. We slipped Gunderman out of his pajamas and put a suit of Doug's on him – dressing a dead man is every bit as unpleasant as it sounds. The shoes and socks were the hardest part. When we were done with him he wouldn't have stood inspection, but then he probably wouldn't have to. The hotel was fairly empty at that hour, and most people don't pay any particular attention to things that don't involve them.

At least that's what we told ourselves. It's not easy to work yourself up to the point where you can cart a corpse around a hotel without losing your air of nonchalance.

Doug checked the corridor. We waited until it was empty, at least on our floor. Then we hoisted him up and each of us draped one of his dead arms over our shoulders. He was supposed to look drunk, or sick, or something, and we were his good friends helping poor Clyde back to his room. This was the script. It wouldn't win Oscars, but it had to do the job.

He was very damned heavy, even with the load shared between us. We got him out into the hallway. I kicked the door shut, and we headed for the stairs. As we got there I heard an elevator coming. We ducked into the stairwell just as the door opened on our floor. Whoever got off, we weren't spotted.

The stairs were easy. We got down them in a hurry, and I stood at the landing with Gunderman draped all over me while Doug checked the traffic on the floor. There was a maid en route, her can of clean linen blocking our way. We waited for her, and she took her time, until finally she busied herself in one of the bathrooms. She couldn't see the hallway from there. Doug grabbed hold of Gunderman and we took him for another walk. We couldn't rush, because the whole scene had to look natural if anyone happened to glance our way.

No one did. We made it to the room and closed the damned door and eased our plucked pigeon down onto the floor. I wanted a cigarette. Instead I lit one of Gunderman's cigars, and so did Doug. We put another one in the pocket of Doug's suit.

The rest was frosting. We unpacked Doug's suitcase and put his clothes away in the dresser and in the closet. With the end of my cigar, I burned a pair of holes in Gunderman's shirt right above the bullet holes. They did not look exactly like .38-caliber powder burns but they were close enough for the time being.

We planted the fake wallet in his pocket, tossed Doug's hat on his dresser, dropped our cigar butts in the ashtrays. Then for a finale, we tucked Gunderman in the closet and closed the door on him.

If the bitch had only shot him once, we could have staged it as suicide. But nobody shoots himself twice in the chest. It was as well to make it a murder and let them figure out why and by whom. We left him in the closet and went back to Gunderman's room.

'Don't get noticed on the way out,' I said.

'Right.'

'I'll catch you at the office.'

'Right.'

I gave him a few minutes. Then I hefted a bag with W.J.G. properly embossed upon it, lifted the phone, told the desk to get my bill ready. They said they would. I gave the room a last check, left it, went to the elevator and rode down to the lobby. I should have been nervous. I wasn't, for some odd reason. Everything was crystal clear now. All I had to do was go by the book. I was Wallace J. Gunderman, and I was checking out of their hotel, and once I was gone they could put me out of their minds forever. They would never fasten my name onto the dead thing a floor away.

I gave the room key to the clerk. He looked up at me brightly. 'You had a call about an hour ago, Mr Gunderman—'

'I know, I was in the shower. Any message?'

'No, he didn't leave his name.'

'Well, I think I know who it was. No problem.'

He had my bill ready. While I checked it over he asked me if I had enjoyed my stay. I said I had. With phone calls and room service the tab came to a little short of twenty bucks. I put Gunderman's Diners Club card on the counter, then snatched it back just as the clerk was reaching for it. I wanted to flash it but I didn't want to risk a phony signature on the hotel books.

'Let me pay cash,' I said. 'I don't want to mix them up with charges in Canadian funds.'

He couldn't argue with logic like that. I gave him a twenty, and he gave me change and stamped my bill and handed it to me. I stuck it to Gunderman's wallet and stuck the wallet in my pocket and picked up my suitcase and headed for the door.

Nobody stopped me.

17

Doug had a few things to do. He had to clear out his apartment, and he had to turn the Barnstable offices into a ghost town. We were on too many official records and we had scattered too much correspondence to strike our sets completely, but Doug could wipe out some of the more obvious traces. This is easy when you have all the time in the world. We had to move fast, and we had to do what we could.

But that was a minor headache. The important thing was something else again. We had two definite facts to contend with – there was a dead man in a closet in the Royal York, and there was a man named Wallace J. Gunderman who had disappeared. If anybody matched the name and the body, then we were in trouble. The longer it took them to put the two together, the better off we were. We had given the body a name and a logical way of dying. Now we had to take the Gunderman identity and find a way to let it trail off and dissolve like smoke.

He had return reservations to Olean for the late afternoon. I called the airport and changed his reservations, asking them for the first plane to Chicago. They had a flight at three-fifteen. I booked a seat on the plane in Gunderman's name.

Doug was waiting for me at the office. He had called Helen Wyatt to tell her that things had gone sour, and that she should let the other hired hands know as much. They didn't stand any chance of getting involved – Gunderman alone had seen them, and he wasn't going to tell anyone – and by the same token they weren't likely to involve us. It was a courtesy call. When the ship sinks, a good captain at least lets the crew know about it.

'I'm packed and ready,' he said. 'Got any cash?'

'A couple of hundred. You?'

'A little more. And there's a little over twelve thou in the bank, the Barnstable account. If we can get it.'

'No problem there. A day or two from now it might be tight, but nobody's going to put a freeze on our account for the time being.'

He whistled soundlessly. 'We can't get rich this way. Anyway, it's a stake. I'm out a few thou but not as much as I expected.'

'You're forgetting something.'

'What?'

'Terry Moscato.'

His face fell. 'That's ten grand.'

'Plus interest Eleven thousand. That leaves us with cabfare.'

'We can't pay him.'

'We damn well have to. You don't cross the man who bankrolls you. That's one thing you don't do. You can lie to your partner—'

'I'm not the only one, Johnny.'

'All right. Put a lid on it. You don't stiff Moscato, not because it's a case of honor among thieves but because you'd wind up dead. I mean it. He's the easiest man to work with as long as you're good, but if you play him bad you've had it. He is hard.'

'Eleven thousand dollars.'

'We've got twelve or so in the bank. And I'm holding Gunderman's check for forty more.'

He'd forgotten about it. This was easy to do. We'd been crossed and skinned and sliced up for bait, and it was hard to regard that cashier's check as anything more than a prop she'd left for the police to play with. Besides, it was a dead man's check. A dead man's check is not negotiable. It's evidence of a receivable asset, and you can hold it as a claim against the estate of the deceased, but you cannot scrawl your name across the back of it and pass it to a friendly neighborhood teller. It's locked up tight. Our check was signed by Gunderman, and he was as dead as you can get.

'But nobody knows this,' I said. 'It's going to be a long time before they know he's dead. We can get rid of the paper long before then.'

'Discount it and sell it?'

'I think it's easier to cash it. Just shove it the hell through the Barnstable account.'

'And when that check works its way back to his bank?'

'That's days from now. And who's going to look at it, anyway?' I crushed a cigarette in the ashtray. 'There's a big unknown here. I'm not sure how she's going to play it. Right now she's sure we're going to get picked up for this one by nightfall. She left a deep wide trail and it leads straight to us and she'll be expecting a call sometime this evening telling her that her husband is dead.'

'That's the part I can't believe.'

'That he married her?'

'Yeah.'

I made him believe it. Then I carried it further. She'd be waiting for that call, and by early evening she'd be starting to sweat. Cool or not, the act of killing was going to get to her sooner or later. And when she had time to think about it, she couldn't miss seeing that it would be tough for her to keep her fingers clean once they picked us up and we talked.

Because we would have to talk, and we would have to sing out her name loud and clear. We might not be able to prove it. If we did, we were still up to our ears in it; as parties to the con game felony we were legally parties to the murder, like it or not. So we were in trouble, but she was going to have some of it rub off on her. She might not do a bit for murder, might not serve any time at all, but she would have it much easier if we escaped free and clear, and she couldn't help figuring that out in time.

All of this left her a handy out. She could sit on her hands for awhile, saying that Gunderman had gone off on a business trip and she didn't know when he would be back. Finally she could report him missing, but by this time she could have all the Barnstable correspondence cleared from his files. If our cashier's check cleared his bank, she could head it off and get rid of it.

They might make the murder connection after awhile, but we'd be light years away by then and she wouldn't steer them toward us. They might not pin the Gunderman label on the Royal York corpse at all. We were trailing Gunderman to Chicago and losing him there. And good hotels don't publicize men who get murdered on the premises. It's bad for business. The Royal York would keep the newspaper publicity to a minimum on their dead man. Gunderman might wind up permanently missing. Evvie would have enough control of his money to live it up for the seven years it would take to declare him legally dead. Then she could take the whole bundle.

She might not like it that way, but she could drift into the pattern very easily. As the wife of a missing man, she could live as lush a life as ever. She didn't have to stay in Olean. And once the seven years played themselves out she was home free.

The bitch didn't have it so bad. She'd spend seven years waiting for an Enoch Arden decree, and they'd go a lot faster and pass a lot more pleasantly than the seven years I had done in Q. When they ran out, she'd pick up the pot of gold. All I'd landed was a brass check and a night-man slot at a bowling alley.

When I ran out of words we stood there smoking and listening to the silence. He broke it first. 'We can come out clean,' he said, and his voice turned it into a prayer.

'Maybe. And probably not. If I had to lay odds I'd guess that they'll tag us for murder inside of a month and spend three months trying to find us before they write us off. Our prints are on file, but that doesn't matter if we never get mugged and printed. We'll be across a national border. We'll have different names and different haircuts. I think we ought to make it, but we won't come up smelling of roses.'

He thought it over. I thought about that warm woman and how well I'd been had. I had never felt so much like a mooch. The depths of her eyes, the little sounds of liquid desperation she made in bed. It was hard to believe that all of these things could have been counterfeit.

Forget it. It was every mark's story, in technicolor on a wide wide screen with a cast of thousands. *He was such a nice man, Mommy. I can't believe such a nice man would steal my candy. He seemed so sincere, Mommy—*

Forget it.

I went to our bank and deposited Gunderman's check to our account. I let the same teller handle a withdrawal for me, and I took an even twenty thousand dollars in cash. This didn't throw her. The cashier's check was as good as gold, and I could have tried to get the full amount in cash if I had wanted to. I didn't. I took the twenty thou from the one girl, and I had another girl certify a check for thirty-one thousand dollars payable to P. T. Parker in U.S. funds. I went to my other bank where I had the Parker account, deposited this check and bought five bank drafts payable to cash for varying amounts ranging from five to ten thousand dollars each.

In a third bank, I used the Canadian cash to buy a few more bank drafts and a handful of traveler's cheques. I held out eleven thousand in U.S. dollars. In the main post office, I packed away the bank drafts in individual envelopes and mailed them off. I shipped a few of them to Robert W. Pattison at the Hotel Mark Twain in Omaha. I scattered the rest around the Midwest, mostly in Kansas and Iowa, sending them to various names at various general delivery offices. I mailed a little less than half of them from the Toronto Post Office and kept the rest aside.

There was just enough time for a telephone call before my plane was ready to go. It took a few tries to reach Terry Moscato. I finally got him.

I said, 'I think you know me. Can you talk now?'

'I know you, and I can talk, but no names or details. Go ahead.'

'It's done. It went to hell, but it's done. I have the goods you want and I'd like to deliver.'

'I'd be glad to have you make delivery. Are you sure you've got the right size?'

'Size eleven,' I said.

'That's fine. Can you come to town for delivery?'

'Not very easily.'

'If I arranged a pick-up,' he said carefully, 'there would be an additional handling charge.'

I didn't want him to send a boy, handling charge or no. 'I was thinking about the mails,' I said.

'I don't like that.'

'Not from this port. A standard interstate shipment, registered and insured.'

The line was silent while he thought this over. There is nothing safer than registered and insured mail. But he still didn't like it.

'Railway Express,' he said.

'Seriously?'

'Definitely. The same drop.' And he rang off. I wondered what he had against the mails.

They were already calling my flight when I remembered two things. The gun and the money. I had the murder gun and a pair of bloody pajamas in my suitcase, and I had eleven thousand dollars of Moscato's money keeping them company.

On an ordinary flight this wouldn't have mattered. It's against some silly law to carry a gun on a plane, but no one normally paws through your baggage or frisks you as you enter the plane. This was not an entirely normal flight. This was a flight from one country to another, and that meant going through Customs.

You lose sight of this when the two countries are the States and Canada. Customs inspections are cursory at best – every fifth car going over a bridge, a quick peek in suitcases on a plane ride. If your contraband is something as innocuous as a fifth of undeclared Scotch, you don't break out in a rash worrying about getting tagged. When you're packing eleven thousand dollars that you can't explain along with a gun that's just been used in a murder, it gets a little sticky.

There was no place to stash the gun, no handy way to conceal the dough. I ducked into the men's room and got the suitcase open. I ripped the pajamas apart, flushed the singed and bloody pieces down the toilet along with the Olean label and tucked the rest in the trashcan. I parceled up the stack of hundred-dollar bills. There were a hundred and ten of them, and by balancing them off in various pockets and lodging a healthy sheaf of them in my wallet, I managed to spread them over my person without bulging anywhere.

That left the gun. And I didn't dare dump it anywhere in Canada, because a ballistics check would tie it to the dead man in the closet, and this would not be good at all. I couldn't know where she bought the gun. It might have come out of Olean originally, and that was the sort of link I did not want to supply. Ideally the gun would be broken down and spread out over a score of sewer systems. In a pinch it would be wiped free of prints inside and out and dropped into a river a thousand miles away from Toronto. But it couldn't stay in the city, and it couldn't ride on my person, and it could not nestle in my suitcase.

They called the flight again. I couldn't miss it or they would start paging Wallace J. Gunderman over the P.A. system. This was not precisely what I had in mind. The Customs inspection wouldn't come now, at least. It would come when we got to O'Hare. I could sneak the gun onto the plane. But I couldn't take it off or leave it behind.

Beautiful. I wedged it into a pocket. It looked as inconspicuous as an albino in Harlem. I grabbed my suitcase and ran for the plane.

The plane was mostly full. I had an aisle seat just forward of the wing. My seat partner was a youngish woman with a sharp nose and acne scars. She read a Canadian magazine and ignored me entirely. I fastened my belt and put out my cigarette and told the stewardess that I did not want a magazine, and we left the ground and aimed at Chicago.

The .38 was burning a hole in my pocket. Literally. There were any number of ways to get rid of it and none of them looked especially attractive. I could stow it under a seat, set it on top of the luggage rack, even make a stab at dumping it into somebody's suitcase. Whatever I did, it was an odds-on bet that the gun would turn up within an hour after landing, and probably before then. I took a hike to the john, and that was no help at all. Just the bare essentials. No handy hiding place for a hunk of steel that was hotter than . . . well, hotter than a pistol.

I tried to think it through and couldn't get anywhere. I kept coming back to the job itself, how smoothly it had gone, how thoroughly it had gone to hell for itself. I was a long time hating a girl named Evelyn Stone. I thought about a hundred different ways to make her dead and couldn't find one mean enough for her. She had conned me as utterly as a man can be conned. She had not merely made me trust her. She had made me love her, and then she stuck it in and broke it off deep.

A funny thing. I wanted badly to hate her, but I kept losing my grip and easing up on all of that hate. I couldn't hold onto it. She had not betrayed any love because she had faked and manipulated that crock of love from the beginning. Ever since she first latched onto Doug in Vegas, long before she ever set eyes on me, I was her pigeon. She never owed me a thing. If I had seen her within the first couple of hours after we found Gunderman's body, I probably would have killed her. The rage was fresh then. Time took the edge off it in a hurry. I couldn't even summon up any really strong craving for revenge. I might never be a charter member of her fan club, but the real gutbucket hate was gone.

Evelyn Stone had played our little game according to the rules; it was only sad that she and I had been on opposite sides, and that I had not known this. But there was one person who had broken the rules. Right at the start he forgot the one cardinal injunction. Never, under any circumstances, do you play fast and loose with your partner.

Doug crossed me from the opening whistle. He must have known all along that I had a weakness for women, an irritating habit of going overboard for them. So he didn't bother telling me that he'd pushed Evvie over on her round little heels. That set everything in motion. Once he established the pattern, she played us off so neatly that we never felt the strings. He had not meant to mess me up. It was just the way he chose to run his show. It had to be his show all the way – his ego wouldn't let go of it – and that made him improvise, keeping part of the picture hidden, keeping me just far enough in the dark so that things had a chance to go to hell for themselves.

You don't do that to your partner. That's the one thing you don't do, and he'd done it and set Evvie up so that I wound up doing the same thing. And if I didn't hate her any more, that didn't mean I was in love with the whole world and at peace with mankind. Not at all.

The sharp-nosed girl beside me stirred in her seat. Down the aisle, the stewardess began serving the meal, the usual airline fare, as sterile and tasteless as the stewardess herself. I broke off my woolgathering and thought about the gun.

There's always a way. I let the girl serve me my dinner. I ate about half of it and drank a cup of lukewarm coffee. When she took my tray away, my knife wasn't on it. It was on my lap.

I reached down between my knees and worked on the front edge of my seat with the knife. It was a steak knife, sharp enough on the edge of the blade but not too keen at the tip, and this made it slow going. Once I broke through the vinyl it got easier. I had to keep stopping; the stewardess was walking back and forth, as busy as a speakeasy on Election Day, and my seatmate had turned restless and was given to looking my way. But before too long I had a good hiding place arranged, with the slit just wide enough to admit the gun but small enough to retain it and to pass unnoticed for a good long time.

I couldn't think of a clever way to pull the gun out of my hip pocket without attracting attention. Finally I went to the john again and came out with the gun wrapped in a paper towel. I sat down again, and when the opportunity came I slipped the gun out of its paper envelope and wedged it into the seat. Someday someone would find it there and wonder how in hell it got there. But they would have no idea what passenger on what flight put it there, and by then it wouldn't matter any more.

We landed five minutes ahead of schedule at O'Hare. The Customs man asked me if I had anything to declare, and I said I hadn't. He asked me how long I had been in Canada. I told him something. He opened my suitcase but didn't do more than glance in it before passing me on. I could have had three pounds of heroin and an M-1 rifle in there and he never would have noticed it.

I stayed at the terminal long enough to practice Gunderman's signature, copying it from his driver's license and a few other cards in his wallet. I'm fair but not perfect with a pen. I would never fool an expert, but I might not have to. I would sign his name once, on the hotel registration card, and that would be all. If I could come fairly close, that would probably be good enough.

I cabbed to the Palmer House. They had a single available and I took it. I signed in, did a fair job with the signature, and went to my room. I had a couple of things to do in Chicago and more than enough time to do them.

I packed eleven thousand dollars in a cigar box and packaged it with tender loving care. At the Railway Express office, I shipped it to Terry Moscato's address and insured it, appropriately enough, for eleven thousand dollars. I told the clerk the parcel contained jewelry. He could not have cared less.

On the way back I called the Palmer House and asked for myself. They rang my room and told me that I wasn't there. I thanked them. I went to the hotel and the clerk told me there had been a call for me, and gave me the message I had left. I thanked him and went to the room to pick up the envelopes from the suitcase, a handful of bank drafts to be mailed to different places. I bought stamps from a machine in the lobby and mailed them. I went to a movie house on South Dearborn and sat through most of a double feature. I had dinner across the street from the theater and decided to use Gunderman's credit card and sign his name a second time. I did an even better job with the signature this time around.

The rest was just putting in time. I hit a couple of bars and sorted things out in my mind. By now Doug was probably in Omaha, waiting for me. I'd get there in time to help him pick up the bank drafts that I was scattering all over the Midwest. I tried to figure out just how much cash I was going to realize on the deal. We'd wind up holding something like forty thou, give or take a little, and Doug would draw ten off the top, the original working capital that he'd contributed. The rest would get cut up straight down the middle. No matter how you counted, that made my end in the neighborhood of fifteen grand.

I had another beer and thought about it. It wasn't all that bad. Getting anything at all was a fluke – hell, beating the murder rap was a fluke, as far as that went.

Fifteen thousand dollars. It was possible. Bannion could give a certain amount of ground; if I played him right, I could get his place for less than I'd figured, and if I couldn't find the right pitch to hand that old lush I might as well call it a day. If I arranged the right sort of financing and played it close to the vest for the first two or three years, I just might manage to handle the deal after all. It would be close, but it might work.

Ideally, I should have more money to play with. But dreams rarely come true, and never materialize without losing a certain amount of their glow. The original dream sparkled like diamonds – plenty of money and a girl to make it all worthwhile. If I could just squeeze by I was still coming out with a rosy smell.

I called the hotel again and found another bar to play in. It turned out to be a long night. Somewhere toward the tail end of it I spent enough time in a joint on North Clark to pick up a semi-pro hooker with oversized breasts and too much makeup. We went to her place and made a brave try, but I couldn't do anything. This didn't come as much of a surprise. I may have stopped hating her, but I hadn't yet lost the taste of her. That would take awhile.

18

I don't know whether they can handle jets at Omaha or not. The plane I took was a prop job, an old DC-7. It got me there fast enough. I'd stayed two nights and a day at the Palmer House before making reservations from Chicago to Buffalo in Gunderman's name. He'd never make that flight, but it could let them think he'd headed back toward Olean, or planned on it, before something went haywire. If they traced it that far. It was mostly just a question of going through the motions, setting up a few false trails partly for insurance and partly for practice. I'd made the reservation, and then I went out to O'Hare and caught a plane, not for Buffalo but for Omaha. I left his suitcase and his clothes in the room. I took the wallet with me, because men do not leave their wallets in their hotel rooms. In the can at O'Hare I burned up what cards and papers he had that would burn, dropped them in the bowl and flushed them away. The wallet was anonymous enough to go in the wastebasket. The various credit cards would neither burn nor flush nor disappear. I bought a small packet of razor blades at the newsstand and used one of them to slice the cards into strips. I threw the strips away and threw the blades away and waited for my plane. I had a few things in a canvas flight bag. The rest of my clothes were in Omaha. I was anxious to get to them. Gunderman's clothes did not fit me, and I'd been wearing one change of clothing for too many days.

The airport was thick with police. A day ago they'd have bothered me. Now I hardly noticed them.

The tension was wearing away. A couple of days ago we had been inches from the pot of gold at the rainbow's end, and my skin had been too tight over my bones and sweat came freely. Then in a few fast minutes the gold faded out and there was nothing but a noose at the end of that rainbow. It got very tight for awhile. I stopped remembering the seven years in Q and started seeing ropes and gas pellets and electrodes attached to the shaved spots on the head. I wondered how they did it in Ontario. Different states have different ways. In Utah you can stand in front of a firing squad, if you want. And wave away the blindfold and look them in their eyes—

The best way to relax a muscle is to tighten it all the way and squeeze as hard as you can and then let it unwind completely. This, essentially, is what happened. By the time I'd cleared the cashier's check through our account I was functioning like a machine, gears meshing precisely, bearings oiled and motor in tune. By the time I was playing Hide-the-Gun on the plane for Chicago I was too preoccupied with doing things properly to worry about what might happen if I blew it. And with Chicago behind me and Omaha coming up I could think about meeting Doug and collecting the bank drafts and cashing them, and how much money we would have and what my end would be and whether or not it would be enough. I could think about these things because I knew we were clear. They were not going to tag us for this one.

Which led right into the part that was there all along, hard to see but never hidden. We were making out on this little deal. Everything had gone wrong, the whole bundle had been snatched away when we were already so close to it that we'd mentally spent it twice over. Even so, we were making out. I was fifteen thousand dollars to the good no matter how you added it up. All of that in a couple of months. Three, four years of the salary they paid me at the Boulder Bowl.

So you figure it. I'd missed the girl and I'd missed more than half of the money. The girl wouldn't bother me long. I love them fast and hard with all the dreamer's desperation, but once they're gone I don't carry their ghosts around. I'd missed the girl and half of the score, but fifteen thou was fifteen thou regardless.

There was a room waiting for me at the Mark Twain. My name was Robert W. Pattison, and they had some letters for me at the desk. I took them upstairs with me. They were one of the batches of bank drafts, all there and all in order, plus a note from Doug telling me where I could find him. He'd left my suitcase with the manager, and I called the desk and asked about it. They apologized and sent a kid upstairs with it and he went back downstairs half a dollar richer. I spent a long time under the shower tap, shaved close and clean, and put on fresh clothes. I picked the one suit I liked, a gray sharkskin with a double vent and patch pockets and just one button in the front. A suit John Hayden never wore in Olean.

I called Doug. He said he'd come around for me.

'I bought a car across the line in Kansas,' he said. 'I had to take a test and get a license and everything all over again. I thought it would come in handy.'

'The car or the license?'

'Both of them.'

I waited out front for him. The car was a Pontiac, two years old, long and low, a very dark green. It was the kind of car a very square businessman buys when he's feeling a little racy. I got in it and he drove while I talked. He seemed to know the city fairly well. It's bigger than it looks. He drove all over it while I talked.

He said, 'You come out of this pretty good, don't you?'

'Do I?'

'Fifteen grand, isn't it? You didn't have a pot or a window a few months ago. Setting pins for a dime a line in Nothing, Colorado.'

'Boulder,' I said. 'I didn't set pins. We had AMF automatic pin-spotters. I was the night man.'

'Uh-huh.'

'So you can just come out and say it, fellow.'

He turned to face me and almost sideswiped a parked Ford. He cursed and I said something about him being lucky to pass the Kansas road test. You could feel it building up inside the car, like steam in a teakettle before it starts to whistle.

'I got a big hate on, Johnny.'

'You've got company.'

'You come off pretty. You can buy that craphouse in the mountains. Your end comes close enough to covering it. You were figuring loose and you know it. You come out fine.'

'You've got the same fifteen I've got,' I said easily. 'On top of all you had to start with.'

'But we missed the score, Johnny. And had to sweat at the end.'

'Sweat never hurt.'

'You let it go sour, Johnny.'

'It started out sour. You crapped in the milk the first day out and now you wonder why it curdled. You got company with that hate, brother.'

'Any time at all, Johnny.'

'The money first.'

It took us a couple of days. I had spread those bank drafts over four states, and we had to drive around and pick them up. It was nothing but mechanical but it had to be done. There was no rush to cash them. They were good any time, and in any place, and they had all been bought with cash. You could trace them to Canada, but you could not trace them to Parker or Whittlief or Rance or Hayden or Barnstable or Gunderman. They were all of them as good as government paper.

We drove around getting them from the post offices and hotels where I had sent them. We did not talk much. At night we took separate motel rooms and drank ourselves to sleep out of separate bottles. When we did talk, we generally got on each other's nerves. I was itching for him and he for me, but it had to wait and we were both of us good at waiting.

Then early one afternoon we picked up the last draft at a post office in a very little Iowa town. He asked me if that was the last one, and I told him it was. He stopped the car and we sliced the pie. We had cashed one of the drafts so that we could even things out properly. He took his expense money out, and the rest divided up into two even piles. My end was a little better than the estimated fifteen. About eight hundred better, plus assorted nickels and dimes.

And he said, 'I'm ready when you are, Johnny.'

'Now's a good time'

There was a motel coming up on the right. He nodded toward it. 'Right here?'

'Cabins would be better.'

'Uh-huh.'

Three miles down the road there was one big shack and eighteen smaller ones. A sign advertised cabins for rent, three dollars for a double. There was one car in front of the office, another parked beside one of the cabins. Evidently they got the motel's overflow and the hot pillow trade and nothing more. Doug pulled off the road and I went into the office and rang for the manager.

He had the too-blue eyes of the alcoholic with a complementary sunburst of broken blood vessels at the bridge of his nose. I told him I wanted a cabin, the farthest one up on the north. He nodded and licked his thin lips.

I gave him three bucks. 'We won't want to be disturbed,' I said. 'You hear any party noises from our cabin, anything at all, you just forget you heard a thing.'

He winked at me. I let him dream his own dreams. Maybe he thought I had a fourteen year old girl in the car, maybe he figured I planned a spirited afternoon of rape. He did not mind.

I left the office and went back to the car. We drove over to the far cabin and parked. I opened the cabin door while Doug locked the car up tight. I flicked a light on. The cabin was stale and cheap. There was a bed, a bureau, and a chair. No rug on the floor. The mirror on the wall had a crack in it. I thought of a man or a woman waking up in a room like that one with a taste of whiskey and stale sex for morning company. A person could commit suicide in a cabin like that one.

Doug came in, closed the door, bolted it. 'Whenever you're ready,' he said, and I hit him in the face.

The punch didn't do much. He was backing up when I threw it and my fist glanced off the side of his face. He missed with a left and threw a right hand into my chest over the heart. I suddenly could not breathe. I ducked away from him and got hit a few times. I got my breath back, ducked under a punch and hit him in the pit of the stomach, hard. He doubled up and almost fell.

I went for him and kept missing. He spun away and ducked and dodged while I threw everything but the bed at him. He said, 'Old man, I'm going to take you apart.' I hit him again and he bounced back off a wall. I moved in low and he chopped me in the side of the head. A slew of colors danced inside my head. I felt myself slipping forward, put my hands out in front of me, caught his knee with the point of my chin. I snapped straight up and started over backward.

Everything was trying like hell to turn black. I wouldn't let go. He was standing over me, and I threw myself at his legs and held on. He tried to kick his way loose but didn't make it, and I got squared away and hauled his feet out from under him. He landed on top of me and threw a barrage of punches that bounced off my shoulders. I spun him around and tried to hit him but my arms wouldn't move all that well. I got up. He came up after me and shoved and I went over on to the bed. I kicked him coming in. The kick didn't have much power in it, but it caught him fairly square between the legs and put him on the floor again.

'You son of a bitch,' he said.

He got up from the floor and I hauled myself off the bed and we stood in the middle of the room hitting each other. Neither of us had the energy to be cute. We had stopped dodging punches. We just kept hitting each other. I don't know if he felt the punches. I know I didn't, not any more. I just stood there taking it and trying to beat the son of a bitch to the ground. I hit him and he hit me and I hit him and he hit me, over and over, just like that. We had screwed each other up but good, and we felt a clean uncomplicated hate for each other.

A heavy could have taken either of us. We were not strong-arm types. We were grifters, and grifters are rarely much help in a back-street brawl. He had some years on me, and maybe a couple of pounds, but we still wound up close to even.

Once his arms dropped and his eyes glazed over, and he stood there taking it while I hit him. He took a lot of punches before he went down. I stood over him, waiting, and he got up shaking his head and I swung and missed and he hit me square in the gut.

A little later he put another blow over the heart and I felt the way men must feel when they have a coronary. Everything froze, time and space, and I hung there breathless until he hit me in the face and put me down on the floor. I had trouble getting up. He asked me if I had had enough, and I pushed myself up and swung at him and missed, and he hit him again and I went down again. He didn't say anything this time. I got up and hit him, and hit him again, and we were back in the swing of things.

All of this seemed to go on forever. I spent more time on the floor than he did, but not too much more. It got so that it took less out of me to get hit than to lift an arm and throw a punch. We were both of us too arm-weary to do a hell of a lot of damage. And it ended finally with me tumbling back against a wall and holding onto it and sliding down it toward the floor while he sagged backward and sat down on the bed and then lay backward, half on the bed and half on the floor. Neither one of us moved after that, not for a long time.

There was no john in the cabin, just a sink. He washed up, went out to the car to get us some fresh clothes. We took our time cleaning up and changing. We were both of us pretty bloody. He had a split lip, a few cuts on his face, swellings under both eyes. I wasn't cut up quite that much but I had managed to lose one tooth somewhere along the line and my jaw was in fairly sad shape.

Doug was the first to talk. He was looking in the mirror, and he shook his head and said, 'Beautiful.'

'We're both pretty.'

'You can sure as hell take a few punches, Johnny.'

'I should have been a boxer.'

'Yeah. Both of us. I can't find my cigarettes.'

I dug out a pair of mine and gave him one. We chucked our dirty clothes in the corner and went out to the car. He headed north, drove slowly.

'It was a good idea, stopping here,' he said after awhile. 'I was aching for a crack at you ever since Toronto.'

'Well, we worked it out.'

'We did at that,' he said.

I smoked my cigarette all the way down and flipped the butt out the window. I asked him what he figured on doing next.

'I suppose I'll head for Vegas,' he said.

'To give the money back across the tables?'

'Part of it. Or I'll beat them for a change. I like it out there. Get some sun, lie around the pool, get a little drunk, rest up while I figure out how to connect for the next one.'

'Sure.'

'I guess I'll drive. I lucked out on the car, bought the first one off the lot and it doesn't ride bad at all. I figure I can drive it to Vegas with no trouble.'

'You'll want a new name.'

'Well, that's no headache, Johnny. Pick a new name and sell it to myself and then register it in Nevada with Nevada plates. I'll probably put it in my own name, I don't know. Maybe not.' He was silent a moment. 'I have to pass through Colorado, I guess. Or close enough to it. If you feel like riding along, feel free.'

I didn't answer him right away. I thought about a lot of things, added them up and checked the addition.

'Maybe I'll ride on through with you,' I said. 'I could use a vacation. I don't even remember what Vegas looks like.'

He looked at me.

'I don't gamble much,' I went on. 'But the sunshine sounds good, and all the rest.'

'I figured you were anxious to get back to your town.'

'Well,' I said.

'And you'll be tight enough on money. You wouldn't want to blow some of it in Vegas. Even without gambling—'

I lit another cigarette. I thought that it was funny how a couple of days took the prison fever right out of a man. Running the risks and being utterly in tune and getting everything right and beating the system did wonders for you. Lost confidence came back. You found out, once again, just who you happened to be.

'I'll just take things easy in Vegas,' I said finally. The words came easy now. 'And we'll both of us keep our eyes open, you and I, and when the right proposition comes along we'll be ready for it. Next time we'll play it straight. We've got enough troubles without conning each other.'

'You—' He stopped, started over. 'You want to work with me again?'

'Why not? We're a good match for each other. We work damned well together. We already proved that much.'

'But—'

'We both made mistakes we won't make again. They don't change the fact that we make a good team.'

He drove a mile or two in silence. 'That roadhouse in Colorado,' he said.

'What about it?'

'You figure you need one more score to afford it?'

It would have been easy to say yes, sure, that was it. But it wasn't, and I was not about to say so. So I thought for a minute or two, and I pictured myself standing behind a bar wiping glasses, or sitting in an office keeping careful records for the tax beagles, or figuring interest rates and depreciation schedules and breakage allowances. I thought about the last few days and I thought too about the weeks before them. The tension, the feeling of running wide open with the gears meshing and all the machinery perfectly aligned. I thought about The Dream, and I thought about The Girl, and about all dreams and all girls. No dreams come true, I guess, and no girls are as perfect as the heart would have them.

And beyond all that, I thought that a man must be what he is and do what he is geared to do. He cannot permit himself to be conned out of what he truly is. Not by the scare of a prison cell. Not by the smell of a woman, or the teasing song of a dream.

So I told Doug this, or most of it, and maybe he understood, and maybe he did not. At least I did. He pulled out to pass another car and put the gas pedal down on the floor. The sun was about gone but we were heading toward where it had disappeared from sight. West, toward Las Vegas.

Deadly Honeymoon

For Don Westlake

1

Just East of the Binghamton city limits he pulled the car off the road and cut the motor. She leaned toward him and he kissed her. He said, 'Good morning, Mrs Wade.'

'Mmmm,' she said. 'I think I like my new name. What are we stopping for, honey?'

'I ran out of gas.' He kissed her again. 'No, they gimmicked the car. Shoes and everything. You didn't notice?'

'No.'

He got out of the car and walked around the back. Four old shoes trailed from the license-plate mounting. On the lid of the trunk someone had painted *Just Married* in four-inch white letters. He got down on one knee and picked at the knots in the shoelaces. They were tight. The car door opened on her side and she got out and came back to watch him. When he looked up at her she was starting to laugh softly.

'I didn't even notice it,' she said. 'Too busy ducking rice. I'm glad we got married in church. Dave, imagine driving all through Pennsylvania with the car like that! It's good you noticed.'

'Uh-huh. You don't have a knife handy, do you?'

'To defend my honor? No. Let me get it. I have long fingernails.'

'Never mind.' He straightened up, the shoes in hand. He grinned at her. 'Those crazy guys,' he said.

'What are we supposed to do with these?'

'I don't know.'

'I mean, is it good luck to keep them?'

'If the shoe fits—'

He laughed happily and tossed the shoes into the underbrush at the side of the road. He unlocked the trunk, hauled out a rag, and wiped at the paint on the trunk lid. It wouldn't come off. There was an extra can of gasoline in the trunk, and he uncapped it and soaked the rag with gas. This time the paint came off easily. He wiped the trunk lid dry with a clean rag to protect the car's finish, then tossed both rags off to the side of the road and slammed the trunk shut.

She said, 'I didn't know you were a litterbug.'

465

'You can't carry them in the trunk, not soaked with gas. They could start a fire.'

'That's grounds for an annulment, you know.'

'Starting a fire?'

'Concealing the fact that you're a litterbug.'

'Want an annulment?'

'God, no,' she said.

She had changed from her wedding dress to a lime-green sheath that was snug on her big body. Her hair was blond, shoulder length, worn pageboy style with the ends curled under. Her eyes were large, and just a shade deeper in color than the dress. He looked at her and thought how very beautiful she was. He took a step toward her, not even conscious of his own movement.

'Dave, we'd better get going.'

'Mmmm.'

'We've got three weeks. We waited this long, we can wait two more hours. And this is an awfully public place, isn't it?'

Her tone was not quite as light as her words. He turned from her. Cars passed them on the highway. He grinned suddenly and got back into the car. She got in on her side and sat next to him, close to him. He turned the key in the ignition and started the car and pulled back onto the road.

From Binghamton they rode south on 81, the new Penn-Can Highway. Jill had a state map spread open on her lap and she studied it from time to time but it was hardly necessary. He just kept the car on the road and held the speed steady between sixty and sixty-five. The car was a middleweight Ford, the Fairlane, last year's model. It was the second week in September now and the car had a shade less than fifteen thousand miles on it.

They crossed the Pennsylvania state line a few minutes after noon. At twelve-thirty they left Route 81 at a town called Lenox and cut southeast on 106 through Carbondale and Honesdale. The new road was narrower, a two-laner that zigzagged across the hills. They pulled into an Esso station in Honesdale and Jill had a chicken sandwich at a diner two doors down from the station. He had a Coke and left half of it.

A few miles further on, at Indian Orchard, they left 106 and continued south on U.S. 6. They were at Pomquit by a quarter to two. Pomquit was at the northern tip of Lake Wallenpaupack, and their lodge was on the western rim of the lake, half a dozen miles south of the town. They found it without stopping for directions. The lodge had a private road. They followed its curves through a thick stand of white pine and parked in front of a large white Victorian house bounded on three sides by a huge porch. They could see the lake from where the car was parked. The water was very still, very blue.

Inside, in the office, a gray-haired woman sat behind a desk drinking whiskey and water. She looked up at them, and Dave told her his name. The woman shuffled through a stack of four-by-six file cards and found their reservation.

'Wade, David. You wanted a cabin, is that right?'

'That's right.'

'Honeymooners, I guess, and I don't blame you. Wanting a cabin, that is. Rooms in the lodge are nice but you don't get the privacy here you would be getting in a cabin. It's an old house. Sounds carry. And privacy is important, God knows. On a honeymoon.'

Jill was not blushing. The woman said, 'You picked a good time of the year now. What with the lake and the mountains it stays pretty cool here most of the time, but this year July and August got pretty hot, pretty hot. And on a honeymoon you don't want it to be too warm. But it's cooled off now.'

She passed the card to him. On a dotted line across the bottom he wrote, 'Mr and Mrs David Wade,' writing the double signature with an odd combination of pride and embarrassment. The woman filed the card away without looking at it. She gave him a key and offered halfheartedly to show them where the cabin was. He said he thought they could find it themselves. She told him how to get there, what path to take. They went back to the car and drove along a one-lane path that skirted the edge of the lake. Their cabin was the fourth one down. He parked the Ford alongside the cabin and got out of the car.

Their suitcases – two pieces, matching, a gift from an aunt and uncle of his – were in the back seat. He carried them up onto the cabin's small porch, set them down, unlocked the door, carried them inside. She waited outside, and he came back for her and grinned at her.

'I'm waiting,' she said.

He lifted her easily and carried her over the threshold, crossed the room, set her down gently on the edge of the double bed. 'I should have married a little girl,' he said.

'You like little girls?'

'I like big blondes the best. But little girls are easier to carry.'

'Oh, they are?'

'It seems likely, doesn't it?'

'Ever carry any?'

'Never.'

'Liar,' she said. Then, 'That drunken old woman has a dirty mind.'

'She wasn't drunk, just drinking. And her mind's not dirty.'

'What is it?'

'Realistic.'

'Lecher.'

'Uh-huh.'

He looked at her, sitting on the edge of the bed, their bed. She was twenty-four, two years younger than he was, and no man had ever made love to her. He was surprised how glad he was of this. Before they met he had always felt that it wouldn't matter to him what any woman of his had done with other men before their marriage, but now he knew that he had been wrong, that he did care, that he was glad no one had ever possessed her. And that they had waited. Their first time would be now, here, together, and after the wedding.

He sat down next to her. She turned toward him and he kissed her, and she made a purring sound and came up close against him. He felt the sweet and certain pressure of her body against his.

Now, if he wanted it. But it was the middle of the afternoon and sunlight streamed through the cabin windows. The first time should be just right, he thought. At night, under a blanket of darkness.

He kissed her once more, then stood up and crossed the small room to look out through the window. 'The lake's beautiful,' he said easily. 'Want to swim a little?'

'I love you,' she said.

He drew the shades. Then he went outside and closed the door to wait on the porch while she changed into her bathing suit. He smoked a cigarette and looked out at the lake.

He was twenty-six, two years out of law school. In a year or so he would be a junior partner in his father's firm. He was married. He loved his wife.

A heavyset man waved to him from the steps of the cabin next door. He waved back. It was a good day, he thought. It would be a good three weeks.

Jill was a better swimmer than he was. He spent most of his time standing in cool water up to his waist, watching the perfect synchronization of her body. Her blond hair was all bunched up under her white bathing cap.

Later she came over to him and he kissed her. 'Let's go sit under a tree or something,' she said. 'I don't want to get a burn.'

'Jesus, no,' he said. 'Sunburned on your honeymoon—'

'You sound like that drunken old woman.'

He spread a blanket on the bank and they sat together and shared a cigarette. Their shoulders were just touching. There were small woodland noises as a background, and once in a while the faraway sound of a car on the highway. That was all. He dried her back and shoulders with a towel and she took off her bathing cap and let her hair spill down.

Around five the man from the cabin next door, the one who had waved, came over to them carrying three cans of Budweiser. He said, 'You kids just moved in. I thought maybe you'd have a beer with me.'

He was between forty-five and fifty, maybe thirty pounds overweight. He wore a pair of gray gabardine slacks and a navy-blue open-necked sport shirt. His forearms were brown from the sun. He had a round face, the skin ruddy under his deep tan.

They thanked him, asked him to sit down. They each took a can of beer. It was very cold and very good. The man sat down on the edge of their blanket and told them that his name was Joe Carroll and that he was from

New York. Dave introduced himself and Jill and said that they were from Binghamton. Carroll said he had never been to Binghamton. He took a long drink of beer and wiped his mouth with the back of his hand. He asked them if they were staying long.

'Three weeks,' Dave said.

'You picked a good spot. We been having good weather, cooler now than it was, with sun just about every day. A little rain the week before last, but not too much.'

'Have you been here long, Mr Carroll?' Jill asked.

'Joe. Yeah, most of the summer. I'm just here by myself. You can go crazy for somebody to talk to. You kids been married long?'

'Not too long,' Dave said.

'Any kids?'

'Not yet.'

Carroll looked off at the lake. 'I never got married. Almost, once, but I didn't. I'll tell you the truth, I never missed it. Except for kids. Sometimes I miss not having kids.' He finished his beer, held the can in one hand and looked at it. 'But what with business and all, you know, a man stays pretty busy.'

'You're in business.'

'Construction.' He waved a hand in the general direction of the lake. 'Out on Long Island, Nassau County, the developments. We built, oh, a whole lot of those houses.'

'Isn't this your busy season?'

He laughed shortly. 'Oh, I'm out of it now, for the time being.'

'Retired?'

'You could call it that.' Carroll smiled as if at a private joke. 'I may relocate,' he said. 'I might pull up stakes, find a better territory.'

They made small talk. Baseball, the weather, the woman who managed the lodge. Carroll said she was a widow, childless. Her husband had died five or six years back, and she was running the place on her own and making a fairly good thing of it. He said she was a minor-league alcoholic, never blind drunk but never quite sober. 'The hell,' he said, 'what else has she got, huh?'

He told them about a steak house down the road where the food wasn't bad. 'Listen,' he said, 'you get a chance, drop over to my place. We'll sit around a little.'

'Well—'

'There's more beer, I got a hot plate for coffee. You know gin rummy? We could play a few hands and pass the time.'

They ate at the steak house that Carroll recommended. It was just outside of Pomquit. The steaks were thick, the service fast, and the place had the atmosphere of a Colonial tavern, authentic without being intrusive. There was an old copper kettle hanging from a hook on one wall, and Jill wanted it. Dave tried to buy it but the manager said it wasn't for sale. They stood outside for a few minutes after dinner and looked up at the moon. It was just a little less than full.

'Honeymoon,' she said. 'Keep a-shining in June. But it's September, isn't it?'

'The drunken old woman said it's better this way. You don't want it too hot on a honeymoon.'

'Oh, no?'

'Now who's the lecher?'

'I'm shameless,' she said. 'Let's go back to the cabin. I think I love you, Mr Wade.'

On the slow ride home she said, 'I feel sorry for him.'

'Who, Carroll?'

'Yes. He's so lonely it's sad. Why would he pick a spot like this to come to all alone?'

'Well, he said the fishing—'

'But all alone? There are livelier spots where the fishing must be just as good as it is here.'

'Listen, he just sold his business. Maybe he's got problems.'

'He should have gotten married,' she said. She rolled down her window, let her arm hang out, tapped against the side of the Ford with her long fingernails. 'Everybody should be married. Maybe he'll marry the drunken old woman and she won't drink any more and they can manage the lodge together.'

'Or tear it down and build up a tract of ugly little split-levels.'

'Either way,' she said. 'Everybody should be married. Married is fun.'

'You're incorrigible,' he said.

'I love you.'

He almost missed the turnoff for the lodge. He cut the wheel sharply to the left and the Ford moved onto the private road. He drove past the lodge itself and followed the path back to the cabin. The lights were on in Joe Carroll's cabin. She said, 'Mr Carroll wanted us to stop in for coffee.'

'Some other time,' he said.

He parked the car and they walked slowly together up the steps to the cabin. He unlocked the door, turned on the light. They went inside and he closed the door and turned the bolt. She looked at him and he kissed her and she said, 'Oh, God.' He turned off the light. The room was not completely dark. A little light came in, from the moon on one side, from Carroll's cabin on the other.

He held her and she threw her arms around his neck and kissed him. She was a tall girl, a soft and warm girl. His. He found the zipper of her dress and opened it partway and rubbed her back with his fingers.

Outside, a car drew up slowly. The motor died and the car coasted to a stop.

She stiffened. 'There's somebody coming,' she said.

'Not here.'

'I heard a car—'

'Probably some friends of Carroll's.'

'I hope it's not some friends of ours,' she said, her voice almost savage. 'I hope this isn't some idiot's idea of a joke.'

'They wouldn't do that.'

'I just hope not.'

He let go of her. 'Maybe I'd better check,' he said.

The bolt on the door was stuck. He wrestled it open, turned the doorknob, opened the door, and stepped outside onto the porch. Jill followed him, stood at his side. The car, empty now, was parked in front of their cabin by the side of the Ford. It was a big car, a Buick or an Olds. It was dark, and he couldn't be sure of the color in the half-light. Maybe black, maybe maroon or dark green. The two men who had been in the car were walking toward Carroll's cabin. They were short men and they wore hats and dark suits.

He turned to her. 'See? Friends of Joe's.'

'Then why didn't they park at his cabin?' He looked at her. 'They drove right past his cabin,' she said, 'and they parked here, and now they're walking back. Why?'

'What's the difference?'

He took her arm and started to lead her inside again. But she shrugged and stayed where she was. 'Just a minute,' she said.

'What's the matter?'

'I don't know. Wait a minute, Dave.'

They waited and watched. Carroll's cabin was thirty or forty yards from theirs. The men covered the distance without making any noise. One of Carroll's porch steps creaked, and just after the creak they could hear movement inside the cabin. The men did not knock. One of them yanked the door open and the other sprang inside. The man on the porch had something in his hand, something that light glinted off, as though it were metallic.

Sounds came from the cabin, sounds that were hard to make out. Then Joe Carroll walked out of the cabin and the man who had remained outside said something to him in a low voice. They could see what he had in his hand now. It was a gun. The other man came out behind Carroll and he was holding a gun in Carroll's back.

They stayed on the porch and they stayed quiet. It wasn't real – that was all he could think, that it was not real, that it was a play or a movie and not something happening before them.

They heard Carroll's voice, crystal clear in the still night air. 'I'll make it good,' he said. 'I swear to God I'll make it good. You tell Lublin I'll make it good, Jesus, just tell him.'

The man behind him, the one jabbing him in the back with the gun, began to laugh quietly. It was unpleasant laughter.

'Oh, sweet Jesus,' Carroll said. His face was awful. 'Listen, please, just a chance, just give me a chance—'

'Crawl,' the man in front said.

'What do you want me to—'

'Get down on your knees and beg, you bastard.'

Carroll sank to his knees. There were fallen leaves on the ground, and pine needles. He was saying something over and over again in a weak voice but they couldn't quite make it out.

The man in front stepped forward and put the muzzle of his gun against Carroll's head. Carroll started to whine. The man shot him in the center of the forehead and he shook from the blow and pitched forward on his face. The other man moved in and shot Carroll four times through the back of his head.

Jill screamed.

It wasn't much of a scream. It broke off in no time at all, and it was neither very loud nor very high-pitched. But the two men in the dark suits heard it. They heard it and they looked up at the porch of the Wade cabin.

And came forward.

They stood, the four of them, in Carroll's cabin. The small room was as neat as if no one had ever lived in it. There was a hot plate on an oak table, with a large jar of Yuban instant coffee beside it and a half-finished cup of coffee off to one side. The bed was neatly made.

The taller of the two men was called Lee. They knew this, but they did not know whether it was his first name or his last name. He was the one who had made Carroll crawl, the one who had killed him with the first shot in the forehead. Lee had large brown eyes and thick black eyebrows. There were three or four thin scars across the bridge of his nose. His mouth was a thin line, the lips pale. He was holding a gun on them now while the other man, whose name they had not heard yet, was systematically going through Carroll's dresser drawers, taking everything out piece by piece, throwing everything on the floor.

'Nothing,' he said finally. 'Just what was in the wallet.'

Lee didn't say anything. The shorter man turned around and nodded toward Dave and Jill. He was heavier than Lee, with a thick neck and a nose that had been broken and imperfectly reset. He looked as though he might have played guard or tackle on some college's junior varsity.

Now he said, 'What about them?'

'They didn't see a thing. They aren't going to talk.'

'What if they do?'

'So? They don't know a thing.'

'We won't make any trouble,' Dave said. His voice sounded odd to him, as though someone else were pulling strings that moved his lips, as though someone else were talking for him.

They didn't seem to have heard him. Lee said, 'If they talk, it doesn't matter. They talk to some hick cop and he writes it all down and everybody forgets it. They put it in some drawer.'

'We could make sure.'

'Just let us alone,' Dave said. Jill was next to him, breathing heavily. He looked at the gun in Lee's hand and wondered whether they were going to die, now, in this cabin. 'Just let us live,' he said.

'We kill 'em,' Lee said, 'it makes too much stink. Him out there, that's one thing, but you kill a couple of kids—'

'Leave 'em alone then?'

'Yeah.'

'Just like that?'

'I don't like killing nobody without I get paid for it,' Lee said. 'I don't like throwing any in for free.'

The man with the broken nose nodded. He said, 'The broad.'

'What about her?'

'She's nice. Stacked.'

Dave said, 'Now listen—'

They ignored him. 'You want her?'

'Why not?'

The man called Lee smiled brutally. He stepped up to Jill and stuck the gun into her chest just below and between her breasts. 'How about that,' he said. 'You don't mind a little screwing just to keep you alive, now, do you?'

Dave stepped out and swung at him. He threw a left, hard, not thinking, just reacting. The man called Lee stepped back and let the punch go over his shoulder. He reversed the gun in his hand and laid the side of the gun butt across Dave's forehead. Dave took one more little step, a half-step, really, and fell to the floor.

His head was spinning. He got to one knee. The shorter man was pushing Jill toward Carroll's bed. She was crying hysterically but was not fighting very hard. There was the sound of cloth ripping, Jill's shrill scream above the tearing of the dress. He pushed himself up and rushed toward the bed, and Lee stuck out a foot and tripped him. He went sprawling. Lee stepped in close and kicked him in the side of the rib cage. He moaned and fell flat on his face.

'You better take it easy,' Lee said.

He got up again. He stood, wavering, and Lee set the gun down on the table. He moved as if he had all the time in the world. Dave stood there, staring dead ahead, and Lee moved in front of him and hit him in the pit of the stomach. He doubled over but he didn't go down. Lee waited, and he straightened up, and Lee hit him twice in the chest and once in the stomach. This time he went down again. He tried to get up but he couldn't. It was as though someone had cut all his tendons. He was awake, he knew what was happening, he just couldn't move.

Jill had stopped crying. The shorter man finished with her and came over to them. He asked Lee whether Dave had tried to be a hero. Lee didn't say anything. Then the shorter man said, 'She was cherry. You believe that?' And he said it as though he had not known virgins still existed.

Lee said, 'She ain't now.' And took off his jacket and went to take the shorter man's place with Jill.

She didn't scream. She lay there, motionless, and Dave thought that they must have killed her. This time his legs worked, this time he got up. The shorter man hit him with the gun and pain split his skull in half. He went down. The world turned gray, and the gray darkened quickly to black.

2

He never remembered going back to the cabin. He had vague memories of walking and falling down, walking and falling down, but they were as dim as vanished dreams. When he did come out of it, he was in their own cabin. He was lying on the bed and Jill was sitting in a chair looking down at him. She was wearing a beige skirt and a dark-brown sweater. Her face was freshly scrubbed, her lipstick unmarred, her hair neatly combed. There was a moment, then, when nothing made sense – the whole thing, Carroll and the two men and the beating and the violation of his wife, none of this could have happened.

But then he felt the pain in his own body and the dull ache of his head and he saw the discoloration over her right eye, masked incompletely by makeup. It had all happened.

'Don't try to talk yet,' she said. 'Take it easy.'

'I'm all right.'

'Dave—'

'I'm all right,' he said. He sat up. His head was perfectly clear now. The pain was still there, and strong, but his head was perfectly clear. He remembered everything up to the blow that knocked him out. The return from Carroll's cabin to their own, that was lost, but he remembered all the rest in awful reality.

'We've got to get you to a doctor,' he said.

'I'm all right.'

'Did they—'

'Yes.'

'Both of them?'

'Both of them.'

'You've got to see a doctor, Jill.'

'Tomorrow, then.' She took a breath. 'I think the police are over in . . . in the other cabin. I heard a car, someone must have called them. It took them long enough.'

'What time is it?'

'After ten. They'll be coming over here, won't they?'

'The police? Yes, I think so.'

'You'd better clean up. I tried to wash your face. Your head is cut a little.

In two places, on top and behind your ear there.' She touched him, her hand light, cool. 'How do you feel?'

'All right.'

'Liar,' she said. 'Wash up and change your clothes, Dave.'

He went into the tiny bathroom and stripped down. There was no tub, just a shower. It was one of those showers in which you had to hold a chain down in order to keep the water running. He showered very quickly and thought about the two men and Carroll and about what they had done to Jill. At first his mind clouded with fury, but he stayed in the shower and the water rained down upon him, and he thought about it, forced himself to think about it. The fury did not go away. It stayed, but it cooled and changed its shape.

While he was drying himself off the bathroom door opened and Jill brought him clean clothes. After she had left he realized, oddly, that she had just seen him naked for the first time. He shrugged the thought away and dressed.

When he came out of the bathroom, the police were there. There were two tall thin men, state troopers, and there was one older man from the Sheriff's Office in Pomquit. One of the troopers took their names. Then he removed his hat and said, 'A man was murdered here tonight, Mr Wade. We wondered if you knew anything about it.'

'Murdered?'

'Your neighbor. A Mr Carroll.'

Jill drew in her breath sharply. Dave looked at her, then at the trooper. 'We met Mr Carroll just this afternoon,' he said. 'What . . . happened?'

'He was shot four times in the head.'

Five times, he thought. He said, 'Who did it?'

'We don't know. Did you hear anything? See anything?'

'No.'

'Whoever killed him must have come in a car, Mr Wade. We found tire tracks. There was a car parked right next to yours outside. That is your car, isn't it? The Ford?'

'Yes.'

'Did you hear a car drive up, Mr Wade?'

'Not that I remember.'

The man from the Sheriff's Office said, 'You would have heard it – it was right outside your window. And the shots, you would have heard them. Were you here all night?'

Jill said, 'We went out for dinner.'

'What time?'

'We left about seven,' she said. 'Seven or seven-thirty.'

'And got back when?'

'About . . . oh, half an hour ago, I guess. Why?'

The man from the Sheriff's Office looked over at the troopers. 'That would do it, then,' he said. 'Carroll's been dead at least an hour, the way my man figures it. Closer to two hours, probably. They must have gotten back just before we got the call, must have come right in without seeing the body. You wouldn't see it from where the car's parked, anyway. Just been back half an hour, Mr Wade?'

'It may have been longer than that,' he said.

'As much as an hour?'

'I don't think so. Maybe forty-five minutes at the outside.'

'That would do it, then. I guess you didn't see anything, then, Mr Wade. Mrs Wade.'

He turned to go. The troopers hesitated, as though they wanted to say something but hadn't figured out the phrasing yet. Dave said, 'Why was he killed?'

'We don't know yet, Mr Wade.'

'He was a very pleasant man. Quiet, friendly. We sat outside this afternoon and had a beer with him.'

The troopers didn't say anything.

'Well,' Dave said, 'I don't want to keep you.'

The troopers nodded shortly. They turned, then, and followed the man from the Sheriff's Office out of the cabin.

It was midnight when the last carful of police was gone. They sat quietly for five or ten minutes. He stood up then and said, 'We're getting out of here tonight. You'd better start packing.'

'We're leaving tonight?'

'You don't want to stay here, do you?'

'God, no.' She reached out a hand. He gave her a cigarette, lit it for her. She blew out smoke and said, 'They won't be suspicious?'

'Of what?'

'Of us, if we leave so quickly. Without staying the night.'

He shook his head. 'We're newlyweds,' he said. 'Newlyweds wouldn't want to spend their wedding night next door to a murder.'

'Newlyweds.'

'Yes.'

'Wedding night. God, Dave, how I planned this night. All of it.'

He took her hand.

'How I would be sexy for you and everything. How I wouldn't mind if it hurt because I love you so much. Oh, and little tricks I read in one of those marriage manuals, I was going to try those tricks. And surprise you with my ingenuity.'

'Stop it.'

He got the suitcases and spread them open on the bed. They packed their clothes in silence. He put the clothes she had worn earlier and his own dirty clothes in the trunk and loaded the two suitcases in the back seat. She got in the car, and he went to the cabin and closed the door and locked it.

As they drove past the lodge, she said, 'We didn't pay. The old woman would want to be paid, for the one night.'

'That's too fucking bad,' he said.

He turned left at the main road and drove to Pomquit. He passed through the town and took a road heading north. 'It's late and I don't know the roads,' he said. 'We'll stop at the first motel that looks decent.'

'All right.'

'We'll get an early start in the morning,' he went on. He was looking straight ahead at the road and he did not glance over at her. 'An early start in the morning, figure out which route to take, all of that. They're from New York, aren't they?'

'I think so. Carroll said he was from New York. And they all had New York accents.'

He slowed the car. There was a motel off to the left, but the 'No Vacancy' sign was lit. He speeded up again.

'We'll go to New York,' he said. 'We'll be there by tomorrow afternoon, Monday. We'll get a room in a hotel, and we'll find out who they are, the two of them. One of them is named Lee. I didn't catch the other one's name.'

'Neither did I.'

'We'll find out who they are, and then we'll find them and we'll kill them, both of them. Then we'll go back to Binghamton. We have three weeks. I think we can find them and kill them in three weeks.'

Up ahead, on the right, there was a motel. He slowed the car. As he pulled off the road he glanced at her face, quickly. Her jaw was set and her eyes were dry and clear.

'Three weeks is plenty of time,' she said.

3

In the diner the waitress said, 'Mondays, how I hate 'em. Give me any other day, but Monday, just never mind. Coffee?'

'One black, one regular,' he told her.

There were two men at the counter who looked like truckers and one who looked like a farmer. The waitress brought the coffee and he carried the two cups over to a table on the side. Some of the coffee in her cup spilled out onto the saucer. He took a napkin from the dispenser and wiped up the coffee. She added sugar, one level spoonful. He drank his straight black.

When the waitress came over he ordered toast and a side order of link sausages. Jill wanted a toasted English muffin, but the diner didn't have any. The waitress said there would be some coming in around nine-thirty. Jill had a cheese Danish instead and managed to eat half of it.

He spread a road map on the table and studied it, marking a route with a pencil. She sipped her coffee and looked across the room while he traced the route they would take. By the time he was finished, she had drunk her coffee. He looked up and said, 'This is how we'll do it. We're on 590 now. We take it to Ford – that's just across the state line – and pick up 97. We go about five miles on 97 to Route 55. That's at Barryville. Then 55 runs just about due north to something called White Lake, where we get 17B. Then we hook up with 17 at Monticello. That carries us all the way to the throughway at Exit 16, and then we just drive down into New York.'

'I never heard of those towns,' she said.

'Well, Monticello you've heard of.'

'I mean the others.'

He sipped his coffee, checked his watch with the electric clock over the counter. 'Twenty to eight,' he said

'Should we get going?'

'Pretty soon.' He got to his feet. 'I'm having another cup of coffee,' he said. 'How about you?'

'All right.'

He carried the two cups back to the counter. The waitress was busy telling one of the truckers what a terrible day Monday was. She was a heavyish woman with stringy hair. When she finished talking to the truck driver Dave got two fresh cups of coffee and carried them back to the table.

They passed through the town, a small one, and a sign told them to resume their normal speed. He bore down on the accelerator. The sun was bright on the road ahead. The sky had been overcast when they got up, but the clouds were mostly gone now.

'That was Forestine,' she said. 'White Lake in three miles.'

'And then what?'

'Then right on 17B.'

He nodded. So far, in close to an hour of driving, they had talked only about the route and the road conditions. She had the road map open on her lap, the map with their route penciled in, and she told him when to slow down and where to turn. But most of the time passed in long silences. It was not for lack of things to say to each other, or because any distance had sprung up between them. Small talk did not fit and larger talk came hard.

The night before they had stayed at a motel called Hillcrest Manor. They slept in a double bed. After he checked in, they left their suitcases in the locked car and went inside. They undressed with the lights on, then he turned off the lights, and they got into the large bed. She took the side near the windows, and he had the side nearer to the door. He waited, and she came to him and kissed him once, on the side of the face. Then she went back to her side of the bed. He asked her if she thought she would be able to sleep and she said yes, she thought so. After about fifteen minutes he heard her easy rhythmic breathing and knew that she was sleeping.

He couldn't fall asleep. The beating had tired him, and his body wanted sleep, but it didn't work. He would manage to relax and would start drifting off and then the memory would come, racing in at his mind, and he would suck in breath and shake his head and sit up in the bed, his heart beating fast and hard. From time to time he got out of the bed and sat in a chair at the window, smoking a cigarette in the darkness, then putting out the cigarette and returning to bed.

Around four, he dozed off. At a quarter to six he heard a frightened yelp and was instantly awake. She lay on her back, her head on a pillow, her eyes closed, and she was crying in her sleep. He woke her up and soothed her and told her that everything was all right. After a few minutes she fell asleep again, and he got up and put clothes on.

Now he talked to her without looking at her, his eyes conveniently fixed on the road ahead. 'When we get to Monticello,' he said, 'you're going to see a doctor.'

'No.'

'Why not?'

He looked at her. She was worrying her lip with her teeth. 'I don't want anyone, oh, touching me. Now. Examining me.'

'Is that all?'

'I just don't want it. And if a doctor could tell anything, wouldn't he have to report it? Like a gunshot wound?'

'I don't know. But if they injured you—'

'They didn't hurt me,' she said. 'I mean, they didn't do any damage. I checked, I know. There were no cuts or bleeding.' Her voice, flat until then, came alive again. 'Dave, those policemen were stupid.'

'Why?'

'They figured it all out. The mess in Carroll's cabin, the way everything was turned upside down. They think Carroll fought with his murderers and then they dragged him outside and shot him.'

'I didn't even think about that. That's what they figure?'

'They were talking outside, before you got out of the shower. Dave, they didn't hurt me. I don't have to see any doctor.'

'Well—'

'There wasn't even that much pain,' she said. 'The doctor I saw, before we were married—'

He waited.

'He told me about some exercises. To make it easier for us to—' She stopped, and he waited, and she caught hold of herself and started in again. '—to consummate our marriage.'

He kept his eyes on the road. He swung to the left, passed a station wagon, cut back to the right again. He looked at his hands on the steering wheel, the knuckles white, the fingers locked tight around the wheel. He moved his hands lower on the steering wheel so that she would not see them.

Suddenly he was grinning.

'Is something funny?'

'I was just picturing you,' he said. 'Doing your exercises.'

He laughed then, and she laughed. It was the first time either of them had laughed since Carroll was murdered.

A little later he said, 'There's another reason you ought to see a doctor.'

'What's that?'

'I don't know how to say it. Well. Suppose you're pregnant?'

She didn't say anything.

'It's no fun to think about,' he said. 'But it could be. Jesus.'

'Oh, Dave—'

He slowed the car. 'It's nothing to worry about,' he said. 'They can always do something about it. The legal question varies from state to state, but I know a dozen doctors who wouldn't worry about the law. If a ... rape victim is pregnant, she can get an abortion. There's no problem.'

'Oh, God,' she said. 'I didn't even think. You've been worrying about this, haven't you? All night, probably.'

'Well—'

'I'm not pregnant. I'm taking these pills, oral contraceptives. That was one of my surprises for you. The doctor gave me pills to take. Little yellow pills. I couldn't possibly be pregnant.'

She began to cry then. He started to pull off the road but she told him to go on driving, that she would be all right. He went on driving, and she stopped crying. 'Don't worry about me,' she said. 'I'm not going to cry any more, at all.'

They made good time. They stopped once on the road for gas and food and were in New York by twelve-thirty. They came in on the Saw Mill River Parkway and the West Side Drive. They took a room with twin beds at the Royalton, on West Forty-fourth Street. The doorman parked their car for them.

Their room was on the eleventh floor. A bellhop carried their luggage, checked the towels, showed them where their closets were, opened a window, thanked Dave for the tip, and left. Dave walked to the window. You couldn't see much from it, just the side of an office building.

'We're here,' he said.

'Yes. Have you spent much time in New York?'

'A couple of weekends during college. And then for six weeks two years ago. I was studying for the bar exams, and there's a course you take just to cram for the bar. A six-week cram course. I stayed downtown at the Martinique and didn't do a thing but eat and sleep and study. I could have been in any city for all the attention I paid to it.'

'I didn't know you then.'

'No, not then. Do you know this city?'

She shook her head. 'I have an aunt who lives here. A sister of my father's. She never married, and she has a job in the advertising department for one of the big department stores. Had, anyway. I don't know if she still does, I haven't seen her in years. Name some department stores.'

'Jesus, I don't know. Saks, Brooks Brothers—'

'She wouldn't work at Brooks Brothers.'

'Well, I don't know anything about department stores. Bonwit? Is there one called Bonwit?'

'It was Bergdorf Goodman. I remember now. We went to visit her, oh, two or three times. I was just a kid then. We didn't see her very often because my mother can't stand her. Do you think she might be a lesbian?'

'Your mother?'

'Oh, don't be an idiot. My aunt.'

'How do I know?'

'I wonder. There was a lesbian in my dormitory in college.'

'You told me.'

'She wanted to make love to me. Did I tell you that, too?'

'Yes.'

'Everybody said I should have reported her, but I didn't. I wonder if Aunt Beth is a lesbian.'

'Call her up and ask her.'

'Some other time. Dave?' Her face was serious now. 'I think we ought to figure out what we're going to do first. How we're going to find them, the two men. We don't know anything about them.'

'We know a few things.'

'What?'

He had a notebook in his jacket pocket, a small loose-leaf notebook for appointments and memos. He sat down in an armchair and flipped the book open to a blank page. He took his pencil and wrote: 'Joe Carroll.'

'They killed a man named Joe Carroll,' he said. 'That's a start.' She nodded, and he said, 'If that was his name.'

'Huh?'

'That was the name he gave us, and that was the name he used at the lodge. But he was running away, trying to hide. He might not have used his own name.'

'What did the men call him?'

'I don't remember. I don't think they called him anything. I couldn't hear that much from where we were.'

'Wouldn't the police know his real name?'

'The troopers?' He thought a minute. 'He might have had some identification on him. They called him Carroll. They might have done that in front of us just to keep from confusing us, but maybe not. Or maybe he wasn't carrying any identification.'

'Or maybe they took his wallet with them.'

'Maybe.' He lit a cigarette. 'But they would fingerprint him,' he said. 'They would do that much automatically, and they would send his prints to Washington, to the FBI. If he's ever been fingerprinted, then, his prints would be on file and they would get a positive identification of him.'

'How could we find out?'

'If he's important, then it would be in the New York papers. If not, it would just be in the local papers. If Pomquit has a paper. Or one of larger cities around there. Scranton – I don't know.'

'Can you get Scranton papers in New York?'

'Yes. There's a newsstand in Times Square. I used to pick up Binghamton papers during that bar-exam stretch. The papers run late, but they would have them.'

In the notebook he wrote: 'Scranton paper.'

He looked up. 'Let's take it from the top. Carroll, whatever his name is, said he was in construction. And semi-retired.'

'He was probably just talking.'

'Maybe. People usually stay close to the truth when they lie. Especially when they're lying just for the sake of convenience. Carroll wanted to be friendly with us, and he had to invent a story, not to keep anything from us, specifically, but because he couldn't tell the truth without drawing the wrong kind of attention to himself. He was probably a criminal. I got that picture from the way he talked with the two of them.'

'So did I.'

'But I think he was probably a criminal with some background in the construction business. A lot of rackets have legitimate front operations. You know the cigar store across from the Lafayette?'

'In Binghamton?'

'Yes. It's a bookie joint.'

'I didn't know that.'

'It's not exactly a secret. Everybody knows it, they operate pretty much in the open. Still, the place is a cigar store. They don't have a sign that says "Bookie Joint," and the man who runs it tells people he runs a cigar store, not a bookie joint. It's probably something like that with Carroll. He was probably in construction, or on the periphery of it, no matter what racket he may have had on the side.'

He was talking as much to himself as to her now. If they were going to find Lee and the other man, they would do it by reasoning from the few facts and nuances at their disposal.

'Carroll did something wrong. That was why the two of them came after him. He double-crossed somebody.'

'He said that he would make it good.'

He nodded. 'That's right. There was a name. Their boss, the one they work for. Carroll told them to tell the boss that he would make it good.'

On the notebook page he changed the first entry to read: 'Joe Carroll – Construction.' Then he wrote: 'Nassau County,' which was where Carroll had said he was in business.

Jill said, 'They mentioned the boss by name. Or Carroll did.'

'I think Carroll did.'

'I can remember it. Just a minute.' He waited, and she closed her eyes and put her hands together, pressing the palms one against the other.

'Dublin,' she said.

'No, that's not it.'

'Dublin, it was Dublin. "Tell Dublin that I'll make it good." No, that's not right either.'

'It's not what they said.'

'Lublin, maybe?'

'I don't know.'

'Well, say the sentence for me. I think I can tell if I hear it, if you say it for me. Like a visual memory, except different. Say the sentence the way he said it.'

'With Lublin?'

'Yes.'

He said, '"Tell Lublin I'll make it good."'

'That's it. I'm positive, Dave. Lublin.'

He wrote: 'Lublin – Boss.'

'They worked for Lublin? Is that it?'

He shook his head. 'I think he hired them. I don't think they were regular ... well, employees of his. They were paid to kill Carroll. And when one of them wanted to kill us, so that we wouldn't be able to tell the police anything, the other said something about not killing anybody unless he was getting paid for it. As if they had been specifically hired to kill Carroll, to do that one job for a set fee.'

'That was Lee who said that. I remember now.'

He wrote: 'Hired Professional Killers. Lee.' He said, 'I know one name – Lee. It could be his first name or his last name.'

'Or a nickname,' she said. 'If his name is LeGrand, or something.'

'It could be anything. That was all he was called, wasn't it? I didn't hear him called anything else. And he didn't call the other one anything.'

'No, he didn't.'

He lit a fresh cigarette. He looked at the notebook, at the neat entries one beneath the other: 'Joe Carroll – Construction. Nassau County. Scranton paper. Lublin – Boss. Hired Professional Killers. Lee.' He went to the window and looked across at the office building. He wanted to look out at the city but the building was in the way. There were eight or nine million people in the city, and he was looking for two of those millions, and he couldn't even see the city itself. There was a building in the way.

'Dave.'

He turned. She was next to him, her hair brushing his cheek. He put an arm around her and she drew close. Her head settled on his shoulder. For a moment he had thought of those two, lost in that huge crowd, and that it was hopeless and ridiculous. But now his arm was around her, and he remembered what they had done to her and what they had taken from her and from him. He closed his eyes and pictured both men dead.

4

He missed the out-of-town-newspaper stand on the first try. He passed it on the wrong side of the street and walked to Seventh Avenue and Forty-second, then got his bearings and retraced his steps. The stand was at Forty-third Street, in the island behind the Times Tower. He asked for a copy of the Scranton morning paper. The newsie ducked into his shack and came back with a folded copy of the Scranton *Courier-Herald*. He looked at the date. It was Saturday's paper.

'This the latest?'

'What is it, Saturday? That's the latest. No good?'

'I need today's.'

The newsie said, 'Can't do it. The bigger cities, Chicago or Philly or Detroit, we get in the afternoon if it's a morning paper or the next day if it's a night paper. The towns, we run about two days behind. You want Monday's *Courier-Herald*, it would be Wednesday afternoon by the time I had it for you, maybe Thursday morning.'

'I need this morning's paper. Even if it's late.'

'You could use it Wednesday?'

'Yes,' he said. 'And tomorrow's, too.'

'Yeah. Say, we only get two or three. You want 'em, I could set 'em aside for you. If you're sure you'll be coming back. Any paper I'm stuck with, then I'm stuck with it. But if you want 'em, I could hold 'em for you.'

'How much are they?'

'Half a buck each.'

'If I give you a dollar now, will you be sure to have a copy of each for me?'

'You don't have to pay me now.'

'I'd just as soon,' Dave said. He gave the man a dollar, then had to wait while the newsie scrawled out a receipt and made a note for himself on a scrap of paper.

Around the corner, he bought the New York afternoon papers at another newsstand. They didn't have any of the morning papers left. But the news of Carroll's murder wouldn't have gotten to New York in time for the morning papers anyway. He took the papers to a cafeteria on Forty-second Street, bought a cup of coffee, and sat down at an empty table. He checked very carefully and found no mention of the shooting in any of the papers. He left them on his table and went out of the cafeteria.

Two doors down, he stopped at an outdoor phone booth and flipped through two telephone directories, the one for Manhattan and the one for Brooklyn. There were seven Lublins listed in Manhattan and nine in Brooklyn, plus 'Lublin's Flowers' and 'Lublin and Devlin – Bakers.' The other local phone books were not there, just Manhattan and Brooklyn. He went to the Walgreen's on the corner of Seventh Avenue and Forty-second, and the store had the books for the Bronx and Queens and Staten Island. There were fourteen Lublins listed in the Bronx, six in Queens, and none in Staten Island. The Walgreen's did not have telephone books for northern New Jersey, Long Island, or Westchester County. And Lublin might live in one of those places. There was no guarantee that he lived in the city itself.

In the classified directory – a separate book in New York, not just a section of yellow pages at the back – he turned to 'Contractors, General.' He looked first for 'Lublin,' because he had grown used to looking for Lublins, but there were no contractors listed under that name. He tried looking for 'Carroll, Joseph.' He found 'Carroll, Jas' and 'Carrel, J.' He waited until one of the phone booths was empty, and then he dropped a dime in the slot and dialed the number for Carroll, Jas in Queens. A man answered. Dave said, 'Is Mr Carroll there?'

'Speaking.'

He hung up quickly and tried another dime. He called Carrel, J., also in Queens, and the line was busy. He hung up. There was a woman waiting to use the booth. He let her wait. He called again, and this time a girl answered.

'Mr Carrel, please,' he said.

'Which Mr Carrel?'

Which Mr Carrel? He said, 'I didn't know there were more than one. Was more than one.'

'There are two Mr Carrels,' the girl said. 'Whom did you wish to speak to?'

'What are their names?'

'We have a Mr Jacob Carrel and a Mr Leonard Carrel. Lennie ... Mr Leonard Carrel, I mean, is the son. He's not in, but Mr Jacob Carrell—'

He hung up the phone. For the hell of it, he looked up 'Joseph Carroll' in the Brooklyn book. There were listings for fourteen Joseph Carrolls in Brooklyn. He did not bother looking in the other books.

The only way was through Carroll, he thought. They had to learn who the man was. If they learned who Carroll was they could find the right Lublin, and once they got Lublin they could find the men he had hired to do the killing. It was impossible to find Carroll or Lublin or anyone else through the phone book. The city was too big. There were thirty-six Lublins listed in New York City and God knew how many more with no phones or unlisted numbers. And he had never heard the name Lublin before, even. A name he'd never heard, and there were too many of them in New York City for him to know where to begin.

She was waiting in the room at the Royalton. He told her where he had gone and what he had done. She didn't say anything.

He said, 'Right now there's nothing to do but wait. There should be a story in one of the morning papers, and then there should be a longer story in the Scranton papers when we get them. Maybe we should have stayed around the lodge for a day or two, maybe we would have found out something.'

'I couldn't stay there.'

'No, neither could I.'

'We could go to Scranton, if you want. And save a day.'

He shook his head. 'That's going around Robin Hood's barn. We wait. We're here, and we'll stay here. Once we find out who Carroll is, or was, then we can think of what to do.'

'You think he was a gangster?'

'Something like that.'

'I liked him,' she said.

Around six-thirty they went across the street and had dinner at a Chinese restaurant. The food was fair. They went back to the hotel and sat in the room but it was too small, they felt too confined. There was a television set in the room. She turned it on and started watching a panel show. He got up, went over to the set, and turned it off. 'Come on,' he said. 'Let's get out of here, let's go to a movie.'

'What's playing?'

'What's the difference?'

They went to the Criterion on Broadway and saw a sexy comedy with Dean Martin and Shirley MacLaine. He bought loge tickets and they shared cigarettes and watched the movie. They got there about ten minutes after the picture started, left about fifteen minutes before it ended. On the way back to the hotel they stopped at a newsstand, and he tried to buy the morning papers. The early edition of the *Daily News* was the only one available. He bought the *News* and they went back to their room.

He divided the paper in half and they went through it. There was nothing about the murder in either section. He picked up both halves and threw them out. She asked what time it was.

'Nine-thirty.'

'This takes forever,' she said. 'Do you want to try getting the *Times* again?'

'Not yet.'

She got up and walked to the window, turned, walked to the bed, turned again and faced him. 'I think I'm going crazy,' she said.

He got up, walked to her. She turned from him. She said, 'Like a lion in a cage.'

'Easy, baby.'

'Let's get drunk, Dave. Can we do that?'

Her face was calm, unreally so. Her hands, at her sides, were knotted into tight little fists with her long fingernails digging into her palms. She saw him looking at her fists, and she opened her hands. There were red marks on the palms of her hands – she had very nearly broken the skin.

He picked up the phone and got the bell captain. He ordered a bottle of V.O., ice, club soda, and two glasses. When the kid brought their order he met him at the door, took the tray from him, signed the tab, and gave the kid a dollar.

'My husband is a big tipper,' she said. 'How much money do we have left?'

'A couple of hundred. Enough.'

He started making the drinks. She said, 'How much is the hotel room?'

'I don't know. Why?'

'We could go to a cheaper hotel. We'll be here a while and we don't want to run out of money.'

'They'll take a check.'

'They will?'

'Any hotel will,' he said. 'Any halfway decent hotel.'

She took her drink and held it awkwardly while he finished making one for himself. He raised his glass toward her and she lowered her eyes and drank part of her drink. When their glasses were empty he took them over to the dresser and added more whiskey and a little more soda.

'I'm going to get drunk tonight,' she said. 'I've never been really stoned in front of you, have I?'

'The hell you haven't.'

'I don't mean parties. Everybody gets drunk at parties. I mean plain drinking where you're just trying to get stoned, like now. We used to at college. My roommate and I, my junior year. My roommate was a girl from Virginia named Mary Beth George. You never met her.'

'No.'

'We would get stoned together and tell each other all our little problems. She used to cry when she got drunk. I didn't. We swore that we would be each other's maid of honor. Or matron, whoever got married first. I didn't even invite her to the wedding. I never even thought to. Isn't that terrible?'

'Is she married?'

'I think so.'

'Did she invite you to her wedding?'

'No. We lost track of each other. Isn't that the worst thing you ever heard of? We drank vodka and water. Did you ever have that?'

'Yes.'

'It didn't have any taste at all. It tasted like water with too much chlorine in it, the way it gets in the winter sometimes. You know how I mean, don't you?'

'Yes.'

'With a little provocation I think I could maybe become an alcoholic. Will you make me another of these, please?'

He fixed her another drink. He made it strong, and he added a little of the V.O. to his own glass. She took several small quick sips from her drink.

She said, 'I didn't even know you then. Both in Binghamton and we never even met. We went to two different schools together. That's a stupid line, isn't it? There was a comedian who used to say that, but I can't remember who. Can you?'

'No.'

'There are some other lines like that. "Would you rather go to New York or by train?" Silly. "Do you walk to school or take your lunch?" I think that's my favorite. I didn't fall in love with you the first time I saw you. I didn't even like you. What dreadful things I'm telling you! But when you asked me out I felt very excited. I didn't know why. I thought, here I don't like him, but I'm excited he asked me out. I can't stop talking. I'm just babbling like an idiot, I can't stop talking.'

She drank almost all of her drink in one swallow and took a step toward him, just one step, and then stopped. There was a moment when he thought she was going to fall down and he started for her to catch her but she stayed on her feet. She had a worried look on her face.

She said, 'I might be sick.'

'Don't worry about it.'

'I want you to make love to me, you know that, don't you? You know I want that, don't you?'

He held her and her face was pressed against his chest. She put her hands on his upper arms and pushed him away a little and looked up into his eyes. Her own eyes were a deeper green than ever, the color of fine jade.

She said, 'I want to but I can't. I love you, I love you more than I ever did, but I just can't do anything. Do you understand?'

'Yes. Don't talk about it.'

'This afternoon I thought I would wait for you and when you came back I would get you to make love to me, and everything would be all right. You haven't tried to make love to me. I think if you'd tried, before, I would have gone crazy. I don't know. But I sat here in this room and I planned it out, all of it, and just what I would do and just how I would feel, and I was all alone in the room, and all of a sudden I started to shake. I couldn't do it. Oh, I'm afraid.'

'Don't be.'

'Will I be all right?'

'Yes.'

'How can you tell?'

'I know.'

'I think you're right. I think everything's just stopped, just shut up in a box, until we do what we have to do. Those men. I can shut my eyes and see their faces perfectly. If I knew how to draw I could draw them, every detail. I'll be all right afterward, I think.'

A few minutes later she said, 'This is some honeymoon, isn't it? I'm sorry, darling.' Then he took her into the bathroom and held her while she threw up. She was very sick and he held her and told her it was all right, everything was all right. He helped her wash up and he undressed her and put her to bed. She did not cry at all through any of this. He put her to bed and covered her with the sheet and the blanket and she looked up at him and said that she loved him, and he kissed her. She was asleep almost at once.

He had one more drink, no soda and no ice. He capped the bottle and put it in the dresser with his shirts. In the morning, he thought, he would have to take a bundle to the laundry, the two shirts he had worn and a pair of slacks. And he would have to buy some things if he got the chance. He had packed mostly sportswear for the stay at the lodge and he would need dress shirts in New York.

The liquor helped him sleep. He woke up very suddenly and looked at his watch and it was seven o'clock, he had slept eight hours. He got dressed and went downstairs and outside. Jill was still sleeping. He bought the morning newspapers and went back to the room, and one of them had the story.

5

PENNSYLVANIA SHOOTING VICTIM
IDENTIFIED AS HICKSVILLE BUILDER

Scranton, Pa. – State police today identified the victim of a vicious gangland-style slaying as Joseph P. Corelli, a Long Island building contractor residing in Hicksville.

Corelli was shot to death late Sunday in an as yet unsolved attack outside his cabin at Pomquit Lodge on nearby Lake Wallenpaupack. 'It has all the earmarks of a professional murder,' stated Sheriff Roy Fairland of Pomquit. 'Corelli was shot five times in the head and two different guns were used.'

The dead man had resided at Pomquit Lodge for almost three months prior to the murder. He was registered at the Lodge as Joseph Carroll and carried false identification in that name. Proper identification of Corelli was facilitated through fingerprint records of the Federal Bureau of Investigation.

Corelli was arrested three times in the past five years, twice on charges of extortion and once for possession of betting slips. He was released each time without being brought to trial, according to New York Police Sgt. James Gregg. 'He [Corelli] had definite underworld connections,' Sgt. Gregg asserted. 'He had several criminal contacts that we know of, and it's a good bet he was operating outside the law.'

Nassau County police officials denied knowledge of any recent criminal activity on Corelli's part. 'We were aware of his record and kept an eye on him,' one officer stated, 'but if he was involved in anything shady, it was going on outside of our jurisdiction.'

Corelli, a bachelor, lived alone at 4113 Bayview Road in Hicksville and maintained an office in the Bascom Building, also in Hicksville. His sole survivor is a sister, Mrs Raymond Romagno of Boston.

When he opened the door of the hotel room she sat up in the bed and blinked at him. Her face was pale and drawn. He asked her if she was all right.

'I'm a little rocky,' she said. 'I drank too much, I got all sloppy. I'm sorry.'

'Forget it. It's in the paper.'

'Carroll?'

'Corelli,' he said. He folded the paper open to the story and handed it to her. She couldn't find it at first and he sat next to her and pointed it out to her. He watched her face while she worked her way through the article. Halfway through she motioned for a cigarette and he lit one for her. She coughed on it but went on reading to the end of the article. Then she set the paper on the bed beside her. She finished the cigarette and put it out in the ashtray on top of the bedside table. She started to say something, then realized for the first time that she didn't have any clothes on. She looked at herself and jumped up and ran into the bathroom.

When she came out she looked reborn. Her face was fresh and clean, the pallor gone from it now. She had lipstick on. He smoked a cigarette while she put on a dress and shoes.

She said, 'Corelli. I didn't think he looked Italian.'

'He could have been almost anything, as far as I could tell. He didn't look Irish, either.'

'Carroll isn't always Irish.'

'I guess not.'

'There was a composer named Corelli. Before Bach, I think. We were right about almost everything, weren't we? About who he was. He was in construction, but he was also a gangster.'

'In a small way.' He thought a minute. 'There are some things that aren't in that article.'

'You mean about us?'

'I mean about Carroll. Corelli. What rackets he was in, who his friends were. They talked a lot about his contacts but they didn't say who they were. It might help to know.'

'How do we find out?'

'From the police,' he said.

'You mean just ask them?'

'Not exactly,' he said.

They skipped breakfast. They left the hotel and found an empty phone booth in a drugstore on Sixth Avenue. He coached her on what to say and she practiced while he looked up the number of police headquarters in the Manhattan book. He wrote the number in his notebook and she said, 'Let me try it now. How does this sound?'

He listened while she went through her speech. Then he said, 'I think that's right. It's hard to tell without hearing it over the phone. Let's give it a try.'

She went into the booth and closed the door. She dialed the number he had written down. A man answered in the middle of the first ring.

She said, 'Sergeant James Gregg, please. Long distance calling.'

The man asked her who was calling. She said, 'The Scranton *Courier-Herald*.'

The man told her to hang on, he'd see if he could find Gregg. There was a pause, and some voices in the distance, and a click and silence, another click and a youngish voice saying, 'Gregg here.'

'Sergeant James Gregg?'

'Speaking.'

'Go ahead, please.' She opened the phone-booth door quickly, stepped outside and handed the receiver to Dave. He took it, ducked into the booth and pulled the door shut.

He said, 'Sergeant Gregg? This is Pete Miller at the *Courier-Herald*. We're trying to work up a background story on the Corelli murder, and I'd like to ask you a couple of questions.'

'Again? I just talked to you people an hour ago.'

'I just came on,' he said quickly. 'What we're trying to do, Sergeant Gregg, what I'm trying to do, is to work up a human-interest piece on Corelli. Gangland killings, in this area, they're exciting—'

'Exciting?'

'—and people are interested. Could you tell me a few things about Corelli?'

'Well, I'm pretty busy now.'

'It won't take a minute, Sergeant. Now, first of all, I think you or somebody else mentioned that Corelli was connected with the underworld.'

'He had connections,' Gregg said guardedly.

'What sort of racket was he in?'

There was a short pause. Then, 'What he was in was construction. We don't know exactly what he did on the side, the illegal side. He knew a lot of gamblers, and his last arrest was here in Manhattan, he was picked up in a gambling raid. We didn't have a case against him and we let him go.'

'I see.'

'His business was all out on Long Island. That's out of our jurisdiction, and we didn't nose around in that connection. We know he was in touch with some people here in the city, some racket people, but we don't know what exactly he was doing. If he was working a racket in Long Island, well, that wasn't our business.'

'Could you tell me some of his associates in New York?'

'Why?'

'It would give the story some color,' he said.

'The names wouldn't mean anything to you,' Gregg said. 'You're out in Scranton and Corelli's friends, the ones we know about, are just small-time gamblers. People like George White and Eddie Mizell, just people nobody ever heard of. No one important.'

'I see,' he said. 'How about a man named Lublin?'

'Maurie Lublin? What about him?'

'Was he an associate of Corelli's?'

'Where did you hear that?'

'The name came up, I don't remember where. Was he?'

'I never heard about it. It might be. People like Corelli know a lot of people, it's hard to say. Offhand I would say Maurie Lublin is too big to be interested in Corelli.'

'Do you know why Corelli was killed?'

'Well, it's not our case. There's nothing certain. Just rumors.'

'Rumors?'

'That's right.'

It was like pulling teeth, he thought. He said, 'What kind of rumors?'

'He was supposed to owe money.'

'To anyone in particular?'

'We don't know, and I wouldn't want to say anyway. Jesus, don't you people ever get together on anything? I talked to one of your men and told him most of this just a little while ago. Can't you get it from him?'

'Well, you probably talked to someone on straight news, Sergeant Gregg. I'm on features.'

'Oh.'

'I don't want to keep you, I know you're busy. Just one thing more. Will you be in charge of the investigation in New York?'

'Investigation?'

'Of the Corelli murder.'

'What investigation?' Gregg seemed almost irritated. 'He was a man from Long Island who got himself killed out of state. We're not doing anything about it. We'll cooperate with Pennsylvania if they ask us to, but we're not doing anything.'

'Will there be an investigation in Hicksville?'

'On the Island? What for? He got shot out of state, for God's sake.'

He thought, Pennsylvania would shelve it because Corelli was from New York, and New York would forget about it because the murder happened in Pennsylvania. He said, 'Thank you very much, Sergeant. You've been a big help, and I didn't mean to take too much of your time.'

'It's okay,' Gregg said. 'We try to cooperate.'

He got out of the booth. She started to ask him a question, but he shook his head and began writing in the little notebook. He wrote: 'Maurie Lublin.' Under that he wrote: 'George White and Eddie Mizell.' On the next line he wrote: 'Corelli owed money.' Then: 'No Investigation.'

The drugstore was too crowded to talk in. He took her arm, put the notebook back in his breast pocket, and led her out of the store. There was a Cobb's Corner across the street. They waited for the light to change, crossed Sixth Avenue and went into the restaurant. It was past nine already. Most of the breakfast crowd had gone to work and the place was near empty. They took a table for two in the rear and ordered orange juice and toast and coffee. He gave her the whole conversation by the time the waitress brought the food.

'You'd make a good reporter,' she said.

'And you'd make a good telephone operator. I kept waiting for him to catch on and start wondering who the hell I was and why I was bothering him, but he believed it all the way. We learned a lot.'

'Yes.'

'A hell of a lot. George White and Eddie Mizell – I don't know what we can do with those names. But there is a Lublin. And he's a crook, and he's in New York somewhere. Maurie Lublin. Maurice, I guess that would be.'

'Or Morris.'

'One or the other. And everything still holds together the way we figured it. That Joe Corelli owed money, I mean. And that was why he was running.'

She nodded and sipped her coffee. He lit a cigarette and set it down in an oval glass ashtray.

'The big thing is that there's no investigation. Not in New York and not in Hicksville. Isn't that a hell of a name for a town?'

'Probably a description.'

'Probably. But the cops there won't bother with the murder. They may close a file on Corelli but that's all. That means we go out there.'

'To Hicksville?'

'That's right.'

'Is that safe?'

'It's safe. There won't be any police there, not at his place and not at his office either. The New York police aren't interested in Corelli any more. And Lublin's men won't be there, either.'

'How do you know?'

'They had about three months to search Corelli's room and office. Maybe that was how they found out where he was, how they got the idea. That lodge was out of the way. They must have had some information or they never would have dug him up. They've probably sifted through his papers and everything else a dozen times already. Now he's out of the way. They won't be interested any more.'

She looked thoughtful. He said, 'Maybe you should stay at the hotel, baby. I'll run out there myself.'

'No.'

'It won't take long. And—'

'No. Whither thou goest and all that. That's not it. I was just wondering what we could find there. If they already searched—'

'They were looking for different things. They wanted to find out where Corelli was hiding, and we want to find out why he was hiding, and from whom. It's worth a try.'

'And I'm going with you, Dave.'

He argued some more and got nowhere with it. He let it go. It seemed safe enough, and perhaps she'd be better off with him than alone with her thoughts at the hotel.

The doorman at the Royalton got the car for them. He told them how to find the Queens-Midtown tunnel and what to do when they were through it. The sky was clouded over and the air was thick with the promise of rain. They drove through the tunnel and cut east across Queens on an expressway. The road was confusing. They missed the turnoff for Hicksville, went five miles out of their way and cut back. At an Atlantic station they filled the gas tank and found out where Bayview Road was. They hit Bayview Road in the 2300 block and drove past numbered streets until they found the address listed in the newspaper story. Hicksville was monolithic, block after block of semidetached two-story brick houses with treeless front yards and a transient air, a general impression that all the inhabitants were merely living there until they could afford to move again, either further out on the Island or closer to the city.

Corelli's building, 4113, was another faceless brick building jammed between 4111 and 4115. There were wash lines in the back. According to the mailboxes, someone named Haas lived upstairs and someone named Penner lived on the ground floor. Dave stepped back into the street to check the address, then dug the newspaper clipping from his wallet to make sure he had read it correctly the first time around: 'Corelli, a bachelor, lived alone at 4113 Bayview Road in Hicksville . . .'

Jill told him to try the downstairs buzzer. 'Probably the landlord,' she said. 'They buy the house and live downstairs and rent out the upstairs. The income covers the mortgage payments.'

He rang the downstairs bell and waited. There were sounds inside the house but nothing happened. He rang again, and a muffled voice called, 'All right, I'm coming, take it easy.'

He waited. The door opened inward and a woman peered suspiciously at him through the screen door. Her face said she thought he was a salesman and she wasn't interested. Then she caught sight of Jill and decided that he wasn't a salesman and her face softened slightly. She still wasn't thrilled to see him, her face said, but at least he wasn't selling anything, and that was a break.

He said, 'Mrs Penner?'

She nodded. He searched for the right phrasing, something that would fit whether or not she knew Corelli was dead. 'My name is Peter Miller,' he said. 'Does a Mr Joseph Corelli live in the upstairs apartment?'

'Why?'

'Just business,' he said, smiling.

'He used to live here. I rented the place after he skipped on me. He lives here for three years, he pays his rent every time the first of the month, and then he skips. Just one day he's gone.' She shook her head. 'Just disappears. Didn't take his things, that's his furniture and he left it, everything. I figured he would be back. Leaving everything, you would think he'd be back, wouldn't you?'

He nodded. She didn't know Corelli was dead, he thought. Maybe that was good.

'But he never shows,' she said, shifting conveniently into present tense again. 'He never shows, and I hold the place a month, waiting for him. That's seventy dollars I'm out plus another week before I could rent it. I don't rent to colored and it took a full week before they moved in, Mr and Mrs Haas. Eighty-five dollars he cost me, Corelli.'

'Do you have his things? His furniture and all?'

'I rented the place furnished,' Mrs Penner said. She was defensive now. 'Mrs Haas, she didn't have any furniture. They just got married. No kids, you know?' She shook her head again. 'There'll be kids, though. A young couple, they'll have kids soon enough, you bet on it. One thing about Corelli, he was quiet up there. What about his things? He send you or something?'

Jill said, 'Mrs Penner, I'm Joe's sister. Joe called me, he's in Arizona and he had to leave New York in a hurry.'

'Cop trouble?'

'He didn't say. Mrs Penner—'

'There was cops came around right after he left. Showed me their badges and went pawing through everything.' She paused. 'They don't look like cops, not them. But they show me their badges and that's enough. I don't like to stick my nose in.'

Jill said, 'Mrs Penner, you know Joe was in business here. There was a lawsuit and he had to leave the state to stay out of trouble. It wasn't police trouble.'

'So?'

'He called me yesterday,' she went on. 'There were some things of his, some things he had to leave here, and he wanted me to get them for him.'

'Sure.'

'If I could just—'

The screen door stayed shut. 'As soon as I get that eighty-five dollars,' she said. 'That's what he cost me, that eighty-five dollars. There was no lease so that's all, just the eighty-five, but I want that before he gets his stuff.'

Jill didn't say anything. Dave took out a cigarette and said, 'You can hold the furniture for the time being, Mrs Penner. In fact I think Joe would just as soon you kept the furniture, and then you can go on renting the flat furnished. It's worth more than eighty-five dollars, but just to make things easier you could keep the furniture for the rent you missed out on.'

He could see her mind working, balancing the extra five or ten dollars a month against the eighty-five dollars Corelli had cost her. She looked as though she wanted a little more, so he said, 'Unless you'd rather have the money. Then I could have a truck here later this afternoon to pick up the furniture.'

He could imagine her trying to explain that to the Haases. Quickly she said, 'No, it's fair enough. And easier all around, right?'

'That's what I thought. Now if we could see Joe's other stuff, his clothes and all. You kept everything, didn't you?'

She had everything downstairs in large cardboard boxes. Suits, ties, slacks, underwear. Corelli had had an extensive wardrobe, sharp Broadway suits with Phil Kronfeld and Martin Janss labels in them. There was one boxful of papers. Dave took the carton and carried it out to the car. Jill waited in the car, and he went back to the house and told Mrs Penner he would send somebody around for the rest of the stuff, the clothes and everything. 'Today or tomorrow,' he said.

That was fine with her. He got into the car and drove off.

At the Bascom Building, in Hicksville's business district, Jill waited in the car with the box of papers while he went inside and managed to get into Corelli's office. This was easier, because they hadn't moved him out for nonpayment of rent. He had been gone for three months but they had left his office as he had left it, the door locked and everything undisturbed. He found the superintendent and told him he wanted to get into Corelli's office, and the old man said he had to have the key or written authorization.

Dave gave him a story off the top of his head – that Corelli had sent him down to pick up copies of a contract, that it would only be for a minute, and that he didn't want to take the time to get a written authorization from Corelli. The super didn't believe it but he just nodded, waiting. Dave gave him ten dollars and the super made the bill disappear and took him upstairs and unlocked the door for him. He seemed to be doing something he had done before – for the men who had been looking for Corelli.

'Don't be long now,' he said. 'And lock the door behind you, hear?'

He wasn't long. The office was a cubbyhole, one window facing out on the main street of Hicksville, a single dark-green filing cabinet, a cheap oak desk, a standing coatrack. The wooden desk chair was padded with a cushion that smelled slightly of old rubber.

There were three drawers to the filing cabinet. The bottom drawer held a half-full bottle of Philadelphia blended whiskey. The middle drawer was empty. In the top drawer there was a disorganized pile of contracts and invoices and letters. The letterheads, as far as he could see, were of various companies in the building trades. He shuffled all the papers into a moderately neat pile and stuffed them into a brown manila envelope.

The desktop was free from clutter. There was a thick layer of dust across it but nothing else. In the top drawer of the desk he found a box of paper clips, a year-old copy of *Argosy* folded open to an article on skin-diving paraphernalia, a memo pad with no entries in it, a Zippo cigarette lighter initialed 'J.C.,' a four- by five-inch glossy print of a girl in panties and bra, a pigskin address book, and a packet of contraceptives. He added the address book to the manila envelope and closed the drawer. In another drawer, far in the rear, he found an unloaded gun and, behind it, a nearly full box of cartridges.

He picked up the gun, then stopped and glanced automatically at the window. No one was watching him, of course. He hefted the gun and felt its weight. He hesitated just a moment, then tucked the gun into his pants pocket, the right-hand pocket. He put the box of shells in his left-hand jacket pocket, stopped, lit a cigarette, and checked the one remaining drawer in the desk. It was empty, and he closed it and straightened up.

Outside, it was getting ready to rain. He got behind the wheel and Jill asked him if there had been anything important in the office. He told her he didn't know yet, that they would have to see. She said she had forgotten how to get back to the city and asked him if he remembered the route. He started the car and told her that he remembered the way.

6

The gun was a Bodyguard, by Smith & Wesson. It was a five-shot revolver that took .38-Special shells, and it was hammerless, so you didn't have to cock it – a pull on the trigger would fire the gun. It had a two-inch barrel, it was black, it was steel, it weighed a pound and a quarter. The grip was textured, and formed to fit the hand.

The purpose of the gun was implicit in its design. Because it was short-barreled, its accuracy was somewhat limited; it would be a poor bet for target shooting or long-range plinking. The short barrel meant that it was designed to be carried easily on the person, probably concealed. The absence of a hammer facilitated quick draws; a hammer might catch on clothing, might leave the gun snagged in a pocket or under a belt. The gun had been made to carry, to fire easily and quickly, to shoot ammunition that would kill a man with a well-placed hit. It was a gun for killing people.

Now, it was unloaded. He sat on the edge of the bed in their hotel room and held the gun in his right hand, his hand curled around the butt, his finger just resting lightly upon the trigger. The box of shells was on the bed beside him. He opened the box and loaded the gun, putting shells in four of the five chambers. He rotated the cylinder so that there was no cartridge under the hammer and so that nothing would happen if the trigger was pulled accidentally.

He looked up. Jill's eyes were on the gun, and they were nervous. She raised her eyes to meet his.

'Dave, do you know how to use that?'

'Yes.' He looked at the gun again, set it down on the bed beside him. He closed the box of ammunition. 'In the army. They taught us guns. In basic training. Mostly rifles, of course, but there was a brief course on handguns.'

She didn't say anything. He picked up a stack of papers and ruffled through them. They had gone through everything in less than an hour, finding almost all of Corelli's papers less than useless. The business papers might have been clues to something, but they couldn't tell – they were just various bills and receipts and letters relating to Corelli's construction business. He had evidently been something of a middleman in construction, setting up jobs and parceling them out among subcontractors.

The personal papers included a slew of IOU's, around a dozen of them representing money owed to Corelli, debts canceled now by his death. They ranged from thirty-five dollars to one for an even thousand, with most of them running around a hundred. There were four rather stiff letters from the sister in Boston, written neatly in dark-blue ink, telling him about her husband and her children and her house and asking him how business was going. There were irritatingly obscure little bits of memoranda – telephone numbers, addresses, names, none linked to anything in particular, each of them standing alone on its own sheet of paper: 'Room 417 Barbizon Plaza'; 'Henrich, 45 @ $7\frac{1}{2}$ = $337.50'; 'Flowers for Joanie' – a few tickets on losing horses that had run at Aqueduct, at Belmont, at Roosevelt.

In the address book, there were more than fifty entries, most of them tersely inscribed with initials or just a first name or just a last name. There were seventeen girls listed only by first name and telephone number, no address, no last name. Maurie Lublin was listed by last name alone, with a phone number and no address.

Several slips of paper contained just numbers – columns of figures, isolated numbers, bits of addition and subtraction. The number 65,000 came up on several sheets, twice with a dollar sign: $65,000.

Dave said, 'Sixty-five thousand dollars. That must be what he owed.'

'To Lublin?'

'I suppose so. I don't know whether he stole it or owed it. Lee and the other one didn't find that money, so he didn't take it with him. If he had it, and he was running away, wouldn't he have taken the money with him? I think he must have owed it to Lublin and then couldn't pay. He left town in a hurry, not as though he had planned it or anything. I think he owed the money and planned on paying it, and then he couldn't pay it and he panicked and ran. And they found him.'

'And killed him.'

'Yes.'

She sat next to him on the bed. The gun was between them, and she looked down at it and said, 'Guns scare me.'

'Pick it up.'

'Why?'

'Pick it up.' She did. He showed her how to hold it and made her curl her index finger around the trigger. 'Aim at the doorknob,' he said.

She aimed. He sighted along the barrel and showed her how her aim was off, and taught her how to line up a target. He took the gun from her and spilled out the shells, clearing all five chambers. Then he made her aim at the doorknob and squeeze the trigger to get the feel of the gun. After she practiced for a few minutes he took the gun from her and loaded it again.

He said, 'There's only one way. We could try to dig up Corelli's life history if we wanted. We could call up each of the girls he knew and find out what they all knew about him. We could look him up in the *New York Times* file, and we could look up all the people in his address book, and we could find out everything there is to know about Joe Corelli.'

'Is that what you want to do?'

'No.' He took out two cigarettes, lit one for himself and offered the other to her. She shook her head and he put the cigarette back in the pack. 'No,' he said again. 'Corelli doesn't matter any more. We're not trying to find Corelli. He's dead, and we don't need him. We're not writing his biography. We're looking for the two other men.'

She didn't say anything.

'Lublin hired those men,' he said. 'We have Lublin's name and we have his phone number. We can find out where he lives. We'll see him, and he'll tell us who the men were who killed Corelli.'

'Why will he tell us?'

'We'll make him tell us.'

Her eyes darted to the gun, then away. She said, 'Now?'

'Now.' He stood up, gun in hand. 'We'll check the drugstore phone books. We'll find the Lublin who matches the number in Corelli's book, and then we'll go see him.'

Dave tried the gun in each of his jacket pockets. In the inside pockets, it made a revealing bulge. In the outside pockets it hung loose and awkward. He jammed it under his belt but it didn't feel right there, either.

Jill said, 'Give it to me.' He gave her the gun and she put it in her purse. The purse was a flat one, black calf, and the gun did not fit well. She got another purse from the dresser, a larger one, and she put the gun and her other things into it. There was no bulge this time.

It was raining now, raining steadily, with a wind whipping the rain into their faces as they walked to the drugstore. Cars streaked by on wet asphalt. She held his arm with one hand and the purse with the other. In the drugstore, he started to look through all the phone books. She saved time by calling Information and asking the operator which borough Lublin's exchange would be in. The exchange was Ulster 9, and the operator told her that would be in Brooklyn.

They found him in the Brooklyn phone book: 'Lublin, Maurice 4412 Nwkrk . . . ULster 9-2459.' He looked at the listing and couldn't figure out what the street was supposed to be. There was a New York street directory on the magazine rack, and he thumbed back to the index and checked the Brooklyn streets in alphabetical order. There was a Newkirk Avenue listed; it was the only street that fit.

He tried Lublin's number, and no one answered. He called again and got no answer, then checked the phone book again to see if there was an office listed. There wasn't.

'He's not home,' he told her.

'Then let's have dinner. I'm starving.'

He was, too. They hadn't eaten at all since morning, and it was almost six already. But he hadn't noticed his hunger until she mentioned it. He interpreted this as a sign of their progress. They were moving now, growing involved in the mechanics of pursuit, and he had been hungry without even realizing it.

They went to an Italian restaurant down the block and ate lasagne and drank bottles of beer. In the middle of the meal he left the table and used the phone to dial Lublin's number. There was no answer. He came back to the table and told her.

'He'll get home eventually,' she said.

'I suppose so.'

After dinner, he called again. There was no answer. They stopped at a drugstore and bought a couple of magazines, and he tried again on the drugstore phone. No answer. They went back to the hotel room. At seven-thirty he tossed a magazine aside and picked up the phone, then cradled it.

'What's the matter?'

'I don't know,' he said. 'Do you suppose they listen in?'

'Who?'

'The hotel operators.'

'Maybe.'

'I'll be back in a minute.'

He went downstairs and around the corner to the drugstore and tried again. There was no answer. In the hotel room, he kept looking at his watch. He went back to the drugstore again at eight, and called, and a man answered.

He said, 'Mr Lublin?'

'Just a minute, I'll get him.' Then, 'Maurie. For you.'

He hung up and went back to the room. He told her, 'Lublin's home now but he's not alone. Somebody else answered the phone.'

'Was it—'

'No, I'm sure it wasn't. I'd remember their voices.' He thought a moment. 'There were noises in the background. They may have been having a party. I don't know. I think there were a lot of people there. But there's at least one other man, the one who answered the phone. And he called Lublin by name. If Lublin were the only other person there, he wouldn't have called him by name, I don't think.'

'What do we do now?'

'I'll call again in a little while. Sooner or later he'll be the only one left, and then I'll go after him.'

She didn't say anything for several minutes. Then she said, 'Don't call again tonight.'

'Why not?'

'Because he'll be suspicious. Calling and then hanging up – if it just happens once he'll shrug it off, but if it happens more than that he'll get suspicious. We can't let him be on guard. The best thing for us right now is that nobody even knows about us. Lublin doesn't know we exist and the two men don't know we're looking for them. We can't afford to let them find out.'

She was right. 'I'll go there around three in the morning,' he said. 'The party'll be over by then.'

'No.'

'Why not, Jill?'

'He might not live alone.' She sat next to him and held his hands in hers. 'Please,' she said. 'We don't know anything about him yet, about the setup there. Let's wait until tomorrow. We can go there after a call, or if nobody's home we can go there and break in and wait for him. Either way. Right now he's there and he has company, and we don't even know if he lives in a house or an apartment, we don't know anything. Can't we wait until morning?'

'Are you nervous?'

'Partly. And I'm exhausted, for another thing. A good sleep wouldn't hurt either of us. Tomorrow—'

He nodded slowly. She was right, there was no sense wasting their major advantage of surprise. And it wouldn't hurt to wait another day. They had plenty of time.

He got the bottle of V.O. from the drawer and lay on the bed with it. She went over and turned on the television set. There was a doctor program on, something about an immigrant who wouldn't consent to surgery, and they watched it together. He didn't pay very much attention to it. He stretched out on the bed and sipped the V.O. straight from the bottle, not working hard at it but just sipping as he watched the program. She said she didn't want anything to drink.

After that, they watched a cops-and-robbers thing for an hour, then caught the eleven o'clock news. There was nothing important on the news. During the weather report she turned off the television set and suggested that they go to sleep. He was tired without being sleepy. He could feel the exhaustion in his body, the need for sleep, but at the same time he felt entirely awake. But sleep was a good idea. He took another long swig from the bottle to make sleep come easier.

They undressed in the same room with no embarrassment, no need for privacy. The adjustment of the honeymoon, he thought wryly. They had accomplished that much, surely. There was no longer any question of embarrassment. He felt that he could not possibly be embarrassed now in front of this woman, that they had lived through too much together, had shared too much, had grown too intimate to be separated by that variety of distance. They undressed, and he switched on the bedside lamp and turned off the overhead light, and they got into bed, and he switched off the bedside lamp and they lay together in darkness.

She was breathing very heavily. He moved toward her and she flowed into his arms and her mouth was warm and eager. He kissed her and felt her warmth against him, and he kissed her again and touched her sleeping breasts and she said his name in a husky whisper. His hands were filled with the sweet flesh.

It didn't work. It began well, but there was tension for him and tension for her and it did not work at all. The desire was there but the capacity was not.

She lay very close to him. 'I'm sorry,' she said.

'Shhhh.'

'I love you. We were married Sunday. What's today? Tuesday night? We've only been married two days.'

He didn't say anything.

'Two days,' she said. 'It seems so long. I don't think I knew you at all when we got married. Not at all. Courtship, engagement, all of that, and I hardly knew you. And two days.'

He kissed her lightly.

'I love you,' she said. 'Sleep.'

He lay in the darkness, sure he wouldn't sleep. Lublin was in Brooklyn, on Newkirk Avenue. He had called him on the phone, had hung up before Lublin could take the call. He should have waited another minute, he thought. Just long enough to hear the man's voice so he would know it.

But it was real now, it was all real. Before there had been the fury, the need to Do Something, but the reality had not been present. And then that day there had been the article in the paper, the visual proof again of Corelli's death. And the trip to Hicksville, to Corelli's home and to Corelli's office.

It was very real. He had a gun now, Corelli's gun, and all he knew about a gun was what he had learned ages ago in basic training. Could he hit anything with a gun? Could he use it properly?

And he had never fired at a human target. Not with a revolver, not with a rifle, not with anything. He had never aimed at a living person and tried to kill that person.

He reached out a hand and lightly touched his wife's body. She did not stir. He drew his hand back, then, and settled himself in the bed and took a deep breath.

He woke up very suddenly. He had fallen asleep without expecting to, and now he woke up as though he had been dynamited from the bed. His mouth was dry and his head ached dully. He sat bolt upright in the bed and tried to catch his breath. He was out of breath, as if he had been running furiously for a bus.

His cigarettes were on the bedside table. He reached out and got the pack, shook out a cigarette, lit it, cupping the flame to avoid awakening Jill. The smoke was strong in his lungs. He smothered a cough, breathed in air, then drew once more on the cigarette.

He looked at her side of the bed and could not see her in the darkness. He reached out a tentative hand to touch her.

She was not there.

In the bathroom, then. He called her name, and there was no answer, no answer.

'Jill!'

Nothing. He got out of bed and went to the bathroom. It was empty. He turned on lights, looked around for a note. No note.

She was gone.

7

The desk clerk said, 'Mrs Wade left about a half hour ago, sir. Or maybe a little more than that. Let me see, I came on at midnight, and then I had a cup of coffee at two-thirty, and then your wife left the hotel just as I was finishing my coffee. It must have been a quarter to three, I would guess.' It was just three-thirty now. Forty-five minutes, he thought. Jill had been gone for forty-five minutes.

'Is anything wrong, Mr Wade?'

'No,' he said. 'Nothing's wrong.' He forced a smile. 'She probably couldn't sleep,' he said. 'Probably went out for coffee.'

He went back upstairs and sat in the room and smoked another cigarette. Jill was gone. Jill had gotten up in the middle of the night, alone, and had dressed and left. For coffee? It was possible, he guessed. But for three-quarters of an hour?

She had left the hotel by herself. The immediate fear, the automatic reaction once he realized she was gone, was the worry that someone had come to take her away. But that was senseless. No one knew about either of them, no one knew where they were staying. And no one had called their room, either. He would have heard the phone no matter how deeply he was sleeping, for one thing. And the desk clerk would probably have mentioned a call.

He checked the whiskey bottle. It was as full as it had been. If she wanted a drink, he thought, she would have had it there. She wouldn't go barhopping by herself in the middle of the night. Coffee, then. Coffee and a sandwich, maybe.

Why hadn't she come back?

He put on a coat and went down to the lobby and out into the night. It was still raining, but the rain had slowed to a drizzle. Most of the lights were out on Forty-fifth Street. He walked to the corner of Sixth. The Cobb's Corner was open, and he went inside and looked around, but she wasn't there. He went out again and stood on the corner in the rain, looking around, trying to figure out where she might be. There were three or four open restaurants that he could see and, along Sixth Avenue, more than a dozen bars. She could be anywhere. Or she could be somewhere else, and not in any of these places.

Check them all? It didn't make any sense. And suppose she wanted to get in touch with him, and called him, and he wasn't there. Or suppose she got back to the hotel while he was out looking for her.

He went back to the Royalton. He sat in a chair, and then he got up suddenly and looked for her purse. The large brown purse was on a chair. He opened it, and saw the gun; she had left it behind. But the purse was empty otherwise, and he guessed that she had transferred everything to the black-calf purse before leaving.

Where could she have gone? Just out for coffee, he told himself. Just out for coffee, and if he would just sit back and relax she would return to the room in no time at all. But he couldn't make himself believe it. She wouldn't be gone this long.

He remembered again, unwillingly now, the sudden rush of reality that had come that night after the call to Lublin. The quick and certain proof that this was no game they were playing, no treasure hunt. That, and then the unsuccessful attempt to make love.

And he thought, we never should have come. We should have left that place and gone somewhere else until the honeymoon was over, and then we should have gone back to Binghamton. No pursuit, no chase, no revenge. We should have gone home.

Because he knew, now, what had happened. Jill had panicked. The initial shock of violation had steeled her, had made her determination for revenge equal to his own, but by now her reactions had cooled and jelled and had changed from determination to panic. He remembered the look in her eyes when he had taught her to use the gun, and he remembered the way she had wanted to wait a day before going after Lublin. Panic, panic. The hunt was wrong for a woman, for a girl; she was no huntress, no killer, and she had not been able to take it, and now she was gone.

Where? Back to Binghamton, he thought. Back to her home, where she knew everyone and where she would be safe. He had misjudged her and now she was running, and he paced the floor of their room and tried to figure out what to do next. At one point he started to pack their clothes into their suitcases, then suddenly changed his mind and put everything back where it had been. He took the gun from her purse and held it first in one hand and then in the other, switching it nervously back and forth, finally sighing and returning it to the large brown bag.

Twice he picked up the bottle of V.O. and each time he put it back without drinking. One time he uncapped it. The other time he just held it in both hands and looked at the amber whiskey.

At twenty minutes after four, the phone rang. He was sitting right next to it, sitting on the edge of the bed. When it rang he dropped a cigarette onto the rug. He didn't bother to pick it up but ground it into the carpet while he reached for the phone.

'Dave? Did I wake you?'

'My God, where are you?'

'I'm calling from a drugstore. Relax, darling. I'm all right. I didn't mean to frighten you, but—'

'Where are you?'

'Get a pencil.'

He started to say something, changed his mind and got up. His pen and his little notebook were on the top of the dresser. He got them and opened the notebook and said, 'All right. Where are you?'

'A drugstore. It's on the corner of Flatbush Avenue and Ditmas Avenue – that's in Brooklyn.'

'What are you—'

She cut in on him. 'Get in a cab,' she said easily. 'Come here as soon as you can. I'll be waiting right here, in the store. And bring the thing in my brown purse. All right?'

'Jill—'

'Flatbush and Ditmas,' she said. 'I'm sorry if I worried you, darling. And hurry.'

8

The drugstore's lunch counter was to the left of the door, separated from the door by a magazine rack and the tobacco counter. She was drinking coffee at the counter, the only customer. He looked at her and, for a second or two, did not recognize her. Then he looked again and saw that it was Jill.

She looked entirely different. Her hair was a different color, a sort of medium brown, and she wore it off her face now, brought back and done up in a French twist. When she turned to him he stared. Her hair style altered the whole shape of her face.

And her face was different for other reasons, too. Her lips looked fuller, redder. Her eyes were deeper, and she seemed to be wearing a lot of makeup. She was only twenty-four but she looked a good three years older now.

He started to sputter questions but she silenced him with a finger to her lips. 'Sit down,' she said. 'Have a cup of coffee. I'll explain it all to you.'

'I think you'd better.'

He sat down, and an old man with thick wire-rimmed glasses came over to take his order. He asked for coffee. He forgot to order it black, and it came with cream in it. He stirred it with a spoon. The counterman went away, and Dave waited.

She said, 'I went to see Lublin.'

'You must be crazy.'

'No,' she said. 'Dave, it was the only way. We couldn't go after him until we knew what his place was like, if he lived alone or with anybody, all of that. And you couldn't go to meet him because he would have been suspicious, you never would have gotten past the door. Suppose he had live-in bodyguards. He does have one man who lives with him, as a matter of fact. If we went there without knowing—'

'But why did *you* go?'

'Because I knew he would let me in.' She drank coffee. 'He wouldn't let a man in, one that he didn't know, on a night when he was having some people over. But a girl is something else again. Almost any man will open a door for a pretty girl. And let her stay as long as she wants. I told him I was supposed to meet a man there. I said—'

'What man?'

'Pete Miller. You've been using the name so much it was the first one that came to mind.' She grinned quickly. 'He said he didn't know any Pete Miller. I stood there looking lost and pathetic and told him I was sure that this was the address, that I was supposed to come there. I guess he decided that I must be a call girl. He said it was probably somebody's idea of a joke but that I should come in out of the rain and have a drink to warm up. It was still raining then.' She patted her hair and grinned again. 'I was afraid it would wash the color out of my hair.'

He pointed to her hair. 'Why?'

'Because I was afraid one of the men might be there, one of the two men. Or anyone who might have seen the two of us this afternoon, in case Corelli's office was watched. But mostly because I thought Lee or the other one might be there. I don't know if they would remember us or not, if they paid any attention to what we looked like. I didn't want to take chances.'

'You took plenty of chances.'

She sipped at her coffee again, finished it. He tried his own. It tasted flat with cream, but at least it was hot.

She said, 'After I left the hotel, I went to a drugstore, the one where you tried to call Lublin before. I bought some makeup and a different shade of lipstick and a color comb. They use them to color gray hair, mostly, but it worked. I went into a restaurant, into the rest room, and I colored my hair and pinned it up like this. And did my lips and used some eye shadow. Do I look very different?'

'I almost didn't recognize you.'

'Like me this way?'

'Not too.'

'I wanted to look different, and I also wanted to look like a girl who might ring a man's doorbell in the middle of the night. Do I look cheap? Not terribly cheap, but slightly tacky?'

'Slightly tacky.'

'Good. Don't worry – the makeup comes off and the hair color will wash right out. It's not a permanent transformation. Do you want to hear about Lublin?'

'Yes.'

'First give me a cigarette.' He gave her one, lit hers and one for himself. 'Lublin lives in a house, not an apartment. A two-story house. His bedroom is upstairs, in the back. He—'

'How do you know?'

She coughed on smoke, laughing. 'Are you jealous? I waited until somebody was in the bathroom downstairs and then I said I had to use the john and they sent me to the upstairs bathroom, and I looked around upstairs. There are three bedrooms up there, one where he sleeps, one that's a television room and one set up as an office. So he sleeps upstairs. He has a man who lives with him, sort of a bodyguard, I guess. Very muscle-bound and not bright. His name is Carl and people carry on conversations in front of him and pretend he isn't there. Nobody talks to him. Like the movies. He sleeps downstairs, on a daybed in the den.'

'Go on.'

'There were half a dozen people there, all men, plus Lublin and Carl. They were doing some fairly heavy drinking and talking about things that I couldn't understand. About horse racing, mostly, and other things, but nothing that I could follow. Nobody mentioned Corelli and nobody mentioned Lee or anything. They all left by the time I did. They left first, as a matter of fact. Lublin told me, very nicely, that he would pay me a hundred dollars if I spent the night with him.'

'He—'

'I told him I couldn't, that I was just supposed to meet this Pete Miller as a favor. He didn't press.' Her face was thoughtful. 'He's a very pleasant man,' she said quietly. 'Very soft-spoken, and he tries very hard to show class. Only the most expensive brands of liquor. And very polite when he propositioned me, and very gracious when I turned him down.'

There were little lines at the corners of her eyes, largely obscured by the eye shadow she wore. They were the only signs of tension he could see. Her voice was a little brittler than usual, but otherwise she spoke as calmly as though she were telling him about some mediocre film she had seen. In the hotel, he had worried about her panicking and rushing back to Binghamton because she was in over her head. He could hardly have been more wrong about her.

How little you know, he thought. How little you know about any other person. You could marry a girl and never realize what she was truly like inside, could not begin to assess her separate strengths and weaknesses. And he had never realized how very strong Jill was. He was learning.

'We can go there now,' she was saying. 'You have the gun, don't you?'

'Yes.' It was tucked under his belt, the butt hidden by jacket and raincoat.

'I think we can take him now. Newkirk is one block over, and then he lives about a dozen blocks down Newkirk. We ought to be able to get a cab outside. This is a busy street, even at this hour. There were cabs cruising by while I was waiting for you.'

'I'll go,' he said.

'Don't be ridiculous. He knows me and Carl knows me. They'll open the door for me without thinking twice about it. If you went alone they would be on guard, but they already know me.'

He opened his mouth automatically, to argue, and changed his mind. She was right, she had to come along. He touched the side of her face with his fingers and grinned at her. 'You're one hell of a woman,' he said.

'Surprised?'

'A little.'

'I surprised myself,' she said.

In the cab he said, 'You never should have left like that. In the middle of the night without saying anything.'

'I had to.'

'Why?'

'Would you have let me go otherwise?'

'No. Why didn't you leave a note?'

'I didn't think you would wake up. I hoped you wouldn't. I thought about leaving a note, anyway, but I was afraid it would worry you.'

'It worried me enough this way.'

'I'm sorry. I thought if I left you a note you would come running straight to Lublin's, and we both would have been in trouble. It's the next block, on the left. Three houses down.'

The cab pulled to a stop. They got out, and he paid the driver and told him not to wait. The cab drove off. They stood on the sidewalk and looked at Lublin's house. All the lights were off.

'They're asleep,' she said.

The house was white clapboard, with a screened-in porch in front. He could see rocking chairs on the porch. A Cadillac was parked in the driveway just in front of the garage. They walked up the driveway to the side door. He reached inside his coat and pulled the revolver from under his belt. The metal of the gun was warm with his body heat. The butt fit snugly in his hand, and his finger moved to the trigger. He stood in darkness at the side of the door. She rang the bell.

'If Carl answers the door,' she whispered, 'let me get inside with him. Then get him from behind. He's big, he must be strong as an ox.'

He could hear nothing inside the house. He nudged her, and she leaned on the doorbell, a little more insistently this time. He heard something. She poked the bell again for emphasis, and inside the house footsteps moved slowly toward them.

'Who's it?'

A voice, deep and guttural. He tensed himself in the shadows, and Jill called, 'It's me, Carl. Rita. You wanna let me come in for a minute?' Her voice, he thought, was as different now as her face and her hair. Harsh and strident, with a New York inflection which sounded utterly foreign coming from her lips.

The curtains parted. He saw a face, large, heavy. A thick nose, a very broad forehead. Carl's eyes did not look at him but stayed on Jill. The doorknob turned, the door opened inward. She stepped inside.

'Whattaya want, Miss Rita?'

'Is Maurie up?'

'Sleeping. You want him?'

Dave moved softly, quickly. Carl had his back to the door now. Dave came through the door, the gun gripped by the barrel. He swung it downward with full strength, and Carl turned toward the sound just in time to catch the butt of the gun on the side of his head instead of at the base of the skull. He blinked dizzily and Dave hit him again, across the forehead. This time he went down.

But not out. He was an ox, a hardheaded ox, and a tap on the head wasn't enough to stop him. He got to his knees and looked at Jill and at Dave. He didn't seem to notice the gun; if he saw it, he didn't pay any attention to it. He pushed himself up into a crouch and lowered his head and charged.

Dave brought up a knee that caught him in the mouth, then smashed the gun down across the broad skull once again. But Carl had momentum working for him. They both went down, with the big man on top. A table tipped and a lamp crashed down and the room went dark. The gun was still in Dave's hand but his arm was pinned to the floor. Carl was on him, too dazed to hit him, too dazed to do anything but wrestle around with his weight as a lever. He had plenty of weight to work with.

Dave heaved, tried to swing free. He drove a knee upward and caught the big man in the groin. Carl didn't seem to notice. Dave twisted, first to the left, then hard to the right. Carl was hitting him in the chest. He let go of the gun and pushed Carl's face back with both hands, then let go with his right hand and hammered at Carl's nose with the side of his palm. Blood came. Carl rolled away, holding his face with both hands. Dave hit him openhanded on the side of the throat. Carl croaked like a frog, slipped forward, fell off to the side.

The room was swaying. Dave's head ached and his mouth was dry. He didn't know where the gun was. Carl was trying to get up again, and Dave moved toward him and kicked him in the side of the head. Carl's nose was bleeding freely now. His head snapped to the side from the force of the kick. He groaned and tried again to get up but he couldn't make it. He slumped forward and lay still.

There were lights on upstairs, and sounds. A loud voice wanted to know what the hell was going on. Carl tried to get up again. Dave looked for the gun and couldn't find it. The room was lighter now with illumination from upstairs. Carl was on his knees, shaking his head and trying to clear it. Dave got the lamp, the one that had spilled from a table earlier in the fight. It was almost too heavy to lift. He picked it up and half-swung, half-dropped it on Carl. There was a thudding sound and Carl sprawled forward again and did not move.

The gun. Where in hell was the gun?

Then he heard Jill's voice, cool and clear. 'You'd better come down those stairs, Maurie,' he heard her say. 'Come down slow and easy or I'll kill you, Maurie.'

Dave turned. There was a short and plumpish man at the head of the stairs, his hands tentatively raised to shoulder height. His bathrobe, belted snugly around his thick waist, was red silk, monogrammed 'ML' over the heart in flowing gold script. He had a moustache, thick and black, about an inch and a half long. His mouth was curled slightly downward at the corners. He was barefoot.

Jill stood at the foot of the stairs. Dave looked at her, then at Lublin. She was holding the gun on the little man, pointing it just as he had taught her to point it that afternoon at the doorknob in their room.

He walked over to her, his head still rocky. He took the gun from her hand and trained it on Lublin. Lublin came down the stairs very slowly, his hands in the air. The whole house was as silent as death.

9

Lublin stood at the foot of the stairs and looked at them, and at the gun. To Jill he said, 'You're a damn fool, Rita. I don't keep cash around the house. Maybe a couple of hundred, no more than that.'

'We're not looking for money.'

'No?' He looked at Dave, eyes wary. 'Then what?'

'Information.'

'Then put the gun away. What kind of information?'

'About Corelli.' He didn't put the gun away.

'Corelli?'

'Joe Corelli.'

'I don't know him,' Dublin said. 'Who is he? And put the gun away.'

The man looked soft, Dave thought, except for the eyes. There was a hardness there that didn't go with the pudgy body or the round face. 'Corelli is dead,' he said.

'I didn't even know he was sick.'

'You had him killed.'

Lublin was smiling now, with his mouth, not with his eyes. 'You made a mistake somewhere,' he said. 'I never heard of this Corelli of yours. How could I have him killed?' He spread his hands. 'You two oughta relax and go home. What do you want to point a gun at me for? You're not going to shoot me. What are you? You're a couple of kids, it's late, you ought to go home. Then—'

Dave thought, he has to believe it. He has to take it seriously, he has to feel it. But the mood wasn't right for violence. A plump little man in a bathrobe, talking easily in a calm voice. You couldn't hit him, not out of the blue.

Jill, he thought. They raped Jill. He fixed the thought very carefully in his mind, and then he stepped forward and raked the barrel of the gun across Lublin's face. Lublin looked surprised. Dave transferred the gun to his left hand and hit Lublin hard in the mouth with his right. He hit him again, in the chest, and Lublin fell back against the stairs. He sat down there, breathing heavily, holding the back of one hand to his mouth. Blood trickled from his face where the gun barrel had cut him.

'You son of a bitch,' he said.

'Maybe you better start talking.'

'Go to hell.'

Dave said, 'Do you think you can take it, old man? You didn't kill Corelli, you had it done. All I want to know is the names of the men who killed him. You're going to tell me sooner or later.'

'What's Corelli to you?'

'He's nothing to me.'

'Then what do you care who killed him?'

'You don't have to know.'

Lublin thought this over. He got to his feet slowly, rubbing his mouth with the back of his hand. He avoided Dave's eyes, centering his gaze a foot below them. He patted the pockets of the robe and said he needed a cigarette. Dave tossed him a pack. Lublin caught the cigarettes, fumbled them, bent to scoop them from the floor. He touched the floor with one hand and came up out of the crouch, leaping for the gun. Dave kicked him in the face, stepped back, kicked him again.

They had to get water from the kitchen and throw it on him. His face was a mess. His mouth was bleeding, two teeth were gone, and one was loose. He got up and found a chair and fell into it. Dave lit a cigarette and gave it to him. Lublin took it and held it, looked at it but didn't smoke it. Dave said, 'Corelli,' and Lublin took a deep drag on the cigarette and coughed.

Then he said, 'I knew Corelli. We had dealings now and then.'

Dave didn't say anything.

'I didn't have him killed.'

'The hell you didn't.'

Lublin's eyes were wide. 'Why would I have him hit? What did he ever do to me?'

'He owed you sixty-five thousand dollars.'

'Where did you hear that?'

'From Corelli.' He thought a minute, then added, 'And from other people.'

Dave watched his face, watched the eyes trying to decide how to manage the lie, whether to tell none or part of the truth. And he thought suddenly of law school. Techniques in Cross-examination. They didn't teach you this, he thought. You learned how to make a witness contradict himself, how to trip him up, how to discredit testimony, all of that. But not how to worm information out of a man when you held a gun on him. They taught you how to do it with words, not how to get along when words didn't work any more.

Lublin said, 'He owed me the money.'

'How?'

'How? In cash.'

'Why did he owe it to you?'

'A gambling debt.'

'So you had him killed when he didn't pay.'

'Don't be stupid,' Lublin said. He was more confident now; maybe his face had stopped hurting. 'He would have paid. The minute he died I was out the money. He can't pay me when he's dead.'

'When did he lose the money?'

'February, March. What's the difference?'

'How?'

'Cards. He got in over his head, he borrowed, he couldn't pay back. That's all she wrote.'

'What kind of game?'

'Poker.'

'Poker. You let him have sixty-five thousand?'

'Fifty. Fifteen gees was interest.'

He thought a minute, and Jill said, 'He's lying, Dave.'

'How do you know?'

'He made two-dollar race bets. You saw the slips. He wouldn't plunge like that at a card table.'

Lublin said, 'Listen, dammit—'

And she said, coolly, 'Hit him again, Dave.'

Techniques in Cross-examination. He used the barrel of the gun, raked it across the side of Maurie Lublin's face. He was careful not to knock him out this time. He just wanted to make it hurt. Lublin winced and tried to shrink back into the chair. Dave hit him again, and the cut bled lightly. It was easy now, mechanical.

'Start over,' he said.

'I loaned him the money. I—'

'The truth, all the way.'

'We were in on a deal.'

'What kind of a deal?'

'Corelli's deal. There was a warehouse robbery in Yonkers. Instant coffee, a hijacking deal. The heavies who took the place came up with a little better than a quarter of a million dollars' worth of instant coffee. That's wholesale. When they got it, they had it set up to push it to an outfit in Detroit for a hundred thou. The thing fell in.'

'So?'

'So they got in touch with Corelli. Joe handled this kind of a deal before. They didn't want to play around with the load, they just wanted their money out. He offered fifty grand for the load but they wanted better, it had to be carved up a few ways. They settled for seventy-five.'

'And?'

'And Joe didn't have the seventy-five. He could raise ten but anything more was scraping, he couldn't make it. He came to me and offered me half the gross for sixty-five thousand. My capital and his connections. He had other people on the line, in Pittsburgh, to take the pile off his hands for a hundred and twenty-five thousand, which meant a gross profit of fifty thousand dollars with the whole play figured to take a little less than a month. My share would be twenty-five, and twenty-five less costs for Corelli.'

'You went in with him?'

Lublin half-smiled. 'For thirty, not for twenty-five. That still gave Corelli twenty thousand for his ten and nobody was going to give him a better deal. Besides, he didn't have that much time to shop around. The hijackers were in a hurry. He took my sixty-five and his ten and bought them out. That gave us half the coffee in the world, and Joe had the place to move it, to Pittsburgh.'

'What happened?'

'The rest made the papers. This was in March. Corelli hired a trucker. The trucker stopped to make time with a waitress, and the other trucks with him got ahead of him, and this one schmuck got nervous and started speeding to catch up. On the Pennsy Turnpike, in a truck, the son of a bitch is speeding. One of those long-distance trucks and they never speed, they always hold it steady.' He shook his head, still angry with the driver. 'So a trooper stopped him and this driver got nervous, and the trooper got suspicious, and the driver pulls a gun and the trooper shoots his head off, like that. They opened the truck and found a load of hot coffee, and they radioed ahead and cut off the other trucks, and that was the shipment, all of it, with the drivers off to jail and the coffee back to the warehouse where it came from in the first place.'

'And you were out the money?'

'We weren't exactly insured.'

'But why did Corelli owe you the dough?'

'Because it was his fault the deal fell in,' Lublin said. 'It was his play. I was investing, and he was supposed to manage it. He was responsible for delivering the load and collecting payment. All I had going was my capital. When it fell in, he owed me my cost, which was sixty-five thousand.' He narrowed his eyes slightly. He said, 'I knew he didn't have it then, because if he had had it he would have carried the deal all by himself, he wouldn't have cut me in. It wasn't the kind of debt where I was going to press him for payment. He didn't have it, and the hell, you don't get blood from a stone. But he would get it, little by little. He would pay up, and I had no instant need for the money. When he got it he would pay me. In the meanwhile, he owed me. If I needed a favor I could go to him because he owed me. Joe was small but not so small it hurt me to have him owe me favors. That never hurts, it can always be handy.'

'Then why have him killed?'

'I didn't. That's the whole point, why I wouldn't be the one to have him killed. There was nothing personal. It was his fault the deal went sour, sure, but that was nothing personal. And killing him could only cost money without getting any money back. Use your head, why would I kill him?'

'Then who did?'

'I don't know.'

'But you have ideas.'

'No ideas,' Lublin said.

'He was out his own ten thousand dollars and he owed you sixty-five thousand on top of it. He must have been hungry for big money, and fast. What was he doing?'

'He didn't tell me.'

'Who was he involved with?'

'I don't know.'

'He mentioned your name when they went to kill him. He said to tell you he would pay up the money, but they shot him anyway.'

'You were there?'

Maybe it was a mistake to let him know that, he thought. The same mistake as Jill's mentioning his name. The hell with it.

'He mentioned your name,' he said again. 'He thought you were the one who had him killed.'

'I don't get it. Where do you and the broad come in?'

'We come in right here. Corelli thought you killed him. Why should I think any different?'

'I told you—'

'I know what you told me. Now you have to tell me something else. You have to tell me who had him killed, because that's something you would know, it's something you would have to know. Corelli left town three months ago, running for his life. He owed you a pile of money. If anybody owed you that kind of money and skipped town you would know why. He was either running from you or running from somebody else, and either way you would damn well know about it.'

Lublin didn't say anything.

'You're going to tell me. I've got the gun, and your man over there isn't going to be any help to you, and I don't care what kind of a job I have to do on you to get you to talk. I'll take you apart if I have to. I mean that.'

'How did you get so hard?' Dave looked at him. 'You talk too clean, you look too clean. You don't come on like a hotster. But you got guts like a hotster. Who the hell are you?'

'Nobody you know. Who was Corelli running from?'

'Maybe his shadow.'

A slap this time, openhanded across the face. Lublin's head snapped back from the blow, and he said something dirty. The back of the hand this time, again across the face, the head snapping back once again, the face flushed where the slaps had landed. Techniques in Cross-examination.

Dave said, 'I don't care who had him killed, whether it was you or somebody else. I'm not looking for the man who gave the order.'

'Then—'

'I'm looking for the two men who did the killing.'

'The guns?'

'Yes.'

'Why?'

He didn't answer. Lublin looked at him, then at Jill, then said, 'I don't get it.'

'You don't have to.'

'You want to know the names of the two men who took Corelli and shot him. The ones hired to hit him.'

'Yes.'

'Well, I don't know that.'

'You don't?'

'If I had him killed,' Lublin said guardedly, 'even then I wouldn't know the actual names of the guns. I would call someone, a friend, and say that there was this Corelli and I wanted him found and killed, and I would pay so much dough to this friend, and that's all I would know. He might fly a couple of boys all the way in from the West Coast, and they would do the job, make the hit, and then they would be on the next plane back to S.F. or somewhere. Or even local boys, I wouldn't know their names or who they were.'

'Then tell me who you called.'

'I didn't call anybody. I was just saying that even if I did I still wouldn't know the guns.'

'Then tell me who did make the call. Who had Corelli killed?'

'I told you. I don't know that.'

'I think you do.'

'Dammit—'

Monotonous Techniques in Cross-examination. It took a long time, a batch of questions, a stonewall of silence, a barrage of pistol-whipping and slapping, a gun butt laid across Lublin's knee, the barrel of the gun slapped against the side of his jaw. There would be a round of beating, and a round of unanswered questions, and another round of beating.

Jill hardly seemed to be there at all. She stood silent, cigarette now and then, went away once to use the bathroom. Carl never moved and never made a sound. He lay inert on the far side of the room and nobody ever went over to look at him. There was Lublin in the chair and there was Dave with the gun, standing over him, and they went around and around that way.

Until Lublin said, 'You'll kill me. I'm not so young, I'll have a heart attack. Jesus, you'll kill me.'

'Then talk.'

'I swear I did not have him hit. I swear to God I did not have that man hit.'

'Then tell me who did.'

'I can't tell you.'

'You know who it was.'

'I know but I can't say.'

Progress. 'You don't have any choice. You have to say, Lublin.'

He did not hit him this time, did not even draw the gun back. Lublin sat for a long moment, thinking. Outside, it was light already. Daylight came in around the edges of the drapes. Maybe Lublin was trying to stall, maybe he thought he could take punishment until somebody showed up. But he was running out of gas. No one had come and he couldn't take it any more.

'If they find out I told you,' he said, 'then I'm dead.'

'They won't find out. And you'll be just as dead if you don't talk.'

He didn't seem to have heard. In a dull dead voice he said, 'Corelli wanted money fast. He owed other people besides me but nothing big, not to anybody else. He was strapped for capital. He couldn't make fast money legit because his construction operation was down to nothing but the office and the name. He was mostly a middleman anyway and everything he had owned before was tied up now or cleared out. He stripped himself pretty badly getting up the ten grand for the instant-coffee deal.'

'Keep talking.'

'He did a stupid thing. He was stuck and he was up against it, and he knew I wasn't going to wait forever for the sixty-five thou, not forever, and he needed maybe a hundred grand or better to be completely out from under and able to operate. He got a smart idea, he was going to middleman a hundred grand worth of heroin to someone with a use for it. You understand what I mean?'

'Yes. Where did he get the heroin?'

'He never had it. That was the stupid idea. He was going to sell it without having it, get the money and deliver something else, face powder, anything. It was stupid and he would have gotten himself killed even if he pulled it off, but he maybe figured that with a hundred grand he could get into something good and double the money and pay back before his man tipped to the play, and then he would be back in the clear. It was risky as hell and it didn't stand a chance. He was sure to get himself killed that way.'

'What happened?'

'The man he was dealing with—'

'Who was he?'

Lublin tensed.

'You'll tell me anyway. Make it easy on yourself.'

'Jesus. It was Washburn. You know him?'

'No. His first name?'

'Ray. Ray Washburn.'

'Where does he live?'

'I don't know. Up in the Bronx.'

He's lying, he thought. He said. 'You've got an address book in the house. Where is it?'

'An address book—'

'Yes. Where is it?'

Lublin was defeated. He said it was upstairs, in the den, and Jill went up for it. He looked under 'W' and found a Frank Washburn listed, with a

Manhattan address and a telephone number. He said, 'You must have gotten the name wrong. It's Frank Washburn, and he lives in Manhattan. That's right, isn't it?'

Lublin didn't answer.

'All right. He went to Washburn. What happened?'

'Washburn said he would let him know. He checked around, and he found out that Corelli was in hock up to his ears and he couldn't have the stuff, that it had to be a con. He didn't let on that he knew, just told Joe he wasn't interested, that he couldn't use the stuff. Joe dropped the price still further and Washburn knew it had to be a con then, it couldn't be anything else at that price, so he just kept on saying he wasn't interested.

'But the word got around, about what Joe had tried to pull, and Washburn saw it was bad to let him get away with it, if people tried to con him like that and got by with it, he would get a bad name. And he was mad, anyway, because he is not the type of man people set up for stupid con games and Joe should have known this. So he marked Joe for a hit.'

'Who did he hire?'

'I don't know. If I knew that I would give it to you. I would give it a long time before I would give you Washburn.'

'Why didn't Corelli know it was Washburn who was after him? Why did he think it was you?'

'Because Washburn turned the deal down. Corelli didn't know Washburn had it in for him. He thought he just turned the deal down because he had no use for the goods.'

'Then why did he get out of town?'

'Because Washburn sent somebody to make a hit, and Corelli was shot at but the gun missed, and he knew somebody was trying to kill him, and he must have figured it was me because I was the one he owed heavy money to. When somebody's shooting at you, you don't look to see the serial number on the gun. You get the hell out of town.'

Dave looked over at Jill. She was nodding thoughtfully. It all made sense. He nodded himself. He looked down at Lublin now and he said, 'You're not calling Washburn. You don't want to warn him.'

Lublin looked up.

'You took a hell of a beating to keep from giving me his name,' Dave went on. 'You don't want him to know you talked to me. He won't find out from me. If he finds out, it'll be from you. You know what he'll do to you if he finds out, so you don't want to tell him.'

'I won't call him.'

'Good.'

'Because I'll get you myself,' Lublin said. 'It may be fast and it may be slow, you son of a bitch, but it is damned well going to happen.' A hand wiped blood from his mouth. 'You are going to catch it, you and your pig of a broad. You better get to Washburn very fast, kid, or you won't get to him at all. Because there's going to be a whole army with nothing to do but kill you.'

Dave knocked him out. He took him out easily, not angry, not wanting to hurt him, just anxious to put him on ice for the time being. He did it with the gun butt just behind the ear and Lublin did not even try to dodge the blow, did not even shrink from it. Lublin took it, and went back and out, and when Dave poked him he didn't move.

An army, Lublin had said.

But the army would not include Carl. They checked him before they left and he was still out, all that time, so they checked a little more closely. They saw that the last blow, with the lamp, had caved in the side of his skull. He was dead.

10

The diner had no jukebox. Behind the counter a radio blared. The song was an old one, Ella Fitzgerald and Louis Jordan doing 'Stone Cold Dead in the Market.' The air was thick with cooking smells. The diner had two booths, and both of them had been occupied when they entered it. They had adjoining seats at the counter. He was drinking coffee and waiting for the counterman to finish making him a bowl of oatmeal. She had coffee too and was eating a toasted English muffin. His cigarette burned slowly in a glass ashtray. She was not smoking.

The diner was on Broadway just below Union Square. When they left Lublin's house, they had walked along Newkirk Avenue as far as Fifteenth, and there was a subway entrance there. They went downstairs and bought tokens and passed through the turnstile and waited in silence for a Manhattan-bound train. The train came after a long wait – the BMT Brighton line, just a few cars at that hour, just a very few passengers. They rode it as far as Fourteenth Street and got out there. From the subway arcade, the diner looked like as good a place as they would be likely to find there. It was around seven when they went into the diner. They had been there for about twenty minutes.

A man who had been sitting next to Jill folded his copy of the *Times* and left the diner. Dave leaned closer to her and said, 'I killed him.' She stared down into her coffee cup and didn't answer. 'I murdered a man,' he said.

'Not murder. It was self-defense. You were fighting and—'

He shook his head. 'If an individual dies in the course of or as a direct result of the commission of a felony, the felon is guilty of murder in the first degree.'

'Did we commit a felony?'

'A batch of them. Illegal entry as a starter, and a few different kinds of aggravated assault. And Carl is dead. That means that I'm guilty of first-degree murder and you're an accessory.'

'Will anything—'

'Happen to us? No.' He paused. 'The law won't do anything. They won't hear about it, not officially at least. I understand there's a standard procedure in cases like this. Lublin will get rid of Carl's body.'

'The river?'

'I don't know how they do it nowadays. I read something about putting them under roadbeds. You know – they have a friend doing highway construction, and they shovel the body into the roadbed during the night and cover him up the next day, and he's buried forever. I read somewhere that there are more than twenty dead men under the New Jersey Turnpike. The cars roll right over them and never know it.'

'God,' she said.

His oatmeal came, finally, a congealed mass in the bottom of the bowl. He spooned a little sugar onto it and poured some milk over the mass. He got a little of it down and gave up, pushed the bowl away. The counterman asked if anything was wrong with it and he said no, he just wasn't as hungry as he had thought. He ordered more coffee. The coffee, surprisingly, was very good there.

He said, 'We're in trouble, you know.'

'From Lublin?'

'Yes. He wasn't just talking. For one thing, we shoved him around pretty hard. He's a tough old man and he took it well but I hurt him, I know that. I messed him up and I hurt him. He's not going to write that off too easily. But more than that, I managed to get Washburn's name out of him, and the whole story of why Corelli was killed. He took a hell of a beating to keep from giving me Washburn's name. He won't want Washburn to find out that he let it out, and he'll be sure that Washburn will find out if we get to him. So he'll want to get us first. To have us killed.'

'Will he be able to find us?'

'Maybe.' He thought. 'He knows my first name. You called me Dave in front of him.'

'It was a slip. Does he still think my name is Rita?'

'I don't know. Maybe.'

'I don't want to be killed.' She said this very calmly and levelly, as though she had considered the matter very carefully before coming to the conclusion that death was something to be avoided if at all possible. 'I don't want him to kill us.'

'It won't happen.'

'He knows your first name, and he's got my name wrong. That's all he knows, and a description of us. But the description doesn't have to fit, does it? Do you think it's time for me to be a blonde again?'

'That's not a bad idea.'

'Pay the check,' she said. 'I'll meet you outside, around the corner.'

He finished his coffee and paid the check. She got up and went to the washroom in the back. He left a tip and went outside. The sky was clear now, and the sun was bright. He lit a cigarette. The smoke was strong in his lungs. Too many cigarettes, too long a time without sleep. He took another drag on the cigarette and walked to the corner of Thirteenth Street. He finished the cigarette and tossed it into the gutter.

When she came to him he stared hard at her. The transformation was phenomenal. She was his Jill again, the hair blond with just a trace of the brown coloring still remaining. She had undone the French twist and the hair was pageboy again, framing her face as it had always done. Her face was scrubbed free of the heavy makeup. She had even removed her lipstick and had replaced it with her regular shade. And, with the transformation, her face had lost its hard angular quality, had softened visibly. She had played the role of cheap chippy so effectively that the performance had very nearly sold him; he had almost grown used to her that way. It was jarring to see her again as she had always been before.

'I didn't do a very good job,' she said. 'I didn't want to soak my hair, and I couldn't get all the brown out. I'll take care of it later, but this ought to do for now. How do I look?'

He told her.

'But it was fun pretending,' she said. 'I liked being Rita, just for a while. I must be a frustrated actress.'

'Or a frustrated prostitute.'

'Frustrated.'

'Jill, I'm sorry.'

'Don't be silly.'

'I was teasing, I didn't think—'

'It's my fault. We ought to be able to tease each other.'

'It was tactless.'

'We should not have to be tactful with each other. Let's forget it. What do you want to do now?'

'I don't know.'

'Where should we go?'

'We could go back to the hotel,' he said. 'You must be exhausted.'

'Not especially.'

'You didn't sleep at all. And you didn't sleep very well the night before last, either. Aren't you tired?'

'Very, but not sleepy. I don't think I could sleep. Are you tired?'

'No.'

'Do you want to go back to the hotel?'

'No.' He lit another cigarette. She took it from him and dragged on it. He told her to keep it and lit another for himself. He said, 'I think we ought to find out a little about Washburn. If he's so important he probably made the papers at one time or another. We could spend an hour at the library. They keep the *New York Times* on microfilm, and it's indexed. It might be worth an hour.'

'All right. Do you know how to get there? The library?'

He had used it once before, during the course for the bar exam, and he remembered where it was. They couldn't get a cab. The morning rush hour had started and there were no cabs. They walked along Thirteenth Street to catch a bus heading uptown.

He said, 'You know, with Carl dead, that's one less person who knows what we look like. Lublin is the only one who can identify us.'

'You're upset, aren't you?'

He looked at her.

'About Carl,' she said.

'That I killed him?'

'Yes.'

'Partly,' he said. He threw his cigarette away.

'And I'm partly upset that I didn't kill Lublin. I should have.'

'You couldn't do that,' she said.

'All I had to do was hit him a little too hard. Later I could tell myself I didn't mean to kill him, that it was just miscalculation on my part or weakness on his. And we wouldn't have anyone after us, we would be in the clear. It would have been logical enough.'

'But you couldn't do it, Dave.'

'I guess not,' he said.

Francis James Washburn had appeared in the *Times* almost a dozen times in the course of the past five years. Twice he had been called to Washington to testify before senatorial investigating committees, once in a study of gangland control of boxing, once in an investigation of labor racketeering. In each instance he had pleaded the Fifth Amendment, refusing to answer any and all questions on the grounds that he might incriminate himself. The questions themselves suggested that Washburn had some hidden connections with a local of a building-trade-workers' union, that he was unofficial president of a local of restaurant and hotel employees, that he owned a principal interest in a welterweight named Little Kid Morton, and that he was otherwise fundamentally involved in the subjects of the senatorial investigations to a considerable degree.

He had been arrested three times. He was charged with conspiracy in a bribery case involving a municipal official. He was charged with suspicion of possession of narcotics. He was picked up in a raid on a floating crap game and was then charged with vagrancy and with being a common gambler. Each time the charges were dropped for lack of evidence and Washburn was released. In one of the stories, the *Times* reported that Washburn had served two years in prison during the Second World War, having been convicted for receiving stolen goods. He had also done time during the thirties for assault and battery, and had been acquitted of manslaughter charges in 1937.

His other mentions in the newspaper were minor ones. He was listed as a major contributor to the campaign fund of a Republican member of the New York State Assembly. He was among those attending a Tammany Hall fund-raising dinner. He was a pallbearer at another politician's funeral.

The overall picture that emerged was one of a man fifty-five or sixty years old, one who had started in the lower echelons of the rackets and who had done well, moving up the ladder to a position bordering upon unholy respectability. Washburn had a great many business interests and a great many political connections. He was important and he was successful. He would be harder to reach than Maurice Lublin.

They spent a little more than a hour in the library's microfilm room. When they got back to the hotel, the night clerk was gone and another man was behind the desk. They went upstairs. They showered, and Jill rinsed the remaining coloring out of her hair and combed and set it. Dave put on a summer suit. Jill wore a skirt and blouse. They were in the room for about an hour, then went downstairs and left the hotel.

Washburn lived at 47 Gramercy Park East. They didn't know where that was, and Dave ducked into a drugstore and looked up the address in a street guide. It was on the East Side, around Twentieth Street between Third and Fourth Avenues.

They took a cab and got off three blocks away at the corner of East Seventeenth Street and Irving Place. They were only a few blocks from the diner where they had had breakfast. The neighborhood was shabby-genteel middle class, unimpressively respectable. The buildings were mostly brownstones. There were trees, but not many of them. The neighborhood picked up as they walked north on Irving Place.

He wondered if Lublin had Washburn's place staked out. It was possible, he thought. He reached under his jacket and felt the weight of the gun tucked beneath his belt. They kept walking.

11

The building at 47 Gramercy Park East was a large four-story brownstone that had been thoroughly renovated around the end of the war. There were four apartments, one to a floor. There was a doorman in front, a tall Negro wearing a maroon uniform with gold piping. No, the doorman told Jill, there was no Mr Watson in the building, but there was a Mr Washburn up on the fourth floor, if that was who she wanted. She said it wasn't and he smiled a servile smile.

So Washburn was on the fourth floor. They crossed the street and moved halfway down the block, out of range of the doorman. The green square of park was bordered on all sides by a high iron fence. There was a gate, locked. A neat metal sign indicated that if you lived in one of the buildings surrounding the park you were given a key to that gate, and then you were allowed to go into the park when you wanted. Otherwise the park was out of bounds. They stood near the gate and Dave smoked a cigarette.

Jill said, 'We can't stand here forever. Lublin will send somebody around sooner or later.'

'Or the police will pick us up for loitering.'

'Uh-huh. What do we do? Can we go up there after him?'

'No. He wouldn't be alone. One of the newspaper stories mentioned a wife, so she would be there with him, I suppose. And he probably has plenty of help. Bodyguards, a maid, all of that.'

'Then what do we do?'

'I don't know,' he said.

They walked to the corner. A uniformed policeman passed them heading downtown. He didn't smile. They stood on the corner while the light changed twice.

'If we could get into the park—' he said.

'We don't have a key.'

'I know,' he said. 'From the park, we could keep an eye on the doorway without being seen. It would be natural enough. We could sit on a bench and wait for something to happen. We don't even know if Washburn's home, or who's with him. Or what he looks like, for that matter. The one picture in the paper wasn't much good. Blurred, the way news photos always are—'

'All those little dots.'

'And not a close-up anyway. We might be able to see him, he might come out alone, we could have a crack at following him. He's the key to it. Unless Lublin was doing an awfully good job of last-minute lying, Washburn is our only connection with the killers.'

'Do you think we could get him to talk?'

'I don't know. For a while I didn't think Lublin would talk.' He looked over at Washburn's building. 'The damn thing would have to face a park,' he said. 'In the movies, they always rent an apartment right across the street from the suspect and set themselves up with binoculars and gun-shot microphones and tape recorders and everything else in the world, and they've got him cold. But what the hell do you do when the son of a bitch lives across from a park that you can't even get into?'

'Maybe next door?'

The buildings on either side of Washburn's were more of the same, renovated brownstones with an air of monied respectability about them. There would be no rooms for rent there, he thought. Not at all. But maybe around in back ... 'Come on,' he said.

A Fourth Avenue office building was around the block from Washburn's brownstone. They looked at the building directory in the lobby. There were three lawyers, two CPA's, one insurance agency, one employment agency, a commercial-art studio, and a handful of small businesses identified in such a way that they might have done anything from advertising layout to import-export. The elevator seemed to be out of order. They walked up steep stairs to the fourth floor. The whole rear wall of the floor was taken up by one business, an outfit called Beadle & Graber. The office door was shut and the window glass frosted. A typewriter made frantic sounds behind the closed door.

He went to the door and knocked on it. The typewriter stopped quickly and a gray-haired woman opened the door cautiously. Dave asked if a Mr Floyd Harper worked there, and the gray-haired woman said no, there was no Mr Harper there. He looked over her shoulder at the window. It faced out upon a courtyard, and across the courtyard he could see the rear windows of Washburn's apartment. The drapes were open, but he didn't have time to see much of anything. But if he were closer to the windows, and if he had a pair of binoculars—

'You can see Washburn's apartment from their window,' he told Jill.

'Then it's a shame they have the office. If it were vacant, we could rent it.'

'There's still a way.'

'How?'

'Wait for me in the lobby,' he said.

They walked as far as the third floor together. Then she went on downstairs while he knocked on the door of one of the CPA's. A voice told him to come in. He went inside. A balding man in his forties asked what he could do for him.

Dave said, 'Just wanted to ask a question, if I could. I was thinking of taking an office in this building. There's space available, isn't there?'

'I think so. On the top floor, I believe.'

'Just one thing I wanted to know. Is this a twenty-four-hour building? Can you get in and out any time?'

You could, the accountant told him. They kept a night man on duty to run the elevator, and from six at night until eight in the morning you had to sign a register if you entered or left the building. 'It's not a bad location,' the accountant said. 'The address has a little more prestige than it used to. It's Park Avenue South now, not Fourth Avenue. Everybody in the city still calls it Fourth Avenue, of course, but it gives you a more impressive letterhead, at least for the out-of-town people. You want the rental agent's phone number?'

'I've already got it,' Dave said.

There was a coffee shop two doors down the street, empty now in the gap between breakfast and lunch crowds. They ate at odd times lately, he thought. They settled in one of the empty booths and ordered sliced-chicken sandwiches. She had coffee, he had milk. The sandwiches were good and he was hungrier than he had thought. And tired, suddenly. He didn't want to sleep, but he felt the physical need for it. A couple of times he caught himself staring dully ahead, his mind neatly empty, as if it had temporarily turned itself off. He ordered coffee after all and forced himself to drink it.

'I can go back there during the night,' he told her. He explained the way the building was kept open. 'I can sign some name to the book and break into that office.'

'Break into it?'

'Pick the lock. Or break the window and unlock it. There won't be anybody around, and once I'm in I can get a good look into his place. Washburn's.' But then he stopped and shook his head. 'No,' he said. 'That's crazy, isn't it?'

'It sounds risky. If anybody heard you—'

'More than that. In the first place, he probably closes his drapes when it gets dark out. Everybody does. Besides, all I could see would be the one room of the apartment, and it's probably a bedroom anyway. I couldn't keep an eye on the front door, and I would never know if he left the building. We have to be able to see the front of his building, not the back of it.'

A few minutes later she looked up and said, 'But there is something we can do, honey.'

'What?'

'Instead of breaking into the office. Or sneaking in. And it should be easier, and less dangerous. We could break into Gramercy Park.'

They waited on the north side of the park, about twenty yards down from the main gate. The privilege of a key to the park was evidently more symbolic than utilitarian. The park was empty except for a very old man who wore a black suit and a maroon bow tie and who sat reading the *Wall Street Journal* and moving his lips as he read. They waited for him to leave the park but he seemed determined to sit on his bench forever. They waited a full half hour before anyone else entered the park. Then a woman came, a very neat and very old woman in a gray tweed suit. She had a cairn terrier on a braided leather leash. She opened the gate with a key and led the dog inside and they watched the gate swing shut behind her.

The woman spent twenty minutes in the park, leading the cairn from one tree to another. The small dog seemed to have an extraordinary capacity for urine. They completed the tour, finally, and woman and dog headed for the gate. Their move was well timed. The two of them reached the gate just as the woman was struggling with the lock. She opened it, and Dave drew the gate open while Jill made a show of admiring the dog. The dog admired them. The woman and the dog passed through the gate, and Jill stepped inside and Dave started to follow her.

The woman said, 'You have your own key, of course.'

'I left it in the apartment,' Jill said. She smiled disarmingly. 'We're right across the street.' She pointed vaguely toward Washburn's building.

The woman looked at them, her eyes bright. 'No,' she said gently, 'I don't think you are.'

The dog tugged at the leash but the woman stood her ground. 'One so rarely sees younger people at this park,' she said. 'Isn't it barbaric, taking something as lovely as a park and throwing a fence around it? The world has too many fences and too few parks. There are times when I think Duncan' – she nodded at the dog – 'has the only proper attitude toward this fence. He occasionally employs it as a substitute tree. You don't live in this neighborhood, do you?'

'Well—'

'You sound as though you're from upstate somewhere. Not native New Yorkers, certainly.' She shook her head. 'Such intrigue just to rest a moment in a pleasant park. You're married, of course. Wearing a wedding ring, both of you are, and the rings seem to match. And even if they didn't I'd be good enough to give you the benefit of the doubt and assume that you're married to each other. From out of town, and anxious to sit together in a park—' The woman smiled pleasantly. 'Probably on a honeymoon,' she said. 'After a year or two of marriage you'll have had your fill of parks, I'm sure. And, probably, of each other.'

'Oh, I hope not,' Jill said.

The woman's smile spread. 'So do I, my dear, so do I. You're quite welcome to the park. My late husband and I used to go to Washington Square when we were courting. Isn't that a dated term? I'm old, aren't I?'

'I don't think so.'

'You're very charming, aren't you? But I very certainly am old, nevertheless. Courting. I understand Washington Square's changed a great deal since then. A great many young persons with leather jackets and beards and guitars. Perhaps that's an argument for gates and fences after all. Every question has so many sides. I am a silly old woman, aren't I?'

'No.'

'Enjoy the park,' the woman said, passing through the gate now. 'And enjoy each other. And don't grow old too quickly, if you'll pardon more advice. Giving unwanted advice is one of the few remaining privileges of the aged, you know. Don't grow old too quickly. Being old is not really very much fun. It's better than being dead, but that's really about all one can say for it.'

The iron gate swung shut. The woman and the dog walked quickly with small and precise steps to the corner and waited for the signal to change. Then they crossed the street and continued down the block.

'We really fooled her,' Jill said.

'Uh-huh.'

They went to a bench on a path running along the western edge of the park. They were almost directly across from Washburn's apartment house. The same doorman still stood at the door.

'We did fool her,' Jill said suddenly.

'That woman? How?'

'She thought we were a nice young couple,' Jill said. 'I guess we used to be.' She looked away. 'I'm not sure we are now,' she said quietly.

12

Their bench was shaded by two tall elms. There, in the park, the air was cleaner and cooler than in the surrounding city. They sat close together on the bench, looking over a stretch of green and through the grating of the fence at the luxury apartment buildings across the small street. The setting did not match the circumstances at all. Too placid, too secure. His mind would wander, and he had to force himself to remember what they were there for, and why. Otherwise he kept relaxing to fit the old woman's image. A couple of honeymooners who wanted a few peaceful moments for themselves away from the hot hurry of New York.

Other images helped him concentrate. The five bullets pumped one after another into Joe Corelli's head. The professionally disinterested beating he himself had taken. The direct and dispassionate rape of Jill. The cold fury of the ride into the city. Carl, Lublin's personal heavyweight, first lumbering like a gored ox, then dead.

The watching was hard. It had seemed direct enough at the beginning, a stakeout straight out of *Dragnet*. You took a position and you held it and you waited for something to happen. But there was one basic difficulty. Nothing happened.

No one left Washburn's building and no one entered it. The doorman stood at his post. At one point he lit a cigar, and after about twenty minutes he threw the cigar into the gutter. Cars drove by, the traffic never very thick. Occasionally someone with a key came into the park, either to walk a leashed dog or to sit reading a book or an afternoon paper. The drapes were still open in Frank Washburn's apartment but it was on the fourth floor, and they were at ground level. They could tell that there were lights on, which meant there was probably someone at home, but that was all they could tell.

So it became hard to concentrate. They talked, but concentration had an unreal quality to it. There wasn't much to say about the job at hand, about Washburn and where he might lead them. Once they had gone over that a few times they were tired of it. And any other conversation was fairly well out of place. Mostly, they sat together in silence. The silence would be broken now and then – she would ask for a cigarette, or one of them would ask a question that the other would quickly answer. Then the silence would come back again.

Until she said, 'That car was here before.'

He looked up quickly. She was nodding toward a metallic-gray Pontiac that was turning west at the corner of Twentieth Street. He caught a quick look at it before another car blocked his view.

'Are you sure?'

'Yes. About five minutes ago. This time it just coasted by slowly, as if they were looking for somebody.'

'Like us?'

'Maybe.'

'Did you—'

'I think there were two people in the car. I'm not sure. The first time, I didn't pay much attention. Who looks at cars? Then the second time, just after they passed us, I remembered the car. There's a spotlight mounted on the hood. That's what I noticed that made me remember the car. You don't see that many of them.'

'And the men?'

'I'm not even sure they were both men. The driver was. By the time I realized that it was the same car they had already passed us and all I saw were the backs of their heads.'

His hand went automatically to the gun, secure under the waistband of his slacks. He patted the gun almost affectionately, a nervous gesture. We are getting close now, he thought. Before we were looking for them, and now people are looking for us.

'I wish you'd had a better look at them.'

'Maybe they'll be back.'

'Yes.' He started to light a cigarette, then changed his mind. Get up and get out, he thought. They could see into the park. This next time, they might get lucky and spot them. And then—

No, they had to stay where they were. If they could get a look at the men in the Pontiac, they were that much ahead of the game. They could not afford the luxury of running scared.

'Lublin must have sent them,' he said.

'I suppose so.'

'It only stands to reason. He doesn't want Washburn to know that he talked, and he knows we're going to try to get information from Washburn. So he would have Washburn's place watched and try to head us off on the way there. It evidently took him a little while to get organized. That was good luck for us. Otherwise they would have seen us wandering around the street and—'

It was a good sentence to leave unfinished. He reached again for a cigarette, the movement an instinctive one, and his hand stopped halfway to his breast pocket. He said, 'That means Washburn doesn't know.'

'You mean about us?'

'Yes. If he knew, he would have men outside, waiting for us. But if Lublin didn't tell him, then Lublin would have to accomplish two things. He would have to keep us from getting to Washburn, and at the same time he would have to watch the place without arousing suspicion. He would want to get to us without Washburn knowing anything about the whole play. Where are you going?'

She was standing, walking toward the fence. 'To see better,' she said. 'In case that car comes back.'

He grabbed her hand and pulled her back. 'Don't be a damned fool. We can see them well enough from farther back. And we can't risk having them see us.'

He led her back across a cement walk and sat down with her on another bench. There was an extra screening of shrubbery now between them and the street. They could see through it, but it would be hard for anyone passing by to get a good look at them.

'It might not have been anything,' he said.

'The Pontiac?'

'It could have been somebody driving around the block and looking for a place to park. You sort of coast along like that when you're trying to find a parking place.'

'Maybe, but—'

'But what?'

'I don't know. Just a feeling.'

And he had the same feeling. It was funny, too – he half-wanted the car to turn out to be innocent, because the idea of being pursued while pursuing added a new and dangerous element to the situation. But at the same time pursuit now would be a good sign. It would mean Washburn didn't know what was happening, which was good. It would mean for certain that Lublin's story was true.

A few minutes later he saw the Pontiac again. Jill nudged him and pointed but he had already noticed the car himself. It was coming from the opposite direction this time, cruising uptown past Washburn's apartment toward Twenty-first Street. It was a four-door car, the windows rolled down, the back seat empty. It was going between fifteen and twenty miles an hour.

There were two men in the front seat. At first he couldn't get a good look at them. He squinted, and as the car drew up even with them he got a good look at the man on the passenger side. He drew in his breath sharply, and he felt Jill's hand on his arm, her fingers tightening, squeezing hard. Then as the car moved off he got a brief glimpse of the man behind the wheel.

The man on the passenger side was thickset and short-necked with a heavy face and a once-broken nose. The man doing the driving had thick eyebrows and a thin mouth and a scattering of thin hairline scars across the bridge of his nose.

The car was gone now. It had turned at the corner, had continued west at

Twenty-first Street, picking up speed once it rounded the corner. He looked after it and watched it disappear quickly from view. He turned to Jill. She had let go of his arm, and both of her hands were in her lap, knotted into tight fists. Her face was a blend of hatred and horror.

Lee and his friend. Corelli's murderers. Their target.

They got out of there in a hurry. He said her name and she blinked at him as though her mind were elsewhere, caught up either in the memory of violation or in the plans for vengeance. He said, 'Come on, we've got to take off.' She got to her feet and they let themselves out of the park and walked off in the opposite direction, toward Third Avenue. An empty cab came by and they grabbed it. He told the driver to take them to the Royalton.

They started uptown on Third. Jill said, 'Suppose they know about the hotel?'

'How?'

'I don't know. I'm just panicky, I guess.'

'They might know,' he said. He leaned forward. 'Just leave us at the corner of Thirty-fourth Street,' he said.

'Not the Royalton?'

'No, just on the corner.'

'Thirty-fourth and where?'

'And Third,' he said.

There was a bar on Third halfway between Thirty-fourth and Thirty-fifth. They got out of the cab and walked to it. He didn't relax until they were inside the bar and seated in a booth in the rear. It was ridiculous, he knew. The Pontiac was nowhere near them, they were safe, they were clear. But he couldn't walk in the open street without the uncomfortable feeling that someone was watching them.

There was no waitress. He went to the bar and got two bottles of Budweiser and two glasses, paid for the beers and carried them to the booth. He poured beer into his glass and took a drink. She let her beer sit untouched on the table in front of her. She opened her mouth as if to speak, then shook her head suddenly and closed her mouth again without saying anything.

Finally she said, 'I don't understand it.'

'What?'

'Lublin didn't know who the killers were. That's what he said, isn't it?'

'Yes.'

'Then he must have been lying. Lee and the other man were in the car. They were driving around looking for us. Is there anyone besides Lublin who knows about us?'

'No. Unless someone recognized you at Lublin's last night.'

'Who? No one could have. So Lublin had to tell them. That meant that he hired them in the first place, and that the whole business about Washburn was a lot of nonsense, and that—'

'He wasn't lying.'

'He must have been. He—'

'No. Wait a minute.' He picked up the glass of beer and took a long drink. The beer was very cold and went down easily. He made rings on the top of the table with the cold glass.

He said, 'Lublin was telling the truth. I think I see it now. After we left, there were two things he had to do. He had to keep us from getting to Washburn, first of all. But he also had to let Lee and the other one know about us, that we were coming. They were the logical people to set after us. They were the ones we were after, first of all, and that would give them a personal stake in nailing us. It would save his hiring men to run us down, too. All he had to do was tell the two of them that a man and a woman were in town looking for Corelli's killers, and then the two of them would handle the rest. If they got to us and killed us, Lublin was in the clear. And if we got to them first, and killed them, he was still in the clear. Because we would pack up and move out without Washburn hearing about the whole deal.'

'Is he really that scared of Washburn?'

'Washburn killed Corelli – had him killed, that is – just because Corelli tried to swindle him. Didn't succeed, just *tried*. Lublin did worse than that. He informed on Washburn. I guess Lublin has a right to be scared.'

She was shaking her head. 'It still doesn't add up,' she said. 'Last night, Lublin didn't know who the killers were. If he had known he would have told us, wouldn't he? I mean, assuming that he was telling us the truth. So how would he know who to call today? How would he know to set them after us?'

'That's easy.'

She looked at him.

'All he had to do was ask Washburn,' he said. 'Jesus, I'm so stupid it's pathetic. He called Washburn and asked him who the men were, and Washburn told him without knowing what it was all about, and then he got in touch with them, with Lee and the other one. We went around playing detective, staking out his apartment, everything. All around Robin's Hood's barn, for God's sake. We missed the shortcut.'

'Where are you going?'

'To call Washburn.'

He made the call from the telephone booth right there in the bar. At first he tried to find Washburn's number in the phone book, but there was no listing. Then he remembered and dug out his notebook. He had copied the number, along with the address, from Lublin's address book. He dropped a dime and dialed the number, and a soft-voiced woman picked up the phone almost immediately and said, 'Mr Washburn's residence.'

He made his voice very New York. He asked if he could speak to Mr Washburn, please. She wanted to know who was calling. Jerry Manna, he said. She asked if he would hold the line, please, and he said that he would.

Then a man's voice said, 'Washburn here. Who's this?'

'Uh, I'm Jerry Manna, Mr Washburn. I—'

'Who?'

'Jerry Manna, Mr Washburn. Mr Lublin said that I should call you. He said that—'

'Maurie?'

'Yes,' Dave said. 'I—'

'Hold it,' Washburn said. He had a very deep voice and spoke quickly, impatiently. 'I don't like this phone. Give me your number, I'll get back to you. What's the number there?'

Could Washburn trace the call? He didn't think so. Quickly, he read off the telephone number. Washburn said, 'Right, I'll get back to you,' and broke the connection.

He sat in the phone booth, the door closed, and he wiped perspiration from his forehead. The palms of his hands were damp with sweat. Right now, he thought, Washburn could be calling Lublin. Lublin would tell him he never heard of a Jerry Manna. And then—

But why should Washburn be suspicious? Unless Lublin had told him everything after all. But Lublin wouldn't do that, because it didn't make any sense, that was the one thing Lublin had to avoid. And it took a long time to take a number and find out who it belonged to, where the phone was. The police could do it. Otherwise the phone company wouldn't give out the information. But Washburn was an important criminal, the kind who would have connections in the police department. One of them could get the information for him. Then he would stall on the phone, and a couple of goons would head for the bar.

They couldn't stay in the bar too long. If Washburn called back right away, they might be all right. But if he took too long it could be a trap.

Jill stood at the door of the phone booth, her eyebrows raised in question. He shook his head and waved her away. She went back to the table and poured beer into her glass, tilting the glass a few degrees and pouring the beer against the side of it. She raised the glass and sipped the beer.

The phone rang.

He reached for the receiver, fumbled it, knocked it off the hook. He grabbed it up and said, 'Hello, Manna speaking.'

Washburn said, 'All right, I can talk now. What's the story?'

'Mr Lublin said I should call you, Mr Washburn.'

'You said that already. What's it about?'

'It's about a builder from Hicksville,' he said carefully. 'A man named Joe. Maurie said—'

'What, again?'

He took a quick breath. *What, again?*

'You want to know the two boys on that, is that right?'

'That's right, Mr Washburn. I—'

'Dammit, Maurie called me already today on that. When did you talk to him?'

'Last night.'

'Well, he called here this morning. Early. He woke me up, dammit. I gave him all of that right then. Didn't you talk to him?'

'I can't reach him, Mr Washburn. I tried him a couple of times. He maybe tried to get me, but I've been out and he couldn't call me where I've been. I thought I could take a chance and call you direct, Mr Washburn, after I couldn't get hold of Maurie.'

There was a long pause. Then Washburn said, 'All right, dammit, but I hate these goddamned calls. They are two New York boys who work out of East New York near the Queens line. Lee Ruger is one, he's the one to talk to, and the other is Dago Krause. The price depends on the job, what they have to do. They get a good price because they do good work, they're reliable. That what you wanted?'

'If you could give me the address, Mr Washburn, I would—'

'Yeah. Jesus, this is all stuff I told Maurie this morning. He got me out of bed for this, and now I've got to go over it all. This is a pain in the ass, you know that?'

'I really appreciate it, Mr Washburn.'

'Yeah. Just a minute.' He waited, and Washburn came back and said, 'I can't find the damned phone number. Krause's address I don't have, I never had it. Ruger's the one you want to talk to anyhow, see. That's 723 Lorring Avenue. There's a phone, you can probably find it. Maurie—'

'Thanks very much, Mr Washburn.'

Washburn wasn't through. 'Maurie's a goddamned idiot,' he said now. 'He gave you my name, is that right?'

'Well, he—'

'He should damn well know better than that. What'd he do, just let it drop out?'

'More or less, Mr Washburn.'

'You tell him he should watch his mouth, you got that? Or I'll tell him myself. What did you say your name was? Manna?'

'Manna,' he said. And, after Washburn rang off, he said, 'From heaven.'

13

The Royalton was probably safe but they didn't go back there. Jill was afraid of the place, which was reason enough. Besides, it was vaguely possible that Ruger and Krause knew their names. The half hour after the murder of Corelli had been a time when everything happened too quickly, when everything was confused; even the memory of it was bright in some parts and hazy in others, and it was possible that the killers knew their names. They had registered under their right names at the Royalton, and if they ran a check from hotel to hotel—

But they had to get some rest. They walked half a block west on Thirty-fourth Street, and Dave went into a leather-goods store and bought a cheap suitcase. There was a haberdashery two doors down; he bought socks and underwear and two shirts there and packed them in the suitcase. Further down the same block they bought underwear and stockings for Jill.

They took a cab to a third-rate hotel on West Thirty-eighth between Eighth and Ninth, a place called the Moorehead. A sallow-faced clerk rented them a double room on the second floor, five-fifty a day, cash in advance. They registered as Mr and Mrs Ralph Cassiday of Albany, Georgia. There was an elevator but no operator to run it. The desk clerk took them upstairs and unlocked the door for them. He didn't wait for a tip.

The room held an old iron bedstead that had been repainted with white enamel long enough ago so that the paint had begun to flake away from the metal. The bed itself was a little smaller than a double, about three-quarter size. It sagged slightly in the middle. The bed linen was clean but old and worn. There was a dresser which had been repainted with brown enamel fairly recently. The painter had covered up the scars of neglected cigarettes without bothering to sand them down. Since then, three more burns had been added to the dresser top.

There was no rug. The floor was covered with brownish linoleum which was cracked in several places. The walls were a greenish gray, and very dirty. A fixture on the high ceiling held three unshaded light bulbs, one of which had burned out. A light cord hung down from the fixture over the center of the bed. The room had one window, which needed washing. It faced out upon a blank brick wall just a few feet away. The desk clerk had said that there was a bathroom down the hall.

He stood in the room, looking for some place to put the suitcase, finally setting it on top of the bed. She walked over to the window and opened it. 'This is a dump,' he said.

'It's all right.'

'We could get out of here and go someplace better. Will you be able to sleep here? It's pretty bad.'

'I don't mind. I think I could sleep anywhere, now.'

He went over to her and put his arm around her. 'Poor kid. You must be dead.'

'Almost.' She yawned. 'This place isn't so bad. There's a bed – that's all I care about right now. What time is it?'

'Dinnertime.'

'I'm not hungry. Are you?'

'No.'

'We'll eat when we wake up. Right now I wouldn't know whether to order breakfast or dinner, anyway, so let's just get to sleep. We couldn't stay at a better hotel anyway, honey. We're such a mess they wouldn't take us in. Don't unpack the suitcase.'

'Why not?'

'Because I wouldn't want to put any clothes in that dresser. None that I ever intended to wear. What are our names, incidentally? I didn't see what you wrote.'

He told her.

'Cassiday,' she said. 'So many different names lately. Did you ever use phony names when you took other girls to motels?'

'Huh?'

'I bet you did. What names did you use?'

'Jesus,' he said.

She grinned suddenly, a quick and wicked grin. Then she stepped away from him and began to unbutton her blouse. She took it off and asked him to unhook her bra. He did this. She took the bra off and crossed the room to set it and the blouse on the room's only chair, and he looked at her and was surprised when a sudden uncontrollable burst of desire shot through him. She began getting out of her skirt. He tried looking away from her but her body drew his eyes magnetically.

For God's sake, he thought. He turned away, toward the door, and said that he had to go downstairs for a minute.

'What for?'

'There's a drugstore on the corner,' he said. 'A few things I wanted to pick up.'

'Just don't pick up any girls.'

'Don't be silly.'

She laughed happily at him. 'First kiss me goodbye,' she said.

He turned again. She was wearing a slip and stockings, nothing else. Her face was drawn with exhaustion and her skin was pale but this only served to make her still more desirable. She held her arms out to him and he caught her and kissed her. She pressed herself tightly against him and held the kiss.

When he let go of her she said, 'I'll wait up for you.'

'Don't.'

'Well—'

'I might be a while,' he said.

He wound up going to the drugstore after all. He bought a street guide there but it didn't do him much good. It told him what streets Lorring Avenue crossed, but he had never heard of any of those streets and wasn't even sure what borough East New York was in, or whether it was a separate suburb on Long Island. There was a West New York, he knew, and it was in New Jersey.

The drugstore had a pocket atlas of New York, with maps of the whole city, and he bought that. East New York turned out to be a part of Brooklyn. Brooklyn was a slightly lopsided diamond, and East New York was just above the eastern point of the diamond, north and west of Canarsie. He managed to find Lorring Avenue but couldn't figure out how to get there.

He bought two packs of cigarettes at the drugstore. He ate a candy bar. He weighed himself on a penny scale. According to the scale, he was a full twelve pounds under his normal weight, but he wasn't sure how accurate the scale might be.

He killed a few minutes that way to give Jill a chance to fall asleep. He could have made love to her, he thought. She would have let him, might even have been able to enjoy it, and God knew he wanted her, the passion no less strong because of its suddenness.

On the way back to the room he stopped at the floor's communal bathroom. He thought of taking a shower but changed his mind when he saw what the tub looked like. He washed his hands and face at the sink and went to the room, let himself in with his key. She was asleep, lying on top of the bedclothes, naked. She slept on her side facing the door with her knees bent, one arm under her head, the other up in front of her face. He saw the curves of her breasts.

He got undressed and lay down beside her, facing away from her. The bed was too small. Their bodies touched. She made a small sound in her sleep. He moved a little away from her and closed his eyes, trying to relax. He lay there for quite a while, wide awake, and then sleep came all at once.

14

There was this dream. In it, he was representing the plaintiff in a negligence action. His client had fallen down a department-store escalator and was suing for damages in the amount of sixty-five thousand dollars. The department-store floorwalker had just finished testifying that Dave's client had not fallen but had been pushed by a companion, as yet unidentified. Dave cross-examined. He argued brilliantly, but the defense witness ducked every question, slipping them off his shoulders and winking surreptitiously at Dave. There was no justice, he thought, frustrated, and he took out a gun and shoved the barrel into the man's slick face. He shouted questions at him and beat him over the head and shoulders with the butt of the gun. The man bled from the wounds and slumped in his chair. The judge pounded with his gavel, and Dave raised the gun and shot him. The bailiff moved toward him, gun drawn, and Dave shot him, too, and turned toward the gallery and fired into the rows of spectators. The faces of the spectators melted away when his bullets hit them.

He woke up bathed in sweat. Jill was sitting on the edge of the bed beside him, holding his shoulder and asking if everything was all right. She was dressed and her face was fresh and alive. The overhead light was on. He turned toward the window. It was dark outside, still. He shook his head to clear the dream away. She asked what was the matter.

'A dream,' he said.

'A bad one?'

'An odd one. Very surrealistic.'

'Dave—'

'It's nothing.' He shook his head again and swung his legs over the side of the bed. She was smoking a cigarette. He took it from her and dragged on it. He asked her how long she had been up.

'Just a few minutes.'

'What time is it?'

'Four-thirty.'

'The middle of the night,' he said. He got dressed and went down the hall to the bathroom to wash up. He had a bad taste in his mouth and he needed a shave, but he hadn't bought a razor or a toothbrush. He washed his mouth with soap and gargled with tap water. He came back to the room, put on a tie and knotted it carefully. 'I look like hell,' he told her.

'You need a shave. That's all.'

Outside, the streets were dark and empty. The corner drugstore was closed. Even the bars were closed. He bought a safety razor and a small pack of blades at an all-night drugstore on Forty-second Street. Down the block, Hector's cafeteria was open, one of four lighted spots on Times Square. The block itself was dark, movie marquees unlighted, almost every place closed. They got coffee and rolls at Hector's and he went upstairs to the men's room and shaved, lathering up with bar soap. He nicked himself, but not badly. When he was done he put the razor and the blades in a wastebasket and went back downstairs. His coffee had cooled off but he drank it anyway.

He said, 'I was just thinking.'

'About what?'

'Going back to Binghamton. It's going to feel funny, don't you think? Moving into the apartment, getting back to work.'

'You mean after all of this?'

'Yes,' he said. He got up and took their coffee cups back to the counter and had them filled again. He came back to the table and stirred his coffee methodically with a spoon. 'Right back to another world,' he said quietly. 'Searching titles and filing deeds and drawing wills.'

'That's not all you do.'

'Well, no, but our kind of law is pretty quiet and orderly. You don't get up in the middle of the night. Or carry a gun.'

She didn't say anything.

He sipped coffee and put the cup back on the saucer. 'You'll be a housewife,' he said.

'With a weekly bridge game, I suppose.'

'Probably.'

'Is it bad?'

'What – your bridge game? It's pretty bad.'

She didn't smile. 'That's not what I mean. Going back, and what our life will be like there.'

'No, it's not bad. Why?'

'The way you were talking.'

'I didn't mean it to sound that way,' he said. 'Just that it's very different from, well, this. What day is it?'

'I think Thursday.'

'I'm supposed to pick up the Scranton papers. At that newsstand. I don't think I'll bother. Are you sure it isn't Friday?'

'No, it's Thursday.'

'It seems longer. We haven't been married a week – can you believe that?'

'It does seem longer.'

'I killed a man yesterday.' He hadn't meant to say it. It had come out all by itself. *Nice day today. Maybe it'll rain. I killed a man yesterday. Want more coffee?*

'Don't think about it.'

'I think I was dreaming about it. No one knows about it. You and I know, and Lublin knows, but no one else knows about it. Back home, nobody would dream it. If they heard about it they wouldn't believe it.'

'So?'

'I was just thinking,' he said.

They had to go back to the Moorehead. The gun was there, tucked between the mattress and the bedspring. The extra shells were in their room at the Royalton and he thought that a maid might stumble across them while she was cleaning the room. And the people at the Royalton might get suspicious if they didn't occupy the room at all. He decided to call the hotel later in the day.

They locked the room door and went through the pocket atlas to try to figure out the best way to get out to Lorring Avenue. Two subways came close. There was an IND train that ran out Pitkin Avenue, but he couldn't make out from the maps how you picked up the train in the first place. It seemed to originate somewhere in Brooklyn. One line of the IRT Seventh Avenue ran as far as Livonia Avenue and Ashford Street, which would put them about a dozen short blocks from Lorring. And he could figure out how to get that train. They could take a cab, of course, but he wasn't sure he could find a driver who would want to go all the way out there, or who would know the route.

Downstairs, he left the key at the desk and paid another five-fifty for the next night. They might return to the hotel and they might not, but this way the room would be there for them if they needed it in a hurry. The five-fifty was insurance.

They got on the subway at Thirty-fourth Street a few minutes before seven. The train was fairly empty at the start. It thinned out even more at the Wall Street stop, and when they crossed over into Brooklyn there were only five other passengers in their car. He got up to check the map on the wall of the car near the door. The train had a full twenty stops to make in Brooklyn. A few people got on while the train followed Flatbush Avenue; most of them left at the Eastern Parkway stop. The .38 was in Dave's pants pocket now. When he sat down his jacket came open, and he didn't want the gun butt to show. The pocket that held the gun bulged unnaturally and he kept fighting the impulse to pat it. No one seemed to notice the bulge.

The ride lasted forever. Once the train came up out of the earth and ran elevated for four stops before disappearing into the ground once more. Then it came up and stayed up. At a quarter after eight they hit the last stop, the end of the line. They were by then the only passengers in their car. They got off the train and walked to the staircase at the end of the subway platform. The sun was out but there was a strong breeze blowing that chilled the air. They went down the stairs and passed through a turnstile.

He found a street sign. They were at the corner of New Lots and Livonia. He dug out the pocket atlas and thumbed to the map of that area, trying to figure out which direction to take next. He knew what route they had to take but he couldn't tell which way they were facing or how to start off. He looked back at the subway platform, trying to orient himself, and Jill nudged him. He looked up and saw a uniformed policeman heading across the intersection toward them. The only thing he could think of was the gun. The cop knew about it, the cop was coming to pick him up. He was almost ready to start running when he realized he was acting crazy. The cop came closer and asked if they were lost, if he could help.

Dave laughed now, unable to help it. The cop looked at him curiously. He broke off the laughter and said yes, they were lost, and asked how to get to Lorring Avenue. The cop gave him directions – two blocks over Ashford to Linden Boulevard, then a dozen or so blocks to the left on Linden and he couldn't miss it. They thanked the cop and left.

The neighborhood was a marginal slum, less densely populated than a Manhattan slum would be, but run-down and dirty, with a similar air of chronic depression. Most of the houses were only two or three stories tall. They were set close together with no driveways and no lawns. Stores were beginning to open, kids walked to school in bunches. About a third of the kids were Negroes.

Further along Linden Boulevard the neighborhood improved a little. The housing there was similar to where Corelli had lived in Hicksville, two-story semidetached brick fronts. The lawns here were smaller, and few of them had more than scattered patches of weeds springing up from hard-packed dirt. There were trees, but they were scrawny.

'I made a mistake,' he told her. They were waiting for a light to change. 'I told that cop Lorring Avenue. He could remember.'

She didn't answer him. He lit a fresh cigarette, thinking that this was something new, another unfamiliar element. The policeman was to be feared, to be avoided. He should have just asked the way to Linden Boulevard and found his own way from there. There were so many things to learn, a whole new approach to social phenomena that had to be fixed in the mind.

At Fountain Avenue, Linden Boulevard cut forty-five degrees to the left. Lorring Avenue started across the intersection from it, running due east. It was almost entirely residential. Here and there an older building remained, with a grocery store or delicatessen on the ground floor and apartments over it. The rest of the homes were semidetached brick fronts, blocks of them, all very much the same. Most of the houses had very tall television antennas. The cars at curbs or in driveways were Fords and Plymouths and

Ramblers and Chevys. There were a lot of station wagons and a few Volkswagens.

When they crossed Grant Street, they moved into an older part of the neighborhood and the scenery changed abruptly. For half a block there were brick fronts on one side of Lorring, but the rest of that block and the other side of the street were made up of older frame houses, larger buildings set somewhat further back from the street. A sign in the front window of one white-clapboard house announced that tourists were welcome.

The block after Grant was Elderts Lane. Lee Ruger lived at 723 Lorring, between Elderts and Forbell. His house, like several others on that block, was three stories tall. A wooden sign on the lawn said 'Rooms,' and a small metal strip on the front of the house beside the door said 'Rooms for Rent.'

They walked past the house and kept walking almost to the end of the block. The Pontiac they had seen yesterday was not at the curb, nor had they seen it alongside the house. It might be at the back, in the rear of the driveway or in a garage.

He said, 'I don't know if he's home or not. I didn't see the car. Of course, it might be Krause's car, the one we saw.'

'They don't live together?'

'I don't think so. They might share an apartment, but this is just a furnished room. They wouldn't share a room. Unless they both have rooms in the same building. There's still a lot we don't know. We have to know whether or not anybody's home.' The gun was still in his pocket, and its weight made him uncomfortable. He looked around quickly to make sure no one was watching him, then took the gun from the pocket and jammed it once again beneath the waistband of his slacks.

'This is crazy,' he said.

'What is?'

'What we're doing now. Standing on the corner waiting for him to come by in a car and blow our brains out. I feel like a target, standing here in the open.'

'We could call up and—'

'The hell with it,' he said. 'I don't want to call him. A phone call would only put him on guard if he is home, anyway. And I'm sick of calling people on the phone. Look, there are two possibilities. He's there or he isn't. If he isn't home, I want to know about it, and I also want to get upstairs and search his room. Or take another room at the house so that we can sandbag him when he comes in.'

'What's sandbag?'

'Surprise him, I don't know. They say it on television. If he *is* home, there's no sense waiting in the shadows for him to leave the house. He might be there now, lying in bed, sound asleep. It's still early. He could be sleeping. If he's home, the only thing to do is go upstairs and kill him.'

She shivered.

'That's what we came for,' he said.

'I know. Would you shoot him in bed?'

'If I got the chance.' Her eyes were lowered. He cupped her chin with his right hand and raised her face so that her eyes met his. 'Listen to me,' he said. 'It's not fair play. Fine. We are not playing. They were not playing before, not with Corelli and not with us, and we are not playing now. I'm not Hopalong Cassidy. I don't want to be a good sport and let that bastard draw against me. I'd much rather shoot him in the back, or while he's sleeping.'

He watched as she put her tongue out to lick her lower lip. 'All right,' she said.

'Do you understand, Jill?'

'I understand.'

'Are you sure?'

'Yes. Only—'

'Only what?'

'Nothing,' she said. He waited, and she started to say something else, then gripped his arm and pointed. He spun around. A car was coming toward them down Lorring, a car the color of the one they had seen at Gramercy Park the day before. He shoved Jill behind him and dropped automatically to one knee. His hand went for the gun. The front sight snagged momentarily on his clothing. Then he got the gun out. The car came closer.

It was a convertible, though, and it wasn't a Pontiac; it was a Dodge, and a woman was driving it. There were two kids and three bags of groceries in the back seat. The car passed them, and he looked at the gun in his hand and felt like an idiot. He shoved it under his waistband and got to his feet. She said, 'I thought—'

'So did I.' He pointed down Forbell Avenue. There were stores a block away at the corner. 'Go down there,' he said.

'Why?'

'Because you'd be in the way now. I have to go inside, and I have to go alone.'

'Now?'

'Now. There's no sense waiting. That car wasn't them, but the next one might be, and we're perfect targets like this. Go on.'

She hesitated, then turned and went. He waited until she was a few doors down the block. Then he went back to 723 and walked quickly to the front door. A sticker on the windowpane said 'We Gave.' There was a red feather under the inscription. There were curtains behind the window and he couldn't see into the house. He tried the door. It was locked. He rang the bell.

Nothing happened. He took a breath and rang the bell again. An angry voice, sounding neither male nor female, said, 'I'm coming!' He waited. There were footsteps, coming closer, and he put his hand inside his jacket and let his fingers settle on the butt of the .38. The metal felt very warm now.

The door opened warily. He saw a face, and for a shadow of a second he thought it was Lee's face and he tensed his hand to draw the gun. Then the door opened wider, and he saw that it was a woman, an old woman with rheumy eyes and a mannish moustache. Her hair was black, sprinkled with flat gray. She looked at him and waited for him to say something.

'Does Lee Ruger live here?'

'Ruger?' She looked at him. 'He's here,' she said. 'Why?'

'Is he home?'

She looked exasperated. 'Eight rooms here,' she said. She drew the door open, stepped back. 'Eight rooms, and seven of 'em rented. You think I own this place? I just run it, I get the rent, I make sure it's clean. You expect me to keep track of who's here and who isn't? I got enough without that.'

He entered the house, looked over her shoulder at the staircase. There was a table at the second-floor landing. On it was a vase of withered flowers. The house smelled of cigarette smoke and old furniture. He said, 'Ruger—'

'Room Six. If he's here he's in it. If he's not he's not. You want to go upstairs, then go. The top floor.'

She didn't wait to be thanked. She turned bulkily and went back to the kitchen and he started up the stairs. They creaked under his feet. At first he tried to walk softly and slowly, placing his feet on the edges of the steps to cut down their creaking. But it didn't matter whether or not anyone heard his approach. Now he was just another man walking up the flight of stairs.

The dying flowers at the second-floor landing were roses, their petals mostly gone. He thought, The woman can be a witness, she can identify me. But that didn't matter either, he decided. Her description would not be enough to lead the police to him, and if he were picked up by them, they wouldn't need her as a witness. If he and Jill were picked up, they would confess. He was fairly sure of this.

He climbed another flight of stairs to the top floor. There were four rooms on the floor, four doors off the small hallway. Room 6 was at the end of the hall away from the staircase. The door was closed. He walked over to the door and tried to listen for movement inside the room. He couldn't hear anything. Downstairs, in another part of the rooming house, someone flushed a toilet. The noise carried clearly. He waited while the plumbing noises died down and listened again at the door. No sounds came from within.

He took the gun out and held it in his right hand. He positioned himself at the side of the door and held the gun so that it was pointed just above and slightly to the side of the knob. His finger curled expectantly around the trigger. He held his breath for a moment, then let it out slowly, then breathed in again. With his left hand he reached for the doorknob.

15

The room was anticlimactically empty. The door was not locked. He turned the knob and threw the door open, gun in hand, like Broderick Crawford bulling his way into George Raft's hideout, and the room was empty. He stood in the doorway looking at an unmade empty bed. Cigar butts filled an ashtray on the bedside table. There were ashes on the floor. He stepped inside and pulled the door shut quickly. He started to bolt the door, then decided that was crazy. He took a deep breath and sat down on the edge of the unmade bed and put the gun down beside him, then remembered and rotated the gun's cylinder so that there was no bullet under the chamber.

Ruger wasn't around. But this was Ruger's room and the man would come back to it, sooner or later. And he would be waiting for him. Ruger would open the door and he, Dave, would be sitting on Ruger's bed with a gun in his hand, waiting.

The bathroom. He remembered the flushing of the toilet and thought that Ruger might still be in the house. He could be in the bathroom on a lower floor. He could bump into the woman and find out that a man had come to his room, looking for him.

He ran his hand over the bed linen. It was cool, and he guessed that it hadn't been slept in for hours. He picked up the ashtray and several of the cigar butts. They were cold and smelled stale. The air in the room was also stale, and there was a thin layer of dust over the chair and dresser and night table. It didn't look as though anyone had been in the room in a day or more. Just to make sure, he slipped out of the room and walked halfway down the stairs. The door of the second-floor bathroom was slightly ajar. He perched himself on the stairs and waited until the bathroom's occupant finished and left. It was a man, a very old man who walked with a slight limp, carrying a towel and a toothbrush and an old-fashioned straight razor down the hall to his room.

So Ruger was out. He got to his feet and went back up to the third floor again and let himself into Ruger's room once more. He closed the door and walked over to the window. There were curtains, lacy ones that didn't quite fit the image of the hired killer. He pushed them apart and looked out through the window. It needed washing, and the room needed airing out. He opened the window three inches at top and bottom and looked out through the glass. A small boy was riding his bicycle in the street, poised precariously on a seat that was too high for him. The boy rode off. A sports car breezed by and cornered sharply at Elderts Lane. A mailman, his leather sack bulging, walked down one driveway and up another.

Perfect, he thought. Ruger was out, and sooner or later Ruger would come back. Alone, or with Dago Krause in tow. Either way, he would be able to see them coming from the window. That was luck, the window facing the street. Ruger couldn't get to the house without being seen on the way. He would be ready for him, ready and waiting.

His mind hurried ahead, sketching in the details. The escape shouldn't be too difficult. There would be no gun battle to draw attention, because Ruger wouldn't know he was there until it was too late for him to do anything about it. There would only be one shot, the one he himself would fire. People would hear it, but few people ever recognized a single shot for what it was. A truck backfiring, a kid with a firecracker – no one ever thought it was a gunshot. And by the time people reacted to the shot he would be on his way out of the house.

Jill, thank God, was out of the way around the corner. He would kill Ruger and get clear of the house. He would hurry around the corner and find her, and then they would grab a cab back to Manhattan or get onto a subway, anything at all. All he had to do was wait.

Fingerprints. With Ruger's body left behind, the police would be all over the place checking for prints. And his were on file. He had been printed in the army, and he had vague memories of his fingerprints having been taken years ago as a matter of course when he held a summer job with the Broome County welfare department. He went around the room wiping the things he had touched – the doorknob, the ashtray, the window. He did a thorough job, then hauled Ruger's chair over to the window and cleared a pile of dirty clothes off the seat. He sat down facing the window and waited.

Time crawled. Three cigarettes later he got up from the chair and began searching Ruger's room. There might be something the police shouldn't find, he thought. A note mentioning Washburn or Lublin or Corelli, anything that would enable the cops to make a connection between Ruger and them. But there was nothing like that. Ruger's room was strangely barren of artifacts of any sort. There were two or three paper-bound books, their bindings cracked and pages dog-eared. There was a mimeographed thirty-page pamphlet of hard-core pornography illustrated with crude drawings and featuring a sadomasochistic theme and a semiliterate prose style. There were clothes, selected with little evident thought for quality or fashion. There were no guns, so Ruger was evidently carrying one – Dave couldn't believe the man could get along without owning one. There was a knife, a switchblade stiletto with a five-inch blade. The edge was quite sharp. There was a homemade blackjack – a length of lead pipe with a leather loop for a handle and several thicknesses of black electrical tape wrapped around the pipe.

No notes, no addresses, no telephone numbers. There was a key, evidently to a safe-deposit box somewhere. Dave pocketed it; there was no telling what the police might find in the box, and he decided it couldn't hurt to keep them from it.

He wiped everything clean of prints and sat down again. Outside, the street was calm and clear. He wondered how long it would be before Ruger came back. If the man had been out hunting them all night long, he would probably be tired, ready to sleep. But he might have slept. He could have spent the night with a girl, or anywhere.

And his mind filled suddenly with a picture of Ruger with a girl and then of Ruger with Jill. He closed his eyes and gritted his teeth painfully. The image passed and he opened his eyes again and gazed again out the window.

How long? It was going slowly enough for him, there in Ruger's room, and he realized how much more slowly it must be going for Jill. She didn't know what was happening, where he was, where Ruger was – she was stuck around the corner and had no idea what was happening or when she would see him again. He pictured her sitting over a cup of coffee and not knowing for certain whether he was alive or dead, and he realized all at once what a bad arrangement this was.

She should have stayed in the hotel, of course. He had suggested that, briefly, but as he said it he had known she wouldn't go along with it. And once he decided to go straight up after Ruger, he should have sent her back to the city to wait for him. She probably would have put up an argument but he might have been able to talk her into it.

This way, everything was up in the air. She was close by but not close enough to know what was going on. He thought of leaving the rooming house for a minute. He could duck around the corner, find her, let her know what was happening, and then get her into a cab headed for their hotel. But if he left the room, how could he get back in? He might not be able to bluff his way past the woman again. Even if he managed that, it would just get her wondering, and if she wondered enough she might make a point of tipping Ruger off when he came through the door.

And if he left the place, Ruger could come back while he was looking for Jill. He wouldn't know about it one way or the other and he could come bouncing up the stairs into a trap he wouldn't be able to get out of. As things stood, he had the advantage, he held all the cards. But if he left the room he would be chancing the loss of that edge. He couldn't risk it.

She would just have to wait.

He reached for a cigarette. There were only two left in his pack, and he didn't have a spare. He hesitated, then shrugged and took out one of the cigarettes and lit it.

They drove up just as he was finishing the cigarette. He saw the car coming down Lorring, moving slowly toward the house, and he dropped his cigarette to the floor and covered it with his foot. He took hold of the gun, spun the cylinder to put a bullet under the hammer once again. It was their car this time. The Pontiac, and the right color, and coasting to a stop in front of the house and across the street.

He opened the window a little wider at the bottom and drew the curtains almost shut. Looking down, he could see them through the front windshield. Ruger was on the passenger side and Krause was behind the wheel. They were sitting there now, making no move to leave the car.

Come on, he thought. Both of you. Come on.

He rested the gun barrel on the windowsill. They were still in the car. They might both drive away, he thought. They might change their minds and drive away and leave him there. His grip tightened on the butt of the gun, and beads of sweat dotted his forehead. He couldn't breathe.

A car door opened, on Ruger's side. One of them spoke in an undertone. They both laughed. Then Ruger was coming and Krause was driving off, he thought. He was both glad and sorry. He wanted them both, right away, but one would be better than none at all.

Hurry up, dammit—

Ruger put a foot out of the car, then drew it back in again. Dave gritted his teeth. Ruger swung the foot out again, then shifted his weight and stepped out of the Pontiac. He stood with one hand on the open door and the other on the roof of the car. He was talking with Krause but Dave couldn't hear anything.

He straightened up, then, and slammed the car door shut. Krause gunned the motor. Ruger nodded to him, and Krause pulled off, slowed down briefly for the stop sign at Forbell and continued east on Lorring. Ruger stood watching the Pontiac until it disappeared from view. He made no move to cross the street.

Dave aimed the gun at him, tentatively. He lowered it and looked at the man. For the first time, he didn't know if he could do it. He did not know if he could shoot him.

His words to Jill: 'Listen to me. It's not fair play. Fine. We are not playing.' But it was less clear-cut when you had time to think about it, less certain when you had the man centered in your sights.

He watched Ruger. The gunman seemed stubbornly determined to wait forever before he crossed the street. He reached into his breast pocket now and drew out a stubby cigar. Dave watched as he unwrapped the cigar slowly, carefully. He dropped the cellophane wrapper. It fell to the sidewalk and the wind played with it. Ruger bit off the end of the cigar, spat it out, took out a windproof lighter, thumbed it open, lit the cigar, closed the lighter, returned it to his pocket, and puffed on the cigar. He moved to the curb and glanced across the street.

Then Dave saw him glance to his right, saw the cigar drop unnoticed to the street. Ruger was staring. Dave grabbed the curtains, tugged them aside.

Jill.

She had just turned the corner. She was walking toward the rooming house, looking straight ahead. He looked at Ruger. The man had a gun in his hand, he recognized her.

He yelled, 'Jill, get back!'

He saw Jill look up, then clap one hand to her mouth. Ruger shot at her, missed, spun around to look up at the window. Dave pointed the .38 and squeezed the trigger. The sound was deafening and the recoil jolted up his arm to his shoulder. Jill had not moved. He yelled at her to get back, to get the hell out of the way. She hesitated and then spun abruptly around and dashed for the corner. Ruger looked at her but did not shoot. He aimed the gun at the third-story window, steadied himself, and fired.

16

Ruger's shot went off to the left. It slammed into the house a few feet to the side of the window and the whole house seemed to rock. Dave kicked the chair back out of his way and dropped into a crouch in front of the window. He looked out. Ruger was crouching, too, trying to present the smallest possible target. He looked around for a place to hide himself but stayed where he was. The trees there were young ones, too small to hide behind, and the nearest parked cars were three doors down the street.

Dave shot at him. This time his arm anticipated the recoil and the gun stayed steady. He missed; the bullet dug into the pavement a few feet in front of Ruger. Ruger snapped off a shot in reply. It shattered the window and glass flew.

Down the street a car stopped with a screech of brakes, spun in a ragged U-turn that took it a few feet over the curb, and sped off in the opposite direction. Somewhere a woman screamed. Ruger ran halfway across the lawn behind him, stopped, crouched, fired. His shot wasn't even close.

Ruger was up again, running in a crouch, zigzagging toward the side of the house behind him. Dave followed him with the gun, his elbows braced on the windowsill, holding the .38 with both hands now. Ruger stopped, and as he started to spin once more around he was no longer a moving target. Dave gave the trigger a gentle squeeze.

He had not really believed the shot would be on target. But the bullet tore into Ruger's arm above the elbow and sent his gun flying. The impact of the shot spun Ruger halfway around and knocked him to the ground. He moved awkwardly there, using his good arm to push himself to his feet. The bad arm hung like deadweight.

He got up and turned toward Dave, then away from him. His arm was leaking blood. He had lost his bearings and looked this way and that like a nearsighted man searching for his eyeglasses.

Dave aimed again and fired again, and the bullet took Ruger in the small of the back. He shrieked like a girl and went down flat on his face and didn't move.

Now the whole house was awake. Dave yanked the door open, tore out of the room. A woman across the hallway was looking at him from her door. He glanced at her and she drew back in terror, slamming the door shut after her. He raced down the stairs. At the second floor, a burly man in his undershirt stepped into his path. Dave hit him across the face with the barrel of the gun, shoved him and sent him flying.

On the ground floor, a woman was shouting. There was nobody in sight. The front door was wide open. He ran through it, down the steps, along the path to the street. Across the street Ruger lay bleeding. Dave ran over to him. Ruger lay on his face, his body twitching spasmodically, a low moan issuing from his lips. Dave knelt momentarily and put the muzzle of the gun to the back of Lee Ruger's head. He barely heard the roar of the gun as his last bullet tore into Ruger's brain.

The neighborhood screamed with excitement. Doors slammed, windows opened. A police siren sounded in the distance. He was running now, not thinking, just running at top speed. His heart pounded violently and there was a constant roaring in his ears, like wind in a tunnel. He turned at the corner and kept running. Jill was up ahead, staring openmouthed at him. He ran to her.

'Dave, I didn't know. Are you all right? Are you all right?'

He couldn't answer her. He turned her around and grabbed her arm and they ran.

17

In the cab he moved the gun from one pocket to the other. He could smell powder burns on his hands and it seemed to him that the whole back seat of the taxi reeked of the smell, that the driver couldn't help noticing it. He sat stiffly in his seat, trying not to look over his shoulder for policemen. They had caught the cab on Linden Boulevard, and they were already approaching the Manhattan Bridge, so they seemed to be in the clear, but he couldn't shake off the feeling that carloads of police were hot on their trail.

They crossed over into Manhattan. He waited for guilt to claim him, waited to be moved once again by a feeling of having crossed a great moral boundary. But this did not happen. He felt that he had been a very lucky bungler. He had very nearly gotten Jill killed, and had watched a prospective one-sided ambush turn into a gun battle. Good shooting and good position had won the battle, and pure blind luck had let them get out uncaught from the mess he had created. He was ashamed of the bungling and grateful for the luck. But the confused guilt that had come over him after he had killed the bodyguard in Lublin's house – this did not come now. He wondered why.

They got out of the cab at Forty-second Street and ducked into a cafeteria. He went to the counter to get coffee and stood in line just long enough to decide that he didn't want coffee. He left the line and took Jill around the corner. There was a bar there, and it was open already. They sat at a table. He had a straight shot of bar rye with a beer chaser. She didn't want anything.

They lit cigarettes, and she said, 'I'm so stupid, I almost ruined everything. I thought I was being so good at all this. And then like an idiot—'

'What happened?'

'I don't know. I kept waiting and waiting and you didn't come. I didn't know what was happening. I couldn't stand it.'

'It's all right now.'

'I know.' She closed her eyes for a moment, then opened them. 'I'm okay. It was the waiting. I thought I was very brave. When I went to Lublin's—'

'You were a little too brave then.'

'But it was easy. I was doing something, I could see what was going on. This time all I could do was stand around and find things to worry about. I had to see what was going on. I picked a hell of a time, didn't I?'

'It was a bad arrangement. Forget it.'

'I'm sorry.'

'Don't be sorry. We're out of it.'

'Are you sure he's—'

'Yes, he's dead.' The *coup de grâce*, the bullet in the back of the skull. Yes, Lee was dead.

'Did anyone see you?'

'Half the world saw me.'

'Will they find us?'

'I don't think so.' He sipped beer. 'They'll know what we look like, but they won't know where to look for us, or who to look for. The big worry was that we might have been picked up on the spot. They would have had us then, and cold. A dozen different people could have identified me. But I think we're out of it now.'

'What now?'

'Now we check out of the Royalton,' he said. 'I was going to call them and tell them to hold our room. But that's silly. If we're not going to stay there, we might as well clear out altogether. And there are things there that we need.'

'What?'

'Our clothes and all. And the rest of the bullets.'

'I forgot that.'

'For Krause,' he said.

There was no problem at the Royalton. They went to their room and packed, and he called the desk and told them to make out the bill and to get the car ready. He packed everything and took the suitcases downstairs himself. The hotel took his check. The doorman brought the Ford around, and Dave gave him a dollar and loaded the suitcases into the back seat. They got into the car. He drove around until he found a Kinney garage on Thirty-sixth Street between Eighth and Ninth and left the car there. They carried the suitcases back to the Moorehead and walked upstairs to their room there instead of waiting for the ancient elevator.

Around four in the afternoon he went around the corner and came back with a deck of cards, a six-pack of ginger ale and a bottle of V.O. They played a few hands of gin rummy and drank their drinks out of water tumblers. There was no ice. At six he found a delicatessen and brought back sandwiches. They ate in the room and drank more of the ginger ale, plain this time. He brought back a paper, but they couldn't find anything about Ruger.

'You never did get those Scranton papers,' she said.

'So we're out a dollar.'

Later he felt like talking about the shooting. He told her how he had sat at the window watching Ruger with the cigar, how he had pointed the gun at him, how he had felt.

'I don't think I could have shot him just like that,' he said.

'But you did.'

'Because all hell broke loose. There was no time to debate the morality of it, not with the bastard shooting at us.'

'You would have killed him anyway.'

'I don't know. I don't feel bad about it. Not even uneasy.'

'How do you feel?'

'I don't know.'

'I feel relieved,' she said.

'Relieved?'

'That we're both alive. And that he's not, too. We came here to do something, and we've done part of it, and we're still safe and all right, and I feel relieved about that.'

They went to sleep early. They had both gotten a little drunk. She didn't get sick, just sleepy. They got undressed and into bed, and the liquor made sleep come easily. And there was no attempt at lovemaking to complicate things, not this time. He held her and kissed her and they were close, and then he rolled aside and they slept.

In the morning she asked what they were going to do now, about Dago Krause.

'Lie low for a little while,' he said.

'Here at the hotel?'

'It's as good a place as any. If we let things cool down, we'll be in a better position. There's the cops to think about, for one thing. With Ruger's murder so fresh, they'll be on their toes. If they have a little time to relax they'll just let it ride in the books as another gang killing. They won't break their necks looking for us or keeping a watch on Krause. You remember the amount of attention they paid to Corelli's death. Everybody was delighted to find an excuse not to try finding Corelli's murderers. It'll be the same here. They'll decide Ruger was killed by a professional, and they'll bury the whole thing in the files.

'The same thing with Krause, in another way. He'll be on guard right now. He won't tell the police anything. He'll be sure we're coming for him, and he'll walk around with eyes in the back of his head. In three days he'll manage to convince himself that one killing was enough to satisfy us or that we panicked once Ruger was dead and beat it out of the city. Let him relax.'

'How will we find him?'

'We'll find him.'

'He won't be in the phone book. I mean, there must be a million Krauses, even if he has a phone, and we don't know his first name. Just a nickname. Why do you suppose they call him Dago? Krause isn't an Italian name, is it?'

'No. We'll find him.'

'How?'

'We'll find him. One way or another, we'll find him.'

They spent the morning in the hotel room. At noon he went to the drugstore and picked up a stack of magazines, plus the morning papers. All the papers had the story, but not even the tabloids gave it a very big play. It wasn't good copy. There had been a gun battle of sorts, which was on the plus side, but no innocent bystanders had been killed, and since no one had spotted Jill there was no sex angle to work on. The prevailing theory seemed to be that Ruger had been killed by a professional killer, a common enough ending for a criminal. The eyewitness reports contradicted one another incredibly, and the composite description of the killer made him about thirty-five, shorter and heavier than Dave. The whole pattern of the killing itself was confused in the papers. One witness insisted that Ruger had been ambushed by two men, one firing from the rooming house and the other gunning him down from behind a parked car. The woman at Ruger's place told reporters that the killer had showed her false credentials and had posed as a federal officer.

They read all the articles together, and he laughed and folded up the papers and carried them down the hall and stuffed them in a large wastebasket. 'I thought so,' he told Jill. 'They would have had to pick us up on the spot in order to get us. Now they're a million miles away.'

They went out for lunch and sat a long time with coffee and cigarettes. They walked up to Forty-second Street. There were a pair of science-fiction movies playing at the Victory, and the daytime rates were less than a dollar. It seemed like too much of a bargain to pass up. They walked in somewhere around the middle of a British import about a lost colony on Alpha Centauri and sat in the balcony. The theater was fairly crowded. They watched the end of that picture, a newsreel, three cartoons, a slew of coming attractions, and the other movie, one in which the fate of the world is menaced by giant lemmings, beasts that rushed pell-mell to the sea and devoured all the human beings in their path. Then there were more trailers, and they saw the Alpha Centauri movie up to the point where they had come in.

There was a comfortable feeling of security in the theater, a feeling of being in a crowd but not of it, of being surrounded by other persons while remaining comfortably anonymous. At first they were tense and on guard, but this stopped, and they got quickly lost in the action on the screen.

He picked up the evening papers on the way back to the hotel. In the room, he checked through them while Jill went down the hall to wash out underwear and stockings in the bathroom sink. He didn't expect to find anything much in the papers, just checked them out methodically as a matter of form. For the most part, the material on the shooting was just a rehash of the stories in the morning papers, with a little extra material on Ruger's background and criminal record and some hints at the police investigation of the murder.

But a final paragraph in one article said:

Philip 'Dago' Krause, described by police as a longtime friend and associate of the murdered man, was among those brought in for questioning. Krause, who lives at 2792 23rd Avenue in Astoria, has a record of arrests dating back to 1948. He was released after close interrogation . . .

He took the paper down the hall to Jill and showed it to her. 'Look at that,' he said, excited. 'I told you we'd find him. The damned fools drew us a map.'

That night they had dinner at a good steak house on West Thirty-sixth Street. They went back to the hotel and drank more V.O. The ginger ale was gone. He drank his straight, and she mixed hers with tap water. They played gin rummy part of the time and spent the rest of the time sitting around reading magazines. She washed out some socks for him and hung them on the curtain rod over the window to dry. She muttered something about playing housewife on her honeymoon, and he smiled thoughtfully. It was the first time in days that either of them had mentioned the word 'honeymoon.'

The next day was Saturday. There was nothing new on Ruger's killing in any of the papers. Most of them had dropped it. One of the tabloids had a brief and pointless follow-up piece, but that was about all there was. They stayed close to the hotel.

By Sunday she was getting impatient, anxious to get it over and done with. 'It's better to wait,' he said. 'Another couple of days. It won't be long now.' They spent the afternoon at another Forty-second Street movie house and had dinner at the Blue Ribbon, on Forty-fourth Street. They had drinks before dinner and steins of Wurzburger with their meal and brandy with the coffee, and they were feeling the drinks by the time they left the place. He wanted to go back to the Moorehead, but she suggested stopping at a jazz place down the street and he went along with it. They sat at a circular bar and listened to a man play piano, until she lowered her head suddenly and fastened her fingers around his wrist.

She said, 'Don't look up. Not now.'

'What's the matter?'

'There's a man across the bar, he was one of the ones at Lublin's that night. I don't remember his name but I met him there. The one with the red tie. Don't look straight at him, but see if he's looking at us.'

He saw the man she meant, watched him out of the corner of his eye. The man hadn't seemed to notice them yet.

'He may not recognize me,' she said softly. 'I looked different then, and I think he was drunk that night, anyway. Is he looking this way?'

'No.'

'We'd better get out of here. Let me go first.' She slipped off her stool. He left change on the bar and followed her out the door. Outside, she stood leaning against the side of the building and breathing heavily. He took her arm and led her down the street. A cab stopped for them. They got in and rode back to the hotel without saying a word.

In the room she said, 'It's dangerous. The more time we spend in this city—'

'I know.' He lit a cigarette. 'Tomorrow.'

'Is that too soon?'

'No. I was going to wait until Tuesday or Wednesday, but you're right, we can't stick around here too long. It was only a matter of time before we bumped into somebody. It was lucky he didn't spot us.'

'Yes.'

'And lucky you recognized him.'

He stayed with her until after midnight. Then he left the hotel and walked downtown for a dozen blocks. On a dark side street he found a two-year-old Chevy with New Jersey license plates. The plates were in frames fastened by bolts. He used a quarter to loosen the bolts, took both plates, and carried them back to the hotel inside his shirt.

They packed up everything except the gun and the box of shells. He loaded the revolver with five bullets and carried the remaining shells outside to another dark street. There were about fifteen shells left in the box. He dropped them one by one into a sewer and chucked the empty carton into a mailbox.

At seven the next morning, he left the hotel again and walked to the Kinney garage. The place was just opening. He got his car, paid the attendant three and a half dollars, and parked the car on the street a few doors down from the hotel. He went upstairs for the luggage. Jill came down with him. She had the gun in her purse. They walked down to where the car was parked and loaded their bags into the trunk and locked it. He drove the car and she sat close beside him. He took the West Side Drive uptown to Ninety-fifth Street, then drove around the side streets between Broadway and West End Avenue until he found what he was looking for, an alleyway alongside a warehouse. He drove through the alley to the back of the warehouse and switched license plates, bolting the New Jersey plates loosely to the car and putting his own plates in the trunk of the Ford. He backed out of the alley and drove up to 125th Street and swung east to the Triborough Bridge.

They crossed the bridge. The heavy traffic was coming across the bridge into Manhattan, rush-hour commuters coming into the city. He drove through Astoria, and she checked the route in the pocket atlas and told him which turns to take. They made only one wrong turn; it took them three blocks out of their way, but they found their mistake and got back where they belonged. He found Krause's block and then Krause's building and drove around looking for a parking place. The only spot was next to a fire hydrant. He drove around the block twice, and by the second time around someone had come out and moved a car. It was a tight fit, but he managed to squeeze the Ford into the space.

He killed the motor, got out of the car. He walked around to the curb side while she moved over behind the wheel. He got in and sat beside her. Her purse, with the .38 in it, was on the seat between them. From where he sat he had a good view of the entrance to Krause's apartment building. It was about half a block away, on their side of the street.

And Krause was home. Dave could see the gunmetal Pontiac just across the street from Krause's building. Krause was inside, and he would not stay there forever.

'This time,' he said quietly, 'we do it right.'

She nodded. Her hands gripped the steering wheel securely and her eyes were fixed straight ahead. He offered her a cigarette but she didn't want one.

His window was up. He rolled it all the way down.

He said, 'The easy way, the simple way. Listen, back up as far as you can, and swing the wheel so that we can get out of here in a hurry. We don't want to be stuck in this spot.'

She did as he told her, backing the car all the way against the car behind them and turning the wheel so that they would be able to pull out quickly when the time came. He smoked his cigarette and flicked the ashes out of the open window.

Waiting, he thought, was always the hardest part. Once things began to happen, a good percentage of your actions were automatic. You didn't have to sit and think, and you had no time to worry, no chance to second-guess yourself. But waiting required a special sort of personal discipline. You had to accept that stretch of time as something to be endured, a wasted period during which you turned yourself off and let the time pass by itself.

His mind went over details. He tested the plan from every angle, and each time it held up. It was simple and direct. There were no little tangles to it, no sharp corners that could catch and snag. It held.

And they waited.

A few people left Krause's building. Two or three entered it. One time he saw a man framed in the doorway who looked very much like Krause, and he had to look a second time before he realized it was someone else. He felt annoyingly conspicuous, sitting like this in a parked car, but he told himself that it was safe enough. No one would pay any attention to them. People sat in parked cars. There was no law against it. And the people who walked past them seemed in too much of a hurry to waste valuable time noticing them.

It was cool out, and once he started to roll up the window. She asked what he was doing, and he caught himself and rolled the window down again. He reached over and opened her purse. The gun was there, waiting.

At twenty-five minutes after ten, Dago Krause came out of the building. They both saw him at the same moment. Krause stepped out of the doorway, a cigarette in one hand, and he took a drag on the cigarette and flipped it toward the curb. He was wearing a tan trench coat, unbelted, the cloth belt flapping. His shoes were highly polished. He moved toward the curb, and Jill turned the key in the ignition and pulled out of the parking space. The Ford rolled forward. Dave took the gun from her purse and held it just below the window on his side.

There were two cars parked in front of Krause's building with a four-foot space between them. Krause stood at the curb's edge between the two cars. He moved out to cross, saw the Ford, and stepped back to let it pass him. The Ford moved even with Krause. Dave braced the barrel of the gun on the window frame. Jill hit the brake, not too hard, and the car slowed.

Krause looked at them. There was an instant of recognition – of the gun, of Dave. Then Dave emptied the gun at him.

One bullet missed and broke glass in the door of the building. The other four bullets were on target. Three hit Krause in the body, one in the stomach and two in the center of the chest. The final bullet caught him as he was falling and took half his head off. The combined force of the shots lifted Dago Krause off his feet and tossed him back on the curb. He never had time to move, never uttered a sound.

Jill's foot left the brake pedal and put the accelerator on the floor. The Ford jumped forward as though startled and raced straight ahead for two blocks. There was a red light at the second intersection. She slowed the car briefly, then took a hard left through the light and sped down that street for two more blocks. She turned again, right this time, and slowed down to normal speed. The .38 was back in her purse, the window rolled up. The car had a heavy gunpowder smell to it, and he opened the vent slightly to let it air out.

On a residential street about a mile away she stopped the car and he got out and switched the plates. The whole operation – removal of the Jersey plates and substitution of his own – took less than five minutes. He got back in the car and she headed for the Triborough Bridge again while he wiped his fingerprints from the stolen license plates. When they passed a vacant lot, she slowed the car and he unrolled the window and threw the plates out into the middle of the field.

They crossed the bridge. She drove the width of Manhattan on 125th Street, then stopped at the entrance to the Henry Hudson Parkway and let him take the wheel. He headed north on the Henry Hudson, picked up the Saw Mill River Parkway and followed the throughway signs. There were three bridges to cross and a lot of tolls to pay, and the traffic was moderately heavy on the Saw Mill River Parkway, but they were on the throughway by noon.

18

The sky was turning dark. They stood together at the crest of the hill and looked out over the rolling countryside. There was very little traffic on the highway. The sun had set minutes ago. There was a red glow to the west. Behind them, the motel's neon sign winked on and off, on and off.

The motel was on Route 28, a two-lane state highway that curved through the Catskills. They had left the throughway at the Saugerties exit and had driven this far before he decided to call it a day. They spent the afternoon by the side of the motel pool, ate dinner at a roadhouse a few miles down the road to the east.

She said, 'I can't believe it, you know.'

'That it's over?'

That it's over. Or that it happened at all, the crime or the punishment. Neither one seems real now. Just eight days, I can't believe any of it.'

He slipped an arm around her waist. She leaned against him and he smelled the fragrance of her hair. 'After a year,' she said, 'we won't be able to believe it at all, any of it. You'll be a very very promising young attorney and I'll be a charming young married in the social swim and it will seem so completely unreal we'll think we dreamed it.'

He kissed her. She looked at him with the biggest eyes on earth and he held her close and kissed her again, and when he released her there was no need to say anything, not a word. Together they turned and walked to their room. The door was not locked. They went inside, and he locked the door while she drew the blinds. Together, they took the spread off the bed and drew the covers down.

They undressed slowly and silently. He took her in his arms and kissed her again, gently, and she sighed, and he drew her down upon the bed and lay down beside her. She was incredibly beautiful.

'My wife,' he whispered. 'My love.'

There were tears in the corners of her eyes. She blinked them away. His hands filled up with the warmth of her body, and desire welled up within him, a living force. He had never wanted anything, ever, as much as he wanted her now.

The bars were gone, the blocks were kicked aside. When it was time, her thighs opened to him and her breasts cushioned him. He took her, and she gave a small sweet cry of joy, and they were together.

Whole concepts fled – time, space, memory, self. Love lived its own life, an island to itself, and sleep came quick on its heels.

They spent four days at the motel. Almost all of that time was spent in the room, in the bed. Their need for each other was overpowering, irresistible. They would laugh about it and tell each other that they had turned into sex maniacs, and suddenly the laughter and the banter would die in the air and they would fall hungrily back into bed.

Once she said, 'I'm very good, aren't I?'

'And modest too.'

'But good,' she said, yawning. 'Am I the best you ever had?'

'The only one I ever had.'

'Ah.' She yawned again, stretching her arms high overhead. 'But I don't mind the others,' she said. 'I'm not even a little jealous. They couldn't make you like this. Only me.'

And another time, after a meeting that was fast and furious, she put her head on his chest and cried. He stroked her hair and asked her what was the matter. She wouldn't tell him. He held her in silence, and after a few minutes she looked up at him with tears in her eyes, tears staining her cheeks.

She said, 'I wish—'

'What?'

'That I could have been a virgin for you.'

'But you were,' he said.

She thought that over for a few minutes. Then, slowly, she nodded. 'Yes,' she said, 'I was, wasn't I?'